OUT OF ___ _____ ___
INTO ___

Armstrong thrus_ ___ ___ _____ ___ ____ed
the other two into ___ ___ ___ ___ ___ ___ell
you to shoot, *do it!*" Then the detective jo___ ___er
into motion once more.

They pelted down the alleyway and into heavy
traffic. Armstrong ran right in front of a taxi. The car
screeched to a halt, the driver cursing. Armstrong
yanked open the driver's door and tossed the cabby
into the street.

"*Get in!*"

Jenna dove for the passenger's door. She barely
had her feet off the pavement before the car
squealed into motion. Armstrong drove like a maniac.
"Forget Europe, kid," he muttered. "They're not
gonna let you get out of New York alive."

Jenna's eyes burned, and she couldn't get enough
air down.

"Ever been time-touring, kid?" Armstrong asked
before she could speak.

"Wh-what?"

"Time-touring. Have you ever?"

She blinked, tried to force her brain to function
again. "No. But . . . Carl and I, we were going to
go . . . through TT-86, to London. Got the tickets
and everything, used false ID to buy them, to keep
it a secret . . ."

The taxi that Armstrong had taken from its driver
slewed around another corner, merged with traffic
on Broadway, slowed to a decorous pace.

"Kid," the detective said softly, "those tickets might
just save your life. Because the only by-God way out
of this city now is through TT-86."

RIPPING TIME

LINDA EVANS
&
ROBERT ASPRIN

RIPPING
TIME

Chapter One

She hadn't come to Shangri-La Station for the usual reasons.

A slight and frightened young woman, Jenna had lost the lean and supple dancer's grace which had been hers . . . God, was it only three days ago? It seemed a year, at least, for every one of those days, a whole lifetime since the phone call had come.

"Jenna Nicole," her aunt's voice had startled her, since Aunt Cassie hadn't called in months, not since before Jenna had joined the Temple, "I want to see you, dear. This evening."

The commanding tone and the use of her full name, as much as the unexpected timing, threw her off stride. *"This evening?* Are you serious? Where are you?" Jenna's favorite aunt, her mother's only sister, didn't live anywhere near New York, only appeared in the City for film shoots and publicity appearances.

"I'm in town, of course," Cassie Tyrol's famous voice came through the line, faintly exasperated. "I flew in an hour ago. Whatever you've got on your calendar, cancel it. Dinner, class, Temple services, anything. Be at Luigi's at six. And Jenna, darling, don't bring your roommate. This is business, family business, understand? You're in deep trouble, my girl."

Jenna's stomach clenched into knots. *Oh, my God. She's found out!* Aloud, she managed to say, "Luigi's at six, okay, I'll be there." Only a lifetime's worth of acting experience and the raw talent she'd inherited from the same family that had produced the legendary Jocasta "Cassie" Tyrol got that simple sentence out without her voice shaking. *She's found* out, *what'll she say, what'll she do, oh my God, what if she's told Daddy? She wouldn't tell him, would she?* Jenna's aunt hated her father, almost as much as Jenna did.

Hand shaking, Jenna hung up the phone and found Carl staring at her, dark eyes perplexed. The holographic video simulation they'd been running, the one they'd been thrown into fits of giggles over, trying to get ready for their grand adventure, time touring in London, flickered silently behind Jenna's roommate, forgotten as thoroughly as last summer's fun and games. Carl blinked, owl-like, through his glasses. "Nikki? What's wrong?" He always called her by her middle name, rather than her more famous given name—an endearing habit that had drawn her to him from the very beginning. He brushed Jenna's hair back from her brow. "Hey, what is it? You look like you just heard from a ghost."

She managed a smile. "Worse. Aunt Cassie's in town."

"Oh, dear God!" Carl's expressive eyes literally radiated sympathy, which was another reason Jenna had moved in with him. Sympathy was in short supply when your father was *the* John Paul Caddrick, the Senator everybody loved to hate.

Jenna nodded. "Yeah. What's worse, she wants me to meet her by six. At Luigi's, for God's sake!"

Carl's eyes widened. "Luigi's? You're kidding? That's *worse* than bad. Press'll be crawling all over you.

Remind me to thank the Lady of Heaven for not giving *me* famous relatives."

Jenna glared up at him. "Some help you are, lover! And just what am I supposed to *wear* to Luigi's? Do you see any six-thousand-dollar dresses in my closet?" Jenna hadn't put on much of anything but ratty jeans since hitting college. "The last time I was seen in public with Aunt Cassie, she had on a *blouse* that cost more than the rent on this apartment for a year! And I still haven't lived down the bad press from that horrible afternoon!" She hid her face in her hands, still mortified by the memory of being immortalized on every television set and magazine cover in the country after slipping headlong into a mud puddle. "Cassie Tyrol and her niece, the mudlark . . ."

"Yep, that's you, Jenna Nicole, the prettiest mudlark in Brooklyn." Jenna put out her tongue, but Carl's infectious grin helped ease a little of the panic tightening down. He tickled her chin. "Look, it's nearly four, now. If you're gonna be in any shape to walk into Luigi's by six, with a crowd of reporters falling all over the two of you—" Jenna just groaned, at which Carl had the impudence to laugh "—then you'd better jump, hon. In case you hadn't noticed, you look like shit." Carl eyed her up and down, wrinkling his nose. "That's what happens when you stay out 'til four A.M., working on a script due at six, then forget to go to bed when you get back from class."

Jenna threw a rolled up sock at him. He ducked with the ease of a born dancer and the forlorn sock sailed straight through a ghostly, three-dimensional simulation of a young woman laced into proper attire for a lady of style, prim and proper and all set to enjoy London's Season. The Season of *1888.* When Jenna's sock "landed" in the holographic teacup, while the holographic young lady continued smiling and sipping her now-contaminated tea, Jenna's roommate fell down on the floor, howling and pointing a waggling finger at her. "Oh, Nikki, three-point shot!"

Jenna scowled down at the idiot, who lay rolling around holding his ribs and sputtering with laughter. "Thanks, Carl. You're all heart. Remind me to lose your invitation to the graduation party. *If* I ever graduate. God, if Simkins rejects *this* script, I'll throw myself in the East River."

Carl chuckled and rolled over, coming to his feet easily to switch off the holoprojector they'd borrowed from the campus library. "Nah. You'll just film it, win an Oscar or two, and take his job. Can you imagine? A member of the Temple on faculty?"

Jenna grinned—and bushwhacked Carl from behind while he wasn't looking, getting in several retaliatory tickles. He twisted around and stole a kiss, which turned into a clutch for solid ground, because she couldn't quite bring herself to tell Carl the worst part of her news, that her aunt *knew.* Just how much Cassie knew remained to be seen. And what she intended to do about it, Jenna didn't even want to think about. So she just held onto Carl for a long moment, queasy and scared in the pit of her stomach.

"Hey," he said gently, "it isn't that bad, is it?"

She shook her head. "No. It's worse."

"Cassie loves you, don't you know that?"

She looked up, blinking hard. "Yes. That's why it's worse."

His lips quirked into a sad, understanding little smile that wrenched at Jenna's heart. "Yeah. I know. Listen, how about I clean up the place while you're out, just in case she wants to visit, then when it's over, I'll give you a backrub, brush your hair, pamper your feet, spoil you silly?"

She gave him a watery smile. "Lover boy, you got yourself a deal."

Then she sighed and stepped into the shower, where she could let the smile pour away down the drain, wishing the fear would drain away with it. Christ, what could she tell Aunt Cassie? She tried to envision the scene, quailed inwardly. Cassie Tyrol, cool and elegant and *very* Parisian, despite her New Hollywood accent and the ranch up in the hills, where Jenna had spent the happiest summers of her life— the only happy ones, in fact, until college and the Temple and Carl. . . . Aunt Cassie was not likely to take the news well. Not at all. Better, of course, than her father.

Two hours later, Jenna was still quailing, despite the outward charm of her smile for the *maitre d'* at Luigi's, the most fashionable of the restaurants owned by increasingly wealthy members of New York's leading Lady of Heaven Temple. It was little wonder her aunt had chosen Luigi's. Given Cassie's prominence in the New Hollywood Temple, she probably had a stakeholder's share in the restaurant's profits. Jenna's only aunt never did anything by halves. That included throwing herself into her latest religion or making money the way Jenna accumulated rejection slips for her screenplays.

The *maitre d'* greeted her effusively, by name. "Good evening, Ms. Caddrick, your aunt's table is right this way."

"Thank you." She resisted the urge to twitch at her dress. Carl had, while she showered and did her hair and makeup with the most exquisite care she'd used in a year, worked a genuine theatrical miracle. He'd rushed over to the theater department and liberated a costume which looked like a million bucks and had only cost a few thousand to construct, having been donated by some New Hollywood diva who'd needed a tax write-off. Jenna, who existed by her own stubborn insistence on a student's budget that did *not* include dinner at Luigi's or the requisite fashions appropriate to be seen there, had squealed with delight at his surprise.

"You wonderful idiot! If they'd caught you sneaking this out, they'd have thrown you out of college!"

"Yeah, but it'd be worth it, just looking at you in it." He ran his gaze appreciatively across her curves.

"Huh. This dress is a lot more glamorous than I am. Now, if I just had Aunt Cassie's nose, or cheekbones, or chin . . ."

"I like your nose and cheekbones and chin just the way they are. And if you don't scoot, you'll be late."

So Jenna had slid gingerly into the exquisite dress, all silken fringe and swaying sheik, and splurged on a taxi, since arriving on a bicycle in a ten-thousand-dollar dress simply would not do. Jenna followed the *maitre d'* nervously into the glitzy restaurant, aware of the stares as she made her way past tables frequented by New York's wealthiest Templars. She did her best to ignore the whispers, staring straight ahead and concentrating on not falling off her high-heeled shoes and damning her father for saddling her with the price of an infamous family face and name.

Then she spotted her aunt at a dim-lit corner table and swallowed hard, palms abruptly wet. *Oh, God, she's got somebody with her and it's* not *her latest.*

If this was family only . . . The only person it *could* be was a private detective. Cassie'd hired more than her share over the years. Jenna knew her style. Which meant Jenna was in *really* serious hot water. Worse, her aunt appeared to be absorbed in a violent argument with whoever it was. The dark circles under Cassie Tyrol's eyes shocked her. When Jenna reached the table, conversation sliced off so abruptly, Jenna could actually hear the echoes of the silence left behind. Her aunt managed a brittle smile as she stooped to kiss one expertly manicured cheek.

"Hello, Jenna, dear. Sit down, please. This is Noah Armstrong."

Jenna shook hands, trying to decide if the

androgynous individual in a fluid silk suit beside her aunt was male or female, then settled for, "A pleasure, Noah." Living in New York for the past four years—not to mention a solid year plunged into Temple life—had been an education in more ways than one.

"Ms. Caddrick." Firm handclasp, no clue from the voice. Noah Armstrong's eyes were about as friendly as a rabid pit bull challenging all comers to a choice cut of steak.

Jenna ignored Armstrong with a determination that matched Armstrong's dark scowl, sat down, and smiled far too brightly as Cassie Tyrol poured wine. Cassie handed over a glass in which tiny motion rings disturbed the wine's deep claret glint. Jenna hastily took it from her aunt before it could slosh onto snowy linen.

"Well, what a surprise, Cassie." She glanced around the elegant restaurant, surreptitiously tugging at her short skirt to be sure nothing untoward was showing, and realized with a start of surprise there were no reporters lurking. "Gawd. How'd you manage to ditch the press?"

Her aunt did not smile. *Uh-oh.*

"This was not an announced visit," she said quietly. "Officially, I'm still in L.A."

Worse, oh, man, she's gonna let me have it, both barrels . . .

"I see. Okay," she sighed, resigned to the worst, "let's have it."

Cassie's lips tightened briefly. The redness in her eyes told Jenna she'd been crying a great deal, lately, which only added guilt to an already-simmering stew of fear and defensiveness. Jenna, wishing she could gulp down the wine, sipped daintily, instead, determined to maintain at least a facade of calm.

"It's . . ." Cassie hesitated, glanced at Noah Armstrong, then sighed and met Jenna's gaze squarely. "It's your father, Jenna. I've discovered something about him. Something you deserve to know, because it's going to wreck all our lives for the next year or so."

Jenna managed not to spray wine all over the snowy linen, but only because she snorted thirty-dollar-a-glass wine into her sinuses, instead. She blinked hard, eyes watering, wineglass frozen at her lips. When she'd regained control, Jenna carefully lowered the glass to the table and stared at her aunt, mind spinning as she tried to reassess the entire purpose for this clandestine meeting. She couldn't even think of a rejoinder that would make sense.

"Drink that wine," her aunt said brusquely. "You're going to need it."

Jenna swallowed hard, just once. Then knocked the wine back, abruptly wishing this meeting *had* been about her highly secret down-time trip with Carl, a trip they'd been planning for more than a year, to Victorian London, where she and her roommate planned to film the East End terror instilled by Jack the Ripper. They'd bought the tickets fourteen months previously under assumed names, using extremely well-made false identifications she and Carl had managed to buy from an underworld dealer in new identities. New York teemed with such dealers, with new identifications available for the price of a few hits of cocaine; but they'd paid top dollar, getting the best in the business, because Jenna Nicole Caddrick's new identity had to be foolproof. *Had* to be, if she hoped to keep the down-time trip secret from her father. And what her father would do if he found out . . .

Jenna had as many reasons to fear her world-famous father as she had to adore her equally famous aunt. Whatever Cassie was about to lay on her, it promised to be far worse than having her father discover she was going time-touring in the face of the elder Caddrick's ultimatums about never setting foot through any time terminal gate, ever. Voice tight despite her relief at the reprieve, Jenna asked, "Dad, huh? What's the son-of-a-bitch done now? Outlaw fun? He's outlawed everything else."

Noah Armstrong glanced sharply into Jenna's eyes. "No. This isn't about his career as a legislator. Not . . . precisely."

Jenna glanced into his—her?—eyes and scowled. "Who the hell are you, Armstrong? Where do you fit into anything?"

Armstrong's lips thinned slightly, but no reply was forthcoming. Not to her, at any rate. The look Armstrong shot Jenna's aunt spoke volumes, a dismissive, superior look that relegated Jenna to the realm of infant toddlers who couldn't think for themselves or be trusted not to piddle on the Persian carpets.

Jenna's aunt said tiredly, "Noah's a detective, hon. I went to the Wardmann Wolfe agency a few months ago, asked for their best. They assigned Noah to the case. And . . . Noah's a member of the Temple. That's important. More important than you can begin to guess."

Jenna narrowed her eyes at the enigmatic detective across the table. Wardmann Wolfe, huh? Aunt Cassie certainly didn't do things by halves. She never had, come to that. Whatever her father had done, it was clearly more serious than the occasional sex scandals which, decades ago, had rocked the careers of other legislators possessing her father's stature. A chill ran through her, wondering just what Daddy Dearest *was* involved in.

Cassie said heavily, "You remember Alston Corliss?"

Jenna glanced up, startled. "The guy in *Sacred Harlot* with you? Blond, looks like a fey elf, loves Manx cats, opera, and jazz dance? Nominated for an Oscar for *Harlot*, wasn't he? And still a senior at Julliard." Jenna had been impressed—deeply so—by her aunt's talented young co-star. And more than a little envious of that Oscar nomination. And with his good looks, Jenna had just about melted all over the theater seats every time he smiled. Guiltily, she remembered a promise to try and get Carl an autograph, via the connection with her aunt. "Wasn't there some talk of you starring in another film with him? Something about *A Templar Goes to Washington*, sort of a new take on that old classic film?

Her aunt nodded. "Alston wanted to spend a semester interning in Congress. Role research. I . . . I set it up, got him a job in your father's office. Asked him to snoop around for us. Find out things Noah couldn't, didn't have access to." Cassie Tyrol bit a well-manicured lip. "Jenna, he's dead."

"*Dead?*"

Cassie was crying, smudging her careful eye makeup into ruins. "Four hours ago. It hasn't hit the press yet, because the FBI's put a press blackout on it. I know because Noah dragged me out of my house, scared spitless because they'll come after *me*."

Jenna couldn't take this in. Alston Corliss dead, Cassie in danger? "But . . ." Nothing intelligent would form coherently enough to say anything else.

Noah Armstrong spoke quietly, with just a hint of anger far back in those piercing grey eyes. "Surely you've heard the scuttlebutt about people close to your father? To know Senator John Paul Caddrick is to inherit a tombstone?"

White-hot anger blazed at the crude insult, jolting her out of shock sufficiently to glare murderously at the detective. There were *plenty* of reasons to hate John Paul Caddrick, Senator from Hell. But murder wasn't by God one of them! Then she saw the sick, anguished pain in her aunt's eyes. Anger slithered to the floor in a puddle at her feet and Jenna was quite suddenly very cold inside.

Cassie Tyrol's lips trembled. "When we leave here, Jenna, we're going to the FBI. What Noah's found, what your father's been doing, who he's involved with and what *they've* been doing . . . it's got to be stopped. Noah didn't want me to tell you, Jenna, I sneaked away to call you, asked you to meet me here . . ."

She was crying harder, voice shaking. Shocked by her collapse into violent tremors, Jenna reached out, grasped her aunt's chilled fingers, held on tight. "Hey. It's okay," she said gently.

Cassie tightened her fingers around Jenna's, shook her head. "No," she choked out, "it isn't. You're his little girl. It's going to hurt you so much when all of this comes out. I thought you deserved to know. If . . ." she hesitated. "If you want to take off for Europe for a while, I'll pay for the tickets. Take Carl with you, if your roommate wants to go."

Jenna had to scrape her lower jaw off the table.

Cassie tried to smile, failed utterly. "You're going to need a friend, someone to protect you, while this is breaking loose, Jenna, and . . . well, your father and I don't see eye to eye on a lot of things. He's never approved of either of us joining the Lady of Heaven Temple or the food I eat or the men I divorced or the way I make my living, any more than he's ever approved of *your* friends or your choice of career. You're growing up, Jenna. Who you're friends with— or sleep with—is your business, not mine or his or anyone else's, and frankly, a blind man could see Carl's good for you, say what your father will. For one thing," she said bitterly, "you're standing up to that bastard for once in your life, insisting on a film career, and I *know* how much Carl's had to do with that. And I know what's in that bank box of yours. Frankly, I approve. It's why I'm sending him with you. I *know* he'll take care of you for me."

"*What?*" Jenna gasped. *Cripes* . . . Where *did* Aunt Cassie get her information from? But her concern was so genuine, Jenna couldn't even take offense at the invasion of privacy which her really serious snooping represented.

Cassie tried to smile, failed. "Don't be angry with me for prying, sweety, please. I'm just trying to look out for you. So." She slid an envelope across the table. "If you want to go, you can probably get out before the press gets wind of this. And don't go all stubborn and proud on me and tell me you've got to do things on your own. You think the press has been savage before? You have no idea how bad it's going to get, hon. They're going to crucify us. *All* of us. So take it, grab your passports, both of you, and get out of town. Okay, Jenna?"

She just didn't know what to say. Maybe that crazy scheme to get down time to film the Ripper terror wasn't so crazy, after all—and here was her aunt, handing Jenna enough cash to keep her hidden safely down time from the press corps for months, if necessary. Carl, too. Maybe they'd win that Kit Carson Prize in Historical Video, after all, with months to complete the filming, rather than a couple of weeks. The envelope she slid into her handbag was heavy. Thick, heavy, and terrifying. She poured another glass of wine and drank it down without pausing.

"Okay, Cassie. I'll go. Mind if I call Carl?"

Her aunt's attempt at a smile was the most courageous thing Jenna ever seen, braver and more real than anything her aunt had ever done in her presence. "Go on, Jenna. I'll order us dinner while you're gone."

She scooted back her chair and kissed her aunt's cheek. "Love you, Cassie. Be right back." She found the phones in the back beside the bathrooms and dug into her purse for change, then dialed.

"Hello?"

"Carl, it's Jenna. You're never going to believe—"

Gunfire erupted in stereo.

From the telephone receiver *and* the restaurant. Carl's choked-off scream, guttural, agonized, cut straight through Jenna. Rising screams out in Luigi's

main dining room hardly registered. "Carl! *Carl!*"
Then, as shock sank in, and the realization that she
was still hearing gunfire from the direction of her
aunt's table: *"Cassie!"* She dropped the receiver with
a bang, ignoring its violent swing at the end of its
cord. Jenna ran straight toward the staccato chatter
of gunfire, tried to shove past terrified patrons fleeing the dining room.

Someone shouted her name. Jenna barely had time
to recognize Noah Armstrong, elegant clothing covered in blood. Then the detective body-slammed her
to the floor. Gunfire erupted again, chewing into the
man behind Jenna. The wall erupted into splinters
behind *him.* The man screamed, jerked like a murdered marionette, plowed into the floor, still screaming. Jenna choked on a ghastly sound, realized the
hot, wet splatters on her face were blood. A booming report just above her ear deafened her; then
someone snatched her to her feet.

"Run!"

She found herself dragged through Luigi's kitchen.
Screams echoed behind them. The gun in Armstrong's
hand cleared a magical path. Waiters and cooks dove
frantically out of their way. At the exit to the alleyway behind the restaurant, Armstrong flung her
against the wall, reloaded the gun with a practiced,
fluid movement, then kicked the door open. Gunfire
from outside slammed into the door. Jenna cringed,
tried to blot from memory the sound of Carl's scream,
tried desperately not to wonder where Aunt Cassie
was and just *whose* blood was all over Armstrong's
fluid silk suit.

More deafening gunfire erupted from right beside
her. Then Armstrong snatched her off balance and
snarled, *"Run, goddamn you!"* The next instant, they
were pelting down an alleyway littered with at least
three grotesquely dead men. All three were dressed
like middle-easterners, wearing a type of headdress

made popular during the late twentieth century by a famous terrorist turned politician, Jenna couldn't recall the name through numb shock. The detective swore savagely, stooped and snatched up guns from dead hands. "It figures! They showed up as *Ansar Majlis!*" Armstrong thrust one salvaged gun into a pocket, shoved the other two into Jenna's shocked hands with a steel-eyed glance. "Don't drop them! If I tell you to shoot, *do it!*"

Jenna stared stupidly at the guns. She'd used guns before, Carl's black-powder pistols, which he carried in action-shooting re-enactments, the ones stored in her bank box along with their time-touring tickets and the diamond ring she didn't dare wear publicly yet, and she'd fired a few stage-prop guns loaded with blanks. The guns Noah Armstrong shoved into her hands were modern, sleek, terrifying. Their last owners had tried to kill her. Jenna's hands shook violently. From the direction of Forty-Second Street, sirens began to scream.

"Come *on,* kid! Go into shock later!"

Armstrong jerked her into motion once more. She literally fell off her high-heeled shoes, managed to kick them off as she stumbled after Armstrong. They pelted down the alleyway and emerged into heavy traffic. Armstrong ran right in front of a yellow taxi-cab. The car screeched to a halt, driver cursing in a blistering tongue that was not English. Armstrong yanked open the driver's door and bodily tossed the cabby onto the street.

"*Get in!*"

Jenna dove for the passenger's door. She barely had her feet off the pavement before the car squealed into motion. Armstrong, whatever his/her gender, was a maniac behind the wheel of a car. If anyone tried to follow, they ended up at the bottom of a very serious multi-car pileup that strung out several blocks in their wake. Jenna gulped back nausea, found herself checking the guns with trembling fingers to see how much ammunition might be left in them, terrified she'd accidentally set one of them off. She'd never used *any* guns like these. She asked hoarsely, "Aunt Cassie?"

"Sorry, kid."

She squeezed shut her eyes. *Oh, God . . . Cassie . . . Carl. . . .* Jenna needed to be sick, needed to cry, was too numb and shocked to do either.

"It's my fault," Armstrong said savagely. "I should *never* have let her meet you. I told her not to wait at Luigi's for you, told her they'd trace her through that goddamned call to your apartment! I *knew* they'd try something, dammit! But Christ, an all-out war in the middle of Luigi's . . . with his own daughter and sister-in-law!"

Wetness stung Jenna's eyes. She couldn't speak, couldn't think. Her hands shook where she gripped the guns Armstrong had shoved at her.

"Forget Europe, kid," the detective muttered. "They're not gonna let you get out of New York alive. They hit your apartment, didn't they? Killed your fiancé? Carl, wasn't it?"

She nodded, unable to force any sound past the constriction in her throat.

Whoever Armstrong was, he or she could out-curse a rodeo rider. "Which means," the detective ended harshly, "they were going to hit you anyway, even if Cassie hadn't met you. Just on the chance she might have *mailed* it to you. And they had to kill Carl, in case you'd said something to *him*. God *damn* them!"

"Who's 'them'?" she managed to choke out, not quite daring to ask what Cassie might have mailed, but hadn't.

Armstrong glanced sidelong at her for just an instant, long enough for Jenna to read the pity in those cold grey eyes. "Your father's business associates. One royal bastard in particular, who's been paying off your father for years. And the goddamned terrorists they're bringing into the country. Right past customs and immigration, diplomatic fucking immunity."

Jenna didn't want to hear anything more. She'd heard all the slurs, the innuendo, the nasty accusations in the press. She hadn't believed any of it. Who would've believed such filth about her own father, for Chrissake, even a father as lousy as hers had been over the years? Jenna had learned early that politics was a dirty, nasty game, where rivals did their damnedest to smear enemies' reputations with whichever reporters they'd paid off that week. It was one reason she'd chosen to pursue a career in film, following her aunt's lead, despite her father's furious opposition. *Oh, God, Aunt Cassie . . . Carl. . . .* Her eyes burned, wet and swollen, and she couldn't get enough air down.

"Ever been time-touring, kid?" Armstrong asked abruptly.

"Wh-what?"

"Time-touring? Have you ever been?"

She blinked, tried to force her brain to function again. "No. But . . ." she had to swallow hard, "Carl and I, we were going to go . . . through TT-86, to London. Got the tickets and everything, used false ID to buy them, to keep it a secret . . ."

The taxi slewed around another corner, merged with traffic on Broadway, slowed to a decorous pace. "Kid," Armstrong said softly, "those tickets might just save your life. Because the only by-God way out of this city now is through TT-86. Where did you hide them? Do you still have the fake ID's you bought?"

She'd begun to shake against the cracked plastic of the taxi's front seat, was ashamed of the reaction, couldn't hide it. "Yeah, we've still—I've still—" she was trembling violently now, unable to block the memory of Carl's agonized screams. "Locked them up in . . . in my lock box . . ." The other secret hidden in that lock box brought the tears flooding despite her best efforts not to cry. Carl's ring, the one she couldn't wear openly, yet, not until she'd turned twenty-one, making her legally and financially independent of her hated father, lay nestled in the lock box beside the tickets.

Noah glanced sharply into her eyes. "Lock box? A bank box? Which bank?"

Jenna told him.

Twenty minutes later, after a brief stop at a back-alley stolen-clothes huckster for new clothes—something without blood on it—Jenna clutched the entire contents of her bank account—which wasn't much—and the false identification papers and tickets she and her secret fiancé had bought to go time-touring, a grand adventure planned in innocence, with dreams of making a film that would launch both their careers . . . and so much more. Jenna rescued the ring from the safe, too, still closed up its little velvet box that had once been Carl's mother's, wanting at least that much of Carl's memory with her.

She also carried a thick case which held Carl's two black-powder 1858 Remington Beale's pistols she'd kept in the vault, the heavy .44 caliber pistols Carl had carried during re-enactments of Gettysburg and First Manassas and the Wilderness campaigns, the ones he'd taught her to use, after he'd won that action-shooting match in up-state New York last month. The ones her father would've exploded over, had he known Jenna was keeping them in her bank box. Armstrong eyed the heavy pistols silently, that glance neither approving nor disapproving, merely calculating. "Do you have ammo for those?"

Jenna nodded. "In the bottom of the gun case."

"Good. We'll have to ditch this modern stuff before we enter TT-86. I'd just as soon be armed with *something*. How do you load them?"

Wordlessly, Jenna began loading the reproduction

antique guns, but Noah's steel-cold voice stopped her. "Not yet."

"Why not?" Jenna demanded shrilly. "Just because it's illegal? My own father wrote those laws, dammit! It didn't stop . . ." Her voice shattered.

Noah Armstrong's voice went incredibly gentle. "No, that isn't it. We just won't be able to take loaded guns through TT-86's security scans. We can take them through as costume accessories, but not loaded and ready to fire. Tell me *how* to load them, and we'll do that the second we're on station."

Jenna had to steady down her thoughts enough to explain how to pour black powder into each cylinder and pull down the loading lever to seat bullets, rather than more traditional round balls, in each chamber of the cylinder, how to wipe grease across the openings to prevent flame from setting off the powder in adjoining chambers, how to place percussion caps . . . The necessity to think coherently helped draw her back from raw, shaking terror.

"They're probably going to figure out where we went," Armstrong said quietly when she'd finished. "In fact, they'll be hitting TT-86, too, as soon as possible." The detective swore softly. "*Ansar Majlis* . . . That's the key, after all, isn't it? After today, it's even money they'll hit *her* the next time Primary cycles. Part of their goddamned terrorist plan."

Jenna glanced up, asking the question silently.

"Those bastards at Luigi's were *Ansar Majlis*. Never heard of 'em? I wish to Christ I hadn't. Your aunt is—was—a prominent public supporter of the Lady of Heaven Temples. So are the owners of Luigi's. And half the patrons. The bastard behind that attack back there sent a death-squad of *Ansar Majlis* to do his dirty work for him. You've heard of Cyril Barris? The multi-billionaire? Believe me, kid, you *don't* want to know how he made all that money. And he can't afford to have your aunt's murder tied to *him*. Or to your father. Getting the *Ansar Majlis* involved makes goddamned sure of that. And *those* bastards have lined up another 'terrorist' hit, aimed right at the very soul of the Lady of Heaven Temples . . ."

Jenna gasped, seeing exactly where Armstrong was going with this.

The detective's glance was grudgingly respectful. "You see it, too, don't you, kid?"

Jenna truly, genuinely didn't want to know anything else about this nightmare.

Armstrong told her, anyway. Showed her the proof, sickening proof, in full color and stereo sound, proof which the elfin actor on the miniature computer screen in Jenna's hands had managed to give Armstrong before his death.

It killed what little respect for her father she'd still possessed.

In the year 1853, a stately man with a high forehead and thick, dark hair that fell down across his brow from a high widow's peak was inaugurated as the 14th US President under the name of Franklin Pierce. Armed conflict between Russia and Turkey heralded the beginning of the disastrous Crimean War. Further south, Britain annexed the Mahratta State of Nagpur, while in the British home islands, Charlotte Bronte published "Villette" and another writer on the opposite side of the Atlantic, American Nathaniel Hawthorne of *Scarlet Letter* fame, brought out the "Tanglewood Tales." Noted historian Mommsen wrote "A History of Rome" and the legendary impressionist painter Vincent Van Gogh was born. European architecture enjoyed a renaissance of restoration as P.C. Albert began the rebuilding of Balmoral Castle, Aberdeenshire, Scotland, and—across the English Channel—Georges Haussmann began the reconstruction of Paris with the Boulevards, Bois de Boulogne.

In New York, Mr. Henry Steinway began

manufacturing fine pianos. On the Continent, Italian composer Verdi wrote his great operas *Trovatore* and *La Traviata* and German composer Wagner completed the text of the masterwork *Der Ring des Nibelungen*. Alexander Wood shot his first patient with a subcutaneous injection from a hypodermic syringe and Samuel Colt, that American legend of firearms design, revolutionized British small-arms manufacture with his London factory for machine-made revolvers.

In London, Queen Victoria ensured the increasing popularity of the previously little-trusted chloroform as a surgical anesthetic by allowing herself to be chloroformed for the birth of her seventh child. Britain established the telegraph system in India and made smallpox vaccinations mandatory by law. In America, the world's largest tree, the *Wellingtonia gigantea,* was discovered growing in a California forest. And in Middlesex Street, Whitechapel— otherwise known as Petticoat Lane, after the famous market which lined that cobbled thoroughfare—a child was born to Lithuanian immigrant Varina Boleslaus and English dock laborer John Lachley.

The child was not a welcome addition to a family of six subsisting on John Lachley's ten shillings a week, plus the shilling or two Varina added weekly from selling hand-crafted items made on her crocheting hook. In fact, in many parts of the world during that year of 1853, this particular child would have been exposed to the elements and allowed to die. Not only could its parents ill afford to feed the baby, clothe it, or provide an education, the child was born with physical . . . peculiarities. And in 1853, the East End of London was neither an auspicious time nor a hospitable place to be born with marked oddities of physique. The midwife who attended the birth gasped in horrified dismay, unable to answer every exhausted mother's first, instinctive question: *boy or girl?*

Statistically, the human gene pool will produce

children with ambiguous genitalia once in every
thousand live births, perhaps as often as once in every
five hundred. And while true hermaphrodites—
children with the genital tissues of both sexes—
account for only a tiny fraction of these ambiguously
genitaled infants, they still can occur once in every
one million or so live human births. Even in modern, more culturally enlightened societies, surgical
"correction" of such children during infancy or early
childhood can give rise to severe personality disorders, increased rates of suicide, a socially inculcated
sense of guilt and secrecy surrounding their true
sexual nature.

In the year 1853, London's East End was an eth-
nically diverse, poverty-stricken, industrial cesspool.
The world's poor clustered in overcrowded hovels ten
and twelve to a room, fought and drank and forni-
cated with rough sailors from every port city on the
globe, and traded every disease known to humanity.

Women carrying unborn children swallowed quack
medical remedies laced with arsenic and strychnine
and heavy metals like sugar of lead. Men who would
become fathers worked in metal-smelting foundries
and shipyards, which in turn poured heavy metals into
the drinking water and the soil. Sanitation consisted
of open ditches where raw sewage was dumped,
human waste was poured, and drinking water was
secured. In such areas, a certain percentage of
embryos whose dividing cells, programmed with
delicate genetic codes, inevitably underwent massive
genetic and teratogenic alterations.

And so it was that in Middlesex Street, Whitechapel,
in that year of 1853, after a protracted debate, many
condemnations of a God who would permit such a
child to be born, and a number of drunken rages cul-
minating in beatings of the woman who had produced
this particular unfortunate offspring, the child was
named John Boleslaus Lachley and reared as a son in

a family which had already produced four dowerless sisters. Because he survived, and grew to manhood in London's East End, where he was tormented into acquiring a blazing ambition and the means to escape, the infant born without a verifiable gender grew in ways no innocent should ever have to grow. And once grown, John Lachley made very certain that the world would never, ever forget what it had done to him.

On a quiet, rainy Saturday morning in the waning days of August, 1888, Dr. John Lachley, who had long since dropped the foreign "Boleslaus" from his name, sat in a tastefully decorated parlour in an exceedingly comfortable house on Cleveland Street, London, opposite his latest patient, and brooded over his complete dissatisfaction with the entire morning while daydreaming about his last encounter with the one client who would finally bring into his life everything his soul yearned to possess.

The room was cold and damp, despite the coal fire blazing in the hearth. August in London was generally a fine month, with flowers in bloom and warm breezes carrying away the fog and coal smoke and damp chill of early autumn with glorious blue skies and sunshine. But rain squalls and thunderstorms and an unseasonable chill had gripped the whole South of England for months, leaving arthritic bones aching and gloomy spirits longing for a summer that had seemed indefinitely postponed and then abruptly at an end before it had properly begun. John Lachley was tired of hearing the week's complaints, never mind those which had been lodged in all the previous weeks since winter had supposedly ceased to plague them.

He had little tolerance for fools and whiners, did John Lachley, but they paid his bills—most handsomely—so he sat in his parlour with the curtains drawn to dim the room and smiled and smiled at the endless parade of complainers and smiled some more as he collected his money and let his mind drift to remembered delights in another darkened room, with Albert Victor's hands and mouth on his body and the rewards of Albert Victor's social status firmly within his grasp.

He had been smiling steadily for the past hour or more, concealing his loathing for his current patient with an air of concerned understanding, while the bloody idiot of a Liverpudlian who'd appeared on his doorstep rambled on and endlessly on about his health, his illnesses, his medicines, his incessant chills and shaking hands, his itching skin and aching head . . .

It was enough to drive a sane man round the twist and gone. Which was where, in John Lachley's private opinion, this pathetic cotton merchant had long since departed. Hypochondria was the least of Mr. James Maybrick's woes. The fool daily swallowed an appalling amount of "medicinal" strychnine and arsenic in the form of powders prescribed by his physician, some doddering imbecile named Hopper, who should have known better than to prescribe arsenic in such enormous quantities—five and six doses a day, for God's sake. And as if that weren't enough, Maybrick was *supplementing* the powdered arsenic with arsenic *pills*, obtained from a chemist. And on top of that, he was downing whole *bottles* of Fellow's Syrup, a quack medicine available over any chemist's counter, liberally laced with arsenic and strychnine.

And Maybrick was so dull of mind, he honestly could not comprehend why he now suffered acute symptoms of slow arsenic poisoning! *Grant me patience*, Lachley thought savagely, *the patience to deal with paying customers who want any answer but the obvious one*. If he simply told this imbecile, "Stop taking the bloody arsenic!" Maybrick would vanish with all his lovely money and never darken Lachley's doorstep again. He would also, of course, die somewhat swiftly of the very symptoms which would kill him,

anyway, whether or not he discontinued the poisonous drug.

Since the idiot would die of arsenic poisoning
either way, he might as well pay Lachley for the
privilege of deluding him otherwise.

Lachley interrupted to give Maybrick the one
medication he *knew* would help—the same drug he
gave *all* his patients before placing them into a
mesmeric trance. Most people, he had discovered,
could easily be hypnotized without the aid of drugs,
but some could not and every one of his patients
expected some spectacular physical sensation or other.
His own, unique blend of pharmaceuticals certainly
guaranteed that. Success as a mesmeric physician
largely depended upon simple slight-of-hand tricks
and the plain common sense of giving his patients
precisely what they wanted.

So he mixed up his potent chemical *aperitif,* served
in a glass of heavy port wine to help disguise the
unpleasant flavor, and said, "Now, sir, drink this
medicine down, then give me the rest of your medical
history while it takes effect."

The drug-laced wine went down in two gulps, then
Maybrick kept talking.

"I contracted malaria, you see, in America, trading
for cotton shares in Norfolk, Virginia. Quinine water
gave me no relief, so an American physician prescribed
arsenic powder. Eleven years, I've taken it and the
malaria rarely troubles me, although I've found I
require more arsenic than I used to. . . . Poor Bunny,
that's my wife, I met her on a return trip from Norfolk, Bunny worries so about me, dear child. She hasn't
a brain in her pretty American head, but she does fret.
God knows I have tried to gain relief. I even contacted
an occultist once, for help with my medical disorders.
A Londoner, the lady was. Claimed she could diagnose
rare diseases by casting horoscopes. Told me to stop
taking my medicines! Can you imagine anything more

absurd? That was two years ago, sir, and my health has grown so alarmingly worse and Dr. Hopper is such a bumbling fool. So when I decided to visit my brother Michael, yes, that's right, Michael Maybrick, the composer, he publishes under the name Stephen Adams, I said to myself, James, you must consult a London specialist, your life is most assuredly worth the time and money spent, what with the wife and children. So when I saw your advert in *The Times,* Dr. Lachley, that you were a practicing physician and an occultist with access to the guidance of the spirit world for diagnosis of difficult, rare illnesses, and that you use the latest techniques in mesmeric therapies, well, I simply knew I must see you . . ."

And on, and on, *ad infinitum, ad nauseum,* about his *nux vomica* medications, his New York prescriptions that Dr. Hopper had so insultingly torn up . . .

John Lachley sat and smiled and thought *If I were to jab my fingers into his larynx, I could put him on the floor without a sound, cut off his testicles, and feed them to him one bollock at a time. If he even has any. Must have, he said he'd fathered children. Poor little bastards. Might be doing them a favor, if I simply slit their father's throat and dumped his body in the Thames. Wonder what Albert Victor is doing now? Christ, I'd a thousand times rather be swiving Victoria's brain-damaged grandson than listening to this idiot. Dumb as a fence post, Albert Victor, but what he can do with that great, lovely Hampton wick of his . . . And God knows, he will be King of England one day.*

A small, satisfied smile stole across John Lachley's narrow face. It wasn't every Englishman who could claim to have balled the future monarch of the British Empire. Nor was it just any Englishman who could tell a future king where to go, what to say, and how to behave—and expect to be slavishly obeyed. Stupider than a stick, God bless him, and John Lachley had him wrapped right around his finger.

Or rather, a point considerably lower than his finger.

Albert Victor, secretly bi-sexual outside certain very private circles, had been ecstatic to discover John's physical . . . peculiarities. It was, as they said, a match created in—

"Doctor?"

He blinked at James Maybrick, having to restrain the instantaneous impulse to draw the revolver concealed in his coat and shoot him squarely between the eyes.

"Yes, Mr. Maybrick?" He managed to sound politely concerned rather than homicidal.

"I was wondering when you might be able to perform the mesmeric operation?"

Lachley blinked for a moment, then recalled Maybrick's request to be placed in a mesmeric trance in order to diagnose his disease and effect a "mesmeric surgical cure." Maybrick was blinking slowly at him, clearly growing muzzy from the medication Lachley had given him.

"Why, whenever you are ready, sir," Lachley answered with a faint smile.

"Then you do think there is hope?"

Lachley's smile strengthened. "My dear sir, there is always hope." *One can certainly hope you will pass into an apoplectic fit while in trance and rid the world of your unfortunate presence.* "Lie back on the daybed, here, and allow yourself to drift with the medication and the sound of my voice." Maybrick shifted from the overstuffed chair where he'd spent the past hour giving his "medical history," moving so unsteadily, Lachley was required to help him across to the daybed.

"Now, then, Mr. Maybrick, imagine that you are standing at the top of a very long staircase which descends into darkness. With each downward step you take, your body grows heavier and more relaxed, your mind drifts freely. Step down, Mr. Maybrick, one step at a time, into the safe and comfortable darkness, warm and cozy as a mother's embrace . . ."

By the end of twenty-five steps, Mr. James Maybrick, Esquire, was in deep trance, having been neatly drugged into a state of not-quite oblivion.

"Can you hear my voice, Mr. Maybrick?"

"Yes."

"Very good. You've been ill, Mr. Maybrick?"

"Yes. Very ill. So many different symptoms, I can't tell what is wrong."

Nothing new, there. "Well, then, Mr. Maybrick, what is it that is troubling you the most, just now?"

It was an innocent question, completely in keeping with a patient suffering from numerous physical complaints. All he was really interested in was narrowing down which symptom troubled the fool the most, so he could place post-hypnotic suggestions in the man's drugged mind to reduce the apparent levels of that symptom, something he had done successfully with a score of other patients suffering more from hysteria and nervousness than real illnesses. He had been following the work of that fellow in Vienna, Dr. Freud, with considerable interest, and had begun a few experiments of his own—

"It's the bitch!"

John Lachley nearly fell backward out of his chair.

Maybrick, his drugged face twisting into a mask of rage, snarled it out. *"She* troubles me! The goddamned *bitch,* she troubles me more than anything in the world! Faithless whore! Her and her whoremaster! I'll kill them both, I swear to God, the way I killed that filthy little prostitute in Manchester! Squeezed the life out of her with my own hands, thinking of that bitch the whole time! Wasn't pleasurable, though, damn her eyes, I wanted it to be pleasurable! I'll squeeze the life out of that bitch, I swear I will, I'll cut her wide open with a knife, god*damn* Brierly, fucking my own wife . . ."

Stunned, open-mouthed silence gripped John Lachley for long moments as he stared at the raving cotton merchant, for once completely at a loss as to how he ought to proceed. He'd never stumbled across anything even remotely like this homicidal fury. What had he said? ... *killed that filthy little prostitute in Manchester ... squeezed the life out of her with my own hands ...* Lachley gripped the upholstered arms of his chair. *Dear God! Should I contact the constabulary? This madman's murdered someone!* He started to speak, not even sure what he was going to say, when a frantic knocking rattled the front door, which was situated just outside the closed parlour. John Lachley started violently and slewed around in his chair. In the hallway just outside, his manservant answered the urgent summons.

"Your Highness! Come in, please! Whatever is wrong, sir?"

"I must see the doctor at once, Charles!"

Prince Albert Victor ... In a high state of panic, too, from the sound of it.

John Lachley glared furiously at the ranting cotton merchant on the daybed, who lay there muttering about ripping his wife open with a knife for sleeping with some arsehole named Brierly, about keeping a diary some servant had almost discovered, nearly ending in a second murder, and something about a room he'd rented in Middlesex Street, Whitechapel, so he could kill more filthy whores, and hated James Maybrick with such an intense loathing, he had to clench his fists to keep from shooting him on the spot. The crisis of his career was brewing outside and this homicidal maniac had to be dealt with first!

Outside, Charles was saying, "Dr. Lachley is with a patient, Your Highness, but I will certainly let him know you're here, immediately, sir."

Lachley bent over Maybrick, gripped the man's shoulders hard enough to bruise, hissed urgently, "Mr.

Maybrick! I want you to be quiet now! *Stop talking at once!*"

The drugged merchant fell silent, instantly obedient.

Thank God . . .

Lachley schooled his features and stilled his hands, which were slightly unsteady, then crossed the parlour in two hurried strides, just as Charles knocked at the door.

"Yes, Charles? I heard His Highness arrive. Ah, Your Highness," he strode forward, offering his hand to the visibly distraught grandson of Queen Victoria, "welcome back to Tibor. You know my house is always open to you, whatever the time of day. Please, won't you come back to the study?"

Charles bowed and faded into the back of the house, his duty having been discharged. Prince Albert Victor Christian Edward was a tall, good-looking young man with an impressive dark moustache, a neck so long and thin he had to wear exaggeratedly high collars to disguise the deformity, and the dullest eyes John Lachley had ever seen in a human face. He was twisting expensive grey kidskin gloves into shreds. He followed Lachley down the corridor into the study with jerky, nervous strides. John closed the door carefully, guided his star client to a chair, and poured him a stiff shot of brandy straight away. Albert Victor, known as Eddy to his most intimate friends—and John Lachley was by far the most intimate of Eddy's current friends—gulped it down in one desperate swallow, then blurted out his reason for arriving in such a state.

"I'm ruined, John! Ruined . . . dear God . . . you must help me, tell me what to do . . ." Eddy gripped Lachley's hands in desperation and panic. "I am undone! He can't be allowed to do this, you know what will become of me! Someone must stop him! If my grandmother should find out—dear Lord, she can't ever find out, it would destroy her good name, bring such shame on the whole family . . . my God, the whole government might go, you know what the situation is, John, you've told me yourself about it, the Fenians, the labor riots, what am I to *do?* Threats—*threats!*—demands for money or else ruination! Oh, God, I am destroyed, should word leak of it . . . Disgrace, *prison* . . . he's gone beyond his station in life! Beyond the bounds of civilized law, beyond the protection of God, may the Devil take him!"

"Your Highness, calm yourself, please." He pulled his hands free of Eddy's grip and poured a second, far more generous brandy, getting it down the distraught prince's throat. He stroked Eddy's absurdly long neck, massaging the tension away, calmed him to the point where he could speak coherently. "Now, then, Eddy. Tell me very slowly just exactly what has happened."

Eddy began in a shaken whisper, "You remember Morgan?"

Lachley frowned. He certainly did. Morgan was a little Welsh nancy boy from Cardiff, the star attraction of a certain high-class West End brothel right here on Cleveland Street, a boulevard as infamous for its homosexual establishments as it was famous for its talented artists, painters, and art galleries. Hard on the heels of learning that his ticket to fame and fortune and considerable political power was banging a fifteen-year-old male whore on Cleveland Street, he had drugged Eddy into a state of extreme suggestibility and sternly suggested that he break off the relationship immediately.

"What about Morgan?" Lachley asked quietly.

"I . . . I was indiscreet, John, I'm sorry, it's only that he was so . . . so damned beautiful, I was besotted with him . . ."

"Eddy," Lachley interrupted gently, "how, exactly, were you indiscreet? Did you see him again?"

"Oh, no, John, no, I wouldn't do that, I haven't been with him since you told me to stop seeing him. Only women, John, and you . . ."

"Then what did you do, Eddy, that was indiscreet?"

"The letters," he whispered.

A cold chill slithered down John Lachley's back. "*Letters?* What letters?"

"I . . . I used to write him letters. Just silly little love letters, he was so pretty and he always pouted so when I had to leave him . . ."

Lachley closed his eyes. *Eddy, you stupid little bastard!*

"*How many letters, Eddy?*" The whiplash of his voice struck Eddy visibly.

"Don't hate me, John!" The prince's face twisted into a mask of terror and grief.

It took several minutes and a fair number of intimate caresses to convince the terrified prince that Lachley did not, in fact, hate him. When he had calmed Albert Victor down again, he repeated his question, more patiently this time. "How many letters, Eddy?"

"Eight, I think."

"You think? You must be certain, Eddy. It's very important."

Eddy's brow creased. "Eight, it must be eight, John, I saw him eight weeks in a row, you see, and I sent him a letter each week, then I met you and didn't need to see him any longer. Yes, it's eight letters."

"Very good, Eddy. Now, tell me what's happened to upset you so deeply about these eight letters."

"He wants money for them! A great deal of money! Thousands of pounds, John, or he'll send the letters to the newspapers, to the Scotland Yard inspectors who arrest men for crimes of sodomy! John, I am ruined!" Eddy covered his eyes with his hands, hiding from him. "If I don't pay him everything he wants . . ."

"Yes, yes, Eddy, he'll make the letters public and

you will go to prison. I understand that part of the situation, Eddy, very thoroughly, indeed. Now then, how has he demanded payment? Where is the money to be delivered and who is to take it there?"

"You know I enjoy little jaunts in to the East End, occasionally, dressed as a commoner? So no one suspects my identity?"

Lachley refrained from making a tart rejoinder that Eddy was the only person in London fooled by those pitiful disguises. "Yes, what about your little trips?"

"I'm to take the money to him there, tomorrow night, alone. We're to meet at Petticoat Lane and Whitechapel Road, at midnight. And I must be there! I must! If I don't go, with a thousand pounds, he'll send the first letter to the newspapers! Do you realize what those newspapermen—*what my Grandmother*—will do to me?" He hid his face in his hands again. "And if I don't pay him another thousand pounds a week later, the second letter will go to the police! His note said I must reply with a note to him today, I'm to send it to some wretched public house where he'll call for it, to reassure him I mean to pay or he will post the first letter tomorrow."

"And when you pay him, Eddy, will he give you back the letters?"

The ashen prince nodded, his thin, too-long neck bobbing like a bird's behind the high collars he wore as disguise for the slight deformity, which had earned Eddy the nickname Collars and Cuffs. "Yes," he whispered, moustache quivering with his distress, "he said he would bring the first letter tomorrow night if he receives my note today, will exchange it for the money. Please, John, you must advise me what to do, how to stop him! *Someone must make him pay for this!*"

It took several additional minutes to bring Eddy back to some semblance of rationality again. "Calm yourself, Eddy, really, there is no need for such hysteria. Consider the matter taken care of. Send the note to him as instructed. Morgan will be satisfied that you'll meet him tomorrow with your initial payment. Lull him into thinking he's won. Before he can collect so much as a shilling of his blood money, the problem will no longer exist."

Prince Albert Victor leaned forward and gripped John's hands tightly, fear lending his shaking fingers strength. Reddened eyes had gone wide. "What do you mean to do?" he whispered.

"You know the energies I am capable of wielding, the powers I command."

The distraught prince was nodding. John Lachley was more than Eddy's lover, he was the young man's advisor on many a spiritual matter. Eddy relied heavily upon Dr. John Lachley, Physician and Occultist, touted as the most famous scholar of antiquities and occult mysteries ever to come up out of SoHo. And while most of his public performances—whether as Johnny Anubis, Whitechapel parlour medium or, subsequent to earning his medical degree, as Dr. John Lachley—were as fake as the infamous seances given by his greatest rival, Madame Blavatsky, not everything Dr. John Lachley did was trickery.

Oh, no, not by any means everything.

"Mesmerism, you must understand," he told Prince Albert Victor gently, patting Eddy's hands, "has been used quite successfully by reputable surgeons to amputate a man's leg, without any need for anesthesia. And the French are working the most wondrous marvels of persuasion one could imagine, making grown men crow like chickens and persuading ladies they have said and done things they have never said or done in their lives."

And in the parlour down the hall from this study, a homicidal Liverpudlian cotton merchant had just been spilling his darkest secrets under Lachley's considerable influence.

"Oh, yes, Eddy," he smiled, "the powers of mesmerism are quite remarkable. And I am, without modesty, quite an accomplished mesmerist. Don't trouble yourself further about that miserable little sod, Morgan. Contact him, by all means, promise to pay the little bastard whatever he wants. Promise him the world, promise him the keys to your grandmother's palace, for God's sake, just so long as we keep him happy until I can act. We'll find your letters, Eddy, and we'll get back your letters, and I promise you faithfully, before tomorrow night ends, there will be no more threat."

His oh-so-gullible, most important client gulped, dull eyes slightly brighter, daring to hope. "You'll save me, then? John, promise me, you will save me from prison?"

"Of course I will, Eddy," he smiled, bending down to plant a kiss on the prince's trembling lips. "Trouble yourself no more, Eddy. Just leave it in my capable hands."

Albert Victor was nodding, childlike, trusting. "Yes, yes of course I shall. Forgive me, I should have realized all was not lost. You have advised me so admirably in the past . . ."

Lachley patted Eddy's hands again. "And I shall continue to do so in future. Now then . . ." He walked to his desk, from which he retrieved a vial of the same medication he had given James Maybrick. Many of his patients preferred to consult with him in a more masculine and private setting such as his study, rather than the more public and softly decorated parlour, so he kept a supply of his potent little mixture in both locations. "I want you to take a draught of medicine before you leave, Eddy. You're in a shocking state, people will gossip." He splashed wine into a deep tumbler from a cut-crystal, antique Waterford decanter, stirred in a substantial amount of the powder, and handed the glassful of oblivion to Eddy. "Sip this. It will help calm your frayed nerves."

And leave you wonderfully suggestible, my sweet and foolish prince, for you must never recall this conversation or Morgan or those thrice-damned letters ever again. Eddy was just sufficiently stupid, he could well blurt out the entire thing some night after a drinking spree in the East End. He smiled as Eddy swallowed the drugged wine. Lachley's one-time public persona, Johnny Anubis, might have been little more than a parlour trickster who'd earned ready cash with the mumbo-jumbo his clients had expected—indeed, demanded. Just as his new clients did, of course.

But Dr. John Lachley . . .

Dr. Lachley was a most accomplished mesmerist. Oh, indeed he was.

He would have to do something about that drugged cotton merchant down the hall, of course. It wouldn't do to leave a homicidal maniac running about who could be associated with him, however innocently; but the man had mentioned an incriminating diary, so Lachley might well be able to rid himself of that problem fairly easily. A man could be hanged even for murdering a whore, if he were foolish enough to leave proof of the crime lying about. And James Maybrick was certainly a fool. John Lachley had no intention of being even half so careless when he rid the world of Eddy's blackmailing little Morgan.

His smile deepened as Prince Albert Victor Christian Edward leaned back in his chair, eyes closing as the drug that would leave him clay in Lachley's hands took hold, allowing him to erase all memory of that frightened, desperate plea:

Make him pay . . . !

Oh, yes. He would most assuredly make young Morgan pay.

No one threatened John Lachley's future and lived to tell the tale.

✧   ✧   ✧

Senator John Paul Caddrick was a man accustomed to power. When he gave an order, whether to a senatorial aide or to one of the many faceless, nameless denizens of the world he'd once inhabited, he expected that order to be executed with flawless efficiency. Incompetence, he simply did not tolerate. So, when word that the hit he'd helped engineer at New York's exclusive Luigi's restaurant had failed to accomplish its primary objective, John Paul Caddrick backhanded the messenger hard enough to break cartilage in his nose.

"*Imbecile!* What the hell do you mean, letting that little bastard Armstrong get away? And worse, with my *daughter!* Do you have any idea what Armstrong and that vindictive little bitch will do if they manage to get that evidence to the FBI? My God, it was bad enough, watching Cassie turn my own daughter into a crusading, stage-struck fool! And now you've let her escape with enough evidence to electrocute the lot of us?"

The unfortunate lackey chosen to carry the bad news clutched at his nose. It bubbled unpleasantly as he whimpered, "I'm sorry, Senator, we sent six men to your daughter's apartment, *ten* into that restaurant! Who'd have figured Armstrong was such a slippery snake? Or that your kid would leave the table just before the hit went down?"

John Caddrick vented his rage with another backhand blow, then paced the dingy little hotel room, muttering curses under his breath and trying to figure out what that little bastard Armstrong would do next. High-tail it to the FBI? Maybe. But with Jenna Nicole in tow? Armstrong was good at disguises—as John Caddrick had discovered, much to his chagrin—but Jenna was instantly recognizable. If they tried to go anywhere near the New York FBI offices, the men he and Gideon Guthrie had hired would nail them. The trouble was, Armstrong was bound to realize that. No, that meddlesome bastard would attempt getting them both out of the city. But how? And where would the detective go? Armstrong was more than smart enough to know they'd be watching the bus stations, the airports, the car rental agencies, the ferry launches, anything and everything that offered a way out of the city.

Caddrick swore explosively again. Dammit! After everything he'd worked to achieve, with the timetable counting down to the final few days, along comes that goddamned, nosy bastard *Armstrong*. . . . He paused in his pacing. Armstrong knew that timetable, knew enough of it, anyway, to calculate their next major move. And the rat-assed little detective was a Templar, too, same as the senator's worthless daughter and now-deceased sister-in-law. If Armstrong and Jenna Nicole didn't try to rescue the next target slated to die, John Caddrick didn't know Templars.

"They'll go to TT-86," Caddrick muttered under his breath. "Get your butt onto that station with a hand-picked team. I want Armstrong dead."

"And your daughter?" the lackey quavered.

John Paul Caddrick shut his eyes, hating Cassie Tyrol for turning his daughter against him, for bringing her into this mess, for showing her the evidence. . . . And John Caddrick's employers would demand blood. At this stage, security leaks had to be plugged. Fast. Regardless of whose family got in the way. So he snarled out, "I won't by God let *anybody* screw this up. Not as close as we've come!"

Speaking through a handful of blood, the messenger asked, "Same M.O. as Luigi's?"

"Hell, yes!" He ran a distracted hand through his hair. "We've already got *Ansar Majlis* on station, thank God. Infiltrated 'em into that construction crew weeks ago. The second your team sets foot on that station, I want them activated. Major blowup. Whatever it takes to make it look good."

"Yes, sir."

"Well, don't just stand there, goddammit! Move!"
The lackey scrambled for the door.

John Caddrick yanked open the hotel room's wet
bar and upended an entire, miniature bottle of scotch,
then hurled the empty against the wall. The thing
didn't even have the decency to shatter. It just
bounced off. His ragged temper left a considerable
hole in the drywall above the television set, along with
a broken lamp and three overturned chairs. *Damn*
that meddling detective! And God damn that brainless bitch, Cassie Tyrol! His only child . . . who'd never
quite forgiven him for all the missed birthday parties and recitals and graduation ceremonies, stranded
on the campaign trail or conducting Congressional
business . . .

But there wasn't a stinking, solitary thing he could
do to save his little girl. And once Jenna knew the
truth, Caddrick's ungrateful wretch of a daughter would
do whatever it took to see her own father behind bars.
If he wanted to keep his butt out of the electric chair,
he'd better make damned sure she died. And before
this business was done, Noah Armstrong would bitterly
regret having ever interfered in Caddrick's business.
The senator ripped out another savage oath, then
stalked out of the hotel.

Cassie had finally been paid in full for the trouble
she'd caused.

All that remained now was to finish the job.

Chapter Two

Of all the souls wandering the Commons of Time Terminal Eighty-Six, none felt as out of place Skeeter Jackson. He wasn't lost, which was more than he could say of three-quarters of the people around him. But his status was so changed, he couldn't help but reflect wryly on how odd it was to be trundling a heavy cart stencilled "Station Maintenance" through Edo Castletown, past crowds of kimono-clad tourists jostling elbows with Victorian gents and bustled ladies and a few forlorn, middle-aged men with paunches, bald knees, and Roman tunics.

Confidence man to bathroom-cleaning man wasn't quite the transition Skeeter had hoped for, when he'd decided to give up his life of petty crime. There wasn't much glamor in a cart full of mops, detergent bottles, and vending-machine supplies. On the other hand, he did *not* miss having to dodge station security every ten minutes, or sweating bullets every time some chance acquaintance glanced his way. And while he didn't eat high on anybody's hog, at least he didn't regularly miss

39

meals, any more, thanks to the uncertainty of a pickpocket's income.

Skeeter was very glad he'd switched careers. But he wasn't quite used to it yet.

A wry smile tugged at the corners of his mouth. As confused as *he* sometimes felt, the other up-time residents were goggle-eyed with shock to find La-La Land's most notorious confidence artist walking the straight and narrow, working the first honest job of his life. It had only taken an act of God and Ianira Cassondra to get him that job. But he couldn't have continued in his old career, not after the pain his greed and stupidity had caused the only friends he possessed in the world. He frequently marveled that he still possessed any friends at all. Never mind ones close enough to help him start his life over again. After what Skeeter had done, he wouldn't have blamed Marcus and Ianira if they'd never spoken to him again. Whatever their reasons, he wouldn't let them down.

As Skeeter maneuvered his cart through the bustling hoards of eminently lost humanity trying to find their way back to hotels, to restaurants that were impossible to find in the station's sprawling maze, or simply standing still and screaming for junior at the top of panic-stricken lungs, the public address system came to life from speakers five stories overhead. "Your attention, please. Gate One is due to open in three minutes. All departures, be advised that if you have not cleared Station Medical, you will not be permitted to pass Primary. Please have your baggage ready for customs inspection by agents of the Bureau of Access Time Functions, who will assess your taxes due on downtime acquisitions . . ."

A familiar voice, the sound of friendship in the middle of all the chaos, sounded at his ear. "Double gate day, yes?"

Startled, Skeeter turned to find Ianira Cassondra smiling up at him.

"Ianira! What are you doing up here in Edo
Castletown?" The lovely *cassondra* of ancient Ephesus
could usually be found at her kiosk down in Little
Agora, surrounded by her adoring up-time acolytes.
Ianira's self-proclaimed worshipers flocked to TT-86
by the thousands each year, on pilgrimage to honor
the woman they considered the Goddess incarnate on
earth.

Ianira, blithely ignoring the adoring worshippers
who trailed her like pilot fish in the wake of an
ancient schooner, swept long strands of glossy, raven's-
wing hair back from her forehead. "I have been to
visit Kit Carson, at the Neo Edo. The Council of
Seven asked him to participate in the Festival of Mars
next week."

Kit Carson, the planet's most famous and successful
individual ever to enter the business of scouting the
gates through time, had retired to TT-86. Having
pushed most of the famous tour gates now operating through the terminal, Kit Carson was one of the
station's major tourist draws, in his own right, despite
his status as essentially a recluse who had vowed never
to return to that up-time world again. Skeeter, however, steered clear of Kit whenever possible, on
general principle. He tended to avoid the older male
relatives of any girl he'd tried to finagle into bed with
him. Kit, he avoided even more cautiously than others.
Kit Carson could seriously cripple a man, just looking crosswise at him. The day Kit had hunted him
down and read him the riot act about staying away
from Kit's granddaughter, Skeeter would've welcomed
a double-gate day. He'd have crawled through an
unstable gate, if one had been available, by the time
Kit had finished with him.

Skeeter smiled ruefully. "Double gate day, is right.
And I've got this funny feeling we'll be neck deep
in lunatics before the day's over. First Primary, then
Britannia, and tomorrow, *another* double gate day."

"Yes," Ianira nodded. "The Wild West Gate opens tomorrow."

"And that new tour gate they're ripping half the station apart over, adding to the Commons."

"At least, there won't be any tourists coming through for it, yet," Ianira smiled.

"No. For now, it's the Britannia tours, packing in the loons. In record numbers." He shook his head. "Between your acolytes and all those crazies coming in for the Ripper Season, this place is turning into the biggest nuthouse ever built under one roof. And those Scheherazade Gate construction workers . . . eergh!" He gave a mock shudder. "What slimy boulder did they turn over, hiring that bunch of thugs?"

As Ianira fell into step alongside Skeeter's push cart, she glanced up with a reproachful glint in her eyes. "You must not be so irritated by the construction workers, Skeeter. Most of them are very good men. And surely you, of all up-timers on station, must understand their beliefs and customs are different? As a down-timer, I understand this very well."

"Oh, I understand, all right. But some of the guys on the Scheherazade Gate crew are throwbacks to the dark ages. Or maybe the Stone Ages. Honestly, Ianira, everybody on station's had trouble with some of them."

She sighed. "Yes, I know. We do have a problem, Skeeter. The Council of Seven has met about them, already. But you, Skeeter," she changed the subject as they navigated a goldfish pond with its ornate bridge and carefully manicured shrubbery, "you are ready for the Britannia? There are only seven hours left. Your case is packed? And you will not be late?"

Skeeter let go the heavy handle of his push cart with one hand and rubbed the back of his neck in embarrassment. "Yes, I'm packed and ready. I still can't believe you pulled off something like that." About seven hours from now, the first official Ripper Watch tour of the season was scheduled to arrive in

London, on the very evening of the first murder officially attributed to Jack the Ripper. And thanks to Ianira, Skeeter would spend the next eight days in London, courtesy of Time Tours, working the gate as a baggage porter. Hauling suitcases wasn't the world's greatest job either; but carrying rich tourists' luggage beat hell out of scrubbing La-La Land's bathrooms for a living. He'd been doing that for weeks, now. And Ripper Watch Tour tickets were selling for five-digit figures on the black market, when they could be found at all. Every one of the Ripper tours had been sold out for over a year.

Skeeter rubbed his nose and smiled wryly. "Time Tours baggage porter. Who'd've believed that, huh? They never would've trusted me, if you hadn't offered to replace anything that went missing on my watch."

"They will learn," she said firmly, giving him a much-needed boost of confidence. Ianira rested a hand on his arm. "You will do well, Skeeter. But will you try to go with the scholars? To see who is this terrible man, the Ripper?"

Skeeter shook his head. "No way. The videotapes will be bad enough."

"Yes," Ianira said quietly. "I do not wish to see any of them."

"Huh. Better avoid Victoria Station, then," Skeeter muttered as he bumped his cart across the division between Edo Castletown and Victoria Station, the portion of Commons which served the Britannia Gate. Bottles of cleaning solution rattled and boxes of toilet paper rolls, feminine supplies, and condoms (latex, spray-on, and natural for those going to appropriate down-time destinations) bounced and jiggled as he shoved the cart across the cobblestones. Mop handles sticking out the top like pungee stakes threatened tourists too slow to dodge—and on every side, pure-bred lunatics threatened everything in sight, including Skeeter and his awkward cart.

"God help us," Skeeter muttered, "Ripper Watch Season is really in full swing."

Ripperoons had come crawling out of the woodwork like swarming termites. So had the crazies preying on them. Saviors of the Gates, convinced the Savior would appear through one of the temporal gates . . . the Shifters, who drifted from station to station seeking Eternal Truth from the manifestations of unstable gates . . . Hell's Minions, whose up-time leader had convinced his disciples to carry out Satan's work with as many unsuspecting tourists and downtimers as possible . . . and, of course, the Ripper Cults.

Those were visible everywhere, holding hand-scrawled signs, peddling cheap literature and ratty flowers, hawking cheap trinkets in the shape of bloody knives. Most of them carried as sacred talismans the authentic surgical knives Goldie Morran was selling out of her shop, and all of them were talking incessantly in a roar of excited conversation about the one topic on *everyone's* mind.

"Do you suppose they'll catch him?"

"—listen, my brothers, I tell you, Jack is Lord, traveling to this world from another dimension to show us the error of our sins! Repent and join with Jack to condemn evil, for He cannot die and He knows the lust in your hearts—"

"No, how can they catch him, no one in 1888 ever discovered who he was."

"—I don't care if you *do* have a ticket for the Britannia, you can't take that surgical knife with you, it's against BATF rules—"

"—let the Sons of Jack show you the way to salvation! Condemn all whores and loose women! A whore is the downfall of righteousness, the destruction of civilization. Follow the example of Jack and rid our great society of the stain of all sexual activity—"

"Yes, but they're putting video cameras at all the

murder sites, so maybe *we'll* find out who he was, at least!"

"—somebody ought to confiscate all those goddamned knives Goldie's selling, before these loons start cutting one another up like Christmas turkeys—"

"—a donation, please, for Brother Jack! He will come to Shangri-La to lead us into the paths of truth. Support his good works with your spare change—"

"A hundred bucks says it's that crazy cotton merchant from Liverpool, what's-his-name, Maybrick."

"Go back up time, you sick lunatics! What kind of idiots are you? Jack the Ripper, an alien from another planet—?"

"Hah! Shows what you know! A hundred-fifty says it was the Queen's personal physician, Sir William Gull, hushing up the scandal over Victoria's grandson and his secret marriage, you know, the Catholic wife and daughter!"

"—you want me to *what*? I'm not following Brother Jack or anybody else in a crusade against evil. My God, mister, I'm an *actress!* Are you trying to put me out of work?"

"—help us, please, Save Our Sisters! S.O.S. is determined to rescue the Ripper's victims before he can strike, they're so unimportant, surely we can change history just this once—"

"Oh, don't tell me you bought that Royal Conspiracy garbage? There's absolutely no evidence to support that cockamamie story! I tell you, it's James Maybrick, the arsenic addict who hated his unfaithful American wife!"

"—all right, dump that garbage into the trash bin, nobody wants to read your pamphlets, anyway, and station maintenance is tired of sweeping them up. We've got parents complaining about the language in your brochures, left lying around where any school kid can find them—"

"No, you're both wrong, it's the gay lover of the Duke of Clarence, the queen's grandson, the tutor with the head injury who went crazy!"

Skeeter shook his head. La-La Land, gone *totally* insane. Everyone was trying to outguess and out-bet one another as to who the real Ripper would turn out to be. Speculation was flying wild, from genuine Scotland Yard detectives to school kids to TT-86's shop owners, restauranteurs, and resident call girls. Scholars had been pouring into the station for weeks, heading down time to cover the biggest murder mystery of the last couple of centuries. The final members of the official Ripper Watch team had assembled three days ago, when Primary had last cycled, bringing in a couple of dandified reporters who'd refused to go down time any sooner than absolutely necessary and a criminal sociologist who'd just come back from another down-time research trip. They'd arrived barely in time to make the first Ripper murder in London. And today, of course, the first hoard of tourists permitted tickets for the Ripper Season tours would be arriving, cheeks flushed, bankrolls clutched in avaricious hands, panting to be in at the kill and ready to descend on the station's outfitters to buy everything they'd need for eight days in London of 1888.

"Who do you think it is?" Ianira asked, having to shout over the roar.

Skeeter snorted. "It's probably some schmuck nobody's ever heard of before. A sick puppy who just snapped one day and decided to kill a bunch of penniless prostitutes. Jack the Ripper wasn't the only madman who ripped up women with a knife, after all. The way those Ripperologists have been talking, there were hundreds of so-called 'rippers' during the 1880s and 1890s. Jack was just better with his PR, sending those horrible letters to the press."

Ianira shuddered, echoing Skeeter's own feelings on the subject.

If Skeeter had still been a betting man, he might have laid a few wagers, himself. But Skeeter Jackson had learned a very harsh lesson about making wagers. He'd very nearly lost his home, his life, and his only friends, thanks to that last ill-considered, ruinous wager he'd made with Goldie Morran. He'd finally realized, very nearly too late, that his life of petty crime hurt a lot more people than just the rich, obnoxious tourists he'd made a living ripping off. For Skeeter, at any rate, ripping time was over. For good.

Unfortunately, for the rest of La-La Land, it was just getting started.

As though on cue, the station's PA system crackled to life as Primary cycled open. The station announcer blared out instructions for the newly arriving tourists—and at Skeeter's side, Ianira Cassondra faltered. Her eyes glazed in sudden pain and a violent tremble struck her, so hard she stumbled against him and nearly fell.

"Ianira!" He caught and held her up, horrified by the tremors ripping through her. All color had drained from her face. Ianira squeezed shut her eyes for a long, terrifying moment. Then whatever was wrong passed. She sagged against him.

"Forgive me . . ." Her voice came out whispery, weak.

He held her up as carefully as he would've held a priceless Ming vase. "What's wrong, Ianira, what happened?"

"A vision," she choked out. "A warning. Such power . . . I have never Seen with such power, never have I felt such fear . . . something terrible is to happen . . . is happening now, I think . . ."

Skeeter's blood ran cold. He didn't pretend to understand everything this seemingly fragile woman he braced so carefully was capable of. Trained in the ancient arts of the Temple of Ephesus as a child, some twenty-five hundred years before Skeeter's birth,

Ianira occasionally said and did things that raised the
hair on the back of Skeeter's neck. Ianira's acolytes,
who followed her everywhere, pressed closer, exclaiming in worry. Those farther back, unable to see clearly,
demanded to know what was wrong.

"Dammit, get back!" Skeeter turned on the whole
lot of them. "Can't you see she needs air?"

Shocked faces gawped at him like so many fish,
but they backed away a few paces. Ianira sagged
against him, trembling violently. He guided her
toward a bench, but she shook her head. "No,
Skeeter. I am fine, now." To prove it, she straightened and took a step under her own power, wob-
bly, but determined.

Worried acolytes formed a corridor for her. Skeeter
glared silently at them, guiding her by the elbow,
determined not to allow her to fall. Speaking as
quietly as possible, in the probably vain hope their
vid-cams and tape recorders wouldn't pick up the
question, he murmured, "What kind of vision was it,
Ianira?"

She shivered again. "A warning," she whispered.
"A warning of dark anger. The darkest I have ever
touched. Violence, terrible fear . . ."

"Sounds like everyday life, up time." He tried to
make light of it, hoping to make her smile.

Ianira, the gifted Cassondra of Ephesus, did not
smile. She shuddered. Then choked out, "It is from
up time the danger comes."

He stared down at her. Then a prickle ran up his
back. It occurred to him that Primary had just cycled.
Skeeter narrowed his eyes, gazing off toward the end
of Commons where Primary precinct would be filled
with tourists shoving their way into the station. *Screw
the bathroom floors. I'm not letting her out of my
sight.*

They reached the junction between five of the
terminal's major zones, a no-man's land where the

corners of Urbs Romae and Victoria Station ran into
El Dorado, Little Agora, and Valhalla, not too far from
the new construction site where the Arabian Nights
sector was going up. It was there in that no-man's
land, with Ianira's acolytes making it impossible to
see for any distance, that Skeeter heard the first
rumbles. An angry swell of voices heralded the
approach of trouble. Skeeter glanced swiftly around,
trying to pin down the source. It sounded like it was
coming from two directions at once—and was apparently triangulating straight toward them.

"Ianira . . ."

Four things occurred simultaneously.

Tourists screamed and broke into a dead run. A full-
blown riot engulfed them, led by enraged construction workers shouting in Arabic. A wild-eyed young kid
burst through the crowd and yelled something that
sounded like, *"No! Aahh!"*—then pointed an enormous
black-powder pistol right at Skeeter and Ianira. Gunfire
erupted just as someone else lunged out of the crowd
and swept Ianira sideways in a flying tackle. The blow
slammed her against Skeeter, knocked them both sideways. They crashed to the floor. The maintenance cart
toppled, spilling ammonia bottles, mop handles, and
toilet paper rolls underfoot. Screams and alarm klaxons
deafened him. Skeeter rolled awkwardly under running feet and came to his hands and knees, searching wildly for Ianira. He couldn't see her anywhere.
Couldn't see anything but fleeing tourists and spilled
cleaning supplies and embattled construction workers.
They were locked in hand-to-hand combat with Ianira's
howling acolytes.

"Ianira!"

He gained his feet, was rocked sideways by a body
blow as a cursing construction worker smashed into
him. They both went down. Skeeter's skull connected
with El Dorado's gold-tinted paving stones. He saw
stars, cursed furiously. Before he could roll to his hands

and knees again, security killed the station lights. The entire Commons plunged into utter blackness. Shrieking riot faded to an uncertain roar. Somebody stumbled over Skeeter in the darkness, tripped and went down, even as Skeeter clawed his way back to his feet.

"Ianira!"

He strained for any sound of her voice, heard nothing but the sobs and cries of frantic tourists, maddened acolytes, and screaming, erstwhile combatants. Somebody ran past him, with such purpose and certainty it could only be security. They must be using that night-vision equipment Mike Benson had ordered before the start of Ripper Season. The riot helmets had their own infrared light-sources built in, for just this kind of station emergency. Then the lights came up and Skeeter discovered himself hemmed in by a solid wall of security officers, armed with night sticks and handcuffs. They waded in, cuffing more rioters, breaking up combatants with scant regard for who was attempting to throttle whom. "Break it up! Move it—"

Skeeter peered wildly through the crowd, recognized the nearest officer. "Wally! Have you seen Ianira Cassondra?"

Wally Klontz stared at him, visibly startled. "What?"

"Ianira! Some crazy kid shot at us! Then somebody else knocked us both down and now she's missing!"

"Oh, Jeezus H., that's *all* we need! Somebody taking pot-shots at the most important religious figure of the twenty-first century!" A brief query over Wally's squawky produced a flat negative. Nobody from security had seen her, anywhere.

Skeeter let loose a torrent of fluent Mongolian curses that would've impressed even Yesukai the Valiant. Wally Klontz frowned and spoke into the squawky again. "Station alert, Signal Eight-Delta, repeat, Signal Eight-Delta, missing person, Ianira Cassondra. Expedite, condition red."

The squawky crackled. "Oh, shit! Ten-four, that's a Signal Eight-Delta, Ianira Cassondra. Condition red. Expediting."

More sirens hooted insanely overhead, a shrieking rhythm that drove Skeeter's pulse rate into the stratosphere and left his head aching. But the pain in his head was nothing to the agony in his heart. Wally let him pass the security cordon around the riot zone, then he fought his way clear of the riot's fringe, searching frantically for a flash of white Ephesian gown, the familiar gloss of her dark hair. But he couldn't find her, not even a trace. Skeeter bit his lip, shaking and sick. He had allowed the unthinkable to happen. *Someone* wanted Ianira Cassondra dead. And whoever that someone was, they had snatched her right out of his grasp, in the middle of a *riot.* If they killed Ianira . . .

They wouldn't get out of Shangri-La Station alive.

No one attacked the family of a Yakka Mongol and lived to boast of it.

Skeeter Jackson, adopted by the Khan of all the Yakka Mongols, a displaced up-time kid who had been declared their living *bogda,* spirit of the upper air in human form, the child named honorary uncle to an infant who one day would terrorize the world as Genghis Khan, had just declared blood feud.

Margo Smith glanced at her wristwatch for the tenth time in three minutes, fizzing like a can of soda shaken violently and popped open. Less than seven hours! Just seven more hours and she would step through the Britannia Gate into history. And, coincidentally, into her fiancé's arms. She could hardly wait to see Malcolm Moore's face when she showed up at the Time Tours gatehouse in London, guiding the final contingent of the Ripper Watch Team. Malcolm had been in London for a month, already, acclimating the other Ripper Watch Team members.

Margo hadn't lived through four longer, lonelier weeks since that gawdawful misadventure of hers in southern Africa, going after Goldie Morran's ill-fated diamonds.

But she'd learned her lessons—dozens of them, in fact—and after months of the hardest work she'd ever tackled, her gruelling efforts had finally paid off. Her grandfather was letting her go back down time again. And not through just any old gate, either. The Britannia! To study the most famous murder mystery since the disappearance of the Dauphin during the French Revolution. All that stood between her and the chance to earn herself a place in scholarly history—not to mention Malcolm Moore's embrace— was seven hours and one shooting lesson.

One she dreaded.

The elite crowd gathered in the time terminal's weapons range talked nonstop in a fashion unique to an assemblage of late-arriving wealthy tourists, world-class scholars, and self-important reporters—each hotly defending his or her own pet theories as to "who-dunnit." They ignored her utterly, even when she stuffed earmuffs and lexan-lensed safety glasses into their gesticulating, waving hands. Most of the students stationed along the firing line were tourists holding ordinary tickets, many of them for the Wild West tour set to leave tomorrow.

The Denver-bound tourists, headed for some sort of action cowboy shoot down time, cast envious glances at the lucky ones who'd managed to beg, borrow, buy, or steal Ripper Watch tickets. *Those* were Margo's new charges, although they didn't know it yet. The mere tourists heading for London, Margo ignored. Her attention was focused on the three individuals with whom she would be spending the next three solid months, as their time guide.

Dominica Nosette, whose name, face, and body seemed quintessentially *French,* yet who was as staidly British as kippers and jellied eels, was chattering away with her partner Guy Pendergast. And Shahdi Feroz . . . Margo gulped, just approaching Dr. Feroz where she stood locked in conversation with a Ripper Watch tourist at the next lane over. Dr. Feroz had spent the past four months studying the rise of cults and cult violence in Imperial Rome, through the Porta Romae. At previous training classes like this one, Margo had met all the other team members now in London, before they'd left the station with Malcolm. But none of the others possessed the credentials or the fieldwork record Shahdi Feroz did. Not even the team's nominal leader, Conroy Melvyn, a seedy-looking Englishman who bore the impressive title of Scotland Yard Chief Inspector.

Looking as Persian as her name and voice sounded, Dr. Feroz *awed* Margo. Not only was she exotic and beautiful in a way that made Margo feel her own youth and inexperience as keenly as a Minnesota winter wind, Shahdi Feroz was absolutely brilliant. Reading Dr. Feroz' work, virtually all of it based on first-hand study of down-time populations, reminded Margo of what she'd seen in New York during her agonizing, mercifully short stay there, and of things she'd seen during her few, catastrophic trips through TT-86's time gates. Not to mention—and she winced from the memory—her own childhood.

Margo's lack of education—a high-school GED and one semester of college which Kit had arranged for up time, augmented with months of intensive study on the station—caused her to stammer like a stupid schoolgirl with stagefright. "Dr. Feroz. Your, uh, safety goggles and muffs, earmuffs, I mean, for your ears, to protect them . . ." *Oh, for God's sake, stop shaking, Margo!*

"Thank you, my dear." The inflection of dismissal in her voice reduced Margo to the status of red-faced child. She fled back down the line of shooting benches, toward Ann Vinh Mulhaney, resident projectile weapons instructor, and the reassuring familiarity of a routine she knew well: preparing for a shooting lesson. Ann, at least, greeted her with a warm smile.

"So, are you all set for London?"

"Oh, boy, am I just! I've been packed for two whole days! I still can't believe Kit managed to swing it with Bax to let me go!" She had no idea what it had taken to convince Granville Baxter, CEO of Time Tours, Inc. on station, to give Margo that gate pass. And not just a one-cycle pass, either, but a gate pass that would let her stay the entire three months of East End Ripper murders.

Ann chuckled. "Grandpa wants you to get some field experience, kid."

Margo flushed. "I know." She glanced at the journalists, at the woman whose scholarly work was breaking new ground in the understanding of the criminal mind in historical cultures. "I know I haven't really got enough experience to guide the Ripper Watch Team through the East End. Not yet, even though I've been to the East End once." *That* trip, and her own greenhorn mistakes, she preferred not to remember too closely. "But I'll get the experience, Ann, and I'll do a good job. I know I can do this."

Ann ruffled Margo's short hair affectionately. "Of course you can, Margo. Any girl who could talk Kit Carson into training her to become the world's first woman time scout can handle mere journalists and eggheads. Bet Malcolm will be happy to see you, too," Ann added with a wink.

Margo grinned. "He sure will! He'll finally have somebody else to send on all the lousy errands!"

Ann laughed. "Let's get this class started, shall we?"

"Right!"

Margo needed to prove to Ann, to Kit, and to Malcolm that she was capable of time scouting. And—

perhaps most importantly—Margo needed to prove it to herself. So she dredged up a bright smile to hide her nervousness, hoped she didn't *look* as young as she felt in such illustrious, enormously educated company, and wondered if the team members could possibly take seriously a hot-headed, Irish alley-cat of a time guide who'd just turned seventeen-and-a-half last week . . .

Her smile, which had been known to cause cardiac arrest, was one of the few weapons currently available in her self-defense arsenal, so she dredged up a heart-stopping one and got to work. "Hi! Is everybody ready to get in some weapons practice?"

Heads swivelled and Margo was the abrupt focus of multiple, astonished stares.

Oh, Lordy, here we go. . . . "I'm Margo Smith, I'll be one of your time guides to London—"

"You?" The sound was incredulous, just short of scathing. Another voice from further down the line of shooting benches said, "What high school is that kid playing hooky from?"

Margo's face flamed. So did her temper. She bit down on it, though, and forced a brittle smile. Ann Mulhaney, the rat, just stood off to one side, waiting to see how she handled herself. *Oh, God, another test. . . .* One she'd better pass, too, drat it. So Margo ignored the incredulous looks and scathing remarks and simply got on with the job. "Most of the other guides are already in London," she said firmly. "I've been assigned the job of shepherding you through weapons training, so let's get organized, shall we? We've got a lot to do. Everyone's signed in, been assigned a lane and a shooting partner? Yes? Good. We'll get started, then."

Dominica Nosette interrupted, in a voice acid enough to burn holes through solid steel. "Why d'you insist we learn to shoot? It isn't proper, isn't decent, handling such things. I'm a photojournalist, not some

macho copper swaggering about and giving orders
with a billycock, nor yet some IRA terrorist. I'm not
about to pick up one of those nasty things."

Hoo boy, here we go . . .

Margo said as patiently as possible—which wasn't
very—"You don't have to carry one with you. But you
will have to pass the mandatory safety class if you
want to be a part of the Ripper Watch Team. Not
my rules, sorry, but I will enforce them. London's East
End is a very dangerous neighborhood under the best
of conditions. We're going into areas that will be
explosive as a powderkeg. Tempers will be running
hot. In the East End, gangs of thieves and cutthroat
muggers routinely knife prostitutes to death, just to
steal the few pence in their pockets. Any stranger will
be singled out by suspicious minds—"

"Oh, sod off, I've never needed a gun, not on a
single one of my photo shoots, and I've trailed mob
hit men!"

Oh, man, it's gonna be a long three months . . .

Margo steeled herself to keep smiling if it killed
her, and vowed to cope. "Ms. Nosette, I am fully
aware of your credentials. No one is questioning your
status as a competent journalist. But you may not
appreciate just how dangerous it's going to be for us,
even for the team members born in England, trying
to blend in with Victorian East End Londoners. It's
your right to choose not to carry a personal weapon.
But the rules of the Ripper Watch Team are clear.
You must be familiar with their use, because many
of us *will* be carrying them. And the more you know
about the kind of gun some Nichol-based gang
member pulls on you, the more likely you'll be to
survive the encounter—"

"Miss Smith," Dr. Shahdi Feroz interrupted gently,
"I am sorry to disagree with you, but I have been to
London's East End, several years ago. Most of the
Nichol gangs did not carry guns. Straight razors were

the weapon of choice. So popular, laws against carrying them were suggested by London constables, even by Parliament."

Margo was left with her mouth hanging open and blood scalding her cheeks until her whole face hurt. She wanted desperately to dig a hole through the concrete floor with the toe of her shoe and crawl down through it, pulling the top in after herself. Before she could recover her shattered composure, never mind think of anything to say that wouldn't sound completely witless, the station's alarm klaxons screamed out a warning that shook through the weapons range like thunder. Margo gasped, jerking her gaze around.

"What's going on?" Dominica Nosette demanded.

"Station emergency!" Margo shouted above the strident *skronkk!* Ann had already bolted toward her office. Margo was right behind, literally saved by the bell. *Oh, God, how'm I ever gonna face that bunch again?* Ann flung open her office door, snatched up the telephone, dialed a code that plugged her into the station's security system. Margo crowded in, then barricaded the doorway so tourists and the Ripper Watch Team couldn't barge in, as well. A moment later, Ann hung up, white-faced and shaken. "There's been a shooting! Skeeter and Ianira! Security's just put out a station-wide alarm. Ianira's *missing!* And there's a station riot underway!"

Her voice carried out through the doorway to the milling throng of tourists and Ripperologists. For one agonizing second, indecision crucified Margo. Ianira was a friend, a good friend, but Margo had a job to do here. And no matter how desperately she wanted to run from her own embarrassing mistake, she had to finish that job.

Dominica Nosette and Guy Pendergast, however, showed no such hesitation.

They grabbed equipment bags and ran.

"Margo! Go after those idiots!" Ann was already striding toward the exit, blocking the way with her body. "Nobody else leaves this range, is that clear? *Nobody!*" Diminuitive as she was, none of the others challenged her. They'd all seen her shoot. And nobody wanted to face down the Royal Irish Constabulary revolvers she abruptly clutched in either hand, rather than wearing benignly in twin holsters.

Margo, however, broke and ran, pounding up the stairs after the fleeing British reporters. "Hey! Wait!" *Yeah, like they're really gonna stop just because I said so . . .*

They didn't even slow down.

Seconds later, Margo—hard on their heels and gaining ground—emerged straight into chaos. A seething mass of frightened, confused tourists tried to rush in fifty-eleven directions at once, kids crying, women shouting for husbands, fathers grimly dragging youngsters toward anything that promised shelter. The awesome noise smote Margo like a physical blow, a fist made up of alarm klaxons, medi-van sirens, and screaming, shouting voices. Security squads raced past. Officers were jamming riot helmets on, even as they ran.

Margo's AWOL reporters surged right into the thick of utter chaos, dragging out cameras and recorders on the fly and pounding along in the wake of security. Margo swore under her breath and darted after them. She was small enough to dodge and weave with all the skill of a trained acrobat. An instant later, however, total darkness crashed down, engulfing the whole Commons. Margo skidded to a halt—or tried to, anyway. She caromed into at least half-a-dozen shrieking people before she managed to stop her headlong rush. Sobs of terror rose on every side. The insane wail of the klaxons shook through the darkness.

Margo stood panting in a film of sweat. The hair on her arms stood starkly erect. Unreasoning fear surged. Booted feet pounded past through the total blackness, startling Margo until she realized those odd helmets she'd seen security putting on were Mike Benson's new night-vision helmets. What seemed hours, but couldn't have been longer than a few minutes later, the lights started coming back up, moving gradually inward from the far edges of Commons. Margo blinked as the overhead lights flickered back to life in banks, illuminating Edo Castletown at one far end of the station and the Anachronism's Camelot sector and Outer Mongolia at the other end, around several twists and turns where Commons snaked through the massive cave system into which TT-86 had been built.

Tourists clung to one another, badly shaken. Margo searched the crowd for her charges and finally caught a glimpse of purposeful movement. The Ripper Watch reporters were on the move again. She swore in gutter Latin that would've shocked Cicero and pounded after them. "Are you crazy?" she demanded, catching up at last. "You can't go in there!"

Dominica Nosette flashed her a pitying smile. "Love, never tell a reporter what she can't do—*can't* is one word we don't understand."

Then they reached the zone of destruction. They'd beat SLUR-TV, the in-station televison news crew, to the punch. Dominica and Guy started filming steadily on every side as more reporters arrived, trailing cameras and lights and microphones. Then Margo caught her first glimpse of the blood and the broken bones.

Oh, my God . . .

While the newsies interviewed shaken eyewitnesses, station security zipped up a body bag with an extremely deceased individual inside. It wasn't the first time Margo had seen a dead person. Not even the second. And her mother's murder had been far more brutal a shock. But blood had stained the golden "bricks" of El Dorado's floor, leaking down between the paving stones in rivulets and runnels, where Margo had never expected to see it. And if that glimpse into the body bag had been accurate, the dead man had been shot in the face, point-blank.

With a very large caliber firearm.

What in God's name happened up here?

Margo began to tremble violently as the remembered smell of burnt toast and spreading, stinking puddles of blood smashed into her from her own childhood, from that long-ago morning when it had been her mother's body zipped up and carted out, and her father led away in handcuffs. . . . She wrapped both arms around herself, biting her lips to keep them from shaking. Violence like this happened in places like New York or London or even Minnesota, where drunkards beat their wives to death. But murder wasn't supposed to happen in a place like La-La Land, not where happy tourists gathered for vacations of a lifetime, where residents pursued dreams that came true every single day, where delightful amounts of money changed hands and everybody had fun in the process. Margo discovered she'd pressed the back of her hand against her mouth, unable to drag her gaze away from the macabre load as security carried away the grey zippered bag with the remains of a stranger inside.

Who is he? she wondered grimly. Or, rather, who had he been? He hadn't been dressed in a tourist costume, or as one of those construction workers building the new section of the station. More than a dozen of the Arabian Nights crewmen, bruised and bleeding, were being dragged off in handcuffs. Then station medical arrived, having to fight their way past newsies filming white-faced, bleeding, dazed survivors. Among the worst injured were the Lady of Heaven Templars, members of the cult which had singled out Ianira as their prophetess. And Ianira was missing, might be dead. . . . Ugly cuts, swollen bruises, and visibly broken bones had so badly injured more than a dozen Templars, medi-vans were required to rush them out of the riot zone.

"Margo!"

She stumbled around, dazed, and found her grandfather cutting through the crowd like an ice-breaking ship plowing through arctic seas. Margo ran to him, threw her arms around him. "Kit!"

Her grandfather hugged her close for a long moment, then murmured, "Hey, it's over, Imp, what's wrong?" He peered worriedly into her eyes.

"I know." She gulped, feeling stupid from lingering shock. "It's just . . . stuff like that isn't supposed to happen. Not *here*."

Lines of grief etched deeper into Kit's lean cheeks. "I know," he said quietly. "It isn't. I hate it, too. Which is why we're going to do something about it."

"Do *what*? I mean, what can we possibly do? And what happened, exactly? I got here a little late."

Kit thinned his lips. "*Ansar Majlis* is what happened."

"Answer who?"

The grim look in his eyes frightened Margo, worse than she was already. "*Ansar Majlis*," he said it again. "The *Ansar Majlis* Brotherhood is one of the most dangerous cults to form up time in the past fifty years. Where's Ann?"

"On the weapons range. She stayed with Dr. Feroz and the tourists, to keep anybody else from leaving. I tried to catch up with the reporters. They went charging straight up here, but they outran me." She ducked her head. "I'm sorry. I did try to stop them."

Kit muttered under his breath. "I'm sure you did. Listen, Imp, we've got *big* trouble on this station, with Ianira Cassondra missing. I don't have to tell you the repercussions of that, both on station and up time.

And with the *Ansar Majlis* involved, this riot may be the first of a whole *lot* of station riots. When word of this gets out . . ." He thinned his lips. "Next time Primary cycles, we are going to be neck deep in more trouble than you can shake an entire tree at. I want you to find Marcus. Try the Down Time Bar & Grill. Tell him we need search parties organized, Found Ones as well as up-time residents. And see if you can find out how Skeeter is."

"Skeeter's hurt? Ann said there'd been a shooting . . ." She swallowed hard, abruptly queasy to her toes. Margo and Skeeter Jackson might have a mutually uncivil history, but the idea of someone having shot the admittedly charming, one-time con artist left Margo sicker and colder than before. She'd gradually been changing her opinion of Skeeter Jackson, particularly since he'd become Marcus and Ianira's latest rescue project. An apparently successful one.

But Kit was shaking his head. "No, not shot, just banged up. Security said he had a lump on his temple the size of a goose egg. Should've had medical look at it, but he bolted into this mess, trying to find Ianira. Get Marcus busy organizing the Found Ones, okay? And find out if Marcus needs help looking after the girls."

Margo drew a shaky breath. "Kit . . ."

If we can't find Ianira, ever . . .

"Yes, I know. When you've got all that set up, meet me at the aerie."

"Bull's office? Won't Bull be busy conducting the official investigation?"

"Yes. Which is why you and I are going to be there." When Margo gave him her best look of blank befuddlement, Kit explained. "In a major station emergency, every single time scout in residence becomes a *de facto* member of station security. Same with the independent guides, the ones not on a company payroll, or with specific tour commitments to meet. And I'd say a riot, a murder, and a kidnapping qualify as a major station emergency in anybody's book. We're going to be busy, Margo, busier than you've been since you arrived on station."

He must have noticed the sudden panic Margo couldn't choke down, try as she might, because he said more gently, "Don't worry about the Ripper Watch tour, kid. You'll get to London, all right. But the Britannia doesn't open for almost six and a half hours and right now, we've got a murderer loose somewhere in this station. A killer who's very likely got Ianira Cassondra in his hands."

Margo shuddered. It was one thing, studying a serial murderer like Jack the Ripper, whose victims were quite well known. Hunting for a madman loose in TT-86 was another prospect altogether—one that terrified her. "Okay, Kit." She managed to keep her voice fairly steady. "I'll find Marcus, get the downtimers organized, try to find out about Skeeter, then meet you at Bull's office."

"Good girl. And for God's sake, Imp, *don't* let those damned newsies follow you!"

She tried to imagine the kind of story *any* reporter would take up time about this disaster, tried to imagine the impact that story would have, particularly the disappearance of the inspiration for the fastest-growing cult religion in the world, and nodded, jaw clenched.

"Right."

"Get moving, then. I'll see you later."

Margo turned her back on the chaos of the riot zone and headed for the popular residents' bar where Marcus worked, wondering how badly Skeeter had been injured and just who had grabbed Ianira—and what they were doing to her, now they had her. Margo bit her lip. What would Marcus do if they couldn't find her? Or if—she swallowed hard at the thought—if they didn't find her *alive?* And their little

girls? They weren't even old enough to understand
what had happened . . .

Margo's fear edged over into terror, mingled with
helpless anger. If those little girls had been left
motherless . . . Today's riot would be small potatoes
compared to the explosion yet to come. And violence
of that magnitude could get a station closed down,
permanently. Even one as famous and profitable as
TT-86. After the bombing destruction of TT-66 by
whichever group of middle eastern religious fanatics
had blown the station sky-high, all it would take was
another major station rocked by violence to shut down
the whole time-tourism industry. There was already
a powerful up-time senator trying to close down the
stations. If TT-86 went under because of riots and
on-station murders, Kit wouldn't need to kick her out
of time-scout training to wreck her dreams.

Up-time politics would wreck them for her.

Chapter Three

Marcus had not known such fear since his one-time master had tricked him through the station's Roman gate and sold him back into a slavery from which Skeeter Jackson had rescued him. Abandoning the Down Time's bar without a backward glance, he bolted into the chaos loose on Commons, hard on the heels of Robert Li, the antiquarian who'd burst into the bar with the white-faced news: "Marcus! Someone's shot at Skeeter and Ianira!"

Ianira! Fear for her robbed breath he needed for running. Everything that was good and beautiful in his life had come through her, through the miracle of a highly-born woman who had been treated cruelly by her first husband, who had still managed, somehow, to love Marcus enough to want his touch, to want the love he had offered as very nearly the only thing in his power to give her. He had been a slave and although Marcus was free now in a way he had never dreamed possible, he would never be a wealthy man, could never give Ianira the kind of life she deserved.

If anything had happened to her, *anything* . . . He

could not conceive of a life without her. And their children, how could he tell their beautiful little girls they would never see their mother again? *Please,* he prayed to the gods of his Gallic childhood, to the Roman gods of his one-time masters, but especially to the many-breasted Artemis of Ephesus, the Great Mother of all living creatures, whose temple Ianira had served as a child in that ancient goddess' holy city, *please let her be unharmed and safe . . .*

Marcus was struggling to thrust himself through a packed crowd at the edge of Urbs Romae when a hand closed around his arm. A voice he didn't recognize said, "As you value your children's lives, come with me."

Shocked, he turned—and found himself staring into haunted grey eyes.

He could not have said if the person watching him so narrowly was male or female. But there was pain in those grey eyes, desperate pain and fear and something else, something dark and deadly that made his pulse shudder.

"Who—?"

"Your wife is safe. For the moment. But I can't keep her safe forever, not from the people who want her dead. And your children are in terrible danger. Please. I can't tell you why, not here. But I swear to you, if you'll just come with me and bring your little girls, I'll do everything in my power to keep all of you alive."

It was insane, this impulse to trust. Too many people had betrayed Marcus over the years, and too much that was precious to him, more precious than his own life, depended on his making the right choice. *This is Shangri-La Station,* he found himself thinking desperately, *not Rome. If I am betrayed here, there are people who will move heaven and stars to come to our aid . . .*

In the end, it came down to one simple fact: this

person knew where Ianira was. If Marcus wanted to see her, he *had* to go. And the girls?

"I will not risk my children until I know Ianira is safe."

Impatience flared in those grey eyes. "There's no time for this! My God, we've already killed one of them, before he could shoot her. They'll murder your little girls, Marcus, in cold blood. I've seen how they kill! Cassie Tyrol died right in front of me and there was nothing I could do to save her—"

Marcus started. "The woman from the movies? Who played the priestess of Artemis, the Temple harlot? She is dead?"

Pain shone in those grey eyes. "Yes. And the same people who killed her are trying to kill Ianira, her whole family. Please, I'm begging you . . . get your little girls out of danger while there's still time. I'll tell you everything, I swear it. But we have to move *now.*"

Marcus pressed clenched fists to his temples, tried to think clearly, wishing he possessed even a hundredth the skill Ianira did in reading people's hearts and intentions. Standing irresolute in the middle of a panic-stricken crowd jammed into Commons, voices echoing off the girders of the ceiling five stories overhead, Marcus had never felt more alone and afraid in his life. Not even as a child, thrust into chains and caged like an animal for sale. Then, the only person at risk had been himself. Now . . .

"They are at the school and daycare center," he decided, voice brusque. "This way."

He still didn't know if the grey-eyed person at his side was a man or a woman.

But when they reached the day-care center and interrupted an ugly, heart-stopping tableau, Marcus discovered that his shaky trust in his new companion was well-founded. They skidded through the day care center's doors at an all-out run—and found an armed Arabian Nights construction worker holding Harriet Banks at gunpoint. Another armed man was dragging Artemisia and Gelasia away from the other children. Rage and terror scalded Marcus, blinded him, sent him forward with fists clenched, even as the grey-eyed person with him erupted with a violence that would have struck terror, had that violence been aimed at his family.

Marcus barely had time to see the gun before it discharged. The roar deafened in the confines of little daycare center. His ears rang even as smoke bellied out from the antique gun's barrel. Children screamed and scattered like frightened ants. The construction worker closest to them, the one holding a gun on Harriet Banks, jerked just once, then fell like a man whose legs have been abruptly jerked out from beneath him. The hole through the back of his skull was far smaller than the one through his face, where the bullet had plowed through on its way out. Shock caught Marcus like a fist against the side of his head— then the black-powder pistol discharged again and the man holding Artemisia's wrist plowed into the floor, obscenely dead.

Marcus snapped out of shock with the grotesque thud as the second body landed on the daycare center's floor. He flung himself toward his screaming children. "Hush . . . it's all right, Daddy's here . . ."

He gathered the girls close, hugged them, wept against their hair.

"Marcus! Come *on,* man! More of the bastards are headed this way!"

Marcus had no time to say anything to Harriet Banks, who was trying to get the other children out through the back door, away from the carnage in the playroom. He simply scooped up his daughters and ran with them, following his unknown benefactor into the chaos on Commons. There were, indeed, more construction workers racing toward them, with weapons clutched in their hands as tourists screamed and scattered.

His benefactor's voice cut through shock and terror. "Do you know any better way to reach the Neo Edo Hotel? They're between us and any safety we've got on this station."

Marcus took one look at the burly construction workers running toward them and swore savagely in the language only he, alone of all residents on TT-86, could understand. His Gaulish tribe was as extinct as the language they'd spoken. But his children were still alive. He intended to keep them that way. "This way," he snarled, spinning around and plunging toward Residential. "Down-timers know *all* the secret ways through this station!"

Skeeter had taught Marcus routes he'd never suspected could be used to get from one side of the station to the other. Those escape routes had proven useful when he and Ianira had needed to slip away from the pressing attentions of her adoring acolytes, trying to gain a little privacy for themselves. Marcus had never dreamed he would need them to save his little family from cold-blooded murder. Why anyone would want to kill them, he could not imagine. But he intended to find out.

Marcus might be nothing more than an ex-slave, a down-timer without legal rights. But he was a husband and a father and an "'eighty-sixer," a member of the insane, fiercely independent, intensely loyal community of residents who called Time Terminal Eighty-Six home. Whoever sought to kill them, they had failed to take that particular fact into account. 'Eighty-sixers took care of their own.

Even if it meant breaking up-time laws to do so.

By the time Skeeter arrived at the aerie, Bull Morgan's glass-walled office was packed, standing room only. And that was *without* the howling mob of reporters trying to get past security to the elevator and stairs that led up to the station manager's ceiling-level office. The elevator had been crowded, too, with 'eighty-sixers responding to the emergency call for search teams. Connie Logan, owl-eyed behind her thick glasses and dressed as outlandishly as ever in bits and pieces of various costumes she'd been testing when the call had gone out, stood crammed into one corner, trying not to jab anybody with the pins sticking out of her clothes. Arley Eisenstein, restauranteur of one of the ten most famous restaurants on the planet and married to the station's head of medicine, stared at the elevator doors with his jaw muscles clenched so tight, Skeeter wondered why his teeth hadn't broken yet. Brian Hendrickson, station librarian and a man who hadn't forgotten the circumstances of Skeeter's disastrous wager with Goldie, any more than he'd forgotten anything else he'd ever seen, heard, or read, was swearing colorfully in a language Skeeter had never heard in his life. Ann Vinh Mulhaney had come upstairs from the weapons range in company with a woman Skeeter recognized as one of the Ripper Watch Team members. Both women were as silent as ghosts and very nearly as pale.

Dr. Shahdi Feroz, Skeeter knew, was not just a world-renowned Ripperologist, she was also the team's cult-phenomena expert. She had made a life's study of criminal cults and intended to research first-hand Victorian London's teeming subculture of spiritualists, occult worshipers, Celtic-revivalists, magic practitioners, and the city's numerous flourishing, quasi-religious cult groups. It had led her to support some rather unusual ideas about the Ripper murders. What she knew about down-time occult groups made for a terrifying parallel to what Skeeter knew of *up*-time cults. He'd seen his share of them in New York. And over the past few years, the new ones popping up like malignant mushrooms made those older ones look positively apple-pie ordinary. Which was doubtless why Bull Morgan had personally requested her presence at this meeting. Shahdi Feroz, as elegant and composed as a Persian queen, dark hair upswept in a mass of thick, raven's-wing waves, glanced at Skeeter, evidently aware of his intent scrutiny, and started to speak—

And the elevator doors slid open onto pandemonium.

Shahdi Feroz turned aside at once, stepping out of the elevator to make room for the others. She glanced over at Ann through dark, worried eyes as they all crowded off the elevator and tried, somewhat vainly, to find space in Bull's packed office.

"I didn't expect quite so many people to be here." Her speech was rich and fluid. Skeeter, fascinated by the rising and falling inflections of her exotic voice, managed to locate a space that hid him from most people's view.

Ann answered in a strained undertone. "I did. In fact, I'm betting we won't be the last to arrive."

When the weapons instructor glanced around, her gaze paused on Skeeter. The look in Ann's eyes caused him to stiffen. Skeeter clenched his jaw and looked away first, unsure which was worse: the pity or the deep, lingering suspicion that Skeeter had only been using Ianira, the way most 'eighty-sixers thought he used everyone he came into contact with. There was nothing he could say, no explanation he could—or cared to—offer that anyone in this room would believe. With the down-timers on station, it was different. But in a room crammed shoulder-to-jowl with *up*-time 'eighty-sixers, Skeeter felt as alone and isolated as he'd felt in Yesukai's felt tent, a lost little boy of eight without the ability to understand a word spoken around him or to go home again to a family that didn't want him, anyway.

He set his jaw and wished to hell Bull would get

this meeting underway. He needed to be down on Commons, searching. He'd only come to this meeting because he was not, by God, going to let them leave him out of whatever decisions were made on where and how to search for her. A door near the back of Bull's office opened and Ronisha Azzan, the deputy station manager, appeared, looking worried. She said something to Bull, too low for Skeeter to overhear. Bull ground his teeth over the stubby end of an unlit cigar, then spat debris into an ornate brass spittoon strategically positioned on one corner of his desk. Margo arrived a moment later via the elevator, breathless, her green eyes clouded with fear. She spotted Ann Vinh Mulhaney and Shahdi Feroz and bit her lower lip, then pushed past to Bull's desk. "I can't find Marcus," she said flatly. "He ran out of the Down Time with Robert Li and nobody's seen him since. Robert said Marcus was behind him one minute and he'd vanished into the crowd the next." Ronisha Azzan stepped into the office behind Bull's, swearing under her breath.

Skeeter knew a moment of fear almost as deep as when Ianira had vanished right in front of *him*. Then reason reasserted itself, helped by the white-knuckled hands he used to push back heavy locks of hair sticking to his damp brow. Marcus would be with other Found Ones, searching, of course, there was no reason to panic, no up-timer on station knew the back routes the way the down-timers did, somebody had obviously got to him and maybe even told him they'd seen her somewhere . . .

Station alarms screamed to life again.

Fear tightened down once more, driving daggers through Skeeter's nerves. He very nearly pulled out two fistfuls of his own hair. Skeeter clenched his jaw and made himself wait, while sweat prickled out over his entire torso. Bull Morgan snatched the security phone off his desk and shouted, "What the hell is it *now*?"

Whatever was said on the other end, Bull's florid face actually lost color. The unlit cigar he chewed went deathly still. Then he spat out the cigar with a furious curse and snarled, "Turn this station upside down, dammit, but *find* them! And I want every construction worker in this goddamned station locked up on suspicion of attempted murder, do you hear me, Benson? *Do it!* Ronisha!" The phone didn't quite bend when he slammed the receiver back down, but a crack appeared in the plastic casing.

The deputy station manager, African-patterned silks swirling around her tall figure, reappeared from the back office, talking urgently to someone via squawky. She was snarling, "I don't care who you have to slap in the brig! Control that mess or find yourself another job! Yes?" she asked, turning her attention to Bull.

"Get down to the war room! Coordinate the search from down there. Have Benson's security teams report directly to you there. We've got another helluva mess breaking loose."

Ronisha fled down the back stairs, squawky in hand. La-La Land's station manager faced the expectant hush from the crowd in his office. The silence in the glass-walled office was as unbearable as the sound of fingernails on a blackboard.

Bull said heavily, "There's been a shooting at the day care center. Two construction workers messily dead, dozens of children in hysterics. Marcus and his little girls vanished in the middle of the shooting." Nausea bit Skeeter's throat. He forced himself not to bolt for the elevator, forced himself to wait, to hear the rest of it. "A couple of Scheherazade construction workers were trying to take his daughters out at gunpoint when Marcus showed up with someone Harriet didn't recognize. Whoever it was, they shot both construction workers dead and took Marcus and the girls out of there." Bull craned to peer through the crowd of white-faced, furious residents. "Is Dr. Feroz here yet?"

Shahdi Feroz pushed through the throng to the front of Bull's office. "Yes, Mr. Morgan, I am here. How may I help?"

"I want to know what we're up against. Kit Carson told security the bastards who've attacked Ianira and her family are members of the *Ansar Majlis* Brotherhood. He's not here yet, or I'd ask him to brief us."

Shahdi Feroz moved sharply at the mention of the Brotherhood, as though wanting to deny what he'd just said. Then she sighed, tiredly. "*Ansar Majlis* . . . This is very bad, very dangerous. The *Ansar Majlis* Brotherhood began when Islamic fundamentalist soldiers began recruiting down-time Islamic warriors for *jihad* through the gates where TT-66 used to be. The station is destroyed, but the gates still function, of course."

She spoke with a bitterness Skeeter understood only too well. He hadn't known anyone personally on the station, but hundreds of innocents had died when the station had been blown sky-high. The elevator's soft *ping!* sent Skeeter two inches straight up the wall. But it was only Kit Carson, face haggard, eyes bleak. He moved quietly into the office as Dr. Feroz continued her explanation.

"Since the station was destroyed, thousands of down-time recruits have been brought through to fight *jihad*. Some of these soldiers have banded together to form a brotherhood. They have styled themselves after the nineteeth-century *Ansar*, fanatical religious soldiers of the Mahdi, an Islamic messiah who drove the British out of the Sudan and killed General Gordon at Khartoum. It operates very much like the social structure of a nomadic tribe. Those in the brotherhood are fully human; those outside are not. And the lowest, least human of all are the women of the Lady of Heaven Temples. Such women are considered evil and heretical by these soldiers. A female priesthood, a female deity . . ." She shook her head. "They have sworn the destruction of the Artemis Temple and all Templars. There has been trouble with them in the Middle East, but they were for many years contained there. It seems they are contained no longer. If they have managed to establish cells in major cities like New York, there will be terrible violence against the Temple and its members. The whole purpose of this cult is to destroy the Lady of Heaven Temples as completely as if they had never existed. It is *jihad*, Mr. Morgan, a particularly virulent, fundamentalist form of hatred."

Skeeter wanted to close his hands around someone's throat, wanted to center the bastards responsible for these attacks on Ianira and her family in the sights of any weapon he could lay hands on. Instead, he forced himself to wait. He had learned patience from Yesukai, had learned that to destroy an enemy, one must first know and understand him.

Bull Morgan clenched his teeth over the stub of his cigar, which he'd retrieved from his desk top and was now shredding between molars once again. "All of which explains the attack on Ianira. And her kids, goddamn it. But those construction workers have been on station for weeks. Why wait until now to attack? Why today?"

Margo spoke up hesitantly. "Maybe someone came through Primary today with orders? I mean, the whole thing blew up within minutes of Primary cycling."

Bull pinned her with a sharp stare. Kit nodded silently, clearly agreeing with that assessment. It made sense to Skeeter, as well. Too much sense. And there was that terrifying vision of Ianira's, right before the violence had erupted. Right *after* Primary had cycled.

Bull picked up his security phone again. "Ronisha, I want a dossier on every man, woman, and child who came through Primary today. Complete history.

Anybody who might have ties to the Middle East or the *Ansar Majlis* Brotherhood, I want questioned."

Skeeter wanted to question two other individuals, too: the wild-eyed young kid who'd shot whoever it was behind Ianira and Skeeter in that riot, and the person who'd knocked both Ianira and Skeeter to the floor in time for that kid to do the shooting. Skeeter wondered which one of that pair had done the killing in the day care center. Whoever they were, they clearly knew about the threat to Ianira and her family. But why were they trying to protect her? Were they Templars? Someone else? Skeeter intended to find out, if he had to take them apart joint by joint to learn the truth.

Only to do that, he had to find them first.

He edged toward the elevator, impatient to do something besides stand here and listen. Bull hung up the phone again and started spitting orders. "All right, I want the biggest manhunt in the history of this station and I want it yesterday. Hotels, restaurants, shops, residential, library, gym, weapons ranges, physical plant and maintenance areas, waste management, storage, *everything*. Organize search teams according to the station's emergency management plan. Presume these bastards are armed and dangerous. Personal weapons are not only permitted, but encouraged. Questions?"

Nobody had any.

Least of all Skeeter.

"Let's move it, then, people. I want Ianira and her family found."

Skeeter got to the elevator before anybody else and found himself sharing a downward ride with Kit Carson, of all people. The retired time scout glanced at him as others crowded into the elevator. "You'll organize the Found Ones?"

The question surprised Skeeter. He and Kit Carson were hardly on civil terms, not after his ill-conceived attempt to get Margo into bed with that ruse about being a time scout, himself. Of course, he hadn't known Margo was Kit's granddaughter at the time. In point of fact, not even Kit had known, then. But when the scout *had* discovered the truth, his visit to Skeeter had been anything but grandfatherly—and nothing even remotely resembling cordial. Kit's concern now surprised Skeeter, until he realized that it had nothing to do with Skeeter and everything to do with how Kit felt about Ianira Cassondra.

So he nodded with a short jerk of his head. "They'll be organized already, but I'll join them."

"Let me know if you need anything."

Again, Skeeter stared. He said slowly, grudgingly, "Thanks. We're pretty organized, but I'll let you know if something comes up we can't handle." Not that he could think of anything. The Found Ones' Council of Seven had made certain the resident down-timers on station were as prepared as possible for any station crisis that threatened them. The down-timers were, in fact, as prepared as Sue Fritchey's Pest Control officers were for an invasion of anything from hordes of locusts to prehistoric flying reptiles—which, in point of fact, TT-86 had been forced to deal with, just a few months previously.

Kit's next question startled the hell out of Skeeter.

"Would you mind if Margo and I joined you and the Found Ones to search?"

Skeeter's brows dove down as suspicion flared. "Why?"

Kit held his gaze steadily. "Because if anyone on this station has a chance of finding them, it's the downtimers. I'm aware of those meetings held in the subbasements. And I know how underground organizations operate. I also want rather badly to be there if and when we *do* find whoever is responsible for this."

Skeeter had known for a long time that Kenneth "Kit" Carson was a thoroughly dangerous old man, the sort you didn't want as an enemy, ever. It came as a slight shock, however, to realize that the retired time scout would relish taking apart whoever had done this as thoroughly as Skeeter, himself, would. He hadn't expected to share anything in common with the world's most famous recluse.

"All right," he found himself saying tightly. "You're on. But when we do find them . . ."

"Yes?"

He looked the man he was mortally afraid of straight in the eye. "They're *mine.*"

Kit Carson's sudden grin was as lethal as the look in his eyes. "Deal."

Skeeter was left with the terrifying feeling that he'd just made a deal with a very formidable devil, indeed. A deal that was likely to lead him places he truly didn't want to go. Before he could worry too intensely about it, however, the elevator bumped to a halt and the doors opened with a swoosh. Five minutes later, he was leading the way through Commons, an unlikely team leader for a search team consisting of himself, Kit Carson, the fiery tempered Margo, and—surprisingly—Dr. Shahdi Feroz.

"The Britannia opens in less than six hours," Margo said pointedly when she insisted on joining them.

"Yes, it does. And I am as ready as I will ever be. I may not know how to shoot a gun yet, but I am certain you can remedy that for me once we reach London, Miss Smith."

The look Margo shot the breathtakingly beautiful older woman wavered somewhere between pleased surprise and wary assessment. Skeeter wondered why, but he didn't have the time to pursue it. Then he spotted Bergitta, a young down-timer who'd fallen through an unstable gate from medieval Sweden. She'd been crying, to judge from her reddened, swollen eyes. She'd hooked up with young Hashim ibn Fahd, a down-time teenager who'd fallen through the Arabian Nights gate, and with Kynan Rhys Gower, whose face was a lethal mask of fury.

Bergitta gave a glad cry when she spotted him. "Oh, Skeeter! We have looked and looked . . ."

Kit was already speaking rapidly in Welsh with the bowman, who had sworn an oath of fealty to Kit down that unstable gate into sixteenth-century Portuguese southern Africa. Skeeter gave Bergitta's hands a swift and reassuring squeeze. "The search teams are organized and out?"

"Yes, Skeeter, and I am told to say to you, please search the escape routes from Little Agora to Frontier Town. You will need a team . . ."

"They're with me," Skeeter said roughly, nodding at the others. "Not my choice, but they're good."

It was a monumental understatement, one of his all-time best, in fact.

Bergitta, who knew their reputations perfectly well, for all that she'd been on station only three months, widened pretty blue eyes; then nodded. "Kynan and Hashim and I go to search also, then." She hugged him, very briefly, but it didn't take more than a fleeting contact to feel the tremors shaking through her.

"We'll find them, Bergitta." Skeeter forced the conviction in his voice. *We have to find them. Dear God, please let us find them soon . . . and safe.*

She nodded and tried to smile, then departed with Kynan Rhys Gower and Hashim, whose glance looked ready to kill anyone who hurt Ianira, despite his youth. Skeeter found Margo's speculative gaze on Bergitta as she moved away into the crowd. What he read in her eyes defied translation for several moments. At first, he thought it was simply distaste for sharing company with a girl who'd been forced by circumstances to sell the only commodity she possessed to make a living on the station: herself. Then he looked again, struck forcibly by the memories lurking in Margo's shadowed green eyes, which had filled with pain, shame, remorse. But for what? He knew how other kids Margo's age had been forced to make a living in New York. He rather doubted Margo had been there long enough to get into serious trouble, given her determination to get onto TT-86 and begin her career as a trainee time scout. But with the kind of pain and the depth of shame he could see in Margo's eyes, Skeeter found himself wondering how she'd raised the money for a ticket through Shangri-La Station's expensive Primary gate.

If Kit's granddaughter *had* resorted to . . . that . . . Skeeter wasn't sure how Grandpa would take the news. Or—Christ, talk about complications—Malcolm, who planned to marry her. *Noneya,* Skeeter told himself severely. Whatever the reason for that look in Margo's eyes, it was very much none of Skeeter's business.

"We'll start in Little Agora," he said gruffly. "It's closer. Let's go, I've waited too long as it is."

Wordlessly, his little search party followed.

Jenna Nicole Caddrick didn't take Ianira to the hotel room she'd reserved nearly a year previously in Carl's married sister's name. She hadn't dared try to check into the luxury hotel, not with Ianira Cassondra draped, unconscious, across her back and shoulders in a fireman's carry where Noah Armstrong had put her. "Get her to the hotel!" the detective had ordered. "Take the stairways to the basement—I've got to find her husband and kids!"

So, staggering with every step, because Jenna was not that much larger than Ianira, herself, she carried the sacred prophetess through the station's Commons during security's riot-control blackout, bumping into people and stumbling into walls until she finally found a staircase, its emergency "Exit" sign glowing in the stygian darkness. The lights down here, at least, hadn't been shut off. Shangri-La Station's basement was a twisting montage of pipes and conduits and crowded storage rooms where, with any luck—and the Lady alone knew they deserved a little of that—the *Ansar Majlis* wouldn't think to look. Or anyone else, for that matter, not right away, at least. Jenna, legs and arms trembling with the effort, joints all but cracking, finally spotted a thick pile of hotel towels, in a big packing crate that someone had pried open to remove part of its contents. Moving gingerly, she lowered Ianira onto the piled towels. The prophetess was still as death, with a nasty bruise along her brow where Noah had slammed her to the floor, saving her life.

Jenna didn't know much about medicine or first aid, but she knew how to test a pulse, anyway, and remembered that a shock victim had to be kept warm. So she covered Ianira with a whole pile of the crated towels and tested her pulse and wondered if slow and regular might be good or bad news. She bit one lip, then wondered how to let Noah Armstrong know where to find them. *We'll meet at the Neo Edo, kid, that's where you've got reservations and they'll expect you to show up.*

Yeah, she thought glumly. But not with an unconscious prophetess across her shoulder. Showing up with Ianira, Cassondra of Ephesus, in a state of coma was a great way to get the attention of all the wrong people, *fast.* When Jenna heard the footfalls and the distant murmur of voices, she spun on her heel, gripping Carl's reproduction pistol in both hands, terrifying herself with that blurred, instinctive reaction. *I don't want to get used to people trying to kill me . . . or having to kill them.* The thundering shock of shooting down a living human being up on Commons would have left Jenna on hands and knees, vomiting, if Ianira Cassondra's life hadn't been in mortal jeopardy with every passing second. She wanted to go into shock now, *needed* to be sick, was

shaking violently with the need, but there was someone coming and she couldn't let them kill Ianira.

The voices drew closer, voices she didn't recognize. Jenna scowled, fist tight on the reproduction
antique weapon in her hand, trying to make sense
of what they were saying. She realized abruptly that
the words weren't *going* to fall into any recognizable patterns because they weren't in English.
Whatever it was, it sounded like . . . Classical Latin,
maybe? Would the *Ansar Majlis* speak Latin? She
couldn't imagine it, not a pack of medieval terrorists imported from the war-wracked Middle East for
the express purpose of destroying the Temple which
formed the bedrock of Jenna's faith.

Then the speakers rounded an abrupt corner and
Jenna gasped, giddy with relief. *"Noah!"*

Armstrong swung around sharply, recognized her,
relaxed a death grip on the trigger. "Kid," Noah
muttered, "you are gonna get yourself shot one of
these days, doing that. Where is she?"

Jenna pointed, eyeing the people who accompanied Noah. The ashen-faced young man in jeans and
an ordinary short-sleeved work shirt, she recognized
as the Cassondra's husband—the Roman slave—and
the two little girls with him looked so much like
their mother it closed Jenna's throat. Another young
man with them was a kid, really, younger than Jenna.
A lot younger. At the moment, Jenna Nicole Caddrick felt about a thousand years old and aging
rapidly.

"Ianira!" Marcus cried, running toward his wife.

"She's unconscious," Jenna said, voice low and
unsteady. "She hit her head on the floor . . ."

Marcus and the teenager broke into a voluble spate
of Latin, Marcus nodding his head vehemently up and
down, the kid looking stubborn. A fragment of historical research for a film class came back to her, that
Romans bobbed their heads up and down to indicate

disagreement, not wagging them from side to side the way moderns did. At length, the younger kid muttered something that sounded foul and trotted away into the dim-lit basement.

"Where's he going?" Jenna asked. What if they brought the station authorities in? If that happened, Ianira and Marcus and those beautiful little girls would die. *Nobody* could protect them, not as long as they remained on this station.

Marcus didn't even glance up. He was stroking his wife's hair back from her bruised forehead, holding her cold hand. Their little girls whimpered and clung to his leg, too young to know or comprehend what was happening around them, but old enough to know terror. "He goes to bring medicine. Food, water, blankets. We will hide her in the Sanctuary."

Jenna didn't know exactly what or where Ianira's Sanctuary might be, although she suspected it was hidden deep under the station. But she knew enough to blurt out, "You can't! It won't be safe there. These bastards will hunt through every inch of this station, looking for her. For you, too, and the children."

Frightened brown eyes lifted, met hers. "What can we do, then? We have friends here, powerful friends. Kit Carson and Bull Morgan—"

Armstrong cut him off. "Not even Kit Carson can stop the *Ansar Majlis,*" Noah bit out, bitterness darkening the detective's voice, leaving it harsh and raw. "You have to get completely off this station. The faster, the better. We sure as hell are," Noah nodded toward Jenna. "The only place that's gonna be safe is someplace down time. There's a whole lot of history to hide in, through this station's gates. We hide long enough, stay alive long enough, I can slip back through the station in disguise—and I'm damned good at disguises—and get the proof of what we know to the up-time authorities. If we're going to stop the bastards responsible for this," Noah jerked a glance toward Ianira, curled up on her side, fragile as rare porcelain, "the *only* way is to destroy them, make sure they're jailed for life or executed. And we can't do that if *we're* dead."

"*Who is it?*" Marcus grated out. "I will kill them, whoever they are!"

Jenna believed him. Profoundly. Imagination failed her, trying to comprehend what this ordinary-seeming young man in blue jeans and a checkered shirt had already lived through. Noah told Marcus what they were up against. All of it. In thorough and revolting detail. The suspicion that flared in Marcus' eyes when he looked at Jenna wounded her.

"I'm not my father!" she snapped, fists aching at her sides. "If that son-of-a-bitch were in front of me right now, I'd blow his head off. He always was a lousy, rotten, stinking bastard of a father. I just never knew how *much*. 'Til now."

The suspicion in the other man's brown eyes melted away while something else coalesced in its place. It took a moment to recognize it. When he did, it shook Jenna badly. *Pity*. This ex-slave, this man whose family was targeted for slaughter, pitied *her*. Jenna turned roughly aside, shoved her pistol through her belt and her hands into her pockets, and clenched her teeth over a flood of nausea and anger and fright that left her shaking. A moment later, Noah settled a hand on her shoulder.

"You never killed a man before." It wasn't a question, didn't have to be a question, because it was perfectly obvious. Jenna shook her head anyway. "No." Noah sighed, tightened fingers against her shoulder for a moment. "They say it's never easy, kid. I hadn't either, you know, until that hit in New York." Jenna glanced up, found deep pain in Noah's enigmatic eyes. "But I always knew I might have to, doing the job I chose. It's worse for you, probably. When a kid comes to the Temple young as you are, she's hurting inside already. You got more reason than most. And Cassie told me you cried when you accidentally ran over a mongrel dog on the road out to the ranch."

She clenched her teeth tighter and tried to hold back tears she did not want the detective to witness. Noah didn't say anything else. Just dropped the hand from Jenna's shoulder and turned away, moving briskly around the confined space Jenna had chosen to defend, making up a better bed for Ianira. That it was necessary only upset Jenna more, because she hadn't done a good enough job of it, herself. The Latin-speaking teenager returned a few silent minutes later, bringing a first aid kit, a heavy satchel that wafted the scent of food when he lifted the flap, blankets piled over one shoulder, and a couple of stuffed toys, which he gave to Ianira's daughters. The children grabbed hold of the shaggy, obviously home-made bears, and hugged them with all their little-girl strength. Jenna's eyes stung, watching it. No child only three years old should ever look at the world through eyes that looked like *that*. And Artemisia's sister was even younger, barely a year old. Barely walking, yet.

"We can't stay here long," Noah was saying, voice low. "They'll be searching for her. We'll have to smuggle her up into the hotel room Jenna's reserved. We can hide there until the Britannia Gate opens." The detective checked a wristwatch. "We won't need to hide long. But we've got to outfit for the gate between now and then. And find a way to smuggle Ianira through."

"Us," Marcus said sharply. "We all go through."

But Noah was shaking a head that ought to've gone grey by now, if the detective's private life was anything like what they'd already lived through. "No. They're going to send a death squad after us, Marcus. They'll send somebody through every gate that opens during the next week, trying to get her. I won't risk all of you anywhere in one group. Just in case the worst happens and the bastards who follow her through the gate *do* catch up."

"Not the Britannia," Marcus insisted stubbornly. "They cannot get through the Britannia. It is Ripper Season. There have been no tickets for today's gate for over a year. I could get through working as a porter hauling baggage, because I am a station resident, but no one else."

"Don't underestimate these people, Marcus. If necessary, they'll kill one of the baggage handlers, take his place, and get through that way, using their victim's ID and timecard."

Marcus' already pale cheeks ran dead white. "Yes," he whispered. "It would be easy. Too easy."

"So." Noah's voice, so difficult to pin down as either a man's light voice or a woman's deep one, was cold and precise. "We put Ianira in a steamer trunk. Same thing for the girls. You," the detective nodded at Marcus, "go through one of the other gates with your children. And we'll disguise you as a baggage handler, since they're almost invisible. The problem is, which gate?"

The teenager spoke up at once. "The Wild West Gate opens tomorrow."

Jenna and Noah exchanged glances. It was perfect. Too perfect. The *Ansar Majlis* would track Marcus and the girls straight through that gate, figuring it would be the one gate Jenna was likeliest to choose. The tour gate into Denver of 1885 was the only gate besides the sold-out Britannia where the natives spoke English. And Carl had been such a nut about that period of American history, the killers tracking them would doubtless figure Jenna had cut and run through the gate she and Carl would've known the most about, the only one she could get tickets for, not knowing, thank the Lady, that Jenna had secretly bought tickets through the Britannia in another name more than a year ago.

Noah, however, was frowning in concentration, studying Marcus closely. "It could work. Put you and the girls down Denver's Wild West Gate, with me as guard, send Jenna and Ianira through to London."

"But—" Jenna opened her mouth to protest, terrified at the prospect of Noah abandoning her.

A dark glance from steel-cold grey eyes shut her up. "There are two of us. And two groups of them." The detective nodded at Marcus and Ianira, who still lay unmoving except to breathe. Fright tightened down another notch, leaving Jenna to wonder if she'd ever be hungry again, her gut hurt so much. Noah said more gently, "We have to split up, kid. If we send Marcus and the girls through without a guard . . . hell, kid, we might as well shoot them through the head ourselves. No, we *know* they're going to follow whoever goes through the Wild West Gate. So I'll go with them, pose as somebody they're likely to think is you, use a name they'll think is something you'd come up with, something you'd think is clever—"

The teenager interrupted. "You don't look like her. Not anything like her. Nobody would believe you *were* her. You are too tall."

For the first time, Jenna Nicole Caddrick saw Noah Armstrong completely flummoxed. The detective's mouth opened onto shocked silence. But the kid who spoke Latin—which probably meant he was a downtimer, too, same as Marcus—wasn't finished. "I look more like her than any of us. I'll go in her place. If I dress up like a rich tourist, wear a wig the color of her hair, pretend to be rude and obnoxious, wear a bonnet low over my eyes and swear a lot, the people hunting *her*," the kid nodded toward Jenna, "will think she's *me*. Or I'm her. It *will* work," he insisted. "There is a tour leaving tomorrow that plans to shoot in a special competition, men and women both. I *have* watched every John Wayne movie ever made, twice, and I have seen thousands of tourists. I can pretend to be a woman cowboy shooter with no trouble at all."

The very fact that he'd come up with the idea in the first place told Jenna a great deal about how much the residents of this time station loathed tourists. Obnoxious and rude . . . It probably would work beautifully, given half a chance. "You realize you're risking your life?" she asked quietly.

The teenager stared her down. "Yes. They have tried to murder Ianira."

It was all that needed to be said.

"Julius—" Marcus started to protest.

"No," Julius swung that determined gaze toward his older friend. "If I die, then I will die with honor, protecting people I love. What more can any man ask?"

How did a kid that young end up that wise? Jenna thought about ancient Rome and what men did to other men there and shuddered inside. The fact that she, herself, had done exactly what this boy was volunteering to do didn't even occur to her. Jenna, too, was risking her own life to save Ianira's.

"That's settled, then," Noah said briskly. "Julius, I don't have words to thank you. Right now, I'd better go up to Commons, check into the hotel under the name on my station pass, find an outfitter. You, too, Jenna. I'll need help getting those steamer trunks back to the hotel, and all the gear we've got to buy along with it." The detective glanced at Marcus and Julius. "We'll bring the steamer trunks back right away, get Ianira and the rest of you into a hotel room until the gate goes. We're going to hide you right in the open, in a perfectly ordinary hotel room, and let them tear the basement and the rest of the station apart, looking for you. Then I'm going to establish my Denver persona with a vengeance, draw the attention of the bastards after us, so they'll concentrate on Denver, rather than London. There's going to be one more rude and obnoxious cowboy added to the station's population, today, I believe, the sooner the better. With a name that ought to grab somebody's attention."

The purloined letter . . . Jenna grimaced. She sure as hell didn't have any better ideas. Noah had gotten her out of New York alive. She was pretty sure Noah could get them all out of the station alive, too. Whether or not she and Ianira stayed that way in London was up to Jenna. She prayed she was up to the job. Because there just wasn't anybody else around to do it. Thoughts of her father brought her teeth together, hard and brutal. *You're gonna pay for this, you son-of-a-bitch. You'll pay, if it's the last thing I ever do on this earth!*

Then she headed up to Commons on Noah Armstrong's heels to fetch a steamer trunk.

Chapter Four

Shangri-La Station was an Escheresque blend of major airport terminal, world-class shopping mall, and miniature city, all tucked away safely inside a massive cavern in the heart of the uplifted limestone massifs of the Himalayan mountains, a cavern which had been gradually enlarged and remolded into one of the busiest terminals in the entire time-touring industry. Portions of the station emerged into the open sunshine on the mountain's flank, or would have, if Shangri-La's engineers hadn't artificially extended that rocky flank to cover the station's outer walls in natural-looking concrete "rock" faces. Because the terminal's main structure followed the maze of the cave system's inner caverns, TT-86 was a haphazard affair that sprawled in unexpected directions, with tunnels occasionally boring their way through solid rock to connect one section of the station with another.

The major time-touring gates all lay in the Commons, of course, a vast area of twisting balconies, insane staircases and ramps, and all the glitter of high-class shops and restaurants that even the most discriminating of billionaires could wish to find themselves surrounded with. But because Commons followed the twists and turns of the immense cavern, there was no straight shot or even line-of-sight view from one end to the other. And station Residential snaked back into even more remote corners and crannies, with apartments tucked in like cells in a beehive designed by LSD-doped honeybees.

The underpinnings of the station descended multiple stories into the mountain's rocky heart, where the nitty-gritty, daily business of keeping a small city operational was carried out. Machinery driven by a miniature atomic pile hummed in the rocky silence. The trickle and rush of running water from natural underground streams and waterfalls could be heard in the sepulchral darkness beyond the station's heating, cooling, and waste-disposal plants. Down here, anybody could hide anything for a period of many months, if not years.

Margo had realized long ago that Shangri-La Station was immense. She just hadn't realized how big it really was. Not until Skeeter Jackson led them down circuitous, narrow tunnels into a maze he clearly knew as well as Margo knew the route from Kit's palatial apartment to her library cubicle. Equally clearly, Skeeter had taken full advantage of this rat's maze to pull swift disappearing acts from station security and irate tourists he'd fleeced, conned, or just plain robbed.

Probably what saved his life when that enraged gladiator was trying to skewer him with a sword, she thought silently. Under Skeeter's direction, their search party broke apart at intervals, combing the corridors and tunnels individually, only to rejoin one another further on. She could hear the footsteps and voices of other search parties off in the distance. The echoes, eerie and distorted, left Margo shivering in the slight underground chill that no amount of central heating could dispel. Occasional screams and girder-bending shrieks drifted down from the enormous *pteranodon sternbergi* which had entered the station through an unstable gate into the era of dinosaurs.

The size of a small aircraft, the enormous flying reptile lived in an immense hydraulic cage that could be hoisted up from the sub-basements right through the floor to the Commons level for "feeding demonstrations." The pterodactyl ate several mountains of fish a day, far more than they could keep stocked through the gates. So the head of pest control, Sue Fritchey, had hatched an ambitious project to keep the big *sternbergi* fed: breeding her own subterranean food supply from an up-time hatchery and any down-time fingerlings they could bring in. The sub-basement corridors were lined with rows and high-stacked tiers of empty aquariums, waiting to be filled with the next batch of live fingerlings. Piles and dusty stacks of the empty glass boxes left the tunnels under Little Agora and Frontier Town looking like the ghost of a pet shop long since bankrupt, its fish sold below cost or dumped down the nearest toilet.

It was a lonely, eerie place to have to search for a missing friend.

Margo glanced at her watch. How long had they been searching, now? Four hours, twenty minutes. Time was running out, at least for her and anyone else heading down the Britannia Gate. She bit one lip as she glanced at Shahdi Feroz, who represented in one package very nearly everything Margo wanted to be: poised, beautiful, a respected professional, experienced with temporal gates, clocking in nearly as much down time as some Time Tours guides. Time Tours had actually approached Dr. Feroz several times with offers to guide "seance and spiritualist tours" down the Britiannia. She'd turned them down flat, each and every time they'd offered. Margo admired her for sticking by her principles, when she could've been making pots and kettles full of money. Enough to fund her down-time research for the next century or two.

And speaking of down-time research . . .

"Kit," Margo said quietly, "we're running short of time."

Her grandfather glanced around, checked his own watch, frowned. "Yes. Skeeter, I'm sorry, but Margo and Dr. Feroz have a gate to make."

Skeeter turned his head slightly, lips compressed. "I'm supposed to work that gate, too, you know. We're almost directly under Frontier Town now. We finish this section of tunnels, then they can run along and play detective down the Britannia as much as they want."

Margo held her breath as Kit bristled silently; but her grandfather held his temper. Maybe because he, too, could see the agony in Skeeter's eyes. Kit said only, "All right, why don't you take that tunnel?" and nodded toward a corridor that branched off to the left. "Dr. Feroz, perhaps you'd go with Margo? You can discuss last-minute plans for the tour while you search."

Margo squirmed inwardly, but she couldn't very well protest. She was going to spend the next three months of her life in this woman's company. She'd have to face her sooner or later and it might as well be sooner.

Kit pointed down one of the sinuous, winding tunnels. "Take that fork off to the right. I'll go straight ahead. We'll meet you—how much farther?" he asked Skeeter.

"Fifty yards. Then we'll take the stairs up to Frontier Town."

They split up. Margo glanced at Shahdi Feroz and felt her face redden. Margo barely had a high school diploma and one semester of college. She had learned more in Shangri-La's library than she had in that stuffy, impossible up-time school. And she had learned, enormously. But after that mortifying mistake, with Shahdi Feroz correcting her misapprehension about Nichol gangs' weapons of choice, it wouldn't matter that Margo had logged nearly two-hundred hours through the Britannia or that she spoke fluent Cockney. Kit had drilled her until she could not only make sense of the gibberish that passed for Cockney dialect, but could produce original conversations in it, too. Without giving herself too savage a headache, remembering all the half-rhymes and word-replacement games the dialect required. None of that would matter, not when she'd goofed on the very first day, not when Margo's lack of a diploma left her vulnerable and scared.

Shahdi Feroz, however, surprised Margo with an attempted first gesture at friendliness. The scholar smiled hesitantly, one corner of her lips twisting in chagrin. "I did not mean to embarrass you, Miss Smith. If you are to guide the Ripper Watch Tour, then you clearly have the experience to do so."

Margo almost let it go. She wanted badly to have this woman think she really did know what she was doing. But that wasn't honest and might actually be dangerous, if they got into a tight spot and the scholar thought she knew more than she did. She cleared her throat, aware that her face had turned scarlet. "Thanks, but I'm not, really." The startled glance Dr. Feroz gave her prompted Margo to finish before she lost her nerve. "It's just that I'm in training to be a time scout, you see, and Kit wants me to get some experience doing fieldwork."

"Kit?" the other woman echoed. "You know Kit Carson that well, then, to use his first name? I wish I did."

Some of Margo's nervousness drained away. If Dr. Shahdi Feroz could look and sound that wistful and uncertain, then maybe there was hope for Margo, after all. She grinned, relief momentarily transcending worry and fear for Ianira's family. "Well, yeah, I guess you could say so. He's my grandfather."

"Oh!" Then, startling Margo considerably, "That must be very difficult for you, Miss Smith. You have my sympathy. And respect. It is never easy, to live up to greatness in one's ancestors."

Strangely, Margo received the impression that Shahdi Feroz wasn't speaking entirely of Margo. "No," she said quietly, "it isn't." Shahdi Feroz remained silent, respecting Margo's privacy, for which she was grateful. She and the older woman began testing doors they came to and jotting down the numbers painted on them, so maintenance could check the rooms later, since neither of them had keys. Margo did rattle the knobs and knock, calling out, "Hello? Ianira? Marcus? It's Margo Smith . . ." Nobody answered, however, and the echoes that skittered away down the tunnel mocked her efforts. She bit her lower lip. How many rooms to check, just like these, and how many miles of tunnels? God, they could be *anywhere*.

No, she told herself, not just anywhere. If they had been killed, the killer would either have needed keys to unlock these doors or would've had to use tools to jimmy the locks. And so far, neither Margo nor Shahdi Feroz had found any suspicious scratches or toolmarks indicating a forced door. So they might still be alive.

Somewhere.

Please, God, let them still be alive, somewhere . . .

Their tunnel twisted around, following the curve of the cavern wall, and re-joined the main tunnel fifty yards from the point they'd left it. Kit was already there, waiting. Skeeter, grim and silent, arrived a moment later.

"All right," Skeeter's voice was weary with disappointment, "that's the whole section we were assigned." The pain in his voice jerked Margo out of her own worry with a stab of guilt. She hadn't lost anything, really, in that goof with Shahdi Feroz, except a little pride. Skeeter had just lost his only friends in the whole world.

"I'm sorry, Skeeter," she found herself saying, surprising them both with the sincerity in her voice.

Skeeter met her gaze steadily for a long moment, then nodded slowly. "Thanks. I appreciate that, Margo. We'd better get back up to Commons, get ready to go through the Britannia." He grimaced. "I'll carry the luggage through, because I agreed to take the job. But I won't be staying."

No, Margo realized with a pang. He wouldn't. Skeeter would come straight back through that open gate and probably kill himself searching, with lack of sleep and forgetting to eat. . . . They trooped wordlessly up the stairs to the boisterous noise of Frontier Town. With the Wild West gate into Denver set to open tomorrow, wannabe cowboys in leather chaps and jingling spurs sauntered from saloon to saloon, ogling the bar girls and pouring down cheap whiskey and beer. Rinky-tink piano music drifted out through saloon doors to mingle with the voices of tourists speculating on the search underway, the fate of the construction workers who'd attacked Ianira, her family, and her acolytes, on the identity of the Ripper, and what sights they planned to see in Denver of 1885 and the surrounding gold-mining towns.

In front of Happy Jack's saloon, a guy with drooping handlebar mustaches, who wore an outlandish getup that consisted of low-slung Mexican sombrero, red silk scarf, black leather chaps, black cotton shirt, black work pants tucked into black, tooled-leather boots, and absurdly roweled silver spurs, was staggering into the crowd, bawling at the top of his lungs. "Gonna win me that medal, y'hear? Joey Tyrolin's the name, gonna win that shootin' match, l'il lady!"

He accosted a tourist who wore a buckskin skirt and blouse. She staggered back, apparently from the smell of his breath. Joey Tyrolin, drunker than any skunk Margo had yet seen in Frontier Town, drew a fancy pair of Colt Single-Action Army pistols and executed an equally fancy roadhouse spin, marred significantly by the amount of alcohol he'd recently consumed. One of the .45 caliber revolvers came adrift mid-air and splashed into a nearby horse trough. Laughter exploded in every direction. A scowl as dark as his clothes appeared in a face that matched his red silk bandanna.

"Gonna win me that shootin' match, y'hear! Joey Tyrolin c'n shoot th' eye outta an eagle at three hunnerd yards . . ." He bent, gingerly fishing his gun out of the horse trough.

Margo muttered, "Maybe he'll fall in and drown? God, am I ever glad we're going to London, not Denver."

Kit, too, eyed the pistolero askance. "Let's hope he confines his shooting to that black-powder competition he's bragging about. I've seen far too many idiots like that one go down time to Denver and challenge some local to a gunfight. Occasionally, they choose the wrong local, someone who can't be killed because he's too important to history. Now and again, they come back to the station in canvas bags."

Shahdi Feroz glanced up at him. "I should imagine their families must protest rather loudly?"

"All too often, yes. It's why station management requires the hold harmless waivers all time tourists must sign. Fools have a way of discovering," Kit added with a disgusted glance toward the drunken Joey Tyrolin, who now dripped water all over the Frontier Town floor and any tourist within reach, "that the laws of time travel, like the laws of physics, have no pity and no remorse."

Skeeter said nothing at all. He merely glared at the drunken tourist and clamped his lips, eyes ravaged by a pain Margo could literally feel, it was so strong. Margo reached out hesitantly, touched his shoulder. "I'm sorry, Skeeter. I hope you find them. Tell them . . . tell them we helped look, okay?"

Skeeter had stiffened under her hand. But he nodded. "Thanks, Margo. I'll see you later."

He strode away through the crowd, disappearing past Joey Tyrolin, who teetered and abruptly found himself seated in the horse trough he'd just fished his pistol out of. Laughter floated in Skeeter's wake. Margo didn't join in. Skeeter was hurting, worse than she'd ever believed it possible for him to hurt. When she looked up, she found Kit's gaze on her. Her grandfather nodded, having read what was in her eyes and correctly interpreted it, all without a word spoken. It was one of the reasons she was still a little in awe of him—and why, at this moment, she loved him more fiercely than ever.

"I'll keep looking, too, Imp," he promised. "You'd better scoot if you want to get into costume and get your luggage to the gate on time."

Margo sighed. "Thanks. You'll come see us off?"

He ruffled her hair affectionately. "Just try and keep me away."

She gave him a swift, rib-cracking hug, having to blink salty water out of her eyes. "Love you, Kit," she whispered.

Then she fled, hoping he hadn't noticed the tears.

Time scouting was a tough business.

Just now, Margo didn't feel quite tough enough.

The night dripped.

Not honest rain, no; but a poisonous mist of coal smoke and river fog and steam that carried nameless scents in the coalescing yellow droplets. Above a gleam of damp roofing slates, long curls of black, acrid smoke belched from squat chimney pots that huddled down like misshapen gargoyles against an airborne, sulphurous tide. Far above, an almost forgotten moon hung poised above the city, a sickle-shaped crescent, the tautly drawn bow of the Divine Huntress of the Night, pure as unsullied silver above the foul murk, taking silent aim into the heart of a city long accustomed to asphyxiating beneath its own lethal mantle.

Gas jets from scattered street lamps stung the darkness like impotent bees. The fog dispersed their glow into forlorn, hopeless little pustules of light along wet cobblestones and soot-blackened walls of wood and stone and ancient, crumbling brick. Diffuse smells lurked in eddies like old, fading bruises. The scent of harbor water thick with weeds and dead things afloat in the night drifted in from the river. Wet and half-rotted timbers lent a whiff of salt and moldering fungus. Putrefied refuse from the chamber pots and privies of five million people stung the throat and eyes, fighting for ascendency over the sickly stench of dead fish and drowned dogs.

The distant, sweet freshness of wet hay and muddied straw eddying down from the enormous hay markets of Whitechapel and Haymarket itself lent a stark note of contrast, reminding the night that somewhere beyond these dismal brick walls, fresh air and clean winds swept across the land. Closer at hand came the stink of marsh and tidal mud littered with the myriad flotsam cast up by the River Thames to lap against the docks of Wapping and Stepney and the Isle of Dogs, a miasma that permeated the chilly night with a cloying stink like corpses too long immersed in a watery grave.

In the houses of respectable folk, rambling in orderly fashion to the west along the river banks and far inland to the north, candleshades and gas lamps had long since been extinguished. But here in the raucous streets of Wapping, of Whitechapel and of Stepney, drunken voices bellowed out the words of favorite drinking tunes. In rented rooms the size of storage bins, huddled in ramshackle brick tenements which littered these darkened streets like cancerous growths, enterprising pimps played the blackmail-profitable game of "arse and twang" with hired whores, unsuspecting sailors, and switchblade knives. Working men and women stood or sat in doorways and windows, listening to the music drifting along the streets from public houses and poor-men's clubs like the Jewish Working Men's Association of Whitechapel, until the weariness of hard work for long, squalid hours dragged them indoors to beds and cots and stairwells for the night. In the darkened, shrouded streets, business of another kind rose sharply with the approach of the wee hours. Men moved in gangs or pairs or slipped singly from shadow to shadow, and plied the cudgels and prybars of their trade against the skulls and window casements of their favorite victims.

Along one particular fog-cloaked street, where music and light spilled heedlessly from a popular gathering place for local denizens, bootheels clicked faintly on the wet cobbles as a lone young man, more a fair-haired boy than a man fully grown, staggered out into the wet night. A working lad, but not in the usual sense of the word, he had spent the better part of his night getting himself pissed as a newt on what had begun as "a quick one down to boozer" and had steadily progressed—through a series of pints of whatever the next-closest local had been selling cheapest—into a rat-arsed drunken binge.

A kerb crawler of indeterminate years appeared from out of the yellow murk and flashed a saucy smile. "You look to be a bloke what likes jolly comp'ny, mate." She took his arm solicitously when he reeled against a sooty brick wall, leaving a dark streak of damp down his once-fine shirt, which had seen far better days in the fashionable West End. She smiled into his eyes. "What about a four-penny knee trembler t' share wiv a comfy lady?" A practiced hand stole along the front of his shapeless trousers.

He grabbed a handful of the wares for sale, since it was expected and he had at least the shreds of a reputation to maintain, then he sighed dolefully, as though a sluggish, drunken thought had come to him. He carefully slurred his voice into the slang he'd heard on these streets for weeks, now. "Ain't got a four-pence, luv. No ackers a'tall. Totally coals an' coke, 'at's what I am, I've spent the last of what I brung 'ome t'night on thirty-eleven pints."

The woman eyed him more closely in the dim light. "I know 'at voice . . ."

When she got a better look, she let out a disgusted screech and knocked his hand away. " 'Oo are you tryin' t'fool, Morgan? Grabbin' like it's me thripenny bits you'd want, when it's cobbler's awl's you'd rather be gropin' after? Word's out, 'bout you, Morgan. 'At Polly Nichols shot 'er mouth good, when she were drunk, 'at she did." The woman shoved him away with a harsh, "Get 'ome t' yer lovin' Mr. Eddy—if th' toff'll 'ave you back, whoever he might be, unnatural sod!" She gave a short, ugly bark of laughter and stalked away into the night, muttering about wasting her time on beardless irons and finding a bloke with some honest sausage and mash to pay her doss money for the night.

The cash-poor—and recently infamous—young drunk reeled at her sharp shove and plowed straight into the damp wall, landing with a low grunt of dismayed surprise. He caught himself ineffectually there and crumpled gradually to the wet pavement. Morgan sat there for a moment, blinking back tears of misery and absently rubbing his upper arm and shoulder. For several moments, he considered seriously what he ought to do next. Sitting in muck on a wet pavement for the remainder of the night didn't seem a particularly attractive notion. He hadn't any place to go and no doss money of his own and he was very far, indeed, from Cleveland Street and the fancy West Side house where he'd once been popular with a certain class of rich toffs—and until tomorrow night, at least, when Eddy would finally bring him the promised money, he would have nothing to buy food, either.

His eyes stung. Damn that bitch, Polly Nichols! She was no better than he was, for all the righteous airs she put on. Just a common slattern, who'd lift her skirts for a stinking fourpence—or a well-filled glass of gin, for that matter. Word on the streets hereabout was, she'd been a common trollop for so many years her own husband had tossed her out as an unfit mother and convinced the courts to rescind the order for paying her maintenance money. Morgan, at least, had plied his trade with respectably wealthy clients; but thinking about that only made the hurt run deeper. The fine West End house had tossed him out, when he'd lost their richest client. *Wasn't my fault Eddy threw me over for that bloody mystic of his, with his fancy ways and fine house and his bloody deformed . . .*

And Polly Nichols, curse the drunken bitch, had found out about that particular house on Cleveland Street and Morgan's place in it, had shoved him against a wall and hissed out, "I know all about it, Morgan. All about what you let a bloke do t'you for money. I've 'eard you got a little rainy day fund put aside, savin's, like, from that 'ouse what tossed you onto the street. You 'and it over, Morgan, maybe I won't grass on you, eh? Those constables in H Division, now, they might just want to know about an 'andsome lad like you, bendin' over for it."

Morgan had caught his breath in horror. The very last thing Morgan needed was entanglements with the police. Prostitution was bad enough for a woman. A lad caught prostituting himself with another *man* . . . Well, the death penalty was off the books, but it'd be prison for sure, a nice long stretch at hard labor, and the thought of what would happen to a lad like himself in prison . . . . But Morgan had come away from the house on Cleveland Street with nothing save his clothes, a half-crown his last client had given him as a bonus, which he'd managed to hide from the house's proprietor, and a black eye.

And Eddy's letters.

"Here . . ." He produced the half-crown, handed it over. "It's everything I've got in the world. Please, Polly, I'm starving as it is, don't tell the constables."

"*An 'alf a crown?*" she screeched. "A mis'rable *'alf crown?* Bleedin' little sod! You come from a fine 'ouse, you did, wiv rich men givin' it to you, what do you mean by givin' me nuffink but a miserly 'alf crown!"

"It's all I've got!" he cried, desperate. "They took everything else away! Even most of my clothes!" A harsh, half-strangled laugh broke loose. "Look at my face, Polly! That's what they gave me as a going away present!"

"Copper's'll give you worse'n bruises an' a blacked eye, luv!" She jerked around and started to stalk away. "Constable!"

Morgan clutched at her arm. "Wait!"

She paused. "Well?"

He licked his lips. They were all he had . . . but if this drunken whore sent him to prison, what good would Eddy's letters do him? And he didn't have to give them all to her. "I've got one thing. One valuable thing."

"What's 'at?" She narrowed her eyes.

"Letters . . ."

"Letters? What sort of fool d'you tyke me for?"

"They're valuable letters! Worth a lot of money!"

The narrow-eyed stare sharpened. "What sort o' letters 'ave you got, Morgan, that'd be worth any money?"

He licked his lips once more. "Love letters," he whispered. "From someone important. They're in his handwriting, on his personal stationery, and he's signed them with his own name. Talks about everything he did to me when he visited me in that house, everything he planned to do on his next visit. They're worth a fortune, Polly. I'll share them with you. He's going to give me a lot of money to get them back, a *lot* of money, Polly. Tomorrow night, he's going to buy back the first one, I'll give you some of the money—"

"You'll give me the letters!" she snapped. "Hah! Share wiv *you?* I'll 'ave them letters, if you please, y'little sod, you just 'and 'em over." She held out one grasping hand, eyes narrowed and dangerous.

Morgan clenched his fists, hating her. At least he hadn't told the bitch how many letters there were. He'd divided them into two packets, one in his trouser pocket, the other beneath his shirt. The ones in his shirt were the letters Eddy had penned to him in English. The ones in his trouser pocket were the *other* letters, the "special surprise" Eddy had sent to him during that last month of visits. The filthy tart wouldn't be able to read a word of them. He pulled the packet from his trouser pocket and handed them over. "Here, curse you! And may you have joy reading them!" he added with a spiteful laugh, striding away before she could realize that Prince Albert Victor had penned those particular letters in *Welsh*.

Now, hours later, having managed to find himself a sailor on the docks who wanted a more masculine sort of sport, Morgan was drunk and bitter, a mightily scared and very lonely lad far away from his native Cardiff. He rubbed his wet cheek with the back of his hand. Morgan had been a fool, a jolly, bloody fool, ever to leave Cardiff, but it was too late, now, to cry about it. And he couldn't sit here on his bum all night, some constable would pass and then he *would* be spending the night courtesy of the Metropolitan Police Department's H Division.

Morgan peered about, trying to discern shapes through the fog, and thought he saw the dark form of a man nearby, but the fog closed round the shadow again and no one approached nearer, so he decided there was no one about to help him regain his feet, after all. Scraping himself slowly together, he elbowed his way back up the wall until he was more or less upright again, then coughed and shivered and wandered several yards further along the fog-shrouded street. At times, his ears played tricks with the echoing sounds that spilled out onto the dark streets from distant public houses. Snatches of laughter and song came interspersed faintly with the nearer click of footfalls on pavement, but each time he peered round, he found nothing but swirling, malevolent yellow drifts. So he continued his meandering way down the wet street, allowing his shoulder to bump against the sooty bricks to guide and steady him on his way, making for the hidey hole he used when there was no money for a doss-house bed.

The entrance to a narrow alley robbed him of his sustaining wall. He scudded sideways, a half-swamped sailboat lashed by a sudden and brutal cross-wise gale, and stumbled into the dark alley. He tangled his wobbling feet, met another wet brick wall face on, and barely caught himself from a second ignominious slide into the muck. He was cursing softly under his breath when he heard that same, tantalizing whisper of faint footfalls from behind. Only this time, they were no trick of his hearing. Someone was coming toward him through the fog, hurrying now as he clung to the dirty brick wall in the darkness of the alley.

Another tart, perhaps, or a footpad out to pinch what he didn't any longer possess. Alarm flared slowly through his drunken haze. He started to turn—but it was far too late. A blow from something heavy smashed across his skull from behind. Light exploded behind his eyes in a detonation of pain and terror. Unable even to cry out, he crumpled straight down into darkness.

As Morgan toppled toward the filthy alley, a wiry man in his early thirties, dark-skinned with the look of Eastern Europe in his narrow face and eyes and dark moustaches, caught him under the arms. This second man grunted softly, curling his lip at the reek of alcohol and sweat which rose from the boy's grimy, once fancy clothes. This was no time, however, for fastidiousness. He twisted the boy around with a practiced jerk and heaved the dead weight over one shoulder. A swift glance told him the thick fog and darkness of the narrow alleyway had concealed the attack from any chance observation.

Well, Johnny my boy, he smiled to himself, *you've made a good start. Now to finish this pathetic little cockerel.* Dr. John Lachley was as pleased with the enshrouding yellow murk as he was with his swift handiwork and the drunken little fool he'd trailed all evening, who'd finally wandered so conveniently close to a place he could strike. He'd feared he might have to trail the boy all the way back to the filthy hole he'd been living in, on the first floor of a ramshackle, abandoned warehouse along the docks, so dilapidated and dangerous it was in the process of being torn down.

Quite a come-down, eh, pretty Morgan?

Dark-haired, dark-eyed, darker-souled, John Lachley moved deeper into the darkness of the alleyway, staggering slightly under his burden until he found his new center of balance. The alley was narrow, clotted with rubbish and stench. A rat's eyes gleamed briefly in the foggy gloom. A street—little wider than the alley he followed—appeared through the murk. He turned to his right, moving toward the invisible docks a mere three blocks away, which were concealed from sight by grim warehouses and tumble-down shacks. Their bricks leaned drunkenly in the night, whole chunks of their walls missing in random patterns of darkness and swirling, jaundiced eddies.

John Lachley's clothes, little cleaner than those of his victim, revealed very little about their current owner; neither did the dark cloth cap he wore pulled low over his eyes. During daylight, his was a face that might well be recognized, even here, where many years ago Johnny Anubis had once been a household name, sought out by the poorest fishwives in search of hope; but in the darkness, in such rough clothing, even a man of his . . . notoriety . . . might go unremarked.

He smiled and paused at the entrance to one of the soot-streaked blocks of ramshackle flats. An iron key from his pocket unlocked a shabby wooden door. He cast a glance overhead and spotted the waning horns of the sickle-shaped moon. He smiled again. "Lovely night for scything, Lady," he said softly to the sharp-edged crescent. "Grant me success in mine, eh?"

Sulphurous fog drifted across the faintly glowing horns of that wicked sickle, seeming almost to catch and tear on the sharp points. He smiled again; then ducked inside, swung his victim's legs and head clear, and locked the door behind him. He needed no light to navigate the room, for it contained nothing but coal dust and scattered bits of refuse. A savage barking erupted from the darkness of the next room, sounding like every hound in hell had been loosed. Lachley spoke sharply. "Garm!"

The barking subsided into low growls. Heaving his burden into a slightly more comfortable position on his shoulder, John Lachley entered the next room and swung shut another heavy door which he located by feel alone. Here he paused to grope along the wall for the gas light. The gas lit with a faint hiss and pop; dim light sprang up. The windowless brick walls were barren, the floor covered with a cheap rug. A wooden bed frame with a thin cotton tick stood along one wall. A battered dry sink held a jug and basin, a lantern, and a grimy towel. An equally battered clothes press leaned drunkenly in one corner. The chained dog crouched at the center of the room stopped growling and thumped its tail in greeting.

"Have a pleasant evening, Garm?" he addressed the dog, retrieving a meat pie from one pocket, which he unwrapped from its greasy newspaper wrapping. He tossed it carelessly to the huge black hound. The dog bounded to its feet and snatched the food mid-air, wolfing it down in one bite. Had anyone besides himself entered this room, the dog would have shredded them to gobbets. Garm had earned his meat pies on more than one occasion.

Lachley dumped his victim onto the bed, then pulled back the rug and prised up a wooden trap door cut into the floorboards. He heaved this to one side, lit the lantern and set it beside the gaping hole in the floor, then retrieved the unconscious boy from the bed and shouldered his inert burden once again. He paused when he approached the edge and felt downward with one foot, finding the top step of a steep, narrow staircase. Lachley descended cautiously into darkness, retrieving his lantern as he moved downward. A wet, fetid smell of mold and damp brick rose to meet him.

Light splashed across a clammy wall where a rusty iron hook protruded from the discolored bricks. He hung the lantern on this, then reached up and dragged the trapdoor back into place. It settled with a scrape and hollow bang. Dust sifted down into his hair and collar, peppering his clothes as well as his victim's. He dusted off his palms, brushed splinters from a sleeve, then rescued his lantern from its hook and continued the descent. His feet splashed at the bottom. Wavering yellow light revealed an arched, circular brick tunnel through the bowels of Wapping, stretching away into blackness in either direction. The filthy brick was chipped and mottled with algae and nameless fungi. He whistled softly as he walked, listening to the echoes spill away like foam from a mug of dark ale.

As Lachley paralleled the invisible Thames, other tunnels intersected the one he'd entered. The sound of rushing water carried through the sepulchral darkness from underground streams and buried rivers— the Fleet River, which had blown up in 1846 from the trapped rancid and fetid gasses beneath the pavements, so toxic was the red muck leaking from the tanneries above; the once-noble Walbrook, which ran through the heart of the City of London; and River Tyburn, which had lent its name to the triple-tree where convicts were hanged at the crossroads— each of them was now confined beneath London's crowded, filthy streets, churning and spilling along their former courses as major sewers dumping into the mighty Thames.

John Lachley ignored the distant roar of water as he ignored the sewer stench permeating the tunnels. He listened briefly to the echoes of his footfalls mingle with the squeals of rats fighting over a dead dog's corpse and the distant sound of mating cats. At length, he lifted his lantern to mark the exact spot where the low entrance loomed. He ducked beneath a dripping brick arch, turned sharp left, and emerged in a narrow, coffin-sized space set with a thick iron door. An brass plaque set into it bore the legend *"Tibor."*

Since the word was not English, the owner of this door had little fear of its meaning being deciphered should anyone chance to stumble across the hidden chamber. Lachley was not Hungarian by birth, but he knew the Slavic tongues and more importantly, their legends and myths, had studied them almost since boyhood. It amused him to put a name that meant "holy place" on the door of his private retreat from workaday London and its prosaic, steam-engine mentality.

Another key retrieved from a coat pocket grated in the lock; then the stout door swung noiselessly open, its hinges well oiled against the damp. His underground Tibor welcomed him home with a rush of dark, wet air and the baleful glow of perpetual fire from the gas jet he, himself, had installed, siphoning off the requisite fuel from an unsuspecting fuel company's gas mains. Familiar sights loomed in the dim chamber: vaulted ceiling bricks stained with moss and patchy brown mold; the misshapen form of gnarled oak limbs from the great, dead trunk he'd sawn into sections, hauled down in pieces, and laboriously fitted back together with steel and iron; the eternal gas fire blazing at its feet from an altar-mounted nozzle; huddled cloaks and robes and painted symbols which crawled across the walls, speaking answers to riddles few in this city would have thought even to ask; a sturdy work table along one wall, and wooden cabinets filled with drawers and shelves which held the paraphernalia of his self-anointed mission.

The reek of harsh chemicals and the reverberations of long-faded incantations, words of power and dominion over the creatures he sought to control, spoken in all-but-forgotten ancient tongues, bade him welcome as he stepped once more across the threshold and re-entered his own very private Tibor. He dumped his burden carelessly onto the work table, heedless of the crack of his victim's head against the wooden surface, and busied himself. There was much to do. He lit candles, placed them strategically about the room, stripped off his rough working clothes and donned the ceremonial robes he was always careful to leave behind in this sanctuary.

White and voluminous, a mockery of priestly vestments, and hooded with a deep and death-pale hood which covered half his face when he lowered it down, the semi-Druidic robes had been sewn to his specifications years previously by a sweatshop seamstress who had possessed no other way to pay for the divinations she'd come to him to cast for her. He slipped into the robes, shook back the deep hood for now, and busied himself with the same efficient industry which had brought him out of the misery of the streets overhead and into the life he now sought to protect at all cost.

John Lachley searched the boy's appallingly filthy, empty pockets, then felt the crackle of paper beneath Morgan's shirt. When he stripped off his victim, a sense of triumph and giddy relief swept through him: Morgan's letters were tucked into the waistband of his trousers, the foolscap sheets slightly grimy and rumpled. Each had been folded into a neat packet. He read them, curious as to their contents, and damned Albert Victor for a complete and bumbling fool. Had these letters come into the hands of the proper authorities . . .

Then he reached the end and stared at the neatly penned sheets of foolscap.

There were only four letters.

John Lachley tightened his fist down, crushing the letters in his hand, and blistered the air. *Four!* And Eddy had said there were *eight!* Where had the little bastard put the other half of the set? All but shaking with rage, he forced himself to close his fists around empty air, rather than the unconscious boy's throat. He needed to throttle the life out of this little bastard, needed to inflict terror and ripping, agonizing hurt for daring to threaten *him*, Dr. John Lachley, advisor to the Queen's own grandson, who should one day sit the throne in Victoria's stead . . .

With a snarl of rage, he tossed Morgan's clothing into a rubbish bin beneath the work table for later burning, then considered how best to obtain the information he required. A slight smile came to his lips. He bound the lad's hands and feet, then heaved him up and hauled him across the chamber to the massive oak tree which dominated the room, its gnarled branches supported now by brackets in ceiling and walls.

He looped Morgan's wrist ropes over a heavy iron hook embedded in the wood and left him dangling with his toes several inches clear of the floor. This done, he opened cabinet doors and rattled drawers out along their slides, laying out the ritual instruments. Wand and cauldron, dagger, pentacle, and sword . . . each with meanings and ritual uses not even those semi-serious fools Waite and Mathers could imagine in their fumbling, so-called studies. Their "Order of the Golden Dawn" had invited him to join, shortly after its establishment last year. He had accepted, naturally, simply to further his contacts in the fairly substantial social circles through which the order's various members moved; but thought of their so-called researches left him smiling. Such simplicity of belief was laughable.

Next he retrieved the ancient Hermetic deck with its arcane trumps, a symbolic alphabetical key to the terrible power of creation and transformation locked away aeons previously in the pharoahonic *Book of Thoth*. After that came the mistletoe to smear the blade, whose sticky sap would ensure free, unstaunchable bleeding . . . and the great, thick-bladed steel knife with which to take the trophy skull . . . He had never actually performed such a ritual, despite a wealth of knowledge. His hands trembled from sheer excitement as he laid out the cards, mumbling incantations over them, and studied the pattern unfolding. Behind him, his victim woke with a slow, wretched groan.

It was time.

He purified the blade with fire, painted mistletoe sap across its flat sides and sharp edge, then lifted his sacred, deep white hood over his hair and turned to face his waiting victim. Morgan peered at him through bloodshot, terrified eyes. Morgan's throat worked, but no sound issued from the boy's bloodless lips. He stepped closer to the sweating, naked lad who hung from Odin's sacred oak, its gnarled branches twisting overhead to touch the vaulted brick ceiling. A ghastly sound broke from his prisoner's throat. Morgan twisted against the ropes on his wrists, to no avail.

Then Lachley shook back his hood and smiled into the lad's eyes.

Blue eyes widened in shock. *"You!"* Then, terror visibly lashing him, Morgan choked out, "What— what'd I ever do to you, Johnny? Please . . . you got Eddy for yourself, why d'you want to hurt me now? I already lost my place in the house—"

He backhanded the little fool. Tears and blood streamed. *"Sodding little ponce! Blackmail him, will you?"*

Morgan whimpered, the terror in his eyes so deep they glazed over, a stunned rabbit's eyes. John Lachley let out a short, hard laugh. "What a jolly little fool you are, Morgan. And look at you now, done up like a kipper!" He caressed Morgan's bruised, wet face. "Did you think Eddy wouldn't tell me? Poor Eddy . . . Hasn't the brains God gave a common mollusk, but Eddy trusts me, bless him, does whatever I tell him to." He chuckled. "Spiritualist advisor to the future King of England. I'm at the front of a very long line of men, little Morgan, standing behind the rich and powerful, whispering into their ears what the stars and the gods and the spirits from beyond the grave want them to say and do and believe. So naturally, when our distraught Eddy received your message, he came straight to my doorstep, begging me to help him hush it all up."

The lad trembled violently where he dangled from the ropes, not even bothering to deny it. Not that denial would have saved him. Or even spared him the pain he would suffer before he paid the price for his schemes. Terror gleamed in Morgan's eyes, dripped down his face with the sweat pouring from his brow. Dry lips worked. His voice came as a cracked whisper. "W-what do you want? I swear, I'll leave England, go back to Cardiff, never whisper a word . . . I'll even sign on as deck hand for a ship out to Hong Kong . . ."

"Oh, no, my sweet little Morgan," Lachley smiled, bending closer. "Hardly that. Do you honestly think the man who controls the future King of England is so great a fool as that?" He patted Morgan's cheek. "The first thing I want, Morgan, is the other four letters."

He swallowed sharply. "H-haven't got them—"

"Yes, I know you haven't got them." He brushed a fingertip down Morgan's naked breastbone. "Who *has* got them, Morgan? Tell me and I may yet make it easier for you."

When Morgan hesitated, Lachley slapped him, gently.

The boy began shaking, crying. "She—she was going to tell the constables—I hadn't any money left, all I had was the letters—gave her half of them to keep her quiet—"

"*Who?*" The second blow was harder, bruising his fair skin.

"Polly!" The name was wrenched from him. He sobbed it out again, "Polly Nichols . . . filthy, drunken tart . . ."

"And what will Polly Nichols do with them, eh?"

he asked, twisting cruelly a sensitive bit of Morgan's anatomy until the boy cried out in sharp protest. "Show them to all her friends? How much will *they* want, eh?"

"Wouldn't—wouldn't do any good, all she has is my word they're worth anything—"

He slapped Morgan again, hard enough to split his lips. "Stupid sod! Do you honestly think she won't read your pitiful letters? You *are* a fool, little boy. But don't ever make the mistake of thinking I am!"

Morgan was shaking his head frantically. "No, Johnny, no, you don't understand, she *can't* read them! They're not in English!"

Surprise left John Lachley momentarily speechless. "Not in English?" It came out flat as a squashed tomato. "What do you mean, not in English? Eddy doesn't have the intelligence to learn another language. I'm surprised the dear boy can speak his *own*, let alone a foreign one. Come, now, Morgan, you'll have to do better than that."

Morgan was crying again. "You'll see, I'll get them for you, Johnny, I'll show you, they're not in English, they're in Welsh, his tutor helped him—"

He backhanded the sniveling liar. Morgan's head snapped violently sideways.

"Don't play me for a fool!"

"Please," Morgan whimpered, bleeding from cut lips and a streaming nose, "it's true, why would I lie to you *now*, Johnny, when you promised you wouldn't hurt me again if I told you the truth? You have to believe me, *please* . . ."

John Lachley was going to enjoy coercing the truth from this pathetic little liar.

But Morgan wasn't done blubbering yet. His eyes, a watery blue from the tears streaming down his face, were huge and desperate as he babbled out, "Eddy *told* me about it, right after he sent the first one in Welsh, asked me if I liked his surprise. He thought

it was a grand joke, because the ever-brilliant Mr.
James K. Stephen—" it came out bitter, jealous,
sounding very much, in fact, like Eddy "—was always
so smart and learned things so easily and made sure
Eddy was laughed at all through Cambridge, because
everybody but a few of the dons knew it was *Mr.
James K. Stephen* writing Eddy's translations in Latin
and Greek for him, so Eddy could copy them out
correctly in his own hand! He *told* me about it, how
much he paid dear Jamesy for each translation his
tutor did for him while they were still at Cambridge!
So when Eddy wanted to write letters nobody else
could read, he got the doting Mr. James K. Stephen
to help him translate *those* for him, too, paid him ten
sovereigns for each letter, so he wouldn't whisper
about them afterwards . . ."

It was, Lachley decided, just possible that Morgan
was telling him the truth. Paying his tutor to translate his Latin and Greek at University was very Eddy-
like. So was paying the man to translate his love
letters, God help them all. He caught Morgan's chin
in one hand, tightened down enough to bruise his
delicate skin. "And how much did Eddy pay his tutor
to keep the secret that he was writing love letters in
Welsh to a male whore?"

"He didn't! Tell him, I mean. That I'm a boy. He
told Mr. Stephen that 'Morgan' was a pretty *girl* he'd
met, from Cardiff, said he wanted to impress her
with letters in her own native Welsh, so Mr. Stephen
wouldn't guess Eddy was writing to *me*. He's not so
very bright, Eddy, but he doesn't want to go to
prison! So he convinced Mr. Stephen I was a girl
and the gullible idiot helped Eddy write them, I
swear it, Eddy said he stood over his shoulder and
told him all the right Welsh words to use, even for
the dirty parts, only when Eddy wrote out the
second copies to me in private, he changed all the
words you'd use for a girl's body to the right ones

for a boy, because he looked that up, himself, so
he'd know—"

"*Second copies?*"

Morgan flinched violently. "*Please, Johnny, please
don't hit me again!* Eddy thought it would be funny,
so he sent me the first copies attached to the ones
he wrote out especially for me . . ."

His voice faded away as Lachley's white-faced
fury sank in, mistaking Lachley's rage honestly
enough. *My God, the royal bastard is stupider than
I thought! If it would do any good, I'd cut off
Eddy's bollocks and feed them to him! Any
magistrate in England would take one look at a
set of letters like that and throw away the bloody
key!*

He no longer doubted Morgan's sordid little tale
about Welsh translations. Eddy was just that much
of a fool, thinking himself clever with such a trick,
just to impress a money grubbing, blackmailing little
whore not fit to sell his wares for a crust of bread,
much less royal largesse.

Morgan was gasping out, "It's true, Johnny, I'll
prove it, I'll get the letters back and *show* you . . ."

"Oh, yes, Morgan. We will, indeed get those letters back. Tell me, just where might I find this Polly
Nichols?"

"She's been staying at that lodging house at 56
Flower and Dean Street, the White House they call
it, rooming with a man, some nights, other nights
sharing with Long Liz Stride or Catharine Eddowes,
whoever's got the doss money for the night and needs
a roommate to share the cost . . ."

"What did you tell Polly Nichols when you gave
her the letters?"

"That they were love letters," he whispered. "I
didn't tell her who they were from and I lied, said
they were on his personal stationery, when they're on
ordinary foolscap, so all she'll know is they've been

signed by someone named Eddy. Someone rich, but just Eddy, no last name, even."

"Very good, Morgan. Very, very good."

Hope flared in the little fool's wet eyes.

He patted Morgan's cheek almost gently.

Then Lachley brought out the knife.

Chapter Five

The reporters were waiting outside his office building, of course.

Senator Caddrick stepped out of his chauffeured limo and faced the explosion of camera flashes and television lights with an expression of grief and shock and carefully reddened eyes.

"Senator! Would you comment on this terrorist attack—"

"—tell us how feels to lose your sister-in-law to terrorists—"

"—any word on your daughter—"

Caddrick held up his hands, pled with the reporters. "Please, I don't know anything more than you do. Cassie's dead . . ." He paused, allowing the catch in his voice to circle the globe live via satellite. "My little girl is still missing, her college roommate has been brutally murdered, that's all I know, really . . ." He was pushing his way through the mob, his aide at his side.

"Is it true the terrorists were members of the *Ansar Majlis*, the down-time organization that's declared *jihad* against the Lady of Heaven Temples?"

"Will this attack cause you to re-open your campaign to shut down the time terminals?"

"Senator, are you aware that Senator Simon Mukhtar al Harb, a known *Ansar Majlis* sympathizer, is spearheading an investigation into the Temples—"

"Senator, what do you plan to do about this attack—"

He turned halfway up the steps leading to his office and faced the cameras, allowing his reddened eyes to water. "I intend to find my daughter," he said raggedly. "And I intend to find the bastards responsible for her disappearance, and for murdering poor Cassie . . . If it turns out these down-timer terrorists *were* responsible for Cassie's murder, if they've kidnapped my only child, then I will do whatever it takes to get every time terminal on this planet shut down! I've warned Congress for years, the down-timers flooding into the stations are a grave threat to the stability of our up-time world. And now this . . . I'm sorry, that's all I can say, I'm too upset to say anything else."

He fled up the steps and into his office.

And deep in his heart, smiled.

Phase Two, successfully launched . . .

Ianira Cassondra regained consciousness while Jenna and Noah were still packing. The faint sound from the hotel bed where she rested brought Jenna around, hands filled with the Victorian notion of ladies' underwear, which she'd purchased specifically for Ianira with Aunt Cassie's money. Jenna would be going through to London in disguise as a young man, something that left her shaking with stage fright worse than any she'd ever experienced. Seeing Ianira stir, Jenna dumped corsets and woolen drawers into an open steamer trunk and hurried over to join Marcus. Noah glanced up from the telephone, where the detective was busy scheduling an appointment with

the station's cosmetologist. Armstrong wanted Jenna
to go in for some quick facial alterations before the
gate opened, to add Victorian-style whiskers to Jenna's
too-famous, feminine face. Noah frowned, more
reflectively than in irritation, then finished making the
appointment and joined them.

Ianira stirred against the pillow. Dark lashes fluttered. Jenna discovered she was clenching her hands
around her new costume's trousers belt. The leather
felt slippery under the sweat. She realized with a
sinking sensation in her gut that it was one thing to
carry the prophetess on earth unconscious through
the station's basement. It was quite another to gaze
eye-to-eye with the embodiment of all that Jenna had
come to believe about life and how it ought to be
lived. Then Ianira's eyelids fluttered open and Ianira,
Cassondra of Ephesus, lay gazing up at her. For a
breathless moment, no intelligence flickered in those
dark eyes. Then an indrawn breath and a lightning
flicker of terror lashed at Jenna. Ianira flinched back,
as though Jenna had struck her. Marcus, who knew
Ianira better than anyone, surely, pressed the tips of
his fingers across her lips.

"Hush, beloved. We are in danger. Cry out and you
warn them."

Ianira's gaze ripped away from Jenna's, met her
husband's. "Marcus . . ." It was the sound of a drown-
ing soul clinging to a storm-battered, rocky shore. His
arms went around her. The former Roman slave lifted
her trembling figure, held her close. Jenna had to turn
aside. The sight of such intimacy tore through her,
a bitter reminder of the emptiness of her own life
before Carl, an emptiness which had brought her,
shaking and sick in her heart, into the Temple in the
first place. The Temple, where she'd found real
friendship for the first time in her life, friendship and
Carl . . . The loss tore through her, still too new and
raw to endure. Across the hotel room, Marcus was

speaking, voice low, the words in some language other than English or the Latin he'd used earlier. Greek, probably, since Ianira had come to the station from Athens.

Someone touched Jenna's arm. She glanced up and found Noah watching her. "Yeah?" she asked, voice roughened, uncertain.

"She's asked for you."

Jenna's pulse banged unpleasantly in the back of her throat as she crouched down at the edge of the hotel bed. Ianira's dark, unearthly gaze shook her so deeply she couldn't even dredge up a greeting. When the prophetess lifted a hand, Jenna very nearly flinched back. Then Ianira touched Jenna's brow, slowly. "Why do you Seek," she murmured, "when you already know the answers in your heart?"

The room closed in around Jenna, dizzy and strange, as though voices whispered to her from out of a shimmering haze, voices whose whispered words she could not quite hear. From the depths of the blackness which filled her mind, a blackness which had swallowed nearly all of her childhood—which was far better forgotten than relived in aching emptiness again and again—a single image blazed in Jenna's mind. A woman's smiling face . . . arms held out to her . . . closing around her with a sense of safety and shelter she had not felt since her mother's death, so many years ago, now, it was blurred in her memory. What this sudden memory meant, Jenna wasn't sure, but it left her gasping and sick on her knees, so violently shaken she couldn't even wipe her burning eyes.

Someone crouched beside her, braced Jenna all along one side, wiped her face with a warm, damp cloth. When the stinging, salty blindness had passed, she found Noah gazing worriedly at her. "You okay, kid?"

"Yeah." The fact that it was true shocked her.

She *was* okay. Then it hit her why: she wasn't
quite alone any longer. She knew almost nothing
about Noah Armstrong, not even the most basic
thing one person can know about another—their
gender—but she wasn't alone, facing this nightmare.
Noah might not be going with her when Jenna
stepped through the Britannia Gate a couple of
hours from now, but Noah *cared*. Somehow, it was
enough. She managed to meet the enigmatic detective's eyes. "Thanks."

"Sure." Noah gave her a hand up, steadied her.

Jenna turned slowly to face the woman whose
presence, whose touch and single question had
triggered . . . whatever it had been. "Did—" Jenna had
to clear her throat roughly. "Did Marcus tell you
what's happened?"

She studied Jenna gravely. "He has told me all that
he knows."

Jenna drew breath, trying to find the words to
make sense of this. "My father . . ." She stopped,
started again, coming at this mess from a different
direction, trying to find the words to explain to a
woman who had never seen the up-time world and
would never be permitted to visit it. "You see, lots
of people don't like the Temples. The Lady of Heaven
Temples. They've got different reasons, but the prejudice is growing. Some people think Templars are
immoral. Dangerous to society. Perverting children,
that kind of garbage.

"There's this one group, though . . . down-timers,
mostly, coming up-time from the remains of TT-66.
They formed a cult to destroy us. The *Ansar Majlis*
hate us, say it's blasphemous to worship a goddess.
Rather than *their* idea of a god." It came out bitter,
shaky. The expression in Ianira's eyes left Jenna gulping, terrified to her bones. She got the rest out in a
rush, trying to hold onto her nerve. "As long as the
Ansar Majlis were kept bottled up in the Middle East,

where they started coming through the down-time
gates, they were pretty much harmless. But a lot of
people would like to see the Temples destroyed, or at
least hurt badly enough they're not a political threat,
anymore. Some of the lunatics who live up time have
been helping that murdering pack of terrorists . . ."

"Your father," she said quietly. "He is among them."

Jenna didn't have to answer; Ianira *knew.* Jenna
bit one lip, ashamed of the blood in her own veins
and furious that she couldn't do anything besides
smash Ianira's world to pieces. "He gave the orders,
yes. To a death squad. They murdered my mother's
sister. And my . . . my best friend from college . . ."
Jenna's voice went ragged.

Ianira reached across, touched Jenna's hand. "They
have taken him from you," she whispered, the sympathy in her voice almost too much to bear, "but you
have his final gift to you. Surely this must bring some
consolation, some hope for the future?"

Jenna blinked, almost too afraid of this woman to
meet those dark, too-wise eyes. "What . . . what do you
mean?"

Ianira brushed fingergips across Jenna's abdomen,
across the queasiness which had plagued her for
nearly a full week, now. "You carry his child," Ianira
said softly.

When the room greyed out and Jenna clutched at
the edge of the bed in stupid shock, the prophetess
spoke again, very gently. "Didn't you know?"

Someone had Jenna by the shoulders, kept her her
from falling straight to the floor. *Dear God . . . it's not
fear sickness, it's morning sickness . . . and I am late,
oh, God, I'm going to Victorian London with Daddy's
killers trying to find me and I'm carrying Carl's
baby. . . .* How long would they have to hide in London? Weeks? Months? Years? *I can't go disguised as
a man, if I'm pregnant!* But she had no real choice
and she knew it. Her father's hired killers would be

searching for a frightened girl in the company of a detective, not a lone young man travelling with several large steamer trunks. When she looked up, she found Ianira's dark gaze fastened on her and, more surprisingly, Noah Armstrong's grey-eyed gaze, filled with worry and compassion.

"You're . . . sure . . . ?" Jenna choked out.

Ianira brushed hair back from Jenna's brow. "I am not infallible, child. But about this, yes, I am certain."

Jenna wanted to break down and cry, wanted to curl up someplace and hide for the next several decades, wanted to be held and rocked and reassured that everything would be all right. But she couldn't. She met Ianira's gaze again. "They'll kill us all, if they can." She wrapped protective arms around her middle, around the miracle of Carl's baby, growing somewhere inside her. A fierce determination to protect that tiny life kindled deep within. "I'd be in a morgue someplace, already, undergoing an autopsy, if Noah hadn't dragged me out of that trap where Aunt Cassie died. I'm not going to let them win. Not if I have to spend the next forty years on the run, until we can find a way to stop them."

"And they have come here," Ianira whispered, fingers tightening around Jenna's arm, "to destroy the world we have built for ourselves."

Jenna wanted to look away from those too-knowing eyes, wanted to crawl away and hide, rather than confirm it. But she couldn't lie to the prophetess, even to spare her pain. "Yes. I'm sorry . . ." She had to stop for a moment, regain her composure. "We can get you off station, make a run for it down time. I don't give a damn about the laws forbidding down-timers to emigrate through a gate."

Ianira's gaze went to her children. Mute grief touched those dark eyes. "They cannot come with me?"

Noah answered, voice firm. "No. We don't dare risk

it. They'll find a way to follow us through every gate that opens this week. If we put your children in the same trunk we smuggle you out of the station in, and their assassins get to Jenna . . ."

Ianira Cassondra shuddered. "Yes. It is too dangerous. Marcus . . ."

He gripped her hands hard. "I will guard them. With my life, Ianira. And Julius has pledged to help us escape. No one else must know. Not even our friends, not even the Council of Seven. Julius only knows because he was using the tunnels to run a message from one end of Commons to the other. He found us."

At the look that came into her eyes, a shudder touched its cold finger to Jenna's spine. Ianira's eyelids came clenching down. "The death that stalks us is worse than we know . . . two faces . . . two faces beyond the gates . . . and bricks enclose the tree where the flame burns and blood runs black . . . be wary of the one with grey eyes, death lives behind the smile . . . the letters are the key, the letters bring terror and destruction . . . the one who lives behind the silent gun will strike in the night . . . seeks to destroy the soul unborn . . . will strike where the newborn bells burn bright with the sound of screams . . ." She sagged against her husband, limp and trembling.

Jenna, too, was trembling, so violently she could scarcely keep her feet where she crouched beside the bed.

Marcus glanced up, eyes dark and frightened. "I have never seen the visions come to her so powerfully. Please, I beg of you, be careful with her."

Jenna found herself lifting Ianira's cold hands to warm them. They shook in Jenna's grasp. "Lady," she whispered, "I'm not much good at killing. But they've already destroyed the two people I cared about more than anything in the world. I swear, I will kill anything or anyone who tries to hurt *you*."

Ianira's gaze lifted slowly. Tears had reddened her eyes. "I know," she choked out. "It is why I grieve."

To that, Jenna had no answer whatever.

Dr. John Lachley had a problem.

A very serious problem.

Polly Nichols possessed half of Eddy's eight letters, written to the now-deceased orphan from Cardiff. Unlike Morgan, however, whom nobody would miss, Polly Nichols had lived in the East End all her life. When she turned up rather seriously dead, those who knew her were going to talk. And what they knew, or recalled having seen, they would tell the constables of the Metropolitan Police Department's H Division. While the police were neither well liked nor respected in Whitechapel, Polly Nichols *was,* despite her infamous profession. Those who liked and respected her would help the police catch whoever did to her what John Lachley intended to do to *anyone* who came into possession of Eddy's miserable little letters.

God, but he had enjoyed carving up that little bastard, Morgan . . .

The very memory made his private and unique anatomy ache.

So . . . he must find Polly Nichols, obtain her letters, then cut her up the same delightful way he had cut Morgan, as a message to all blackmailing whores walking these filthy streets, and he must do it without being remarked upon or caught. He would disguise himself, of course, but John Lachley's was a difficult face to disguise. He looked too foreign, always had, from earliest childhood in these mean streets, a gift from his immigrant mother. Lachley knew enough theatrical people, through his illustrious clientele, to know which shops to visit to obtain false beards and so on, but even that was risky. Acquiring such things meant people would recall him as the foreigner who had bought an actor's bag of makeup and accouterments. That was nearly as bad as being recalled as the last man seen with a murdered woman. Might well prove worse, since being remembered for buying disguises indicated someone with a guilty secret to hide. How the devil did one approach the woman close enough to obtain the letters and murder her, afterwards, without being *seen?*

He might throw suspicion on other foreigners, perhaps, if he disguised himself as one of the East End's thousands of Jews. A long false beard, perhaps, or a prayer shawl knotted under his overcoat . . . Ever since that Jew, what was his name, Lipski, had murdered that little girl in the East End last year, angry Cockneys had been hurtling insults at foreigners in the eastern reaches of London. In the docklands, so many refugees were pouring in from the Jewish communities of Eastern Europe, the very word "foreigner" had come to mean "Jew." Lachley would have to give that serious consideration, throwing blame somehow onto the community of foreigners. If some foreign Jew hanged for Lachley's deeds, so much the better.

But his problem was more complicated than simply tracing Polly Nichols, recovering her letters, and silencing her. There was His Highness' tutor to consider, as well. The man knew too much, far too much for safety. Mr. James K. Stephen would have to die. Which was the reason John Lachley had left London for the nearby village of Greenwich, this morning: to murder Mr. James K. Stephen.

He had made a point of striking up an acquaintance with the man on the riding paths surrounding Greenwich just the morning previously. Lachley, studying the layout of the land Stephen preferred for his morning rides, had casually trailed Stephen while looking for a place to stage a fatal accident. The path Eddy's tutor habitually took carried the riders out into fields where farm workers labored to bring in the harvest despite the appalling rain squalls, then wandered within a few feet of a large windmill near the railway line. Lachley gazed at that windmill with a faint smile. If he could engineer it so that Stephen rode past the windmill at the same time as a passing train . . .

So he followed Stephen further along the trail and cantered his horse up alongside, smiling in greeting, and introduced himself. "Good morning, sir. John Lachley, physician."

"Good morning, Dr. Lachley," Eddy's unsuspecting tutor smiled in return. "James Stephen."

He feigned surprise. "Surely not James K. Stephen?"

The prince's former tutor stared in astonishment. "Yes, in fact, I am."

"Why, I am delighted, sir! Delighted! Eddy has spoken so fondly of you! Oh, I ought to explain," he added at the man's look of total astonishment. "His Highness Prince Albert Victor is one of my patients, nothing serious, of course, I assure you. We've become rather good friends over the last few months. He has spoken often of you, sir. Constantly assigns to you the lion's share of the credit for his success at Cambridge."

Stephen flushed with pleasure. "How kind of His Highness! It was my priviledge to have tutored him at university. You say Eddy is quite well, then?"

"Oh, yes. Quite so. I use certain mesmeric techniques in my practice, you see, and Eddy had heard that the use of mesmeric therapy can improve one's memory."

Stephen smiled in genuine delight. "So naturally Eddy was interested! Of course. I hope you have been able to assist him?"

"Indeed," John Lachley laughed easily. "His memory will never be the same."

Stephen shared his chuckle without understanding Lachley's private reasons for amusement. As they rode on in companionable conversation, Lachley let fall a seemingly casual remark. "You know, I've enjoyed this ride more than any I can recall in an age. So much more refreshing than Hyde Park or Rotten Row, where one only appears to be in the countryside, whereas this is the genuine article. Do you ride this way often?"

"Indeed, sir, I do. Every morning."

"Oh, splendid! I say, do you suppose we might ride out together again tomorrow? I should enjoy the company and we might chat about Eddy, share a few amusing anecdotes, perhaps?"

"I should enjoy it tremendously. At eight o'clock, if that isn't too early?"

"Not at all." He made a mental note to check the train schedules to time their ride past that so-convenient windmill. "Eight o'clock it shall be." And so they rode on, chatting pleasantly while John Lachley laid his plans to murder the amiable young man who had helped Eddy with one too many translations.

Early morning light, watery and weak, tried vainly to break through rainclouds as Lachley stepped off Greenwich pier from the waterman's taxi he'd taken down from London. The clock of the world-famous Greenwich observatory struck eight chimes as Lachley rented a nag from a dockside livery stable and met James Stephen, as agreed. The unsuspecting Stephen greeted him warmly. "Dr. Lachley! Well met, old chap! I say, it's rather a dismal morning, but we'll put a good face on it, eh? Company makes the gloomiest day brighter, what?"

"Indeed," Lachley nodded, giving the doomed tutor a cheery smile.

The scent of the River Thames drifted on the damp breeze, mingling with the green smell of swampy ground from Greenwich Marshes and the acrid, harsh smell of coal smoke, but Dr. John Lachley drew a deep, double-lungful and smiled again at the man who rode beside him, who had but a quarter of an hour to live.

Riding down the waterfront, past berths where old fashioned, sail-powered clipper ships and small, iron-hulled steamers creaked quietly at anchor, Lachley and Mr. Stephen turned their nags up King William Walk to reach Greenwich Park, then headed parallel to the river past the Queen's House, built for Queen Anne of Denmark by James the First in 1615. Greenwich boasted none of London's stink, smelling instead of fresh marshes and late-autumn hay and old money. Tudor monarchs had summered here and several had been born in Greenwich palaces. The Royal Naval College, once a Royal Hospital for Seamen, shared the little village on the outskirts of London with the Royal Observatory and the world-famous Greenwich Meridian, the zero line of oceanic navigation.

As they left behind the village with its royal associations, riding out along the bridle path which snaked its way between Trafalgar Road and the railway line, Lachley began sharing an amusing story about Eddy's latest forays into the East End, a low and vulgar habit Eddy had indulged even during his years at Cambridge, in order to drink and make the rounds of the brothels, pubs, and even, occasionally, the street walkers and fourpence whores who could be had for the price of a loaf of bread.

" . . . told the girl he'd give her quid if she'd give him a four-penny knee-trembler and the child turned out to be an honest working girl. Slapped his face so hard it left a hand-print, little dreaming she'd just struck the grandson of the queen. And poor Eddy went chasing after her to apologize, ended up buying every flower in her tray . . ."

They were approaching the fateful windmill Lachley had spied the previous morning. The screaming whistle of a distant train announced the arrival of the diversion

Lachley required for his scheme. He smiled to himself and slowed his horse deliberately, to be sure of the timing, leaning down as though concerned his horse might be drawing up lame. Stephen also reined in slightly to match pace with him and to hear the end of the story he was relating.

The train whistle shrieked again. Both horses tossed their heads in a fretting movement. *Good* . . . Lachley nodded approvingly. A nervous horse under Mr. James K. Stephen was all the better. The sorrel Stephen rode danced sideways as the train made its roaring, smoking approach. A moment later they were engulfed in a choking cloud of black smoke and raining cinders.

Lachley whipped his hand into his coat pocket and dragged out the lead-filled sap he'd brought along. His pulse thundered. His nostrils dilated. His whole body tingled with electric awareness. His vision narrowed, tunnelling down to show him the precise spot he would strike. They passed the whirling blades of the windmill, engulfed in the deafening roar of the passing train. *Now!* Lachley reined his horse around in a lightning move that brought him alongside Stephen's sweating mount. Excitement shot through him, ragged, euphoric. He caught a glimpse of James Stephen's trusting, unsuspecting face—

A single, savage blow was all it took.

The thud of the lead sap against his victim's skull jarred Lachley's whole arm, from wrist to shoulder. Pain and shock exploded across Stephen's face. The man's horse screamed and lunged sideways as its rider crumpled in the saddle. The nag bolted straight under the windmill, crowded in that direction by Lachley's own horse and the deafening thunder of the passing train. Stephen pitched sideways out of the saddle, reeling toward unconsciousness. And precisely as Lachley had known it would, one of the windmill vanes caught Stephen brutally across the back of the skull. He was thrown violently to one side by the turning blade. The one-time tutor to Prince Albert Victor Christian Edward landed in a crumpled heap several feet away. Lachley sat watching for a long, shaking moment. The sensations sweeping through him, almost sexual in their intensity, left him trembling.

Then, moving with creditable calm for a man who had just committed his second murder with his own hands—and the first in open view of the public eye—John Lachley wiped the lead sap on his handkerchief and secreted his weapon in his pocket once more. He reined his horse around and tied it to the nearest tree. Dismounting from the saddle, he walked over to the man he'd come here to kill. James K. Stephen lay in a broken heap. Lachley bent down . . . and felt the pulse fluttering at the man's throat . . .

The bastard was still alive! Fury blasted through him, brought his vision shrieking down to a narrow hunter's focus once more. He stole his hand into his pocket, where the lead sap lay hidden—

"Dear God!" a voice broke into his awareness above the shriek and rattle of the train. Lachley whirled around, violently shaken. Another man on horseback had approached from the trail. The stranger was jumping to the ground, running towards them. Worse, a striking young woman with heavy blond hair sat another horse on the trail, watching them with an expression of shock and horror.

"What's happened?" the intruder asked, reasonably enough.

Lachley forced himself to calmness, drew on a lifetime's worth of deceit and the need to hide who and what he was in order to survive, and said in a voice filled with concern, "This gentleman and I were riding along the trail, here, when the train passed. Something from the train struck him as it went by, I don't know what, a large cinder perhaps, or maybe someone threw something from a window. But his

horse bolted quite abruptly. Poor devil was thrown
from the saddle, straight under the windmill blades.
I'd just reached him when you rode up."

As he spoke, he knelt at Stephen's side, lifted his
wrist to sound his pulse, used his handkerchief to bind
the deep wound in his head, neatly explaining away
the blood on the snowy linen. The stranger crouched
beside him, expression deeply concerned.

"We must get him to safety at once! Here . . . cradle
the poor man's head and I'll lift his feet. We'll put
him in my saddle and I'll ride behind, keep him from
falling. Alice, love, don't look too closely, his head's
a dreadful sight, covered in blood."

Lachley ground his teeth in a raging frustration and
gave the man a seemingly relieved smile. "Capital
idea! Splendid. Careful, now . . ."

Ten minutes later the man he'd come all this way
to murder lay in a bed in a Greenwich Village doctor's
cottage, in a deep coma and not—as the doctor said
with a sad shake of his head—expected to survive.
Lachley agreed that it was a terrible tragedy and
explained to the village constable what had occurred,
then gave the man his name and address in case he
were needed again.

The constable said with genuine concern, "Not that
there's likely to be any inquest, even if the poor chap
dies, it's clearly an accident, terrible freak of an
accident, and I appreciate your help, sir, that I do."

The bastard who'd come along at just the wrong
instant gave the constable his own name, as well, a
merchant down from Manchester, visiting London with
his younger sister. Lachley wanted to snatch the lead
sap out of his pocket and smash in the merchant's skull
with it. Instead, he took his leave of the miserable little
physician's cottage while the constable arranged to
contact James Stephen's family. It was some consolation, at least, that Stephen was not likely to survive
much longer. And, of course, even if Stephen did live,

the man would not realize that the blow which had struck him down had been an intentional one. The story of the accident would be relayed to the victim by the constable, the village doctor, even his own family. And if Stephen did survive . . .

There were ways, even then, of erasing the problem he still represented.

The matter being as resolved as he could make it at this juncture, John Lachley set his horse toward Greenwich Village pier for the return trip to London and set his seething mind toward Polly Nichols and the problems *she* represented.

He was still wrestling with the problem when he returned home to find a letter which had arrived, postmarked, of all places, Whitechapel, London, Liverpool Street Station. "My dearest Dr. Lachley," the missive began, "such a tremendous difference you have made! Many of my symptoms have abated immeasurably since my visit to your office, Friday last. I feel stronger, more well, than I have in many months. But I am still troubled greatly by itching hands and dreadful headaches. I wondered if you would be so good as to arrange another appointment for me in your surgery? I am certain you can do me more good than any other physician in the world. As I have returned to London on business, it would be most kind of you to fit me into your admittedly busy schedule. I eagerly await your response. Please contact me by return post, general delivery, Whitechapel."

It was signed James Maybrick, Esquire.

John Lachley stared at the signature. Then a slow smile began to form. James Maybrick, the murderous cotton merchant from Liverpool . . . With his delightful *written* diary and its equally delightful confession of murder. And not just any murder, either, but the murder of a *whore*, by damn, committed by a man with all the motive in the world to hate prostitutes! Maybrick wasn't a Jew, didn't look even remotely foreign. But if Lachley recruited Maybrick into this hunt for Polly Nichols, worked with him, there would be *two* descriptions for eyewitnesses to hand police, confounding the issue further, throwing the constables even more violently off Lachley's trail. Yes, by damn, Maybrick was just the thing he required.

It was so simple, he very nearly laughed aloud. He would meet the man in Whitechapel this very night, by God, induce a state of drugged mesmeric trance, then turn that lethal rage of his into the perfect killing machine, a weapon he could direct at will against whatever target he chose. And the diary would ensure the man's death at the end of a rope. Lachley chuckled, allowing the seething frustration over his failure to silence the prince's tutor to drop away. He would encourage Maybrick to dutifully record every sordid detail of Polly Nichols' murder, would even place mesmeric blocks in Maybrick's mind to prevent the imbecile from mentioning *him* in the diary.

James Maybrick was a godsend, by damn, a genuine godsend!

But as he turned his thoughts toward the use he would make of Maybrick, the enormity of the threat Polly Nichols represented drained away his jubilant mood. God, that Nichols bitch had been in possession of the letters long enough, she might have found someone to translate the bloody letters into English! He had to move quickly, that much was certain. Tonight. He would risk waiting no longer than that.

Lachley opened his desk and removed pen, paper, and penny-post stamps, then composed a brief reply to his arsenic-addicted little cotton merchant. "My dear sir, I would be delighted to continue your treatment. It is an honor to be entrusted with your health. I am certain I can make a changed man of you. Please call upon me in my Cleveland Street surgery this evening by eight P.M. If you are unable to keep this appointment, please advise me by telegram and we will arrange a mutually agreeable time."

He left the house to post the letter, himself, wanting to be certain it would go out in plenty of time for the late afternoon mail delivery bound for Liverpool Street Station, Whitechapel—no more than a handful of miles from his house in Cleveland Street. London was the envy of Europe for its mail service, with multiple pickups a day and delivery times of only a few hours, particularly for general delivery mail service. Lachley smiled to himself and whistled easily as he strolled past the fashionable artists' studios which lined Cleveland Street, giving it the air of respectability and fashion its other, less reputable inhabitants could never hope to achieve. Men of wealth and high station patronized the studios on Cleveland Street, commissioning paintings for their homes, portraits of their wives and progeny, immortalizing themselves on the canvasses of talented artists like Walter Sickert and the incomparable Vallon, who'd recently painted a canvas which the Prime Minister, Lord Salisbury, had just purchased for the astonishing sum of five hundred pounds, merely because members of his family were included in the work.

John Lachley had chosen Cleveland Street for his residence because of its association with the highly fashionable artistic community. Here, a mesmeric physician and occultist appeared to his wealthy clientele as a model of staid respectability compared with the somewhat more Bohemian artists of the district. Lachley knew perfectly well he would have been considered outlandish in more sedate surroundings such as Belgravia. So to Cleveland Street he had come, despite the reputations of one or two of its pubs and houses, which catered to men of Eddy's persuasion. And it was in Cleveland Street where he had first met the darling prince Albert Victor Christian

Edward and turned that chance meeting to his considerable advantage. His scheme was certainly paying handsome dividends.

All he had to do now was protect his investment.

Polly Nichols didn't yet know it, but she had less than a day to live. Lachley hoped she spent it enjoying herself. He certainly intended to enjoy her demise. He hastened his footsteps, eager to post his letter and set into motion the events necessary to bring him to that moment. James Maybrick would make the perfect weapon. Why, he might even let Maybrick have the knife, once Lachley, himself, had vented his rage.

He chuckled aloud and could have kissed the fateful letter in his gloved hand.

Tonight, he promised Polly Nichols. *We meet tonight.*

When Margo arrived at the Britannia Gate's departures lounge, Victoria Station had taken on the chaotic air of a tenting circus in the process of takedown for transit to the next town. Not a cafe table in sight, either on the Commons floor or up on one of the balconies, could be had for less than a minor king's ransom and it was standing room only on every catwalk and balcony overlooking Victoria Station. If many more spectators tried to crowd onto the concrete and steel walkways up there, they'd have balconies falling three and four stories under the weight.

Besides the ordinary onlookers, the loons were out in force, as well, carrying placards and holding up homemade signs. Delighted news crews filmed the chaos while Ripperoons and assorted lunatics gave interviews to straight-faced camera operators about how Lord Jack was going to appear through an unstable gate created by a passing meteor and step off into the open Britannia amidst a host of unheavenly demons charged with guarding his most unsacred person from all earthly harm . . .

It might almost have been funny if not for the handful of real crazies demanding to be allowed through, tickets or no tickets, to serve their lord and master in whatever fashion Jack saw fit. Margo, jockeying for position in the crowd, trying to get her luggage cart through, stumbled away from one wild-eyed madman who snatched at her arm, screaming, "Unchaste whore! Jack will see your sins! He will punish you in this ripping time . . ." Margo slipped out of his grasp and left him windmilling for balance, unprepared for someone who knew Aikido.

Security arrived a moment later and Margo waved at Wally Klontz as the nutcase came after her again. "Wally! Hey! Over here!"

"What's the prob—oh, shit!" Wally snatched out handcuffs and grabbed the guy as he lunged again at Margo and screamed obscenities. More security waded in as a couple of other frenzied nutcases protested the man's removal. Violence broke out in a brief, brutish scuffle that ended with Margo gulping down acid nervousness while security agents hauled away a dozen seriously deranged individuals—a couple of them in straightjackets. Standing in the midst of a wide-eyed crowd of onlookers and glassy camera lenses, Margo brought her shudders under control and shoved her way past news crews who thrust microphones and cameras into her face.

"Aren't you Margo Smith, the Time Tours special guide for the Ripper Watch—"

"—true you're training to become a time scout?"

"—give us your feelings about being accosted by a member of a 'Jack is Lord' cult—"

"No comment," she muttered again and again, using the luggage cart as a battering ram to force the newsies aside. If things were this bad on station . . . What was it really going to be like in London's East End, when the Ripper terror struck?

And what if it'd been one of those madmen who'd

grabbed Ianira? As a sacrifice to Jack the Ripper? It didn't bear thinking about. Margo thrust the thought firmly aside and turned her luggage over to Time Tours baggage handlers, securing her claim stubs in her reticule, then lunged for the refuge of the departures lounge, where the news crews could follow her only with zoom lenses and directional microphones. It wasn't privacy, but it was the best she could do under the circumstances and Margo had no intention of giving anybody an interview about anything.

Once in the Time Tours departures lounge, she searched the crowd, looking for her new charges, Shahdi Feroz and the two journalists joining the Ripper Watch Team. She'd made one complete circuit of the departures area and was beginning to quarter it through the center when the SLUR-TV theme music swelled out over the crowds jamming Commons and a big screen television came to life. Shangri-La's new television anchor, Booth Hackett, voiced the question of the hour in booming tones that cut across the chaos echoing through Commons.

"It's official, Shangri-La Station! Ripper Season is underway and the entire world is asking, who really was Jack the Ripper? The list of suspects is impressive, the theories about conspiracies in high-government offices as convoluted as any modern conspiracy theorist could want. In an interview taped several hours ago with Dr. Shahdi Feroz, psycho-social historical criminologist and occult specialist for the team . . ."

Margo tuned it out and kept hunting for the Ripper scholar and wayward journalists, who should've been here by now. She wasn't interested in what that ghoul, Hackett, had to say and she already knew all the theories by heart. Kit had made sure of that before consenting to send her down the Britannia. First came the theories involving cults and black magic—hence

Shahdi Feroz's inclusion on the team. Robert Donston Stephenson, who had claimed to know the Ripper and his motives personally and was at the top of several suspect lists, had been a known Satanist and practitioner of black magic. Aleister Crowley was on the cult-member suspect list, as well, although the evidence was slim to non-existent. Neither man, despite individual notoriety, fit the profile of a deranged psychopathic killer such as the Ripper. Margo wasn't betting on either of them.

She didn't buy any of the Mary Kelly theories, either—and some of them were among the weirdest of all Ripper theories. Honestly, Queen Victoria ordering the Prime Minister to kill anyone who knew that her grandson had secretly married a Catholic prostitute and fathered a daughter by her, guaranteeing a Catholic heir to the throne? Not to mention the Prime Minister drafting his pals in the Masonic Temple to re-enact some idiot's idea of Masonic rituals on the victims? It was just too nutty, not to mention the total lack of factual support. And she didn't think Mary Kelly's lover, the unemployed fish porter Joseph Barnett, had cut her up with one of his fish-gutting knives, either, despite their having quarrelled, or that he'd killed the other women to "scare" her off the streets. No, the Mary Kelly theories were just too witless . . .

"You are looking very irritated, Miss Smith."

Margo jumped nearly out of her skin, then blinked and focused on Shahdi Feroz' exquisite features. "Oh! Dr. Feroz . . . I, uh, was just looking . . ." She shut up, realizing it would come out sounding like she was irritated with the scholar if she said "I was looking for you," then turned red and stammered out, "I was thinking about all those stupid theories." She nodded toward the big-screen television where Dr. Feroz' taped interview was still playing, then added, "I mean, the ones about Mary Kelly."

Shahdi Feroz smiled. "Yes, there are some absurd ones about her, poor creature."

"You can say that again! You're all checked in and your luggage is ready?"

The scholar nodded. "Yes. And—oh *bother!*"

Newsies. Lots of them. Leaning right across the departures lounge barricades, with microphones and cameras trained on Shadhi Feroz and Margo. "This way!" Margo dragged the scholar by the wrist to the most remote corner of the departures lounge, putting a mass of tourists between themselves and the frustrated news crews. As Margo forced their way through, speculation flew wild amongst the tourists milling around them in every direction, eager to depart.

"—I think it was the queen's grandson, himself, not just some alleged lover."

"The queen's grandson? Duke of Clarence? Or rather, Prince Albert Victor? He wasn't named Duke of Clarence until after the Ripper murders. Poor guy. He's named in at least three outlandish theories, despite unshakable alibis. Like being several hundred miles north of London, in *Scotland*, for God's sake, during at least one of the murders . . ."

A nearby Time Tours guide in down-time servant's livery, was saying, "Ducks, don't you know, just *everybody* wants it to've been a nice, juicy royal scandal. Anytime a British royal's involved in something like the Ripper murders or the drunk-driving death of the Princess of Wales, back near the end of the twentieth century, conspiracy theories pop up faster than muckraking reporters are able to spread 'em round."

They finally gained the farthest corner, out of sight of reporters, if not out of earshot of the appalling noise loose in Victoria Station. "Thank you, my dear," Shadhi breathed a sigh. "I should not be so churlish, I suppose, but I am tired and reporters . . ." She gave an elegant shrug of her Persian shoulders, currently clad in Victorian watered silk, and added with a twinkle in her dark eyes, "So you believe none of the theories about Mary Kelly?"

"Nope."

"Not even the mad midwife theory?"

Margo blinked. *Mad midwife?* Uh-oh . . .

Shahdi Feroz laughed gently. "Don't be so distressed, Miss Smith. It is not a commonly known theory."

"Yes, but Kit made me study this case inside out, backwards and forwards—"

"And you have been given, what? A few days, at most, to study it? I have spent a lifetime puzzling over this case. Don't feel so bad."

"There really is a mad midwife theory?"

Shahdi nodded. "Oh, yes. Mary Kelly was three months pregnant when she died. With a child she couldn't afford to feed. Abortions were illegal, but easily obtained, particularly in the East End, and usually performed by midwives, under appalling conditions. And midwives could come and go at all hours, without having to explain blood on their clothing. Even Inspector Abberline believed they might well be looking for a woman killer. This was based on testimony of a very reliable eyewitness to the murder of Mary Kelly. Abberline couldn't reconcile the testimony any other way, you see. A woman was seen wearing Mary Kelly's clothes and leaving her rented room the morning she was killed, several hours *after* coroners determined that Mary Kelly had died."

Margo frowned. "That's odd."

"Yes. She was seen twice, once between eight o'clock and eight-thirty, looking quite ill, and again about an hour later outside the Britannia public house, speaking with a man. This woman was seen both times by the same witness, a very sober and reliable housewife who lived near Mary Kelly, Mrs. Caroline Maxwell. Her testimony led Inspector

Abberline to wonder if the killer might perhaps be a deranged midwife who dressed in the clothing of her victim as a disguise. And there certainly were clothes burned in Mary Kelly's hearth, shortly after the poor girl was murdered."

"But she died at four A.M.," Margo protested. "What would've kept her busy in there for a whole four hours? And what about the mutilations?"

"Those," Shahdi Feroz smiled a trifle grimly, "are two of the questions we hope to solve. What the killer did between Mary Kelly's death and his or her escape from Miller's Court, and why."

Margo shivered and smoothed her dress sleeves down her arms, trying to smooth the goose chills, as well. She didn't like thinking about Mary Kelly, the youngest and prettiest of the Ripper's victims, with her glorious strawberry blond hair. Margo's memories of her mother were sharp and terrible. Long, thick strawberry blond hair, strewn across the kitchen floor in sticky puddles of blood . . .

The less Margo recalled about what her mother had been and how she'd died, the better. "A mad midwife sounds nutty to me," she muttered. "As nutty as the other theories about Mary Kelly. Besides, there probably was no such person, just a police inspector groping for a solution to fit the testimony."

Shahdi Feroz chuckled. "You would be wrong, my dear, for a mad midwife did, in fact exist. Midwife Mary Pearcey was arrested and hanged for slashing to death the wife and child of her married lover in 1890. Even Sir Arthur Conan Doyle suggested the police might have been searching for a killer of the wrong gender. He wrote a story based on this idea."

"That Sherlock Holmes should've been searching for *Jill* the Ripper, not *Jack* the Ripper?"

Shahdi Feroz laughed. "I agree with you, it isn't very likely."

"Not very! I mean, women killers don't do that sort

of thing. Chop up their victims and eat the parts? Do they?"

The Ripper scholar's expression sobered. "Actually, a woman killer is quite capable of inflicting such mutilations. Criminologists have long interpreted such female-inflicted mutilations in a psychologically significant light. While lesbianism is a perfectly normal biological state for a fair percentage of the population and lesbians are no more or less likely than heterosexuals or gays to fit psychologically disturbed profiles, nonetheless there is a pattern which some lesbian killers do fit."

"*Lesbian* killers?"

"Yes, criminologists have known for decades that one particular profile of disturbed woman killer, some of whom happen to be lesbians, kill their lovers in a fit of jealousy or anger. They often mutilate the face and breasts and sexual organs. Which the Ripper most certainly did. A few such murders have been solved only after police investigators stopped looking for a male psychotically deranged sexual killer and began searching, instead, for a female version of the psychotic sexual killer."

Margo shuddered. "This is spooky. What causes it? I mean, what happens to turn an innocent little baby into something like Jack the Ripper? Or Jill the Ripper?"

Shahdi Feroz said very gently, "Psychotic serial killers are sometimes formed by deep pyschological damage, committed by the adults who have charge of them as young children. It's such a shocking tragedy, the waste of human potential, the pain inflicted. . . . The adults in such a person's life often combine sexual abuse with physical abuse, severe emotional abuse, and utter repression of the child's developing personality, robbery of the child's power and control over his or her life, a whole host of factors. Other times . . ." She shook her head. "Occasionally, we run across a serial killer who has no such abuse in his background. He simply enjoys the killing, the power. At times, I can only explain such choices as the work of evil."

"Evil?" Margo echoed.

Shahdi Feroz nodded. "I have studied cults in many different time periods, have looked at what draws disturbed people to pursue occult power, to descend into the kind of killing frenzy one sees with the psychotic killer. Some have been badly warped by abusers, yet others simply crave the power and the thrill of control over others' lives. I cannot find any other words to describe such people, besides a love of evil."

"Like Aleister Crowley," Margo murmured.

"Yes. Although he is not very likely Jack the Ripper."

Margo discovered she was shuddering inside, down in the core of herself, where her worst memories lurked. Her own father had been a monster, her mother a prostitute, trying to earn enough money to pay the bills when her father drank everything in their joint bank account. Margo's childhood environment had been pretty dehumanized. So why hadn't *she* turned out a psychopath? She still didn't get it, not completely. Maybe her parents, bad as they'd been, hadn't been quite monstrous enough? The very thought left her queasy.

"Are you all right?" Shahdi asked in a low voice.

Margo gave the scholar a bright smile. "Sure. Just a little weirded out, I guess. Serial killers are creepy."

"They are," Shahdi Feroz said softly, "the most terrifying creation the human race has ever produced. It is why I study them. In the probably vain hope we can avoid creating more of them."

"That," Margo said with a shiver, "is probably the most impossible quest I've ever heard of. Good luck. I mean that, too."

"What d'you mean, Miss Smith?" a British voice said in her ear. "Good luck with what?"

Margo yelped and came straight up off the floor, at least two inches airborne; then stood glaring at Guy Pendergast and berating herself for not paying better attention. *Some time scout trainee you are! Stay this unfocused and some East End blagger's going to shove a knife through your ribcage....* "Mr. Pendergast. I didn't see you arrive. And Miss Nosette. You've checked in? Good. All right, everybody's here. We've got—" she craned her head to look at the overhead chronometers "—eleven minutes to departure if you want to make any last-minute purchases, exchange money, buy a cup of coffee. You've all got your timecards? Great. Any questions?" *Please don't have any questions...*

Guy Pendergast gave her a friendly grin. "Is it true, then?"

She blinked warily at him. "Is what true?"

"Are you really bent on suicide, trying to become a time scout?"

Margo lifted her chin a notch, a defiant cricket trying to impress a maestro musician with its musicality. "There's nothing suicidal about it! Scouting may be a dangerous profession, but so are a lot of other jobs. Police work or down-time journalism, for instance."

Pendergast chuckled easily. "Can't argue that, not with the scar I've got across me arse—oh, I beg pardon, Miss Smith."

Margo almost relaxed. Almost. "Apology accepted. Whenever I'm in a lady's attire," she brushed a hand across the watered silk of her costume, "please watch your speech in my presence. But," and she managed a smile, "when I put on my ragged boy's togs or the tattered skirts of an East End working woman, don't be shocked at the language I start using. I've been studying Cockney rhyming slang until I speak it in my dreams at night. One thing I'm learning as a trainee scout is to fit language and behavior to the role I play down time."

"I don't know about the rest of the team," Dominica

Nosette flashed an abruptly dazzling smile at Margo and held out a friendly hand, completely at odds with her belligerence over the shooting lesson, "but I would be honored to be assigned to you for guide services. And of course, the *London New Times* will be happy to pay you for any additional services you might be willing to render."

Margo shook Dominica's hand, wondering what, exactly, the woman wanted from her. Besides the scoop of the century, of course. "Thank you," she managed, "that's very gracious, Ms. Nosette."

"Dominica, please. And you'll have to excuse my scapegrace partner. Guy's manners are atrocious."

Pendergast broke into a grin. "Delighted, m'dear, can't tell you how delighted I am to be touring with the famous Margo Smith."

"Oh, but I'm not famous."

He winked, rolling a sidewise glance at his partner. "Not yet, m'dear, but if I know Minnie, your name will be a household word by tea time."

Margo hadn't expected reporters to notice her, not yet, anyway, not until she'd really proved herself as an independent scout. All of which left her floundering slightly as Dominica Nosette and Guy Pendergast and, God help her, Shahdi Feroz, waited for her response. *What would Kit want me to do? To say? He hates reporters, I know that, but he's never said anything about what I should do if they talk to me . . .*

Fortunately, Doug Tanglewood, another of the guides for the Ripper Watch tour, arrived on the scene looking nine feet tall in an elegant frock coat and top hat. "Ah, Miss Smith, I'm so glad you're here. You've brought the check-in list? And the baggage manifests well in hand, I see. Ladies, gentlemen, Miss Smith is, indeed, a time scout in training. And since we will be joining her fiancé in London, I'm certain she would appreciate your utmost courtesy to her as a lady of means and substance."

Guy Pendergast said in dismay, "Fiancé? Oh, bloody *hell!*" and gave a theatrical groan that drew chuckles from several nearby male tourists. Doug Tanglewood smiled. "And if you would excuse us, we have rather a great deal to accomplish before departure."

Doug nodded politely and drew Margo over toward the baggage, then said in a low voice, "Be on your guard against those two, Miss Smith. Dominica Nosette and Guy Pendergast are notorious, with a reputation that I do not approve of in the slightest. But they had enough influence in the right circles to be added to the team, so we're stranded with them."

"They were very polite," she pointed out.

Tanglewood frowned. "I'm certain they were. They are very good at what they do. Just bear this firmly in mind. What they do is pry into other people's lives in order to report the sordid details to the world. Remember that, and there's no harm done. Now, have you seen Kit? He's waiting to see you off."

Margo's irritation fled. "Oh, where?"

"Across that way, at the barricade. Go along, then, and say goodbye. I'll take over from here."

She fled toward her grandfather, who'd managed to secure a vantage point next to the velvet barricade ropes. "Can you believe it? Eight minutes! Just eight more minutes and then, wow! Three and a half *months* in London! Three and a half very *hard* months," she added hastily at the beginnings of a stern glower in her world-famous grandfather's eyes.

Kit kept scowling, but she'd learned to understand those ferocious scowls during the past several months. They concealed genuine fear for her, trying to tackle this career when there was so much to be learned and so very much that could go wrong, even on a short and relatively safe tour. Kit ruffled her hair, disarranging her stylish hat in the process. "Keep that in mind, Imp.

Do you by any chance remember the first rule of surviving a dangerous encounter on the streets?"

Her face went hot, given her recent lapses in attention, but she shot back the answer promptly enough. "Sure do! Don't get into it in the first place. Keep your eyes and ears open and avoid anything that even remotely smells like trouble. And if trouble does break, run like hel—eck." She really was trying to watch her language. Ladies in Victorian London did not swear. *Women* did, all the time; *ladies,* never.

Kit chucked her gently under the chin. "That's my girl. Promise me, Margo, that you'll watch your back in Whitechapel. What you ran into before, in the Seven Dials, is going to look like a picnic, compared with the Ripper terror. *That* will blow the East End apart."

She bit her lower lip. "I know. I won't lie," she said in a sudden rush, realizing it was true and not wanting to leave her grandfather with the impression that she was reckless or foolhardy—at least, not any longer. "I'm scared. What we're walking into . . . The Ripper's victims weren't the only women murdered in London's East End during the next three months. And I can only guess what it's going to be like when the vigilance committees start patrolling the streets and London's women start arming themselves out of sheer terror."

"Those who could afford it," Kit nodded solemnly. "Going armed in that kind of explosive atmosphere is a damned fine idea, actually, so long as you keep your wits and remember your training."

Margo's own gun, a little top-break revolver, was fully loaded and tucked neatly into her dress pocket, in a specially designed holster Connie Logan had made for her. After her first, disastrous visit to London's East End with this pistol, Margo had drilled with it until she could load and shoot it blindfolded in her sleep. She just hoped she didn't need to use it, ever.

Far overhead, the station's public address system

crackled to life. "Your attention please. Gate Two is due to cycle in two minutes. All departures . . ."

"Well," Margo said awkwardly, "I guess this is it. I've got to go help Doug Tanglewood herd that bunch through the gate."

Kit smiled. "You'll do fine, Imp. If you don't, I'll kick your bustled backside up time so fast, it'll make your head swim!"

"Hah! You and what army?"

Kit's world-famous jack-o-lantern grin blazed down at her. "Margo, honey, I *am* an army. Or have you forgotten your last Aikido lesson?"

Margo just groaned. She still had the bruises. "You're mean and horrible and nasty. How come I love you?"

Kit laughed, then leaned over the barricade to give her a hug. "Because you're as crazy as I am, that's why." He added in a sudden, fierce whisper, "Take care of yourself!"

Margo hugged him tight and gave him a swift kiss on one lean, weathered cheek. "Promise."

Kit's eyes were just a hint too bright, despite the now-familiar scowl. "Off with you, then. I'll be waiting to test you on everything you've learned when you get back."

"Oh, God . . ." But she was laughing as she took her leave and found Douglas Tanglewood and their charges. When the Britannia Gate finally rumbled open and Margo started up the long flight of metal stairs, her computerized scout's log and ATLS slung over her shoulder in a carpet bag, Margo's heart was pounding as fast as the butterflies swooping and circling through her stomach. Three and a half months of Ripper Watch Tour wasn't exactly scouting . . . but solving the most famous serial murder of all time was just about the next best thing. She was going to make Kit proud of her, if it was the last thing she ever did. Frankly, she could hardly wait to get started!

Chapter Six

Polly Nichols needed a drink.

It'd been nearly seven hours since her last glass of gin and she was beginning to shake, she needed another so badly. There was no money in her pockets, either, to buy more. Worse, trade had been miserably slow all day, everywhere from the Tower north to Spitalfields Market and east to the Isle of Dogs. Not one lousy whoreson during the whole long day had been willing to pay for the price of a single glass of gin to calm her shaking nerves. She hadn't much left to sell, either, or pawn, for that matter.

Polly wore cheap, spring-sided men's boots with steel-tipped heels, which might've been worth something to a pawn broker, had she not cut back the uppers to fit her small legs and feet. Worse, without boots, she could not continue to ply her trade. With rain falling nearly every day and an unnatural chill turning the season cold and miserable, she'd catch her death in no time without proper boots to keep her feet warm and dry.

But, God, how she needed a drink...

Maybe she could sell her little broken mirror. Any

mirror was a valuable commodity in a doss house—
which made Polly reluctant to give it up. For a woman
in her business, a mirror was an important professional
tool. She frowned. What else might she be able to sell?
Her pockets were all but empty as she felt through
them. The mirror . . . her comb . . . and a crackle of
paper. *The letters!* Her fingers trembled slightly as she
withdrew the carefully folded sheets of foolscap. That
miserable little puff, Morgan, had lied to her about
these letters. There was no name on the paper, other
than a signature. She suspected she could figure out
who the letter-writer was if she could only get the
letters translated from Welsh into English. A translation
would make Polly a rich woman. But that wouldn't get
her a drink right now.

Well, she could always sell some of the letters,
couldn't she? With the agreement that as soon as they
found out the identity of the author, they would share
the spoils between them. Or, if Polly found out
quickly enough, she might simply buy them back by
saying she'd had them translated and Morgan had lied
to her and the letters were worthless. Yes, that was
what she would do. Sell three of the four now, to get
her gin money, then get them back with a lie and
figure out who to blackmail with the whole set of four.
But who to convince to buy them in the first place?

It must be someone as desperate for money as
herself, to buy into the scheme. But it couldn't be
anyone like an ordinary pawn broker. No, it had to
be someone she could trust, someone who would trust
her. That left one of a few friends she had made on
the streets. Which meant she wouldn't be able to get
much up front. But then, Polly didn't need much right
now, just enough to buy herself a few glasses of gin
and a bed for a night or two. She could always get
the letters back the moment she had money from her
next paying customer, if it came to that.

The decision as to which of her friends to approach

was made for her when Polly saw Annie Chapman walking down Whitechapel Road. Polly broke into a broad smile. Annie Chapman was a prostitute, same as herself, and certainly needed money. Dark Annie ought to buy into a blackmail scheme, all right. Annie was seriously ill, although to look at her, a body wouldn't guess it. But she was dying slowly of a lung and brain ailment which had put her into workhouse infirmaries occasionally and siphoned much of what she earned on the streets for medicines.

Yes, Annie ought to be quite interested in making a great deal of money quickly.

"Well, if it isn't Annie Chapman!" she said with a bright smile.

The other woman was very small, barely five feet tall, but stoutly built, with pallid skin and wide blue eyes and beautiful teeth that Polly, herself, would have given much to be able to flash at a customer when she smiled. Annie's dark brown hair was wavy and had probably been lustrous before her illness had struck. Her nose was too thick for beauty and at forty-five she was past her best years, but she was a steady little individual, meeting life quietly and trying to hold on in the face of overwhelming poverty, too little to eat, and an illness that sapped her strength and left her moving slowly when she was able to walk at all.

Annie Chapman smiled, genuinely pleased by the greeting. "Polly, how are you?"

"Oh, I'm good, Annie, I'm good. I'd be better if I 'ad a gin or two, eh?"

The two women chuckled for a moment. Annie was not the drinker Polly was, but the other woman enjoyed her rum, when there was enough money to be spared for it, same as most other women walking these dismal streets.

"Say, Annie, 'ow's your 'ealth been these past few weeks?"

The other woman's eyes darkened. "Not good," she

said quietly, with a hoarse rasp in her voice. "It's this rain and cold. Makes my lungs ache, so it's hard to breathe." She *sounded* like it hurt her to breathe.

"I'd imagine a good bit more money would 'elp, eh? Maybe even enough to take you someplace warm and dry, right out o' London?"

"Daft, are you, love?" Annie laughed, not unkindly. "Now, just tell me Polly, how would I get that sort of money?"

Polly winked and leaned close. "Well, as it 'appens I just might be set to come into a small fortune, y'see. And I might be willin' to share it." She showed Annie the letters in her pocket and explained her scheme— and let on like she knew who the author was and was only willing to share the money because she was totally broke, herself, and needed a bed for the night. When she finished her proposition, Annie glared at her. "But Polly! That's blackmail!" The anger in the other woman's eyes and rasping voice astonished Polly.

She drew herself up defensively. "An' if it is? Bloke should 'ave thought of that before 'e went about dippin' 'is Hampton into a bloke's arse'ole! Besides, Annie, this 'ere bastard's rich as sin. And what've you got, eh? A dead 'usband and a sickness eatin' away at you, 'til you can't 'ardly stand up. If we went to a magistrate, this 'ere bloke would go t'prison. I'm not talkin' about 'urting a decent sort of chap, I'm talkin' about makin' a right depraved bastard pay for 'is crimes against God an' nature. An' 'ow better *should* 'e pay, than to 'elp a sick woman? I ask you that, Annie Chapman, 'ow better to pay for 'is sins than to 'elp a woman 'oo needs it most? Think of it, Annie. Enough money t'go someplace where it don't rain 'alf the year an' the fogs don't make it near impossible to breathe of a night. Someplace warm, even in winter. A decent 'ouse wiv a roof over and enough to eat, so's you aren't weak all the time, wot lets the sickness gets a better grip than ever. Annie,

think of it, enough money to pay a real doctor an'
get the sort of medicines rich folk 'ave . . ."

Annie's expression had crumpled. Tears filled her
eyes. "You're right," she whispered. "Isn't my fault
I'm sick. Not my fault this nasty chap went out and
seduced a half-grown boy, either. God, to have enough
money for real medicine. A warm place to live . . ."
She coughed, swaying weakly. Misery and longing
ploughed deep gullies into her face.

Polly patted her shoulder. "That's right, Annie. I'll
share wiv you. There's four letters. You take three of
'em. All I need's enough money to pay me doss 'ouse
for a few nights. Can you spare that much, Annie?
A few pence for now . . . and a lifetime of medicine
and rest in warm beds, after?"

Annie was searching through her pockets. "I've got
to have enough for my own doss house tonight," she
muttered, digging out a few coins. "I've had some luck
today, though. Made enough money to pay for almost
a week's lodging. Here." She gave Polly a shilling.
"That's fourpence a letter. Is it enough?" she asked
anxiously.

Polly Nichols had to work hard not to snatch the
shilling out of Annie's hand. She was looking at
enough money to buy four brimming *glassfuls* of gin.
"Oh, Annie, that's a gracious plenty." She accepted
the shilling and handed over three of her precious
letters. "An' 'ere you are, luv, three tickets to the life
you deserve."

Annie actually hugged her.

Polly flushed and muttered, "I'll not forget this,
Annie. An' we'll send the letter to this nasty Mr. Eddy
together, eh? Tomorrow, Annie. Meet me at the
Britannia pub tomorrow an' we'll compose a lovely
letter to Mr. Eddy an' send it off. You got a better
education than I 'ave, you can write it out all posh,
like, eh?"

By tomorrow she would have found someone to

translate her remaining letter for her and be able to
keep that promise. And she just might let Annie keep
one of the letters, after all, rather than buying them
all back.

Annie smiled at her, eyes swimming with gratitude.
"You're a grand friend, Polly Nichols. God bless you."

They said their goodbyes, Annie tucking three of
the letters into her pockets while Polly pocketed the
remaining letter and her precious shilling. As they
went their separate ways, Polly smiled widely. Then
she headed for the nearest public house as fast as
her steel-capped boots would carry her there. She
needed a drink, all right.

To celebrate!

Skeeter wasn't certain what, exactly, he was looking for as he worked the Britannia Gate's baggage
line. But the Britannia was the first gate to cycle
since Ianira's disappearance. If Skeeter had kidnapped someone as world-famous as Ianira Cassondra, intending something more subtle than simply
killing her and dumping the body somewhere, he'd
have tried to smuggle her out through the first open
gate available.

For one thing, it would be far easier to torture a
victim down a gate. Fewer people to hear—or at least
care about—the screams. And if her abductor really
was the person who'd shoved her out of the way of
an assassin's bullet, if he actually was interested in
keeping her alive, then getting her off the station
would be imperative. Too many people had far too
many opportunities to strike at Ianira on station, even
if her rescuer tried to keep her hidden. In a gossip-
riddled place like La-La Land, *nothing* stayed secret
for long. Certainly not an abduction of someone as
beloved and strikingly recognizable as Ianira.

So Skeeter had abandoned his search of the station, donned a shapeless working man's shirt and the

creaseless trousers of the Victorian era—the costume worn by all Time Tours baggage handlers working the Britannia—and reported for work, as planned. As Ianira had planned . . . He couldn't think about that now, couldn't dwell on the fear and the dull, aching anger, not if he hoped to catch what might be a very fleeting, subtle clue betraying a smuggler.

How someone might successfully sneak someone through a gate occupied Skeeter's thoughts as hotel bellhops arrived in steady streams from hotels up and down Commons, bringing cartloads of luggage tagged for London. Tourists generally carried no more on their person than an average passenger was permitted to carry aboard a jetliner, which meant—and Skeeter stared in dismay at the flood of baggage carts on direct approach to the Britannia's lounge—that bellhops and baggage handlers had to transport every last trunk, carpet bag, portmanteau, and ladies' toiletry case from hotel room door to down-time destination, through a gate which opened only so wide and stayed open only so long.

Sloppy handling, broken contents, and lost luggage had resulted in the firing of many a baggage handler, not to mention four baggage *managers* in just the past few months. And Celosia Enyo, the latest in that dismal line of unhappy managers, was not the kind of woman to tolerate mistakes by anyone, not on this gate's cycle, anyway. After all, this wasn't just *any* gate opening. This was a Shangri-La Event: Ripper Season's official kick-off. And true to 'eighty-sixer predictions, the social gala on the other side of the departures-lounge barricades had roared to boisterous, ghoulish life.

"I don't care what those experts say," a severely dressed woman was saying as she passed through the check-in procedures, "I think it was that barber-surgeon, the bigamist. George Chapman."

Her companion, an equally severe woman with upswept, greying hair, said, "Chapman? His real name was Severin Klosowski, wasn't it? I don't think he was a very likely suspect."

"Well, Inspector Abberline named him as a leading candidate! Klosowski killed lots of women. Wives, mistresses, girlfriends—"

"Yes, but he didn't use a knife, my dear, he poisoned them. The Ripper wasn't that devious. Klosowski killed his women when they got too inconvenient. Or too expensive to keep. Jack the Ripper killed for the pleasure of it."

And behind those two, a professorial-looking little man in a seedy suit was holding forth at length to a drab little woman with a dumpy build and a rabbitty, frightened look in her eyes: "A serial killer needs to punish the woman or women he hated in his own life. He acts out the violence he wished he'd had the nerve to commit against the women who injured him. Jack the Ripper simply transferred that violence to the prostitutes of London's East End. That's why it can't be Klosowski," he added, nodding at the two severely dressed women in line ahead of him. "Personally, I favor the Mysterious Lodger, that Canadian chap, G. Wentworth Bell Smith. He went about in rubberized boots, changing clothes at all hours, railing against loose women. I'd stake my reputation on it, Bell Smith's the man . . ."

The nearest of the ladies championing Chapman rounded on the Bell-Smith supporter. "A killer proven is a killer proven!" she insisted, refusing to be swayed in her convictions by any amount of evidence or reason. "Mark my words, Claudia," she turned back to her friend, "Chapman or Klosowski, whichever name you prefer, he'll turn out to be the Ripper! I'm sure of it . . ."

While overhead, on the immense SLUR television screen, the scholarly debate raged on. "—a very common pattern," Scotland Yard Inspector Conroy Melvyn was saying in a taped interview with fellow

Ripper Watch Team member Pavel Kostenka, "for a male serial killer to attack and kill prostitutes. Bloke sees 'em as a substitute for the powerful woman in 'is life, the one 'e feels powerless to strike at, instead."

"Indeed," Dr. Koskenka was nodding. "Not only this, but a prostitute represents a morally fallen woman. And prostitutes," Dr. Kostenka added heavily, "were and still are the most easily available women to such killers. Add to that the historical tendency of police to dismiss a prostitute's murder as less important than the murder of a 'respectable' woman and streetwalkers surge into prominence as victims of mass murderers—"

Skeeter tuned out the debate as best he could and grunted under the weight of massive steamer trunks, portmanteaus, carpet bags, leather cases, smaller trunks and satchels until his back ached. The arriving luggage was transferred case by case to a growing pile at the base of a newly installed, massive conveyor system which Time Tours' new baggage manager had finally had the good sense to install. Skeeter glanced up to the gate platform, five stories overhead. Thank God for the conveyer. Some of those steamer trunks weighed more than Skeeter did. Considerably more. He eyed the gridwork stairs he'd be climbing soon and blessed that conveyer system fervently.

Geographically speaking, the Britannia was the highest of Shangri-La's active tour gates. When it opened, tourists climbed up to an immense metal gridwork platform which hovered near the steel beams and girders of the ceiling. Until the advent of that conveyer, sweating baggage handlers and porters had climbed that same ramp, gasping and hurrying to make it through before the gate disappeared into thin air once more.

"Sheesh," Skeeter muttered, grabbing another trunk by its leather handles and hauling it over to the conveyer, "what's in some of these monsters? Uranium bricks?" One of the other baggage handlers, a down-timer who worked most gate openings as a porter, grunted sympathetically as Skeeter groused, "They're only staying in London eight days, for Chrissake. And they'll be bringing back more than they left with!"

They would, too. Right down to the last yammering, whining kid in line. Parents had to pay a hefty amount of extra cash demanded by Time Tours, Inc. for children's tickets, a policy put into place after a couple of kids had managed to get themselves fatally separated from tours out of other stations. Children on a time tour were like gasoline on an open camp-fire. But parents still brought their brats with them in droves, and a surprising number paid the extra fees for kids' tickets. Others simply dropped the kids off at the station school to "have fun" in the zany world of the station while Mommy and Daddy went time hopping.

Skeeter dragged over another portmanteau. Why anybody would take a child into something like the Ripper terror . . . He could see it now. *My summer vacation: how a serial killer cut up women who make their living sleeping with strangers for money.* And kids had grown up fast in *his* day.

"C'mon, Jackson," an angry voice snapped practically in his ear, "enough goofing off! Put your back into it! Those baggage carts are piling up fast. And more are coming in from the hotels every minute!"

Skeeter found the baggage manager right behind him, glaring at him through narrowed, suspicious eyes. He resisted the urge to flip her a bird and said, "Yes, ma'am!" Just exactly how he was supposed to work faster than top speed, Skeeter wasn't quite sure, but he made a valiant effort. He cleared the cart in front of him and shoved it out of the way so another could take its place. Celosia Enyo watched him sharply for the next couple of minutes, then stalked further down the line, browbeating some other unfortunate. At least she was impartially horrible to everyone. Of course, after the miserable track record her four immediate predecessors had compiled between them, Enyo doubtless sweat bullets every time a gate opened, hoping she'd still have a job when it closed again. Skeeter could sympathize. Not much, maybe— anybody that universally rude deserved a dose of unpleasantness right back, again. But he could sympathize some.

Of course, Skeeter grunted sharply and dropped another case onto the stack, by that same logic, he'd still be working off his own karma when he was four-hundred ninety. *Yeah, well, at least I was never obnoxious to anybody I ripped off. . . .* A polite thief, that's what he'd been, by God. But no longer a thief, thanks to Marcus and Ianira.

Skeeter blinked sweat out of his eyes, fighting a sudden tightness in his chest as he emptied yet another baggage cart. Surely Marcus realized he could trust Skeeter? After what Skeeter'd gone through in Rome, damn near dying in that gladiatorial combat in the Circus Maximus before wrenching Marcus out of slavery again, surely Marcus could've trusted him enough to let him know they were alive, at least? Whoever was trying to kill them, he had to realize that Skeeter, of all people, wouldn't betray him and his daughters?

He ground his teeth in silent misery. If somebody had tried to shoot *his* wife, if he'd walked into *his* daughters' daycare center to find two armed thugs trying to drag off *his* kids, would *he* have risked contacting anybody? Just on the remote chance they might be followed, trying to bring help? Skeeter knew he wouldn't have. Wouldn't have dared risk his loved ones, no matter what risks he, himself, might have been willing to run. The realization hurt, even as he was forced to admit he understood the silence. But the girls were just babies, Artemisia not yet four, Gelasia barely turned one. Marcus couldn't stay in hiding with them, not for long. Which was doubtless what the faceless bastards trying to kill them were counting on. If Skeeter were Marcus, he'd seriously consider trying to jump station. Through *any* gate that opened.

Skeeter closed his hands around the stout handles of yet another steamer trunk and heaved it into place, wishing bitterly he could get his hands on whoever had dragged Ianira away through that riot. It must have been staged. Create a perfect diversion, shoot her down in the midst of the chaos . . . Only somebody had interrupted the attempt. Had the shooter dragged her off? To finish the job at his leisure? Or someone else? Skeeter couldn't bear to keep thinking in ragged circles like this, but he couldn't *not* think about her, either, not considering what he owed her.

Skeeter wiped sweat from his forehead. Just another few minutes, he told himself fiercely. Another few minutes and the gate would have cycled, all this ridiculous luggage would be on the other side of the Britannia, and he could get back to combing the station with the finest-toothed comb ever invented by humanity.

Meanwhile . . .

Watching the freakshow beyond the barricades helped keep his mind off it and watching the tourists inside the barricades occupied the rest of his mind, searching faces for clues, for any similarity to the face in his memory, that wild-eyed kid with the black-powder pistol. Gawkers formed an impenetrable barrier around the edges of the departures lounge, so thick, security had formed cordons to permit ticketed tourists, uniformed Time Tours employees, freelance guides, baggage handlers, and supply couriers to reach the roped-off lounge. The noise was appalling. Troops of howler monkeys had nothing on the mob of humanity packed into the confined spaces of Victoria Station. And every man-jack one of 'em wanted to be able to tell his grandchildren some day, "I was there, kids, I was there when the first Ripper tour went through, let me tell you, it was *something . . .*"

It was something, all right.

There weren't words disgusting enough to describe it, that electric air of anticipation, of excitement that left the air supercharged with the feeling that a major event is happening right before your eyes, an excitement sensed in the nerve endings of skin and hair, completely independent of sight and sound and smell. Skeeter was the kind of soul who loved excitement, thrived on it, in fact. But this . . . this kind of excitement was a perversion, even Skeeter could sense that, and Skeeter Jackson's moral code, formed during his years with the Yakka Mongols, didn't exactly mesh with most of up-time humanity's. What was it going to be like when *next* week's gate opened? When all these people and probably a couple hundred more, besides, newly arrived through Primary, jammed in to learn who the ghoul *really* was?

Maybe after he dragged all this luggage through the Britannia and came back to look for Ianira some more, he'd volunteer to haul baggage to Denver for a couple of weeks, just to miss out on the whole sordid thing? The Wild West Gate opened tomorrow, after all, and Time Tours was perennially short of baggage handlers. If only they'd found Ianira by then, and Marcus, and little Artemisia and bright-eyed, laughing Gelasia.

If, *if*, IF!

It was the not knowing that was intolerable, the not knowing or being able to find out. He wanted this job over with, so he could get back to searching. Skeeter stared intently through the crowd, trying to spot anybody he might recognize from The Found Ones. Any news was better than none. But he couldn't see a single down-timer in that crowd who wasn't already busy to distraction hauling luggage. Which meant they wouldn't know spit about the search underway, either.

God, how much longer until this blasted gate cycled?

He peered up at the huge chronometer boards suspended from the distant ceiling, picking out the countdown for Gate Two: five minutes. At the rate time was creeping past, it might as well be five years.

"Jackson! Do you really like scrubbing toilets that much?"

He started so violently he nearly dropped the carpet bag dangling from his hands. Celosia Enyo was glaring at him, lips thinned to a murderous white line.

"Sorry, ma'am," he muttered. "I was hoping I might see someone who'd heard about Ianira—"

"We're all worried! But that gate doesn't give a damn who's missing or found. We get that—" she jabbed a finger toward the small mountain of luggage "—through the gate on time or some millionaire will have your head on his dinner platter for having to buy a new wardrobe in London. Worry about your friends on your own time. Or by God, your own time is all you'll have!"

She was absolutely right, in a cold-blooded, mercenary sense. The moment she turned away to snarl at someone else, Skeeter gave her a flying eagle salute and dragged another portmanteau off a groaning luggage cart. He scowled at the enormous stack of luggage on the conveyer already, mentally damning Time Tours for insane greed. No wonder the last four baggage managers had failed disastrously with gate logistics. Time Tours was sending through too many blistering tourists at once.

Never mind *way* too many trunks per tourist.

If he'd kept accurate count, the last five steamer trunks and three portmanteaus alone had belonged to the same guy. Benny Catlin, whoever the hell he was. Rich as sin, if he could cart that much luggage through in just one direction. The big conveyer rumbled to life with one jolting squeal and a grating of metal gears. Then the rubberized surface began moving upward, ready to carry all that luggage to the platform overhead. Skeeter glanced around to look for the boss. Enyo wasn't in sight, but the shift supervisor was busy sending handlers aloft. He caught Skeeter's eye and said, "Get up top, Jackson. Start hauling that stuff off the conveyer as it arrives."

"Yessir!"

The climb up to the Britannia platform was a long one, particularly after all the hauling he'd done in the past few minutes, but the view was spectacular. Commons spread out beneath his feet, a full five stories deep, riotous with color and sound. Costumed tourists scurried like rainbow-hued bugs whipped around in the currents and eddies of a slow-motion river. Great banners—bright holiday-colored ribbons curling and floating through a hundred-foot depth of open air from balconies and catwalks—proclaimed to the world that Ripper Season had begun, and advertised other not-to-be-missed down-time events. A cat's-cradle tangle of meshwork bridges stretched right across Commons from one side to the other, supported from below by steel struts or suspended from above by steel cables disappearing into the ceiling. The noise from hundreds of human throats lapped at the edges of the high platform like crashing surf against jagged rocks, leaping and splashing back again, indistinct and unintelligible from sheer distance.

And booming above it all came the voice of the public address system, echoing down the vast length of Commons: "Your attention, please. Gate Two is due to open in two minutes . . ."

The first luggage on the conveyor belt arrived with a jolt and scrape against the gridwork platform. Skeeter joined a human-chain effort, hauling luggage clear of the moving conveyor and piling it on the platform. Railings ran all the way around, with a wide metal gate set into one side. Until the Britannia actually opened, that wide metal gate led to a sheer, hundred-foot drop to the cobblestones of Victoria Station. Despite the railing, Skeeter stayed well away from the edge as he hauled, piled, and stacked a steadily increasing jumble of trunks, cases, and soft-sided carpet bags across the broad stretch of platform.

At the far corner, a second conveyor system rumbled to life, moving downward rather than up. Celosia Enyo was testing the system, making sure everything was ready for the returning tour and all of *its* luggage. So engrossed was Skeeter in the monumental task of shifting the arriving baggage, the gate's opening took him by surprise. A skull-shaking backlash of subharmonics rattled his very bones. Skeeter jumped, wanting instinctively to cover his ears, although that wouldn't have done any good. The gate's frequency was too low for actual human hearing. He glanced around—and gasped.

A kaleidoscope of shimmering color, dopplering through the entire rainbow spectrum, had appeared in the middle of empty air right at the edge of the platform. The colors scintillated like a sheen of oil on water, sunlight on a raven's glossy feathers. The hair on Skeeter's arms stood starkly erect. He'd seen gates open hundreds of times, had stepped through a number of them, when he'd had the money for a tour or had conned someone else into paying for it. But he'd never been this close to the massive Britannia as it began its awe-striking cycle a hundred feet above the Commons floor.

From below, a wall of noise came surging up to

the platform, gasps and cries of astonishment from hundreds of spectators. A point of absolute darkness appeared dead center in the wild flashes of color. The blackness expanded rapidly, a hole through time, through the very fabric of reality . . . Something hard banged into Skeeter's elbow. He yelped, jumped guiltily, then grabbed the steamer trunk thrust at him. It went awkwardly onto the top of the stack, canted at an angle, too unstable for anything else to go on top. The next portmanteau to arrive thudded against the steel gridwork, starting a new pile.

Skeeter rearranged wetness on his brow with a limp, soaked sleeve, then straightened his aching back and started piling up the next stack, all while keeping one eye on the massive gate rumbling open behind him. The blackness widened steadily until it stretched the full width of the platform. A Time Tours guide climbed up from the Commons floor and opened the broad metal gate at the edge of the platform to *its* full extent, as well.

A blur of motion caught his eye and the first returnee arrived, rushing at them with the speed of a runaway bullet train. Skeeter resisted the urge to jump out of the way. Then the apparent motion slowed and a gentleman in fancy evening clothes, protected by a wet India-rubber rain slicker, stepped calmly onto the platform and turned to assist the returning tourists through. Men and women in silks and expensively cut garb, most of them holding 1880's style umbrellas and brushing water off their heavy cloaks, jostled their way through, many chattering excitedly. Quite a few others had gone slightly greenish and stumbled every few steps. Guides in servants' uniforms and working men's rougher clothes helped those who seemed worst off to stagger through the open gate. Porters rushed through on their heels, tracking mud onto the platform, then a mad scramble ensued to get all the arriving luggage—every bit of it slick with what must be a drenching downpour on the other side of the gate—onto the downward-rumbling conveyer. Below, tourists raced up the five flights of stairs to hurry through in the other direction. Skeeter worked fiendishly. He hauled trunks which arrived from down time onto the downward-rumbling conveyer, in an effort to clear the jam at the gate. Then the Britannia was finally clear and outbound tourists rushed past, laughing excitedly and squealing as they stepped off the edge of the platform into what their hindbrains insisted was a hundred-foot sheer drop to the floor below.

"Get that outbound baggage moving!"

Skeeter lunged to the task, along with a dozen other porters. He staggered through the open gate and emerged into a rain-lashed garden. It was nearly dark. Worse, the ground was cut up from all the foot traffic across it, muddy and treacherous with slick leaves. There was a flagstone path, but that was crowded with tourists and guides and gatehouse staff holding umbrellas. The porters didn't have time to wait for them to clear out of the way. Following the lead of more experienced baggage handlers in front of him, Skeeter plunged into the muddy grass and slogged his way toward the gatehouse. The rain was icy, slashing against his clothing and soaking him to the skin. He dumped his first load at the back door of the three-story gatehouse and pelted back through the open gate to grab another load. The sensation was dizzying, disorienting.

Then he was through and staggering a little, himself, across the platform. His muddy shoes slipped on wet metal. Skeeter windmilled and lurched against a stack of luggage waiting to be ferried through. The topmost steamer trunk, a massive thing, slid sideways and started to topple toward the edge of the platform. The corner of the trunk was well out beyond the periphery of the open Britannia gate, teetering out where it would plunge the full hundred feet to the Commons floor. As Skeeter went to one bruised knee, furious shouts and blistering curses erupted. Then somebody lunged past him to grab the steamer trunk by the handle before it could fall.

"Don't just sit there, goddamn you!" A short, skinny tourist stood glaring murderously down at him, arms straining to keep the trunk from falling. The young man's whiskered face had gone ashen under the lights overhead. "Grab this trunk! I can't hold the weight!" The kid's voice was light, breathless, furious.

His whole knee ached where he'd landed on it, but Skeeter staggered back his feet and leaned over the piles of trunks and cases to secure a wet-handed grip on the corner that had already gone over the end of the platform. Hauling together, Skeeter and the tourist pulled the heavy trunk back onto the platform. The tourist was actually shaking, whether with fright or rage, Skeeter wasn't certain.

But he wasn't so shaken he didn't blow up in Skeeter's face. *"What the hell did you think you were doing?* Were you *trying* to shove that trunk over the edge? Goddammit, do you have any idea what would've happened if that trunk had gone over? If you've been drinking, I'll make sure you never work on this station again!" The young man's face was deathly pale, eyes blazing against the unnatural pallor of his skin and the dark, heavy whiskers of his mutton-chop sideburns and mustache, which he must've acquired from Paula Booker's cosmetology salon, because up-time men didn't grow facial hair in that quantity or shape any more. The furious tourist, fists balled up and white-knuckled, shrilled out, "My God, *do you realize what you almost caused?"*

"Well, it didn't fall, did it?" Skeeter snapped, halting the tirade mid-stream. "And if you stand there cursing much longer, you're gonna miss your stinking gate!" Skeeter shouldered the trunk himself, having to carry it across his back, the thing was so heavy. The short and brutish little tourist, white-lipped and silent now, stalked through the open gate on Skeeter's heels, evidently intent on following to make sure Skeeter didn't drop it again. *So much for my new job. After this guy gets done complaining, I'll be lucky if I still have the job scrubbing toilets.*

It was, of course, still raining furiously in the Spaldergate House garden. Skeeter did slip again, the muddy ground was so churned up beside the crowded flagstone walkway. The furious man on his heels grabbed at the trunk again as Skeeter lurched and slid sideways. "Listen, you drunken idiot!" he shouted above steady pouring of the rain. "Lay off the booze or the pills before you show up for work!"

"Stuff it," Skeeter said crudely. He regained his feet and finally gained the house, where he gratefully lowered his burden to the floor.

"Where are you going?" the irate young man demanded when Skeeter headed back into the downpour.

He flung the answer over one aching shoulder. "Back to the station!"

"But who's going to cart this out to the carriage? Take it to the hotel?"

"Carry it yourself!"

The skinny, whiskered little tourist was still sputtering at the back door when Skeeter re-entered the now-visibly shrunken Britannia Gate. He passed several other porters bent double under heavy loads, trying to get the last of the pile through, then was back on the metal gridwork platform. All that remained of the departing tour was a harried Time Tours guide who plunged through as Skeeter reappeared. Then he was alone with the mud and a single uniformed Time Tours employee who swung shut the big metal safety gate as the Britannia shrank rapidly back in on itself and vanished for another eight days.

Skeeter—wet, shivering, exhausted—slowly descended the stairs once again and slid his timecard through the reader at the bottom, "clocking out" so his brief stay in the London timestream would be recorded properly. The baggage manager was waiting, predictably irate. Skeeter listened in total, sodden silence, taking the upbraiding he'd expected. This evidently puzzled the furious Enyo, because she finally snapped, "Well? Aren't you going to protest your innocence?"

"Why bother?" Skeeter said tiredly. "You've already decided I'm guilty. So just fire me and get it over with so I can put on some dry clothes and start looking for my friends again."

Thirty seconds later, he was on his way, metaphoric pink slip in hand. *Well, that was probably the shortest job on record. Sixty-nine minutes from hired to fired.* He never had liked the idea of hauling luggage for a bunch of jackass tourists, anyway. Scrubbing toilets was dirtier, but at least more dignified than bowing and scraping and apologizing for being alive. And when the job was over, *something,* at least, was clean.

Which was more than he could say of himself at the moment. Mud covered his trousers, squelched from his wet shoes, and dripped with the trickling rainwater down one whole sleeve where he'd caught himself from a nasty fall, that last time through. *Wonder what was in that lousy trunk, anyway? The way he acted, you'd've thought it was his heirloom china. God, tourists!*

Maybe that idiot would do them all a favor and get himself nice and permanently lost in London? But that thought only brought the pain surging back. Skeeter blinked away wetness that had nothing to do with the rainwater dripping out of his hair, then speeded up. He had to get out of these wet, filthy

clothes and hook up with the search teams again. Very
few people knew this station the way Skeeter did. If
he couldn't find her . . .

He clenched his jaw muscles.

He had to find her.

Nothing else mattered at all.

Chapter Seven

Rain had stopped falling over the slate rooftops and crockery chimney pots of London by the time the arriving tour sorted itself out at the Time Tours Gatehouse and departed via carriages to hotels, boarding houses, and rented flats—a British word for apartment that one of the guides had needed to explain to her. Jenna Nicole Caddrick sat hunched now in a rattling carriage, listening to the sharp clop as the horses, a teamed pair of them in harness, struck the cobblestoned street with iron-shod hooves in a steady rhythm.

She shivered and hugged her gentleman's frock coat more tightly around her, grateful for the first time that she was less well endowed than she'd have liked through the chest, and grateful, too, for the simple bulkiness of Victorian men's clothing, which helped disguise bulges that shouldn't have been there. Jenna huddled into her coat, miserable and scared and wishing like anything that Noah had come through with her. She hadn't expected London to be so cold or so wet. It was only the end of August here, after all; but the guides back at the gatehouse had told them London's entire summer had been cold and wet, so there wasn't any use complaining to *them* about the miserable weather.

Miserable was right. The ride jounced her sufficiently to shake her teeth loose, if she hadn't been clenching them so tightly. The air stank, not like New York, which smelt of car exhaust fumes and smog, but rather a dank, bleak sort of stench compounded of whatever was rotting in the River Thames and coal smoke from hundreds of thousands of chimneys and horse dung scattered like shapeless anthills across the streets and a miasma of other stinks she couldn't identify and wasn't sure she wanted to, either. Everything was strange, even the lights. Gaslight didn't look like electric light, which was a phenomenon all those period-piece movies hadn't been able to capture on film. It was softer and yellower, adding a warm and yet alien color to everything where it spilled out across window sills or past half-closed shutters.

What the jouncing, jarring ride was doing to Ianira Cassondra, folded up like last week's laundry and nestled inside an enormous steamer trunk, Jenna didn't even want to consider. They'd cushioned her with blankets and fitted her with a mask for the oxygen canisters supplied in every hotel room in Shangri-La, in case of a station fire. Every hotel room stocked them, since TT-86 stood high in the Himalayas' rarified air. Ianira had clung briefly to Marcus, both their faces white with terror, had kissed her little girls and whispered to them in Greek, then she'd climbed into the trunk, folded herself down into the makeshift nest, and slipped on the oxygen mask.

Noah had been the one to close and latch the lid.

Jenna couldn't bring herself to do it, to lock her in, like that.

She'd wanted to call in a doctor, to look at the nasty bruise and swelling along Ianira's brow where the Prophetess had struck her head on the concrete floor. But risking even a doctor's visit, where questions *would* be asked, meant risking Ianira's life, as well as risking her whole family. And Noah and Jenna's lives, too . . . She clenched down her eyelids. *Please, Goddess, there's been enough killing, let it stop. . . .*

Jenna refused to let herself recall too acutely those ghastly seconds on the platform high above the Commons floor, when Ianira's trunk had teetered and nearly fallen straight off the edge. Jenna's insides still shook, just remembering. She'd have blamed the baggage handler for being a member of the death squad on their trail if the man hadn't obviously been a long-time station resident. And the guy had gone back to the station, too, in a state of churlish rage, which he wouldn't have done, if he'd been sent to murder Jenna and Ianira. No, it'd just been one of those nightmarish, freakish near-accidents that probably happened every time a gate opened and too many people with too much luggage tried to cram themselves through a hole of finite dimensions and duration.

Don't think about it, Jenna, she didn't fall, so don't think about it. There's about a million other things to worry about, instead. Like, where to find refuge in this sprawling, sooty, foul-smelling city on the Thames. She was supposed to stay at the Piccadilly Hotel tonight, in her persona as Mr. Benny Catlin, up-time student doing post-doctoral work in sociology. "Benny" was supposed to be filming his graduate work, as part of the plan she and Carl had come up with, a lifetime ago, when the worst terror she'd had to face was having her infamous father find out she planned to go time touring.

Carl should've been the one playing "Benny Catlin," not Jenna. If Noah'd been able to go with her, the detective would've played the role of the non-existent Mr. Catlin. But they *had* to split up, so Jenna had exchanged identification with Noah. That way, the female "tourist" using the persona she and Carl had bought from that underworld identity seller in New York would cash in her Britannia Gate ticket, then buy one for Denver, instead, leading the *Ansar Majlis* on a merry chase down the wrong gate from the one Jenna and Ianira had really gone through. With any luck, Jenna and the Prophetess would reach the Picadilly Hotel without incident.

But they wouldn't be staying in the Picadilly Hotel for long, not with the probability that they'd been followed through the Britannia Gate by *someone* topping out somewhere around a hundred ten percent. Jenna knew she'd have to come up with some other place to stay, to keep them both safe. Maybe she should check into the Piccadilly Hotel as scheduled, then simply leave in the middle of the night? Haul their luggage down the back stairs to the hotel livery stable and take off with a wagon. Maybe vanish into the East End somewhere for a while. It was the least likely place any searchers would think to look for them, not with Jack the Ripper stalking those dismal streets.

Jenna finally came up out of her dark and miserable thoughts to realize that the carriage driver—a long-term Time Tours employee—was talking steadily to someone who hadn't been listening. The man was pattering on about the city having taken out a whole triangular-shaped city block three years previously. "Demolished the entire length of Glasshouse Street, to cut Shaftesbury Avenue from Bloomsbury to Piccadilly Circus. Piccadilly hasn't been a true circus since, y'see, left it mighty ugly, most folks are saying, but that new Shaftesbury Avenue, now, it's right convenient, so it is . . ."

Not that Jenna cared a damn what streets were brand new, but she tried to pay more attention, because she was going to have to get used to living here, maybe for a long time. Longer than she wanted to think about, anyway. The carriage with its heavy load of luggage passed through the apparently blighted Piccadilly Circus, which looked perfectly fine to Jenna, then jolted at last to a halt in front of the Piccadilly Hotel, with its ornate wrought-iron dome rising like the bare ribs of Cinderella's pumpkin coach. The whole open-work affair was topped by a rampant team of horses drawing a chariot. Wet streets stood puddled with the recent rain. As Jenna climbed cautiously down, not wanting to fall and break a bone, for God's sake, thunder rumbled overhead, an ominous warning of more rain squalls to come.

The driver started hauling trunks and cases off the luggage shelf at the back of the carriage while Jenna trudged into the hotel's typically fussy Victorian lobby. The room was dark with heavy, ornately carved wood and busy, dark-hued wallpaper, crowded with breakables and ornate ornamentation in wrought iron. Jenna went through the motions of signing the guest register, acquiring her key, and climbing the stairs to her room, all in a daze of exhaustion. She'd been running ever since Luigi's in New York, didn't even want to think about how many people had died between then and now. The driver arrived on Jenna's heels and waited with a heavy load of luggage while Jenna unlocked her stuffy, overly-warm room. A coal fire blazed in a hearth along one wall. The driver, puffing from his exertions, was followed in by a bellman who'd assisted the driver in lugging up the immense trunk where Ianira Cassondra lay safely hidden. At least, Jenna hoped she was safe inside that horrible cocoon of leather and brass fittings. When the bellman nearly dropped one end, Jenna's ragged temper exploded again.

"Careful with that!" It came out far more sharply than she'd meant it to, sharp and raggedly frightened. So she gulped and tried to explain her entirely-too-forceful concern. "It has valuable equipment inside. Photographic equipment."

"Beggin' your pardon, sir," the uniformed bellman huffed, gingerly setting down his end, "no wonder it's so heavy, cameras are big things, and all those glass plates and suchlike."

"Yes, well, I don't want anything in that trunk damaged."

The Time Tours driver gave Jenna a sour look. Clearly he'd been on the receiving end of too many tourists' cutting tongues. Driver and bellman vanished downstairs to fetch up the rest of the baggage, making short work of it. Jenna tipped the hotel employee, who left with a polite bow, closing the door after himself. The driver showed her how the gas lights worked, lighting them, then turning one of them out again, the proper way. "If you just blow it out, gas'll still come flooding out of the open valve. They haven't started putting in the smelly stuff yet, so you'd never even notice it. Just asphyxiate yourself in your sleep, if you didn't accidentally strike a spark and blow yourself out of this room."

Jenna was too tired for lectures on how the whole Victorian world operated, but she made a valiant effort to pay attention. The Time Tours driver was explaining how to summon a servant and how to find "Benny Catlin's" rented flat in Cheapside, across the Holborn Viaduct—whatever that was. Jenna didn't know enough about London and hadn't been given a chance to finish her library research for the trip she and Carl had planned to make. "We'll send an express wagon round in the morning, Mr. Catlin, help you shift to your permanent lodgings. Couldn't have you arriving at the flat this late in the evening, of course, the landlady would have a cultured fit of apoplexy, having us clatter about and disturb her seances or whatever she'll have there tonight, it's always something new . . ."

A polite tap at the door interrupted. "Mr. Catlin?" a man's voice inquired.

"Yes, come in, it isn't locked." *Yet* . . . The moment the driver was gone, Jenna intended locking the door and putting a small army of little up-time burglar alarms she'd brought with her on every windowsill and even under the doorknob. The door swung open and Jenna caught one glimpse of the two men in the hallway. Jenna registered the guns they held faster than with the driver. Jenna dove sideways with a startled scream as the pop and clack of modern, silenced semi-autos brought the driver down with a terrible, choked sound. Jenna sprawled to the floor behind the bed, dragging frantically at the Remington Beale's revolver concealed in her coat pocket. The driver was screaming in pain on the far side of the bed. Then Jenna was firing back, bracing her wrists on the feather-ticking of the mattress to steady her hands. Recoil kicked her palms, jarred the bones of her wrists. The shattering noise of the report left Jenna's ears ringing. But one of the bastards went down with a surprised grunt and cry of pain.

Jenna kept shooting, trying to hit the other one. The second shooter had danced into the corridor again, cursing hideously. Smoke from her pistol hung like fog, obscuring her view of the doorway. The wounded driver, gasping with the effort, managed to grab the leg of a nearby washstand. He brought the whole thing crashing down across the wounded gunman's head. The crockery basin shattered, leaving a spreading pool of blood in its wake. Then bullets slammed into the wallpaper beside Jenna's head. She ducked, doing some swearing of her own, wet and shaky with raw terror. Jenna fired and the pistol merely clicked. Hands trembling, she fumbled for her other pre-loaded revolver.

The driver, grey-faced and grunting with the effort, was dragging himself across the floor. He left a sickening trail of blood, as though a mortally wounded garden snail had crawled across the carpets. Jenna fired above the man's head, driving the gunman in the doorway back into the corridor again, away from the open door. Then the driver was close enough. He kicked the door shut with his feet, hooked an ankle around a chair and gave a grunting heave, dragged it in front of the door. Then collapsed with a desperate groan.

Jenna lunged over the top of the bed, scrambled across the floor on hands and knees to avoid the bullets punching through the wooden door at head height, and managed to snap shut the lock. Then she grunted and heaved and shoved an entire bureau across the door, toppling it to form a makeshift barricade. The door secured, Jenna dragged the driver's coat aside. What she found left her shaking and swearing under her breath. She didn't have time, dammit . . . but she couldn't just let the man lie there and bleed to death, could she? It was all Jenna's fault the man had been shot at all. She stripped a coverlet off the bed, managed to tear it into enough strips and pieces to form a tight compress. She had to yank off her gentleman's gloves to tie knots in the makeshift bandages.

"What in hell's going on, Catlin?" the driver gasped out, breathing shallowly against the pain.

"Long story," Jenna gasped. "And I'm really sorry you got dragged into it." She ran a distracted hand through her cropped and Macassar-oiled hair, felt the blood on her hands, wiped them on the remnants of the coverlet. A pause in the shooting outside indicated the gunman's need to change magazines or maybe even guns, temporarily stopping him from turning the solid wooden door into a block of swiss cheese. Jenna bit one lip, then scrambled across the floor on hands and knees. "Look, I can't do much for you. I've got to get the hell out of here. I'm really sorry." She handed the driver a pistol scavenged from

the dead gunman. Then Jenna retrieved the
Remington she'd emptied at their attackers and
wished there was time to reload it, but the gun was
so slow and difficult to load, she just shoved it into
the waistband of her trousers beside the partially
loaded one.

Then she wrenched up the nearest window sash
and let in a flood of relatively fresh, wet air. It stank,
but coal smoke smelled better than the coppery
stench of blood and burnt gunpowder in the room's
close confines. Jenna glanced down, judged the drop.
Even with Ianira, she ought to be able to manage it
without injury. Maybe ten feet. She opened the trunk,
barely able to control her fingers. Holding the trunk
lid open with one hand, she dragged Ianira up out
of the protected cocoon in which she'd traveled. The
Prophetess was fumbling with the oxygen mask and
bottle, clumsy and slow from the cramped confines
of the trunk. Jenna tore them loose and dropped them
back in. "Trouble," she said tersely. "They hit us faster
than I expected."

Ianira was taking in the blood, the corpse on the
carpet, the wounded driver. Her eyes had gone wide,
dark and terrified. She had to lean against Jenna just
to remain on her feet, which terrified *Jenna*.

"What the hell—?" The driver was staring. "Who's
that?"

Jenna gave him a sharp stare. "You don't know?"

"Should I? Been living in London for the past eight
years. Haven't been back on the station in at least
seven . . ."

If this guy didn't know who Ianira Cassondra was,
Jenna wasn't about to tell him.

"I'm going to lower you out the window," Jenna
whispered tersely, so her voice wouldn't carry beyond
the door. "Hold onto my wrists *tight*." Ianira climbed
over the sill and held onto Jenna's wrists with enough
force to leave bruises. Jenna grunted and shifted her

weight, swinging Ianira out, lowering her as far down along the wall as she could reach. "Now! Jump!"

Ianira plunged downward, staggered, landed. "Hurry!" the prophetess called up.

Jenna climbed cautiously across the windowsill, carefully balancing herself, and inched around until she was facing the hotel room. Bullets had started punching through the stout wooden door again. The gunman was shoving at it, too, trying to break it down or splinter the lock out of the doorframe. Thank God for solid Victorian construction, plaster and lathe walls and genuine wooden doors, not that hollow-core modern crap.

"Sorry, really," Jenna gasped, meeting the driver's bewildered, grey-faced gaze. "If he gets through that door, shoot him, will you? If you don't, he'll kill you." Then she scraped her way down until she was just hanging by her fingertips and let go her hold on the window. Jenna shoved outward slightly to keep her face from bashing against the wall on the way down. The drop was longer than she expected, but she landed well. Only went to one knee, jarring the soles of her feet up through her ankles. When she straightened with a pained gasp, her legs even condescended to work. Ianira grabbed her hand and they stumbled toward the carriage.

And the gunman charged out of the hotel's entryway. Gun in hand, he was heading for the window they'd just jumped from. But he hadn't seen them yet . . . Jenna dragged her loaded gun out of her waistband again, cursing herself for not holding onto it, and shoved Ianira behind her. The gunman saw them just as Jenna fired. She managed to loose off a couple of shots that drove their pursuer back into the hotel while smoke bellied up from her pistol and hung in the air like wet fog.

Jenna didn't wait for a second opportunity. She turned and ran, dragging Ianira with her, unable to

reach the carriage without exposing them both to fatal
fire. Ianira couldn't run very fast at first, but found
her stride as they whipped through an alleyway,
dodged into the street beyond, and gained speed. "Is
he still back there?" Jenna gasped, not wanting to risk
a wrenched ankle despite a driving terror that she
would feel a bullet through her back at any second.

"Yes . . . I cannot see him . . . but he still comes, not
far behind . . ."

Jenna decided she didn't want to know how Ianira
knew that. She cut down side streets, running flat out,
then heard a bullet ricochet off the wall beside her.
Jenna shoved Ianira ahead, whirled and snapped off
a couple of wild shots, then ducked down another
street with one hand around Ianira's wrist. They wove
in and out between horse-drawn phaetons and heavier
carriages, running flat out. Drivers and passengers
shouted after them, stared open-mouthed and hurled
curses as horses reared in surprised protest. Then they
were running down yet another street, dodging past
the biggest greenhouse Jenna had ever seen.

They were nearly to a columned portico beyond,
which offered better cover, when something slammed
against her hips. Jenna screamed in pain and fright.
She crashed to the ground, trying to roll onto her
back. Jenna jerked the gun around, fired point-blank
into the gunman's belly—

And the pistol clicked over an empty chamber.
She'd shot it dry.

"*Run!*" Jenna kicked and punched whatever she
could reach, scrambled to hands and knees, saw Ianira
racing for the shelter of the portico. Shadowy movement behind the columns suggested someone watching. *Please God, let it be someone who can help.* Jenna
gained her feet, staggered forward a single stride. A
hand around her ankle brought her down again. The
glint of a knife caught her peripheral vision. Jenna
kicked hard, felt bone crunch under the toe of her

boot. The gunman screamed. Jenna rolled frantically, tried to free herself as the bastard swung the knife in a smashing blow toward her unprotected belly—

A gunshot exploded right above Jenna. She screamed, convinced she'd just been shot. Then she realized she wasn't hit. A stranger had appeared from the darkness. The newcomer had fired that shot, not the man trying to murder her. The bullet had plowed straight through the back of the paid assassin's head. The hitman who'd hunted them through the Britannia was dead. *Messily* dead. The explosive aftermath left Jenna shuddering, eyes clenched shut. Blood and bits of human brain had spattered across her face and neck and coat. She lay on her side, panting and shaking and fighting back nausea. Then she looked up, so slowly it might've taken a week just to lift her gaze from the wet street to the stranger's face. She expected to find a constable, recalled a snatch of memory that suggested London constables had not carried firearms in 1888, and found herself looking up into the face of a man in a dark evening coat and silk top hat.

"Are you unharmed, sir? And the lady?"

Ianira had fallen to her knees beside Jenna, weeping and touching her shoulder, her arm, her blood-smeared face. "I . . ." Jenna had to gulp back nausea. "I think I'm okay."

The stranger offered a hand, calmly putting away his pistol in a capacious coat pocket. Jenna levered herself up with help. Once on her feet, she gently lifted Ianira and checked her pulse. Jenna didn't like the look of shock in the Cassondra's eyes or the desperate pallor of her skin, which was clammy and cold under her touch.

The stranger's brows rose. "Are you a doctor, sir?"

Jenna shook her head. "No. But I know enough to test a pulse point."

"Ah . . . As it happens, I *am* a medical doctor. Allow me."

The down-timer physician took Ianira's wrist to test her pulse, himself. And the Prophetess snapped rigid, eyes wide with shock. The Cassondra of Ephesus uttered a single choked sound that defied interpretation. She lifted both hands—gasped out something in Greek. The doctor stared sharply at Ianira and spoke even more sharply—also in Greek. While Jenna was struggling to recall a snatch of history lesson, that wealthy men of society had learned Greek and Latin as part of a gentleman's education, the physician snarled out something that sounded ugly. Naked shock had detonated through his eyes and twisted his face.

The next moment, Jenna found herself staring down the wrong end of his gun barrel. "Sorry, old chap. Nothing personal, you know."

He's going to kill me!

Jenna flung herself sideways just as the gun discharged. Pain caught her head brutally and slammed her to the street. As the world went dark, she heard shouts and running footsteps, saw Ianira's knees buckle in a dead faint, saw the stranger simply scoop her up and walk off with her, disappearing into the yellow drizzle.

Then darkness crashed down with a fist of brutal, black terror.

Chapter Eight

Malcolm Moore had done a great deal of hard work during his career as freelance time guide. But nothing had come even remotely close to the bruising hours he'd put in setting up a base camp in a rented hovel in Whitechapel Road, guiding scholars and criminologists through the East End from well before sunup until the early morning hours, sleeping in two and three-hour snatches, assisting them in the task of learning everything the scholars and Scotland Yard Inspectors wanted to know before the terror broke wide open on the final day of August.

The last thing Malcolm expected when the Britannia cycled near dusk, just nine hours before the first Ripper murder was what he found in the Spaldergate parlour. Having rushed upstairs from his work with the scholars ensconced in the cellar, he stood blinking in stupid shock at the sight of her. *"Margo?"*

"Malcolm!" His fiancée flung herself toward him, arms outstretched, eyes sparkling. "Oh, Malcolm! I *missed* you!"

The kiss left his head spinning. Giddy as a school-boy and grinning like a fool, Malcolm drew back at last, reluctant to break away from the vibrant warmth of her, and stared, amazed, into her eyes. "But Margo, whatever are you *doing* here?"

"Reporting for duty, sir!" she laughed, giving him a mock salute. "Kit worked it out with Bax," she said in a rush, eyes sparkling. "I'll be guiding for the rest of the Ripper Watch tour, whatever you think I can handle, and Doug Tanglewood came through to help out, too, your message asking for assistance came through loud and clear!"

Malcolm grinned. "Bloody *marvelous!* It's about time those dratted johnnies at Time Tours listened to me. How many additions to the Team did you bring through?"

Margo grimaced expressively.

"Oh, dear God," he muttered, "that many?"

"Well, it's not too bad," Margo said guardedly. "Dr. Shahdi Feroz finally made it in. Mostly, it's those reporters. Guy Pendergast and Dominica Nosette. I don't know which is worse, honestly, the scholars or the newsies. Or the tourists," she added, rolling her eyes at the flood of Ripperoons crowding into Spaldergate's parlour.

"That, I can believe," Malcolm muttered. "We haven't much time to get them settled. Polly Nichols is scheduled to die at about five o'clock tomorrow morning, which means we'll have to put our surveillance gear up sometime after two A.M. or so, when the pubs close and the streets grow a little more quiet. Daren't put up the equipment sooner, someone might notice it. It's not likely, since the wireless transmitters and miniaturized cameras and microphones we'll be setting up are so small. Still and all . . . Let's get them settled quickly, shall we, and take them downstairs to the vault. We've a base camp out in White-chapel, but the main equipment is here, beneath

Spaldergate, where we've the power for computers and recording equipment."

Margo nodded. "Okay. Let's get them moving. And the sooner we get those reporters under wraps, the better I'll feel. They don't listen at all and don't follow rules very well, either."

Malcolm grunted. "No surprise, there. The tourists the past few weeks have been bad enough, trying to duck out on their tour guides so they can cheat and stay long enough to see one of the murders. I expect the reporters will be even more delightful. Now, let's find Mrs. Gilbert, shall we, and assign everyone sleeping quarters . . ."

An hour later, Malcolm and his fiancée escorted the newly arrived team members down into the vault beneath the house, where a perfectly ordinary wooden door halfway across a perfectly standard Victorian cellar opened to reveal a massive steel door that slid open on pneumatics. Beyond this lay a brightly lit computer center and modern infirmary. The scholars greeted one another excitedly, then immediately fell to squabbling over theories as well as practical approaches to research, while the newly arrived reporters busied themselves testing their equipment. Technicians nodded satisfactorily at the quality of the images and sound transmitted by cable from the carefully disguised receiving equipment on the roof of the house above this bubble of ultra-modern technology.

While the scholars and journalists worked, Margo quietly brought Malcolm up to date about events on the station. The news left Malcolm fretting, not just because the station was in danger if the riots continued, but because there was literally nothing he could do to help search for Ianira or her family while trapped on this side of the Britannia Gate. "I've heard about the *Ansar Majlis*," Malcolm said tiredly, rubbing his eyes and the bridge of his nose. "Too much, in fact."

"You had friends on TT-66, didn't you?" Margo asked quietly, laying one gentle hand on his sleeve.

Malcolm sighed. "Yes. I'm afraid I did."

"Anyone . . ." she hesitated, looking quite abruptly very young and unsure of herself.

Malcolm stroked her cheek. "No, Margo. No one like that." He drew her close for a moment, blessing Kit for sending her here. He'd have to turn around and send her into danger out on the streets, he knew that, it was part of the dream which burned inside her and made her the young woman he loved so much; but for the moment, he was content merely to have her close. "Just very good friends, guides I'd known for years."

She nodded, cheek rubbing against the fine lawn of the expensive gentleman's shirt he'd put on to greet the new team members. "I'm sorry, Malcolm."

"So," he sighed, "am I. How much of the station had they managed to search before you had to leave?"

Margo's description of search efforts on station was interrupted by the shrill of the telephone on the computer console behind them. Hooked into a much more antique-looking telephone in the house above, it was a direct link between the outside world and the vault. Malcolm pulled reluctantly away and snagged the receiver. "Yes?"

It was Hetty Gilbert, co-gatekeeper of the Time Tours Gatehouse. The news she had was even worse than Margo's. All color drained from Malcolm's cheeks as he listened. "Oh, dear God. Yes, of course. We'll come up straight away."

"What is it?" Margo asked breathlessly as he hung up again.

"Trouble. Very serious trouble." He glanced at the monitor where, a few hours from now, they hoped to record the identity of Jack the Ripper. Weeks, he'd put in, preparing for that moment. And now it would have to wait. Reluctantly, Malcolm met Margo's gaze again.

"What *is* it?" Margo demanded, as if half-afraid to hear the answer.

"We have a tourist missing," he said quietly. "A male tourist."

"Oh, my God."

"Yes. His name is Benny Catlin. The Gilberts are asking for our help with the search teams. Evidently, he has already killed someone in a brutal shooting at the Piccadilly Hotel. A Time Tours driver is in critical condition, should be arriving within minutes for surgery. He managed to telephone from the hotel before he collapsed."

The animated excitement of the anticipated search for the Ripper's identity drained from Margo's face. Malcolm hated seeing the dread and fear which replaced it. Missing tourist . . . any time guide's worst nightmare. And not just any tourist, either, but one who'd already committed murder in a quiet Victorian hotel. A missing and homicidal tourist, search teams combing London at the beginning of the Ripper's reign of terror . . . and back on the station, riots and murders and kidnappings . . . Malcolm met Margo's frightened gaze, read the same bleak assessment in her eyes which coursed through his entire being. Margo's budding career as a time scout, her dreams, were as much on the line as his own. Malcolm hadn't seen Margo look so frightened since that horrible little prison cell in Portuguese Africa.

Wordlessly, he took her hand, squeezed her fingers. "We'd better get up there."

They headed upstairs at a dead run.

John Lachley hadn't planned to walk down past the Royal Opera, tonight.

But he'd emerged from his lecture at the Egyptian Hall to find the street blocked by an overturned carriage, which had collided with a team of drays, spilling the contents of a freight wagon and several screaming, hysterical ladies into the street, more frightned than injured. Glancing impatiently at his pocket watch, he'd determined that there was time, after all, before meeting Maybrick at his surgery in Cleveland Street, and rendered medical assistance, then pushed his way through the crowd and snarled traffic in search of a hansom he might hire.

It was sheer, blind chance which sent him down toward the Opera, where a rank of cabs could normally be found waiting for patrons. Sheer, bloody chance that had sent him straight into the path of a young woman who appeared from the murk of the wet night, gabbling out a plea for help. John Lachley had been at the wrong end of many an attack from vicious footpads, growing up in the East End, a target for nearly everyone's scorn and hatred. Rage had detonated through him, watching an innocent young man struggle with a knife-wielding assailant, fighting for his life.

So Lachley drew the pistol he'd concealed for the night's work with Maybrick and strode forward, ridding the street of this particular vermin with a single shot to the back of the skull. He expected the young man's shock, of course, no one reacted well to having blood and bits of brain spattered across his face, and he even expected the young woman's distraught reaction, nearly fainting under the strain of their close call.

But he did not expect what happened when he sounded the beautiful young woman's pulse. The words came pouring out of her, in flawless Greek, *ancient* Greek, even as she snapped rigid, straining away from him: *Death hangs on the tree beneath the vault . . . down beneath the bricks where the boy's sightless skull rests . . . and six shall die for his letters and his pride . . .*

This girl could not *possibly* know about the letters, about Tibor, about Morgan's skull, sitting as a trophy atop the flame-ringed altar, or the massive oak on which the little bastard had died. But she did. And more, she had prophesied that five *others* should die for the sake of Eddy's accursed letters . . .

Who?

He couldn't even hazard an educated guess. But he intended to find out. Oh, yes, he most certainly intended to find out. He reacted with the swiftness a childhood in the East End had taught him, brought up the pistol to eliminate the young man whose life he'd just saved. "Sorry, old chap. Nothing personal . . ."

He discharged the gun at the same instant the shaken young man realized Lachley's intent. The blood-spattered man flung himself violently sideways, trying to save himself. The bullet grazed the side of his skull, sending him reeling, wounded, to the ground. Lachley snarled out an oath and brought the pistol up to fire again, while the girl screamed and fainted—

"Jenna!"

The shout was from almost directly in front of him. Lachley jerked his gaze up and found a wild-eyed woman in a shabby dress racing toward him, twenty yards away and closing fast. She had an enormous revolver in one hand and was pointing it right at Lachley. With only a split-second to decide, Lachley loosed off a wild shot at the approaching woman to delay her and snatched up the unconcious girl at his feet. A gunshot ripped through the damp night and a bullet whipped past his ear, knocking his top hat to the street. Lachley swore and bolted with his prize, flung her across one shoulder and ran down toward Drury Lane and SoHo's maze of mean, narrow streets.

He fully expected to hear the hue and cry sounded as constables were summoned; but no cry came, nor did any footsteps chase after him. Lachley slowed to a more decorous pace, discovering he was halfway down Drury Lane, and allowed his pulse to drop from its thunderous roar in his ears. With the panic of flight receding, rational thought returned. He paused for a moment in a narrow alley, shaking violently, then mastered himself and drew deep, gulping lungfuls of wet air to calm the tremors still ripping through him. *Dear God . . .* What was he to make of this?

He shifted the unconcious girl, cradled her in both arms, now, as though he were merely assisting a young lady in distress, and stared down at her pallid features. She was a tiny little thing, delicate of stature. Her face was exquisite and her rich black hair and olive cast of skin bespoke Mediterranean heritage. She'd gabbled out her plea for help in English, but the words spoken in shock—almost, he frowned, in a trance—had been the purest Greek he'd ever heard. But not modern Greek. *Ancient* Greek, the language of Aristotle and Aristophanes . . . yet with a distinctive dialectic difference he couldn't quite pin down.

He'd studied a great deal, since his charity school days, educated as a scholarship pupil at a school where the other boys had tormented him endlessly. He'd learned everything he could lay hands on, had drunk in languages and history the way East End whores downed gin and rum, had discovered a carton of books in the back of the school's dingy, mouldering library, books donated by a wealthy and eccentric patroness who had dabbled in the occult. John Lachley's knowledge of ancient languages and occult practices had grown steadily over the years, earning him a hard-earned reputation as a renowned SoHo scholar of antiquities and magical practices. Lachley could read three major ancient dialects of Greek, alone, and knew several other ancient languages, including Aramaic.

But he couldn't quite place the source of this girl's phrasing and inflections.

Her half-choked words spilled through his memory again and again, brilliant as an iron welder's torch.

Who *was* this insignificant slip of a girl? As he peered
at her face, stepping back out into Drury Lane to find
a gaslight by which to study her, he realized she
couldn't be more than twenty years of age, if that.
Where had she learned to speak ancient Greek?
Ladies were not routinely taught such things, particularly in the Mediterranean countries. And where in
the names of the unholy ancient gods which Lachley
worshiped had she acquired the clairvoyant talent he'd
witnessed outside the Opera House? A talent of that
magnitude would cause shockwaves through the
circles in which Lachley travelled.

He frowned at the thought. Revealing her might
prove dangerous at this juncture. Surely someone
would miss the girl? Would search for her? No matter.
He could keep her quite well hidden from any search
and he intended to exploit her raw talent in every
possible way he could contrive. His frown deepened
as he considered the problem. It would be best to
drug her for a bit, keep her quietly hidden at the top
of the house, locked into a bedroom, until he could
determine more precisely who she was, where she'd
come from, and what efforts would be made to locate
her by the young man and the poorly dressed woman
with the revolver.

Beyond that, however . . .

Lachley smiled slowly to himself. Beyond that, the
future beckoned, with this girl as the instrument by
which he viewed it and Prince Albert Victor as the
key to controlling it. John Lachley had searched for
years, seeking a true mystic with such a gift. He'd
read accounts in the ancient texts, written in as many
languages as he had been able to master. His fond-
est dream had been to find such a gifted person
somewhere in the sprawling metropolis that was
capitol city to the greatest empire on earth, to bring
them under his mesmeric control, to use their powers for his own purposes. In all his years of searching,

he had found only charlatans, like himself, tricksters
and knaves and a few pathetic old women mumbling
over tea leaves and cut crystal spheres in the backs
of Romany wagons. He had all but lost hope of finding a real talent, such as the ancient texts had
described. Yet here she was, not only vibrantly alive,
she'd quite literally run straight into his arms, begging his help.

His smile deepened. Not such a bad beginning to
the evening, after all. And by morning, Eddy's letters would be safely in his hands.

Really, the evening was turning out to be most
delightful, an adventure truly worthy of his skills and
intellect. But before he quite dared celebrate, he had
to make certain his prize did not succumb to shock
and die before he could make use of her.

Lachley's hands were all but trembling as he carried her through increasingly poorer streets, down
wretched alleyways, until he emerged, finally, with
many an uneasy glance over his shoulder, onto the
broad thoroughfare of the Strand, where wealth
once again flaunted its presence in the houses of
the rich and the fine shops they patronized. He
had no trouble, there, flagging down a hansom cab
at last.

"Cleveland Street," he ordered curtly. "The young
lady's quite ill. I must get her to my surgery at once."

"Right, guv," the cabbie nodded.

The cab lurched forward at an acceptably rapid
pace and Lachley settled himself to sound his prize's
pulse and listen to the quality of her breathing. She
was in deep shock, pulse fast and thready, skin
clammy and chill. He cradled her head almost ten-
derly, wondering who the young man with her had
been and who had attacked them. A Nichol footpad,
most likely. They prowled the area near the Opera,
targeting the wealthy gentlemen who frequented the
neighborhood, so close to the slums of SoHo. That

particular footpad's fatal loss, however, was his immense gain.

The cab made excellent time, bringing him to his doorstep before she'd even regained consciousness from her dead faint. Charles answered the bell, since fumbling for his key was too awkward while carrying her. His manservant's calm facade cracked slightly at the sight of his unconscious prize. "Whatever has happened, sir?"

"The young lady was attacked by footpads on the street. I must get her to the surgery at once."

"Of course, sir. Your scheduled patient has arrived a little early. Mr. Maybrick is waiting in the study."

"Very good, Charles," Lachley nodded, leaving the butler to close and lock the door. James Maybrick could jolly well wait a bit longer. He had to secure this girl, quickly. He carried her back through the house and set her gently onto the examining table, where he retrieved his stethoscope and sounded her heartbeat. Yes, shock, right enough. He found blankets, elevated her feet, covered her warmly, then managed to rouse the girl from her stupor by chafing her wrists and placing warm compresses along her neck. She stirred, moaned softly. Lachley smiled quietly, then poured out a draught of his potent aperitif. He was lifting the girl's head, trying to bring her round sufficiently to swallow it, when Charles appeared at the door to the surgery.

"Dr. Lachley, I beg pardon, sir, but Mr. Maybrick is growing quite agitated. He insists on seeing you immediately, sir."

Lachley tightened his hands around the vial of medicine and forcibly fought back an unreasoning wave of rage. *Ill-timed bastard! I'll bloody well shoot him through the balls when this night's business is done!* "Very well!" he snapped. "Tell him I'll be there directly."

The girl was only half conscious, but more than

awake enough to swallow the drug. He forced it past her teeth, then held her mouth closed when she struggled, weak and trembling in his grasp. A faint sound of terror escaped from between ashen lips before she swallowed involuntarily. He got more of the drug down her throat, then gave curt instructions to the waiting manservant. "Watch her, Charles. She's quite ill. The medicine should help her sleep."

"Of course, sir."

"Move her to the guest room as soon as the medicine takes hold. I'll check on her again after I've seen Mr. Maybrick."

Charles nodded and stepped aside to let him pass. Lachley stormed past, vowing to take a suitable vengeance for the interruption. Then he drew multiple calming breaths, fixed in place a freezing smile, and steeled himself to suffer the slings and arrows of a fortune so outrageous, even the bloody Bard would've been driven to murder, taking up arms against it. *One day,* he promised himself, *I shall laugh about this.*

Preferably, on the day James Maybrick dropped off a gallows.

Meanwhile . . .

He opened the door briskly and greeted the madman waiting beyond. "My dear Mr. Maybrick! So delighted to see you, sir! Now, then, what seems to be the trouble this evening . . ."

Beyond James Maybrick's pasty features, beyond the windows and their heavy drapes and thick panes of wavy glass, lightning flickered, promising another storm to match the one in Lachley's infuriated soul.

Kit Carson knew he was a hopelessly doting grandfather when, twenty-four hours after Margo's departure for London, he was seriously considering going through the Britannia the next time it opened, just to be near her. He missed the exasperating little minx more than he'd have believed possible. The apartment they shared was echoingly empty. Dinner was a depressingly silent affair. And not even the endless paperwork waiting for him at the Neo Edo's office could distract him from his gloom. Worse, they'd found no trace of Ianira Cassondra, her husband Marcus, or the *cassondra's* beautiful children, despite the largest manhunt in station history. Station security hadn't been any more successful finding the two people who'd shot three men on station, either, despite their being described in detail by a full two-dozen eyewitnesses.

By the next day, when the Wild West Gate cycled into Denver's, summer of 1885, tempers amongst the security squads were running ragged. Ianira's up-time acolytes—many of them injured during the rioting— were staging protests that threatened to bring commerce in Little Agora to a screeching halt. And Kit Carson—who'd spent a fair percentage of his night working with search teams, combing the rocky bowels of the station for some trace of the missing down-timers—needed a drink as badly as a dehydrated cactus needed a desert rainstorm in the spring.

Unshaven and tired, with a lonely ache in his chest, Kit found himself wandering into Frontier Town during the pre-gate ruckus, looking for company and something wet to drown his sorrows. He couldn't even rely on Malcolm to jolly him out of his mood— Malcolm was down the Britannia with Margo, lucky stiff. A sardonic smile twisted Kit's mouth. Why he'd ever thought retirement would be any fun was beyond him. Nothing but massive doses of boredom mingled with thieving tourists who stripped the Neo Edo's rooms of everything from towels to plumbing fixtures, and endless gossip about who was doing what, with or to whom, and why. *Maybe I ought to start guiding, just for something to do?* Something that didn't involve filling out the endless government paperwork required for running a time-terminal hotel . . .

"Hey, Kit!" a familiar voice jolted him out of his gloomy maunderings. "You look sorrier than a wet cat that's just lost a dogfight."

Robert Li, station antiquarian and good friend, was seated at a cafe table outside Bronco Billy's, next to the Arabian Nights contruction crew foreman. Li's dark eyes glinted with sympathetic good humor as he waved Kit over.

"Nah," Kit shook his head, angling over to grab one of the empty chairs at Robert's table, "didn't lose a dogfight. Just missing an Imp."

"Ah," Robert nodded sagely, trying to look his inscrutable best. A maternal Scandinavian heritage had given the antiquarian his fair-skinned coloring, but a paternal Hong Kong Chinese grandfather had bequeathed Li his name, the slight almond shape of his eyes, and the self-ascribed duty to go inscrutable on command. "The nest empties and the father bird chirps woefully."

Kit smiled, despite himself. "Robert?"

"Yeah?"

"Save it for the tourists, huh?"

The antiquarian grinned, unrepentant, and introduced him to the foreman.

"Kit, meet Ammar Kalil Ben Mahir Riyad, foreman of the Arabian Nights construction team. We've just been discussing pre-Islamic Arabian artwork. He's worried about the Arabian Nights tourists, because they're going to try smuggling antiquities out through the gate and he wanted to know if I could help spot the thefts."

"Of course," Kit nodded, shaking hands across the table and greeting him in Arabic, of which he knew only a few words. The foreman smiled and returned the greeting, then his eyes turned serious. "I will stay only a moment longer, Mr. Carson, our work shift begins again soon." He hesitated, then said, "I wish to apologize for the problems some of my workers have caused. I was not given any choice in the men I brought into TT-86. Others did the hiring. Most of us are Suni, we have no quarrel with anyone, and even most up-time Shi'ia do not agree with this terrible Brotherhood. I did not know some of the men were members, or I would have refused to take them. If I could afford to send away those who started the fighting, I would. But it is not in my power to fire them and we are already behind schedule. I have docked their wages and written letters of protest to my superiors, which I will send through Primary when it opens. I have asked for them to be replaced with reliable workers who will not start riots. Perhaps," he hesitated again, looking very worried, "you could speak with your station manager? If the station deports them, I cannot be held responsible and my superiors will have to send reliable men to replace them, men who are not in the *Ansar Majlis*."

"I'll talk to Bull Morgan," Kit promised.

Relief touched his dark eyes. "Thank you, Mr. Carson. Your word means a great deal." He glanced at Robert and a hint of his smile returned. "I enjoyed very much discussing my country's ancient art with you, Mr. Li."

"The pleasure was mine," Robert smiled. "Let's meet again, when you have more time."

They shook hands, then the foreman took his leave and disappeared into the crowds thronging Frontier Town. Robert said, "Riyad's a good man. This trouble's really got him upset."

"Believe me, I'll take it up with Bull. If we don't stop this trouble, there won't be a station left for Riyad to finish working on."

Robert nodded, expression grim, then waved over a barmaid. "Name your poison, Kit. You look like you could use a dose. I know I could."

"Firewater," Kit told the barmaid. "A double, would you?"

"Sure, Kit." She winked. "One double firewater, coming right up. And another scotch?" she added, glancing at Robert's half-empty glass.

"No, make mine a firewater, too."

Distilled on station from God alone knew what, firewater was a favorite with residents. Tourists who'd made the mistake of indulging had occasionally been known to need resuscitation in the station infirmary. As they waited for their drinks to arrive, a slender young man in black, sporting a badly stained, red silk bandana, reeled toward them in what appeared to be the terminal stages of inebriation. His deeply roweled silver spurs jangled unevenly as he staggered along and his Mexican sombrero lay canted crookedly down over his face, adding to his air of disconsolate drunkenness.

"I'd say that kid's been tippling a little too much firewater, himself," Li chuckled.

The kid in question promptly staggered against their table. Robert's drink toppled and sloshed across the table. A lit candle dumped melted wax into Robert's plate and silverware scattered all over the concrete floor. The *caballero* rebounded in a reeling jig-step that barely kept him on his feet, and kept going, trailing a stench of whiskey and garlic that set both Kit and Robert Li coughing. A baggage porter, bent nearly double under a load of luggage, trailed gamely after him, trying to keep his own course reasonably straight despite his employer's drunken meanderings through the crowd.

"Good God," Kit muttered, picking up scattered silverware as Robert mopped up the spill on the table, "is that idiot *still* drunk?"

"Still?" Robert Li asked as the waitress brought their drinks and whisked away the mess on the table.

"Yeah," Kit said, sipping gingerly at his firewater,

"we saw him yesterday. Kid was bragging about winning some shooting competition down the Wild West Gate."

"Oh, that." Robert nodded as the drunken tourist attempted to navigate thick crowds around the Denver Gate's departures lounge. He stumbled into more people than he avoided, leaving a trail of profanity in his wake and more than a few ladies who made gagging noises when he passed too close. "Yes, there's a group of black-powder enthusiasts from up time going through this trip, mostly college kids, some veteran shooters. Plan to spend several weeks at one of the old mined-out ghost towns. They're running a horseback, black-powder competition, one that's not bound by Single Action Shooting Society rules and regulations. Paula Booker, of all people, came in the other day, told me all about it. She's taking a vacation, believe it or not, plans to compete for the trophy. Bax told the tour organizers they had to take a surgeon with 'em, in case of accidents, so Paula made a deal to trade her skills in exchange for the entry fee and a free gate ticket."

Kit chuckled. "Paula always was a smart lady. Good for her. She hasn't taken a vacation in years."

"She was all excited about the competiton. They can't use anything but single-action pistols in up-time sanctioned competitions any more, which kind of takes the variety out of a shooting match that's supposed to be based on actual historical fact."

Kit snorted. "I'd say it would. Well, if that idiot," he nodded toward the wake of destruction the drunken tourist was leaving behind him, "would sober up, maybe he'd have a chance of hitting something. Like, say, the side of a building. But he's going to waste a ton of money if he keeps pouring down the whiskey."

Li chuckled. "If he wants to waste his money, I guess it's his business. I feel sorry for his porter, though. Poor guy. His boss already needs a bath and they haven't even left yet."

"Maybe," Kit said drily, "they'll dump him in the ghost town's gold-mining flume and scrub him off?"

Robert Li lifted his glass in a salute. "Here's to a good dunking, which I'd say he deserves if any tourist ever did."

Kit clinked his glass against his friend's and sipped, realizing as he did that he felt less lonely and out of sorts already. "Amen to that."

Bronco Billy's cafe was popular during a cycling of the Wild West Gate because its "outdoor" tables stood close enough to the departures lounge, they commanded a grand view of any and all shenanigans at the gate. Which was why Robert Li had commandeered this particular table, the best of the lot available. They spotted Paula in the departures lounge and waved, then Kit noticed Skeeter Jackson working the crowd. "Now, there's a kid I feel for."

Robert followed his gaze curiously. "*Skeeter?* For God's sake, why? Looks like he's up to his old tricks is all."

Kit shook his head. "Look again. He's hunting, all right. For Ianira and Marcus and their kids."

Robert glanced sidelong at Kit for a moment. "You may just be right about that."

Skeeter was studying arrivals intently, peering from face to face, even the baggage handlers. The expression of intense concentration, of waning hope, of fear and determination, were visible even from this distance. Kit understood how Skeeter felt. He'd had friends go missing without a trace, before. Scouts, mostly, with whom the odds had finally caught up, who'd stepped through a gate and failed to return, or had failed to reach the other side, Shadowing themselves by inadvertently entering a time where they already existed. It must be worse for Skeeter, since no one expected resident down-timers to go missing in the middle of a crowded station.

Kit sat back, wondering how long Skeeter would push himself, like this, before giving up. Station security already had. The wannabe gunslinger approached the ticket counter to present his ticket and identification. He had to fish through several pockets to find it.

"Joey Tyrolin!" he bellowed at a volume loud enough to carry clear across the babble of voices to their table. "Sharpshooter! Gonna win me tha' shootin' match. Git me that gold medal!"

The unfortunate ticket agent flinched back, doubtless at the blast of garlic and whiskey fired point-blank into her face. Kit, who'd been able to read lips for several decades, made out the pained reply, spoken rapidly and to all appearances on one held breath: "Good-evening-Mr.-Tyrolin-let-me-check-you-in-sir-yes-this-seems-to-be-in-perfect-order-go-right-on-through-sir . . ."

Kit had never seen any Time Tours employee check any tourist through any gate with such speed and efficiency, not in the history of Shangri-La Station. Across the table, Robert Li was sputtering with laughter. The infamous Mr. Tyrolin, weaving on his cowboy-booted feet, turned unsteadily and peered out from under his cockeyed sombrero. He hollered full blast at the unfortunate porter right behind him. "Hey! Henry or Sam or whoever y'are! Get m'luggage over here! Li'l gal here's gotta tag it or somethin' . . ."

The poor baggage handler, dressed in a working man's dungarees and faded check shirt, staggered back under the blast, then ducked his head, coughing. His own hat had already slid down his brow, from walking bent double. The brim banged his nose, completely hiding his face as the unlucky porter staggered up to the counter and fumbled through pockets for his own identification. He presented it to the ticket agent along with Mr. Tyrolin's baggage tags and managed, in the process, to drop half his heavy load. Cases and leather bags scattered in a rain of destruction. Tourists in line behind him leaped out of the way, swearing loudly. The woman directly behind the hapless porter howled in outrage and hopped awkwardly on one foot.

"You *idiot!* You nearly broke my foot!" She hiked up a calico skirt and peered at her shoe, a high-topped, multi-buttoned affair with a scuff visible across the top where a case had crashed down on top of it. Tears were visible on her face beneath the brim of her calico sunbonnet. "Watch what you're doing, you fumble-fingered moron!"

The porter, mouthing abject apologies, was scrambling for the luggage while the ticket clerk, visibly appalled, was rushing around the counter to assist the injured tourist.

"Ma'am, I'm so dreadfully sorry—"

"You ought to be! For God's sake, can't you get him out of the way?" The unfortunate porter had lost his balance again and nearly crashed into her a second time. "I paid six thousand dollars for this ticket! And that clumsy jackass just dropped a trunk on my foot!"

The harried ticket agent was thrusting the porter's validated ticket into the nearest pocket she could reach on his dungarees, while waving frantically for baggage assistance and apologizing profusely. "I'm terribly sorry, we'll get this taken care of immediately, ma'am, would you like for me to call a doctor to the gate to see your foot?"

"And have them put me in a cast and miss the gate? My God, what a lot of idiots you are! I ought to hire a lawyer! I'm sorry I ever signed that stupid hold harmless waiver. Well don't just stand there, here's my ticket! I want to sit down and get off my poor foot! It's swelling up and hurts like hell!"

Time Tours baggage handlers scrambled to the porter's assistance, hauling scattered luggage out of the way so the irate, foot-sore tourist could complete her check-in procedure and hobble over to the nearest chair. She sent endless black and glowering glares at the drunken Joey Tyrolin and his porter, who was now holding his employer's head while that worthy was thoroughly sick into a decorative planter. Another Time Tours employee, visibly horrified, was fetching a wet cloth and basin. Paula Booker and the other Denver-bound tourists crowded as far as possible from Joey Tyrolin's corner of the departures lounge. Even Skeeter Jackson was steering clear of the mess and its accompanying stench.

"Oh, Kit," Robert Li was wiping tears, he was laughing so hard. "I feel sorry for Joey Tyrolin when he sobers up! That lady is gonna make his life one miserable, living nightmare for the next two weeks!"

Kit chuckled. "Serves him right. But I feel sorrier for the porter, poor sap. *He's* going to catch it from both of 'em."

"Too true. I hope he's being well paid, whoever he is. Say, Kit, I haven't had a chance to ask, who do *you* think the Ripper's going to turn out to be?"

"Oh, God, Robert, not you, too?" Kit rolled his eyes and downed another gulp of firewater.

"C'mon, Kit, 'fess up. Bets are running hot and heavy it turns out to be some *up*-timer. But I know you. *I'm* betting you won't fall for that. Who is it? A deranged American actor appearing in *Dr. Jekyll and Mr. Hyde*? Mary Kelly's lesbian lover? Francis Tumblety, that American doctor who kept women's wombs pickled in jars? Aaron Kosminski or Michael Ostrog, the petty thief and con artist? Maybe Frederick Bailey Deeming, or Thomas Neil Cream, the doctor whose last words on the gallows were 'I am Jack—'? Or maybe a member of a Satanic cult, sacrificing victims to his

Dark Lord? Like Robert Donston Stephenson or Aleister Crowley?"

Kit held up a hand, begging for mercy. "Please, enough! I've heard all the theories! I'd as soon believe it was Lewis Carroll or the queen's personal physician. The evidence is no better for them than for anybody else you've just named. Personally? If it wasn't James Maybrick, and the case against him is a pretty good one, if you don't discount the diary as a forgery—and the forensic and psychological evidence in favor of the diary are pretty strong—then I think it was a complete stranger, someone none of our Ripperologists has identified or even suspected."

"Or the Ripperoons who *think* they're Ripperologists," Li added with a mischievous glint in his eye. Every resident on station had already had a bellyful of the self-annointed "experts" who arrived on station to endlessly argue the merits of their own pet theories. "Well," Robert drawled, a smile hovering around the corners of his mouth, "you may just be right, Kit. Guess we'll find out next week, won't we?"

"Maybe," Kit chuckled. "I'd like to see the faces of the Ripper Watch Team if it *does* turn out to be somebody they've never heard of."

Robert laughed. "Lucky Margo. Maybe she'll take pictures?"

Kit gave his friend a scowl. "She'd better do more than take a few snapshots!"

"Relax, Grandpa, Margo's a bright girl. She'll do you proud."

"That," Kit sighed, "is exactly what I'm afraid of."

Robert Li's chuckle was as unsympathetic as the wicked twinkle in his eyes.

When, Kit wondered forlornly, did he get to start *enjoying* the role of grandpa? *The day she gives up the notion of scouting,* his inner voice said sourly. Trouble was, the day Margo gave up the dream of

scouting, both their hearts would break. Sometimes—
and Kit Carson was more aware of the fact than most
people—life was no fair at all. And, deep down, he
knew he wouldn't have wanted it any other way.
Neither would Margo. And that, Kit sighed, was one
reason he loved her so much.

She was too much like him.

God help them both.

Ianira Cassondra did not know where she was.

Her mind was strangely lethargic, her thoughts slow
and disjointed. She lay still, head aching, and knew
only cold fear and a sickening sense of dislocation
behind her eyelids. The smells and distant sounds
coming through the fog in her mind were strange,
unfamiliar. A harsh, acrid stink, like black dust in the
back of her throat . . . a rhythmic ticking that might
have been an old-fashioned clock like the ones in
Connie Logan's shop or perhaps the patter of rain
against a roof . . . That wasn't possible, of course, they
couldn't hear rain in the station.

Memory stirred, sharp and terrible despite the
lassitude holding her captive, whispered that she
might not be in the station. She'd been smuggled out
of TT-86 in Jenna Caddrick's steamer trunk. And
something had gone terribly wrong at the hotel, men
had come after them with silenced, up-time guns,
forcing them to flee through the window and down
the streets. She was in London, then. But where in
London? Who had brought her to this place? One
of the men trying to kill them? And why did she feel
so very strange, unable to move or think clearly?
Other memories came sluggishly through the murk.
The attack in the street. Running toward the stranger
in a top hat and coat, begging his help. The belch
of flame and shattering roar of his pistol, shooting
the assassin. The touch of his hand against her wrist—

Ianira stiffened as shock poured through her, weak

and disoriented as she was. *Goddess!* The images
slammed again through her mind, stark and terrible,
filled with blood and destruction. And with that
memory came another, far more terrible: their benefactor's pistol raised straight at Jenna's face, the
nightmare of the gun's discharge, Jenna's long and
terrible fall to the pavement, blood gushing from her
skull . . .

Ianira was alone in London with a madman.

She began to tremble and struggled to open her
eyes, at least.

Light confused her for a moment, soft and dim and
strange. She cleared her vision slowly. He had brought
her to an unknown house. A fire burned brightly in
a polished grate across from the bed where she lay.
The room spoke of wealth, at least, with tasteful
furniture and expensive paper on the walls, ornate
decorations carved into the woodwork in the corners
of the open, arched doorway leading to another room,
she had no idea what, beyond the foot of her bed.
Gaslight burned low in a frosted glass globe set into
a wall bracket of polished, gleaming brass. The covers
pulled up across her were thick and warm, quilted
and expensive with embroidery.

The man who had brought her to this place, Ianira
recalled slowly, had been dressed exceedingly well.
A gentleman, then, of some means, even if a total
madman. She shuddered beneath the expensive covers
and struggled to sit up, discovering with the effort
that she could not move her head without the room
spinning dizzily. *Drugged* . . . she realized dimly. *I've
been drugged.* . . . Fear tightened down another
degree.

Voices came to her, distantly, male voices, speaking somewhere below her prettily decorated prison.
What does he want of me? She struggled to recall
those last, horrifying moments on the street with
Jenna, recalled him snarling out something in her

own native language, the ancient Greek of her childhood, realized it had been a curse of shock and rage. *How did a British gentleman come to know the language of ancient Athens and Ephesus?* Her mind was too slow and confused to remember what she had learned on station of Londoners beyond the Britannia Gate.

The voices were closer, she realized with a start of terror. Climbing toward her. And heavy footfalls thudded hollowly against the sound of stairs. Then a low, grating, metallic sound came to her ears and the door swung slowly open. "—see to Mr. Maybrick, Charles. The medication I gave him will keep him quiet for the next several hours. I'll come down and tend to him again in a bit, after I've finished here."

"Very good, sir."

Their voices sounded like the Time Tours Britannia guides, like the movies she and Marcus had watched about London. About—and her mind whirled, recalling the name this man had spoken, the name of Maybrick, a name she recognized with a chill of terror—about Jack the Ripper . . .

Then the door finished opening and he was there in the doorway, the man who had shot Jenna Caddrick and brought Ianira to this place. He stood unsmiling in the doorway for a long moment, just looking down into her open eyes, then entered her bedroom quietly and closed the door with a soft click. He turned an iron key in the lock and pocketed it. She watched him come with a welling sense of slow horror, could see the terrible blackness which hovered about him like a bottomless hunger . . .

"Well, then, my dear," he spoke softly, and pulled a chair close to sit down at her side. "I really didn't expect you to awaken so soon."

She would have cowered from the hand he rested against her temple, had she been able to move. The rage surrounding this man slammed into her senses. She cried aloud, as though from a physical blow.

"No need to be afraid, my dear. I certainly won't be harming you." He laughed softly, at some joke she could not fathom. "Tell me your name."

Her tongue moved with a will of its own. "Ianira . . ." The drugs in her veins roared through her mind, implacable and terrifying.

"Ianira? Where are you from? What last name have you?"

They called her Cassondra, after her title as priestess of Artemis. She whispered it out, felt as well as saw the surprise that rippled through him. "Cassondra? Deuced odd surname. Where the devil did you come from?"

Confusion tore through her. "The station—" she began.

"No, not the bloody train station, woman! Where were you born?"

"Ephesus . . ."

"*Ephesus?*" Shock tore through his eyes again. "You mean from the region of Turkey where that ancient place used to be? But why, then, do you speak Greek, when Turkestani is the language of that part of the world? And how is it you speak the Greek of Pericles and Homer?"

Too many questions, blurring together too quickly . . . He leaned across, seizing her wrist in a brutal grip. "Answer me!"

She cried out in mortal terror, struggled to pull away from the swamping horror of what she sensed in his soul. "Artemis, help me . . ." The plea was instinctive, choked out through the blackness flooding across her mind. His face swam into focus, very close to hers.

"Artemis?" he whispered, shock blazing through his eyes once more. "What do you know of Artemis, the Many-Breasted Goddess of Ephesus?"

The pain of his nearness was unendurable. She lapsed into the language of her childhood, pled with him not to hurt her, so . . .

He left her side, allowing relief to flood into her senses, but was gone only for a moment. He returned with a leather case, which he opened, removing a heavy, metal tube with a needle protruding from one end. "If you are unable to speak with what I've given you already," he muttered, "no power of hell itself will keep you silent with this in your veins."

He injected something into her arm, tore the sleeve of her dress to expose the crook of her elbow and slid the needle in. New dizziness flared as the drug went in, hurting with a burning pain. The room swooped and swung in agonizing circles.

"Now then, Miss Cassondra," the voice of her jailor came through a blur, "you will please tell me who you are and where you come from and who the man was with you . . ."

Ianira plunged into a spinning well of horror from which there was no possible escape. She heard her voice answer questions as though in a dream, repeated answers even she could not make sense of, found herself slipping deep into prophetic trance as the images streamed into her mind, a boy hanging naked from a tree, dying slowly under this man's knife, and a pitiful young man with royal blood in his veins, whose need for love was the most tragic thing about him, a need which had propelled him into the clutches of the man crouched above her now. Time reeled and spun inside her mind and she saw the terrified face of a woman, held struggling against a wooden fence, and other women, hacked to pieces under a madman's knife . . .

She discovered she was screaming only when he slapped her hard enough to jolt her from the trance. She lay trembling, dizzy and ill, and focused slowly on his eyes. He sat staring down at her, eyes wide and shocked and blazing with an unholy sort of triumph. "By God," he whispered, "what else can you do?"

When she was unable to speak, he leaned close. "Concentrate! Tell me where Eddy is now!"

The tragic, lonely young man flashed into her mind, surrounded by splendour such as Ianira had never dreamed might exist. He was seated at a long table, covered with gleaming silver and crystal and china edged in gold. An elderly woman in black Ianira recognized from photographs presided over the head of the table, her severe gaze directed toward the frightened young man.

"You are not to go wandering about in the East End again, Eddy, is that understood? It is a disgrace, shameful, such conduct. I'm sending you to Sandringham soon, I won't stand for such behavior . . ."

"Yes, Grandmama," he whispered, confused and miserable and frightened to be the object of her displeasure.

Ianira did not realize she had spoken aloud, describing what she saw until her jailor's voice shocked her back into the little room with the expensive coverlets and the gas lights and the drugs in her veins. "*Sandringham?*" he gasped. "The queen is sending him to Scotland? Bloody *hell* . . ." Then the look in his eyes changed. "Might be just as well. Get the boy out of the road for a bit, until this miserable business is finished. God knows, I won't risk having him connected with it."

Ianira lay trembling, too exhausted and overwhelmed by horror to guess at her fate, trapped in this madman's hands. He actually smiled down at her, brushing the hair back from her brow. "Your friends," he whispered intimately. "Will they search for you?"

Terror exploded. She flinched back, gabbled out the fear of pursuit, the gunmen in the hotel, the threat to her life from faceless men she had never met . . . Fear drained away at the sound breaking from him. *Laughter.* He was staring down into her eyes and laughing with sheer, unadulterated delight. "Dear God," he wheezed, leaning back in his chair, "they *daren't* search for you! Such a bloody piece of luck! No doubt," he smiled, "someone influential was disquieted by what you can do, my dear lady. Never fear, I shall protect you from all harm. You are much too precious, too valuable a creature to allow anyone to find you and bring you to grief." He leaned close and stroked the back of her hand. "Mayhap," he chuckled, "I'll even take you to wife, as an added precaution."

She closed her eyes against horror at such a fate.

He leaned down and brushed his lips to hers, then murmured, "I've work to do, this evening, my lovely pet, very serious work, which must take me from your side. And you must rest, recover from the shocks to your system. Tomorrow, however . . ." He chuckled then stroked her brow, the chill of her wet cheek. "Tomorrow should prove most entertaining, indeed."

He left her, drugged and helpless, in the center of the bed and carefully locked the door behind him. Ianira lay weeping silently until the medication he had given her dragged her down into darkness.

They didn't intend to stay long.

In fact, they hadn't intended to take the train to Colorado Springs with the rest of the tour group, or ride all the way out to the derelict mining camp in the mountains far to the west of the train station, not at all. Not with Artemisia and Gelasia asleep in a big, awkward trunk, sedated and breathing bottled oxygen from the same type of canisters they'd sent with Ianira into London. Marcus, terrified for his children's safety, had packed away a spare oxygen bottle for each of the girls, just in case something went wrong. And it had. Badly wrong.

They'd been followed through the Wild West Gate.

Just as Noah had predicted.

"His name's Sarnoff," Noah Armstrong muttered, pointing him out with a slight nod of the head. "Chief of security for a real bad sort named Gideon Guthrie. And Guthrie's specialty is making people disappear when they're too much of a threat. Real sweet company, Jenna's Daddy keeps. We can't do a damned thing yet. If we bolt now, he's just going to follow us. Then *he'll* choose the time and place, when there aren't a truckful of witnesses nearby. But if we head for that mining camp with the rest of the shooting competition tour, he'll *have* to follow us, with all those up-time witnesses lurking everywhere. Then *we* can choose the time and place, jump *him* when he's not expecting it."

"I can stick a knife through his ribs," Julius offered, glaring out from under the calico bonnet he'd donned in his role doubling for Jenna.

The detective said sharply, "No, not here!" When Julius looked like arguing, Noah shot a quelling look at the down-time teenager. "Too many witnesses. If we have to explain why murder is really self-defense, it'll just give the next death squad they send after us the chance they need to hit us while we're cooling our heels in the station's jail. So we wait until we're up in the mountains. Marcus, you'll be riding with the baggage mules when we leave the train station. Keep the trunk with the girls at the very back of the mule train. It's a long ride out there, so we'll have to switch out the oxygen canisters partway. Tell the other porters the mule's thrown a shoe or something, just get that trunk open and switch out the bottles. They'll both sleep until sometime tonight, but they'll need air in a few hours."

So that was what they did, Marcus trembling at the thought of the danger to his little girls. And he had no assurance that Ianira was safe, either, that no one had followed her to London. He bit one lip, wishing desperately they had all been able to go through one gate together as a family. But Jenna Caddrick and Noah Armstrong had argued the point forcefully.

Unfortunately, they hadn't brought anything like enough supplies to take his precious children all the way out to the rugged mining camp where the shooting competition was to be held. They'd planned for Marcus and the girls to bolt out of Denver, to ditch the tour and take a train east into the Great Plains which he had seen in so many cowboy movies. They would hide in one of the big cities like Chicago or St. Louis for three or four cycles of the Wild West Gate, just long enough for Noah to eliminate any threat which might come through from up time on the next cycle of the gate.

Then they could slip back onto the station, after Noah had gone back up time, taking to the legal authorities the proof which the detective had brought onto the station. Only when the men responsible for the murderous attacks had been jailed, would Marcus and his little family be safe again. And Julius, too. The teenage leader of Shangri-La's Lost and Found Gang had come through the Porta Romae, same as Marcus had. Julius was playing his part as Jenna's double with superb skill, laying a false trail for their pursuers to follow. His act at the departures lounge, dressed as an aggrieved lady tourist bawling about her injured foot had convinced onlookers, while Noah, acting the role of the drunken Joey Tyrolin, had drawn all attention away from Marcus, who'd needed to remain anonymous until safely on the other side of the gate.

Marcus had taken Julius' own station identification, so he could act as "Joey Tyrolin's" baggage porter to disguise his own identity. Julius had used a fake ID produced by the ever-resourceful Noah Armstrong. Jenna Caddrick had furnished it, as well

as the money for the Denver Gate tickets. Marcus'
throat closed, just thinking of the risk Noah and
Jenna and young Julius were running to keep his
family safe. Ianira and his children had never
seemed so fragile to Marcus, never more precious
to him. They had agreed to the charade, because
they'd had no other choice.

But Marcus had never ridden a horse in his life.
And while he had once been accustomed to the
burning brilliance of a Mediterranean sun, he'd lived
for several years in the sunless world of TT-86.
Despite the broad-brimmed hat which shaded his
face, by the time they were an hour out on the trail,
Marcus was sunburnt, sore in more places than he'd
realized his body possessed, and miserably homesick
for the station and his wife and his many 'eighty-sixer
friends.

"We'll go through with the itinerary we set up,"
Noah Armstrong told them on the trail. "That way,
the bastard following us will think we haven't twigged
to who he is. Any edge we can find, we need."
Dressed in a cowboy's gear, Noah Armstrong was
more difficult than ever to pigeonhole as a man or
a woman. Each time Marcus thought he'd gathered
enough clues to decide, the up-time detective did or
said something which threw all his theories into chaos
again.

Marcus had seen individuals like Noah Armstrong
before, in the slave markets of Rome. Ambiguous
in the way their bodies grew into adulthood, developing into neither man nor woman, such people
were exceedingly rare in nature. But they were
pitifully common on auction blocks. Boys in Roman
slave markets were routinely castrated as children
to preserve a child's sexless features and manner-
isms, so they would grow into eunuchs. Neither male
nor female, such artificially created eunuchs were
valuable slaves. But those *born* that way fetched

astronomical prices in Roman slave pens. Marcus had seen one such slave fetch half-a-million sesterces at auction—ten times the going rate for a highly educated scribe or Greek tutor. Romans, Marcus had learned over the years, were avaricious collectors. And the more unusual the item, or the individual, the greater the status in claiming its ownership. Whoever Noah was, the detective was luckier than he or she knew, to've been born up time, not down the Porta Romae.

As they rode out of Colorado Springs with dust from the horses' hooves hanging on the hot air, Julius frowned slightly under his calico bonnet brim. "Do you want me to go ahead and enter the shooting contest, then? I've watched a lot of movies, but I don't really know how to shoot a black-powder pistol."

"Don't worry about that," Armstrong reassured Marcus' young friend. "I'll show you how to load and operate the pistols tonight at camp, and I'll teach you to fire them. You don't have to shoot well enough to win or even qualify. Just make it look good, that's all we need. Long before the competition's over, we'll have nailed this bastard Sarnoff, so we can go back to Denver. When we've eliminated him, I'll want you to go with Marcus and the girls to the nearest train station. As soon as the men responsible for this have been arrested, I'll send word and we can bring everyone home again."

It sounded so simple . . .

But Marcus had learned the hardest way possible that nothing in life was ever simple, least of all a high-stakes game in which religion, political power, and human life were the stakes. During the long hours it took them to reach the mining camp, refurbish the ghost town to a livable state, and set up the shooting course, with Marcus periodically checking on his precious little girls to be sure they still slept and breathed comfortably in their snug cocoon, Marcus couldn't help glancing over his shoulder every few minutes, expecting disaster to strike them down at any moment.

He searched the faces of the others on the tour, the eager college-age kids who had gathered for a try at the medal, the older shooters who'd clearly been at this sport longer than the kids had been alive; he studied the guides supplied by Time Tours, the baggage handlers and mule drovers who tended the line of stubborn, slack-eared mules which had toted the equipment and personal baggage of the entire competition; and wondered what it must be like to be free to come and go as one pleased through the up-time world, through any gate, so long as the money was there to pay for a ticket. And each time the silent, hired killer who'd come through the gate with them glanced sidelong at Julius and himself, Marcus sweat into his dungarees and swallowed back sour fright.

Some of the tourists were talkative, laughing and bragging or sharing stories about other competitions they'd participated in. Some of them talked about re-enactments of historical battles involving thousands of people and weapons ranging from pistols to full-sized cannons. Marcus had seen cannons only in photographs and movies. Other tour members were loners, keeping to themselves, cleaning and oiling their guns regularly, working hard at tasks assigned to get the competition's complex course of fire laid out and the buildings refurbished, speaking little and wolfing down their supper in silence at mealtime. Impromptu sing-alongs and amateur musicians provided entertainment for those with the desire to socialize.

There was even—and their happiness left Marcus feeling more lonely and isolated than ever—a young couple who planned to marry during the competition. They had brought along a wedding dress, a bridesmaid, a best man, an officiant, and photographer for the happy occasion. The photographer snapped pictures of everything and everyone in sight with a digital camera, much to the irritation of Noah Armstrong. The one person in the tour Marcus avoided like plague was Paula Booker, the station's cosmetic surgeon. She was preoccupied, at least, by the fun of her vacation, and paid little attention to the baggage handlers where they sat in the shadows, eating their meal in silence.

But when Artemisia and Gelasia woke up from their long, drugged sleep, all hell broke loose—and Paula Booker recognized him. Her eyes widened in shock and she opened her mouth to speak . . . then closed it again, looking abruptly frightened. *She understands,* he realized with a jolt of hope, *she understands we are in danger, even if she is not sure of the cause.*

Meanwhile, the whole camp had erupted and the baggage manager, who was not an 'eighty-sixer, but an up-timer hired by the tour organizers, demanded to know what insanity had prompted him to bring two toddlers off the station. The uproar echoed off the black-shadowed mountains hemming them in.

Nearly stammering under the close scrutiny of Sarnoff, aware that Noah Armstrong's hand was poised on the grip of a pistol at the detective's side, Marcus offered the only explanation he could: "I am a down-timer and we are never allowed off the station, sir. My little girls have never seen the sun . . ."

It was true enough and more than a plausible reason. In fact, several women burst into tears and offered the sleepy girls candy and ribbons for their hair while other tourists, irate at such a notion, vented their wrath on the head baggage handler, protesting the cruelty of enforcing a law that didn't even permit down-timers' *children* to leave the station.

"It's not healthy!" one woman glared at the hapless Time Tours guides, men who lived full time down the Denver Gate, rarely returning to the station. They did not recognize him, thank all the gods. One woman in particular, the wedding photographer, was thoroughly incensed. "I've never heard of such an awful thing in all my life! Not letting little children go through a gate for some real sunshine! When I get home, you can believe I'm writing my congresswoman a nasty letter about this!"

Julius, playing the part of Cassie Coventina, added, "You certainly can't expect two little girls to sleep in that disgusting, filthy livery stable!" The disguised down-timer boy glanced at him, giving him and the children a winning smile, "They can stay in my cabin tonight. Every night, in fact. I've got plenty of room."

"Thank you," Marcus said with an exhausted, grateful smile.

So the girls moved into Julius' protective custody and Marcus and Noah watched the killer sent to stalk them, tracking him during their every waking moment, and Paula Booker followed them silently with her gaze, biting her lip now and again, clearly wanting to approach him and fearing to jeopardize his life, or perhaps her own, by doing so, while all of them, killer included, waited for the chance to strike. The man stalking them was too clever to wander off alone, where one or more of them could have sent him back to whatever gods had created him. They couldn't strike in front of witnesses any more than he could, but the chance everyone was waiting for came all too soon, during the endurance phase of the shooting games.

Marcus, burned to lobster red by the sun, was assigned the job of riding shadow on Julius' heels for this portion of the competition. The "endurance round" involved riding a looping, multiple-mile trail through the sun-baked mountains around the dusty gold-mining camp. The competitors were to pause at predetermined intervals to fire at pop-up targets placed along the trail like ambushes. Noah, deeply wary of Julius riding alone through the wild countryside, told Marcus quietly, "I want you to trail him, just far enough behind to stay in earshot. I'll trail you, same way."

Marcus, heart in his throat, just nodded. He couldn't keep his hands from trembling as he mounted his stolid plug of a horse and urged the animal into a shambling trot. He set a course that took him away from camp on a tangent, allowing him to loop back around and pick up Julius' trail just beyond the first ridge outside camp.

The sun blazed down despite the earliness of the hour. At least Julius' persona, Cassie Coventina, had drawn one of the early slots for riding the endurance course, so it wasn't too unbearably hot, yet. Dust rose in puffs where Marcus' horse plodded along the narrow, twisting trail. He urged the nag to a slightly faster shamble until he caught sight of "Miss Coventina" ahead, riding awkwardly in a high-pommeled side saddle. Marcus eased back, cocking his head to listen, reassured when Julius began to whistle, leaving him an audible trail to follow. Marcus glanced back several times and thought he caught a glimpse of "Joey Tyrolin" once or twice through the heat haze behind him.

Saddle leather squeaked and groaned under his thighs. Marcus began to sweat into his cotton shirt. He worried about the girls, back at camp, even though they were surrounded by fifteen adoring women who weren't riding the endurance trail until later in the afternoon, or who were part of the wedding and weren't competing at all. The mingled scent of dust and sweating horse rose like a cloud, enveloping his senses and drawing his mind inexorably back to the years he'd spent as a slave working for the master of the chariot races and gladiatorial games and bestiaries at the great Circus Maximus. The scent of excited, sweating race horses and dust clogged his memory as thoroughly as the scream of dying animals and men—

The sharp animal scream that ripped through the hot morning was no memory.

Marcus jerked in his saddle. Blood drained from his face as the scream came again, a horse in mortal agony. Then a high, ragged shriek of pain, a *human* shriek, tore the air . . . and the booming report of a gun firing shook the dusty air . . .

Marcus kicked his horse into a startled canter. He wrenched at the gun on his hip. From behind him, a clatter of hooves rattled in a sudden burst of speed. Noah Armstrong swept past as though Marcus' horse were plodding along at a sedate walk. Another gunshot split the morning air. Then Marcus was around the bend in the trail and the disaster spread out in front of him.

Julius was down.

His horse was down, mortally wounded.

Dust rose in a cloud along the trail, where Noah pursued whoever had shot down Marcus' friend. He hauled his own horse to a slithering halt and slid out of the saddle, then flung himself to the young Roman's side. Julius was still alive, ashen and grey-lipped, but thank the gods, still alive . . .

"Don't move!" Marcus was tearing at the boy's clothing, ripping open the dress he wore as disguise. The calico cotton was drenched with dark stains that weren't sweat. The bullet had gone in low, missing the heart, plowing instead through the gut. The boy moaned, gritted his teeth, whimpered. Marcus was already stripping off his own shirt, tearing it into strips, placing compresses to staunch the bleeding. In the distance, a sharp report floated back over the rocky hills, followed by three more cracking gunshots. Then hoofbeats crashed back toward them. Marcus snatched up his pistol again. Noah Armstrong appeared, riding hell for leather toward them. Marcus dropped the gun from shaking hands and tied the compresses tighter.

The detective slithered out of a sweaty saddle and

crouched beside the fallen teenager. "Hold on, Julius, do you hear me? We'll get you back to camp. To that surgeon, Paula Booker."

"No . . ." The boy was clawing at Noah's arm. "They'll just kill you . . . and Marcus . . . the girls . . . he'll kill you . . ."

"Not that one," Noah said roughly. "He's dead. Shot the bastard out of his saddle. Left him for the buzzards."

"Then they'll send someone else!"

If they hadn't already . . .

The unspoken words hung in the air, as hot and terrifying as the coppery smell of Julius' blood. "Please . . ." Julius was choking out the words, "you can't afford to take me back. I'll only slow you down. Just get the girls and run, please. . . ." Marcus tried to hush the frantic boy. Guilt ripped through him. He'd allowed Julius to help—this was his fault. "Please, Julius, do not speak! You have not the strength. Here, can you swallow a little water?" He held his canteen to the boy's lips.

"Just a sip," Noah cautioned. "There, that's enough. Here, help me get him up. No, Julius, we have to go back to camp anyway, to rescue the kids. You're coming with us, so don't argue. Marcus, we'll put him on your horse." The detective glanced up, met Marcus' gaze. "He's right, you know. They will send someone else. And someone after that."

"What can we do?" Marcus felt helpless, bitterly afraid, furious with himself for bringing his young friend into this.

"We leave Julius with the camp surgeon, that's what. As soon as we get back to camp, you get the girls and take them back to the livery stable with you. During the confusion, you and I will leave camp with the kids. Take our horses and our gear and ride out. By the time they figure out we're gone, we'll be far enough away to catch a train out of the territory."

Marcus swallowed exactly once. "And go where?" he whispered.

"East. *Way* East. To New York." Noah held Marcus's gaze carefully, reluctance and regret brilliant in those enigmatic eyes. "And eventually," the detective added softly, "to London. Jenna and your wife will be there. We'll meet them."

Three *years* from now . . .

Marcus looked down into his young friend's ashen face, his pain-racked eyes, and knew they didn't have any choice. Three years in hiding . . . or this. When next Ianira saw their children, just hours after dropping them off at daycare, from her perspective, Artemisia would be nearly seven, Gelasia almost four. Gelasia might not even *remember* her mother. Ianira might well never forgive him. But he had no choice. They couldn't risk going back to the station, not even long enough to crash through the Britannia Gate. And crashing it was the only way they could get through the Britannia, because there wasn't a single ticket available for months, not until after the Ripper Season closed. Marcus bowed his head, squeezed shut his eyes. Then nodded, scarcely recognizing his own voice. "Yes. We will go to London. And wait." Three entire *years*. . .

Wordlessly, he helped the detective lift Julius to Marcus' saddle. Wordlessly, he climbed on behind his dying friend, steadied him and kept the boy from falling. Then turned his horse on the dusty, blood-spattered trail and left Julius' groaning, gut-shot mount sprawled obscenely across the path. A sharp report behind him, from Noah's gun, sent his pulse shuddering; but the agonized sounds tearing from the wounded horse cut off with that brief act of mercy. He tightened his hands around the sweaty wet leather of his reins.

And swore vengeance.

◆   ◆   ◆

Jenna woke to the sensation of movement and the deep shock that she was still alive to waken at all. For a moment, the only thing in her mind was euphoria that she was still among the breathing. Then the pain hit, sharp and throbbing all along the side of her skull, and the nausea struck an instant later. She moaned and clenched her teeth against the pain—which only tightened the muscles of her scalp and sent the pain mushrooming off the scale. Jenna choked down bile, felt herself swoop and fall . . .

Then she lay propped across something hard, while she was thoroughly sick onto the street. Someone was holding her up, kept her from falling while she vomited. Memory struck hard, of the gun aimed at her face, of the roar and gout of flame, the agony of the gunshot striking her. She struggled, convinced she was in the hands of that madman, that he'd carried her off to finish her or interrogate her . . .

"Easy, there."

Whoever held her was far stronger than Jenna; hard hands kept her from moving away. Jenna shuddered and got the heaves under control, then gulped down terror and slowly raised her gaze from the filthy cobblestones. She lay propped across someone's thigh, resting against rough woolen cloth and a slim torso. Then she met the eyes of a woman whose face was shadowed by a broad-brimmed bonnet which nearly obscured her face in the darkness. Through the nausea and pain and terror, Jenna realized the woman was exceedingly poor. Her dress and coat were raggedy, patched things, the bonnet bedraggled by the night's rain. Gaslight from a nearby street lamp caught a glint of the woman's eyes, then she spoke, in a voice that sounded as poor and ragged as she was.

"Cor, luv," the woman said softly, "if you ain't just a sight, now. I've 'ad me quite a jolly time, so I 'ave, tryin' t' foller you all the way 'ere, an' you bent on getting yourself that lost and killed."

Jenna stared, wondering whether or not the woman had lost her mind, or if perhaps Jenna might be losing hers. Mad, merry eyes twinkled in the gaslight as a sharp wind picked up and pelted them with debris from the street. The shabby woman glanced at the clouds, where lightning flared, threatening more rain, then frowned. "Goin' t'catch yer death, wivout no coat on, and I gots t'find a bloody surgeon what can see to that head of yours. It's bled a fright, but in't as bad as it seems or likely feels. Just a scrape along above the ear. Bloody lucky, you are, *bloody* lucky." When Jenna stared at her, torn by nausea and pain and the conviction that she was in the hands of yet another down-time lunatic, the madwoman leaned closer still and said in a totally different voice, "Good God, kid, you really don't know me, do you?"

Jenna's mouth fell open. "*Noah?*"

The detective's low chuckle shocked her. Jenna had never heard Noah Armstrong laugh. They hadn't found much to laugh about, since their brutal introduction three days previously. Then she blinked slowly through the fog in her mind. *Three days?* But Noah and Marcus had gone down Denver's Wild West Gate. Or rather, *would* be going down the Wild West Gate. Tomorrow morning, on the station's timeline. Noah Armstrong shouldn't be *here* at all, on the night of Jenna's arrival. The night *before* Noah and Marcus were due to leave the station for Denver . . .

Mind whirling, Jenna asked blankly, "Where did you come from? How did you get here?"

The detective was pulling off a shabby black coat, which served to protect Jenna's head from the cold, damp wind. When Jenna touched gingerly, she found rough, torn cloth tied as makeshift bandages. They were wet and sticky. Noah said, "Let me carry you again, kid. You're just about done in from exhaustion and shock. I'll get you someplace safe and warm as soon as I can."

Jenna lay in a daze as Noah gently lifted her and started walking steadily eastward. "But—how—?"

"We came across from New York, of course. Hopped a train in Colorado and lost ourselves nice and thoroughly in Chicago and points east." The detective's voice darkened. "That down-timer kid from the station, Julius? He was disguised as you, Jenna, dressed in a calico skirt, wearing a wig." Noah paused, eyes stricken in the light streaming from a nearby house window. "They shot him. My fault, dammit, I shouldn't have let that kid out of my sight! I knew Sarnoff would follow us, I just didn't figure he'd slip ahead and ambush the kid so fast. We got him back to the camp surgeon, but . . ."

"No . . ." Jenna whimpered, not wanting to hear.

"I'm sorry, Jenna. He didn't make it. Poor bastard died before we could slip out of camp. I had a helluva time getting us out in the middle of the uproar, with Time Tours guides and the surgeon demanding to know exactly what had happened."

Jenna's vision wavered. "Oh, God . . ." She didn't want to accept the truth. Not that nice kid, the down-timer she'd met in the basement under the Neo Edo hotel. Julius was younger than she was. . . . Her eyes burned and she nearly brought up more acid from her stomach as she fought not to sob aloud. How many people were going to die, trying to keep her alive?

Then she remembered Ianira. "Oh, God! *Ianira!*"

Noah's stride faltered for just a moment. "I know." The detective's voice was rough. "I tried to follow him, the instant I knew you weren't critically wounded. But he disappeared into that rat's maze of streets down in SoHo. Which, coincidentally, is exactly the same thing we did. I had to get us out of there fast, after all the shooting left that hit-man dead in front of the Opera House. The door man and some people in a passing carriage went shouting for a constable."

"But—but Noah, he's got her—"

"Do you have any idea who he was?"

She gulped down terror, tried to think past the memory of that gun levelled at her face, that mad, calm voice telling her it was nothing personal. "He said he was a doctor. Ianira found him, while I was struggling with that killer. I think he was down by those columns."

Noah nodded. "That'd be the Opera House, it's just down the way from where you were attacked."

"He took Ianira's pulse and she . . . she went into shock. Tried to get away from him, starting ranting something that sounded awful. In ancient Greek. Whatever she said, he understood it and his face . . . he *snarled* at her. I've never seen such hatred, such murderous fury . . ."

Noah's quiet voice intruded. "That's damned odd, don't you think?"

Jenna just shivered and huddled closer to the detective's warmth. "He looked at me. Just looked at me and said, 'Sorry, old chap, nothing personal,' and shot me."

"*Damned* odd," Noah muttered. "Doesn't sound like an up-time hit at all."

"No." Then, voice breaking, "*We have to find her!* I let him . . . let him take her away . . ."

"No, you didn't. Don't argue! For Christ sake, Jenna, you've been on the run for three solid days, in shock from the murders in New York, and the shock of being pregnant and shooting a man to death in TT-86, and you damned near got shot at the Picadilly Hotel, then almost knifed to death in front of the Opera, then some lunatic down-timer shot you in the head, and you blame yourself? After all that? Kid, you did one helluva job. And you're not even a pro. I *am*. And I screwed up royally. I didn't manage to grab you aside at Spaldergate House, damn near got caught stealing a horse to follow the carriage you

took, and still arrived at the Picadilly Hotel too
damned late to do you any good. And by the time
the shooting started outside the hotel, I'd tied that
damned horse up a block down the street and had
to chase after you on foot, in these heavy, damned
wet skirts. Kid, I fucked up, plain and simple, and
ended up letting that guy shoot you and kidnap Ianira.
Don't you *dare* blame yourself, Jenna Caddrick. You
did one helluva job getting her out of that hotel in
one piece."

Very quietly and very messily, Jenna began to cry
down the front of Noah's rough woolen dress.

"Aw, shit . . ." Noah muttered, then speeded up. "I
gotta get you out of this raw air." Noah braced her
head against a solid shoulder, easing the coat to
protect her face from the cold, and hurried through
the darkened city. Occasional carriages rattled past,
a greyed-out blur to Jenna's overtaxed senses. Pain,
dull and endless, throbbed through her head. Nausea bit the back of her throat, without letup. *God,
if I really am pregnant, please let the baby be all
right . . .*

At least half-an-hour later, Noah Armstrong carried
Jenna into a snug little house near Christ Church,
Spitalfields. Marcus, who seemed to have aged ter-
ribly since the last time she'd seen him, greeted them
with a cry of fear. "*What has happened?* Where is
Ianira?"

Noah spoke curtly. "Jenna ran into bad trouble,
getting away from the gatehouse. I've got to carry her
upstairs to bed. Heat a water bottle and bring up
some extra blankets, then go out and ask Dr. Mindel
to come. Jenna's been shot, not seriously, but she
needs medical attention and she's in shock."

"Ianira?" Marcus whispered again.

The detective paused. "She's alive. Somewhere. It's
complicated. A man helped them, shot one of the hit-
men. But when he touched her, she went into

prophetic trance and whatever she said, it really upset him. He shot Jenna without warning and was about to finish her off when I finally caught up. He took a potshot at me and I fired back, but missed, dammit, and he grabbed Ianira and took off down Drury Lane. I'm sorry, Marcus. We'll find her. I swear it, we *will* find her."

The ex-slave had gone ashen, stood trembling in the shabby house they'd rented, eyes wet and lips unsteady. At a slight sound behind him, he turned his shaken gaze downward.

"Daddy?" A beautiful little girl of about seven had appeared in the doorway from the back of the house. "Daddy, did Noah bring Mama?"

Jenna had to grasp Noah's shoulders as the whole room spun. Ianira's little girl, Artemisia . . . only she was too old, much too old, and Marcus had aged, as well, there was grey in his hair and she didn't understand . . .

"No, Misia," Marcus choked out, going to his knees to hug the little girl close. "Noah and Jenna tried, honey, but something went wrong and a bad man took Mama away. We'll find her, sweetheart, we'll look all through London and find her. But Jenna's been hurt, trying to protect your mother, and we have to help her, now. I need to go for a doctor, Misia, and Noah has to watch Jenna until the doctor comes, so we all need you to help us out, tonight, okay? Can you watch Gelasia for us, make sure she's had her milk and biscuits?"

The little girl nodded, wide eyes wet and scared as she stared up at Jenna.

"This is Jenna," Noah said gently. "She helped me save your mommy's life tonight. The bad men we ran away from a long time ago chased her, honey, then another man hurt her and took your mother. I'm sorry, honey. We'll get her back."

No child of seven should possess eyes like

Artemisia's, dark as mahogany and too wise and haunted for her age, eyes which had, like her mother's, seen far too much at far too early a point in life. She disappeared into the back of the house. Marcus said raggedly, "I will bring the hot water bottle, then go for Dr. Mindel."

"Good. And take my Colt Thunderer with you. Put it up, when you get back, someplace where the girls can't reach it."

Marcus took Noah's revolver and disappeared into the kitchen.

Noah carried Jenna up a narrow, dark staircase that smelled of dampness and recent, harsh soap. "Noah?" she whispered, still badly shaken.

"Yeah?" The detective carried her into a neat, heartlessly plain bedroom and settled her gently into a deep feather bed.

"Why . . . why is Artemisia so much older? I don't understand . . ."

Noah dragged off the wet, bedraggled bonnet which hid the detective's face, pulled blankets up across her, then gently removed Jenna's makeshift bandages and peered anxiously at the side of her head before pouring out a basin of water and wetting a cloth to sponge away dried blood, all without answering. Jenna found herself staring into Noah's eyes, which had gone dark with an even deeper sorrow Jenna didn't want to know the reasons for. Noah met her frightened stare, paused, then told her.

"You're too foggy to work it out, aren't you? The Denver Gate opens into 1885. The Britannia opens into 1888. It's been three years for us, kid. There wasn't any other way."

The whole bed came adrift under Jenna's back. She found herself a foggy stretch of time later floating in a grey haze while Noah very gently removed her clothing and eased her into a nightshirt, then replaced the blankets. Jenna slowly focused on the detective's

haunted eyes. "Three *years?*" she finally whispered,
her foggy mind catching up at last. "My God . . . Even
if we find her . . . Ianira's little girls won't even know
their own mother. And poor Ianira . . . God, three
years of their lives, gone . . ."

"I know." Quiet, that voice, filled with regret and
hushed pain. "Believe me, we wanted there to be
some other way. There wasn't." The detective kept
talking, voice low, giving Jenna a lifeline to cling to
while her world swung in unpredictable circles all over
again. "We've been in London for nearly two-and-a-
half years, now. Waiting for you. I showed up at
Spaldergate tonight, hoping to catch your attention,
but . . . You know how that ended."

The shock, the misery of what Jenna had caused,
was too much. She squeezed shut her eyes over hot
tears. *What else could I have done? Could any of us
have done?* They could've brought the girls through
with Ianira, at least. But Noah'd been right to guess
hit men would be sent through both gates after them.
If they *had* brought the little girls through with Ianira,
none of them would have escaped the Picadilly Hotel
alive. There really hadn't been any other choice.
Knowing that didn't help much, though, with Ianira
missing somewhere in this immense city, in the hands
of God alone knew what kind of madman, and those
beautiful little girls downstairs, unable to remember
the mother they'd waited three years to meet again
and deprived of her once more by violence and death.
None of them had expected Marcus and the children
to have to stay down time in Denver long enough
to catch up to the Britannia Gate.

The knowledge that none of them were safe, yet,
after everything they'd already been through, was a
pain too deep to express. So Jenna just lay there, staring blankly at the stained ceiling, waiting for the doctor
to arrive while Noah slipped a hot water bottle under
the blankets to warm her and brought a basin full of

hot, steaming water that smelled strongly of disinfectant to wash the gash in her head. She was grateful that Noah Armstrong had managed, at least, to set up a hiding place in London, ready and waiting for her. Outside, lightning flared and thunder rumbled through the dismal streets of Spitalfields as rain poured from leaden skies.

Their safe haven was at least well hidden by grinding poverty. It was probably the last place on earth her father's hired killers would think to look for them. London's violent and poverty-stricken East End during the middle of the Ripper horror . . .

When Dr. Mindel finally arrived, he praised Noah's "nursing" and sutured up Jenna's scalp, then fed her some foul-tasting medicine that left her drifting in darkness. The final awareness to impinge on her exhausted mind was the sound of Marcus in the hallway, talking quietly with Noah, with the cold and granite sound of murder in his voice as they made plans to find his missing wife.

Then she drifted into pain-free oblivion and knew no more.

Malcolm tilted his pocketwatch toward the light of a gas lamp on the street corner, putting the time at half-past eight when he alighted from his hansom cab at the corner of Bow and Hart Streets. Clouds, shot through with lightning, swirled in thick drifts and eddies above the rooftops, muting the sounds of a boisterous Thursday evening with the imminent threat of more rain. Although they were past the official end of the annual London social season, cut short yearly when Parliament adjourned each August 12th, not everyone was fortunate enough to escape London immediately for their country homes or the rural estates of friends. Business matters had to be wound up and some gentlemen remained trapped in London year-round, particularly those of the aspiring middle classes, who had acquired the tastes and pursuits of the wealthy without the means of fleeing London at the end of the social season.

As a result, cultured male voices the length of Bow Street could be heard discussing theater and dinner plans, birds they planned to shoot on favorite grouse moors up in Scotland now that grouse season had opened, or the ladies who inhabited the country houses they would visit during the fall's leisurely hunting seasons, beginning with grouse, graduating to partridge and pheasant, and ending lastly—but perhaps most importantly—with the noble fox.

Also drifting through the damp night came the light laughter of women Malcolm could not actually see, whose carriages rattled invisibly past in the murk that was not quite rain but not quite fog, either. The jingle of harness and the sharp clopping of horse's hooves struck the lime-rock gravel bed of the street with a thick, thumping sound, carrying the hidden ladies off to bright dinner parties. Carefully orchestrated affairs, such dinners were designed to bring together eligible young ladies and equally eligible gentlemen for the deadly serious purpose of finding suitable spouses for the unmarried daughters of the house.

It being a Thursday evening, many such dinner parties throughout the ultra-fashionable west end would be followed by musical and other soirees, theater or the opera, and after that, the final, few elegant balls of the year, at which silk-clad young ladies still unmarried and desperate would swirl across dance floors and sip wine with smartly dressed young gentlemen until three in the morning, with a fair number of those young gentlemen equally desperate to find an heiress, even from a fortune made in *trade*, God help them all for having to stoop to such measures, just to bolster the finances of blue-blooded but cash-poor noble houses.

Above the jingle of harness as carriages rattled past,
filtering through the sounds of gay laughter and
merrymaking, came other, more plaintive cries, the
calls of flower girls and eel-pie vendors hawking their
wares to the genteel folk who frequented this fashionable district on such evenings. Malcolm could just
make out one such girl, stationed beneath the nearest street lamp where she would be most visible in
the drizzle and murk. She held a heavy tray of car-
nations and pinks suspended from cords around her
neck. Her dress, damp in patches from the raw night,
was made of cheap, dark cotton, much mended and
several years out of fashion. The toes of the shoes
peeping out from beneath her skirts had been cut
open to accommodate the growth of her feet.

As Malcolm watched, three gentlemen emerged
from the darkness and paused briefly to purchase
boutonnieres for their lapels. They strolled on
toward Malcolm, nodding and smiling as they
passed, locked deep in conversation about the best
methods of cubbing the young foxes and adolescent fox hounds once cub season opened. Malcolm
nodded in return, wishing them a pleasant, "Good
evening" as they crossed Bow Street and moved
past the looming edifice of the Royal Opera House
down Hart Street in the direction of Covent Garden Theater.

Then he was alone again on the pavement, turning over in his mind everything the Spaldergate staff
had learned about Mr. Benny Catlin's disappearance.
Foul play was now the major fear consuming everyone at Spaldergate. Catlin's abandoned luggage, the
corpse in Catlin's hotel room, and the wounded Time
Tours carriage driver had led police constables straight
to Spaldergate House, asking about the body at the
Picadilly Hotel and a second grisly corpse found
outside the Royal Opera. The police, comparing
witness descriptions, had concluded that the Picadilly

Hotel shooting and the Opera House shooting had been committed by the same desperate individual.

The Time Tours driver injured at the Piccadilly Hotel had, thank God, arrived at the gatehouse unconscious but still alive, driven by one of the gatehouse's footmen dispatched to fetch him back. Catlin's luggage had been impounded, but the footman had managed to secure Catlin's bloodstained gloves from the room before police could arrive, giving the Spaldergate staff at least some chance of tracing Catlin with bloodhounds. Weak from shock and blood loss, the wounded driver had barely been alive by the time he'd been rushed downstairs to surgery.

A massive police manhunt was now on for the missing Mr. Catlin and for anyone who might have been involved in the fatal shootings. Marshall Gilbert, gatehousekeeper, was faced with the worst crisis of his career, trying to assist the police while keeping the secrets of Spaldergate House very much under wraps.

Malcolm dreaded the coming night's work and the lack of sleep this search would mean. At least—and he consoled himself with the prospect—he wouldn't be searching alone. For good or ill, Margo would be assisting him. He needed her close, tired and soul-sore as he was from weeks spent plunged into the misery of the East End, preparing for the coming horror.

When two hansom cabs traveling close behind one another pulled up and halted at the corner of Bow and Hart, Malcolm pocketed his watch and moved rapidly forward to greet the occupants alighting on the pavement. "Ah, Stoddard, very good, I've been awaiting your arrival. Miss Smith, I'm so dreadfully sorry about this trouble, I do wish you had reconsidered coming along this evening. Madame Feroz, frightfully decent of you to accompany her, I know the demands upon your time are keen. And this must be Mr. Shannon?"

The man who had jumped to the pavement behind Spaldergate's stable master, hanging slightly back as Malcolm greeted Margo and Shahdi Feroz in turn, was a temporal native, a stringy, tough old Irishman in an ill-cut suit. He was assisting another passenger to alight, a striking young woman in very plain garments. The girl's skirt was worn but had been made of good quality cloth when new, and her coat, also faded, was neat and clean. Her hair was a glorious copper in the gaslight, her face sprinkled with far too many freckles for her to be considered a beauty by Victorian standards. But she had a memorable face and a quiet air of utter and unshakable self-confidence. She'd wrapped one hand around the leash of a magnificent Alsatian or—had Malcolm been in America—a beautiful black-and-tan German Shepherd dog with bright, intelligent eyes.

The grizzled Irishman, who was doubtless far stronger than his slight frame suggested, shook Malcolm's hand. "That's me, sir, Auley Shannon. This is me granddaughter, Maeve Shannon, Alfie's 'er dog, trained 'im she did, 'er own self, won't find a better tracker in London."

"Malcolm Moore," he smiled in return, offering his hand. "My pleasure, Mr. Shannon, Miss Shannon."

The inquiry agents whom Stoddard had been sent to fetch shook Malcolm's hand firmly. Miss Shannon kept her dog on a short leash, even though the animal was immaculately behaved, sitting on his haunches and watching the humans with keen eyes, tongue lolling slightly in the damp air.

Malcolm turned to Spaldergate's stable master. "Stoddard, you have the gloves that were found when poor Mr. Catlin disappeared from his hotel?"

"I do, sir." He produced a small cloth bag, inside which nestled a gentleman's pair of kid gloves.

Relatively fresh blood stains indicated that they had, in fact, been on Catlin's person when the shootout at the Piccadilly Hotel had occurred and Catlin had rendered life-saving first aid, just as the wounded driver had described via telephone before losing consciousness.

Malcolm nodded briskly. "Very good. Shall we give the dog the scent, then? I'm anxious to begin. Poor Miss Smith," and he bowed to Margo before returning his attention to the Shannons, "is understandably distraught over her fiancé's absence and who can blame the dear child?"

Margo was doing a very creditable job, in fact, of imitating someone in deep distress, shredding her own gloves with jerking, nervous movements and summoning tears through God-alone knew what agency. "Please, can't you find him?" Margo gasped out, voice shaking, one hand clutching at Mr. Shannon's ill-fitting jacket sleeve.

His granddaughter spoke, not unkindly. "Now, then, get 'old of yourself, miss, wailin' and suchlike won't do 'im a bit o' good an' you're like t'give yourself a fit of brain fever."

"Maeve," her grandfather said sharply, "the lady 'as a right to be upset, so you just give Alfie the scent an' mind your tongue! Or I'll give yer me German across yer Hampsteads, so I will."

"You an' what army, I'm wonderin'?" she shot right back, not cowed in the slightest by her grandfather's uplifted hand. "Give Alfie a sniff o' them gloves, now," she instructed Stoddard briskly.

"Where were the chap last spotted?" the elder Shannon wanted to know as the dog thrust an eager nose into the gloves held out to him.

Malcolm nodded toward the opera house across the road. "There, between the Opera and the Floral Hall. The doorman caught a glimpse of him engaged in what he described as a desperate fight

with another man and ran to fetch the constables
he'd just seen pass by. This other man was evidently shot dead and abandoned by Mr. Catlin in
his terror to escape. Probably one of those desperate, criminal youths in one of those wretched,
notorious Nichol gangs. Their depredations have all
London in an uproar. God help us, what are we
coming to when young boys no older than fourteen or fifteen roam the streets as armed thugs and
break into homes, stealing property and dishonor-
ing women—" he lifted his hat apologetically to the
ladies "—and attacking a man in front of the Floral
Hall, for God's sake? The last time anyone saw Mr.
Catlin, he was down Bow Street that way, just past
the Floral Hall, fighting for his life."

"Let's cross, then," Maeve Shannon said briskly, "an'
we'll give Alfie the scent off them gloves again when
we've got right up to where 'e were at the time."

They dodged carriages and ghostly, looming shapes
of horses across the road, carriage lamps and horses'
eyes gleaming in the raw night. Clouds of white
vapour streamed from the horses' distended nostrils,
then they were across and the copper-haired girl
held the gloves to her dog's nose again while her
grandfather tapped one impatient foot. The shepherd sniffed intently, then at a command from his
trainer began casting along the pavement. A sharp
whine reached them, then Alfie strained out into the
road, following the scent. The dog paused at a dark
stain on the cobbles, which, when the elder Shannon crouched down and tested it, proved to be
blood.

Margo let out an astonishing sound and clutched
at Malcolm's arm. "Oh, God, poor Benjamin . . ."

"There, there," Mr. Shannon soothed, wiping his
sticky hand on a kerchief, "it's most like the blagger
wot attacked 'im, 'oo bled on these 'ere cobbles.
Police took 'is body away to the morgue, so it's not

like as to be Mr. Catlin's blood. Not to fret, Miss, we'll find 'im."

Miss Shannon said, "Alfie, seek!" and the dog bounded across the road and headed down a drizzle-shrouded walk which passed beneath the graceful colonnaded facade of the Royal Opera House. The dog led the way at a brisk walk. Malcolm and Philip Stoddard, escorting Margo and Shahdi Feroz solicitously, hastened after them. The darkened glass panes of the Floral Hall loomed up from the damp night. The high, domed roof of the magnificent glasshouse glinted distantly in the gaslights from the street, its high, curved panes visible in snatches between drifting eddies of low-blown cloud.

The eager Alsatian, nose casting along the pavement as the dog traced a scent mingled with thousands of other traces where gentlemen, ladies, horses, dogs, carters, and Lord knew what all else had passed this way today, drew them eagerly to Russell Street, where Alfie cast sharp left and headed rapidly away from Covent Garden. They moved down toward the massive Drury Theater, which took up the better part of the entire city block between Catherine Street and Drury Lane. The drizzling fog swirled and drifted across the heavy stone portico along the front, with its statue at the top dimly lit by gaslight from hanging lamps that blazed along the entrance. Malcolm worried about the scent in weather like this. If the drizzle turned to serious rain, which rumbled and threatened again overhead, no dog born could follow the scent. The deluge would wash it straight into the nearest storm sewer. Which, upon reflection, might be why the dog was able to follow Catlin's trail so easily—most of the competing scents *had* been washed away, by the night's earlier rainstorm.

God alone knew, they needed a piece of luck, just now.

More carriages rattled past in the darkness, carrying

merry parties of well-to-do middle class theater goers
to the Drury's bright-lit entrance. Voices and laughter reached across the busy thoroughfare as London
prepared for yet another evening of sparkling gaiety.
The straining shepherd, however, ignored Catherine
Street altogether and guided the way down Russell
Street along the huge theater's left-hand side, where
a portico of Ionic columns loomed like a forest of stone
trees in the darkness. Malcolm felt his hopes rise at
the dog's sharp eagerness and ability to discern Catlin's
trail. *Good idea, Margo,* he approved silently, grateful to her for thinking of a bloodhound when the rest
of them had been struck stupid with shock.

Their footsteps echoed eerily off tall buildings when
the dog led them straight down Drury Lane. The fact
that Benny Catlin had come this way suggested to
Malcolm he *had* been forced away by someone with
a weapon. The Royal Opera House, Drury Lane Theater, and the Covent Garden district stood squarely in
a well-to-do, middle-class neighborhood, eclipsed in
finery only by the wealthiest of the upper-class districts
to the west. But once into Drury Lane itself, wealth
and even comfort dropped away entirely. As the eager
shepherd drew them down the length of that famous
street, poverty's raw bones began to show. These were
the houses and shops of London's hard-working poor,
where some managed to eke out moderate comfort
while others descended steeply into want and hunger.

Piles of wooden crates stood on the pavements
outside lower-class shops, where wagons had made
daytime deliveries. The deeper they pressed into the
recesses of Drury Lane, which dwindled gradually
in width as well as respectability, the meaner and
shabbier grew the houses and the residents walking the pavements. Pubs spilled piano music and
alcoholic fumes into the streets, where roughly clad
working men and women gathered in knots to talk
and laugh harshly and stare with bristling suspicion

at the well-dressed ladies and frock-coated gentleman passing in the company of a liveried servant,
with an older man and younger woman of their own
class controlling a leashed dog.

Malcolm made mental note of where the pubs lay,
to locate potential witnesses for later questioning, and
pressed his arm surreptitiously against the lump of
his concealed pistol, making certain of it. Margo, he
knew, also carried a pistol in her pocket, as did Philip
Stoddard. He wished he'd thought to ask Shahdi
Feroz whether or not she was armed, but this was
neither the time nor the place to remedy that lack.
Preternaturally aware of the shabby men and women
watching them from shadows and from the lighted
doorways of mean houses and rough pubs, Malcolm
followed the eager dog and his mistress, listening to
the click of their footfalls on the pavement and the
scrape and scratch of the dog's claws.

Whatever Benny Catlin's motive, whether flight from
trouble or the threat of deadly force taking him deeper
into danger, it had carried him the length of Drury
Lane. The dog paused briefly and sniffed again at a
dark spot on the pavement. This time, Mr. Shannon
was not able to explain away the spots of blood so
glibly. Margo clutched at Malcolm, weeping and gulping back evident terror. Malcolm watched Shannon
wipe blood from his hand again, knowing, this time,
it must be Benny Catlin's blood, and was able to console himself only with the fact that not enough had
been spilled here to prove immediately fatal. But
untended, with wounds of unknown severity . . . and
perhaps in the grip of footpads who would kill him
when they had obtained what they'd forced him here
for . . .

Grimly, Malcolm signalled to continue the hunt.
Even Shahdi Feroz's eyes had taken on a strained,
hopeless look. The Ripper scholar clearly knew
Catlin's odds as well as Malcom did.

They reached the final, narrow stretches of Drury Lane where Wych Street snaked off to the left, along a route that would eventually be demolished to create Aldwych. That upscale urban renewal was destined to gobble up an entire twenty-eight acres of this mean district. They kept to the right, avoiding the narrow trap of Wych Street, but even this route was a dangerous one. The buildings closed in, ill-lit along this echoing, drizzle-shrouded stretch, and still the Alsatian shepherd strained eagerly forward, nose to the pavement. When they emerged at last into the famous Strand, another juxtaposition of wealth in the midst of slums, their first sight was St. Mary le Strand church, which stood as an island in the middle of the broad street.

Philip Stoddard muttered, "What the devil was after him, to send him walking down this way in the middle of the night?"

Malcolm glanced sharply at the stable master and nodded warningly toward the Shannons, then said, "I fear Miss Smith is greatly distressed."

Margo was emitting little sounds of horror as she took in their surroundings. She had transferred her act to the Ripper scholar and clung to Shahdi Feroz' arm as though to a lifeline, tottering at the end of her strength and wits. "Where can he be?" Margo was murmuring over and over. "Oh, God, what's happened to him? This is a terrible place, dreadful . . ."

Auley Shannon glanced over his shoulder. "Could be another answer, guv, if 'e never got clean away from th' blokes wot attacked 'im outside the opera. Alfie's 'eadin' straight for 'olywell Street. Might've been brought down 'ere for reasons I'd as soon not say in front o' the ladies."

A chill touched Malcolm's spine. Dear God, not *that*. . . . The dog was dragging them past Newcastle Street directly toward the cramped, dark little lane known as Holywell, which ran to the left of the narrow St. Mary le Strand church on a course parallel to the Strand. On the Strand itself, Malcolm could just see the glass awning of the Opera Comique, a theater sandwiched between Wych and Holywell Streets, reachable only through a tunnel that opened out beneath that glass canopy on the Strand. The neighborhood was cramped and seemingly picturesque, with exceedingly aged houses dating to the Tudor and Stuart periods crowding the appallingly narrow way.

But darkened shop windows advertising book sellers' establishments the length of Holywell were infamous throughout London. In the shops of "Booksellers' Row" as Holywell was sometimes known, a man could obtain lewd prints, obscene books, and a pornographic education for a mere handful of shillings. And for a few shillings more, a man could obtain a young girl—or a young boy, come to that, despite harsh laws against it. The girls and young men who worked in the back rooms and attics of these nasty, crumbling old shops had often as not been drugged into captivity and put to work as whores, photographed nude and raped by customers and jailors alike. If some wealthy gentleman, with or without a title, had requested a proprietor on Holywell Street to procure a young man of a specific build and coloring, Benny Catlin might well have been plunged into a Victorian hell somewhere nearby.

Although the shops were closed for the night and certainly would have been closed when Benny Catlin had passed this way earlier in the evening, women in dark skirts were busy carrying out hasty negotiations with men in rough workingmen's garments. Several of the women cast appraising glances at Malcolm, who looked—to them—like a potential wealthy customer passing by in the close darkness, despite the presence of ladies with him.

"What does Mr. Shannon mean?" Margo whispered

sotto voce. "What is it about Holywell Street that's so awful he won't say?"

Malcolm cleared his throat. "Ah . . . perhaps some other time might be better for explanations, Miss Smith? I rather doubt that what Mr. Shannon referred to is what has actually happened." Malcolm wished he could be as certain as he sounded, but he had no intention of requiring Margo to play out her role by displaying complete hysterics over the notion of her fiancé having been sold to someone to be photographed and raped by a dealer in pornographic literature.

The rough-clad women watching them so narrowly were clearly trying to judge whether or not to risk openly approaching him with *their* business propositions. Had Malcolm been quite alone, he suspected he would have been propositioned no fewer than a dozen times within fifty paces. And had he been quite alone, Malcolm's hand would never have left the pocket concealing his pistol. A man dressed as Malcolm was, venturing unaccompanied into the deep, semi-criminal poverty of Holywell, would be considered fair game by any footpad who saw him. There was more safety in numbers, but even so, Malcolm's hand never strayed far from the entrance to his pocket.

When Malcolm spotted a woman lounging by herself against a bookshop wall, standing directly beneath a large, projecting clock that stuck out perpendicularly from the building, Malcolm paused, carefully gesturing the ladies on ahead with Mr. Stoddard. A gas street lamp nearby shed enough light to see her worn dress, work-roughened hands, and tired face beneath a bedraggled bonnet.

"Good evening, ma'am."

She stood up straighter, calculation jumping into her eyes. "Evenin', luv. Whatcher' wantin', then?"

"I was wondering if you might have seen someone

pass this way earlier this evening? A gentleman dressed much the same way I am? My cousin's gone missing, you see," he added at the sharp look of distrust in her face. "I'm quite concerned over my cousin's safety and his fiancée, there, is in deep distress over it." He gestured toward Margo, who was clinging to Shahdi Feroz and biting her lip, eyes red and swollen. He must remember to ask her how she managed to conjure tears on command.

"Yer cousin, eh? Well, that's diff'rent, innit?" She shrugged. "Right about when might 'e 'ave gone by, luv?"

"Half-eight or shortly thereafter."

"I weren't 'ere at 'alf-eight, tonight nor any other. I got a job at the Black Eagle Brewery, I 'ave, what I gets up at six o'clock of a morning for, t' earn shilling an' sixpence a week, an' I don't leave brewery 'ouse til nigh on 'alf-nine of a night. Weren't 'ere at 'alf-eight, luv."

A shilling and sixpence. Eighteen cents a week, for a job that started at six A.M. and ran fifteen hours or more a shift. It was little wonder she was out here on the street after dark, trying to earn a few extra pence however she could. He sighed, then met her narrow-eyed gaze. "I see, madame. Well, thank you, anyway." He held up a shining silver florin. "If you could think of anyone who might have been hereabouts at that hour?"

She snatched the coin—nearly two weeks' wages—from his fingers. "G'wan down to Davy's, ask round there. Pub's open til all hours, anybody could've seen 'im. Ain't like we see gents every night o' th' week, these parts."

"Indeed? Thank you, ma'am, and good evening."

He was aware of her stare as he rejoined the ladies and followed the straining Alfie at the end of his leash. By dawn, the story of the missing gent and his grieving fiancée would be news from one end of the

district to the other. With any luck, word of Benny
Catlin might yet shake loose—particularly in the hopes
of a cash "donation" for information given. Meanwhile,
Alfie was whining and straining in the direction of
Davy's Pub at the end of Holywell Street where it
rejoined the Strand once more. Music and laughter
reached up the narrow lane as they approached the
busy public house, brightly lit by a multitude of gas
lamps. Its windows and placard-plastered walls advertised Scotch and Irish Whiskeys . . . Wainey, Comb,
and Reid fine ales . . . favorite brands of stout . . . and,
of course, Walker's.

Malcolm wasn't dressed for mingling in such a
crowd, but Auley Shannon was. He nodded slightly
at Malcolm, then disappeared into the packed pub.
Malcolm waited patiently with Margo and Shahdi
Feroz and the others, noting the location of another
pub, The Rising Sun, across the road where Wych
Street emerged just the other side of Davy's. Beyond,
in the wide avenue that lay beyond the conjunction
of the two narrow, old streets, lay the ancient facade
of St. Clement Danes Church, another island church
built in the center of the Strand. Its high steeple was
topped with what appeared to be a miniature, columned Greek temple, barely visible now between
drizzle-laden clouds and streaks of jagged lightning.

And in another of London's abrupt transitions,
where glittering wealth shared a line of fenceposts
with criminal poverty, where the narrow Wych and
Holywell Streets intersected the Strand, a sharp line
of demarcation divided the dark poverty-stricken
regions behind them, separating it from the expensive, well-to-do houses and shops right in front of
Malcolm, shops and houses that stood in a stately
double row to either side of the street, lining the
Strand, itself. Such abrupt changes from deepest
poverty to startling wealth, within half-a-block of one
another, placed destitute men and women with no

hope at all side-by-side with socially ambitious businessmen and their ladies, ensconced in fine houses, with servants and carriages and luxuries their neighbors could never aspire to owning through any means except thievery.

And thievery was exactly how many a denizen of SoHo obtained such items.

Studying the intersection and judging the lay of the land and the inhabitants of the various buildings within view, Malcolm realized they'd need to field a good-sized search party through this area just to question all the potential witnesses. Five minutes later, Shannon emerged from Davy's, looking hopeful. "Blokes are suspicious o' strangers," he said quietly, "an' rightly so, what wiv coppers lookin' t'nick 'alf the blokes in there, I'd reckon, but I pointed out Miss Smith, 'ere, give 'em the bare bones of what's 'appened. Got a few of 'em t'thaw a bit, seein' the lady cryin' and all. Must be 'alf a dozen blokes said they saw a bloke wot might've been 'im." He paused, with a glance toward Margo, then cleared his throat. "Wot they saw was a woman walk past, Mr. Moore, carryin' a wounded gentleman. Walkin' quick-like, as if to find a surgeon. Blokes remembered, on account of that poor street-walker, Martha Tabram, 'oo got 'erself stabbed to death August Bank 'oliday, an' on account of it were so queer, seein' a woman in a patched dress and ragged bonnet, carryin' a gentleman in a fine suit wiv a shabby old coat wrapped round 'is head."

Malcolm paled, even as Margo blanched and clutched at Shahdi Feroz. "Odd," Malcolm muttered, "How deuced *odd.*"

"You've the right o' that, sir."

"It's unlikely a woman would have attacked Mr. Catlin. Perhaps she found him lying on the street, injured, and was, indeed, carrying him to safety with a surgeon. Mr. Catlin was a slightly built young man, after all, and wouldn't have proved difficult to lift and

carry, for a stout woman." Margo nodded, wiping tears
from her face with the back of one gloved hand. "Mr.
Shannon, Miss Shannon, lead on, please. Let's see
how much farther this trail will take us."

As it happened, that was not much farther at all.
Alfie crossed the Strand right along the front of the
old Danish church, where the street curved around
to the south. Tailors' establishments and boot sellers'
shops advertised their wares to wealthy families able
to afford their trade. But where Millford Lane cut
off to the south near the rear corner of St. Clement Danes, the skies cut loose with a stinging downpour of rain and Alfie lost the trail. The dog hesitated,
cast about the wet pavement in confusion and ever-
widening circles, and finally sat back on its haunches,
whining unhappily while runoff poured, ankle deep,
past their feet in the gutters. Maeve pulled her coat
collar up around her neck, then bent and patted the
dog's shoulder and ruffled its wet, clamped back ears,
speaking gently to it.

Malcolm noted the presence of a few hansom cabs
along the Strand, waiting hopefully for customers from
amongst the wealthier gentlemen Malcolm could see
here and there along the street, some of them escorting
well-dressed ladies out to carriages under cover of taut
umbrellas, and said, "Well, perhaps Mr. Catlin's bene-
factress hired a cab?"

It was, at least, worth the asking, although he
doubted a woman as shabbily clad as the one the men
in Davey's pub had described would've been able to
afford the cost of a hansom cab fare.

Miss Shannon patted her dog's wet side and glanced
around. "Pr'aps, sir. I'm that sorry, I am, 'bout the rain.
'E's a good tracker, Alfie is, but no dog born wot'll trace
a man through a downpour like this."

"I fear not. Very well," Malcolm said briskly, "we
shall simply have to proceed along different lines.
Mr. Shannon, I believe the terms of our agreement

include pressing inquiries amongst potential witnesses at whatever point your fine Alsatian lost the trail? If you and your granddaughter would be so good as to assist us, I feel we might yet make good progress this evening. Try the cabbies, there, if you please. Stoddard, if you'll broach the denizens of the Rising Sun Pub, I'll endeavor to strike up a conversation with some of the gentlemen out for the evening's merriment and dinner parties. Ladies, if you would be so good as to secure a hansom cab? I hope we may need one shortly."

"Yes, sir."

"Of course, Mr. Moore."

"Right, sir. Let's give 'er a go, then, Maeve."

Over the course of the next half-hour, Malcolm spoke with dozens of gentlemen and their stout, respectable wives, the latter dressed in satins and bonnets with drooping feathers under widespread umbrellas, inquiring politely about an ill-dressed woman assisting a wounded gentleman of their class. The answers he received were civil, concerned, and entirely negative, which left Malcolm increasingly frustrated as well as thoroughly soaked. Lightning flared overhead, sizzled down to strike chimney pots and church steeples with crashes of thunder that sent the well-dressed citizenry scrambling for doorways and covered carriages.

They couldn't stay out in this kind of weather any longer, searching.

London was a vast maze of streets and lanes. The number of places an unwary time tourist could go fatally astray would have sobered the most optimistic of searchers. Malcolm hurried back down the Strand, calling for Stoddard and the Shannons. They rejoined Margo and Shahdi Feroz, who had secured the services of the nearest hansom cab and were huddled inside it, out of the downpour. None of the others had found so much as a trace, either.

"There's nothing more to be done, here, in this weather," Malcolm shouted above the crash of thunder.

Margo's performance inside the hansom cab, weeping distraughtly and leaning against Shahdi Feroz, left Mr. Shannon clearing his throat in sympathy. Maeve Shannon stepped up onto the running board and leaned in to put a comforting hand on Margo's shoulder, said something too low for Malcolm to hear, at which Margo nodded and replied, "Thank you, Miss Shannon. Thank you . . ."

"I'm that sorry, I am, miss, but I'm sure it'll come right." Maeve smiled at Margo, then stepped back down to the pavement and called her dog to heel. Malcolm handed over Mr. Shannon's fee for the night's work and a bonus for Maeve's unexpected sympathy to Margo, which he felt deserved recognition of some kind. The Shannons might be accustomed to the harshness of life in Whitechapel, where they kept their inquiry agency, but they were good and decent people, nonetheless. The inquiry agent and his granddaughter wished him luck and hurried off into the downpour with Alfie trotting between them, seeking shelter from the rising storm. Malcolm sighed heavily, then secured a cab of his own to follow Margo and Shahdi Feroz back to Spaldergate, and settled down for a clattering ride through night-shrouded streets. Stoddard, riding silently beside him, was grim in the actinic glare of lightning bolts streaking through London's night sky.

Somewhere out there, Benny Catlin *was* known, to someone.

Malcolm intended finding that someone. All it required was a bit of luck added to the hard work ahead. In the swaying darkness of the hansom, Malcolm grimaced. This was not a good time for reminding himself that before Margo had come into his life, Malcolm's luck had run to the notoriously bad. Malcolm Moore was not a superstitious man by nature, but he couldn't quite shake the feeling that on this particular hunt, luck just might not be with him.

He could only pray that it *had* been with Benny Catlin.

If not, they might yet locate him in a morgue.

Chapter Nine

Gideon Guthrie poured a drink from an expensive cut-crystal decanter and moved quietly to the window. Night had fallen across the city, turning the filthy sprawl of New York into a fairy-land jewel at his feet. Behind him, the television flickered silently, sound muted. Gideon frowned slowly, then sipped at his scotch. John Caddrick had given quite a performance for the press today. How the sociopathic bastard was able to summon tears for the cameras, Gideon didn't know. But the press had eaten it up, delighted with the ratings points Caddrick's grief gave them. Which played quite nicely into Gideon's plans. What worried Gideon, however, and it worried *his* boss, as well, was Caddrick's tendency to explosive fits of temper. They played a very delicate game, Gideon and Cyril Barris and the senator, a damned delicate game. Caddrick's notorious temperament was just as likely to prove a liability as an asset.

It was too bad about the girl, in a sense, although Caddrick didn't seem to give a damn that Gideon had ordered a fatal hit on the Senator's own daughter. Of course, Caddrick wasn't stupid and there'd never been any love lost between those two. If Gideon and his political ally played it right, Cassie Tyrol's impulsive decision to tell her niece would play into Cyril Barris' long-range plans brilliantly. All Gideon had to do was keep Caddrick's temper from screwing things up. A man like John Caddrick was priceless in Congress, where that temper and his ruthless ability to play the filthy game of politics made him a devastating enemy and a cunning advocate. But Caddrick's flair for playing the press could easily backfire, if they weren't incredibly careful. The senator's call for investigating the *Ansar Majlis*, claiming they'd kidnapped his daughter, worked wonders for television ratings. And it would doubtless fire up a world-wide demand for the destruction of the very terrorists Gideon had chosen to further his employer's plans. Which was, ultimately, the precise outcome both Cyril Barris and Gideon, himself, wanted.

But too close an investigation into the *Ansar Majlis* could prove risky.

Very risky.

He'd have to keep a close watch on John Caddrick, all right. Their timetable was moving along right on schedule, with only one minor hitch, which ought to've been effectively eliminated, by now. He'd sent a good team onto TT-86 to destroy Ianira and her whole family, not to mention finishing up the job with Jenna Caddrick and that miserable, meddlesome detective, Noah Armstrong. Gideon scowled and poured himself another scotch. *That* was one complication he hadn't anticipated. Cassie Tyrol, actress, six-time divorcee, and scatter-brained Templar, was the last person Gideon had expected to hire a detective, for God's sake, to investigate her own brother-in-law's business practices. And who'd have guessed she would come so damned unglued over the seemingly accidental death of that little bastard, Alston Corliss, who'd taped all the evidence on Caddrick?

How, in fact, had she even known about it, so soon? She'd bolted *hours* before the FBI had leaked word to the press. Armstrong again, no doubt.

Alston Corliss was yet another reason to worry about the senator. If a goddamned *actor* could ferret out that kind of evidence on the senator's activities. . . .When this was over and done with, maybe it would be a good idea to bring about Caddrick's political downfall. Do it subtly, so Caddrick would never suspect Gideon had orchestrated it. Yes, he'd have to look into that. Suggest it to Cyril Barris as a potential course of action for the future, after they'd culled everything useful they could from Caddrick's position in government. Meanwhile, Noah Armstrong had somehow absconded with a copy of that goddamned, incriminating tape, the original of which they'd found and destroyed. Maybe Corliss had used the stinking Internet to send it, with streaming video technology. However he'd gotten the tape to Armstrong, out in California, it spelled certain disaster for their plans if they didn't get it back before Armstrong found a way to contact the authorities.

Gideon knocked back the scotch and swore under his breath. Complications like this, he did not need. But he had the situation under control again, thank God, so all he had to do now was keep an eye on John Caddrick and make sure nothing else went wrong. If anything else did . . . Heads would by God roll. Gideon scowled. The senator had believed for years *he* was calling the shots. Fine. Let him. If Caddrick screwed up one more time, he'd find out the bitter truth, fast. It would almost be worth the trouble, to see the shock on his face.

Gideon switched off the television and settled himself to set in motion the events necessary to bring about the end of a powerful politician's career.

Chapter Ten

It was a vastly subdued Margo who returned to Spaldergate House in a driving downpour, with lightning sizzling in the night skies and Benny Catlin missing and wounded somewhere beyond their reach. After the preoccupation of their abortive search, it was actually a shock to return to the warmth and brightness of Spaldergate and the lively discussion amongst the Ripper scholars, who cared absolutely nothing about a missing time tourist. All except Shahdi Feroz. Margo still wondered why she'd volunteered to accompany them.

An argument broke out the moment they returned, as to which scholars would go into the East End to help place the final surveillance equipment at the first murder scene. Not to be outdone, Dominica Nosette and Guy Pendergast joined the fray.

"We're coming along, as well."

Pavel Kostenka said, "You are not qualified—"

"I've been on more undercover photoshoots than you have credentials strung out behind your name!"

"And you are a two-bit, muckraking—"

"Two-bit my arse! I'll have you know—"

"Enough!" Malcolm's stern voice cut through the babble and silenced the entire lot of them. "*I'll* make the decision as to who goes and who stays! Is that clear?"

Even Margo gulped, staring wide-eyed at her infuriated fiancé.

"Now. Miss Nosette, Mr. Pendergast, the terms of the Ripper Watch contract include you as the only journalists. It would be remiss of us if you did not accompany the team members placing the equipment, tonight, to record the attempt for posterity. I presume you've brought low-light, miniaturized cameras?"

"I know my trade," the blond reporter said with an icy chill in her voice, glaring at Kostenka. "And my equipment."

Kostenka just shrugged and pretended to find the carpet utterly absorbing.

"Very well. I would suggest you go and get that equipment ready. We'll leave the house at two A.M. If you're not dressed for the East End and waiting in the carriage drive, we'll leave without you. Now then, Margo, please be good enough to help them select costumes. They haven't been into the East End. Assist Dr. Feroz with that as well. I'll want you along, Inspector," he glanced at Conroy Melvyn, the Scotland Yard chief inspector who'd been named head of the Ripper Watch team, "and the others can prepare the relay and recording equipment on the roof and down in the vault."

There were grumbles, but clearly, the Ripper Watch team had grown accustomed to taking Malcolm's orders when it came to his decisions as head guide.

"Very good. I expect you all have someplace better to be than standing about in the parlour, with your mouths hanging open."

The assembled scholars and journalists dispersed quickly. Only Conroy Melvyn seemed to find the situation humorous. The police inspector winked at

Malcolm as he strolled out in the wake of the disgruntled scholars. Then Margo was alone with Malcolm, at last.

"Margo, I'm afraid you're not going to like what I have to say next."

"Oh, no, Malcolm, please let me come with you!"

He grimaced. "That isn't it. Quite the opposite, in fact." He rubbed the back of his neck distractedly. "It's this blasted business with Catlin. Thank God you've come. I've got to work with the Gilberts, organize some plan of attack to search for him. We'll try the hospitals, the workhouse infirmaries, anywhere Catlin might have gone seeking medical attention."

Margo gulped, seeing abruptly where this was leading. "Malcolm . . . I—I'm not ready to guide that bunch by myself—"

Malcolm grinned. "Good. I'm glad you've the sense to admit it. I didn't intend sending you alone. Tanglewood's a good man, an experienced guide, and he's been in the East End a fair bit."

Margo frowned. "Isn't that kind of an odd place for tourists to go?"

Malcolm merely cleared his throat. "Zipper jockey tours."

Oh. "That's disgusting!"

"It isn't his fault, Margo. He's a Time Tours employee. If he wants to keep his job, he goes where the paying customers want to visit. Even if it's some back-alley brothel in Wapping."

"Huh. I hope they catch a good dose of something nasty!"

"Occasionally," Malcolm said drily, "they do. Spaldergate's resident surgeon keeps rather a generous supply of penicillin on hand. There is a reason London's courtesans wore death's-head rings, even as early as the eighteenth century."

Margo shivered. Poor women, reduced to such poverty they'd no choice but to risk syphillis and its slow, certain deterioration toward madness and death in an era predating antibiotics.

"Very well," Malcolm said tiredly, "that's settled, then. I would suggest you go in costume as a girl, rather than a street ruffian. You'll be less apt to run into serious trouble, particularly in company with the members of the Ripper Watch team. But go armed, love. It's no busman's holiday I'm sending you into, out there."

She nodded. "Believe me, I will be. I'll watch over them, get them back here safe again, as soon as their equipment is in place."

Malcolm held out his arms and she walked into his embrace, just holding onto him tightly for a long moment. He kissed her with such hunger, it left her head swimming. Then he broke the contact and leaned his brow against hers and sighed. "I would give anything . . . But I must get on with the search for Benny Catlin."

"I know."

He kissed her one last time, then went in search of the Spaldergate House gatekeepers. Margo found her way upstairs and helped the new arrivals pick out costumes ragged enough for the East End, then showed Dominica Nosette how to get into the costume. Shahdi Feroz had, at least, been down the Britannia before.

"In the West End, mostly" she said with a slight smile, glancing at the garments Margo had authorized. "But I do know how the underthings, at least, go on."

Dominica Nosette expected Margo to assist her as lady's maid, a task she did not relish. *Three months of this?* Margo groused silently, yanking at the strings on Miss Nosette's stays. *I'll lop off her pretty blond hair and put her in a boy's tog's, first!*

By the time the mantle clocks throughout Spaldergate chimed two A.M. and they were ready to leave in one of the Time Tours carriages, which would take them as far as the Tower of London, Malcolm had been gone for hours, out combing the hospitals and work-house infirmaries for some trace of their missing tourist. Douglas Tanglewood ushered them all into a stylish Calash Coach, which possessed a hard, covered roof and curtains to screen them from outside scrutiny, since they were dressed as roughly as any dockhand out of Stepney. They rode in a silence electric with anticipation. Even Margo, who fretted over Malcolm's safety, searching for a man who had already been involved in two fatal shootings, found herself caught up in the air of excitement.

In three hours, they would *know*.

After more than a century and a half of mystery, they would finally *know*.

If nothing went wrong. If she did her job right. If the equipment didn't fail . . .

When they finally alighted at the Tower, which stood at the very gateway to the East End, dividing it from more prosperous areas to the west, Dominica Nosette gasped in astonishment and pointed through the darkness toward a misshapen silhouette outlined now and again by flashes of lightning.

"The Bridge!" she gasped. "What's wrong with the Bridge? Who's destroyed it?"

Douglas Tanglewood chuckled softly. "Miss Nosette, Tower Bridge hasn't suffered any damage. They simply haven't finished building it, yet." Flickers of lightning revealed naked iron girders which only partly spanned the River Thames in the darkness. The famous stone covering had not yet been put into place. "There's been quite a controversy raging about the Bridge, you know. Stone over iron, unheard of, risky."

"Controversy?" the blonde sniffed, clearly thinking Tanglewood was feeding her a line. "Absurd. Tower Bridge is a national monument!"

"Will be," Margo put in. "Right now, it's just another bridge. Convenient for trans-shipping cargo from the docks on this bank to the docks on the South Side, since it'll cut five miles out of the draymen's one-way journey, but just a bridge, for all its convenience."

"Nonsense!"

Margo shrugged. "Suit yourself. This isn't the London you left a couple of days ago, Miss Nosette. I'd advise you to keep that in mind. Let's get moving, all right? We don't have any time to waste, standing around arguing about a stupid bridge that isn't even finished, yet."

They set out, Doug Tanglewood in the lead, Margo and Shahdi Feroz bringing up the rear, while Dominica Nosette and Guy Pendergast, voices low, deadlocked in a debate with Conroy Melvyn of Scotland Yard as they walked through the dark, rainy streets. Pubs had just closed down and houses were mostly dark, gas lights turned out while the working poor found what sleep they could before dawn sent them reeling out once more to earn a living however they could manage.

"There's a lot of evidence against Frederick Bailey Deeming, isn't there?" Pendergast asked softly.

"A small-time swindler with brain fever," Conroy Melvyn said with a dismissive air. "Killed his wife and children, slashed their throats. They hanged him in '92."

"Didn't the press dub him the official Ripper, though?" Dominica Nosette pressed the argument. "And Scotland Yard, as well? For years, the Yard exhibited his death mask as the Ripper's."

Conroy Melvyn shrugged. "Well, he was a right popular chap at the time, so he was, violent and known t'be in Whitechapel during the murders. Carried knives, so witnesses told police. Not," the up-time Scotland Yard inspector added drily, "that anybody had any real evidence against him. Prob'ly just an epileptic, drunken lout of a sailor with a violent temper and a nasty habit of killing off family when they got inconveniently expensive to support."

"Nice guy," Margo muttered, earning a sardonic glance from Shahdi Feroz.

Dominica Nosette, who had secreted a miniature video camera system under her clothing and bonnet, turned to glance at the Scotland Yard inspector—thus adroitly filming the "interview" as well.

"Who do *you* think did it, then?"

"I dunno, ma'am, and that's what we're doin' tonight, innit? Taking a bit of a look-see for ourselves, eh?"

Dominica Nosette, clearly not one to be dismissed so easily, dropped back to where Margo and Shahdi Feroz walked behind the chief inspector and Guy Pendergast. "Who do you think did it, Dr. Feroz? You never did name your top suspect, back on the station, despite all those marvelous theories about Satanists and mad lesbian midwives. Come, now, Dr. Feroz, who's your favorite suspect?"

Neither Shahdi Feroz nor Dominica Nosette noticed the sharp stare from a roughly dressed man nearly invisible in the shadows of a dark alleyway. A man who abruptly changed course to follow them. But Margo did. And she noticed the heavy sap in his hand and the covetous look he cast at Shahdi Feroz and her carpet bag. He'd clearly heard Dominica Nosette call Shahdi Feroz "doctor" and doubtless figured there was something valuable in her satchel. Medicines, maybe, which could be sold for cash. Margo rounded on him in scalding language that brought the ill-dressed villain—and the entire Ripper Watch Team—to a screeching halt in the middle of Whitechapel Road.

"Cor, 'ave a nice butcher's, will you?" Margo shrilled, fists clenched as she advanced menacingly on him. "Ain't you never clapped yer bleedin' minces on no missionary doctor before, you gob-smacked lager lout? Takin' 'er to London Horse Piddle, so I am, an' you lay a German on 'er, I'll clout you upside yer pink an' shell-like, so I will! I ain't no gormless git, I ain't, I know wot a blagger like you is up to, when 'e follows a lady, so g'wan, then, 'ave it away on yer buttons! Before I smack you in the 'ampsteads wiv a bleedin' sap! C'mon, get yer finger out!"

Margo was, in fact, gripping a lead-filled leather sap of her own, so hard her knuckles stood out white. The shabbily dressed man following them had halted, mouth dropping open as he stared. Then he let out a bark of laughter past blackened teeth.

"Grotty-mouthed bit, ain't yer? Don't want no bovver, not 'at bad, I don't. Sooner go back to me cat an' face me ruddy knife, so I would, after she's copped an elephant."

The man faded back into the darkness, his harsh laughter still floating back to them. Margo relaxed her grip on the lead-filled sap one finger joint at a time, then glanced up to discover Douglas Tanglewood hovering at her side, pistol concealed behind one hip. "Well done," he said quietly, "if a bit theatrical. Ladies, gentlemen, we have a schedule to keep. Move along, please."

It was only then, as Margo herded the Ripper Watch team members down the street, casting uneasy glances over her shoulder, that she noticed the open-mouthed stares from Guy Pendergast, Dominica Nosette, and— of all people—Shahdi Feroz, who broke the stunned silence first. "I am amazed! Whatever did you say to that man? It wasn't even in English! Was it?" she added uncertainly.

Margo cleared her throat self-consciously. "Well, no, it wasn't. That was Cockney dialect. Which isn't exactly English, no."

"But what did you *say?*" the Ripper scholar insisted. "And what did *he* say?"

"Well . . ." Margo tried to recall, exactly, what it was she'd actually said. "I asked him if he'd had a good look, hadn't he ever laid eyes on a missionary doctor, and I was taking you to London Hospital. So if he laid a hand on you, I'd hit him across the ear with a sap.

Told him to go away, or I'd smack him in the teeth, and told him to hurry it up. Then he said I had a dirty mouth and told me he didn't want any trouble. Said he'd rather go home and face his wife after she'd been drinking than mix it up with me." Margo smiled a little lamely. "Actually, he was right about the dirty mouth. Some of what I said was really awful. Bad enough, a proper lady would've fainted from the shock, if she'd understood half of it."

Dominica Nosette laughed in open delight. "My dear, you are a treasure! Really, you've a splendid career ahead. What made you want to scout? Following in your grandfather's footsteps, no doubt?"

Margo didn't really want to talk about her family. Too much of it was painful. So she said, "We really shouldn't discuss anything from up time while we're here, Miss Nosette. That jerk started following us because he overheard what we were saying. You called Madame Feroz, there, by her professional title, which left him dangerously curious about us and the contents of her bag. There are very few women doctors in 1888 and it caught his attention. If you want to talk about scouting later, at the gatehouse, we can talk about it then, but not now. And please don't ask so many questions about the suspects while we're out on the streets. You-know-who hasn't even struck yet, despite the deaths on Easter Monday and August Bank Holiday, both of which will be attributed to him by morning. And since the nickname isn't made public in the newspapers until after September 30th, with the Dear Boss letter that's published after the double murders, conversation on that subject should be confined strictly to the gatehouse."

Dominica gave her one rebellious glance, then smiled sweetly. "Oh, all right. I'm sure you're only trying to watch out for our safety, after all. But I will get that interview, Miss Smith!"

Margo didn't know whether to feel flattered or alarmed.

Then they reached the turn-off for Buck's Row and all conversation came to a halt as the Ripper Watch team went to work. They set up their surveillance equipment efficiently, putting in place miniature cameras, low-light systems, tiny but powerful microphones, miniaturized transmitters that would relay video and audio signals up to the rooftops and across London. They worked in silent haste, as the factory cottages terraced along the road were occupied by families who slept in the shadow of the factories where they worked such long and gruelling shifts. Conroy Melvyn had just finished putting the last connection in place when the constable assigned to this beat appeared at the narrow street's end, sauntering their way with a suspicious glance.

"Wot's this, then?" the policeman demanded.

"Don't want no barney, guv," Doug Tanglewood said quickly, "just 'aving a bit of a bobble, ain't we? C'mon, mates, let's 'ave a pint down to boozer, eh?"

"Oh, aye," Margo grumbled, "an' you'll end pissed as a newt again, like as not!"

"Shut yer gob, eh? Bottle's goin' t'think you ain't got no manners!"

The constable watched narrowly as Douglas Tanglewood and Margo herded the others out of Buck's Row and back toward Whitechapel Road. But he didn't follow, just continued along his assigned beat. Margo breathed a sigh of relief. "Whew . . ."

And did her dead-level best to keep the scholars and journalists out of trouble the whole way back to Spaldergate House, where Margo grew massively absorbed in the unfolding drama in the East End. They did a test recording, which captured a disturbance underway in one of the terraced cottages. The screaming fight which erupted on the heels of a drunken man's return home was not in English. Or

Cockney, either. Bulgarian, maybe . . . Lots of immigrants lived in the East End, so many it was hard to distinguish languages, sometimes. The fight flared to violence and breaking crockery, then subsided with a woman sobbing in despair.

The street and the houses lining it grew quiet again. The constable walked his beat past the cameras several times during the next three hours, virtually alone on the dark stretch of road where no public gas lights burned anywhere within reach of the camera pickups. The silence in the street was mirrored by a thick silence in the vault, as they waited, downing cupfuls of coffee, fidgeting with the equipment, occasionally muttering and adjusting connections. As the clock ticked steadily toward Zero-Hour, the excitement, the electric tension in the vault beneath Spaldergate House was thick enough to cut with the Ripper's knife. Ten minutes before the earliest estimated time of death, they switched on the recording equipment, videotaping the empty stretch of cobbled street.

"Check those backup recordings," Conroy Melvyn muttered. "Be bloody sure we're getting multiple copies of this."

"Number two recording."

"Number three's a go."

"Four's copying just fine."

"Got a sound-feed problem on number five. I'm on it."

Margo, who had nothing to do but watch the others huddle tensely over consoles, fiddling with computer controls and adjusting sound mixers, wondered with a lonely pang what Malcolm was doing and why he hadn't returned, yet. Hours, it'd been, since he'd left on the search of London's hospitals. How many were there in London? She didn't know. After all the work he'd put in during the past weeks, setting up the base camp and helping the scholars learn their way around the East End, he was missing the historical moment when they would finally discover who Jack the Ripper really was. Lousy idiot of a tourist! Why Benny Catlin had chosen tonight, of all nights, to get himself into a gunfight at the Piccadilly Hotel . . .

"Oh, my God!" Pavel Koskenka's voice sliced through the tense silence. "There they are!"

Margo's breath caught involuntarily.

Then Jack the Ripper walked calmly into view, escorting Polly Nichols, all unknowing, to her death.

The night resembled the entire, waning summer: wet and cold. Rain slashed down frequently in sharp gusting showers which would end abruptly, leaving the streets puddled and chilly, only to pour again without warning. Thunder rumbled through the narrow cobbled streets like heavy wagon wheels laboring under a vast tonnage of transport goods. Savage flares of lightning pulsed through low-lying clouds above the wet slate rooftops of London. For the second time that night, a hellish red glow bathed the underbellies of those clouds as another dock fire raged through the East End. It was nearly two-thirty in the morning of a wet, soggy Friday, the last day of August.

James Maybrick paused in the puddled shadows along Whitechapel Road, where he watched the exceedingly erratic progress of the woman he had been following all evening, now. His hands, thrust deep into the pockets of his dark overcoat against the chill of the wet night, ached for the coming pleasure. His right hand curled gently around the hard wooden handle of the knife concealed in his coat's deep pocket. He smiled and tugged down his dark felt cap, one of many caps and hats he had purchased recently in differing parts of the city, preparing for this work.

The woman he followed at a discreet distance staggered frequently against the wall as she made her way east down Whitechapel Road ahead of him. She was a small woman, barely five feet two inches in height, with small and delicate features gone blowzy and red from the alcohol she had consumed tonight. High cheekbones, dark skin, and grey eyes, framed by brown hair beginning to show the signs of age . . . She might have been anywhere from thirty to thirty-five, to look at her, but Maybrick knew her history, knew everything it was possible to discover about this small, alcoholic woman he stalked so patiently. John Lachley had told Maybrick all about Polly Nichols. About her years of living as a common whore on the streets of White-chapel.

She was forty-four years old, this "Hooker" as the Americans in Norfolk would have called her, after the general who had supplied such women in the camps during the Civil War. Not a handsome woman, either. She must have a dreadful time luring customers to pay for the goods she offered up for sale. Polly's teeth were slightly discolored when she smiled and just above her eyes, Polly's dark complexion was marred by a scar on her brow. She was married, was "Polly" Nichols, married and a mother of five miserable children, God help them, to have such a mother. Mary Ann Walker, as Lachley had told him was her maiden name, had married William Nichols, subsequently left him five or six times (by William Nichols' own disgusted admission), and had finally left him for good, abandoning her children to take up a life of itinerant work "in service" between stints in workhouses and prostitution. William, poor sod, had convinced the courts to discontinue her maintenance money by proving that she was, in fact, living as a common whore.

Not even her father, Edward Walker, a respectable blacksmith in Camberwell, had been able to live with her during her slide into the miserable creature James Maybrick stalked through this rainy and unseasonably chilly August night. Her own father had quarreled violently with her over her drunkenness, precipitating her departure from his doorstep. Her most recent home—and Maybrick curled his lip at the thought of calling such lodgings home—had been the cold, unheated rooms she'd paid for in various "doss" houses along the infamous Flower and Dean Street and the equally notorious Thrawl Street, establishments which catered primarily to destitute whores. Hundreds of such lodging houses existed in Whitechapel, some of them even permitting men and women to share a bed for the night, as scandalous a notion as that was. The "evil quarter mile" as the stretch of Commercial Road from Thrawl Street to Flower and Dean was known, had for years been vilified as the most dangerous, foul street in London.

James Maybrick knew this only too well, for he had lived, briefly, in Whitechapel during the earliest years of his career as a cotton merchant's clerk, had met and married a pretty working girl named Sarah here, where she had still lived, unknown to the wealthy and faithless bitch he'd married many years later and settled in a fine mansion in Liverpool. Florie, the whore, had discovered Sarah's existence not so many weeks ago, had dared demand a divorce, after what she, herself, had done with Brierly! James had laughed at her, told her to consider her own future carefully before taking such a step, to consider the massive debts she'd run up at dressmakers' shops, debts she could not pay. If she hoped to avoid disgrace, to avoid bringing shame upon herself and her innocent children, she would jolly well indulge his appetites, leave poor Sarah in peace, and keep her mouth shut.

James had visited Sarah tonight, before arriving at Dr. Lachley's. He had enjoyed the conjugal visit with his precious first wife, who bore his need for Florie's money and social position stoically and lived frugally on the money Maybrick provided for her. Sarah was a good, God-fearing girl who had refused to leave Whitechapel and her only living relatives and ruin his social chances. Sarah, at least, would never have to walk these streets. Even the local Spitalfields clergy despaired of the region and its violent, criminal-minded denizens.

James Maybrick smiled into the wet night. They would not despair over one particular denizen much longer. Three and a half hours previously, he had quietly followed Polly Nichols down Whitechapel Road as she set out searching for her evening's doss money, the four-pence needed to secure a place to sleep, and had watched from the shadows as his guide, his mentor, Dr. John Lachley, had accosted her. The disguise his marvelous teacher wore had changed his appearance remarkably, delighting James to no end, as much as the secret retreat beneath the streets had delighted him. The false theatrical beard Maybrick had obtained for him from a cheap shop in SoHo and the dye used to color it left Lachley as anonymous as the thousands of other shabbily dressed working men wandering Whitechapel, wending their way from one gin palace to the next on a drunken pub crawl.

Lachley, stepping out into Polly Nichols' path, had smiled into her eyes. "Hello, my dear. It's a raw evening, isn't it?"

The doctor, whose medical treatments had left Maybrick feeling more powerful, more vigorous and invincible than he'd felt in years, glanced briefly past the whore's shoulder to where Maybrick stood in concealment, nodding slightly to indicate that this was Polly Nichols, herself, the woman he had brought James here to help murder. Dressed in a brown linsey frock, Polly Nichols had smiled up at John Lachley with a whore's calculating smile of greeting.

"Evening. Is a bit wet, innit?"

"A bit," Lachley allowed. "A lady such as yourself shouldn't be out with a bare head in such weather."

"Ooh, now aren't you the polite one!" She walked

her fingers coyly up his arm. "Now, if I were to 'ave
the coin, I might buy me a noice, fancy bonnet and
keep the rain off."

"It just so happens," Lachley smiled down into her
brown eyes, "that I have a few coins to spare."

She laughed lightly. "An' what might a lady need
t'do to share that wealth, eh?"

"Consider it a gift." The physician pressed a silver florin into her palm.

She glanced down at the coin, then stared, open-
mouthed, down at her grubby hand. "A *florin*?" This
pitiful alcoholic little trollop now held in her hand
a coin worth twenty-four pence: the equivalent of
six times the going rate for what she was selling
tonight. Or, marketed differently, six glasses of gin.
Polly stared up at Lachley in sudden suspicion.
"What you want t'give me an whole, entire florin
for?" Greed warred with alarm in her once delicate
little face.

John Lachley gave her a warm smile. "It's a small
token of appreciation. From a mutual friend. Eddy
sends his regards, madam." He doffed his rough cloth
cap. "It has come to his attention that another mutual
friend, a young man by the name of Morgan, loaned
you a few of his personal letters. Eddy is desirous
of re-reading them, you see, and asked me if I might
not do him the favor of speaking with you about
obtaining them this evening."

"*Eddy?*" she gasped. "Oh, *my!* Oh, blimey, the
letters!"

Deep in his pocket, Maybrick gripped the handle
of his knife and smiled.

John Lachley gave the filthy little trollop a mocking
little bow. "Consider the florin a promise of greater
rewards to come, in appreciation of your discretion
in a certain, ah, delicate matter."

"Oh, I'm most delicate, I am, and it's most generous of Mr. Eddy to send a token of 'is good faith.

But you see, I don't exactly 'ave those letters on me person, y'see. I'd 'ave to go an' fetch them. From the safe place I've been keepin' 'em 'idden, y'see, for Morgan," she added hastily.

"Of course, madam. Shall we meet again when you have obtained them? Name the time and place and I will bring a far better reward than that paltry florin, there."

"Oh, yes, certainly! Give me the night, say? Maybe we could meet in the morning?"

Maybrick tightened his hand on the knife handle again, in anger this time. *No!* He would *not* wait a whole day! The bitch must be punished now! Tonight! Visions of his wife, naked in her lover's arms, tormented James Maybrick, drove him to a frenzy of hatred, instilled in him the burning desire to kill this filthy prostitute posturing in front of them as though she were someone worthy of breathing the same air they did. Polly Nichols was nothing but a blackmailing, dirty little whore . . .

"You must understand," John Lachley was saying to her, "Eddy is most anxious to re-read his letters. I will meet you again here, later tonight, no later than, say, three-thirty in the morning. That should give you more than adequate time to fetch the letters, buy yourself something to drink at a public house and get a little something to eat, perhaps even buy yourself a nice new bonnet to keep this miserable rain off your lovely hair."

She bobbed her head in excitement, now. "Oh, yes, that'd be fine, three-thirty in the morning, no later. I'll be 'ere, I will, with them letters."

"Very good, madam." Lachley gave her another mocking bow. "Be sure, now, to find yourself a nice bonnet, to keep out the wet. We don't want you catching your death on a raw night like this." Lachley's lips twitched at the silent joke.

The doomed whore laughed brightly. "Oh, no, that

would never do, would it? Did you want to go someplace dry and comfy, then?" She was caressing
Lachley's groin vulgarly.

The thought tickled Maybrick's sense of humor, that
this dirty little trollop would sell herself to the very
man who was bringing about her murder. The thought
excited him, almost as much as the thought of killing her did. He hoped Lachley dragged her to the
nearest private spot and commenced banging her as
hard as possible, toothless blackmailing bitch that she
was.

John Lachley gave her a wry little smile. "Indeed,
madam," he lifted his cap again, "little would give me
greater pleasure, but duty recalls me to Eddy's side,
I fear."

"Oh! Well, then, tell Mr. Eddy I'm that grateful
for the money and I'll buy a proper bonnet before
we meet again."

Maybrick reined in his seething frustration and
disappointment with barely restrained violence. He
gripped the wicked new knife inside his pocket until
his whole hand ached. He wanted to strike *now,* curse
it! But he had to wait until the tart found Lachley's
letters, had hours to wait, yet. *I will rip her apart,*
he thought savagely, *rip her wide open and let the
rain wash the filth from the bleeding womb she sells
so freely . . .*

Lachley gave her a courteous bow she did not
merit and left her walking down Whitechapel Road.
Maybrick's clever mentor had carefully instructed him
in the exact method he must use to murder this bitch,
to keep the blood from splashing across his clothes
when he struck. The brilliant physician and occultist had guided him to the worst of the slatterns
walking these streets—deserving targets of the monumental rage he carried against the bitch who lay with
her lover, tonight, in Liverpool. Maybrick almost loved
his mentor, in that moment, as he thought of what

delights lay ahead. As Polly wobbled drunkenly off into the night, Lachley circled around silently, sent a secretive little smile in Maybrick's direction, and followed Polly Nichols once again.

Maybrick trailed at a leisurely distance, smiling to himself, now, and caressed the handle of his concealed knife with loving fingertips. Polly Nichols, stumbling ahead of them, first visited an establishment that sold clothing of dubious origins. There she acquired a reddish brown ulster to keep off the rain, which fastened up with seven large brass buttons, and a fetching little black straw bonnet with black velvet trim and lining. She giggled as she put it on, then paraded down the wet streets to pub after pub, steadily drinking the remaining change from the silver florin.

Twice, both he and Lachley paused in dense, wet shadows while she disappeared into a secluded spot with a customer to earn three or four pence "for my doss money" she explained each time. And twice, after she had earned a few more pence, they followed along behind again as she found yet another pub in which to spend the money on gin. Well past midnight, she staggered out of the locally famous Frying Pan Public House, just one more in a long series of pubs, and found herself another customer with whom to earn another fourpence. She spent this money just as quickly as she had the rest, pouring it down her alcoholic gullet.

And so the night waned into the small hours. At nearly one-thirty in the morning, she returned to a lodging house at 18 Thrawl Street and remained inside its kitchen for several minutes, until the lodging house deputy escorted her to the door and said, "Get your doss money, ducks, an' don't come back 'til you 'ave it."

"Won't you save a bed for me?" she asked the man. "Never mind! I'll soon get my doss money. See what a jolly bonnet I've got now?" And she touched the black, velvet-lined straw hat with caressing fingers. "I've 'ad money tonight and I'll get more just as easy, I will, an' I'll be back wiv my doss money soon enough."

And so out onto the streets she wandered again, clearly searching for another customer to procure more gin to while away the time before their three-thirty appointment—presumably having retrieved the letters Lachley sought from the room she was not yet able to pay for and would not be needing, ever again. Maybrick followed her silently, as did the all-but-invisible John Lachley, a mere shadow of a shape in the darkness ahead, the paler blur of Lachley's skin lit now and again by the lightning flaring across the sky. The rumble of thunder threatened more rain. It would need rain, to wash away the blood James would spill into these streets . . .

Polly Nichols stumbled and staggered her way through the better part of an hour, approaching and being turned down by one prospect after another, leading James and his mentor eventually toward the corner of Whitechapel Road and Osborn Street. There, she put out a hand to brace herself and greeted a woman coming up Osborn. "Well, if it in't Emily 'olland," she slurred, "where you been?"

Emily Holland was a woman considerably older than Polly Nichols, closer to Maybrick's own age, he suspected, although she looked considerably older than Maybrick's fifty years. Emily greeted the drunken prostitute with considerable surprise. "Polly? I didn't expect to find you at this hour! Whatever are you doing wandering around so late? Me, I've been down to Shadwell Dry Dock. To see the fire." Emily gestured toward the distant docks, where the sky glowed a sullen red from the dockside disaster. It was the second fire that night which had reddened the clouds scudding so low above Whitechapel's broken and dilapidated rooftops. "What are you doing out at this hour, Polly? I thought you were coming back down to Flower and Dean Street, with Annie and Elizabeth and me. You were at the White House with us last night."

"'At's right," Polly nodded, slurring the words. "But I've got to get me doss money, yet. Bastard wouldn't let me stay 'til I've got it."

"Polly, it's two-thirty in the morning!" Almost as an echo, a nearby church clock struck the time. "Hear that? Why don't you have your doss money by now?"

"Oh, I *'ad* it. Three times today, I've 'ad it." She touched her pretty new bonnet in an absent little gesture. But she didn't explain about the florin and the letters, which was just as well, since that would have required Maybrick to murder this new trollop, Holland, also. Lachley had made it clear that none of these filthy whores must be allowed to know about such important letters. Truly, Maybrick was doing all England a great service, ridding the streets of the kind of filth Polly Nichols represented.

Polly was saying in a deeply slurred voice, "Three times, Emily, I've 'ad me doss money, but I've drunk it all. Every las' penny of it. Three times. Never you fret, though. I'll 'ave my doss money before long, I will, and I'll be back wiv you and the girls." She patted her pocket and let out a drunken giggle. "Won't be long at all, now."

Whereupon Polly took her leave of Emily Holland and staggered away on a new course, down Osborn Street in the direction of the Shadwell dock fire, where she might presumably find paying customers in abundance. The other woman called a low-voiced "Good night!" after her and watched Polly for a moment longer, shaking her head sadly, then shrugged and pulled her shawl more tightly about her shoulders and continued on her way, down Osborn Street in the opposite direction. James Maybrick waited impatiently until Emily Holland had disappeared into the wet night before moving down Whitechapel Road in pursuit, once more. John Lachley also broke from hiding.

Polly's voice, badly slurred, drifted back to Maybrick. "Be nice, 'aving an 'ot fire to warm me cold fingers by." She laughed drunkenly and reached the edge of the crowd which had gathered at Shadwell to watch the docks burn. Utter chaos reigned. Firemen swept continuous streams of water back and forth across the blazing dry dock and several doomed warehouses. Fire boats in the river added their drenching spray, trying to contain the inferno before it spread to any other warehouses with valuable contents.

More than two centuries might have passed since the Great Fire, but London had never forgotten the devastation which had destroyed all but one tiny corner of Britain's capital city. The only good to come of *that* fire, which had forced thousands to flee, only to watch their homes and livelihoods burn to ashes, had been the complete eradication of the Black Death. Afterwards, plague had never broken out in London again.

Not a plague of *that* sort, in any case. A plague of whores and prostitutes and bitches, however, had swelled to number in the thousands. Tonight, Maybrick would begin his campaign to eradicate this latest deadly plague to strike the greatest city in the greatest Empire on the earth. He smiled, marshaled his patience, and kept watch on Polly Nichols as she trolled for customers.

Despite the late hour, thousands of spectators jammed the narrow streets to watch this latest London fire. The electric thrill of danger was a tangible presence in the wet night. Maybrick hung well back, as did Lachley, losing sight of the drunken Polly Nichols in the crowd. The atmosphere in Shadwell was a carnival madness. Alcohol flowed in prodigious quantities. Maybrick, seething like the jagged lightning overhead, downed pint after pint of dark ale, himself, feeding his rage, nursing the hunger in his soul. John Lachley, too, had vanished through the crowd, leaving Maybrick to wait. He wanted to shout obscenities, he was so weary of walking and endlessly *waiting*. He gripped the handle of his knife so tightly he was sure there would be bruises across his palm by morning.

Nearly an hour later, with the fire still blazing furiously, Maybrick finally caught another glimpse of Polly Nichols' black, velvet-trimmed bonnet. She was just emerging through the door of a jam-packed public house which had thrown open its doors in all defiance of the closing-hour laws. She staggered mightily under the influence of God-only-knew how much more alcohol. She passed Maybrick without even seeing him, stumbled straight past a doorway from which John Lachley subsequently emerged, and headed down Osborn Street toward Whitechapel Road.

It was time for her to keep her rendezvous with murder.

The game was in Maybrick's blood, now, the stop and start of shadowing his prey down wet streets with the growl of thunder snarling overhead like a savage beast loose in the night. They waited, strolling quietly along, until they were well away from the crowd at the fire. Polly reached the now-deserted Whitechapel Road and turned east, moving unsteadily toward the spot they'd agreed to meet. John Lachley started out into the open, making his move to retrieve the letters. Then halted abruptly. So did Maybrick, cursing their foul luck. A rough man dressed like a dockhand, also coming from the direction of the Shadwell Dry Dock fire, had appeared at the end of the block and accosted her first.

Maybrick and his mentor melted back into the

shadows of dark overhanging doorways, on opposite sides of the narrow street. The dockhand and the drunken whore bent their heads together and spoke quietly. A low laugh broke from the man and Maybrick heard Polly say, "Yes." A moment later, the two of them sought deeper shadows, so close to James Maybrick's hiding place, he could literally *smell* them from where he stood.

Maybrick's pulse flared like the lightning overhead as he stood there in the darkness, listening to the rustle of skirts and clothing hastily switched about, the sharp sounds of the dockhand shifting his hobnailed boots on the pavement as he pressed the cheap trollop back into a convenient corner, the heavy breaths and meaty sounds of flesh coming together, slow and rhythmic and hard. Maybrick's nostrils flared. He gripped the wooden handle of his knife, listened eagerly to the gasp of breath as the whore ground her hips against her customer's. He could all but see the clutch of the dock worker's hands against a straining breast, a naked thigh, skirts and petticoats lifted high to either side to accommodate him. He imagined his wife's face where the strumpet's was, saw his wife's glorious, strawberry blond hair falling down across her naked breasts as the unwashed dockhand shoved into her, took her right here on the street like the slut she was, heard his wife's voice gasping in the close darkness . . .

Low, breathy obscenities drifted on the night air, his voice, then hers, encouraging him. *Hurry,* she must be thinking, *hurry up and finish, I'm drunk and need a bed for the night and they'll be along with the money for the letters soon, so get on with it and spend your spunk, you great ugly lout of a dockhand . . .*

Maybrick clutched his knife, hand thrust deep in his pocket, and breathed hard as she whispered to the man using her. "'At's right, lovey, 'at's good, Friar me right good, you do, 'at's grand . . ."

Friar Tuck . . . the rhyming slang of the streets . . .

A low, masculine grunt finally drifted past Maybrick's hiding place.

He waited for their breaths to slow from the frantic rush.

Waited for the sounds of clothing going back down, the jingle of coins in a pocket, the whisper of, "'Ere's three-pence, pet, and a shiny penny besides." The sound of a wet kiss came, followed by the muffled smack of a hand against a cloth-covered backside. "An' a right nice trembler it was, too."

Maybrick waited, pulse pounding like the thunder overhead, as the dockhand's hobnailed boots clattered away down the pavement in the direction of the docks and the still-burning fire. As his footfalls died away, Polly's low, slurred voice drifted to Maybrick. "Eh, then, got my doss money, just like I told Emily I would. I've 'ad a lovely new bonnet tonight and a warm new ulster and thirty-eleven pints and still got my doss money. And there's still the money for the letters to collect, too!" A low laugh reached Maybrick's hiding place.

He waited in a fever of impatience while she staggered out into the open again, heading down Whitechapel Road with the money she'd just earned in her pocket. Across the street, Lachley, silent on the rubberized overshoes they'd both bought, the same shoes worn by several million ordinary domestic servants to silence their footfalls, stole after her down Whitechapel Road. They crept up behind . . .

"Hello, love," Lachley whispered.

She gave a tiny, indrawn shriek and whirled, with semi-disastrous results.

Lachley steadied the small woman easily. "There, now, I didn't mean to terrify you. Steady."

She peered up at him, face pinched from the shock. "Oh, it's you," she breathed out, "you give me such a fright!" She smiled happily, then, and touched her bonnet. "See? I got me that bonnet, just like you said. Innit a fine one?"

"Very fine. Very becoming. Velvet-trim, isn't it? A lovely bonnet. I trust you have the letters we discussed earlier?"

A crafty smile stole across the woman's face. "I've got one of 'em, so I 'ave."

Only Maybrick saw the flicker of murderous wrath cross Lachley's face. Then he was smiling down at her again. "*One* of them? But, my dear, there were four! Mr. Eddy really is most anxious to obtain the full set."

"Course 'e is, an' I don't blame 'im none, I don't, but y'see, I only 'ad the one letter. An' I've looked for my friend, looked an' looked everywhere, what 'as the other three—"

"Friend?" Lachley's voice came to Maybrick as a flat, blank sound of astonishment. "*Friend?*"

The stupid whore didn't even notice the cold rage in her murderer's voice.

"I 'adn't so much as a single 'apenny to me name and it were ever so cold an' raining ever so 'ard. An' I 'adn't drunk no gin in an whole day, y'see, so I give three of the letters to Annie an' she give me a shilling, so I could pay for a doss 'ouse an' not be caught by some constable sleepin' rough and get sent back to Lambeth Work'ouse. She's only 'olding 'em for me, like, 'til I get the shilling back to repay 'er the loan . . ."

Lachley touched her gently, tipping up her chin. "Who is this friend, Polly? What is her name?"

"Annie. I said that, Annie Chapman, what lives in the doss 'ouses over to Flower and Dean Street, same as me. She's 'oldin' the other three letters for me, but I'll 'ave 'em back by tomorrow morning, swear I will."

"Of course you will." Lachley was smiling again.

Maybrick's hand was sweaty where he gripped his knife.

Polly blinked anxiously up into Lachley's face. "Say, you finish up your business with Mr. Eddy for the night?" She leaned against Lachley, still reeking of the dockworker's sweat. "Maybe we could go someplace b'fore I go back to me doss 'ouse an' find Annie?"

"No, my business tonight is not quite finished," Lachley said with fine irony. Maybrick admired the man more and more. He gestured Maybrick forward with a motion of his head. "But I've a friend here with me who has a little time in hand."

Polly turned, so drunk on the gin she'd guzzled that Lachley had to keep her from falling. "Well, then, 'ello, luv."

"Good evening, ma'am." Maybrick tipped his hat.

"Polly," John Lachley said with a faint smile, "this is James. He is a dear friend of mine. James will take care of you this evening. Now. Here is the money for the letter you have with you." Lachley held out a palmful of glittering sovereigns.

Polly gasped. Then fumbled through her pocket and produced a crumpled letter.

Lachley took it gently from her, swept his gaze across what had been written on the grubby sheets of foolscap, and put the money in her hand, then glanced up at Maybrick with a quirk of his lips. Polly wouldn't be keeping her money long.

"There, now. First payment, in good faith. Payment in full very soon. Shall Mr. James, here, escort you someplace quiet?"

Polly smiled up at Maybrick in turn and moved her hand downward along the shapeless workmen's trousers he wore. "Grand."

Maybrick's breaths came faster. He smiled down into her eyes, pulse beating a savage rhythm at his temples. He said to his whore, "This way, my dear."

They had timed the rounds of the constables of

the H Division all through this area, he and Lachley. Maybrick knew very well that the next few minutes would provide him with exactly the opportunity he needed. Lachley doffed his cap and bid Polly good-night and disappeared down Whitechapel Road at a brisk walk, whistling merrily to himself. James knew, of course, that his mentor would circle around to Buck's Row by way of quiet little Baker's Row and meet him again soon . . . very soon.

Maybrick took Polly's arm and gave her a brilliant smile, then guided her off the main road, down Thomas Street, a narrow bridge road which led across the rail line of the London and Northern Railway, twenty feet below. Beyond the railway line lay the exceedingly narrow street known as Buck's Row, lined by high brick warehouses, a board school, and several terrace houses, which served as cottages for the tradesmen who worked in Schneiders Cap Factory and several high, dark warehouses: the Eagle Wool Warehouse, which supplied fabric for the cap factory, and the massive warehouse called Essex Wharf.

James knew Schneider of old, a dirty little foreigner, which in this dismal region meant only one thing: Jew. James had chosen his killing ground carefully, most carefully, indeed. It was the filthy foreigners flooding into London who were destroying the moral fibre of the English Empire, bringing in their foreign ways and unholy religious practices and speaking every tongue heard at the Tower of Babel except the Queen's good English. Yes, James had chosen this spot with great care, to leave a message on the very doorstep of the bastards destroying all that was English.

The place he wanted was an old stableyard which stood between the school and the workers' cottages. The only street lamp was at the far end of Buck's Row, where it met Baker's Row to the west. As they entered the cramped, cobbled street, which was no

more than twenty feet wide from housewalls on the
one hand to warehouse walls opposite, Maybrick
slipped his right hand into his coat pocket again. He
closed his hand around the handle of the beautiful,
shining knife and gripped it tightly. His pulse raced.
His breath came in short, unsteady gasps. The smell
of cheap gin and sex and greed was a poison in his
brain. Her whispered obscenities to the dockworker
rang in his ears. His hand sweat against the wood.
Here, his mind shrieked. *Quick, before the bloody
constables come back!* He drew another breath, seeing
in his mind his beautiful, faithless wife, naked and
writhing under the lover who impaled her in that
hotel he'd seen them coming out of together, the one
in Liverpool's fashionable Whitechapel Street.

Maybrick glanced toward Baker's Row. Saw Lachley
appear from the blackness at the end of Buck's Row.
Saw him nod, giving the signal that all was clear.
Maybrick's breath whipsawed, harsh and urgent. He
tightened his left hand on the whore's arm. Moving
her almost gently, Maybrick pressed her back against
the stableyard gate. It was solid as iron. She smiled
up at him, fumbling with her skirts. He slid his hand
up her arm, toyed with a breast, slipped his fingers
upwards, toward her neck—

Then smashed a fist into her face.

Bone crunched. Several of her teeth broke loose.
She sagged back against the fence, stunned motionless. Maybrick tightened a savage grip around her
throat. Her eyes bulged. Her abruptly toothless mouth
worked. Shock and terror twisted across her once-
delicate face. High cheekbones flushed dark as he cut
off her air. His wife's face swam before his eyes,
gaping and toothless and terror stricken. He dug his
thumb into dear, faithless Florie's jaw, bruising the
right side of her face. The bitch struggled feebly as
he tightened down. He dented and bruised the flesh
of her throat, the left side of her face with his fingers,

ruthless and drunk with the terror he inflicted. *She* was so drunk, she wasn't able to do more than claw weakly at his coat sleeve with one hand.

James Maybrick smiled down into his whore's dying eyes . . .

. . . and brought out his shining knife.

Skeeter Jackson pushed his heavy maintenance cart toward the men's room in Little Agora, bottles rattling and mops threatening to crash against the protestors who screamed and carried signs and picketed fifteen feet deep around Ianira's vacant booth, threatening to shut down commerce with their disruptive presence and threatening to shut down the station with the violence that broke out between them and the Arabian Nights construction workers at least once every couple of hours.

Nuts, he groused, maneuvering with difficulty through the packed crowd, *we are neck deep in nutcases.* He finally gained the bathroom, which he was already fifteen minutes overdue to scrub, slowed down on his schedule by the crowds of protestors and uneasy tourists, and turned on the hot water to fill his mop bucket. He'd just added soap when the trouble broke loose.

A sudden scuffle and a meaty smack and thump shook the whole bank of stalls behind him. Skeeter came around fast, mop gripped in both hands like a quarterstaff. A pained cry, high-pitched and frightened, accompanied another thud and violent slap. Then a stall door burst open and a burly guy with Middle Eastern features, who wore jeans and a work shirt and a burnoose-style headdress, strode out. He looked smug and self-satisfied. He was still zipping his fly. A muffled, startlingly feminine sob came from the now-open stall.

Skeeter narrowed his eyes at the construction worker, who wore a wicked linoleum knife in a sheathe on his belt. These creeps had been involved in the attacks on Ianira and her family. He was convinced they might yet know where she was, despite their protests of innocence to station security. They were trouble, wherever they went on station and it looked very much like more trouble was breaking loose right in front of him.

"You want to tell me what that was all about?" Skeeter asked quietly, placing himself carefully between the heavily muscled worker and the exit.

The dark-eyed man smirked down at Skeeter, measuring his shorter height and lighter frame contemptuously. "Little girls should not demand more money than they are worth."

"Is that a fact?" Skeeter balanced lightly on the balls of his feet, aware that he played a potentially lethal game. These guys carried tools that doubled as deadly weapons. But he wasn't going to let this creep just walk out of here, not with somebody back there crying in that stall like a hurt child. "Hey, you okay in there?" he called out to the pair of grubby tennis shoes visible under the partially open door. "I'll call the station infirmary if you need help."

"S-Skeeter?" The voice was familiar, quavering, terrified.

When the voice clicked in Skeeter's memory, the anger that burst through him was as cold and deadly as the winter winds howling down off the mountains onto the plains of the Gobi. "*Bergitta?*" The girl huddled in the back of the stall was younger than Skeeter. She'd helped search for Ianira, that first terrible day, had searched along with the other downtimers long after station security had given up the job. The Found Ones had been teaching her modern technical skills so she could make a living doing something besides selling herself.

"Skeeter, please . . . he . . . he will hurt you . . ."

Skeeter had no intention of abandoning a member

of his adopted down-timer family to the likes of this smirking lout. "How much did he agree to give you, Bergitta?" he asked, carefully keeping his gaze on the construction worker who now eyed him narrowly.

"T-twenty—but it is okay, please . . ."

Skeeter gave the angry construction worker a disgusted glare. "*Twenty?* Geez, last of the big spenders, aren't we? You can't hardly buy a *burger* around here for that. Listen, asshole, you pay my friend, there, what you promised and get the hell out of here, maybe I won't get nasty."

Incredulous black eyes widened. "*Pay* her?" His laugh was ugly, contemptuous. "Out of my way, you stupid little cockerel!"

Skeeter stood his ground. The other man's eyes slitted angrily. Then the construction worker started forward, moving fast, one fist cocked, the other reaching for his belt. Skeeter caught a glint of light off that wicked linoleum knife—

He whirled the mop handle in a blurred, sweeping arc.

It connected solidly with a solar plexus that came to an abrupt halt.

A sharp, ugly grunt tore loose. The knife clattered to the tiled floor. The would-be knife-fighter folded up around the end of Skeeter's mop, eyes bugged out. Skeeter kicked the knife away with one foot. It clattered across the floor and skidded into a puddle under a distant urinal, then Skeeter assisted the gagging construction worker face-first into the steaming mop bucket at his feet. He landed with a *skloosh!* While he was upended, Skeeter lifted his wallet with light-fingered skill and extracted its contents. Curses gurgling underwater blew the most interesting soap bubbles Skeeter had ever seen.

As soon as he'd secured Bergitta's money, Skeeter hauled the former customer up by the shirt collar.

"Now," he said gently, "you want to tell me about Ianira Cassondra?"

The reply was in Arabic and doubtless obscene. Skeeter fed him more soap bubbles.

By the fourth dunking, the man was swearing he'd never laid eyes on Ianira Cassondra and would've strewn petals at her feet, if it would've helped keep his head above water. Reluctantly, Skeeter decided the bastard must be telling the truth. He shoved the guy's wallet between soapy teeth and said, "Twenty for services rendered and the rest for damages wrought. Now get the hell out of here before I break ribs. Or call security."

One twist of the mop handle and the dripping construction worker found it necessary to launch himself across the tiled floor, out the doorway, and past the "Slippery When Wet" sign just beyond. From the startled shrieks and angry shouts outside, he cannoned straight into a group of protestors. A moment later, security whistles sounded and a woman's voice drifted in, shrill with indignation. "He knocked me down! Yes, he ran that way . . ."

Skeeter crossed the bathroom, flexing a slightly strained shoulder, and peered into the open stall. Bergitta had clutched one side of her face, which was already swollen and turning purple. The simple dress she wore was torn. Anger started a slow burn as he gazed down at his terrified friend. "Are you okay?" he asked gently.

She nodded. Then burst into tears and slid to the tiled floor, trembling so violently he could hear the scrape of her identification bracelet—a gift from the Found Ones—against the wall. Skeeter bit his lip. Then sighed and waded in to try and pick up the shattered pieces. He crouched beside her, gently brushed back Bergitta's hair, a glorious, platinum blond, thick and shining where the lights overhead touched it.

"Shh," he whispered, "he's gone now. You're safe, shh . . ." When she'd stopped crying, he said gently, "Bergitta, let's take you down to the infirmary."

She shook her head. "No, Skeeter, there is no money . . ."

Skeeter held out the cash he'd liberated. "Yes, there is. And I've got some money put aside, too, so don't you worry about that, okay?" He'd been saving that cash for his rent, but what the hell, he could always sleep in the Found Ones' council chamber down in the station's sub-basement until he could afford to rent another apartment.

Bergitta was crying again, very quietly and very messily down her bruised face. Skeeter retrieved a towel from his push cart and dried her cheeks, then helped her to her feet. When she wobbled, shaking violently, Skeeter simply picked her up and carried her. She clung to his shoulders and hid her face from the curious onlookers they passed. When he carried her into the infirmary, Rachel Eisenstein was just stepping out of her office.

"Skeeter! What's happened? Not another riot?" she asked worriedly.

"No. Some asshole construction worker blacked Bergitta's face and God knows what else before I interrupted. Tried to disembowel me with a linoleum knife when I protested."

Rachel's lips thinned. "Bring her into the back, Skeeter, let's see how badly hurt she is. And we'd better file an official complaint with security. The more complaints we log, the more likely Bull is to push the issue and toss the men responsible for all this trouble through Primary, schedule or no schedule. Kit's already been after Bull to do just that."

So Rachel took charge of Bergitta, and Skeeter found himself giving a statement to security. He identified the man from a file of employment photos. "That's him. Yeah, the creep came at me with a linoleum knife."

"You realize we can't press charges for what he did to Bergitta?" the security officer said as he jotted down notes. "She's a down-timer. No legal rights."

"Yeah," Skeeter muttered darkly, "I know." They'd search for Ianira Cassondra, move heaven and earth to find her, because of the Templars and the phenomenal popularity and power of the Lady of Heaven Temples, but Bergitta was just another down-timer without rights, trapped on the station with no way off and no protection from the people who ran her new world. Worse, she was a known prostitute. Security didn't give a damn when a girl like Bergitta got hurt.

The guard said, "If *you* want this creep charged with assault and battery with a deadly weapon, plus anything else I can think up, you got it, but that's all we can nail him for, Skeeter."

"Yes, I want him charged," Skeeter growled. "And tossed off station, if you can swing it. Along with his pals."

"Don't hold your breath. That crew's already running behind schedule and the first tour's slated for next month. We might be able to work out a trial up time after the new section of Commons is finished, but getting him tossed off station before that job's done is flogging a dead horse. Not my idea, but that's how it is. Just figured you'd want to know up front."

Skeeter muttered under his breath. "Thanks. I know you're doing your best."

Rachel put in appearance just then, returning from the exam room where Bergitta rested. "She's badly shaken up and her face is going to be sore for a while, along with some other nasty bruises he left, but she's basically all right. No internal hemorrhaging, no broken bones."

Skeeter relaxed marginally. "Thank God."

Rachel eyed him curiously. "You fought a man with a knife, protecting her?"

Skeeter shrugged. "Wasn't much of a contest, really. I had a mop, he never got close to me with it."

"Well, whatever you think, it was still a risky thing to do, Skeeter."

He realized she was trying to thank him. Skeeter felt his cheeks burn. "Listen, about the bill, I've got some money—"

"We'll talk about that later, all right? Oh-oh . . ."

Skeeter glanced around and blanched.

His boss was in-bound and the head of station maintenance did not look happy.

"Is it true?" Charlie Ryan demanded.

"Is what true?" Skeeter asked, wary and on his guard.

"That you beat up a construction worker over a goddamned down-timer whore? Then brought her up here while you're still clocked in officially on my dime?"

Skeeter clenched his fists. "Yes, it's true! He was beating the shit out of her—"

"I don't pay you to rescue your down-timer pals, Jackson! I looked the other way when it was Ianira Cassondra, but this by God tears it! And I sure as hell don't pay you to put hard-working construction professionals in the brig!"

Rachel tried to intervene. "Charlie, everyone on station's had trouble with those guys and you know it."

"Stay out of this, Rachel! Jackson, I pay you to mop bathrooms. Right now, there's a bathroom in Little Agora that's not getting mopped."

"I'll clean the stinking bathroom!" Skeeter growled.

Charlie Ryan look him up and down. "No, you won't. You're fired, Jackson."

"Charlie—" Rachel protested.

"Let it go, Rachel," Skeeter bit out. "If I'd known I was working for a stinking bigot, I'd've quit weeks ago."

He stalked out of the infirmary and let the crowds on Commons swallow him up.

What he was going to do now, he honestly did not know.

He walked aimlessly for ages, hands thrust deep into his pockets, watching the tourists practice walking in their rented costumes and laughing at one another's antics and buying each other expensive lunches and souvenirs, and wondered if any of them had the slightest notion what it was like for the down-time populations stranded on these stations?

He was sitting on the marble edging of a fountain in Victoria Station, head literally in hands, when Kynan Rhys Gower appeared from out of the crowd, expression grim. "Skeeter, we have trouble."

He glanced up, startled to hear the Welshman's voice. "Trouble? Oh, man, *now* what?"

"It is Julius," Kynan said quietly. "He is missing."

Skeeter just shut his eyes for a long moment. "Oh, no . . ." Not another friend, missing. The teenager from Rome had organized the down-timer kids into a sort of club known affectionately as the Lost and Found Gang. Under Ianira's guidance, the "gang" had turned its attention to earning money guiding lost tourists back to their hotel rooms, serving as the Found Ones' eyes and ears in places where adults would have roused suspicion, running errands and proving their value time and again. The children's work had allowed the Found Ones to learn rather a good bit more about the cults active on station than Mike Benson or anyone in security had managed to discover.

"How long has he been missing?" Skeeter asked tiredly.

"We are not sure," Kynan sighed. "No one has seen him since . . ." The Welshman hesitated. "He was supposed to be running an errand for the Found Ones, just before the riot broke out, the one Inaira disappeared in. No one has seen him, since."

"Oh, God. What's going on around this station?"

Kynan clenched his fists in visible frustration. "I do not know! But if I find out, Skeeter, I will take apart whoever is responsible!"

Of that, Skeeter had no doubt whatsoever. Skeeter intended to help. "Okay, we've got to get another search organized. For Julius, this time."

"The Lost and Found Gang are already searching."

"I want them to get as close to those creeps on the Arabian Nights construction crew as they can. And those crazy Jack the Ripper cults, too. *Any* group of nuts on this station who might have a reason to want Ianira to disappear, to stir up trouble, is on the suspect list."

Kynan nodded. "I will get word to the children. They are angry, Skeeter, and afraid."

"Huh. So am I, Kynan Rhys Gower. So am I."

The Welshman nodded slowly. "Yes. A brave man is one who admits his fear. Only a fool believes himself invincible. The Council of Seven has called an emergency meeting. *Another* one."

"That's no surprise. What time?"

"An hour from now."

Skeeter nodded. At least he wouldn't have to worry about losing his job, sneaking off to attend it. Kynan Rhys Gower hesitated. "I have heard what happened, Skeeter. Bergitta is all right?"

"Yeah. Bruised, scared. But Rachel said she's okay."

"Good." The one-time longbow-man's jaw muscles bunched. "Charlie Ryan is a pig. He hires us because he does not have to pay, what is the up-time word? Union wages."

"Yeah. Tell me about it."

"Skeeter . . ."

He glanced up at the ominous growl in the other man's voice.

"Accidents happen."

"No." Skeeter shoved himself to his feet, looked

the Welshman straight in the eyes. "No, it's his right to fire me. And I *was* doing a lousy job, spending all my time looking for Ianira and Marcus instead of working. I happen to think he's got his priorities screwed up, but I won't hear of anything like that. I appreciate it, but it'd just be a waste of effort. Guys like Charlie Ryan are like mushrooms. Squash one, five more pop up. Besides, if anybody's going to loosen his teeth, it's gonna be me, okay?"

Kynan Rhys Gower clearly considered arguing, then let it go. "That is your right," he said quietly. "But you have earned more this day than you have lost."

Skeeter didn't know what to say.

"I will see you at the Council meeting," the Welshman told him quietly, then left him standing in the glare and noise of Commons, wondering why his eyes stung so harshly. "I'll be there," Skeeter swore to empty air.

How many more of his friends would simply vanish into thin air before this ugly business was done? What had Julius seen or overheard, to cause someone to snatch him, too? When Skeeter got his hands on whoever was responsible for this . . . That someone would learn what it meant to suffer the summary justice of a Yakka Mongol clansman. Meanwhile, he had another friend missing.

Skeeter had far too few friends to risk losing any more of them.

Margo craned forward, so excited and repelled at the same time, she felt queasy. Then she saw the face and gasped as she recognized him. "*James Maybrick!*" she cried. "It's James Maybrick! The cotton merchant from Liverpool!"

"Shh!" The scholars motioned frantically for silence, trying to hear anything the murderer and his victim might say, even though everything was being recorded, including Polly Nichols' final footfalls. Margo gulped back nausea, watched in rising horror as Maybrick escorted his victim down to the gate where he would strangle and butcher her. When he struck with his fist, Margo hid her face in her hands, unable to watch. The sounds were bad enough . . .

Then Conroy Melvyn burst out, "Who the bloody hell is *that*?"

Margo jerked her gaze up to the television screen . . . and found herself staring, right along with the rest of the shocked Ripper Watch Team. A man had crept up behind Jack the Ripper, who was still hacking away at his dead victim.

"James . . . enough." Just the barest thread of a whisper. Then, when Maybrick continued to hack at the dead woman's neck, as though trying to cut loose her entire head, *"She's dead, James. Enough!"*

Whoever this man was, he clearly knew James Maybrick. More importantly, Maybrick clearly knew *him.* The maniacal rage in Maybrick's eyes faded as he glanced around. Maybrick's lips worked wetly. "But I wanted the head . . ." Plaintive, utterly mad.

"There's no time. Fetch me the money from her pockets. Be quick about it, the constable will be arriving momentarily."

The Buck's Row cameras, fitted with low-light equipment, picked up the lean, saturnine face, the drooping mustaches of a total stranger who stepped up to peer at Polly Nichols. As Maybrick stooped to crouch over the dead woman, the newcomer closed a hand around Jack the Ripper's shoulder, a casual gesture which revealed a depth of meaning to anyone who knew the stiff etiquette of Victorian Britain. These men knew each other well enough for casual familiarities. Maybrick was wiping his knife on Polly's underskirts.

"Very good, James. You've done well. Strangled her first, as instructed. Not more than a wineglass of blood. Very good." Voice pitched to a low whisper,

the tones and words were clearly those of an educated man, but with hints of the East End in the
vowels, hints even Margo's untrained ear could pick
out. Then, more sharply, "The money, James!"

"Yes, doctor!" Maybrick's voice, thick with sexual
ecstasy, trembled in the audio pickup. The arsenic-
addicted cotton merchant from Liverpool bent over
the prone remains of his victim and searched her
pockets, retrieving several large coins that glinted gold
like sovereigns. "No other letters, doctor," he whispered.

"Letters?" Pavel Kostenka muttered, leaning closer
to the television monitor to stare at the stranger's face.
"What letters? And Dr. *Who?*"

Across the room, the British police inspector Conroy
Melvyn choked with sudden, silent laughter for some
completely unfathomable reason. Margo resolved to
ask him what he could possibly find funny, once this
macabre little meeting in Bucks Row had ended.

On the video monitor, the stranger muttered impatiently, "No, of course there won't be any other letters. She said she'd sold them, drunken bitch, and
I believed her when she said it. Come, James, the
H Division Constables will be along momentarily.
Wipe your shoes clean, they're bloody. Then come
with me. You've done well, James, but we have to
hurry."

Maybrick straightened up. "I want my medicine,"
he said urgently.

"Yes, I'll be sure and give you more of the medicine you need, before you catch your train for home.
After we've reached Tibor."

Maybrick's eyes glittered in the low-light pickup.
He gripped the other man's arm. "*Thank you,* doctor! Ripping the bitch like that . . . she opened like
a ripe peach . . . so bloody wonderful . . ."

"Yes, yes," the narrow-faced man said impatiently.
"You can write it all down in your precious diary.

Later. Now, you must come with me, we haven't much time. This way . . ."

The two men moved away from the camera's lens, walking quickly but not so fast as to arouse suspicion should anyone happen to glance out a window. The crumpled body of Polly Nichols lay beside the gate where she'd died, her disarranged skirts hiding the ghastly mutilations Maybrick's knife had inflicted. Margo stared after the two men who—clearly—were conspirators in some hideous game that involved unknown letters, payments made to prostitutes, and murder. The game made no rational sense to Margo, any more than it did to the openly stunned Ripper scholars. Who was this mysterious doctor and why was Maybrick involved with him? And why hadn't Maybrick's diary even once hinted at such a turn of events? That diary, explicit as to detail, with its open, candid mention of the many people in Maybrick's life—his unfaithful American wife, their young children and the little American girl staying with the Maybrick family, his brothers, employees, murder victims, friends—that diary had never even once hinted at a co-conspirator in the murder of the five Whitechapel prostitutes Maybrick had taken credit for killing.

Who, then, was this dark-skinned, foreign-looking man? A man who, Margo realized abruptly, fit perfectly some of the Ripper eyewitness descriptions. And Maybrick, with his fair skin and light hair and thick gold watch chain, fit other eyewitness descriptions to the last detail. The many witnesses questioned by London police had described two very different-appearing men—for the perfectly simple reason that there'd been *two* killers. "The eyewitness accounts," Margo gasped, "no wonder they differed, yet were so consistent. There *were* two of them! A dark-haired, foreign-looking man *and* a fair-haired one. And Israel Schwartz, the Jewish merchant who'll see Elizabeth Stride attacked, he saw *both* of them! Working together!"

She grew aware of startled stares from the Ripper Watch scholars. Shahdi Feroz, in particular, was frowning; but not, Margo sensed, in disapproval. She looked merely thoughtful. "Yes," Dr. Feroz nodded, "that would certainly account for much of the confusion. It is not so unheard of, after all."

Margo gulped. "What's not so unheard of?"

Shahdi Feroz glanced up again. "Hmm? Oh. It is not unheard of, this collusion between psychopaths. A weaker psychopathic serial killer will sometimes attach himself to a mentor, a personal god, if you will. He worships the more powerful killer, does his bidding, learns from him." She was frowning, dark eyes agitated. "This is very unexpected, very serious. It is, indeed, possible that more of the murders during this time period *should* be attributed to the Ripper, if the Ripper was, in fact, *two* men. Two very disturbed men, working as a team, master and worshiper. They might well have struck in different *modus operandi*, which would explain the confusion over which women were killed by the Ripper."

"Yes," Inspector Melvyn broke in, "but what about these letters? What letters? And just who *is* this bloke? Doesn't fit any of the known profiles. Not a bloody, damned one of 'em!"

Dr. Kostenka shook his head, however. "Not one of the named profiles, no; but a profile, yes. He is a doctor. A man with medical knowledge. It is this doctor, clearly, who warned James Maybrick to strangle his victims first, to avoid drenching his clothing with blood from arterial spurts. If Maybrick's victim had been alive when he slashed her neck and throat, he would have ended covered in the 'red stuff' of which he writes in his diary."

The passages to which Kostenka referred had been labeled as damning Americanisms, which had caused some experts to call the diary a hoax. Of course, Maybrick had lived for years in Norfolk, Virginia and married an American girl, so he would've been intimately familiar with American slang from the late Victorian period. Sometimes, so-called experts could be as blind as an eyeless cave shrimp.

Kostenka was frowning thoughtfully at the TV monitor. "Whoever he is, the man is foreign-looking and of genteel appearance, just as the witnesses described. A man of education."

Margo heard herself say, "And he's spent time in the East End. You can hear it in his voice."

Once again, she was the abrupt focus of startled stares from the Ripper Watch experts. Then Guy Pendergast grinned. "She's right, y'know, Melvyn. Rerun the tape. Heard it, meself. Just didn't twig to it quite so fast. Used to hearing that sound, hear it every day, just about, on a job."

Shahdi Feroz was nodding. "Yes, whereas Miss Smith has needed to listen very carefully to East End accents, to pick up the vowel sounds and the rhythms of the speech. Very well done, Margo."

A warm glow ignited in her middle and spread deliciously through her entire being. She smiled at the famous scholar, so proud of herself, she felt like she must be floating a couple of inches above the floor.

Dominica Nosette said abruptly, "Well, I intend to find out who our mystery doctor is! Anybody else game to give it a go?"

Guy Pendergast lunged for cameras and recorders.

"Oh, no you don't!" Margo darted squarely in front of the exit to Spaldergate House's main cellar. "I'm sorry," she said firmly, "but there will be an official police investigation getting underway in Bucks Row a few minutes from now. And no one, *not one member of this tour,* is going to be anywhere near that spot when the police arrive. We have remote cameras and

microphones in place and every second of this is being recorded."

"Listen," Guy Pendergast began, "you can't just keep us locked up in this cellar!"

"I have no intention of locking anybody in this cellar!" Margo shot back, trying to sound reasonable as well as authoritative, when she felt neither. "But there's no point in leaving Spaldergate for the East End right now. Maybrick has been positively identified. His companion has remained a mystery for nearly a hundred fifty years. We'll certainly begin working to identify him. Carefully. Discreetly. Word of this murder is going to send shockwaves through Whitechapel. Especially the mutilations, when the workhouse paupers who clean the body tomorrow finally remove Mrs. Nichols' clothing and discover them. It's been less than a month, after all, since Martha Tabram was savagely slashed to death in the East End."

"August seventh," Shahdi Feroz put in, "August Bank Holiday. And don't forget Emma Smith, stabbed to death Easter Monday. To the residents of the East End, April fourth wasn't all that long ago. Not when women are being cut to pieces and nobody feels safe walking the streets."

"Yes," Margo said forcefully. "So everyone out there will assume this is the *third* murder, not the first. We are *not* going to go charging into the East End asking, 'Say, have you seen a foreign-looking doctor hereabouts, friend of James Maybrick's?' The investigators of the day had no inkling that James Maybrick was involved, let alone this other guy, whoever he turns out to be. So we'll use extreme caution in proceeding with this investigation. Do I make myself perfectly clear on that point?"

Dominica Nosette looked petulant, but nodded. Slowly, her partner agreed, as well, grumbling and visibly irritated, but compliant. At least for the moment.

"Good. I'd suggest we analyze the tapes we've got for further clues. Inspector Melvyn, if you would rewind one of the backup copies while the master tape and other backups continue running?"

As they viewed the footage again, Shahdi Feroz pursed her lips thoughtfully. "He is familiar to me. The face is not quite right, but the voice . . . I have heard it somewhere. I would swear that I have." She shook her head, visibly impatient with her own memory. "It will come to me, I am certain. There are so many I have studied in so many different places and time, over the past few years. I spent several weeks in London, alone, looking into occult groups such as the Theosophical Society and various Druidic orders. And if he is a friend to James Maybrick, he, too, may be a Liverpudlian, not a Londoner. But I know that I have seen or heard him before. Of that, I am completely certain."

What Shahdi Feroz might or might not have remembered at that moment would never be known, however, because the telephone rang with the news that Malcolm and the search teams had returned for the night. There was no news of Benny Catlin, although from the sound of Malcolm's voice, there was something worse which he wasn't telling her. Margo narrowed her eyes and frowned at the monitors where the Ripperologists were studying their tapes. At least Benny Catlin didn't look anything like their unknown Ripper, thank God. And an American graduate student wouldn't sound like an East End Londoner, particularly not one who'd taken pains to train poverty from his voice. The notion that they were facing *two* wrenching murder mysteries, an up-time shootout *and* the Ripper slayings, left Margo deeply disturbed as she quietly left the vault to meet her fiancé in the house upstairs.

"What's wrong, Malcolm?" Margo whispered after he'd hugged her close and buried his face in her hair.

"Oh, God, Margo . . . we are in a great deal of trouble with Catlin."

She peered up into his eyes, alarmed by the exhaustion she found there. "What now?"

"The men who were killed? At the hotel and the opera? They're not down-timers, as we'd all assumed. Not Nichol gang members or any other native foot-pads."

Margo swallowed hard. "They're not?"

He shook his head. "No. The constables of the Metropolitan police asked Mr. Gilbert and me to come to the police morgue, to see if we might be able to identify either man, since Mr. Catlin had been a guest in Spaldergate for a brief time." He paused fractionally. "Margo, they're up-timers. Baggage handlers from TT-86. Gilbert recognized them, said they came through with your group, he saw them earlier in the evening hauling steamer trunks out to carriages for the newly arrived tour group. Then they vanished, abandoned a wagonload of luggage and half-a-dozen tourists at Paddington Station and went haring off on their own. The Spaldergate footman in charge of the wagon thought perhaps they were reporters who'd slipped through as baggage handlers and tried to follow, but lost them within minutes and returned to help the stranded tourists."

Margo rubbed her eyes with the heels of her hands. "I don't get it, Malcolm," she moaned softly, "why would a couple of baggage handlers ditch their jobs to chase halfway across London and try to murder a graduate student at the Picadilly Hotel?"

"And failing that, chase him all the way to the Royal Opera?" Malcolm added. "I don't know, Margo. I haven't the faintest bloody idea. It simply makes no rational sense."

"Maybe Catlin's involved somehow with organized crime?" Margo wondered with a shiver.

"God knows, it could be anything. I don't want to

think about it for a while. What's the news from the Ripper Watch?" he added quietly, drawing her closer to him and burying his lips in her hair once again.

"You're not gonna believe it," Margo muttered against his coat.

Malcolm's face, wet from the rain that had been falling again, drew down into a whole ladder of exhausted lines and gullies. "That bad?"

"Bad enough." She told him what they'd just discovered, down in the vault.

Malcolm let out a low whistle. "My God. A ruddy pair of them? And you're sure the other chap isn't Catlin?"

"Not unless he brought a plastic surgeon with him. And knows how to walk on stilts. This guy's a lot taller than Benny Catlin."

"Well, that's one breath of good news, anyway. Whatever's up with Catlin, he's not a psychopathic serial murderer."

"No," Margo said quietly. "Given what's happened on station, though, and what you just found out about the guys he killed tonight, quite frankly, I'd feel better if Catlin *had* turned out to be the Ripper."

"My dear," Malcolm sighed, "I wish it weren't so distressing when you're right."

To that, Margo said nothing at all. She simply guided her weary fiancé up to bed and did what she could to help them both forget the night's horrors.

Chapter Eleven

Kit Carson was in the back room of the Down Time Bar & Grill, doing his best to beat Goldie Morran at pool—and losing his shirt, as usual—when Robert Li appeared, dark eyes dancing with an unholy glee.

"What's up?" Kit asked warily as Goldie sank another ball in the corner pocket with a rattle like doom.

The antiquarian grinned. "Oh, goodie! You haven't heard yet!"

"Heard what?" Goldie glanced up before pocketing another fifty bucks of Kit's money. "We didn't get a riot when Primary opened, did we?"

"No," Robert allowed, eyes twinkling. "But you're not gonna believe the news from up time!"

Kit scowled. "Oh? Don't tell me. Some up-time group of nuts sent an official protest delegation to the station?"

Li's eyes glinted briefly. "As a matter of fact, they did, but not about Jack the Ripper or his victims."

Kit grunted. A vocal group calling themselves S.O.S.—Save Our Sisters—had been lobbying for the right to intervene and save the London prostitutes the Ripper would kill, despite the fact that it wasn't possible to alter important historical events. Their argument went that since these women were nobodies, the effort ought to at least be made, but Kit didn't see how, since Jack the Ripper was one of the most important murder cases in the past couple of centuries.

"Well," Kit said as Goldie lined up another shot, "if it's not the S.O.S. or some group like Jack is Lord, what is it?"

Robert grinned. "Those *Ansar Majlis* Brothers involved in the riot, the ones Mike Benson threw in the brig? Their up-time brothers have been raising holy hell. Attacks on the Lady of Heaven Temples and important Templars, riots in the streets, you name it. And a whole bunch of somebodies figured out trouble was likely to break out here, because of Ianira Cassondra. The first group through is already demanding the release of the creeps Mike Benson jailed. Seems it's a violation of their human rights to throw in jail a pack of down-time terrorists who left their home station illegally and came to another station to commit murder."

Kit just grimaced. "Why am I not surprised?" Behind him, another fifty bucks of his hard-earned cash dropped into a little round hole. He winced. "But," he added hopefully, "that's not what you came to tell us, is it?"

Li's glance was sympathetic as Goldie dropped yet another ball with a fateful clunk, into a side pocket this time. "Well, no, actually. That news is even better."

Goldie glanced up from lining up her next shot. "Oh, my. Something even better than a bunch of nuts who want to protect the non-existent rights of down-time terrorists?"

Li nodded. "Yep. Better, even, than the arrival of

an Angels of Grace Militia Squadron. First thing *they* did was pick a fight with the idiots agitating for the release of the Brothers in jail. A *big* fight. Wrecked three kiosks, a lunch stand, and the costume Connie Logan was modeling. She's suing for damages. The costume was a custom order, worth eight grand."

Kit just groaned.

Goldie muttered, "Lovely, this is all we need. What could possibly be worse than a pack of militant feminists whose sole aim in life is to ram their religion down other people's throats at the point of a bayonet?"

Li let the bombshell drop just as Goldie lined up another shot. "You remember Senator John Caddrick, don't you? That nut who outlaws everything he doesn't agree with? The one who's been agitating about the dangers to modern society from time tourism? Well, it seems the *Ansar Majlis* have kidnapped his only kid. *After* killing his sister-in-law and about sixty other people in a New York restaurant. He's threatening to shut down every time terminal in the business unless his little girl's returned to him alive and well."

Goldie's shot went wild. So wild, in fact, the five ball jumped *off* the table and smacked into the floor with a thud. Goldie's curse peeled paint off the ceiling.

"Ooh, Goldie," Robert looked about as contrite as a well-fed cat, "sorry about that, Duchess."

The hated nickname which Skeeter Jackson had given La-La Land's most infamous money changer, combined with the ruin of her game, sent Goldie into a rage so profound, she couldn't even squeeze sound past the purple-hued knot of distended veins in her throat. She just stood there glaring at the antiquities dealer, cue in hand, sputtering like a dying sparkler.

Kit threw back his head and crowed. "Robert, you are a prince among men!" He snatched up his pool cue, replaced the five ball on the felt, and calmly ran the table while Goldie stood flexing the narrow end of her pool cue until Kit feared the wood would crack. When the final ball rattled into the far corner pocket, Kit bowed, sweeping his arm around in a courtly flourish. "Goldie, thank you for a *lovely* game."

He stuck out a hand to collect his winnings.

She paid up with a seething glare and stalked stiff-legged out of the pool room, a wounded battle destroyer running under the gun for home port. Her deflated reputation trailed after her like the tail of a broken kite. Kit pocketed Goldie's money with a broad grin, then danced a jig around the pool table, whooping for sheer joy. "I did it! Damn, I finally did it! I beat Goldie at pool!"

Robert chuckled. "Congratulations. How many decades have you been waiting to do that?"

Kit refused to be baited. "Noneya, pal. Buy you a drink?"

"Sure!"

They ambled out into the main room of the bar, where an astonishing amount of money was changing hands in the aftermath of Kit's unexpected victory. Excited laughter echoed through the Down Time Bar & Grill as 'eighty-sixers celebrated, relishing the victory almost as much as Kit. La-La legend held that Goldie Morran had never lost a game of pool in the entire millennium or so she'd been on station.

As they fought their way through the crowd toward the bar, Kit had to raise his voice to be heard. "Listen, were you serious about Caddrick threatening to shut down the time terminals?"

Robert Li's smile vanished. "As a heart attack, unfortunately."

"Damn. That man is the most dangerous politician of this century. If he's declared war on us, we're all in trouble. Big trouble."

Li nodded. "Yeah, that's how I've got it figured. And the riots on station won't play in our favor, either.

We're going to look like a war zone, with the whole station out of control. Every news crew on station sent video footage up time with couriers."

Kit scowled. "Once the newsies get done with us, Caddrick won't need to shut us down. The tourists will just stay home and do it for him."

Robert Li's worried gaze matched Kit's own. They both had too much to lose, to risk letting anyone shut down Shangri-La Station. Shangri-La was Robert's life as much as it was Kit's. For one thing, they both owned priceless objects which neither could take up time, not legally, anyway. And what *was* legal to take with them, would break them financially with the taxes BATF would impose. Never mind that Shangri-La was *home*, where they had built dreams and brought something good and beautiful to life, where Kit's only grandchild was building her own dreams and trying to build something good for *herself*.

"Molly," Kit muttered, sinking into a seat at the bar, "we need a drink. Make it a double. *Two* doubles. Apiece."

The down-timer barmaid, who had come into Shangri-La Station through the Britannia Gate, gave them a sympathetic smile and poured. Despite the impromptu party roaring all around them, somehow Molly knew *they* were no longer celebrating Kit's victory over Goldie Morran. Kit watched her pour the drinks with a sinking sensation inside his middle. If the station were closed, where Molly would go? Molly and the other down-timer residents? Kit didn't know. "Those idiots demanding human rights for the *Ansar Majlis* are defending the wrong down-timers. Doesn't anybody up time give a damn about folks like Molly and Kynan Rhys Gower?"

Robert Li muttered into his glass, "Not unless it makes for good press, no."

That was so depressingly true, Kit ordered another double.

And wondered when somebody would figure out that the down-timer problem facing every time terminal in the business would have to be solved one of these days. He just hoped Shangri-La Station was still open for business when it happened.

When Skeeter heard that Charlie Ryan had hired Bergitta to take his place on the station maintenance crew, his first thought was that maybe Ryan had a soul, after all. Then he wondered if maybe Kynan Rhys Gower hadn't paid him a little visit anyway? Whatever the case, Bergitta finally had a job that would give her enough income to pay for her closet-sized apartment and food and station taxes.

But when she learned that she'd been hired only because he'd been fired, she showed up on his doorstep in tears, vowing to quit.

"No," he insisted, "don't even think such a thing. It is not your fault I lost my job."

"But Skeeter . . ."

"Shh." He placed a fingertip across her lips. Her face was still bruised where that creep had hit her, but the swelling along her eye had gone down, at least. "No, I won't hear it. You need the job, Bergitta. I can get work doing anything. I only took the maintenance job because it was the first one they offered me."

Her stricken expression told Skeeter she knew full well it had been the only job anyone had offered him. What he was going to do to earn enough money to pay rent, buy food, keep the power turned on, and pay his own station taxes, Skeeter had no idea. But that wasn't important. Taking care of the few friends he had left was. So he locked up his dreary little apartment and placed Bergitta's hand through his arm. "Let's go someplace and celebrate your new job!"

Commons was still Skeeter's favorite place in the world, despite the loneliness of knowing that Marcus

and Ianira weren't anywhere to be found on station.
The bustle of excited tourists, the vibrant colors of
costumes and bright lights and glittering merchandise
from around the world and from Shangri-La's many
down-time gates, the myriad, mouth-watering scents
wafting out of restaurants and cafes and lunch stands,
all washed across them like a tidal wave from heaven
as soon as Bergitta and Skeeter emerged from Residential.

"How about sushi?" Skeeter asked teasingly, since
Bergitta adored fish but could not comprehend the
desire to eat it raw.

"Skeeter!"

"Okay," he laughed, "how about yakitori, instead?"

The little bamboo skewers of marinated chicken
had become one of the Swedish girl's all-time favorite up-timer foods. "Yes! That would be a real
celebration!"

So they headed up toward Edo Castletown,
where the Japanese lunch stands were concentrated.
Skeeter paused as they shouldered their way
through Victoria Station and bought a single rose
from a flower girl, another down-timer who had
sewn her own street-vendor costume and grew her
flowers in the station's lower levels. The Found
Ones had set up hydroponics tanks to supplement
their diets with fresh vegetables, and to grow flowers as a cash crop. They kept the crops healthy
with special grow lights Ianira had purchased with
money made at her kiosk.

Skeeter's throat tightened at the thought of Ianira
and everything she'd done for these people, but he
made himself smile and handed the rose to Bergitta.
She dimpled brightly, then hugged him on impulse.
Skeeter swallowed hard, then managed, "Hey, I'm
starved. Let's go find that yakitori."

They were halfway through Victoria Station, with
Bergitta sniffing at her flower's heady perfume every

few moments—the down-time varieties of roses the Found Ones grew had been carefully chosen for scent, as well as beauty—when they came upon Molly, the London down-time barmaid, surrounded by an improbable hoard of reporters.

"I dunno 'oo 'e is," Molly was protesting, "an' I don't want ter know! G'wan, now, I got a job to get back to, don't want t'be late or they'll dock me wages . . ."

"But you're a down-timer from the East End!" a reporter shouted, shoving a microphone into Molly's face.

"And didn't you earn your living as a streetwalker?" another newsie demanded. "What's your opinion on prostitution in the East End?"

"How would you feel if you were back in London now?"

"Did any of your customers ever rough you up? Were you ever attacked?"

At Skeeter's side, Bergitta began to tremble. She clutched at Skeeter's arm, holding on so tight, blood stopped flowing down to his hand. "Do something, Skeeter! How can they ask her such things? Have they no heart?"

Molly, sack lunch in hand and clearly on break from her job at the Down Time Bar & Grill, glared at the reporters hemming her in. "Blimey, 'ark at the lot of you! Arse about face, y'are, if you Adam I'll give it some chat! Don't give me none of your verbals, I'll clout you round the ear'ole, I will, you pack o' bloody wind-up merchants! Clear off, the rabbitin' lot of you!"

When Molly plowed straight through the pack of gaping newsies, not one of whom had understood a single word in five, given their round eyes and stunned silence, Skeeter burst into laughter. "I think Molly can fend for herself," he chuckled, patting Bergitta's hand. "I'll wager she's the stroppiest bit they've seen in a while. Come on, let's go find that lunch stand."

Bergitta waved at Molly as the other woman sailed past, trailing uncertain reporters after her, then she turned a smile up at Skeeter. "Yes, I feel sorry now for the newsies!"

Skeeter bought yakitori skewers for both of them and brimming cups of hot green tea, which they carried with them, sipping and munching as they strolled Commons, just taking in the sights. Frontier Town was quiet, but Camelot was gearing up for an impending invasion by re-enactors of the Society for Creative Anachronism, since the Anachronism Gate was scheduled to cycle in a few days. Floods of tournament-bound pseudo-medievalists would pour through the station, complete with horses, hooded hunting falcons, and all the attendant chaos of two separate month-long tournaments trying to flood through one gate, moving in opposite directions.

"I heard BATF plans to start watching the Mongolian Gate more closely," Skeeter said as they passed a shop where a Camelot vendor was putting up advertisements for falconry equipment. "Word is, that pair who went through last time are bird smugglers. Mongolian falcons are worth a fortune up time, especially to Arab princes. Some of the species have gone extinct, up time. Monty Wilkes wants to make sure those two don't try to smuggle out a suitcase load of rare falcons or viable eggs."

"Skeeter," Bergitta frowned, dabbing at her mouth with a paper napkin to wipe sauce off her lips, "why do they worry so about it? If there are no such birds on the other side of Primary, would it not be good to bring them through?"

Skeeter snorted. "You'd think so. Actually, if you get the special permits, you *can* bring extinct birds and animals back through a gate. What's illegal is *smuggling* them through to sell them to rich collectors, without paying taxes on them. First law of time travel: Though Shalt Not Profit from the Gates."

Bergitta shook her head, clearly baffled by the up-time world. "My brother is a trader," she said, eyes dark with sorrow. Bergitta would never again be able to see her family. "He would say such a law is not sane. If no one is to profit, how can the world do business?"

"My dear Bergitta," Skeeter chuckled, "you just asked the sixty-four-million-dollar question. Me, I think it's crazy. But I'm just an ex-thief, so who's going to listen to me?"

"I would," Bergitta said softly.

A sudden lump blocked Skeeter's throat. He gulped tea just to hide the burning in his eyes, and nearly strangled, because his throat was still too constricted to swallow. He ended up coughing while Bergitta thumped his shoulder blades. "Sorry about that," he finally wheezed. "Thanks."

Their wandering had brought them down into Little Agora, where Skeeter and Bergitta ran into total chaos. The news-hungry reporters up in Victoria Station were small potatoes compared with Little Agora's cult lunatics and militant groups like—God help them all—the Angels of Grace Militia, which had so recently arrived amid a flurry of violence. The Angels were determined to protect the station's down-timers and Lady of Heaven Templars, whether they wanted protection or not.

Everywhere Skeeter glanced, Templars were picketing and shouting, many of them reading from scriptural compilations of Ianira's recorded "words of wisdom." Angels of Grace strutted in black uniforms, their red emblems resembling a running Mirror of Venus which had mated with a swastika, prowling like rabid wolves, moving in packs. Some of them resembled female linebackers or maybe animated refrigerators in jackboots; others were lithe and deadly as ferrets. The psychological effect of all those black

uniforms was undeniable. Even Skeeter shivered in
their presence. Monty Wilkes had ordered his BATF
agents to break out their "dress uniforms"—the red
ones with black chevrons on the sleeves—to keep BATF
agents from being mistaken for Angel Squads.

Nutcases in sympathy with the *Ansar Majlis* Brotherhood picketed the picketing Templars, chanting for
the release of their oppressed Brothers. Other up-time
protesters who didn't agree with terrorism in any
form, but wanted the Temples shut down for reasons
of their own, stalked through Little Agora with hand-
lettered signs that read, "MY GOD'S A FATHER—YOURS
IS A WHORE!" and "DRIVE OUT THE MONEYCHANGERS IN
THE TEMPLE! THE LADY OF HEAVEN IS A FRAUD AND A
FRONT FOR ORGANIZED CRIME!"

And seated on the floor by the dozens, locked in
human protest chains around the shops and kiosks
of Little Agora, blocking exits to Residential and
public bathrooms, were shocking *droves* of keening,
disconsolate acolytes. Everywhere Skeeter turned his
glance, security was running ragged, trying to keep
fights from exploding out of control every half hour
or so.

"I wonder," Skeeter muttered, "how soon the violence on this station is going to close Shangri-La down
for good?"

Bergitta's rosy cheeks lost color. "Would they really
do this, Skeeter? Everyone says it could happen, but
there are so many people here, so much business and
money . . . and where could we go? They will not let
us walk through Primary and it is not legal for us to
go to live down another gate, either. And my gate will
never open again. It was unstable."

"I know," Skeeter said quietly, trying to hide his
own worry. The thought of living somewhere else—
anywhere else—stirred panic deep in his soul. And
the thought of what might become of his friends, his
adopted family, left him scared spitless. He'd heard

rumors that Senator Caddrick was talking internment camps, run like prisons . . .

Bergitta peered toward the ceiling, where immense chronometers hanging from the ceiling tracked date and time on station, down each of the station's multiple active gates, and up time through Primary. "Oh," she exclaimed in disappointment, "it is time for me to go to work!" She hugged Skeeter again, warm and vibrant against him for a brief moment. "Thank you, Skeeter, for the yakitori and the beautiful rose. I . . . I am still sorry about the job."

"Don't be." He smiled, hoping she couldn't sense his worry, wondering where he was going to line up another job, when his search for *that* job had broken world records for the shortest job interview category. "You'd better scoot. Don't want *you* to be late."

When she reached up and kissed his cheek, Skeeter reddened to his toes. But the warmth of the gesture left him blinking too rapidly as she hurried away through the crowds, still clutching her single rose. He shoved hands into pockets, so abruptly lonely, he could've stood there and cried from the sheer misery of it. He was turning over possibilities for job applications when a seething whirlwind of shrieking up-timer kids engulfed him. Clearly dumped by touring parents, the ankle-biters, as Molly called them, were once again playing hooky from the station school. Screaming eight- through eleven-year-olds swirled and foamed around Skeeter like pounding surf, yelling and zooming around, maddened hornets swarming out of a dropped hive. Skeeter found himself tangled up in the coils of a lasso made from thin nylon twine. He nearly fell, the coils wound so tightly around his body and upper legs. Skeeter muttered under his breath and yanked himself free.

"Hey! Gimme that back!" A snot-mouthed nine-year-old boy glared up at him as Skeeter wound the

lasso into a tight coil and stuffed it into his pocket.
Skeeter just grabbed the kid by the collar and dragged
him toward the nearest Security officer in sight, Wally
Klontz, whose claim to fame was a schnoz the size
of Cyrano de Bergerac's. "Hey! Lemme go!" The kid
wriggled and twisted, but Skeeter had hung onto far
slipperier quarries than this brat.

"Got a delinquent here," Skeeter said through
clenched teeth, hauling the kid over to Wally, whose
eyes widened at the sight of a screeching nine-year-
old dangling from Skeeter's grasp. "Something tells
me this one is supposed to be in school."

Wally's lips twitched just once, then he schooled
his expression into a stern scowl. "What did you catch
him doing, Skeeter?"

"Lassoing tourists."

Wally's eyes glinted. "Assault with a deadly weapon,
huh? Okay, short stuff. Let's go. Maybe you'd prefer a night in jail, if you don't want to sit through
your classes."

"Jail? You can't put me in jail! Do you have any
idea who my daddy is? When he finds out—"

"Oh, shut up, kid," Wally said shortly. "I've hauled
crown princes off to the brig, so you might as well
give it up. Thanks, Skeeter."

Skeeter handed the wailing brat over with satisfaction and watched as Wally dragged the kid away,
trailing protests at the top of his young lungs. Then
Skeeter shoved hands into pockets once again, feeling more isolated and lonely than ever. For just a
moment, he'd felt a connection, as though Wally
Klontz had recognized him as an equal. Now, he was
just Skeeter the unemployed mop man again, Skeeter
the ex-thief, the man no one trusted. Unhappiness
and bitter loneliness returned, in a surge of bilious
dissatisfaction with his life, his circumstances, and his
complete lack of power to do the one thing he needed
to do most: find Ianira Cassondra and her little family.

So he started walking again, heading up through Urbs Romae into Valhalla, past the big dragon-prowed longship that housed the Langskip Cafe. Skeeter tightened his fingers through the coils of the plastic lasso in his pocket and blinked rapidly against a burning behind his eyelids. *Where is she? God, what could have happened, to snatch them all away without so much as a trace? And if they slipped out through a gate opening, how'd they do it?* Skeeter had worked or attended every single opening of every single gate on station since Ianira and Marcus' disappearance, yet he'd seen and heard nothing. If they'd gone out in disguise, then that disguise had been good enough to fool even him.

He cut crosswise down the edge of Valhalla and shouldered past the crowd thronging around Sue Fritchey's prize *Pteranodon sternbergi*. Its enormous cage could be hoisted up from the basement level—where it spent most of its noisy life—to the Commons "feeding station" which had been built to Sue's specifications. The flying reptile's wing span equaled that of a small aircraft, which meant the cage was a big one. Expensive, too. And that enormous *pteranodon* had literally been eating Pest Control's entire operations budget. So the creative head of Pest Control had devised a method whereby the *tourists* paid to feed the enormous animal. Every few hours, tourists lined up to plunk down their money and climb a high ramp to dump bucketloads of fish into the giant flying reptile's beak. The sound of the *sternbergi's* beak clacking shut over a bucketload of fish echoed like a monstrous gunshot above the muted roar on Commons, two-by-fours cracking together under force.

Ianira had brought the girls to watch the first time the ingenious platform cage had been hoisted up hydraulically through the new hole in the Commons floor. Skeeter had personally paid for a couple of bucketloads of fish and had hoisted the girls by turns, helping them dump the smelly contents into the huge pteranodon's maw. They'd giggled and clapped gleefully, pointing at the baleful scarlet eye that rolled to glare at them as the gigantic reptile tried to extend its wings and shrieked at them in tones capable of bending steel girders. Skeeter, juggling Artemisia and a bucketful of fish, had sloshed fish slime down his shirt, much to his chagrin. Ianira had laughed like a little girl at his dismayed outburst . . .

Throat tight, Skeeter clenched his fists inside his jeans pockets, the plastic lasso digging into his palm, and stared emptily at the crowd thronging into Valhalla from El Dorado's nearby gold-tinted paving stones. And that was when he saw it happen. A well-timed stumble against a modestly dressed, middle-aged woman . . . a deft move of nimble fingers into her handbag . . . apologies given and accepted . . .

You rat-faced little—

Something inside Skeeter Jackson snapped. He found himself striding furiously forward, approached close enough to hear, "—apologize again, ma'am."

"It is nothing," she was saying as Skeeter closed in. *Spanish,* Skeeter pegged the woman, who was doubtless here for the next Conquistadores Gate tour. *Doesn't look rich enough to afford losing whatever's in that wallet, either. Probably spent the last five or six years saving enough money for this tour and that fumble-fingered little amateur thinks he's going to get away with every centavo she's scraped up!* Skeeter closed his fingers around the loops of plastic lasso in his pocket and came to an abrupt decision.

"Hello there," Skeeter said with a friendly smile dredged up from his days as a deceitful confidence artist. This screaming little neophyte didn't know the first thing about the business—and Skeeter intended to impart a harsh lesson. He offered his hand to the pickpocket. Startled eyes met his own as the guy shook Skeeter's hand automatically.

"Do I know you?"

"Nah," Skeeter said, still smiling, looping the plastic lasso deftly through the pickpocket's nearest belt loop with his other hand, "but you will in a minute. Care to explain what you're doing with the lady's wallet in your back pocket?"

He bolted, of course.

Then jerked to a halt with a startled *"Oof!"* as the lasso snapped taut at his waist. Skeeter grabbed him and trussed him up, wrists behind his back, in less time than it took the man to regain his balance. The pickpocket stood there sputtering in shock, completely inarticulate for long seconds; then a flood of invective broke loose, crude and predictable.

Skeeter cut him off with a ruthless jerk on his bound wrists. "That's about enough, buddy. We're going to go find the nearest Security officer and explain to him why you've got this lady's property in your pocket. Your technique stinks, by the way. *Am-a-teur.* Oh, and by the way? You're gonna love the isolation cells in this place. Give you plenty of time to consider a career change." Skeeter turned toward the astonished tourist. "Ma'am, if you'd be good enough to come with us? Your testimony will see this rat behind bars and, of course, you'll have your property returned. I'm real sorry this happened, ma'am."

Her mouth worked for a moment, then tears sprang to her eyes and a torrent of Spanish flooded loose, the gist being that Skeeter was the kindest soul in the world and how could she ever repay him and it had taken her ten years to save the money for this trip, *gracias, muchas, muchas gracias, señor . . .*

The stunned disbelief in Mike Benson's eyes when Skeeter handed over his prisoner and eyewitness at the Security office was worth almost as much as the woman's flood of gratitude. Skeeter swore out his deposition and made certain the lady's property was safely returned, then turned down the reward she tried to give him. Broke he might be, but he hadn't done it for the money and did not want to start accepting cash rewards for one of the few decent things he'd ever done in his life. Mike Benson's eyes nearly popped out of his skull when Skeeter simply smiled, kissed the lady's hand gallantly, leaving the proffered money in her fingers, and strode out of Security HQ feeling nine feet tall. For the first time since Ianira's disappearance, he didn't feel helpless. He might never be able to find Ianira Cassondra or Marcus and their children; but there was something he *could* do, something he knew she'd have been proud of him for doing.

His throat tightened again. It was probably the least likely occupation he could have stumbled across. And the station wasn't likely to give him a salary for it. But Skeeter Jackson had just discovered a new purpose and a whole new calling. Who better to spot and trip up pickpockets, thieves, and con artists than a guy who knew the business inside out? *Okay, Ianira,* he promised silently, *I won't give up hope. And if there's the slightest chance I can find you, I'll jump down an unstable gate to do it. Meanwhile, maybe I can do some good around here for a change. Make this a better place for the Found Ones to raise their kids . . .*

Skeeter Jackson found himself smiling. La-La Land's population of petty crooks had no idea what was about to hit them. For the first time in days, he felt good, really and truly good. Old skills twitching at his senses, Skeeter headed off to start the unlikeliest hunt of his life.

Margo Smith had spent her share of rough weeks down temporal gates. Lost in Rome with a concussion, that had been a bad one. Lost in sixteenth-century Portuguese Africa had been far worse, stranded on the flood-swollen Limpopo with a man dying of fever hundreds of miles from the gate, followed by capture and rape at the hands of Portuguese traders . . . At seventeen, Margo had certainly lived through her fair share of rough weeks down a gate.

But the first week after their arrival in London was right up there with the best of them. The Ripper Watch team's second foray into the East End, the morning after Polly Nichols' brutal murder, put Margo in charge of security and guide services for the up-time reporters Guy Pendergast and Dominica Nosette, as well as Ripper scholars Shahdi Feroz and Pavel Kostenka. Doug Tanglewood was going along, as well, but Malcolm, swamped with the search for Benny Catlin, not to mention demands from the rest of the Ripper Watch team, couldn't come with them.

So Malcolm, eyes glinting, told Margo, "They're all yours, Imp. Handle them, you can handle anything."

Margo rolled her eyes. "Oh, thanks. I'll remember to send you invitations to the funeral."

"Huh. Theirs or yours?"

Margo laughed. "With your shield or on it, isn't that what the Roman matron told her son? You know, as he went off to die gloriously in battle? The way I figure it, any run-in with that crew is gonna be one heck of a battle."

"My dear girl, you just said a bloody mouthful. Give 'em hell for me, too, would you? Just get them back in one piece. Even," he added with a telling grimace, "those reporters. Those two are a potential nightmare, snooping around for the story of the century, with the East End set up blow like a powder keg on a burning ship of the line. Doug's good in a routine tour and he's taken a lot of zipper jockeys into the East End, but frankly, he hasn't the martial arts training you do. Remember that, if it comes to a scrap."

"Right." It was both flattering and a little unsettling to realize she possessed skills that outranked a professional guide's. Doug Tanglewood, one of those nondescript sort of brown fellows nobody looks at twice, or even once, and who occasionally shock their neighbors by dismembering small dogs and children, was delighted that he wouldn't have to shepherd the Ripper Watch Team through the East End by himself.

"You handle the reporters," Margo told him as they left the gatehouse to climb into the carriage that would take them to the East End. "I'll tackle the eggheads."

Hitching up her long, tattered skirts, Margo clambered awkwardly up into the carriage in predawn darkness, just an hour after Polly Nichols' murder, then assisted Shahdi Feroz up into the seat. Pavel Kostenka and Conroy Melvyn climbed up and found seats, as well. As soon as everyone was aboard, the driver shook out his whip and they pulled away from the dark kerb and headed east.

Margo still couldn't quite believe that she was herding world-class scholars into the East End on such an important guiding job. She'd ordered the whole crew dressed in Petticoat Lane castoffs, once again. They looked as bedraggled as last year's mudhens. Margo, as disreputable as the rest in a streetwalker's multiple layers and fifth-hand rags, complete with strategic mud smears, carried a moth-eaten haversack which concealed her time scout's computerized log. A tiny camera disguised as one of several mismatched coat buttons transmitted data which her log converted to digitized and compressed video, allowing her to record every moment of their excursion. By popping out and replacing the google-byte disks, Margo could extend her recording capacity almost infinitely, limited only by the number of google disks she could carry.

And, of course, limited by the simple opportunity
to switch them out without being caught at it. The
Ripper scholars and newsies also carried scout's logs
and a large supply of spare googles, as did Doug
Tanglewood, who remained typically reserved and
quiet during the ride. Dominica chatted endlessly as
the carriage rattled eastward through London, navi-
gating in the near darkness of predawn, asking questions that Doug answered in monosyllables whenever
possible. Clearly, the Time Tours guide didn't think
much of up-time newsies, either. Margo sighed
inwardly. *It's going to be a long day.*

By the time they reached the dismal environs of
Whitechapel and Wapping, the sun was just climbing above the slate and broken tar-paper rooftops, all
but invisible through a haze compounded of fog,
drizzle, and acrid, throat-biting coal smoke. As the
carriage rattled to a halt in the stinking docklands,
the black smoke they were all breathing had already
dulled Margo's shapeless white bodice to a smudged
and dirty grey. She apologized to her lungs, wriggled
her toes inside her grubby boots to warm them, and
said, "All right, first stop, Houndsditch and Aldgate.
Everybody out, please."

Watching the Spaldergate carriage vanish back
through the murk toward the west, leaving them
bereft as orphans, Margo's pulse lurched slightly. Her
long, entangling skirts hampered her as they started
walking, but not as much as they might've had she
chosen a more current fashion. She'd opted, instead,
for a dress ten years out of style, one that gave her
leg room. And if need be, running and fighting room.

The reporters were eager, eyes shining, manner
alert. The scholars were no less eager, they were
simply more restrained, or maybe just more conscious
of their stature as dignitaries. Margo had long since
lost any idea that dignity was anything important while
down a gate. What mattered was getting the job done

with the least amount of damage to her person, not what her person looked like. Dignity, like vanity, did not rank as a survival trait for a wannabe time scout.

As they set out through the early dawn murk, the clatter and groaning of heavy wagons rumbled down Commercial Road, only a couple of blocks farther east. Margo couldn't even guess at the raw tonnage of finished goods, coal, grain, brick, lumber, and God knew what else, transported from the docks through these streets on any given day. Shops were already throwing back their shutters and smoke belched from factory chimneys.

The roar of smelting furnaces could be heard and the scent of molten metal, rotting vegetables, and dung from thousands of horses hung thick on the air. Human voices drifted through the murk as well. Dim shapes resolved occasionally into workmen and flower girls and idle ruffians lurking in dark alleyways. The East End was getting itself busily up and at its business, right along with the chickens cackling and clucking and crowing mournfully on their way to the big poultry markets further west or scratching for whatever scraps might've been left from breakfast in many a lightless, barren kitchen yard.

Dogs slunk past, intent on canine business as muddy daylight slowly gathered strength. Cats' eyes gleamed from alleyways, their shivery whiskers atwitch in the cold air, paws flicking in distaste as they navigated foul puddles of filthy rainwater from the previous night's storm. Along those same alleyways, ragged children sat huddled in open doorways. Most of the children clustered together for warmth, faces dirty and pinched with hunger, eyes dull and suspicious. Their mothers could be heard inside the dilapidated cribhouses they called home, often as not shouting in ear-bending tones at someone too drunk to respond. "Get a finger out, y' lager lout, or there'll be no supper in this cat an' mouse, not tonight nor any other . . ."

Margo glanced at her charges and found a study in contrasts. The reporters were taking it all in stride, studying the streets and the people in them with a detached sort of eagerness. Conroy Melvyn looked like the police inspector he was: alert, intelligent, dangerous, eyes taking in minute details of the world unfolding around him. Pavel Kostenka was not so much oblivious as simply unmoved by the shocking poverty spreading out in every direction. He was clearly intent on objective observation without the filter of human emotion coloring his judgements.

Dr. Feroz, on the other hand, was as quietly alert as the chief inspector from Scotland Yard, her dark eyes drinking in the details as rapidly as her miniature, concealed camera, but there was a distinctive shadow of grief far back in her eyes as she recorded the same details: children toting coal in wheelbarrows, tinkers with their donkey carts crying their trade, knife grinders carrying their sharpening wheels on harnesses strapped to their shoulders, little boys with leashed terriers and caged ferrets heading west to the neatly kept squares and tree-lined streets of the wealthy to offer their services as rat catchers.

Margo said quietly, "We'll want to be outside the police mortuary when the news breaks. When the workhouse paupers clean her body, they'll tell half of London's reporters what they found. We'll have to walk fast to make it in time—"

"In time?" Dominica Nosette interrupted, eyes smouldering as she rounded on Margo like a prize-fighter coming in for the kill. "If we're likely to be late, why didn't the carriage take us directly there? What if we miss this important event because you want us to *walk?*"

Margo had no intention of standing on a White-chapel street corner locked in argument with Dominica Nosette, so she kept walking at a brisk clip, ushering the others ahead of her. Doug Tanglewood took Miss

Nosette's arm to prevent her being separated from the group. The photographer took several startled, mincing steps, then jerked her arm loose with a snarled, "Take your hand off me!" She favored Margo with a cool stare. "Answer my question!"

"We did not take the carriage," Margo kept her voice low, "because the last thing we want to do is attract attention to ourselves. Nobody in this part of London arrives in a chauffeured carriage. So unless you enjoy being mugged the instant you set foot on the pavement, I'd suggest you resign yourself to hoofing it for the next three months."

As the poisonous glare died away to mere hellfire, Margo reminded herself that Dominica Nosette's work in clandestine photography had been done in the comfortable up-time world of air-conditioned automobiles and houses with central heating. Margo told herself to be charitable. Dominica Nosette's first daylight glimpse of London's East End was probably going to leave her in deep culture shock—she just didn't know it, yet.

When they reached the corner of Whitechapel and Commercial Roads, one of the busiest intersections in all London, they ran afoul of one of the East End's most famous hallmarks: the street meeting. Idle men thrown out of work by the previous night's dock fire had joined loafing gangs of the unemployed who roamed the streets in loose-knit packs, forming and breaking and reforming in random patterns to hash through whatever the day's hot topic might be, at a volume designed to deafen even the hardest of hearing at five hundred paces. From the sound of it, not one man—or woman—in the crowd had ever heard of Roberts' Rules of Order. Or of taking turns, for that matter.

"—why should I vote for 'im, I wants t'know? Wot's 'e goin' t'do for me an' mine—"

"—bloody radicals! Go an' do good to somebody

wot might appreciate it, over to Africa or India, where
them savages need civilizing, an' leave us decent folk
alone—"

"—let the bloke 'ave 'is say, might be good for a
laugh, eh, mate—"

"—give me a job wot'll put food in me Limehouse Cut, I'd vote for 'im if 'e were wearin' a
devil's 'orns—"

"—say, wot you radical Johnnies in this 'ere London County Council goin' to do about them murders,
eh? Way I 'eard it, another lady got her throat cut
last night, second one inside a month, third one since
Easter Monday, an' me sister's that scared to walk out
of a night—"

Near the edge of the crowd, which wasn't quite
a mob, a thin girl of about fifteen, hair lank under
her broken straw bonnet, leaned close against a man
in his fifties. He'd wrapped his hand firmly around
her left breast. As Margo brushed past, she heard the
man whisper, "Right, luv, fourpence it is. Know of
anyplace quiet?"

The girl whispered something in his ear and giggled,
then gave the older man a sloppy kiss and another
giggle. Margo glanced back and watched them head
for a narrow gate that led, presumably, to one of the
thousands of sunless yards huddled under brick walls
and overlooked by windows with broken glass in their
panes and bedsheets hung to keep the drafts out. As
the girl and her customer vanished through the gate,
a sudden, unexpected memory surged, broke, and
spilled into her awareness. Her mother's voice . . . and
ragged screams . . . a flash of bruised cheek and bleeding lips . . . the stink of burnt toast on the kitchen
counter and the thump of her father's fists . . .

Margo forcibly thrust away the memory, concentrating on the raucous street corner with its shouting voices and rumbling wagons and the sharp clop
of horses' hooves on the limerock and cobbled

roads—and her charges in the Ripper Watch Team.
Furious with herself, Margo gulped down air that
reeked of fresh dung and last week's refuse and the
tidal mud of the river and realized that no more than
a split second had passed. Dominica Nosette was
stalking down Whitechapel Road, oblivious to everything and Doug Tanglewood was hot on her trail so
she wouldn't step straight in front of an express wagon
loaded with casks from St. Katharine's Docks. Guy
Pendergast was still talking to people at the edge of
the crowd, asking questions he probably shouldn't
have have been asking. Dr. Kostenka was intent on
recording the political rally, a historic one, Margo
knew. The speaker at the center of the crowd was
supporting the first London County Council elections,
a race hotly contested by the radicals for control of
London's East End. Conroy Melvyn was staring, fascinated, at the man speaking.

Only Shahdi Feroz had noticed Margo's brief distress. Her dark-eyed gaze rested squarely on Margo.
Her brows had drawn down in visible concern. "Are
you all right?" she asked softly, moving closer to touch
Margo's arm.

"Yes," Margo lied, "I'm fine. Just cold. Come on,
we'd better get moving."

She genuinely didn't have time to deal with *that;*
certainly not here and now. She had a job to do.
Remembering her mother—anything at all about her
mother—was worse than useless. It was old news,
ancient history. She didn't have time to shed any more
tears or even to hate her parents for being what they'd
been or doing what they'd done. If she hoped to work
as an independent time scout one day, she had to
keep herself focused on *tomorrow.* Not to mention
today . . .

"Come on," she said roughly, all but dragging Guy
Pendergast and Conroy Melvyn down the street. "We
got a schedule, mates, let's 'ave it away on our

buttons, eh? Got a job waitin', so we 'ave, time an' tide don't wait for nobody."

They were amenable to being dragged off, at least, clearly eager to get the story they'd come here for, rather than intriguing side stories. They reached the police mortuary in time, thank God, and contrived to position themselves outside where a whole bevy of London's native down-time reporters had gathered. Several of them added foul black cigar smoke to the stench wafting out of the mortuary. Margo took up a watchful stance where she could record the events across the street, yet keep a cautious eye on her charges, not to mention everyone else who'd joined the macabre vigil, waiting for word about the third woman hideously hacked to death in these streets since spring.

The native reporters, every one of them male, of course, were speculating about the dead woman, her origins, potential witnesses they'd already tracked down and plied with gin—"talked to fifty women, I tell you, fifty, and they all described the same man, big foreign looking bastard in a leather apron." Everyone wondered whether or not the killer might be caught soon, based on those so-called witness accounts. The man known as "Leather Apron," Margo knew, had been one of the early top suspects. The unfortunate John Pizer, a Polish boot finisher who also happened to be Jewish, and a genuinely innocent target of East End hatred and prejudice, would find himself in jail shortly.

Of course, he would soon afterward collect damages from the newspapers who had libeled him, since he'd been seen by several witnesses including a police constable, at the Shadwell dock fire during the time Polly Nichols had been so brutally killed. But this morning, nobody knew that yet—

A male scream of horror erupted from the mortuary across the road. "Dear God, oh, dear God, constable, come quick!"

Reporters broke and ran for the door, which slammed abruptly back against the sooty bricks. A shaken man in a shabby workhouse uniform appeared, stumbling as he reached the street. His face had washed a sickly grey. He gulped down air, wiped his mouth with the back of his hand in a visible effort not to lose the meager contents of his stomach. Questions erupted from every side. The workhouse inmate shuddered, trying to find the words to describe what he'd just witnessed.

"Was 'orrible," he said in a hoarse voice, "ripped 'er open like a . . . a butchered side of beef . . . from 'ere to 'ere . . . dunno 'ow many cuts, was 'orrible, I tell you, couldn't stay an' look at 'er poor belly all cut open . . ."

Word of the mutilations spread in a racing shock-wave down the street. Women clutched at their throats, exclaiming in horror. Men stomped angrily across the pavement, cursing the news and demanding that something be done. A roar of angry voices surged from down the street. Then Margo and Doug Tanglewood and their mutual charges were buried alive by the mob which had, just minutes previously, been heckling the radical politicians running for council office. Angry teenage boys flung mud and rocks at the police mortuary. Older men shouted threats at the police officials inside. Margo was shoved and jostled by men taller and heavier than she was, all of them fighting for the best vantage points along the street. The sheer force of numbers thrust Margo and her charges apart.

"Hold onto one another!" Margo shouted at Shahdi Feroz. "Grab Dominica's arm—and I don't care what she says when you do it! Where's Doug?"

"Over there!" The wide-eyed scholar pointed.

Margo found the Time Tours guide trying to keep Guy Pendergast and Conroy Melvyn from being separated. Margo snagged the police inspector's coat sleeve, getting his shocked attention. "Hold onto Guy!

Grab Doug Tanglewood's arm! We can't get separated in this mob! Follow me back!" She was already fighting her way back to the women and searching for Dr. Kostenka, who remained missing in the explosive crowd. She'd just reached Shahdi Feroz when new shouts erupted not four feet distant.

"Dirty little foreigner! It's one o' your kind done 'er! That's wot they're sayin', a dirty little Jew wiv a leather apron!"

Margo thrust Shahdi Feroz at the Time Tours guide. "Get them out of here, Tanglewood! I've got a bad feeling that's Dr. Kostenka!"

She then shoved her way through the angry mob and found her final charge, just as she'd feared she would. Pavel Kostenka clutched at a bleeding lip and streaming nose, scholarly eyes wide and shocked. Angry men were shouting obscenities at him, most of them in Cockney the scholar clearly couldn't even comprehend.

Oh, God, here we go.... "Wot's this, then?" Margo shouted, facing down a thickset, ugly lout with blood on his knuckles. "You givin' me old man wot for, eh? I'll give you me Germans, I will, you touch 'im again!" She lifted her own fist, threatening him as brazenly as she dared.

Laughter erupted, defusing the worst of the fury around them at the sight of a girl who barely topped five feet in her stockings squaring off with a man four times her size. Voices washed across her awareness, while she kept her wary attention on the man who'd punched Kostenka once already.

"Cheeky little begger, in't she?"

"Don't sound like no foreigner, neither."

"Let 'er be, Ned, you might break 'er back, just pokin' at 'er!" This last to the giant who'd smashed his fist into Pavel Kostenka's face.

Ned, however, had his blood up, or maybe his gin, because he swung at Margo anyway. The blow didn't

connect, of course. Which infuriated the burly Ned.
He let out a roar like an enraged Kodiak grizzly and
tried to close with her. Margo slid to one side in a
swift Aikido move and assisted him on his way.
Whereupon Ned was obliged to momentarily mimic
the lowly fruit bat, flying airborne into the nearest
belfry, that being the brick wall of the church across
the street. Ned howled in outraged pain when he
connected with a brutal thud. A roar of angry voices
surged. So did the mob. A filthy lout in a ragged coat
and battered cap took a swing at her. Margo ducked
and sent him on his way. Then somebody else took
offense at having his neighbor come careening head
first into the crowd. Margo dodged and wove as fists
swung like crazed axes in the hands of drunken lum-
berjacks. Then she grabbed Kostenka by the wrist and
yelled, "Run, you bloody idiot!"

She had to drag him for two yards. Then he was
running beside her, while Margo put to use every
Aikido move Kit and Sven had ever drilled into her.
Her wrists and arms ached, but she did clear a path
out. The riot erupting behind them engulfed the
entire street. Margo steered a course toward the spot
where she'd last seen the other members of her little
team. She found them, wide-eyed in naked shock,
near the edge of the crowd. Doug Tanglewood had
wisely dragged them clear as soon as she'd yelled at
him to do so.

"Dr. Kostenka!" Shahdi Feroz cried. "You're injured!"

He was snuffling blood back into his sinuses. Margo
hauled a handkerchief out of one pocket and thrust
it into his hand. "Come on, let's clear out of here. We
got what we came for. Pack this into your nostrils, hold
it tight. Come *on!*" That, to Guy Pendergast, who was
still intent on filming the riot with his hidden camera.
"If we get to the Whitechapel Working Lads' Institute
now, we can scramble for the best seats at the inquest."

That got the reporter's attention. He turned,

belatedly, to help steer Dr. Pavel Kostenka down the
street and away from the mortuary riot. Margo escorted
her shaken charges several blocks away before pausing at a coffee stall to buy hot coffee for everyone.
"Here, drink this," she said, handing Dr. Kostenka a
chipped earthenware mug. "You're fighting shock. It'll
warm you up."

Dominica Nosette too, was battling shock, although
hers was emotional rather than from physical injuries
sustained. Margo got a mugful of coffee down her, as
well, and Doug bought crumpets for everyone. "Here
you go. Carbs and hot coffee will set you to rights,
mates." Pavel Kostenka had seated himself on the chilly
stone kerb, elbows propped on knees, shabby boots
in the gutter. He was trembling so violently, he had
trouble holding Margo's now-stained handkerchief
against his battered nose. Margo crouched beside him.

"You okay?" she asked quietly.

He shuddered once, then nodded, slowly. When
he lowered the handkerchief to his lap, he left a
smear of blood down his chin. "I do believe you saved
my life, back there."

She shrugged, trying to make light of her own role
in the near-disaster. "It's possible. That flared up a
lot faster than I expected it to. Which means you got
hurt and you shouldn't have. I knew people would
be in a mean mood. And I knew about the anti-
Semitism. But I didn't figure on a full-blown riot that
fast."

He stared for a long moment into the cup Margo
handed him, where dark and bitter coffee steamed
in the cold morning air. "I have seen much anger
in the world," he said quietly. "But nothing like this.
Such murderous hatred, simply because I am
different . . ."

"This isn't the twenty-first century," she said in a
low voice. "Not that people are perfect in our time,
they're not. But down a gate, you *can't* expect people

to behave the way up-timers do. Socials norms do change over a century and a half, you know, more than you realize, just reading about it. Me? I'm just glad I was able to pull you out of there in one piece. Next time we come out here, we're gonna be a whole lot more careful about getting boxed into potential riots."

He finally met her gaze. "Yes. Thank you."

She managed a wan smile. "You're welcome. Ready to tackle that inquest?"

His effort to return the smile was genuine, even if the twist of his lips was a dismal failure in the smile department. "Yes. But this time, I think I shall not say anything at all, even if my foot is trod on hard enough to break the bones."

"Smart choice. Through with that coffee yet?"

The shaken scholar drained the bitter stuff—what did the British *do* to coffee, to produce such a ghastly flavor?—then climbed to his feet. "Thank you. From now on, whatever you suggest, I will do it without question."

"Okay. Let's find the Working Lads' Institute, shall we? I want us to keep a low profile." She glanced at the reporters. "No interviewing potential mobs, okay? You want this story, you get it by keeping your mouth shut and your cameras rolling."

This time, none of her charges argued with her. Even Guy Pendergast and Dominica Nosette, whose dress was torn, were momentarily subdued by the flash-point riot. For once, Margo actually felt in *charge*.

She wondered how long it would last.

Chapter Twelve

The smell of tension was thick in Kit's nostrils as he threaded his way through Edo Castletown, answering a call from Robert Li to meet him for the antics at Primary and to ask his expert opinion on a recent aquisition he'd made. So Kit abandoned several stacks of bills and government forms in his office at the Neo Edo Hotel and set out, curious about what the antiquities dealer might have stumbled across this time and wondering what new horror Primary's cycle might bring onto the station.

Kit had never seen a bigger crowd for a gate opening and that was saying a lot, after being caught in the jam-packed mass of humanity which had come to see the last cycling of the Britannia. Kiosks that hadn't existed just a week previously cluttered the once-wide thoroughfares of Commons, overflowing into Edo Castletown from its border with Victoria Station. Their owners hawked crimson-spattered t-shirts and tote bags, Ripper-suspect profiles, biographies and recent photos of the victims, anything and everything enterprising vendors thought might sell.

Humanity, he thought darkly—watching a giggling woman in her fifties plunking down a wad of twenties for a set of commemorative china plates with hand-painted portraits of victims, suspects, police investigators, and crime scenes—*humanity is a sick species.*

"Is she honestly going to display those hideous things in her house?"

Kit glanced around at the sound of a familiar voice at his elbow. Ann Vinh Mulhaney was gazing in disgust at the woman buying the plates.

"Hello, Ann. And I think the answer's yes. I'm betting she'll not only display them, she'll put them right out in the middle of her china hutch."

Ann gave a mock shudder. "God, *Ripperoons . . .* You wouldn't believe the last class of them I had to cope with." She glanced up at Kit, who gave her a sardonic smile. Kit had seen it all—and then some. "On second thought, you probably would believe it. Have you seen Sven yet? He came up before I did."

"No, I just got here. Robert said something about finding a spot to watch Primary go and said he wanted my opinion on something."

"Really?" Ann's eyes glinted with sudden interest. "That something wouldn't have anything to do with Peg Ames, would it?"

Kit blinked. "Good God. Have I missed something?"

Ann laughed, pulling loose the elastic band holding her long dark hair, and shrugged the gleaming tresses over one shoulder. She'd clearly just come from class, since she still wore a twin-holster rig with a beautiful pair of Royal Irish Constabulary Webley revolvers. Unlike the big military Webleys, which came open on a top-break hinge for reloading and were massive in size, the little RIC Webley was a solid-frame double-action that loaded like the American single-action Army revolver through a gate in the

side, and came in a short-barrelled, concealable
version popular with many time tourists heading to
London. At .442 caliber, they packed a decent punch
and were easier to hide than the much larger standard Webleys. Kit had shot them several times during his down-time escapades—and had cut his finger
more than once on the second trigger, a needle-type
spur projecting down behind the main trigger.

As she pocketed her hair band, Ann glanced sidelong at Kit. "You really have been moping with Margo
gone, haven't you? Honestly, Kit, they've been thick
as mosquitoes in a swamp for *days*. Rumor has it,"
and she winked, "that Peg had a line on a Greek
bronze that was going up for auction in London and
Robert was just about nuts, trying to find somebody
to snitch it quietly for him the night the auction
warehouse goes up in smoke. Or rather, went up in
smoke. It burned the night of Polly Nichols' murder,
in a Shadwell dry-dock fire."

Kit grinned as he escorted Ann through the crowds.
Robert Li was engaged in an ongoing, passionate love
affair with any and all Greek bronzes. "I hope he gets
it. Peg Ames will make him the happiest man in La-
La Land if he can lay hands on another one for his
collection."

The IFARTS agent and resident antiquarian had
personally rescued from destruction a collection of
ancient bronzes that most up-time museum directors
would've gnashed their teeth over, had they known
about them. Rescuing artwork from destruction was
perfectly legal, of course, and constituted one of the
major exceptions to the first law of time travel.
Collectors who salvaged such art could even sell it
on the open market, if they were willing to pay the
astronomical taxes levied by the Bureau of Access
Time Functions. Many an antiquarian and art dealer
made a good living doing just that.

But Robert Li would sooner have sold his own

teeth than part with an original Greek bronze, even one acquired through perfectly legitimate means. Of course, snitching one from a down-time auction warehouse before it burned did *not* qualify as a "legitimate" method of acquisition. To rescue a doomed piece of art, one had to rescue it during the very disaster destined to destroy it. Li was a very honest and honorable man. But when it came to any man's abiding passion, honesty occasionally went straight out the nearest available window. Certainly, many another antiquarian had tried smuggling out artwork that was not destined for down-time destruction. Hence the existence of the International Federation for Art Temporally Stolen, which tried to rescue such purloined work and return it to its proper time and place of origin. Robert Li was the station's designated IFARTS agent, a very good one. But if he had a line on a Greek bronze that was scheduled to be destroyed by some method it couldn't easily be rescued from, or one that had just disappeared mysteriously, he wouldn't be above trying to acquire it for his personal collection, whatever the means.

"Wonder which bronze?" Kit mused as they threaded their way toward Primary.

"Proserpina, actually," Robert Li's voice said from behind him.

Kit turned, startled, then grinned. "Proserpina, huh?"

"Yeah, beautiful little thing, about three feet high. Holding a pomegranate."

"Is that what you wanted to ask me about?"

The antiquities dealer chuckled and fell into step beside them. "Actually, no." He held up a cloth sack. "I wondered if you might know more about these than I do. A customer came into the shop, asked me to verify whether or not they were genuine or reproduction. He'd bought 'em from a Templar who came through with a suitcase full of 'em and is selling them down in Little Agora to anyone who'll pony up the bucks."

Curious, Kit opened the sack and found a pair of late twentieth-century, Desert Storm-era Israeli gas masks, capable of filtering out a variety of chemical and nerve agents.

"Somebody," Kit muttered, "has a sick sense of humor."

"Or maybe just a psychic premonition," Ann put in, eyeing the masks curiously. "It's illegal to discharge chemical agents inside a time terminal, but nothing would surprise me around here, these days."

As Kit studied the gas masks, looking for telltale signs of recent manufacture, he could hear, in the distance, the sound of live music and chanting. Startled, Kit glanced up at the chronometers. "What's going on, over toward Urbs Romae?"

"Oh, that's the Festival of Mars," Ann answered, just as Kit located the section of the overhead chronometers reserved for displaying the religious festivals scheduled in the station's timeline.

Kit smacked his forehead, belatedly recalling his promise to Ianira that he'd participate in the festival. "Damn! I was supposed to be there!"

"All the down-timers on station are participating," Robert said with a curious glance at Kit.

Ann's voice wobbled a little as she added, "Ianira was supposed to officiate, you know. They're holding the festival anyway. The way I hear it, they plan on asking the gods of war to strike down whoever's responsible for kidnapping Ianira and her family."

A chill touched Kit's spine. "With all the crazies we've got on station, that could get ugly, fast." Before he'd even finished voicing the thought, shouts and the unmistakable sounds of a scuffle broke out close by. Startled tourists in front of them scrambled in every direction. A corridor of uninhabited space opened up. Two angry groups abruptly faced one another down.

Kit recognized trouble when he saw it—and this was *Trouble*.

Capital "T" that rhymed with "C" and that stood for Crazies.

Ann gasped. A group of women in black uniforms and honest-to-God jackboots formed an impenetrable wall along one flank, blocking any escape in that direction. *Angels of Grace Militia*... And opposing the Angels ranged a line of burly construction workers, the very same construction workers who'd been involved in the *last* station riot.

"*Unchaste whores!*"

"*Medieval monsters!*"

"*Feminazis!*"

"*Get out of our station, bitches!*"

"You're not *my* goddamned brothers!"

"Go back to the desert and beat up your own women, you rag-headed bastards! Leave ours alone!"

Kit had just enough time to say, "*Oh, my God...*" Then the riot exploded around them.

To Margo's relief, they found the Working Lads' Institute without further incident. When the doors were finally opened for the inquest into Polly Nichols' brutal demise, the Ripper scholars and up-time reporters in her charge surged inside with the rest of the crowd. The room was so jam-packed with human bodies, not even a church mouse could have forced its way into the meeting hall. The coroner was a dandified and stylish man named Wynne Edwin Baxter, who arrived with typical flair, straight from a tour of Scandinavia, dressed to the nines in black-and-white checked trousers, a fancy white waistcoat, and a blood-red scarf. Baxter presided over the inquest with a theatrical mien, asking the police surgeon, Dr. Llewellyn, to report on his findings. The Welsh doctor, who had been dragged from his Whitechapel surgery to examine the remains at the police mortuary, cleared his throat with a nervous glance at the crowded hall, where reporters hung expectantly on every word spoken.

"Yes. Well. Five teeth were missing from the victim's jaw and I found a slight, ah, laceration on the tongue. A bruise ran along the lower part of the lady's jaw, down the right side of her face. This might have been caused by a fist striking her face or, ah, perhaps a thumb digging into the face. I found another bruise, circular in nature, on the left side of her face, perhaps caused by fingers pressing into her skin. On the left side of her neck, about an inch below the jaw, there was an, ah, incision." The surgeon paused and cleared his throat, a trifle pale. "An, ah, an incision, yes, below the jaw, about four inches in length, which ran from a point immediately below the ear. Another incision on this same side was, ah, circular in design, severing tissues right down to the vertebrae."

A concerted gasp rose from the eager spectators. Reporters scribbled furiously with pencils, those being far more practical for field work than the cumbersome dip pens which required an inkwell to resupply them every few lines.

Dr. Llewellyn cleared his throat. "The large vessels of the neck, both sides, were all severed by this incision, at a length of eight inches. These cuts most certainly were inflicted by a large knife, a long-bladed weapon, moderately sharp. It was used with considerable violence . . ." The doctor shuddered slightly. "Yes. Well. Ah, there was no blood on the breast, either her own or the clothes, and I found no further injuries until I reached the lower portion of the poor lady's abdomen." A shocked buzz ran through the room. Victorian gentlemen did not speak about ladies' abdomens, not in public places, not anywhere else, for that matter. Dr. Llewellyn shifted uncomfortably. "Some two to three inches from the left side of the belly, I discovered a jagged wound, very deep, the tissues of the abdomen completely cut through.

Several other, ah, incisions ran across the abdomen as well, and three or four more which ran vertically down the right side. These were inflicted, as I said, by a knife used violently and thrust downward. The injuries were from left to right and may possibly have been done by an, ah, left-handed person, yes, and all were without doubt committed with the same instrument."

A reporter near the front of the packed room shouted, "Dr. Llewellyn! Then you believe the killer must have stood in front of his victim, held her by the jaw with his right hand, struck with the knife in his left?"

"Ah, yes, that would seem to be indicated."

Having watched the brutal attack in Buck's Row via video camera, Margo knew that was wrong. James Maybrick had strangled his victim, then shoved her to the ground and ripped her open with the knife gripped in his right hand. Criminologists had long suspected that would be the case, just from the coroners' descriptions of wound placement and surviving crime scene and mortuary photos. But in London of 1888, the entire science of forensics was in its infancy and criminal psychology hadn't even been invented yet, never mind profiling of serial killers.

"Dr. Llewellyn . . ."

The inquest erupted into a fury of shouted questions and demands for further information, witness names, descriptions, anything. It came out that a coffee-stall keeper named John Morgan had actually seen Polly Nichols shortly before her death, a mere three minutes' walk from Buck's Row where she'd died. Morgan said, "She were in the company of a man she called Jim, sir."

Whether or not this "Jim" had been James Maybrick, Margo didn't know and neither did anybody else, since they hadn't rigged a camera at Morgan's coffee stall. But the description Morgan gave didn't match Maybrick's features, so it might well have been another "Jim" who'd bought what poor Polly had been selling, as well as her final cup of bitter, early-morning coffee. If, in fact, Morgan wasn't making up the whole story, just to gain the momentary glory of police and reporters fawning over him for details.

Margo sighed. *People don't change much, do they?*

Once the inquest meeting broke up, Margo and Doug Tanglewood parted company. Tanglewood and the reporters, accompanied by Pavel Kostenka and Conroy Melvyn, set out in pursuit of the mysterious doctor they'd captured on video working with James Maybrick. Margo and her remaining charge, Shahdi Feroz, plunged into the shadowy world inhabited by London's twelve-hundred prostitutes.

"I want to walk the entire murder area," Shahdi said quietly as they set out alone. Most of this lay in the heart of Whitechapel, straying only once into the district of London known as The City. Margo glanced at the older woman, curious.

"Why the whole area now? We'll be rigging surveillance on each site."

Shahdi Feroz gave Margo a wan smile. "It will be important to my work to get a feel for the spatial relationships, the geography of the killing zone. What stands where, how the pattern of traffic flows through or past the murder sites. Where Maybrick and his unknown accomplice might meet their victims. Where the prostitutes troll for their customers."

When Margo gave her a puzzled stare, she said, "I want to learn as much as I can about the world the prostitutes live in. To me, that is the important question, the conditions and geography of their social setting, how they lived and worked as well as where and why they died. This is more important than the forensics of the evidence. The basic forensics were known *then;* what is not known is how these women were treated by the police sent undercover to protect them, or how these women coped with the terror and the stress of having to continue working with such a monstrous killer loose among them. We have studied such things in the modern world, of course; but never in Victorian England. The social rules were so very different, here, where even the chair legs are covered with draperies and referred to as limbs, even by women who sell their bodies for money. It is this world I need to understand. I have worked in middle class London and in areas of wealth, but never in the East End."

Margo nodded. That made sense. "All right. Buck's Row, we've seen already. You want to do the murder sites in numerical order, by the pattern of the actual attacks? Or take them as we come to them, geographically? And what about the murder sites on the question list? The ones we're not sure whether they were Jack's or not? Like the Whitehall torso," she added with a shudder. The armless, legless, headless woman's body, hacked to pieces and left in the cellar of the partially constructed New Scotland Yard building on Whitehall, would be discovered in October, during the month-long lull between confirmed Ripper strikes.

"Yes," Shahdi Feroz said slowly, narrowing her eyes slightly as she considered the question. "With two men working in tandem, it would be good, I think, to check all the murder sites, not just the five traditionally ascribed to the Ripper. And I believe we should take the sites in order of the murders, as well. We will follow the killer's movements through the territory he staked out for himself. Perhaps we might come to understand more of his mind, doing this, as well as how he might have met his victims. Or rather, how they met their victims, since there are two of them working together." Her smile was rueful. "I did not expect to have the chance to study such a dynamic in this particular case. It complicates matters immensely."

Even Margo, with no training in psychology or criminal social dynamics, could understand that. "Okay, next stop, Hanbury Street." Margo intended to get a good look at the yard behind number twenty-nine Hanbury. Seven days from now, she'd be slipping into that yard under cover of darkness, to set up the Ripper Watch team's surveillance equipment.

Number twenty-nine Hanbury proved to be a broken-down tenement in sooty brick. It housed seventeen souls, several of whom were employed in a nearby cigar factory. It was a working-man's tenement, not a doss house where the homeless flopped for the night. Two doors led in from the street. One took residents into the house proper and another led directly to the yard behind the squat brick structure. Margo and Shahdi Feroz chose this second door, opening it with a creaking groan of rusting hinges. The noise startled Margo.

And brought instant attention from an older woman who leaned out a second-story window. "Where d'you think you're going, eh?" the irate resident shouted down. "I know your kind, missies! How many times I got to tell your kind o' girls, keep out me yard! Don't want nuffink to do wiv the likes o' you round me very own 'ouse! Go on wiv you, now, get on!"

Caught red-handed trying to sneak into the yard, Margo did the only thing she could do, the one thing any East End hussy would've been expected to do. She let the door close with a bang and shouted back up, "It's me gormless father I'm after, nuffink else! Lager lout's said 'e 'ad a job, workin' down to Lime'ouse docks, an' where do I see 'im, but coming out the Blue Boy public 'ouse, 'at's where! Followed 'im I did, wiv me ma, 'ere. Sore 'im climb over the fence into this 'ere yard. You seen 'im, lady? You do, an' you shout for a bottle an' stopper, y'hear?"

"Don't you go tellin' an old woman any of your

bloody Jackanories! Off wiv you, or I'll call for that copper me own self!"

"Ah, come on, ma," Margo said loudly to Shahdi Feroz, taking her arm, "senile owd git ain't no use. We'll catch 'im, 'e gots to come 'ome sometime, ain't 'e?"

As soon as they had gained enough distance, Shahdi Feroz cast a curious glance over her shoulder. "How in the world will Annie Chapman slip through that door with seventeen people asleep in the house and *nobody hear a thing?*"

Margo shot the scholar an intent glance. "Good question. Maybe one of the working girls got tired of having that busybody interfere with using a perfectly suitable business location? One of them could've poured lamp oil on the hinges?"

"It's entirely possible," Dr. Feroz said thoughtfully. "Pity we haven't the resources to put twenty-four hour surveillance on that door for the next week. That was quick thinking, by the way," she added with a brief smile. "When she shouted like that, I very nearly lost my footing. I had no idea what to say. All I could imagine was being placed in jail." She shivered, leaving Margo to wonder if she'd ever seen the inside of a down-time gaol, or if she just had a vivid imagination. Margo, for one, had no intention of discovering what a Victorian jail cell looked like, certainly not from the inside. She had far too vivid a memory of sixteenth-century Portuguese ones.

"Huh," she muttered. "When you're caught stealing the cookies, the only defense is a counterattack with a healthy dose of misdirection."

Shahdi Feroz smiled. "And were you caught stealing the cookies often, my dear Miss Smith?"

Margo thrust away memory of too many beatings and didn't answer.

"Miss Smith?"

Margo knew that tone. That was the *Something's*

wrong, can I help? tone people used when they'd
inadvertently bumped too close to something Margo
didn't want bumped. So she said briskly, "Let's see,
next stop is Dorset Street, where Elizabeth Stride was
killed in Dutfield's Yard. We shouldn't have any
trouble getting in there, at least. Mr. Dutfield has
moved his construction yard, so the whole place has
been deserted for months." She very carefully did not
look at Shahdi Feroz.

The older woman studied her for a long, dangerous moment more, then sighed.

Margo relaxed. She'd let it go, thank God. Margo
didn't want to share those particular memories with
anyone, not even Malcolm or Kit. Especially Malcolm or Kit. She realized that Shahdi Feroz, like
so many others since it had happened, meant well;
but raking it all up again wouldn't help anyone or
solve anything. So she kept up a steady stream of
chatter about nothing whatsoever as her most useful barrier to well-intentioned prying. She talked all
the way down Brick Lane and Osborn Street, across
Whitechapel Road, down Plumber Street, past
jammed wagon traffic on Commercial Road, clear
down to Berner Street, which left her badly out of
breath, since Berner Street was all the way across
the depth of Whitechapel parish from number
twenty-nine Hanbury.

Dutfield's Yard was a deserted, open square which
could be reached only by an eighteen-foot alleyway
leading in from Berner Street. A double gate between
wooden posts boasted a wooden gate to the right and
a wicker gate to the left, to be used when the main
gate was closed. White lettering on the wooden gate
proclaimed the yard as the property of W. Hindley,
Sack Manufacturer and A. Dutfield, Van and Cart
Builder. The wicker gate creaked when Margo pushed
it open and stepped through. She held it for Shahdi
Feroz, who lifted her skirts clear of the rubbish blown

against the base by wind from the previous night's storm.

The alleyway, a dreary, dim passage even in daylight, was bordered on the north by the International Workers' Educational Club and to the south by three artisans' houses, remodeled from older, existing structures. Once into the yard proper, Margo found herself surrounded by decaying old buildings. To the west lay the sack factory, where men and teenaged boys could be seen at work through dull, soot-grimed windows. Beside the abandoned cart factory stood a dusty, dilapidated stable which clearly hadn't been used since Arthur Dutfield had moved his business to Pinchin Street. Terraced cottages to the south closed in the yard completely. The odor of tobacco wafted into the yard from these cottages, where cigarettes were being assembled by hand, using sweatshop labor. The whir of sewing machines, operated by foot treadles, floated through a couple of open windows in one of the cottages; a small sign announced that this establishment was home to two separate tailors. The rear windows of the two-story, barn-like International Workers' Educational Club overlooked the yard, looming above it as the major feature closing in this tiny, isolated bit of real estate. The club, a hotbed of radical political activity and renowned for its Jewish ownership, also served as a major community center for educational and cultural events.

Standing in the center of the empty construction yard, Margo gazed thoughtfully at the rear windows of the popular hall. "Bold as brass, wasn't he?" she muttered.

Shahdi Feroz was studying the yard's only access, the eighteen-foot blind alley. She glanced up, first at Margo, then at the windows Margo was gazing at. "Yes," the scholar agreed. "The hall was—will be—filled with people that night."

It would be the Association's secretary, in fact, jeweler Louis Diemshutz, who would discover Elizabeth Stride's body some four weeks hence. Margo frowned slowly as she gazed, narrow-eyed, at the ranks of windows in the popular meeting hall. "Doesn't it strike you as odd that he chose this particular spot to kill Long Liz Stride?"

Shahdi frowned. "Odd? But it is a perfectly natural spot for him to choose. It is completely isolated from the street. And it will be utterly dark, that night. What more natural place for a prostitute to take her customer than a deserted stable in an abandoned yard?"

"Yes . . ." Margo was trying to put a more concrete reason to the niggling feeling that this was still an odd place for Jack to have killed his victim. "But she didn't want to come back here. She was struggling to escape when Israel Schwartz saw her. Given the descriptions he gave of the two men, I'm betting it's our mystery doctor who knocked her to the ground and Maybrick who ran Schwartz off."

Shahdi turned her full attention to Margo. "You know, that has always puzzled me about Elizabeth Stride," the Ripper scholar mused. "Why she struggled. As a working prostitute, this is not in character. And she had turned down a customer earlier that evening."

Margo stared. "She had?"

Shahdi nodded. "One of the witnesses who remembered seeing her said this. That a man had approached her and she said, 'No, not tonight.' And yet we know she needed money. She had quarreled with the man she lived with, had been seen in a doss house, admitted to a friend that she needed money. Why would she have refused one customer, then struggled when a second propositioned her? What did they discuss, that he attacked her?"

"Maybe," Margo said slowly, narrowing her eyes slightly, "she didn't need the money as much as we thought she did."

Shahdi's eyes widened. "The letters," she whispered, abruptly excited. Her eyes gleamed with quick speculation. "Perhaps these mysterious letters are worth a great deal of money, yes? Clearly, our friend the doctor is most anxious to retrieve them. And he recovered several gold sovereigns from Polly Nichols' pockets, which she must have been given by him earlier in the evening, as payment for these letters."

"Blackmail?" Margo breathed. "But blackmail against who? Whom, I mean. And if all these penniless women are being systematically hunted down because they've got somebody's valuable letters, why didn't they cash in on them? Every one of Jack's victims was drunk and soliciting just to get enough money for a four penny bed for the night."

Shahdi Feroz shook her, visibly frustrated. "I do not know. But I intend to find out!"

Margo grinned. "Me, too. Come on, let's go. My feet are freezing and it's a long walk to Mitre Square and Goulston Street."

To reach Mitre Square, they traced one of the possible routes the Ripper might have taken from Berner Street where his bloody work with Elizabeth Stride had been—would be—interrupted by Louis Diemshutz. "One thing I find interesting," Margo said as they followed Back Church Lane up to Commercial Road and from there hiked down to Aldgate High Street and Aldgate proper, further west. "He knew the area. Knew it well enough to pull a stunt like switching police jurisdictions after getting away from Dutfield's Yard. He knew he was going to kill again. So he deliberately left Whitechapel and Metropolitan Police jurisdiction and hunted his second victim over in The City proper, where The City police didn't get on with Scotland Yard at all."

The "City of London" was a tiny district of government buildings in the very heart of London. Fiercely independent, The City maintained its own

Lord Mayor and its own police force, its own laws and jurisdictions, separate from the rest of London proper, and was exceedingly jealous about maintaining its autonomy. It was confusing from the get-go, particularly to up-time visitors. In the case of Jack the Ripper's murder spree on the night of September 30th, it would confuse the devil out of London's two rival constabularies, as well. And it would lead to destruction of vital evidence by bickering police officials trying to keep the East End from exploding into anti-Semitic riots.

"That," Shahdi mused, "or he simply didn't meet Catharine Eddowes until he'd reached The City's jurisdiction. She had just been released from jail and was heading east, while Jack was presumably heading west."

"Well, even if he did just happen to meet her in The City, he doubled back into Whitechapel again, so it'd be the Metropolitan Police who found the apron he left for them under his chalked message, not constables from The City police. Somehow, Maybrick doesn't strike me as quite that clever."

"Perhaps, perhaps not," Shahdi said thoughtfully. "But one thing is quite clear. Our doctor is *very* clever. How has he managed, I wonder, to work so closely with Mr. Maybrick, yet keep all mention of himself out of Maybrick's incriminating diary?"

"Yeah. And why did Maybrick write a diary like that at all? I mean, that's tempting fate just a little too much, isn't it? His wife knew he was married to another woman, that he was a bigamist *and* having other affairs, probably with his own maidservants. At Florie's trial, everybody commented on how gorgeous all the Maybrick maids were. Florie might have gone looking for clues to who the other women were and found the diary. Or one of those nosy maids might have. They certainly helped themselves to Mrs. Maybrick's clothes and jewelry."

Shahdi Feroz was shaking her head in disagreement. "Yes, they did, but you may not realize that Maybrick kept his study locked at all times with a padlock. He kept the only key and straightened the room himself. Very peculiar for a businessman of the time. And he threatened to kill a clerk who nearly discovered something incriminating. Presumably the diary, itself. As to why he wrote the diary, many serial killers have a profound need to confess their crimes. A compulsion to be caught. It is why they play taunting games with the police, with letters and clues. A serial killer is under terrible pressure to murder his victims. By writing down his deeds, he can relieve some of this pressure, as well as relive the terrible thrill and excitement of the crime. Maybrick is not alone, in this. The risk of being caught, either through the diary or at the crime scene, is as addictive to the serial killer as the murder itself, is."

"God, that's really sick!" Margo gulped back nausea.

Shahdi nodded, eyes grim. "Maybrick's diary has always rung with authenticity on many levels. To forge such a thing, a person would have needed to comprehend a vast array of information, technical and scientific skills ranging from psychopathic serial killer psychology to the forensics of ink and handwriting and linguistic styles. No, I never believed the diary to be a forgery, even before we taped Mr. Maybrick killing Polly Nichols, although many of my colleagues have believed it to be, ever since it was discovered in the twentieth century. The thing I find most intriguing, however, is his silence in the diary about this doctor who works with him. Through the whole diary, he names people quite freely, including doctors he has consulted, both in Liverpool and London. Why, then, no mention of *this* doctor?"

"He mentions a doctor in London?" Margo said eagerly. "That's the guy, then!"

"No," Shahdi shook her head. "There are records of this doctor. He does not fit the age or physical description profile of the man on our video. I had already thought of this, of course, but we brought with us downloaded copies of everything known on this case. It is not the same man."

"Oh." Margo couldn't hide the disappointment in her voice.

Shahdi smiled. "It was a good thought, my dear. Ah, this is where we turn for Mitre Square."

They had to dodge heavy freight wagon traffic across Aldgate to reach Mitre Street, from which they could take one of the two access routes into the Square. This was a rectangle of buildings almost entirely closed in on four sides by tall warehouses, private residences, and a Jewish Synagogue. The only ways in and out lay along a narrow inlet off Mitre Street and through a covered alleyway called Church Passage, which ran from Duke Street directly beneath a building, as so many odd little streets and narrow lanes in London did. Empty working men's cottages rose several stories along one side of the square. School children's voices could be heard in one corner, reciting lessons through the open windows of a small boarding school for working families with enough income to give their children a chance at a better future.

As they studied the layout of the narrow square, a door to one of the private houses opened. A policeman in uniform paused to kiss a woman in a plain morning dress. "Good day, m'dearie, an' keep the doors locked up, what with that maniac running about loose, cutting ladies' throats. I'll be back in time for supper."

"Do take care, won't you?"

"Ah, Mrs. Pearse, I always take care on a beat, you know that."

"Mr. Pearse," his wife touched his face, "I worry

about you out there, say what you will. I'll have supper waiting."

Margo stared, not so much because Mr. and Mrs. Pearse had addressed one another so formally. That was standard Victorian practice, using the formal address rather than first names in public. The reason Margo stared was because Mr. Pearse was a police constable. "My God," Margo whispered. "Right across the street from a *constable's* house!"

Shahdi Feroz was also studying the policeman's house with great interest. "Yes. Most interesting, isn't it? Playing cat and mouse with the constables on the very night he was nearly caught at Dutfield's Yard. Giving the police a calculated insult. I am willing to bet on this. Maybrick hated Inspector Abberline already, by the night of the double murder."

"And one of them had already started sending those taunting letters to the press, too," Margo muttered. "No wonder the handwriting on the Dear Boss letters and note didn't match Maybrick's. This mysterious doctor of ours must have written them."

Shahdi Feroz gave Margo a startled stare. "Yes, of course! Which raises very intriguing questions, Miss Smith, most intriguing questions. Such letters are almost always sent by the killer to taunt police with his power. Yet the letters do *not* match Maybrick's handwriting, even though they use the American phrases Maybrick certainly would have known."

"Like the word boss," Margo nodded. "Or the term 'red stuff' which isn't any kind of Britishism. But Maybrick didn't need to disguise his handwriting, because Maybrick didn't send them, the *doctor* did. But why?" Margo wondered. "I mean, why would he write letters taunting the police using language deliberately couched to sound like an American had written them? Or somebody who'd been to America?"

Shahdi's eyes widened. "Because," she said in an excited whisper, "he *meant to betray James Maybrick*!"

Margo's mouth came open. "My God! He sent them to *frame his partner*? To make sure Maybrick was hanged? But . . . surely Maybrick would've turned him in, if he'd been arrested? Which he wasn't, of course. Maybrick dies of arsenic poisoning next spring." Margo blinked, thoughts racing. "Does this mean something happens to the partner? To stop him from turning Maybrick over to the police?"

Shahdi Feroz was staring at Margo. "A very good question, my dear. We *must* find out who this mysterious doctor is!"

"You're telling me! The sooner the better. We've only got a week before he kills Annie Chapman." Margo was staring absently at the building across the square, while something niggled the back of her mind, some little detail she was missing. "If he knew the East End as well as I'm guessing—" She broke off as it hit her, what she was seeing. "*Oh, my God!* Look at that! The *Great Synagogue*! Another *Jewish connection*! First the Jewish Workingmen's Educational Club, then he kills Catharine Eddowes practically on the doorstep of a *synagogue*. And then he chalks anti-Semitic graffiti on a tenement wall on Goulston Street!"

Shahdi stared at the synagogue across Mitre Square. "Do you realize, this has never been noticed before? That a synagogue stood in Mitre Square? I am impressed, Miss Smith. Very much impressed. A double message, with one killing, leaving her between a policeman's home and a Jewish holy place of worship. A triple message, if one considers the taunt to police represented in his crossing police jurisdictions to chalk his message of hatred."

Margo shivered. "Yeah. All this gives me the screaming willies. He's *smart*. And that's scary as hell."

"My dear," Shahdi said very softly, "all psychopathic serial murderers are terrifying. If only we could only eliminate the abuse and poverty and social sickness that create such creatures . . ." She shook her head. "But that would leave the ones we cannot explain, except through biology or a willful choice to pursue evil pleasure at the expense of others' lives."

"No matter how you look at it," Margo muttered, "when you get down to it, human beings aren't really much better than killer plains apes, are they? Just a thin sugar-coating of civilization to make 'em look prettier." Margo couldn't disguise the bitterness in her voice. She'd had enough experience with human savagery to last a lifetime. And she wasn't even eighteen years old yet.

Shahdi's eyes had gone round. "Whatever has happened to you, my dear, to make you say such things at so young an age?"

Margo opened her mouth to bite out a sharp reply; then managed to bite her tongue at the last instant. "I've been to New York," she said, instead, voice rough. "It stinks. Almost worse than this." She waved a hand at the poorly dressed, hard-working people bustling past, at the women loitering in Church Passage, women eyeing the men who passed, at the ragged children playing in the gutter outside the Sir John Cass School, children whose parents couldn't afford to send them for an education, children who couldn't even manage to be accepted as charity pupils, as Catharine Eddowes had been many years previously, whose parents kept them out of compulsory public-sector schools in defiance of the new laws, to earn a little extra cash. How many of those dirty-faced little girls tossing a ball to one another would be walking the streets in just a few years, selling themselves for enough money to buy a loaf of bread and a cupful of gin?

They left Mitre Square and headed east once more, crossing back into Metropolitan Police jurisdiction, and made their way up Middlesex Street, jammed with the clothing stalls which had given the street its nickname of Petticoat Lane. Margo and Shahdi pushed their way through the crowd, recording the whole scene on their scout logs. Women bargained prices lower on used petticoats, mended bodices and skirts, on dresses and shawls and woolen undergarments called combinations, while men poked through piles of trousers, work shirts, and sturdy boots. Children shouted and begged for cheap tin toys their mothers usually couldn't afford. And men loitered in clusters, muttering in angry tones that "somefink ought to be done, is wot I says. We got no gas lamps in the streets, it's dark as pitch, so's anybody might be murdered by a cutthroat. And them constables, now, over to H Division, wot they care about us, eh? Me own shop was robbed three times last week in broad daylight by them little bastards from the Nichol, and where was a constable, I ask you? Don't care a fig for us, they don't. Ain't *nobody* gives a fig for us, down 'ere in the East End . . ."

And further along, "Goin' to be riots in the streets again, that's wot, mate, goin' to be riots in the streets again, an' they don't give us a decent livin' wage down to docks. I got a brother in a factory, puts in twelve hours a day, six days a week, an' don't bring 'ome but hog an' sixpence a week, t' feed a wife an' five children. God 'elp if 'e comes down ill, God 'elp, I say. Me own sister-in-law might 'ave to walk the streets like that poor Polly Nichols, corse I can't feed 'er, neither, nor 'er starvin' dustpan lids, I got seven o' me own an' the shipyard don't pay me much over a groat more'n me brother brings 'ome . . ."

Margo cut across to Bell Lane, just to get away from the press of unwashed bodies and the miasma of sweat and dirt and despair rising from them, then led the way north along Crispin to Dorset Street, one of London's most infamous thoroughfares, lined with shabby, unheated doss houses. It was even money that every second or third woman they saw on the street was up for sale at the right price. "Dosset Street," as it was nicknamed by the locals, was still half asleep despite the fact that the sun had been high over London's rooftops for hours. Many of the women who used these doss houses worked their trade until the early hours of the morning, five and six A.M., then collapsed into the first available bed and slept as late as the caretakers would let them.

Miller's Court, site of the fifth known Ripper murder, lay just off Dorset Street, through an archway just shy of Commercial Road. Directly across the street from the entrance to Miller's Court lay Crossingham's Lodging House, where Annie Chapman stayed by preference when she possessed the means. The killer had chosen his victims from a very small neighborhood, indeed.

Margo and Shahdi Feroz ducked beneath the archway, passing the chandler shop at number twenty-seven Dorset Street. This shop was owned by Mary Kelly's landlord, John McCarthy. Six little houses, each whitewashed in a vain attempt to make them look respectable, stood in the enclosed court where the final Ripper murder would take place, some three months from now. McCarthy's shop on the corner did a brisk business, it being a Friday. The younger McCarthys' voices were audible through the open windows, squabbling in a boisterous fashion.

At one of the cottage windows, a strikingly beautiful young woman with glorious strawberry blond hair leaned out the window to number thirteen. "Joseph! Come in for breakfast, love!"

Margo started violently. Then stared as a thickset man hurried across the narrow court to open the door to number thirteen. He gave the beautiful blonde girl a hearty kiss. *My God! It's Mary Kelly! And her unemployed lover, the fish-porter, Joseph Barnett!* Mary Kelly's laughter floated out through the open window, followed by her light, sweet voice singing a

popular tune. "Only a Violet I Plucked From My
Mother's Grave . . ." Margo shuddered. It was the
same song she'd be heard singing the night of her
brutal murder.

"Let's get out of here!" Margo choked out roughly.
She headed for the narrow doorway that led back to
Dorset Street. She had barely reached the chandler's
shop when Shahdi Feroz caught up to her.

"Margo, what is it?"

Margo found dark eyes peering intently into her
own. Shadows of worry darkened their depths even
further. "Nothing," Margo said brusquely. "Just a little
shook up, that's all. Thinking about what's going to
happen to that poor girl . . ."

Mary Kelly had been the most savagely mutilated
of all, pieces of her strewn all over the room. And
nothing Margo could do, no warning Margo could
give, would save her from that. She understood, in
a terrible flash of understanding, how that ancient
prophetess of myth, Cassandra of Troy, for whom
Ianira Cassondra was named, must have felt, looking into the future and glimpsing nothing but death—
with no way to change any of it. The feeling was far
worse than during Margo's other down-time trips,
worse, even, than she'd expected, knowing it was
bound to strike at some point, during her Ripper
Watch duties.

Margo met Shahdi Feroz's gaze again and forced
a shrug. "It just hit me a lot harder than I expected,
seeing her like that. She's so pretty and everything . . ."

The look Shahdi Feroz gave her left Margo's face
flaming. *You're young,* that look said. *Young and
inexperienced, for all the down-time work you've
done . . .*

Well, it was true enough. She might be young, but
she wasn't a shrinking violet and she wasn't a quitter,
either. Memory of her parents had not and *would not*
screw up the rest of her life! She shoved herself away

from the sooty bricks of McCarthy's chandler shop. "Where did you want to go, now? Whitehall? That's where the torso will be found in October." The decapitated woman's torso, discovered between the double-event murders of Elizabeth Stride and Catharine Eddowes and the final murder of Mary Kelly, generally wasn't thought to be a Ripper victim. The *modus operandi* simply wasn't the same. But with two killers working together, who knew? And of course, the rest of London would firmly believe it to be Jack's work, which would complicate their task enormously as hysteria and terror deepened throughout the city.

Shahdi Feroz, however, was shaking her head. "No, not just yet. To reach Whitehall, we must leave the East End. I have other work to do, first. I believe we should go to the doss houses along Dorset Street, listen to what the women are saying."

Margo winced at the idea of sitting in a room full of street walkers who would remind her of what she'd fought so hard to escape. "Sure," she said gamely, having to force it out through clenched teeth. "There's only about a million of 'em to choose from."

They set out in mutual silence, walking quickly to keep warm. Margo would've faced the prospect of viewing piles of people left dead by the Black Death with less distaste than the coming interview with doss-house prostitutes. But there literally wasn't a thing she could do to get out of it. *Chalk it up to the price of your training,* she told herself grimly. After all, it wasn't nearly as awful as being raped by those filthy Portuguese traders and soldiers had been. She'd survived Africa. She'd survive this. Her life—and Shahdi Feroz's—might well depend on it. So she clenched her jaw and did her best to stay prepared for whatever might come next.

Chapter Thirteen

Cold and rainy weather inflicts enormous suffering on those with lung ailments. The dampness and the chill seep down into the chest, worsening congestion until each breath drawn is a struggle to lift the weight of a boulder which has settled atop the ribcage, crushing the lungs down against the spine. Worse than the aching heaviness, however, are the prolonged coughing spells which leave devastating weakness in their wake, transforming a simple stroll across six feet of floor space into a marathon-distance struggle.

Cold, wet weather is bad enough when the air is clean. Add to it the smoke of multiple millions of coal-burning fireplaces and stoves, the industrial spewage of factory smokestacks, smelting plants, and iron works, and the rot and mold of anything organic left lying on the ground or in the streets or stacked along water-logged, dockside marshes, and the resulting putrid filth will irritate already-burdened lungs into a state of chronic misery. Toss in the systemic, wasting effects of tuberculosis and the slow deterioration of organs, brain tissues, and mental clarity brought on by advanced syphilis and the result is a slow, pain-riddled slide toward death.

Eliza Anne Chapman had been sliding down that fatal slope for a long time.

The summer and early autumn of 1888 had broken records for chilly temperatures and heavy rainfall. By the first week of September, Annie was so ill, she was unable to pay for her room at Crossingham's lodging house on Dorset Street with anything approaching regularity. Most of what she earned or was given by Edward Stanley—a bricklayer's mate with whom she had established a long-term relationship after the death of her husband—went to pay for medicines. A serious fight with Eliza Cooper, whom Annie had caught trying to palm a florin belonging to a mutual acquaintance, substituting a penny for the more valuable coin, had left Annie bruised and aching, with a swollen temple, blackened eye, and bruised breast where the other woman had punched her.

She had confidently expected to receive money soon for the letters she'd bought from Polly Nichols, to pay for the medicines she desperately needed. But no money was forthcoming from Polly or from the anonymous writer of the letters she carried in her pocket. Then, to Annie's intense shock, Polly was brutally murdered, more hideously stabbed and mutilated than poor Martha Tabram had been, back on August Bank Holiday. Even if Annie had wanted to ask Polly who the letter writer had been, it was now impossible. So Annie had dug out the letters to look at them more closely—and realized immediately there would *be* no money coming, either, not anytime soon. Had Annie been able to read Welsh, she might have been able to turn the letters into a substantial amount of cash very quickly. But Annie couldn't read Welsh. Nor did she know anyone who could.

Which left her with a commodity worth a great

deal of money and no way to realize the fortune it represented. So she did the only thing she could. She sold the letters, just as Polly had sold them to her. One went to a long-time acquaintance from the lodging houses along Dorset Street. Long Liz Stride was a kind-hearted soul born in Sweden, who bought the first letter for sixpence, which was enough for Annie to go to Spitalfields workhouse infirmary and buy one of the medications she needed.

The second letter went to Catharine Eddowes for a groat, and the third Annie sold to Mr. Joseph Barnett, a fish-porter who'd lost his job and was living in Miller's Court with the beautiful young Mary Kelly. Mr. Barnett paid Annie a shilling for the last letter, giving her a wink and a kiss. "My Mary lived in Cardiff, y'know, speaks Welsh like a native, for all she was born in Ireland. Mary'll read it out for me, so she will. And if it's as good as you say, I'll come back and give you a bonus from the payout!"

The groat, worth four pence, and the shilling, worth twelve, bought Annie the rest of the medicine she needed from Whitechapel workhouse infirmary, plus a steady supply of beer and rum for the next couple of days. Alcohol was the only form of pain medication Annie could afford to buy and she was in pain constantly. She felt too ill most of the time to walk the streets, particularly all the way down to Stratford, where she normally plied her trade; but the medicine helped. If only the weather would clear, she might be able to breathe more easily again.

Annie regretted the sale of the letters. But a woman had to live, hadn't she? And blackmail was such a distasteful trade, no matter how a body looked at it. Polly had dazzled her with fanciful dreams of real comfort and proper medicines, but in Annie's world, such dreams were only for the foolish, people who didn't realize they couldn't afford to indulge their fancies when there was food to be gotten into the stomach and medicine to be obtained and a roof and bed to be paid for, somehow . . .

Being a practical woman, Annie put those brief, glittering dreams firmly behind her and got back to the business of staying alive as long as humanly possible in a world which did not care about the fate of one aging and consumptive widow driven to prostitution by sheer poverty. It wasn't much of a life, perhaps. But it was all she had. So, like countless thousands before her, "Dark Annie" Chapman made the best of it she could and kept on living—without the faintest premonition that utter disaster hung over her head like the executioner's sword.

Skeeter Jackson had an uncanny nose for trouble.

And this time, he landed right in the middle of it. One moment, he was intent on reaching Urbs Romae to join the Festival of Mars procession, having been delayed by a man moving suspiciously behind a woman gowned in expensive Japanese silk. The next, Skeeter found himself stranded between a solid wall of Angels of Grace Militia on his left and a whole pack of *Ansar Majlis* sympathizers and construction workers to his right.

He tried to backpedal, but it was far too late. Somebody's fist connected with an *Ansar Majlis* sympathizer's nose. Blood spurted. A roar went up from both sides, *Ansar Majlis* Brotherhood *and* Angels of Grace Militia. The crowd surged, fists swinging. A kiosk full of t-shirts and Ripper photo books toppled. Someone yelled obscenities as merchandise was trampled underfoot. A reek of sweat abused Skeeter's nostrils. Combatants plunged, dripping, into Edo Castletown's goldfish ponds, sending prehistoric birds flapping and screeching in protest from the trampled shrubbery. Then a hamhanded fist clouted his shoulder and the riot engulfed him.

Skeeter spun away from the blow. He tripped and teetered over the edge of the overturned kiosk, trying to keep his balance. Somebody hit him from the side. Skeeter yelled and slammed face first into a total stranger. He found himself tangled up with a viciously swearing woman, who sported a bleeding nose and a black uniform. Her eyes narrowed savagely. Angels of Grace hated *all* men, unless they worshipped the Lady of Heaven, and even then, they were suspicious of treason. Skeeter swore—and ducked a thick-knuckled fist aimed at *his* nose. He twisted, using moves he'd learned scrapping in the camp of the Yakka Mongols, trying to stay alive when the camp's other boys had decided to test the fighting skills and agility of their newly arrived *bogdo*.

Skeeter's lightning move sent the screeching woman into the waiting arms of a roaring *Ansar Majlis* construction worker. The collision was spectacular. Skeeter winced. Then yelped and ducked behind the toppled kiosk, dodging another pair of locked, grappling combatants. He stared wildly around for a way out and didn't find anything remotely resembling an escape route. Not four feet away, Kit Carson stood calmly at the center of the riot, casually tossing bodies this way and that, regardless of size, mass, onrushing speed, or religious and political affiliations. The retired scout's expression wavered between disgust and boredom. A whole pile of bodies had accumulated at his feet, growing steadily even as Skeeter watched, awestruck.

Then a crash of drums and a screaming wail from a piper jerked Skeeter's attention around. The Festival of Mars processional had arrived. Just in time to be engulfed in battle. Skeeter caught a confused glimpse of misshapen, shaggy shapes like hirsute kodiak bears. Women in ring-mail armor who resembled a cartoonist's vision of ancient *valkyries* staggered into view, complete with shields, spears, and swords.

Mixed in were several keen-eyed old women in ragged skins, whose screeches in Old Norse lifted the hair on Skeeter's nape.

Kynan Rhys Gower appeared from out of the melee, dressed in the uniform he'd been wearing when the Welsh bowman had stumbled through that unstable gate into the Battle of Orleans, fighting the French army under the command of Joan of Arc. Several other down-timers sported Roman-style armor, hand-made for this very festival out of metal cans and other scraps salvaged from the station's refuse bins. There was even a Spaniard clutching a blunderbuss, wild-eyed and shouting in medieval Spanish as the procession slammed headlong into the riot.

The shock of collision drove tourists scattering for their very lives.

Shangri-La's down-timers fought a pitched battle—and they fought *dirty*.

A wild-eyed construction worker reeled back from a sword blow, blood streaming down his face from the gash in his scalp. A black-unformed ferret staggered past, locked in mortal combat with a six-foot bearskin draped over the head and down the back of a six-foot-eight Viking berserker. Skeeter dimly recognized the man under the bearskin as Eigil Bjarneson, a down-timer who'd stumbled through Valhalla's Thor's Gate several months previously. A sushi lunch stand swayed and crashed to the floor, spilling water and live fish underfoot. Several combatants slipped on the wriggling, slippery contents of the broken aquarium and fell. Skeeter caught a glimpse of onrushing motion from the corner of one eye and jumped back instinctively. A spear missed his midriff by inches, whistling past to embed itself in the wooden slats of a bench behind him

The spear's intended victim, a roaring *Ansar Majlis* sympathizer, pulled a mortar trowel from his tool belt and launched himself at the ring-mail clad woman who'd thrown the spear. Then a giant Angel in black, screaming obscenities in tones to bend metal, lunged right at Skeeter. Obligingly, Skeeter grasped the woman's outstretched arms and assisted her on her way, planting one foot and turning his hip in an effortless Aikido move he'd been practicing for months, now. For just an instant, the startled Militia Angel was airborne. Then the park bench behind Skeeter, complete with protruding spear, splintered under the Angel's landing. If Skeeter hadn't been practicing—and teaching his down-time friends— martial arts moves like that one, he'd have been *under* that mountain of curse-spitting Angel.

Then a man in a red shirt and burnoose, eyes wild and distorted, came in from Skeeter's off-side, and caught him while he still teetered off balance. Skeeter went down hard. He knew, at least, how to fall without doing himself injury, another legacy of scrapping fights with Yakka Mongol youngsters heavier and stronger than he was. Unfortunately, the man in red was heavy, too. A great deal heavier than Skeeter. And he landed right on top of Skeeter's chest, fists pounding everything within reach. Which mainly constituted Skeeter. A blow caught his ribs. Skeeter grunted, half-stunned. His own jab at the man's eyes narrowly missed the mark, but he raked the bastard's nose with a fist and popped his Adam's apple with the side of his arm. Blood welled from both nostrils. The man roared, even as Skeeter twisted under him, trying to wriggle free. Another smashing blow landed against Skeeter's ribs. He gasped, trying to breathe against blossoming pain—

And somebody snatched the bastard up by his red shirt and dragged him off. Skeeter heard a meaty blow and a howl of pain, a curse in Arabic . . . Skeeter rolled to his hands and knees, gasping and cursing a little, himself. His ribs ached, but nothing felt broken. He staggered to his feet, aware of his exposed vulnerability on the floor. Then he blinked. The roar of battle had died away, almost to a whimper. Security had arrived in force. Several dozen uniformed officers were tossing weighted nets and swinging honest-to-God lassos, bringing down combatants five and six at a time. And the Arabian Nights construction foreman was directing more of his crew to help Security, throwing nets across enraged construction workers and dragging them out none too gently, holding them for security to handcuff. In seconds, the fight was effectively over.

Skeeter caught his breath as uniformed bodies waded in, yanking combatants off balance and cuffing them with rough efficiency. Weapons clattered to the cobblestones and lay where they'd fallen, abandoned by owners who found themselves abruptly under arrest. As Skeeter stood swaying, his shirt in shreds where he'd tried to wriggle away from the guy in the red shirt, he realized who'd helped him out. None other than Kit Carson was standing over the fallen *Ansar Majlis* sympathizer, breathing easily, gripping a cotton rag mop in both hands like a quarterstaff. An overturned mop bucket spread a puddle of dirty water behind the retired time scout, where someone on the maintenance crew had been caught up in the riot, as well. At least it wasn't Bergitta—she wasn't anywhere in sight. Judging from the trail of bruised, groaning figures behind Kit, leading from the jumbled pile of combatants Kit had already put down, the retired time scout knew how to use a quarterstaff effectively, too. The jerk in red on the floor was moaning and not moving much.

Then Kit glanced up, caught Skeeter's gaze, and relaxed fractionally. "You okay, Skeeter?"

He nodded, then winced at the bruising along his ribs. "Yeah. Thanks."

"My pleasure." He said it like he meant it. Literally. A feral grin had begun to stretch his lips.

"Whoops, here comes Mike Benson. *Him,* you don't need breathing down your neck. Scoot, Skeeter. I'll catch you later."

Skeeter blinked, then made tracks. Kit was right about one thing. The last person Skeeter wanted to tangle with was Mike Benson cleaning up a riot. Skeeter disappeared into the stunned crowd as Rachel Eisenstein's medical team arrived, setting broken bones and sewing up gashes. Fortunately, from the look of things, they wouldn't be dealing with anything fatal. *How,* he wasn't sure. Spears, swords, knives, construction tools of half-a-dozen shapes and lethal potentialities . . . He shook his head in amazement. One member of the Angels of Grace Militia sported gashes down her face from a fistful of bear claws, where she'd made the mistake of taking a swing at Eigil Bjarneson.

And right at the edge of the riot zone, down at the border between Edo Castletown and Victoria Station, Skeeter found Ann Vinh Mulhaney, totally unscathed despite her tiny size. The petite firearms instructor was sitting calmly atop a wrought iron lamp post, with a small, lethal-looking revolver clutched in each hand. It was clear from the path of wreckage that no one had cared to challenge either her position or her person. Skeeter grinned and waved. Ann smiled and nodded, then holstered her pistols and slithered down the lamp post, lithe and agile as a sleek hunting cat. She landed lightly on the cobbles and headed Skeeter's way.

"Good God, Ann," he said, eying the guns she'd used to defend her perch, "you could've held off an army from up there. Those pistols of yours are cute little things. What are they?"

The petite instructor chuckled. "Webleys, of course. The Royal Irish Constabulary Webley, a different animal altogether from your later military Webley. Pack quite a punch for their size, too, in a delightfully concealable package. Lots of Britannia tourists have been renting them for the Ripper tours."

"No wonder nobody challenged you up there."

She laughed easily. "Occasionally, we get a tourist or two with brains. I don't know about anybody else, but after all that excitement, I could use a drink to cool my throat. Come with us, why don't you, Skeeter?"

He flushed crimson, aware that what little money he had left wouldn't even cover the cost of a beer. "Uh, thanks, but I've got work to do. I'll, uh, take a raincheck, okay?" She probably knew he'd been fired, the whole station knew that, by now, but a guy had his pride, after all.

"Well, all right," she said slowly, studying him with her head tilted to one side. "See you around, then, Skeeter. Hey, Kit! Over here! I saw Robert headed toward Urbs Romae. What say we stop at the Down Time for a quick drink before Primary cycles? We'll probably catch up to Robert there and I heard they had a cask of Falernian . . ."

Skeeter edged his way deeper into the crowd as Kit exclaimed, "Falernian? When did they bring in a cask of heaven?"

Even Skeeter knew that Falernian was the Dom Perignon of ancient Roman wines. And Kit Carson was a connoisseur of fine wines and other potent potables. Skeeter sighed, wondering how marvellous it really tasted, aware that he wouldn't have been able to afford a glass of Falernian even if he had still been employed. But since he wasn't . . .

He cut around the damaged riot zone the long way, heading for Primary again. Skeeter dodged around one corner of the Shinto Shrine which had been built in the heart of Edo Castletown, and wheeled full-tilt into a short, stout woman. The collision rocked her back on her heels. Skeeter shot out a steadying hand to keep her from falling. Familiar blue eyes flashed indignantly up at him. "Cor, blimey, put a butcher's out, won't you, luv? Right near squashed me thrip'nny bits, you 'ave!"

That patter identified her faster than Skeeter could focus on her features. Molly, the down-timer Cockney barmaid who worked at the Down Time Bar & Grill, favorite haunt of station residents, was rubbing her substantial chest with one arm and grimacing. "Molly! What are you doing halfway to Primary Precinct?" Skeeter had to shout above the roar of voices as she tugged her dress to rights and glared sourly up at him. "I thought you were working late today? Did you get caught up in the Festival of Mars procession after all?"

Molly's expressive grimace encapsulated a wealth of disdain, loathing, and irritated anger into one twist of her mobile face. "Nah. Bleedin' newsies invaded, bad as any whirlin' dervishes, they are, wot broke a British square. Devil tyke 'em! I'd like t'see 'em done up like kippers, so I would. Got the manners of a gutter snipe, won't let a lady put 'er past be'ind 'er, not for all the quid in the Owd Lady of Threadneedle Street." When Skeeter drew a blank on that reference, as he often did with Molly's colorful Cockney, she chuckled and patted his arm. "Bank of England, me owd china, that's wot we called 'er, Owd Lady of Threadneedle Street."

"Oh." Skeeter grinned. "Me owd china, is it? I'm honored, Molly." She didn't admit friendship to many, not even among the down-timers. He wondered what he'd done to earn her good opinion. Her next words gave him the answer.

"I come up 'ere t'find Bergitta. Needs a place t'stay, is afraid o' that blagger wot blacked 'er face, livin' alone an' all, an' I got room in me flat, so I 'ave. It'd be cheaper, too, wiv two of us sharin' the bills."

Skeeter didn't know what to say. He found himself swallowing hard.

"You ain't seen 'er, then?"

He shook his head. "No. I was heading for Primary, when that riot broke out."

"Might come along, me own self," Molly mused. "Got nuffink better to do, 'til I finds Bergitta, anyway."

Skeeter grinned. "I'd be honored to escort you, Molly."

She fell into step beside him.

"I've *never* seen this many people at an opening of Primary." Skeeter had to shout above the roar of voices. Using elbows and a few underhanded moves, Skeeter shoved his way through the mob until he found a good vantage point where he and Molly could settle themselves to wait.

Gaudy splashes of color marked long lines of departing tourists and the hundreds of spectators arriving just to watch the show. Montgomery Wilkes, ruling head of BATF on station, wasn't in sight yet. Security officers were scarce, too, in the wake of the riot.

BATF carels, manned by tax-collection agents of the Bureau of Access Time Functions, carefully clad in dress-uniform red, lined the route into and out of Primary Precinct. Once past the BATF carels, inbound tourists and visitors arriving at TT-86 had to run a gauntlet of medical stations, a whole double row of them, which formed the entryway into the time terminal.

Tourists inbound had to scan their medical records into the station's database files before entering Shangri-La. This gave station medical baseline data to compare the tourists' health with, once they returned from their time tours. All departing tourists were required to undergo an intensive physical before leaving the station, as a quarantine procedure against exporting anything nasty up time. The system had stopped an outbreak of black death a couple of years back on TT-13, keeping the deadly plague from reaching the up-time world. The medical screening system wasn't foolproof, of course—nothing in life was—but it kept time tourism operational, which was the lifeblood of a station like Shangri-La.

Skeeter just hoped, with a superstitious shiver, that the irate up-time senator whose daughter had been kidnapped failed to swing enough votes to shut down the time terminals. If station violence on TT-86 continued much longer, he just might get those votes. If BATF was worried about it, however, that worry didn't show in the attitudes of its agents. They were as rude as ever, from what Skeeter could see of the check-out procedures underway. BATF agents ignored the increasing crush of onlookers, busy valuing souvenirs brought back from down-time gates. The agents' main job on station was to establish taxes due on whatever was brought up time from the gates and to levy fines for anyone caught smuggling out contraband. They searched luggage—and occasionally, the tourists and the couriers who ran supplies and mail back and forth through Primary—for anything undeclared that might be considered taxable. At one tax kiosk, a middle-aged lady with diamonds on every finger was protesting loudly that she hadn't any idea how those granulated Etruscan gold earrings and necklaces had come to be sewn into her Victorian corset. *She* hadn't put them in her suitcase, why, they must have been planted in her luggage by some ruffian . . .

"Tell it to the judge," the red-clad BATF agent said in a bored tone, "or pay the taxes."

"But I tell you—"

"Lady, you can either pay the five-thousand-dollar tax fine due on this jewelry, or you can turn it over to a representative of the International Federation of Art Temporally Stolen, to see that it's returned to its proper place of origin, or you can go to prison for

violating the Prime Rule of time travel. You can't profit
illegally from a time gate. Robert Li is the designated
IFARTS agent for Shangri-La Station. His studio is in
Little Agora. You have exactly a quarter of an hour to
dispose of it there or pay the taxes due here."

The woman sputtered indignantly for a long
moment, then snapped, "Oh, all right! Will you take
a check?"

"Yes, ma'am, if you have three forms of identification with a permanent address that matches the
information you gave in your records when you
entered Shangri-La Station. Make it payable to the
Bureau of Access Time Functions."

"Fine!" She was digging into a large, exquisitely
wrought handbag. That bag had walked out of some
designer's studio in Paris, or Skeeter didn't know high
fashion. And since Skeeter had made it a lifelong
practice to keep tabs on *haute couture* as well as
cheap knock-offs, as a way of distinguishing rich,
potential marks from wannabe pretenders, he was
pretty sure it was the real McCoy. She dragged out
a checkbook cover made from genuine ostrich leather
with a diamond insignia in one corner and scribbled
out a check. Five thousand was probably what she
dropped on restaurant tables as tips in the course of
an average month. Skeeter shook his head. The richer
they were, the more they tried to pull, sneaking out
contraband past customs.

The BATF agent verified her identification and
accepted the check.

The lady stuffed her Etruscan gold back into her
corset with wounded dignity and snapped shut the
case, moving deeper into the departures area with an
autocratic sniff.

"Next!"

Gate announcements sounded every ten minutes
until the five-minute mark, after which the loud-
speaker warnings began coming every minute,

reminding stragglers they were running out of time. At the three-minute warning, a familiar voice from somewhere behind him startled Skeeter into glancing around.

"Skeeter!"

He caught a glimpse of Rachel Eisenstein pushing through the crowd. She was panting hard, clearly having run most of the way from the infirmary.

"Rachel? What's wrong?" He entertained momentary, panic-stricken visions of Bergitta having thrown a blood clot from that beating or something else equally life threatening. As Shangri-La's Station's chief of medicine pushed her way through to Skeeter and Molly, he grasped her hand. "What is it? What's *wrong*?"

Rachel blinked in startled surprise. "Wrong? Oh, Skeeter, I'm sorry, of course you'd think something's happened to Bergitta. Nothing's wrong at all, other than I just finished triage from that riot and decided I'd better work Primary, too, just in case." She patted a heavy hip pack. "Brought all the essentials. I was just trying to get here before the gate opened, hoping I might find someone I recognized who already had a good spot. Hi, Molly!"

Skeeter drew a long, deep breath and slowly relaxed. "Well, we've got a decent spot. You're welcome to share."

"Thanks, this *is* a great spot." Rachel pushed back damp hair from her brow. "God, I hope we don't have another riot on the heels of that mess."

"Me, either," Skeeter muttered. "Because now I've got *two* ladies to look out for, if the fists start flying."

The slim surgeon smiled, dark eyes sparkling. "Skeeter, I'm touched, really. I didn't know you cared. What brings *you* out here in all this madness?"

"Me?" Skeeter shrugged, wondering if she'd believe the truth. "I, uh, was wondering how many pickpockets and con artists I might spot on their way in."

Rachel Eisenstein shot him a surprisingly intent stare. "I have been paying attention, you know, Skeeter. I'm not sure, exactly, what triggered it, although I suspect it had something to do with Ianira."

He flushed. "You could say that." Skeeter shrugged. "I'm just trying to make things better around here. For the down-timers." He glanced at Molly, whose eyes reflected a quiet pride that closed his throat. "Folks like Molly, here, they've got a rough enough time as it is, trying to survive, without some jerk stealing them blind." Skeeter shrugged again and changed the subject. "I've been keeping count of outgoing departures. I was up to nearly a hundred before you got here. Want to bet we get more inbound than we send back outbound?"

Rachel chuckled. "No bets!"

Skeeter grinned. "Wise woman."

The klaxon sounded again, blasting away at Skeeter's eardrums. *"Your attention please.* Gate One is due to open in one minute. All departures, be advised that if you have not cleared Station Medical, you will not be permitted to pass Primary. Please have your baggage ready for customs . . ."

The departures in line hastily gathered up their luggage. Those still at the customs tables scrambled to pay the astromical taxes demanded as a condition of departure. Then the savage lash of subharmonics which heralded the opening of a major temporal gate struck Skeeter square in the skull bones. A fierce headache comprised of equal parts low blood sugar, stress, and gate subharmonics blossomed, causing him to wince. Skeeter resisted the urge to cover his ears, knowing it wouldn't shut out the painful noise that wasn't a noise, and simply waited.

The sight was always impressive as Primary opened up out of thin air. A point of darkness appeared five feet above the Commons floor. It grew rapidly, amoeba-like, its black, widening center an oil stain spreading across the air. The outer edges of the dark hole in reality dopplered through the whole visible spectrum, with the spreading fringes shimmering like a runaway rainbow. A stir ran through the spectators. Every person in the station had seen temporal gates open before, of course, but the phenomenon never failed to raise chill bumps or the fine hairs along the back of the neck as the fabric of reality shifted and split itself wide open . . .

A flurry of startled grunts and a rising flood of profanities sounded behind them. Skeeter turned to crane his head above the crowd. "Aw, nuts . . ."

Literally.

The Angels of Grace Militia, at least the portion that had escaped arrest during the riot, was on a crash-course drive for Primary, shoving their way through by brute force.

"What is it?" Rachel asked, trying to see.

"Angel Squad, inbound."

Molly's comment was in obscure Cockney, defying translation.

Rachel rolled her eyes. "Oh, God. Please don't tell me *they're* expecting reinforcements from up time, too?"

"Well," Skeeter scratched his ear, "scuttlebutt has it their captain was seen buying a ticket for some general of theirs who's coming in for a Philosopher's Gate tour. Wants to see the city where Ianira lived in subjugation to an evil male of the species."

"Oh, God, Skeeter, I *told* you not to tell me they were bringing in reinforcements!"

"Sorry," he grinned sheepishly.

Rachel scowled up at him and stood on tiptoe, trying to spot the onrushing Angels. Molly just thinned her lips and moved into a slightly aggressive stance, waiting for whatever might come next. Moving in a close-packed wedge, the Angel Squad drove through the waiting crowd on an unstoppable course, shoving and bullying their way through. One brief altercation ended with a tourist clutching at a bloodied nose while Angels burst past him on a course that would bring them out right about where Skeeter stood with Molly and Rachel. He braced for bad trouble for the second time in a quarter hour, wondering whether it might not be wiser to simply cut and run, taking himself, Molly, and Rachel out of their path, or whether he ought to stand his ground on general principles.

At that instant, an ear-splitting klaxon shattered the air.

Skeeter jerked his gaze around just in time to see it. Primary had opened wide enough to begin the transfer of out-bound tourists. Only they hadn't gotten very far. A writhing, entangled mass of humanity crashed straight through Primary, *inbound.*

Rachel gasped. "What in the world—? *Nobody* crashes Primary!"

But a howling swarm of people had done just that, shoving through into Shangri-La Station before the outgoing departures could get off to a good start. Klaxons blared insanely. The mad, hooting rhythm all but deafened. Nearly a hundred shouting people stormed into Shangri-La Station in a seething mass, rushing past medical stations, past screaming tourists and howling BATF agents, past everything in their path, as though they owned the entire universe.

"Has every nut in the universe decided to converge on Primary today?"

"I don't know!" Rachel shook her head. "But this could get ugly, whoever they are."

Skeeter agreed. Whoever the new arrivals were, they were headed right this way. And where were those damned Angels? He tried to peer back through the crowd where the Angels of Grace still plowed toward them, a juggernaut at full steam. At that moment, Montgomery Wilkes shot from his office at a dead run, driving forward like a hurtled war spear straight into the boiling knot of close-packed humanity crashing through Primary. The head of BATF wielded his authority like a machete. "HALT! Every one of you! Stop *right now!* And I mean—"

Monty never finished.

Someone in that on-rushing maelstrom shoved him. *Hard.*

The seething head of BATF slammed sideways, completely out of the swarm inbound through Primary. Wilkes careened headlong into the chaos of the departure line. Windmilling wildly, he inadvertently knocked down a woman, three kids, and a crate of sixteenth-century Japanese porcelain which had just been valued and taxed by Monty's agents. Its owner, a departing businessman, teetered for an instant, as well. Monty, staggering and stumbling in a half circle, caromed off the businessman and continued on through the line into the concrete wall beyond. They connected—Monty's face and the wall—with a sickening SPLAT!

Wilkes slid, visibly dazed, to the floor just as the Japanese businessman went down. He landed as badly as his irreplacable porcelain. *That* didn't fare nearly as well when it hit the concrete. Japanese curses—which followed the confirmation of utter ruin—poured out above the noise of yelling voices and screaming klaxons. Monty Wilkes simply sat on the floor blinking wet eyes. His agents gaped, open-mouthed, for a long instant, motionless with shock. Then they scattered, antlike. Some broke toward the gate crashers and others raced to their employer's rescue. Sirens and klaxons wailed like storm winds on the Gobi—

Skeeter abruptly found himself tangled up in the outer edges of a churning cyclone of vid-cam crews, remote-lighting technicians, and shouting newsies. Skeeter staggered. A long boom microphone attached to a human being slammed violently sideways. It very nearly knocked him off his feet. Pain blossomed down the side of his head and through his shoulder. Skeeter spat curses and tried to protect Rachel's head when a heavy camera swung straight toward her skull. Molly went spinning under a body slam from someone twice her height.

Then another jostling, shouting mob slammed into them from *behind*.

The Angels of Grace had arrived.

The seething chaos crashing Primary staggered as the juggernaut of black-clad Angels crashed into it, full speed. Skeeter heard shouts and threats and screeches of protest. A fist connected with someone's nose. An ugly exchange of profanity exploded into the supercharged air . . .

"*Armstrong!*"

Hard, grasping hands forcibly jerked Skeeter around. A tall, powerful stranger yanked him forward. "*Armstrong, you son-of-a-bitch! Where's my daughter?*"

Over the shoulder of the gorilla breaking his arm, Skeeter glimpsed a living wall of newsies and camera operators. They stared right at him, eyes and mouths rounded. Skeeter blinked stupidly into a dimly familiar face . . .

One that darkened as sudden shock and anger registered. "You're not Noah Armstrong! Who the hell are *you?*"

"Who am I?" Skeeter's brain finally caught up. He dislodged the man's grip with a violent jerk of his arm. "Who the hell are *you?*"

Before anybody could utter a single syllable, the embattled Angels exploded.

"*Death to tyrants!*"

"*Get him!*"

For just an instant, Skeeter saw a look of stupe-fied surprise cross the stranger's face. The man's mouth sagged open. Then his whole face drained absolutely white. Not in fear. In *fury*. The explosion went off straight into Skeeter's face. "*What in hell is going on in this God-cursed station?*"

Skeeter's mouth worked, but no sound emerged.

"What are those *lunatics*"—he jabbed a finger at the Angels—"doing brawling with my staff? Answer me! Where's your station security? You!" The man who'd mistaken him for somebody named Noah Armstrong grabbed Skeeter's arm again, yanked him off balance. "Take me to your station manager's office! Now!"

"Hey! Take your hands off me!" Skeeter wrenched free. "Didn't anybody teach you assault's illegal?"

The stranger's eyes widened fractionally, then narrowed into angry grey slits. "Just who do you think you're talking to? I'd better get some cooperation out of this station, starting with *you*, whoever you are, or this station's jail is going to be full of petty officials charged with obstruction of justice!"

Skeeter opened his mouth again, not really sure what might come out of it, but at that moment, Bull Morgan, himself, strode through the chaos at Primary. The station manager moved with jerky strides as he maneuvered his fireplug-shaped self on a collision course with Skeeter and the irate stranger.

"Out of the way," Bull growled, shouldering aside newsie crews and BATF agents with equal disregard for their status. He puffed his way up like a tugboat and stuck out one ham-sized hand. "Bull Morgan, Station Manager, Time Terminal Eighty-Six. I understand you wanted to see me?"

Skeeter glanced from Bull's closed and wary expression to the stranger's flushed jowls and seething grey eyes and decided other climes were doubtless healthier places to take himself . . .

"Marshal!" the stranger snapped.

A red-faced bull moose in a federal marshal's

uniform detached itself from the chaos boiling around them. Said moose produced a set of handcuffs, which he promptly snapped around Bull Morgan's wrists.

Skeeter's jaw dropped.

So did Bull's. His unlit cigar hit the floor with an inaudible thud.

"Mr. Clarence Morgan, you are hereby placed under arrest on charges of kidnapping, misuse of public office, willful disregard of public safety, violation of the prime directive of temporal travel—"

"*What?*"

"—and tax evasion. You are hereby remanded to federal custody. You have the right to remain silent. Anything you say can and will be used against you in a court of law—"

From somewhere directly behind Skeeter, a woman in a black uniform let out a strangled bellow. "*You slimy little dictator!* Take your trumped up charges and your Stalinist terror tactics off our station!"

Somebody threw a punch . . .

The riot erupted in every direction. A camera smashed to the concrete floor. Somebody sprawled into Skeeter's line of vision, clutching at a bloody nose and loosened teeth. Another black-clad Angel loomed out of the crowd, fists cocked. Molly's gutter Cockney scalded someone's ears. A newsie went flying and somebody screamed—

The tear gas hit them all at the same instant.

Riot turned abruptly to rout.

Skeeter coughed violently, eyes burning. Rachel Eisenstein staggered into him, bent almost double. A ring of uniformed federal officers materialized out of the spreading cloud, masked against the gas, spewing chemical spray from cannisters in a three-sixty degree swath. They surrounded Bull Morgan and the infuriated, cursing stranger, making sure the latter didn't collapse onto the floor. Moving with neat, deadly calm, more than a dozen federal agents took charge. Snub-nosed riot guns flashed into a bristling circle, muzzles pointed outward.

Newsies fell over one another as they tried to evade armed feds, livid BATF officers, residents trying to get away through the chaos, Shangri-La Security arriving too late to prevent disaster, screaming Angels, and panic-stricken tourists. As the tear gas spread, the inbound traffic arriving through Primary disintegrated into a shambles.

Skeeter grabbed Rachel's wrist and hauled her bodily toward Edo Castletown. They had to get clear of this insanity. Weird, distorted shouts and cries rose on all sides. He couldn't see Molly anywhere. He could barely see, at all. They slithered feet-first into a goldfish pond and nearly fell, then splashed through knee-deep water and ran into screaming, wailing tourists and floating timbers where one of the Edo Castletown bridge railings had collapsed. Skeeter scrambled up the other side of the pond, pulling Rachel up behind him, and half-fell through a screen of shrubbery, then they stumbled into a miraculous pocket of clear air. Skeeter dragged down a double lungful of it, coughing violently. He tried to keep Rachel on her feet, but was hardly able to keep his own.

"Let me help!"

The familiar voice rang practically in his ear. Someone got an arm around Rachel and drew her forward, then somebody grasped Skeeter's elbow and hauled him out of the chaos on tottering feet. Blinded by the tear gas, Skeeter allowed himself to be propelled along. Noise and confusion faded. Then someone else got an arm around him and a few moments later, he found his face buried in blessedly cool, running water. He coughed again and again, blinked streaming, burning eyes. He managed to choke out, "Rachel?"

"She's all right, Skeeter. Damned good job you did, getting her out of that mess."

He heard her coughing somewhere beside him and wondered with an anxious jolt what had become of Molly. Skeeter rinsed his eyes again, swearing under his breath, furious with himself for failing yet again to protect a friend in the middle of a station riot. He was finally able to blink his eyes and keep them open without burning pain sending new tears streaming down his face.

Skeeter was standing, improbably, in what looked like the bathrooms off the Neo Edo Hotel lobby. The mirror showed him a sodden mess that had once been his face. He shook his head, spraying water, and started to scrub his face with both hands. Someone grabbed his wrists and said hastily, "Wash them off, first. They're covered with CS." Slippery liquid soap cascaded across his fingers.

That voice sounded so familiar, Skeeter glanced up, startled. And found himself staring eyeball to reddened eyeball with Kit Carson.

Skeeter's mouth fell open. The lean and grizzled former time scout smiled, a trifle grimly. "Wash your hands, Skeeter. Before you rub tear gas into your eyes again." Behind Kit's shoulder, Robert Li, the station's resident antiquarian, bent over another sink, helping Rachel rinse tear gas out of her eyes. Belatedly, Skeeter noticed the floppy rubber gas mask dangling from Kit's neck. Where the devil had Kit Carson found a gas mask? Surely he hadn't bought one from that Templar selling them down in Little Agora? Wherever he'd stashed it—probably that fabled safe of his, up in the Neo Edo Hotel's office—there'd been two of 'em, because Robert Li wore one, too. Well, maybe Kit had bought them from that Templar, after all. He was smart enough to prepare for any kind of trouble. Wordlessly, Skeeter washed his hands.

When he'd completed the ritual, which helped him regain his composure and some measure of his equilibrium, he straightened up and met Kit's gaze again. He was startled by the respect he found there. "Thanks," Skeeter mumbled, embarrassed.

Kit merely nodded. "Better strip off those clothes. The Neo Edo's laundry staff can clean the tear gas out of them."

Well, why not? Skeeter had done stranger things in his life than strip naked in front of Kit Carson and the station's leading antiquities expert in the middle of the most expensive bathroom in Shangri-La Station while a riot raged outside. He was down to his skivvies when Hashim Ibn Fahd, a down-time teenager who'd stumbled, shocked, through the new Arabian Nights gate, arrived. Dressed in Neo Edo Hotel bellhop livery, which startled Skeeter, since Hashim hadn't been employed two days previously, the boy carried a bundle of clothing under one arm and a large plastic sack.

"Here," Hashim said, holding out the sack. "Put everything inside, Skeeter."

"Have you seen Molly?"

"No, Skeeter. But I will search, if Mr. Carson allows?"

Kit nodded. "I didn't realize she was caught in that mess, too, or I'd have pulled her out along with Skeeter and Rachel."

The down-timer boy handed over his plastic sack and ran for the door. Skeeter dumped in his dress slacks and his shirt, the one the irate construction worker had ripped not thirty minutes previously. The jingle of important things rattled in his pockets. "Uh, my stuff's in there."

"We'll salvage everything, Skeeter," Kit assured him. "There's an emergency shower in that last stall, back there. Sluice off and get dressed. This is going to get mighty ugly, mighty fast. I don't want you anyplace

where that asshole out there," he nodded toward the
riot still underway outside the Neo Edo, "can lay
hands on you. Not without witnesses."

That sounded even more ominous than the riot.
"Uh, Kit?" he asked uncertainly.

The retired time scout glanced around. "Yes?"

Skeeter swallowed nervously. "Just who was that
guy, anyway? He looked sorta familiar . . ."

Kit's eyes widened. "You didn't recognize him?
Good God. And here I thought you had a set the size
of Everest. That was Senator John Caddrick."

Skeeter's knees jellied.

Kit gripped his shoulder. "Buck up, man. I don't
think you'll be going to jail anytime in next ten
minutes, anyway, so shower that stuff off. We'll con-
vene a council of war, after, shall we?"

There being nothing of intelligence Skeeter could
say in response to that, he simply padded off bare-
footed across the marble floor of the Neo Edo's
luxurious bathroom, wondering how in hell Kit Carson
proposed to get Skeeter out of *this* one. He groaned.
Oh, God, this was *all* they needed, with Ianira
Cassondra's suspicious disappearance, fatal shootings
on station during two major station riots, *not* counting
today's multiple disasters . . .

Why *Senator Caddrick,* of all people? And why
now? If Caddrick was here, did that mean his missing, kidnapped kid had been brought here, too? By
the *Ansar Majlis?* Skeeter held back a groan. He had
an awful feeling Shangri-La Station was in fatal
trouble.

Where that left Skeeter's adopted, down-timer
family . . .

Skeeter ground his molars and turned on the
emergency shower. Shangri-La Station wasn't going
down without a fight! If Senator Caddrick meant to
shut them down, he was in for the biggest battle of
his life. Skeeter Jackson was fighting for the very

survival of his adopted clan, for everything he held
sacred and decent in the world.

Yakka Mongols, even adopted ones, were notoriously dirty fighters.

And they did not like to lose.

Chief Inspector Conroy Melvyn, as head of the
Ripper Watch Team, had the right to tell Malcolm
what he wanted to try when it came to searching for
the Ripper's identity, and what Conroy Melvyn wanted
was to know who this mysterious doctor was, assisting James Maybrick. Malcolm, exhausted by days of
searching for Benny Catlin, didn't think Melvyn's latest
scheme was going to work. But he was, as they said
in the States, the boss, and what the boss wanted . . .

Nor could Margo tackle this particular guiding job.
Not even Douglas Tanglewood was properly qualified.
But Malcolm was. So Malcolm Moore dressed to the
nines and ordered the best carriage Time Tours'
Gatehouse maintained, and set his teeth against wea-
riness as they jolted through the evening toward Pall
Mall and the gentlemen's clubs for some trace of a
doctor answering their mystery Ripper's description.

Conroy Melvyn, Guy Pendergast, and Pavel Kostenka rode with him, the latter agreeing to remain silent
throughout the evening, since men of foreign birth
were *not* welcomed in such clubs unless they were
widely known as prominent international celebrities,
which Pavel Kostenka was not—at least, not in 1888.
And he was still very much shaken by the riot which
had endangered his life in Whitechapel earlier in the
week. Conroy Melvyn would also have to remain close-
mouthed in these elite environs, given his working-class
accent; if pressed, Malcolm would explain that he was
with the police, investigating a case, but hoped to avoid
any such scene, which would irretrievably damage his
own reputation. No gentleman would be forgiven for
bringing a low and vulgar creature like a policeman into

an establishment such as the Carlton Club, their first destination for the evening.

Of the three men Malcolm would be guiding this evening, Guy Pendergast would be the least restrained by circumstances. And he remained the most ebulliently convinced of his own immortality, as well, constantly suggesting mad "research" schemes which Malcolm and Douglas and Margo had to veto, sometimes forcefully. Undaunted, Pendergast chatted amiably the whole ride, trying to draw out the Ripper scholars on the subject of the evening's search and chuckling at their close-mouthed irritation.

They finally reached Robert Smirke's famous clubhouse of 1836, which was fated for destruction by Nazi bombs in 1940, and Malcolm told the carriage driver to wait for an hour, then entered the ornately popular Carlton Club, which lay situated beautifully between ultra-fashionable St. James's Square—with its statue of William III and the minaret-steepled church of St. James's Piccadilly visible above the tall, stately buildings—and Carlton House Terrace on the opposite side. The lovely Carlton Gardens ran along Carlton Club's open, easterly facing side, completing the stately club's picturesque, fashionable setting.

Malcolm was known here, as he was in all of the gentlemen's clubs of Pall Mall and Waterloo Place, having procured memberships in each for business purposes as a temporal guide. He greeted the doorman with a nod and introduced his guests, anglicizing Dr. Kostenka's name, then ushered them into the familiar, tobacco-scented halls of the gentleman's private domain. Massive mahogany furniture and dark, rich colors dominated. There was no trace of feminine frills, of the crowding of bric-a-brac, or the typical housewifely clutter which dominated most gentlemen's private homes. Malcolm and his guests

checked their tall evening hats, canes, and gloves,
but Malcolm declined to check his valise, which held
his log and ATLS, pleading business matters.

"I would suggest, gentlemen," he told his charges,
"that we begin in one of the gaming rooms where
card tables have been set up."

Conversation flowed thick as the brandy and the
heavy port wines in evidence at every elbow. Voices
raised in laughter swirled around others engaged in
conversation which was not deemed socially proper
for mixed company, accompanied by blue-grey clouds
of tobacco smoke. Copies of infamous publications
such as *The Pearl,* a short-lived but popular pornographic magazine, could be seen in a few hands where
gentlemen lounged beneath gas lights, reading and
trading jokes.

"—meeting of the Theosophists, this evening?" a
passing gentleman asked his companion.

"Where, here? No, I hadn't realized. What an
intriguing set of gentlemen, although I daresay they
would do well to be rid of that horrid Madame
Blavatsky!"

Both gentlemen laughed and climbed an ornate
staircase for the second floor of the club. Malcolm
paused, wondering if he ought not follow his instincts.

"What is it?" Pendergast asked.

"Those gentlemen just spoke of a Theosophical
meeting here this evening."

Pendergast frowned. "A what meeting?"

"Theosophical Society. One of London's foremost
occult research organizations."

Pendergast chuckled. "Bunch of lunatics, no doubt.
Too bad Dr. Feroz couldn't accompany us, eh?"

Conroy Melvyn, keeping his voice carefully low,
said, "You thinkin' what I am, Moore? Our man might
be a member, eh? Respected doctor, what? Any
number of medical men were attracted to such
groups."

"Precisely. I believe it might be worth our while to attend this evening's meeting."

They fell in behind a group of gentlemen heading for the same staircase, following a snatch of conversation which marked them as probable Theosophists.

"—spoke to an American fellow once, from some cotton-mill town in South Carolina. Claimed he'd spoken to an elderly gentlemen who raised the dead."

"Oh, come now, what guff! It's one thing to debate the existence of an ability to *converse* with the departed. I've seen what a spiritualist medium can do, in seances and with automatic writing and what have you, but *raise* the dead? Stuff and falderol! I suppose next you'll be claiming this Yank thought himself Christ Jesus?"

Malcolm moved his hand unobtrusively, very carefully switching on the scout's log concealed in the valise he carried, with its tiny digital camera disguised as the stickpin in his cravat. He followed the gentlemen, listening curiously as they crossed a grand lounge and neared the staircase.

"No, no," the first gentleman was protesting, "not literally raise the dead, raise the *spirit* of the dead, to converse with it, you know. Without a medium or a mysteriously thumping table tapping out inscrutable messages. To accomplish the feat, one had to procure the rope used to hang a man, stake it out around the grave of the chap you wished to raise and repeat some gibberish in Latin, I don't recall what, now, then the poor sod's spirit would appear inside the rope and *voila!* You're able to converse at your leisure until cock crow. Of course, the spirit couldn't leave the confines of the roped-off ground . . ."

"And you didn't tumble to the fact that this Yank was having you on?"

A low rumbling chuckle reached through the pall of smoke. "No, I assure you, he was not. Senile as they come, I daresay, the chap was ninety if he was a day, but perfectly sincere in his beliefs."

Malcolm was about to take his first step toward the second floor when a voice hailed him by name. "I say, it's Moore, isn't it!"

The unexpected voice startled him into swinging around. Malcolm found himself looking into the bemused and vivid blue eyes of a gentleman he vaguely thought he was supposed to know. He was a young man, barely past his early twenties, handsome in a Beau Brummel sort of fashion, with wavy dark hair, the brilliant blue eyes and fair skin of an Irishman, and the same elegant, almost effete fastidiousness of the trend setter whose name had been synonymous with fashion during the Regency period some sixty-eight years previously.

"It *is* Malcolm Moore, isn't it?" the young man added with a wry smile. A trace of Dubliner Irish in the man's voice echoed in familiar ways, telling Malcolm he was, indeed, supposed to know this friendly faced young man.

"Yes, I am, but I fear you've the advantage of me, sir."

"O'Downett's the name, Bevin O'Downett. We met, let me see, it would have been nearly a year ago, I believe, at last summer's Ascot Races." Eyes twinkling merrily, Mr. O'Downett chuckled, a good-natured sound. "I recall it quite distinctly, you see. We bet on the same rotten nag, came in dead last."

The face and name clicked in Malcolm's memory. "Of course! Mr. O'Downett, how good to see you again!" They shook hands cordially as Malcolm grimaced in rueful remembrance. He, too, had excellent cause to recall that race. He'd placed that losing bet on behalf of a client who'd hired him as guide, a millionaire who considered himself an expert on sport, particularly on the subject of horse racing. Malcolm had warned the fool not to bet on that particular horse, aware as he was of its record in past races, but the client is, as they say, always right . . . Both Malcolm and this young Irishman, Mr. O'Downett, here, had lost spectacularly.

Malcolm introduced his unexpected acquaintance to his guests. "Mr. O'Downett, may I present Mr. Conroy Melvyn and Mr. Guy Pendergast, of London, and Dr. Kosten, of America."

"Pleasure to meet you," O'Downett smiled, shaking hands all around. "I say," he added, "where've you been keeping yourself, Moore? Oh, wait, I recall now, you're from the West Indies, knock about the world a good bit. Envy you that, you know."

Malcolm was trying for the life of him to recall anything about Mr. O'Downett, other than one illplaced bet. "And you?" he asked a bit lamely.

"Ah, well, fortune smiles and then she frowns, as they say. But I did manage to publish a volume of poetry. A slim one, true, but published, nonetheless." His eyes twinkled again, laughing at himself, this time. "Druidic rubbish, nothing like the serious verse I prefer, but it sells, God knows, it does sell. This Celtic renaissance will make gentlemen of us Dubliners, yet." He winked solemnly.

Malcolm smiled. "It does seem to be rather popular. Have you been to the Eisteddfod, then, since Druidic verse appeals to the book-buying masses?"

"Hmm, that Welsh bardic thing they put together over in Llangollen? No, I haven't, although I suppose if I'm to represent the Celtic pen, I had probably ought to go, eh? Have you attended one?"

"As a matter of fact, no, although I intend to do so when they hold another." Malcolm laughed easily. "Moore's a French name, you know, originally, anyway. It's whispered that the back of our family closet might have contained a Gaulish Celt or two rattling round as skeletons."

O'Downett clapped him heartily on the shoulder.

"Well said, Moore! Well said! It is, indeed, the day of the Celtic Fringe, is it not? I've spoken to gentlemen whose grandsires were Prussian generals who were 'Celts' and pure London Saxons who were 'Celts' and, God forbid, a half-caste Indian fellow in service as a footman who was a 'Celt' at least on his father's side!"

Malcolm shared the chuckle, finding it doubly humorous, since there was a wealth of evidence—linguistic, literary, musical, legal, and archaeological—to suggest that the Celtic laws, languages, customs and arts of Ireland, Wales, Cornwall, Scotland, and Gaulish France bore direct and striking ties to Vedic India.

"And speaking of grand and glorious Celts," Mr. O'Downett said, eyes twinkling wickedly, "here comes the grandest of all us Celtic poets. I say, Willie, have you come for our little meeting this evening? I'd thought you would be haunting Madame Blavatsky's parlour tonight."

Malcolm Moore turned . . . and had to catch his breath to keep from exclaiming out loud. His chance acquaintance had just greeted the most profoundly gifted poet ever born in Ireland, the soon-to-be world-famous William Butler Yeats.

"Willie" Yeats smiled at O'Downett, his own eyes glowing with a fire-eaten look that spoke of a massively restless intellect. "No, not tonight, Bevin. The good lady had other plans. Occasionally, even our peripatetic madame pursues other interests." Yeats was clearly laughing at himself. The Dubliner Irish was far more pronounced in the newcomer's voice. Yeats was still in his twenties, having arrived with his parents from Dublin only the previous year, 1887.

Bevin O'Downett smiled and made introductions. "Willie, I say, have you met Mr. Malcolm Moore? West Indian gentleman, travels about a good bit, met him at Ascot last year. Mr. Moore, my dear friend, Mr. William Butler Yeats."

Malcolm found himself shaking the hand of one of the greatest poets ever to set pen to paper in the English language. "I'm honored, sir."

"Pleasure to meet you, Mr. Moore," Yeats smiled easily.

Malcolm felt almost like the air was fizzing. Yeats was already considered an occult authority, despite his relative youth. Malcolm thanked that unknown American ghost-summoner for inducing him to turn on the scout's log in his valise. He managed to retain enough presence of mind to introduce his own companions, who shook Yeats' hand in turn. Guy Pendergast didn't appear to have the faintest notion who Yeats was—or would be—but Conroy Melvyn's face had taken on a thunderstruck look and even Pavel Kostenka was staring, round-eyed, at the young poet who would legitimize Irish folk lore as a serious art form and subject of scholarly interest, as no other Irishman had managed in the stormy history of Irish-Anglo relations, and would be branded the most gifted mystic writer since William Blake.

Bevin O'Downett winked at his fellow Irishman. "Mr. Moore, here, was just sharing a piece of his family history," he chuckled. "A Gaulic Celt or two, he says, rattled about in earlier branches of the family's gnarled old tree."

Yeats broke out into an enthusiastic smile. "Are you a Celtic scholar, then, Mr. Moore?" he asked, eyes alight with interest.

"No, not really." Malcolm smiled, although he probably knew more about Celtic and Druidic history than any expert alive in Great Britain tonight. "My real interest is antiquity of another sort. Roman, mostly."

O'Downett grinned, bending a fond look on his friend. "Willie is quite the antiquarian, himself."

Yeats flushed, acutely embarrassed. "Hardly, old bean, hardly. I dabble in Celtic studies, really, is all."

"Stuff and nonsense, Willie here is a most serious scholar. Helped co-found the Dublin Hermetic Society, didn't you? And Madame Blavatsky finds your scholarship most serious, indeed."

Malcolm, anxious to put the young poet at ease, gave Yeats a warm, encouraging smile. "You're interested in Theosophy, then, Mr. Yeats?" He knew, of course, that Yeats pursued a profound interest in Theosophy and any other studies which touched on the occult. The new and wildly popular organization established by Madame Blavatsky devoted itself to psychical and occult studies along the lines of the "Esoteric Buddhism" which she and so many other practitioners were popularizing.

Clearly uncertain where Malcolm stood on the issue, the young Irish poet cleared his throat nervously. "Well, sir, yes, I am, sir. Most interested in Theosophy and, ah, many such studies."

Malcolm nodded, endeavoring to keep his expression friendly, rather than awestruck. "You've read Wise's new *History of Paganism in Caledonia*? Intriguing ideas on the development of religion and philosophy."

The young poet brightened. "Yes, sir, I have, indeed, read it! Borrowed a copy as soon as I arrived in London last year, as it had just been published. And I've read Edward Davies, of course, and D.W. Nash on Taliesin."

"Ah, the British druid who was said to have met Pythagoras. Yes, I've read that, as well."

Malcolm did not share his opinion on Nash's theories about the so-called British druid, whose existence had been fabricated whole cloth. Probably not by Nash, for the myth was widespread and persistent, but it was myth, nonetheless. "And have you read Charles Graves' latest work?"

"The Royal Commission's study of ancient Irish Brehon laws? Absolutely, sir!"

And the young poet's smile was brilliant, filled with understandable pride in the accomplishments of his forebears, who had been recognized throughout the western world in past centuries as the finest physicians, poets, musicians, and religious scholars of medieval Europe. The Brehon legal system of medieval Ireland had included such "modern" concepts as universal health care and even workman's compensation laws.

"Excellent!" Malcolm enthused. "Marvellous scholarship in that work. Graves is expanding the knowledge of ancient Britain tremendously. And do you, Mr. Yeats, hold that the Druids built Stonehenge?"

Yeats flushed again, although his eyes glowed with delighted interest. "Well, sir, I'm not an archaeologist, but it strikes me that the standing stones must be of considerable antiquity. At least centuries old, I should think?"

Malcolm smiled again. "Indeed. Millennia, to be more precise. Definitely pre-Roman, most definitely. Even the greatest Egyptologist of our day, Mr. W.M. Flinders Petrie, agrees on that point. Keep up the scholarship, Mr. Yeats. We need good, strong research into our own islands' histories, eh? By God, ancient Britain has a history to be proud of! This Celtic revival is a fine thing, a very fine thing, indeed!"

Bevin O'Downett nodded vehement agreement. "Quite so, sir! I say, have you heard that fellow speak down at the Egyptian Hall? That Lithuanian-looking chap, although he's as British as a gold sovereign, what's he calling himself? I heard some reporter say he used to go by some Egyptian sounding moniker, back in his younger days over in SoHo, before he studied medicine and the occult and became a respectable mesmeric physician."

Malcolm hadn't the faintest idea who O'Downett might mean, although he did notice Guy Pendergast lean forward, sudden interest sharp in his eyes. Once a reporter, always a reporter, although Malcolm couldn't imagine why Guy Pendergast would be so acutely interested in a SoHo occultist.

Yeats, however, nodded at once, clearly familiar with the fellow Bevin O'Downett had mentioned. "Yes, I have seen him speak. Intriguing fellow, although he hasn't actually gone by the name of Johnny Anubis in several years. Oh, I know it's an absurd name," Yeats said, noticing the amused tilt of Bevin O'Downett's brows, "but a man must have some way to attract the attention of the public when he's come up from that sort of background. And despite the theatrics of his early career, his scholarship really is sound, astonishing for a self-made man from Middlesex Street, Whitechapel."

Malcolm paused, caught as much by the edge of bitterness in the young poet's voice as by the niggling suspicion that he was missing something important, here. He glanced into Yeats' brilliant, fire-eaten eyes—and was struck motionless by the pain, the anger and pride that burned in this young Irishman's soul. Forthright fury blazed in those eyes for every slight ever made by an Englishman against the Irish race, fury and pain that the achievements of the Celtic peoples were only now, in the latter half of the nineteenth century, being hailed as genius by overbearing English scholars—and then, only by *some* scholars, in a decade when Welshmen, descendants of the original Celtic settlers of Britain, were still belittled as savage subhumans and advised to give up their barbarous tongue if they would ever redeem themselves into the human race, while the Irishman was kicked and maltreated as the mangiest dog of Europe. Yet despite the kicks and slurs, there blazed in Yeats' brilliant, volcanic eyes a fierce, soul-igniting pride, lightning through stormclouds, a shining pride for the history of a nation which for centuries had carried the torch of civilization in Europe.

Malcolm stood transfixed, caught up in the power of the young poet's presence, aware with a chill of awe that he was witnessing the birth of an extraordinary religious and literary blaze, one which would sweep into its path the ancient lore, the mysterious rite and religious philosophy of the entire world, a blaze which would burn that extraordinary learning in the crucible of the poet's fiery and far-reaching intellect, until what burst forth was not so much resounding music as rolling, thunderous prophecy:

> *Mere anarchy is loosed upon the world,*
> *The blood-dimmed tide is loosed, and everywhere*
> *The ceremony of innocence is drowned;*
> *The best lack all conviction, while the worst*
> *Are full of passionate intensity . . .*
> *Now I know*
> *That twenty centuries of stony sleep*
> *Were vexed to nightmare by a rocking cradle,*
> *And what rough beast, its hour come*
> *   round at last,*
> *Slouches toward Bethlehem to be born?*

Malcolm's favorite Yeats poem, "The Second Coming," could easily have been written in prophecy of Malcolm's own time, when mad cults multiplied like malignant mushrooms and insanity seemed to be the rule of the day. To be standing here, speaking with Yeats, before the poem had even been written . . .

"I say, Mr. Moore," Bevin O'Downett chuckled, shattering with a shock like icewater the spell of Yeats' as-yet-embryonic power, "you might want to close your mouth before a bird seizes the chance to perch on your teeth!"

Malcolm blinked guiltily. Then gathered his wits and composure with profound difficulty. "Sorry. I've just been trying to recall whether I'd read anything by this fellow you were just mentioning. Er, what's his name, did you say? Anubis?"

Yeats nodded. "Yes, but he doesn't use that name any longer. The man's a physician, actually, an accomplished mesmerist, Dr. John Lachley. Holds public lectures and spiritualist seances at places like the Egyptian Hall, but he keeps a perfectly ordinary medical surgery in his rooms in Cleveland Street, calls his house Tibor, I believe, after some ancient holy place out of East European myth. He's quite a serious scholar, you know. An acquaintance of mine, Mr. Waite, invited him to join an organization he's recently founded, and was absolutely delighted when Dr. Lachley agreed. He's been awarded Druidic orders, at the Gorsedd, carries the Druidic wand, the *slat an draoichta*. Lachley's been called the most learned scholar of antiquities ever to come out of SoHo."

Malcolm's gaze sharpened. *Waite?* The famous co-founder of the Hermetic Order of the Golden Dawn? Waite had helped develop the most famous Tarot deck in existence. This mesmeric scholar moved in most intriguing circles. "John Lachley, you say? No, I'm afraid I haven't heard of him. Of course," Malcolm gave the intense young Irishman a rueful smile, "I travel so widely, I often find myself having to catch up on months of scholarly as well as social activities which have transpired in my absence. I shall certainly keep his name in mind. Thank you for bringing his work to my attention."

"Well, that's grand," Bevin O'Downett smiled, visibly delighted at having introduced Malcolm to his scholarly young friend. "I say, Moore, you were just on your way up when I detained you. Have I interrupted any plans?"

Malcolm smiled. "Actually, we'd heard there was

to be a meeting here this evening, of Theosophists, and wanted to learn a bit more."

Yeats brightened. "Splendid! We'll be meeting upstairs, sir, in a quarter of an hour."

Malcolm glanced at Conroy Melvyn, who nodded slightly. "Excellent! I believe I'll tell my carriage driver to return rather later than I'd anticipated. We'll join you shortly, I hope?"

The two Irish poets took their leave, heading upstairs, and Malcolm turned towards the entrance, intent on letting the driver know they'd be longer than an hour—and paused, startled. Their party was one short. "Where the devil is Mr. Pendergast?"

Conroy Melvyn, who had been peering up the staircase after the poets, started slightly. The police inspector looked around with a sheepish expression. "Eh?"

"Pendergast," Malcolm repeated, "where the deuce has he gone?"

Pavel Kostenka swallowed nervously and said in a whisper that wouldn't carry very far, "I cannot imagine. He was here just a moment ago."

"Yes," Malcolm said irritably, "he was. And now he isn't. Bloody reporters! We'd better search for him at once."

Within ten minutes, it was clear that Guy Pendergast was no longer anywhere inside the Carlton Club, because he had been seen retrieving his hat, cane, and gloves. The doorman said, "Why, yes, Mr. Moore, he left in a tearing hurry, caught a hansom cab."

"Did you hear him give the driver directions?"

"No, sir, I'm afraid I didn't."

Malcolm swore under his breath. "Damn that idiot journalist! Gentlemen, I'm afraid our mission on your behalf will simply have to wait for another evening. Dr. Kostenka, Mr. Melvyn, we must return to Spaldergate immediately. This is very serious. *Bloody* damned serious. A reporter on his own without a guide, poking about London and asking questions at a time like this . . . He'll have to be found immediately and brought back, before he gets himself into fatal trouble."

The Ripper scholars were visibly furious at having their evening's mission cut short, particularly with the meeting getting underway upstairs, but even they realized the crisis another missing up-timer represented. The Scotland Yard inspector at least had the good grace to be embarassed that he'd allowed the reporter to give them the slip so easily. The driver of the Time Tours carriage which had brought them to the Carlton Club hadn't noticed Pendergast leave, either, and berated himself all the way back to Spaldergate House for his careless inattention. "Might've followed the bloody fool," the driver muttered under his breath every few moments. "Dammit, why'd the idiot go and hire a hansom cab? I'd have taken him anywhere he wanted to go!"

Malcolm had his own ideas about that, which were confirmed less than half an hour later, when they re-entered Time Tours' London gatehouse. Guy Pendergast had returned to Spaldergate, very briefly. Then he and Dominica Nosette had left again, taking with them all their luggage and one of Spaldergate's carriages—without obtaining the Gilberts' permission first.

Fresh disaster was literally staring them square in the face.

Not only had they lost the tourist Benny Catlin, they had now lost two members of the Ripper Watch team, who clearly had defected to pursue the case on their own. Malcolm, operating on less than three hours' sleep a night for several weeks straight, tried to think what Guy Pendergast might possibly have seen or heard tonight to send him haring off on his own, defying all rules set for members of the Ripper Watch tour. Malcolm had been so focused on Yeats, he hadn't been doing his job. And that was inexcusable. Only once before had Malcolm lost a tourist: Margo, that ghastly day in Rome, in the middle of the Hilaria celebrations. It did not improve his temper to recall that both times, he'd been focused on his own desires, rather than the job at hand.

Without the faintest idea where to begin searching for the renegade reporters, Malcolm did the only thing he *could* do and still remain calm. He stalked into the parlour, poured himself a stiff scotch, and started reviewing potential alternative career options.

Crossingham's doss house smelled of mildew and unwashed clothes, of sweat and stale food and despair. When Margo and Shahdi Feroz stepped into the kitchen, it was well after dark and bitterly cold. They found a sullen, smoking coal fire burning low in the hearth and nearly twenty people crowded nearby, most of them women. There were no chairs available. Most of the room's chairs had been dragged over to the hearth by those lucky enough to have arrived early. The rest of the exhausted, grubby occupants of Crossingham's kitchen sat on the floor as close to the fire as they could manage. The floor was at least neat and well-swept despite its worn, plain boards and deep scuffs from thousands of booted feet which had passed across it.

Margo paid the lodging house's caretaker, Timothy Donovan, for a cuppa and handed it over to Shahdi, then paid for another for herself. "'ere, luv," Margo said quietly to the Ripper scholar, using her best Cockney voice, "got a cuppa tea for you, this'll warm you up nice."

The tea was weak and bitter, with neither sugar nor milk to alter the nasty flavor. Margo pulled a face and sipped again. Recycled tea leaves, no doubt—if there was even any real tea in this stuff. The demand for tea was so high and the price of new leaves so steep, an enormous market existed for recycled tea. Used leaves, carefully collected by housewives and servants, were sold to the tea men who came door-to-door, buying them up in bulk. The tea men, in turn, redried them, dyed them dark again, pressed them into "new" bricks, and resold them to cheaper chandlers' shops scattered throughout the East End. There was even a black market in counterfeit tea, with leaves of God-alone knew what and even bits of paper dyed to look like tea, sold in carefully pressed little bricks to those unable to afford real tea often enough to know the difference in taste.

Margo tucked up her skirts and found a spot as close to the fire as she could manage, then balanced Shahdi's teacup for her so the scholar could sit down. Both of them carefully adjusted their frayed carpet bags with the irreplaceable scout logs inside, so they lay across their laps and out of reach of anybody with lighter-than-average fingers. Margo noticed curious—and covetous—glances from several nearby women and most of the men. Very few of the people in Crossingham's owned enough goods in this world to put *into* a carpet bag.

"Wotcher got in the bag, eh, lovie?" The woman beside Margo was a thin, elderly woman, somewhere in her mid-sixties, Margo guessed. She stank of gin and spilt ale and clothes too many months—or years—unlaundered.

Margo made herself smile, despite the stench. "Me owd clothes, wot I'm aimin' to pawn, soon's I got a place to sleep. That an' me lovin' father's shirts, may God send 'im to burn, drunken bastard as 'e is. Was, I mean. They 'anged 'im last week, for 'is tea leafin' ways."

"Never easy, is it," another woman muttered, "when the owd bastard thieves 'is way through life 'til 'e's caught an' 'anged, leavin' a body to make 'er own way or starve. Better a live blagger, I says, than a dead 'usband or father wot ain't no use to anybody. Nobody save the grave digger an' the bleedin' worms."

"Least 'e won't black me face never again," Margo muttered, "nor drink me wages down to boozer. Good riddance, I says, good riddance to the owd bastard. Could've 'anged 'im years ago, they could, an' I'd 'ave been that 'appy, I would, that I would 'ave."

"You got a job, then?" a girl no older than Margo asked, eyes curious despite the fear lurking in their depths. She reminded Margo of a rabbit hit once too often by a butcher's practice blows.

"Me?" Margo shrugged. "Got nuffink but me own self, that an' me mother, 'ere." She nodded to Shahdi Feroz. "But we'll find something, we will, trust in that. Ain't afraid t' work 'ard, I ain't. I'll do wot a body 'as t' do, to keep a roof over an' bread in me Limehouse an' a bite or two in me ma's, so I will."

A timid looking girl of fourteen swallowed hard. "You mean, you'd walk the streets?"

Margo glanced at her, then at Shahdi Feroz, who—as her "mother"—cast a distressed look at her "daughter." Margo shrugged. "Done it before, so I 'ave. Won't be surprised if it comes to the day I 'as to do it again. Me ma ain't well, after all, gets all tired out, quick like, an' feels the winter's cowd more every year. Me, I'd sleep rough, but me ma's got to 'ave a bed, don't she?"

Over in the corner, a woman in her forties who wore a dress and bonnet shabby as last summer's grubby canvas shoes, started to rock back and forth, arms clenched around her knees. "Going to die out there," she moaned, eyes clenched shut, "going to die out there and who'd care if we did, eh? Not them constables, they don't give a fig, for all they say as how they're here to protect us. We'll end like poor Polly Nichols, we will." Several women, presumably Irish Catholics, crossed themselves and muttered fearfully. Another produced a bottle from her pocket and upended it, swallowing rapidly. "Poor Polly..." the woman in the corner was still rocking, eyes shut over wetness. Her voice was rough, although she'd clearly had more education than the other women in the room. Margo wondered what had driven her to such desperate circumstances. "Oh, God, poor Polly... Bloody constable saw me on the street this morning, told me to move on or he'd black my eye for me. Or I could pay him to stay on my territory. And if I hadn't any money, I'd just have to give him a four-penny knee-trembler, for free. Stinking bastards! They don't care, not so long as they get theirs. As for us, it's walk or starve, with that murdering maniac out there..." She'd begun to cry messily, silently, rocking like a madwoman in her corner beside the hearth.

Margo couldn't say anything, could scarcely swallow. She clenched her teeth over the memories welling up from her own past. No, they didn't care, damn them... The cops never cared when it was a prostitute lying dead on the street. Or the kitchen floor. They didn't give a damn what they did or said or how young the children listening might be...

"I knew Polly," a new voice said quietly, grief etched in every word. "Kinder, nicer woman I never knew."

The speaker was a woman in her fifties, faded and probably never pretty, but she had a solemn, honest face and her eyes were stricken puddles, leaking wetness down her cheeks.

"Saw her that morning, that very morning. She'd been drinking again, poor thing, the bells of St. Mary Matfellon had just struck the hour, two-thirty it was, and she hadn't her doss money yet. She'd drunk it, every last penny of it. How many's the time I've told her, 'Polly, it's drink will be the ruin of you'?" A single sob broke loose and the woman covered her face with both hands. "I had fourpence! I could've loaned it to her! Why didn't I just give her the money, and her so drunk and needing a bed?"

A nearby woman put an arm around her shoulders. "Hush, Emily, she'd just have drunk it, too, you know how she was when she'd been on the gin."

"But she'd be alive!" Emily cried, refusing to be comforted. "She'd be alive, not hacked to pieces . . ."

This was Emily Holland, then, Margo realized with a slow chill of shock. One of the last people to see Polly Nichols alive. The two women had been friends, often sharing a room in one of the area's hundreds of doss houses. How many of these women knew the five Ripper victims well enough to cry for them? Twelve hundred prostitutes walking the East End had sounded like a lot of people, but there'd been more students than twelve hundred in Margo's high school and she'd known all of them at least by sight. Certainly well enough to've been deeply upset if some maniac had carved them into little bits of acquaintance.

Margo gulped down acrid tea, wishing it were still hot enough to drive away the chill inside. At least they were gathering valuable data. She hadn't read anywhere, for instance, about London's constables shaking down the very women they were supposed to be protecting. So much for the image of British police as gentlemen. Margo snorted silently. From what she'd seen, most men walking the streets of Great Britain tonight viewed any woman of lower status not decently married as sexually available. And in the East End and in many a so-called "respectable" house, where young girls from streets like these went into service as scullery maids, the gentlemen weren't overly fussy about taking to bed girls far too young to be married. It hadn't been that long since laws had been passed raising the age of consent from *twelve*.

No, the fact that corrupt police constables were forcing London's prostitutes to sleep with them didn't surprise Margo at all. Maybe that explained why Jack had been able to strike without the women raising a cry for help? Not even Elizabeth Stride had screamed out loudly enough to attract the attention of a meeting hall full of people. A woman in trouble couldn't count on the police to be anything but worse trouble than the customer.

Shahdi Feroz, with her keen eye for detail, asked quietly, "Are you cold, my dear?"

Margo shook her head, not quite willing to trust her voice.

"Nonsense, you are shaking. Here, can you scoot closer to the fire?"

Margo gave up and scooted. It was easier than admitting the real reason she was trembling. Sitting here surrounded by women who reminded her, with every word spoken, exactly how her entire world had shattered was more difficult than she'd expected it would be, back on station studying these murders. And she'd known, even then, it wouldn't be easy. *Get used to it,* she told herself angrily. Because later tonight, Annie Chapman was going to walk into this kitchen and then she was going to walk out of it again and end up butchered all over the yard at number twenty-nine Hanbury Street. And Margo would just have to cope, because it was going to be a long, *long* night. Somehow, between now and five-thirty tomorrow morning, she would have to slip into that pitch-dark yard and set up the team's low-light surveillance equipment.

Maybe she'd climb the fence? She certainly didn't want to risk that creaking door again. Yes, that was what she'd better do, go over the wall like a common thief, which meant she'd need to ditch the skirts and dress as a boy. Climbing fences in this getup was out of the question. She wondered bleakly what Malcolm was doing, on his search for their unknown co-killer, and sighed, resting her chin on her knees. She'd a thousand times rather have gone with Malcolm, whatever he was doing, than end up stuck on the kitchen floor in Crossingham's, trying vainly to ignore how her own mother had died.

As she blinked back unshed tears, Margo realized she had one more excellent reason she couldn't risk falling apart, out here. Kit might—just might—forgive her for screwing up on a job, might chalk it up to field experience she had to get some time. But if she came completely unglued out here, Malcolm would know the reason why or have her skin, one or the other. And if she was forced to tell Malcolm that she'd messed up because she couldn't stop thinking about how her mother had died, he was going to discover the truth about that, too.

Try as she might, Margo simply could not imagine that Malcolm Moore would be willing to marry a girl whose drunken father had died in prison while serving a life sentence for murder, after beating to death his wife in front of his little girl because he'd discovered she was a whore. Far worse than losing Malcolm, though—and Margo loved Malcolm so much, the thought of losing him left her cold and bleak and empty—would be the look in her grandfather's eyes if Kit Carson ever found out how and why his only daughter had really died.

For the first time in her young life, Margo Smith discovered that hurting the people you loved was even worse than being hurt, yourself. Which was why, perhaps, in the final analysis, her mother and so many of the women in this room and out on these streets had sunk to the level of common prostitute. They were trying to support families any way they could. Margo's mouth trembled violently. Then she simply squeezed shut her eyes and cried, no longer caring who saw the tears. She'd think up a good reason to give Shahdi Feroz later.

Just now, she needed to cry.

She wasn't even sure who she was crying for.

When Shahdi Feroz slipped an arm around her shoulder and pulled her close, just holding her, Margo realized it wasn't important at all, knowing who her tears were for. In the end, it didn't matter. The only thing that really mattered was protecting the people you cared about. In that moment, Margo forgave her mother everything. And cried harder than she had since those terrible moments in a blood-spattered Minnesota kitchen, with the toast burnt on the counter and the stink of death in her nostrils and her father's rage pursuing her out the door into the snow.

I'm sorry, Mom, I'm sorry . . .
I'm sorry I couldn't stop him.
I'm sorry I hated you . . .

Did Annie Georgina Chapman, Dark Annie Chapman's daughter, who'd run away from her poverty-stricken, prostituted mother to join a French touring circus, hate her mother, too? Margo hoped not. She blinked burning salt from her eyes and offered up one last apology. *And I'm sorry I can't stop him from killing you, Annie Chapman . . .*

Margo understood at last.

Kit had warned her that time scouting was the toughest job in the world.

Now she knew why.

Chapter Fourteen

Skeeter Jackson was just climbing into the clothes Kit had loaned him, in the Neo Edo bathrooms, when a slim, wraith-like little girl named Cocheta, a mixed-blood Amer-Indian who'd stumbled through the Conquistadores Gate and joined the Lost and Found Gang of down-timer children, skidded into the Neo Edo men's room, out of breath and ashen. Her dark eyes had gone wide, glinting with terror. "Skeeter! Hashim sent me for you! There is bad trouble! Please hurry!"

"What's wrong?"

"It is Bergitta! They have taken her away—the men from the construction site!"

The roar of insanity outside the Neo Edo, where the riot was still spreading, faded to a whisper. Skeeter narrowed his eyes over a surge of murderous rage. *"Show me!"*

Cocheta snatched his hand, led him through the craziness running amok in Edo Castletown. "The Lost and Found Gang is following them! Hurry, Skeeter! They took her from the bathroom they just finished building in the new part of the station, when she went to clean the floor."

419

"How many?" Dammit, he didn't have any weapons with him, not even a pocket knife, and those construction workers would all be carrying heavy tools. Any one of which could cut a man's throat or spill his intestines with a single swiping blow.

"Twenty! They knocked unconscious the foreman and several of the other men who did not agree with them, locked them into a supply room. We sent word to the Council for help. I was told to find you, Skeeter, and Hashim said where you were."

As soon as they cleared the mob in Edo Castletown, Skeeter and the girl tugging at his hand broke into a dead run. Cocheta led him through Victoria Station and Urbs Romae, through Valhalla, down toward the construction site, which was ominously silent. There should've been an ear-splitting roar of saws, drills, and pneumatic hammers echoing off the distant ceiling, but they found only silence and a deserted construction zone, tasks left abandoned on every side. The timing of the attack on Bergitta left Skeeter scowling. With the antics at Primary to preoccupy station security and most of the tourists, nobody was likely to notice the work stoppage. Or the disappearance of one downtimer from her job scrubbing bathroom floor tiles.

"Hurry, Skeeter!"

Cocheta didn't need to urge him again. He'd seen enough to leave his whole throat dry with fear. "Which way did they take her?"

"Through there!" Cocheta pointed to a corridor that led into a portion of the station where new Residential apartments were being assembled, back in another of the caverns in which the station had been built. Clearly, they were taking her where nobody could hear the screams. He was just about to ask Cocheta to get word to someone in Security, preferably Wally Klontz, when someone shouted his name.

"Skeeter! Wait!"

A whole group of down-timers pounded his way,

with Kynan Rhys Gower in the lead. The Welsh
soldier carried his war mallet. Molly was hot on his
heels. Where she'd obtained that lethal little top-break
revolver, Skeeter wasn't sure. Maybe she'd brought
it with her from London. Or liberated it from Ann
Vinh Mulhaney's firing range—or some tourist's
pocket. Eigil Bjarneson towered over the whole
onrushing contingent of angry Found Ones. He'd
managed to reclaim his sword from Security after
getting out of jail. Or quite possibly he'd just *broken* out and reconfiscated it? Skeeter wouldn't have
wanted to argue with Eigil in this mood, if he'd been
working the Security desk, which was probably in
chaos anyway, after Bull's arrest . . .

"Cocheta says they took her through there," Skeeter
pointed the way.

"Let's go," Kynan nodded, voice tight, eyes crack-
ling with murderous fury.

Skeeter turned to the girl who'd brought him here.
He said tersely, "Cocheta, stay here and wait for other
Found Ones who might be coming. Send them in
after us. Give us twenty minutes to get in there and
get into position, then start yelling for station security. By then, the mess at Primary should've settled
down enough, Security might actually listen and send
someone."

"Yes, Skeeter. The Lost and Found Gang has followed the men who took her. They will tell you which
way to go. Hurry!"

He signaled for silence, gratified when his
impromptu posse obeyed instantly, and led the way
back into the incomplete section of Commons at a
flat-out run. They entered the tunnel which led to
the new area of Residential and Skeeter slowed to
a more cautious pace, silent as shadows chased by
a hunter's moon. The concrete floors had already been
poured and drywall had gone up in many places.
Work lights rigged high overhead cast unnatural pools

of light and shadow through the incomplete Residential section, where bare two-by-fours marked out rooms and corridors not yet closed in with wallboard. Skeeter listened intently, but heard nothing. This section of station snaked back into the heart of the mountain, twisting and turning unpredictably.

They found a teenager at a major junction where two Residential corridors would intersect when completed. The boy was dancing with impatience, but remained silent when Skeeter raised a finger to his lips in warning. *That way,* the boy pointed. Skeeter nodded, jerked a thumb over his shoulder to indicate that more hunters were on the way, and motioned for the boy to wait for reinforcements. The boy nodded and settled in to wait. Skeeter stole forward, leading his war party down the indicated corridor. Dust from the construction lay thick on every surface, wood dust and debris from particle board. The chalky scent of gypsum drywall clogged his nostrils as they pushed forward.

Skeeter paused to retrieve an abandoned claw hammer. It wasn't his weapon of choice, but offered lethal potentialities he could certainly make use of, and was better than bare fingernails. When they came to a door marking a stairwell, they found another member of the Lost and Found Gang, a girl of thirteen who stood watch with tears streaming down her face.

"They went down," she whispered, pointing to the stairs. "They had hit her, Skeeter, were laughing about raping her and killing her when they were done . . ."

"We'll stop them," Skeeter promised. "Stay here. More are coming." He glanced at the grim men and women of his posse. "I'd prefer live witnesses to testify against their up-time cronies in the *Ansar Majlis*. Maybe we can crack their terrorist gang wide open. But if we have to spill blood to get Bergitta out of there alive, we'll hit 'em hard and worry about the body count and station management's reaction later. The main thing is, we get her out of there."

Kynan Rhys Gower and the others nodded silently, understanding exactly what he meant and accepting whatever happened. Pride in Ianira's achievement, building this community, flared hot in Skeeter's awareness, pride and a determination not to let anything happen to a single one of his new-found friends.

The girl guarding the stairwell held the door open for them.

Skeeter's pulse thundered as he eased silently down the dim concrete steps. Naked light bulbs glared where ceiling panels had not yet been installed. When they reached the bottom of the stairs, another member of the Lost and Found Gang waited silently. The boy stationed here was only eleven, but had the quick presence of mind to signal for silence. He pointed to the left, mimed following the tunnel around to the right. Skeeter nodded and made sure his entire posse was out of the stairwell before continuing. The rear guard had swelled by three new arrivals, easing so silently down the stairs after them, Skeeter hadn't even heard them join up.

Chenzira Umi, the ancient Egyptian who sat on the Council of Seven, must have been in his apartment when the call went out, because he carried the hunting-dart thrower he'd made for himself. Shaped something like an atl-atl, it could throw a lethal projectile with enough penetrating force to bring down a hippo or a Nile croc. The Egyptian had brought with him the Spaniard Alfonzo Menendez, who'd liberated a steel-tipped pike from the decorative wall of the restaurant where he worked. Young Corydon, a Greek hoplite of twenty-three who excelled at the sling as a weapon of war, had joined them as well. Corydon clutched an entire handful of rounded stones, still dripping from the goldfish pond

he'd stolen them from, and was busy unwinding his
sling from under his shirt, where he'd doubtless worn
it in honor of the Festival of Mars.

Skeeter acknowledged the newcomers with a brisk
nod, then motioned the way and set out in pursuit.
And this time, he heard the quarry. Rough male
voices drifted through the subterranean corridors,
punctuated by distant, feminine cries of pain. He
tightened his grip around the lethal claw hammer and
eased forward, stealing softly across the concrete floor
toward the inhuman sport underway somewhere
ahead. Before this business was done, Skeeter vowed,
these construction workers would bitterly rue their
decision to indulge an appetite for revenge on a
member of his adopted family.

As a boy, he'd never been allowed to join a Yakka
war party bent on vengeance.

Now he led the raid.

Guide me, Yesukai . . .

The corridor they followed twisted and turned
through a maze of partially completed Residential
apartments, storage warehouses for equipment, pumping stations to bring water into the new section of
station, stacks of dusty lumber, drywall, and cement
bags, and tangles of electrical wiring and cables.
Skeeter's little band of rescuers, seven strong, now,
crept closer to the distorted sounds of merriment from
twenty burly construction workers somewhere ahead.
God, seven against twenty . . .

They rounded a final corner and found two more
Lost and Found members crouched in the corridor,
peering anxiously their way. One of the boys, eight-
year-old Tevel Gottlieb, had been born on station.
Hashim Ibn Fahd, a cunning little wolf of thirteen,
still wearing Neo Edo livery, beckoned Skeeter forward, then placed his lips directly against Skeeter's
ear and breathed out, "They are in the warehouse just
beyond this corner. They have posted no guards."

Skeeter risked a quick look, ducking low to the floor to minimize the chances of being seen by anyone who cast a casual glance their way. The warehouse where they'd dragged their victim was an open bay some fifty feet across, piled high with lumber and construction supplies, coils of copper wire and crates of plumbing and electrical fixtures, preformed plastic sink basins, miniature mountains of PVC pipe. Two walls were solid concrete, marking the boundary with the cavern walls just beyond. The other two were gypsum board tacked to wooden two-by-fours. One of these gypsum walls, which Skeeter crouched behind, had been completed already, awaiting only the installation of electrical outlet covers. The other was only partially complete, with drywall up along half its length. Bare wooden uprights comprised the balance of its span.

Bergitta lay on the concrete floor along this stretch of wall, wrists wired to thick two-by-fours. Another cruel twist of wire, tightened down around her throat, prevented her from lifting her head. They'd ripped her shirt open, had cut away her bra. They hadn't bothered to tie a gag. Her skirt lay in twists around her waist. One of them was busy raping her while others waited their turn, speaking tensely amongst themselves in what looked almost like an argument. Hashim Ibn Fahd, who'd stumbled through the Arabian Nights gate in the middle of a howling sandstorm, having become separated from the caravan he'd been traveling with, pressed his lips against Skeeter's ear once again.

"They argue about bringing the woman here. Some say their brothers in the *Ansar Majlis* will reward them when they have killed this one. Others say raping a prostitute has nothing to do with the cause and the leaders of the *Ansar Majlis* will be angry, for that and for attacking the foreman and others of the faith. They say the leaders came through Primary today and will punish those who take such chances at being caught. The others say it does not matter, because now that their brothers have come to the station, Mike Benson and all who run the jail will die. Soon their brothers will be free again to hunt the Templars who flock to the whore's shrine in Little Agora. Their leader says to hurry with the woman, his balls ache and he wants his turn on her before she is dead from too many men inside her."

The freezing hatred in young Hashim's eyes sent a chill down Skeeter's back. He beckoned the two boys away from the corner, then led his band several yards back further still, well out of earshot. Speaking in the barest whisper, Skeeter outlined his plan, such as it was. "There's too many of them to rush in there the way we are. We'll just get Bergitta killed and maybe us, too. We've got to lure some of them out here, away from the others, split them up. We've got reinforcements coming, but we don't know how many or when. All we can count on is ourselves."

Seven adults and two kids . . .

Not the best odds he'd ever faced.

But it would have to do. God help them all, it would have to do, because they were out of time—and so was poor Bergitta.

They met in a dingy, drab little pub called the Horn of Plenty on the corner of Dorset Street and Chrispin. As he had been the night of Polly Nichols' murder, John Lachley was once again in deep disguise. James Maybrick was proving most useful in procuring theatrical disguises for him, at the same shops patronized by one of Lachley's new clients, a popular actor at the Lyceum Theater where the infamous American play *Dr. Jekyll and Mr. Hyde* was packing in sellout crowds bent on vicarious thrills.

The thrills Lachley and James Maybrick sought tonight were anything but vicarious. Lachley made eye contact with Maybrick across the smoke-filled pub, making certain his disciple recognized him through the false beard, sideburns, and scar, then nodded toward the door. Maybrick, eyes glittering with intense excitement, paid for his pint of bitters and exited. Lachley finished his stout leisurely, then sauntered out into the night. Maybrick waited silently across the street, leaning one shoulder against the brick wall of a doss house opposite the pub.

Lachley's pulse quickened when Maybrick glanced into his eyes. Maybrick's excitement was contagious. The cotton merchant's color was high, even though he didn't know, yet, the identity of the woman they were to kill tonight. The knowledge that Lachley meant to guide him to his next victim was clearly sufficient to excite the man beyond the bounds of reason. The telegram which had summoned Maybrick back to London from Liverpool had read: "Friday appointment. Arrange as before."

That telegram, which had triggered this meeting, would—at long last—culminate in the final episode of Lachley's quest for Prince Albert Victor's eight indiscreet letters. Four obtained from Morgan . . . one from Polly Nichols . . . and the final three would be in his hands by night's end, obtained from Annie Chapman. Three murders—Morgan, Polly Nichols, and Annie Chapman—were already two more than he'd anticipated needing to wind up this sordid little affair. He very carefully did not think about the prophetic words his lovely prisoner had choked out: *and six shall die for his letters and his pride . . .*

He could not afford to indulge doubt on a job of this magnitude, whatever its source. James Maybrick, at least, was a good deal more than satisfactory as a tool to accomplish Lachley's goals. In fact, Maybrick was proving to be a most delightful tool in John Lachley's capable hands. Completely mad, of course, behind those merry eyes and mild smile, but quite an effective madman when it came to dispatching witnesses and blackmailers. What he'd done to Polly Nichols after choking her death with his bare hands inspired awe. The newspapers were still bleating about "The Whitechapel Murderer" and speculation was running wild through the East End's sordid streets. The terror visible in the eyes of every dirty whore walking these streets was music in Lachley's soul. He had more than good reason to wish a calamitous end on such women. Tormenting, small-minded trollops that they were, pointing at him and laughing through their rotting teeth, calling out filthy names when he passed them on the kerb . . .

Lachley wished he'd taken the satisfaction of punishing that blackmailing little bitch, Polly Nichols, himself. He'd enjoyed Morgan's final hours, had enjoyed them immensely, and regretted having allowed Maybrick all the fun in killing the loathsome Polly Nichols. He wondered what it had felt like, ripping her open with that shining, wicked knife, and found that his pulse was pounding raggedly. *This time,* he promised himself, *I'll do the killing myself this time, I'm damned if Maybrick shall have all the fun, curse him for the maniac he is.*

Lachley's lethal little merchant with the unfaithful wife might be dull as a butter knife when it came to social matters, but give him a belly full of hatred, an eight-inch steel gutting blade, and a hapless target upon which to vent that explosive rage, and James Maybrick was a man transformed. A true *artiste* . . . It was almost a pity Lachley had to ensure the man's execution by hanging. Controlling a mind like James Maybrick's was intoxicating, far more satisfying than controlling a dullard like Eddy—even if Albert Victor Christian Edward did have prospects far beyond anything the Liverpudlian social climber could ever hope to achieve.

Men in the baggy clothes of the common factory laborer and women in the shabby dresses of cheap kerb crawlers prowled up and down Dorset Street, intent on enacting mutually attractive financial transactions. Maybrick, Lachley noted, followed the prostitutes with a hungry, predatory gaze that boded ill for Annie Chapman once Lachley turned his killer loose on the owner of Eddy's final letters.

But to do that, they first must *find* Dark Annie. And that, Lachley had discovered over the course of the previous week, was no easy task. Annie Chapman did not normally travel from doss house to doss house, as many another destitute street walker did, but she had not been seen in Crossingham's—the house she had made her more-or-less permanent home—in well over a week. Lachley *had* seen her during that week, but only twice. And both times she had looked alarmingly ill. During the past two days, he had not seen her at all. Rumor held that she had been injured in a fight with another whore over the attentions of the man who paid a fair number of Annie's bills. He suspected she had spent the two days in the casual ward of Spitalfields workhouse infirmary, since the last time he'd spotted her, near Spitalfields Church, she had been telling a friend that she was seriously ill and wanted to spend a couple of days in the casual ward, resting and getting the medical help she needed.

Her friend had given her a little money and warned her not to spend it on rum.

John Lachley had not seen Dark Annie since.

So he set out down Dorset Street, casting about like a hound seeking the fox, and led James Maybrick into the opening steps of the hunt. And on this night, after many dark and frustrating hours, luck finally returned to John Lachley. He and Maybrick, on edge and all but screaming their tense frustration, returned to Dorset Street shortly after one-thirty in the morning and caught sight of her at long, bloody last.

Annie Chapman was just entering Crossingham's

lodging house by the kitchen entrance, badly the worse for drink. John Lachley halted, breathing hard as excitement shot through his belly and groin. He glanced across the street at Maybrick, then nodded toward the short, stout woman descending the area steps to the kitchen entrance of her favorite doss house.

Maybrick slipped his hand into his coat pocket, where he kept his knife, and smiled slowly. Mr. James Maybrick had seen the face of his new victim. Maybrick's face flushed with sexual excitement in the light from the gas lamp on the street corner. Lachley restrained a slow smile. *Soon . . .* They waited patiently across from Crossingham's and within minutes, their quarry came out again, evidently not not in possession of enough money to pay for the room. They heard her say, "I won't be long, Brummy. See that Tim keeps the bed for me." Whereupon she left Crossingham's and turned down Little Paternoster Row, toward Brushfield Street, where she headed out towards Spitalfields Market.

They followed her quietly on the same rubberized servants' shoes they'd worn the night they'd stalked Polly Nichols to her death. It was clear to Dr. John Lachley that Annie Chapman was seriously ill and in a great deal of pain. She moved slowly, but was still successful in collaring a customer outside the darkened hulk of Spitalfields Market, frustrating them in their intention to waylay her, themselves. The man disappeared with her into some refuse-riddled yard full of shadows. Lachley stood in his hiding place, breathing rapidly. Tension tightened down through him until he needed to shout out his impatience. Soon—very soon, now—poor little Dark Annie Chapman would earn a greater notoriety in death than she had ever earned in life. She was about to become the third mutilated victim of John Lachley's ambition. And the second dead London whore in a week. The anticipation of the terror that would explode through the East End was nearly as potent a delight as controlling the fates of his chosen victims.

Playing God was a sweetly addictive game.

John Lachley was well on his way to becoming a sweetly addicted player.

From where he stood in a grimy doorway, John Lachley couldn't hear anything of Annie's encounter with her customer, but twenty minutes later, they emerged, the man breathing heavily and Annie Chapman flushed, her skirts disarranged. They went together to the nearest pub. Lachley and Maybrick entered the pub, as well, finding separate places at the bar, where they drank a pint and watched the woman they had come to kill.

Annie's customer bought her a hearty meal and several glasses of rum, which she downed quickly, like medicine. John Lachley suspected she was using the rum in precisely that fashion, to kill the pain he could see in her eyes and her every slow, awkward movement. From the cough she tried to suppress while in her customer's company, he suspected consumption, which meant she would be suffering considerable pain in her lungs, as well as difficulty breathing. Clearly she hadn't the means to buy proper medications. Doubtless why she had resorted to blackmail, buying Eddy's letters from Polly Nichols. Lachley hid a smile behind his carefully disguised face and wondered how much terror Dark Annie had felt upon learning of poor Polly's violent end?

She remained with her customer from Spitalfields Market for the whole frustrating night, drinking and eating at his expense, disappearing with him once for nearly half an hour, presumably to renew their intimate acquaintance. Then she and her customer sat down to another round of rum, listening to the piano and the pub songs sung by drunken patrons, watching other prostitutes enter the place and find customers of their own and disappear outside again to conduct their sordid business, until the pub closed its doors. When Annie Chapman and her customer left the public house, he took her through the dark streets to what was presumably his own house, a miserable little factory cottage on Hanbury Street, which she entered and did not leave again until very nearly five-thirty in the morning, at which time her customer emerged dressed for work.

He gave her a rough caress and said, "You ought to see a doctor about that cough, luv. I'd give you sixpence if I 'ad it, but I spent all me ready cash on your supper."

"Oh, that's all right, and thank you for the food and the rum."

"Well, I've got to be off or they'll lock the factory yard gates and dock me wages."

They separated, the man hurrying away down Hanbury Street while Annie Chapman lingered at his doorstep, visibly exhausted.

"Well," she muttered to herself, "you've had a good supper and the rum's been a great help with the pain, but you've still got no money for your bed, Annie Chapman."

She sighed and set out very slowly, moving in the general direction of Dorset Street once more. John Lachley glanced quickly along the street and saw no sign of anyone, so he stepped out of the doorway he'd been leaning against and crossed the street toward her. Since he didn't want to startle her into crying out and waking anyone, he began whistling very softly. She turned at the sound and sent a hopeful smile his way.

"Good morning," John said quietly.

"Good morning, sir."

"You seem to be in something of a bind, madam."

She glanced quizzically into his eyes.

"I couldn't help but overhear you, just now. You need money for your lodging house, then?"

She nodded slowly. "I do, indeed, sir. You realize, I wouldn't ask, if I weren't desperate, but . . . well, sir, I can be very agreeable to a gentleman in need of companionship."

John Lachley smiled, darting a quick glance at Maybrick's place of concealment.

"I'm certain you can, madam. But surely you have in your possession something of value which you might sell, instead of yourself?"

Her cheeks flushed, the right one bruised from the fist fight she'd been in with the other whore earlier in the week. "I've already sold everything of value I own," she said softly.

"Everything?" He stepped closer. Dropped his voice to a mere whisper. "Even the letters?"

Annie's blue eyes widened. "The *letters?*" she breathed. "How—how did you know about the letters?"

"Never mind that, just tell me one thing. Will you sell them to me?"

Her mouth opened, closed again. From the distant tower of the Black Eagle Brewery, the clock struck five-thirty A.M. "I can't," she finally said. "I haven't got them any longer."

"Haven't got them?" he asked sharply. "Where are they?"

Misery pinched her face, turned her complexion sallow. "I've been ill, you see, with a cough. I needed money for medicine. So I sold them, but I could get them back or tell you who bought them, only . . . could you give me a few pence for a bed, if I do? I need to sleep, I'm so unwell."

"You could *maybe* get them for me?" he repeated. "*Will* you?"

"Yes," she answered at once. "Yes," she whispered, leaning against the brick wall in visible weariness, "I will."

He dropped his voice to a whisper and asked, "Who's got them?"

"I sold them to Elizabeth Stride and Catharine Eddowes . . ."

Footsteps behind him told Lachley they were not alone. He swore under his breath, careful not to turn his head, and listened with a trip-hammering pulse until whoever it was continued on their way, rather than interrupt what must look to any observer like a whore and her customer in serious negotiations. When the footsteps had died away again in the distance, Lachley took Annie Chapman by the arm, pressed her back against the shutters of the house they stood in front of, bent down to whisper, "All right, Annie, I'll give you the money you need for your bed . . . and enough to re-acquire the letters."

He dug into his pocket and pulled out two shining shillings, which he handed over.

She smiled tremulously. "Thank you, sir. I'll get the letters back with this, I promise you."

The passing of the money between them was the signal James Maybrick had been waiting for all through the long night. He appeared from the darkness and walked toward them as Lachley caressed Annie's breast through her worn, faded bodice and murmured, "Shall we go someplace quiet, then? You do seem a most agreeable lady on a cold night like this." He smiled down into her eyes. "A mutually delightful few moments of pleasure now, then I'll meet you this evening at Crossingham's," Lachley lied. "And I'll buy the letters from you, then."

"I'll have them," she said earnestly. "There's a nice, quiet yard at number twenty-nine," she added softly, nodding down the street toward a dilapidated tenement. "One of the girls I know oiled the hinges," she added with a wink, "so there's no chance of waking anybody. The second door, there, leads through the house to the yard."

"Lovely," Lachley smiled down at her. "Perfect. Shall we?"

Lachley eased open the door, aware that Maybrick trailed behind, silent as a shadow. Lachley escorted Annie through the black and stinking passage, then down the steps to the reeking yard behind. Very gently, he pressed her up against the high fence. Very gently, he bent, caressed her throat . . . nuzzled her ear. "Annie," he murmured. "You really shouldn't have sold those letters, pet. Give my love to Polly, won't you?"

She had just enough time to gasp out one faint protest. "No . . ."

Then his hands were around her throat and she fell against the fence with a thud, all sound cut off as he crushed her trachea. Her terrified struggles spiraled through his entire being, a giddy elixir, more potent than raw, sweating sex. When it was over, the shock of disappointment was so keen he almost protested the end of the pleasure. Morgan had lasted much longer, struggled much harder, giving him hours of intense pleasure. But they couldn't afford the risk out here in the open, where all of London might hear at any moment. So Lachley drew several deep, rasping breaths to calm himself, then lowered her lifeless corpse to the filthy ground beside the fence. He stepped back, giving her to the impatient Maybrick, who gripped his knife in eager anticipation. The sound of that knife ripping her open was the sweetest sound John Lachley had heard all day.

He bent low and breathed into Maybrick's ear, "Return to Lower Tibor when you've finished. Use the sewers, as I showed you. I'll be waiting in the secret room."

Then he slipped from the yard, leaving the maniacal Maybrick to vent his rage on the lifeless corpse of Annie Chapman. He was not pleased that he must track down and kill two *more* dirty whores, two *more* potential blackmailers in a position to destroy his future. In fact, as the trembling delight of stalk and strike and murder gradually waned in his blood, he cursed the foul luck that had prompted Annie to sell her precious letters to raise money for medicine, cursed it with every stride he took, cursed Prince Albert Victor for writing Morgan's goddamned letters in the first place, and cursed brainless whores who acquired them only to sell them off for ready cash. Two *more* women to locate and silence! Dear God, would this nightmare never end? *Two!*

His beautiful Greek prisoner had known, somehow; had seen clairvoyantly into his future and known he would not succeed tonight. *Curse it!* He would have to question Ianira more closely about what she had seen in that vision of hers. Clearly, he could do nothing further today. It would be getting light soon and Maybrick had to return to Liverpool today, to meet social and family obligations.

Lachley was tempted to find these women himself, to end their miserable lives with his own hands, without waiting for Maybrick's return. But that was far too risky. Maybrick *must* be involved; that was critical to his plans. He must have a scapegoat on which to pin blame for these murders. *All* of them, including the next two. He narrowed his eyes. Elizabeth Stride and Catharine Eddowes . . . He'd never heard of either woman, but he was willing to bet they were common prostitutes, same as the recently departed Polly Nichols and the even more recently departed Annie Chapman. Which meant they ought to be quite easy to trace and just as easy to silence. Provided the bitches didn't tumble to the truth of what they possessed and run, bleating, with it to the constables or—worse—the press.

It was even possible that someone would connect "Eddy" and Prince Albert Victor Christian Edward. Lachley shuddered at such a monstrous vision of the future. These filthy whores must be silenced, whatever the cost. He made for his own little hovel in Wapping, beneath which was the entrance to the sewers which led to his underground sanctuary. James Maybrick knew the way there, already. Lachley had shown him the route shortly before Polly Nichols' murder, introducing him to Garm, to help him escape detection. Since Maybrick couldn't very well walk around with blood on his sleeves, he'd needed an escape route that was certain. The sewers were the most sure escape route possible.

So he'd showed Maybrick how to find his hideaway where Morgan had passed his last hours screaming out his miserable little life, and had arranged to meet Maybrick there again, after Annie Chapman's murder. Maybrick ought to be arriving there shortly to change his clothes and rid himself of any physical evidence connecting him with the murders, including the knife. He'd left the long-bladed weapon at Lower Tibor after Polly's death and collected again this evening, before setting out in pursuit of Annie. Lachley had *planned* to drug Maybrick after this latest murder, to use his mesmeric skills to erase the merchant's memory of Lachley's involvement, then send the knife and an anonymous tip to the Metropolitan Police's H Division with the instructions that a search of Battlecrease House in Liverpool would yield written evidence of the identity of the Whitechapel Murderer.

Putting that plan into action was clearly out of the question, now, at least until he had obtained the letters from Stride and Eddowes, curse them. It was now September the 8th, nearly two *weeks* since he'd first determined to kill Morgan and finish up this sordid business. Yet he was no closer to ending this miserable affair than he'd been the day Eddy had arrived at his house with the unpalatable news in the first place. He wanted this over with! Finished once and for all!

When James Maybrick finally arrived in his underground sanctuary, only to break the news that he couldn't possibly return to London until the end of the month, due to business and social commitments, it was all John Lachley could do not to shoot the maniac on the spot. He stood there breathing hard, with the gnarled oak limbs of his sacrificial tree spreading toward the brick vault of the underground chamber's ceiling and the smell of gas flames and fresh blood thick in the air, and clenched his fists while James Maybrick changed his clothes, burned the coat and shirt and trousers he'd been wearing, and secreted some hideous package that reeked of blood in an oilcloth sack.

"Took away her womb," Maybrick explained with a drunken giggle. "Threw her intestines over her shoulder, cut out her womb and her vagina." He giggled again, hoisting the grotesque oilcloth sack. "Thought I'd fry them up for my supper, eh? Took her wedding rings, too," he added, eyes gleaming in total madness. He displayed his trophies proudly, two cheap brass rings, a wedding band and a keeper. "Had to wrench them off, didn't want to leave holy rings on a dirty whore's hand, eh? Went back for a second helping of her, took part of the bladder, when I realized I'd forgotten my chalk. Wanted to chalk a message on the wall," he added mournfully. "To taunt the police. That fool, Abberline, thinks he's so very clever . . . not nearly so clever as Sir Jim, ha ha ha!"

Lachley thinned his lips into a narrow line, wishing to hell the maniac would simply shut up. God, the man was sick . . .

"Can't be here next week," Maybrick added, pulling on clean clothes Lachley had laid out for him. "But we will kill the other dirty whores, won't we? You'll let me rip them?"

"Yes, yes!" Lachley snapped. "When *can* you be

back, dammit? I'm tired of waiting for you! This business is urgent, Maybrick, dammed urgent! You'd bloody well *better* be here the first day you can get away!"

Maybrick drew on his overcoat, left behind earlier. "Saturday the 29th," Maybrick replied easily. "You have my medicine ready?"

Lachley thrust the stoppered bottle into Maybrick's hand and watched narrowly as he drank it down. The potent mixture which allowed Lachley to place his patients into such a deep trance was even more critical with this patient, giving Lachley the means by which to accomplish his murderous ends without being mentioned in Maybrick's written record of his deeds. "Lie down on that bench," Lachley said impatiently when Maybrick had finished it all.

The cotton merchant slid up onto Lachley's long work bench and lay back with a smile, clearly pleased with the night's work and equally clearly looking forward to another two repeat performances of the evening's fun. Lachley stared down at the insane insect and loathed him so intensely, he had to clench his fists to keep from closing his hands around the man's throat and crushing the life from him, as he'd crushed it from Annie Chapman. Maybrick's eyelids gradually grew heavy and sank closed.

Lachley took Maybrick through the standard routine to bring about trance, went through the litany designed to abate his physical complaints, then repeated his injunction against ever mentioning or even hinting that Lachley existed when he wrote out his diary entries. "You will wake naturally in several hours, feeling refreshed and strong," Lachley told the drugged murderer. "You will leave this place and go to Liverpool Street Station and take the train for home. You will remember nothing of your visits to Dr. John Lachley, nothing except that he is helping you with your illness. You will not mention Dr.

Lachley to anyone you know, not even members of your family. You will remember nothing about this room until the twenty-ninth of September, when you will receive a telegram from your physician informing you of an appointment. You will then come here and meet me in this room and we will kill more whores and you will enjoy it immensely. You will write of your enjoyment in your diary, but you will mention nothing about your London physician or the help I give you. In your diary, you will write of how pleasurable it was to rip your whores, how much you look forward to ripping more of them . . ."

Maybrick, lying there in a drugged stupor, smiled. *Maniacal bastard.*

Lachley flexed his hands, clenching them into fists and glared down at the pathetic creature on his work table. *I'll personally certify your death after they've hung you on the gallows. It can't be too soon, either, damn your eyes.*

Two bloody weeks . . . and two more dirty whores to be killed. Preferably, in one night. If he didn't destroy them both on the same night, God alone knew how long it would be before Maybrick could tear himself away from business and family in Liverpool and return to finish this up. Yes, they would have to die on the same night, next time. Bloody hell . . . and they would have constables crawling like roaches through these streets, by then.

But it had got to be done, regardless, too much depended on it. All told, it was enough to drive a sane man into an asylum.

The message arrived on Gideon Guthrie's computer via e-mail.

Trouble brewing, TT-86. Targets have escaped via two separate gates, Denver and London. Senator Caddrick has departed for terminal with entourage, vowing to close station. Please advise your intentions.

It had been relayed through so many servers, rerouted across so many continents, tracing it back to the original sender would have stymied the efforts even of the CIA and Interpol. When Gideon read Cyril Barris' message, he swore explosively. That goddamned, grandstanding *idiot*! He'd *told* Caddrick, dammit, to stay out of this! Did the jackass really *want* to end up in prison?

He sent a reply: *Will handle personally. Do nothing. Timetable still on schedule.*

Then he deleted the original message from his hard drive and blistered the air with another savage curse. God*dammit*! With Caddrick on the warpath, Gideon would have to go there, himself, clean up this whole God-cursed mess the hard way. Time Terminal Eighty-Six . . .

Gideon Guthrie swore viciously and tapped keys on his computer, opening the program which allowed him to make airline reservations. Just as with the e-mail message and its multitude of rerouting server connections, his request for airline tickets hopped the globe before reaching the airlines reservations computer. He typed in the requisite identification information, then calmly assumed the identity of Mr. Sid Kaederman, the name he'd given Caddrick to use as the "detective" hired to trace his missing kid.

Damn that girl! She was a twenty-year-old, wet-behind-the-ears rich man's brat, with her head stuck in a bunch of history books. Even her boyfriend had played dress-up cowboy, for God's sake, when he hadn't been cozying up to Jenna's film-making friends. But the little bitch had slipped right through their fingers, thanks to Noah Armstrong, and now Caddrick had gone ballistic. The suicidal *idiot!* Trying to play to the press and gain voter sympathy, when the very last thing they needed was Caddrick on *any* warpath.

Once again, Caddrick had failed to use the few brains God had given him, leaving Gideon no choice

but to wade in and try to salvage the mess. Therefore, Mr. Sid Kaederman, detective with the world-
famous, globe-spanning Wardmann Wolfe agency,
would be taking an unplanned time tour. Gideon's lips
twisted in a sardonic smile at the notion of posing
as a detective from Noah Armstrong's own agency. But
he did not find the idea of taking a time tour amusing.
He was a fastidious man by nature, fond of his creature comforts, of up-time luxuries. He hadn't done
real fieldwork in fifteen years and had vowed never
to set foot down a time touring gate, where filth and
disease and accident could rob him of everything he'd
built over his career.

God, *time touring*!

The only question was, *which* of Shangri-La Station's
gates would Mr. Sid Kaederman be touring? Which
one, exactly, had Jenna Caddrick disappeared down,
and which had Ianira Cassondra and her family gone
through? Denver? Or London?

He intended to find out.

With that promise to himself foremost in his
mind, Gideon Guthrie started reviewing methods by
which he would slowly dismember Ms. Jenna Nicole
Caddrick, and began packing his luggage. He was
still reviewing delightfully bloodthirsty methods, up
to the ninety-ninth and counting, when he snatched
up a pre-prepared portfolio with Sid Kaederman's
identification, medical records, and credit cards, and
headed grimly out the door.

Chapter Fifteen

Skeeter knew they didn't have much time. The men who'd kidnapped Bergitta would kill her if they weren't stopped, and stopped fast. Making use of what he had ready at hand, Skeeter deployed part of his forces—the closest thing he possessed to shock troops—in an ambush where the corridor turned, forming a blind corner with a partially constructed apartment along one approach and a storage room along the other, providing two doorways strategically positioned for attack.

Skeeter then led his light, mobile infantry—such as it was—back toward the preoccupied construction crew, in what he hoped would be a maneuver worthy of Yesukai the Valiant himself, or maybe Francis Marion, the Swamp Fox. Having selected the least threatening of his troops to accompany him, Skeeter jogged straight into the big open bay warehouse, with Molly and the two kids from the Lost and Found gang hard on his heels.

"There they are!" Skeeter yelled. "Molly, quick! Go call Security!"

Eight-year-old Tevel, playing his role with enthusiasm, taunted, "Boy, are you gonna get yours! They'll throw away the key! Drop you down an unstable gate! Nyah-nyah, you're all going to jail! Come on, Molly, let's tell on 'em!"

Hashim, not to be outdone, was shouting something that sounded scurrilous. Whether it was the teenager's Arabic taunts or Tevel's threats or Skeeter's shout for Molly to call Security, six of the burliest, nastiest, angriest members of the construction crew charged right at them. Screwdrivers and wicked knives glinted in the work lights dangling from the unfinished ceiling. The man in the lead was shouting, "Don't let them get away! Kill them all!"

Skeeter whipped around, bolting back the way they'd come. *"Run!"*

Hashim was still yelling taunts in Arabic as they pounded through a series of twists and turns in the corridor. Molly passed Skeeter, as planned, while eight-year-old Tevel shot into the lead, on a mission of his own. When they plunged through the blind corner, Skeeter turned on his heel and waited, claw hammer clutched in one hand. He could hear the pounding of their feet, could smell the stench of their sweat—

All six of them piled into the blind corner, running full tilt.

"NOW!"

Kynan Rhys Gower lunged through an open doorway, war hammer gripped over his head for a striking blow. The heavy wooden mallet whistled in a short arc. The lead man ran full tilt into it. His skull caved in with a sickening crunch. The man behind him screamed and tripped over the body, trying to dig a heavy Egyptian hunting dart out of his left kidney. A rock whizzed from the doorway nearest Skeeter. It stuck the throat of the man next to the pincushion. The man gave out a gurgling scream and went down, clutching his crushed trachea. Eigil Bjarneson's screaming war cry sent one man racing in retreat—

straight onto Alfonzo's pike. Another man screamed and fell to his knees when Eigil severed his hand with a single blow of his sword. A sharpened screwdriver clattered to the floor from the twitching, disconnected fingers. The final man was hit with double blows in the chest, once from a spinning rock, once when a heavy hunting dart embedded itself between ribs.

When Eigil would have finished off the man whose hand lay beside him on the concrete, Skeeter rushed in. "Wait! I want one of 'em alive!"

The man on the floor was pleading for mercy, promising anything, if only they would let him live, if only they'd bring medical help to reattach his hand . . . Rushing footfalls from behind brought Skeeter around in a crouch. But it wasn't an enemy, it was more down-timers, six of them, and the enraged construction foreman, whose face was bruised and scabbed with dried blood.

"How can I help?" Riyad snarled.

"Find out what that bastard knows about the *Ansar Majlis*. Their leaders arrived through Primary today. I want to know *everything* he knows about the *Ansar Majlis* and their plans to invade the station!"

"With pleasure! Get a tourniquet on that arm!" Then he switched to Arabic and Skeeter switched his attention to the rest of his war party.

"Kynan, Eigil, Alfonzo, get moving! Frontal assault. Corydon, Molly, Chenzira, back them up! And somebody get Security down here! Hashim, you're with me!" He scooped up a heavy concrete trowel from one of the dead men. With a blade like a hoe, one which stuck straight out from the handle, rather than bending down at an angle, its edge had been sharpened wickedly. It made a conveniently lethal weapon to back up his claw hammer.

Skeeter sent his troops into the open bay warehouse. He put Molly in the lead, since she had the only pistol, with Corydon and Chenzira Umi backing her up

with the other two projectile weapons. Skeeter charged
past the open bay's door and raced down the corridor
toward the unfinished section of wall where Bergitta
lay bound to the uprights. Hashim, too, had confiscated
an abandoned weapon: a sharpened screwdriver. They
crept past the last of the drywall, then crouched low
to peer into the warehouse beyond.

About half of the fourteen remaining men had run
toward the doorway, shouting obscenities at Skeeter's
attacking troops and charging to the attack. Several
others had taken refuge behind stacked supplies,
wailing—or so Hashim whispered—that they should
never have attacked the crew foreman and brought
the woman down here, that they hadn't counted on
killing so many people, couldn't they just abandon the
whore and run? Only two men had been left behind
to guard Bergitta. She was barely conscious, face
swollen and bruised, mouth and nose bleeding where
they'd hit her repeatedly. Neither guard was paying
any attention to her, which meant they weren't looking
at the open "wall" behind her, either.

Hashim slipped through first, easing past the two-
by-fours on Bergitta's left, while Skeeter edged past
on her right. When Molly started shooting, the guards
left with Bergitta moved even further away. That gave
Skeeter and Hashim the chance they needed. The
down-time boy struck first. He drove the sharpened
screwdriver into the nearest guard's back with a snarl
of hatred. The man screamed. The other guard
whirled, bringing up a knife—

Skeeter slashed with the sharpened trowel. The
blow severed fingers. The man screamed and fell to
his knees beside the clattering knife. A kick to the
man's head sent him sprawling. "Wire his hands!" he
yelled to Hashim, who was already crouching low over
Bergitta. A twist of Skeeter's claw hammer served to
break the wires around her wrists and throat. Skeeter
picked her up, then shouted at the embattled

construction workers, "I've got your hostage! You might as well give it up and surrender! Security's on the way and there's no way off this station! Surrender now and maybe these down-timers won't kill you like they did your pals just now!"

Hashim translated into Arabic for good measure.

Moments later, it was over. Security did, in fact, arrive in force, led by Wally Klontz and the crew foreman, Riyad, along with several of his enraged crew who'd been jumped and knocked out. They started cleaning up the mess. Skeeter carried Bergitta up to the infirmary, himself, not trusting the job to anyone else. He ran the whole way, while Bergitta lapsed into unconsciousness. He skidded, out of breath, into the infirmary, where battered tourists and the irate Senator Caddrick were being treated for injuries from the riot at Primary.

Rachel Eisenstein, who was busy rinsing tear gas out of Caddrick's reddened eyes, took one look at Bergitta, blanched, and abandoned Caddrick. "What's happened?"

"Some of the Arabian Nights crew dragged her down to the basement, beat her nearly to death, gang-raped her . . ."

"I need a trauma team, stat!" Rachel shoved past the shocked and red-faced senator, who sputtered an outraged protest at being abandoned.

Skeeter carried Bergitta in Rachel's wake, shoving his own way past the angry senator, and followed the station's chief of medicine into a treatment room. Skeeter turned Bergitta over to Rachel's care, gratified by the swiftness of the trauma team's arrival, and found himself abruptly trembling from head to toes with the aftershock of battle. He dragged his hands across his face, decided he'd better find someplace to sit down, and stumbled back toward the front of the infirmary.

And ran slap into Mike Benson.

"Jackson!"

He glanced up just in time to see the handcuffs. He was so off-balance and exhausted from the fight, from the desperate rush to get Bergitta to a doctor, he didn't even have the strength or presence of mind to slip out of the way. Benson slapped the cuffs around his wrists, cold and terrifying, and tightened them down with a savage twist. "We've got a basement full of bodies, Jackson! And for once, you're not gonna wriggle out of it! Not with Caddrick on station, threatening to shut us down!"

Too badly shaken to do more than stumble, Skeeter followed numbly when Benson hauled him past gaping orderlies, nurses, newsies, and injured tourists. Ten minutes later, Skeeter was in the aerie high above Commons, facing down Ronisha Azzan, Shangri-La's tall deputy station manager. She'd clearly taken over when the feds had dragged Bull Morgan away to jail. Like Time Tours CEO Granville Baxter, Ronisha Azzan claimed Masai heritage and wore richly patterned African textiles done up in expensive suits. At the moment, she towered over Skeeter, glowering down at him from the other side of Bull's desk, while Benson blocked the exit, standing between Skeeter and the elevator doors. Skeeter stood swaying, wrists aching where the too-tight cuffs were cutting the skin, badly shaken and beginning to despair.

Ronisha Azzan said coldly, "We've taken into custody half-a-dozen down-timers on murder charges, Skeeter. What I want to know is—"

The elevator doors slid open with a soft *ping!* and Kit Carson crashed the party.

"Move it, Mike," Kit growled, facing down Benson when the head of security thought twice about letting him into the aerie. Kit brought one arm up to keep the elevator doors from closing again. "I'm in no mood to play games with *anybody.*"

Benson locked eyes with the retired scout, then

grunted once and wisely stepped aside. Skeeter sank, shaking, into the nearest chair, having been on the receiving end of Kit's rage once before, but after a moment's utter panic, he realized what Kit's presence here meant.

Kynan Rhys Gower had sworn an oath of fealty to Kit, several months back. The retired time scout had rescued him from Portuguese traders intent on burning the Welshman and Margo as witches on a beach in sixteenth-century East Africa. Kit was therefore obligated to speak on his behalf as the Welshman's liege lord. Kit Carson might, yet, take Skeeter apart for involving his vassal in something as serious as murder, but for the moment, his attention was rivetted on Ronisha Azzan.

Then he spoke, voice flat with anger, and darted a glance at Skeeter's manacled wrists. "Was it really necessary to cuff him?"

Benson snapped, "I thought so! There's half a dozen dead men down there—"

"*And damned near a dead little girl!*" Kit's lean face ran white with barely controlled fury. "That poor kid's been raped and beaten unconscious! Rachel's staff said they're not even sure she'll come out of surgery alive!"

Skeeter blanched.

"Take the cuffs off, Mike! Skeeter's not going to attack one of us. And even if he did, I could throw him through the nearest window without batting an eyelash, which he knows!"

Skeeter knew, all right.

He had no intention of going one-on-one with Kit Carson under *any* circumstances. But thanks to Kit, Mike Benson grudgingly unlocked the handcuffs, freeing Skeeter's wrists. He flexed them gingerly and rubbed the chafed skin.

"Thanks."

Benson just glowered at him and retreated to a watchful stance between Skeeter and the elevator door.

Ronisha slowly seated herself in Bull Morgan's chair,
studying Skeeter intently. "All right, Kit. He's uncuffed.
Now. You want to explain this mess, Skeeter? If I didn't
have my phones forwarded down to the war room, I'd
have every reporter on station demanding to know why
half-a-dozen construction workers were just murdered
on a station totally out of control. Not to mention
Senator Caddrick, who's demanded to see me the
minute he's released from the infirmary, and I think
we can all guess what *he* wants. This isn't going to play
well in the press, Skeeter. The station's in very serious trouble, even without Caddrick on the warpath
down in station medical."

"Yeah," Skeeter muttered, "that's old news, around
here." Kit's unexpected support gave him the courage to say it right out. "Look, I'm not in any mood
for games, either. Those bastards timed their hit
perfectly, snatching Bergitta during the chaos at
Primary. They knew Security would be run ragged,
trying to control that mess, and frankly, they were
counting on the fact that Bergitta's only a down-timer.
She's not Ianira Cassondra, not somebody we'd tear
the station apart to find, she's just a worthless, down-
timer ex-prostitute, a kid nobody'd miss. If you sit
there and tell me you'd have pulled a single security officer off riot duty at Primary to hunt down those
bastards or even mount a search for her, right in the
middle of this mess, I'll call you a liar, Ronisha
Azzan."

Ronisha's brows arched, but the deputy station
manager said nothing, merely tapped long, elegant
fingernails against the desktop and waited for Skeeter
to finish.

Skeeter shrugged. "I figured the only chance she
had was the down-timers. It was the little ones, the
Lost and Found Gang, who saw them snatch her out
of the bathroom she was cleaning. They came for me,
ran to warn the others. The kids *heard* those creeps

boasting, talking about how they were going to beat her and rape her and then kill her in cold blood when they'd had their fun. When we went in, down there, it was twenty to seven. Twenty, dammit, all of them intent on committing murder. They'd already jumped their own foreman, knocked him out and locked him up along with anybody who disagreed with their idea of fun. And the minute they laid eyes on us, their ringleader started yelling at his men to kill all of us. You tell me what we should've done, under the circumstances. Let them rape to death an innocent girl? Let 'em butcher those kids who led us down there? Tevel Gottlieb is only eight, for Chrissake. Folks around here may not think a helluva lot of me, but goddammit, if you think I was going to stand by with a finger in my ear and do *nothing,* you're as crazy as those idiots out there worshiping Jack the Ripper!"

Before Ronisha Azzan could do more than draw a single breath, Kit Carson said quietly, "I'd have done the same thing, Ronnie. In a second. And I've talked to Mr. Riyad. He supports Skeeter fully."

She glanced sharply at Shangri-La's most famous, influential resident, then sighed and rapped her knuckles agitatedly against the desktop. "Huh. Frankly, if I'd been in Skeeter's place, I might have done what he did, too. Mike, as far as I'm concerned, every one of these people acted in self-defense, saving the life of a station resident. And don't quote up-time law at me, either! I know most of them are down-timers without rights. On this station," she jabbed a finger downward for emphasis, "a resident is a resident. At least they are on *my* watch and I'm pretty sure Bull would back me up, if he weren't in jail with those damned feds holding the keys. So . . . The question is, what to tell those vultures in the press, or that maniac, Caddrick?"

Skeeter's jaw dropped, trying to take in the fact that he wasn't going to jail, after all. Then Skeeter realized he had another ace up his sleeve, one he knew for sure Ronisha Azzan would be interested in. "Well, you might try giving them the story of the week. We've got the key to destroying the *Ansar Majlis,* after all."

"*What?*" The word echoed in triplicate.

Skeeter indulged a brief, satisfied grin. It wasn't every day a guy could shock the likes of *that* trio. Skeeter leaned forward. "The guy who lost his hand? He offered to sing like a caged canary. And according to Hashim, part of what he's offered to sing about is the *Ansar Majlis.* Namely, their plans to invade this station, break their riot-happy Brothers out of jail, and kill off every Security officer in their way and every Templar they can lay hands on, doing it. Their leaders came through Primary today."

Ronisha snatched up the telephone. "Azzan, here. Release every down-timer involved in that fight down in Arabian Nights. Yes, dammit, *now.* And ask that kid, Hashim, and Mr. Riyad to translate for us. Interrogate those construction workers Wally Klontz and Mr. Riyad brought in. I want to know everything *they* do about the *Ansar Majlis.*" Then, to Skeeter, "With a little luck, we may yet blow that terrorist group wide open. Good work, Skeeter. Damned good work, in fact. The station owes you. Go on, get out of here. Get over to the infirmary and see how she's doing."

Skeeter was in such a state of shock, he could scarcely mumble out his thanks. He bolted for the elevator, gratified when Mike Benson merely stepped aside, his own jaw scraping the floor. The head of station security sent an unhappy scowl after him, but that was all. *Good God,* he thought on the way down to Commons, *I'm not going to jail! None of us is going to jail!* Because of Kit Carson. Or was it only that Ronisha Azzan was, in the final analysis, a fair woman, interested in justice? Even though she had to be tough, doing a job like hers, particularly with a whole new stack of corpses to explain to Senator John

Caddrick? Skeeter wasn't sure, but he certainly wasn't going to look a gift horse in the mouth.

When he reached the infirmary, he found Wally Klontz there ahead of him, along with Mr. Riyad and Hashim, taking statements from the injured construction workers. Wally glanced up when Skeeter came in. "Hey, Skeeter! Rachel said to tell you, Bergitta's in surgery, but it looks like she'll make it, after all. You got her up here just in time." Skeeter had to lean against the nearest wall, the relief was so profound. "And these birds," Wally nodded at the construction workers he was questioning, "are giving us enough information to arrest the whole up-time *Ansar Majlis* operation. We've already identified their ringleaders and sent out teams to arrest them at their hotels. Seems the leadership decided to come here and supervise the search for Ianira in person, after their underlings screwed up the mission. Once they're in custody, it'll just be a matter of mopping up the cells scattered in various up-time cities. Good work, Jackson."

He couldn't quite believe his ears. Two 'eighty-sixers in a row, *thanking* him!

But the jubilant mood was short-lived. When Bergitta came out of surgery, and Rachel allowed him to step into the recovery room, Skeeter's warm glow of accomplishment drained away so fast, he had to grip the door frame to steady himself. Bergitta was awake, but only just. Rachel had sedated her heavily for the emergency surgery and she was just coming out from under the anesthesia. The injuries looked even worse against the stark white of hospital bed and bandages than they had down in that nasty, half-finished warehouse in the basement. When Skeeter paused, stricken, beside her bed, Bergitta's bruised and swollen eyes focused slowly on his face. "Skeeter . . ." Tears trickled down her blackened cheeks.

"Shh, don't try to talk. You're safe, now. You've just

come out of surgery, Bergitta. Rachel says you're going to be all right, but you need to rest, save your strength." Moving gingerly, he took her hand. Heavy bandages covered raw cuts from the wire. Her elbow trailed IV lines.

"Thank you," she whispered anyway, throat working to swallow past hideous bruises from more of their damned wire.

"Don't thank me," he insisted quietly. "Thank the kids. They spotted you, when those animals dragged you out of the bathroom. If it hadn't been for the kids . . ." He forced a smile. "But they *did* see you, didn't they? And sounded the alarm. So we got you out of there, thanks to the little ones. And some who aren't so little," he added with a watery smile. "Eigil Bjarneson sent a few to the gods, today."

Her fingers tightened around Skeeter's.

"Listen, you get some rest, okay? Nobody's going to hurt you again, I promise. The ones who aren't dead are under arrest. They'll be kicked off station in handcuffs and tried for attempted murder and ties to the *Ansar Majlis*. You're safe, Bergitta, I promise you are. And Molly wants you to move in with her, when you're stronger, so you won't have to live alone any more." Over at the doorway, a nurse high-signed him. "I have to go now, the nurse says you need to sleep. Close your eyes, I'll come back and see you when you're feeling a little better."

By the time Skeeter extricated his fingers from hers, tucked her hand beneath the blankets, and reached the door, she was sound asleep. He stood in the doorway for a long moment, just watching her, then turned on his heel and headed out into the Commons once again. Bergitta was alive, thank all the Yakka gods of the upper air, and with a little luck, the *Ansar Majlis* wouldn't ever threaten anybody again.

But he still had to find a job, doing *something* to

pay for his apartment and groceries, and he still intended to spot and turn in every pickpocket and confidence artist he could find. And somewhere, down one of the station's gates, his dearest friends in the world were hiding for their very lives. Marcus and Ianira and their beautiful little girls . . .

He didn't yet know *how,* exactly.

But Skeeter intended to find them.

And bring them safely home once more.

Jenna Caddrick sat beside the window of her bedroom in the little house in Spitalfields, listening to the angry shouts in the streets outside, as word of the latest murder in Whitechapel spread through the East End. She'd sat in almost this same spot for a whole week, now, exhausted and trying to recover from the gunshot to her skull. Jenna could no longer doubt Ianira's pronouncement that she was carrying a baby, either. Even with the stress of the past few days, she should've started her period by now and hadn't. And she'd never felt so monstrously queasy in all her life, had been feeling nauseated for days, right through the pain medication Dr. Mendel had prescribed. She hadn't wanted anything more than dry toast in days, had been forcing herself to eat, terrified that she'd lose the baby if she didn't choke food down.

Below her window, angry working men shouted at a police constable, demanding better patrols through the area, and frightened women huddled in doorways, clutching shawls about their shoulders and crying while they talked endlessly of the madman stalking these streets. Jenna brought her eyelids clenching down over wetness. *What am I going to do?* She was in disguise as a man, with fake mutton chops and moustaches which the time terminal's cosmetologist had implanted. That false hair would require a cosmetic surgeon to remove. Not a single doctor anywhere in this city would begin to understand if a seemingly male individual showed up ready to deliver a baby, for God's sake. Talk about attracting unwanted attention . . .

And she couldn't go home to deliver her baby, either, might *never* be able to go home. That was something else she'd been running away from, these last few days, sitting in this chair and staring out this window while her scalp wound healed. She didn't want to face the knowledge that the faceless men her father worked with might never stop trying to kill her, even if Noah managed to destroy her father's career and bring down the men paying him.

None of them might ever be able to go home again, not Jenna or Noah Armstrong or Ianira's beautiful, precious family . . . And they didn't even know where Ianira was, or what had become of her in the hands of the lunatic who'd shot Jenna down in cold blood. Jenna's lips trembled and tears came again, a flood of them as bitter anger threatened to choke her. Somehow, her father was going to pay for this. All of this . . . She didn't hear the first knock at her door and only looked up when someone cleared a throat and said, "Hey, mind if I come in?"

Jenna, eyes streaming, looked around. It was Noah Armstrong. The detective, still playing the role of Marcus' sister, was dressed in a plain cotton skirt and worn bodice, leaving Armstrong's gender even more a mystery than ever. Jenna couldn't even bring herself to care. Noah lifted a tray with several slices of dried toast, a hot meat pie, and a steaming mug of tea. "I bought you something to eat."

Jenna swallowed against the nausea any smell of food brought. She wasn't hungry, hadn't been hungry in so long, she'd forgotten what hunger felt like. "Thanks," she made herself say.

Noah set the lunch tray on the table at Jenna's elbow. As she choked down the first bites, the detective rested a hand on her brow. The gesture was so caring, Jenna's eyes stung and the tears came again. She set down her fork and covered her face with her hands.

"Hey," Noah hunkered down beside her, grey eyes revealing a surprising depth of concern, "what's this? I won't let anyone hurt you, kid. Surely you know that?"

Jenna bit her lip, then managed to choke out, "I . . . I know that. It's why . . . I mean . . . everybody who ever cared about me died," she gulped. "Noah, I'm so scared . . ."

"Sure you are, kid," Noah said quietly. "And you've got every right to be. But look at this another way, Jenna." Noah traced the line of fake whiskers down her jaw, brushed limp hair back from her brow, the gesture curiously gentle. "As long as you're alive, as long as your baby's alive, then at least a part of Carl's still aliv e, too. And that means they've lost. They've failed to destroy the witnesses, failed to destroy quite *everything* you love." Noah took her hand, rubbed her fingers and palm with warm fingertips. "You're not alone, hear? We're all with you in this. And we'll need your help, Jenna. To find Ianira."

Jenna looked up at that, met Noah Armstrong's gaze. The concern, the steely determination to keep her alive gave Jenna a renewed sense of strength. She found herself drying her wet cheeks. "All right," she said, voice low. "All right, Noah. I'll do whatever it takes. Maybe we can try hunting the gentlemen's clubs over in Pall Mall, find some trace of him that way. We have to find her."

"And we will."

"Noah . . ." She bit her lip, half afraid to broach the subject they'd all been avoiding.

"What?" the detective asked gently.

"When you go back up time with that evidence? I want you to do me a favor, will you?" The bitterness in her voice would have shocked her, once, long ago, at least a week previously, before her father had destroyed her entire world. "*Don't* put a bullet between my father's eyes for me."

Noah's grey eyes showed surprise.

She grated out harshly, "I want to do it, myself."

The lunch Noah had brought, forgotten on the table at her elbow, slowly cooled while Noah gathered her in and let her cry. One day, she didn't yet know how, she *would* make her father pay. She had never been more certain of anything in her life.

to be continued in:

THE HOUSE THAT JACK BUILT

Excerpt from

FORTUNE'S STROKE

part of the Belisarius series by

ERIC FLINT &
DAVID DRAKE

*Available May 2000
in hardcover from
Baen Books*

Prologue

The best steel in the world was made in India. That steel had saved his life.

He stared at a drop of blood working its way down the blade. Slowly, slowly. The blood which covered that fine steel was already drying in the sun. Even as he watched, the last still-liquid drop came to a halt and began hardening.

He had no idea how long he had been watching the blood dry. Hours, it seemed. Hours spent staring at a sword because he was too exhausted to do anything else.

But some quiet, lurking part of his battle-hardened mind told him it had only been minutes. Minutes only, and not so many of those.

He was exhausted. In mind, perhaps, even more than in body.

In a life filled with war since his boyhood, this battle had been the most bitter. Even his famous contest against one of India's legends, fought many years before, did not compare. That, too, had been a day filled with exhaustion, struggle, and fear. But it had been a single combat, not this tornado of mass melee. And there had been no rage in it, no murderous bile. Deadly purpose, yes—in his opponent as much as in himself. But there had been glory, too, and the exultation of knowing that—whichever of them triumphed—both their names would ring down through India's ages.

There had been no glory in this battle. His overlords would claim it glorious, and their bards and chroniclers give it the name. But they were liars. Untruth came as naturally to his masters as breathing. He thought that was perhaps the worst of their many crimes, for it covered all the rest.

His staring eyes moved away from the sword, and fixed on the body of his last opponent. The corpse was a horror, now, what with the mass of flies covering the entrails which spilled out from the great wound which the world's finest steel had created. A desperate slash, that had been, delivered by a man driven to his knees by his opponent's own powerful sword-stroke.

The staring eyes moved to the stub still held in the corpse's hand. The sword had broken at the hilt. The world's finest steel had saved his life. That and his own great strength, when he parried the strike.

Now, staring at the man's face. The features were a blur. Meaningless. The life which had once animated those features was gone. The man who stared saw only the beard clearly. A heavy beard, cut in the square Persian style.

He managed a slight nod, in place of the bow he was too tired to make. His opponent had been a brave man. Determined to exact a last vengeance out of a battle he must have already known to be lost. Determined to kill the man who led the invaders of his country.

The man who stared—the *invader*, he named himself, for he was not given to lies—would see to it that the Persian's body was exposed to the elements. It seemed a strange custom, to him, but that was the Aryan way of releasing the soul.

The man who stared had invaded, and murdered, and plundered, and conquered. But he would not dishonor. That low he would not stoop.

He heard the sound of approaching footsteps behind him. Several men. Among those steps he recognized those of his commander.

He summoned the energy to rise to his feet. For a moment, swaying dizzily, he stared across the battlefield. The Caspian Gates, that battlefield was called. The doorway to all of Persia. The man who stared had opened that doorway.

He cast a last glance at the disemboweled body at his feet.

Yes, he would see to it that the corpse was exposed, in the Persian way.

All of the enemy corpses, he thought, staring back at the battlefield. The stony, barren ground was littered with dead and dying men. Far beyond the grisly sight, rearing up on the northern horizon, was the immense mountain which Persians called Demavend. An extinct volcano, its pure and clean lines stood like some godly reproach to the foul chaos of mankind.

Yes. All of them.

His honor demanded it, and honor was all that was left to him.

That, and his name.

Finally, now, he was able to stand erect. He was very tall.

Rana Sanga was his name. The greatest of Rajputana's kings, and one of India's most legendary warriors.

Rana Sanga. He took some comfort in the name. A name of honor. But he did not take much comfort, and only for an instant. For he was not a man given to lies, and he knew what else the name signified. Malwa bards and chroniclers could sing and write what they would, but he knew the truth.

Rana Sanga. The man—the legend, the Rajput King—who led the final charge which broke the Persians at the Caspian Gates. The man who opened the door, so that the world's foulest evil could spill across another continent.

He felt a gentle touch on his arm. Sanga glanced down, recognizing the pudgy little hand of Lord Damodara.

"Are you badly injured?"

Damodara's voice seemed filled with genuine concern. For a moment, a bitter thought flitted through Sanga's mind. But he dismissed it almost instantly. Some of Damodara's concern, true, was simply fear of losing his best general. But any commander worthy of the name would share that concern. Sanga was himself a general—and a magnificent one—and knew full well that any general's mind required a capacity for calculating ruthlessness.

But most of Damodara's concern was personal. Staring down at his commander, Sanga was struck by the oddity of the friendship in that fat, round face. Of all the highest men in the vast Malwa Empire, Damodara was the only one Sanga had ever met for whom he felt a genuine respect. Other Malwa overlords could be capable, even brilliant—as was Damodara—but no others could claim to be free of evil.

Not that Damodara is a saint, he thought wryly. *"Practical," he likes to call himself. Which is simply a polite way of saying "amoral." But at least he takes no pleasure in cruelty, and will avoid it when he can.*

He shook off the thought and the question simultaneously.

"No, Lord Damodara. I am exhausted, but—" Sanga shrugged. "Very little of the blood is mine. Two gashes, only. I have already bound them up. One will require some stitches. Later."

Sanga made a small gesture at the battlefield. His

voice grew harsh. "It is more important, this moment, to see to the needs of honor. I want all the Persians buried—exposed—in their own manner. *With* their weapons."

Sanga cast a cold, unyielding eye on a figure standing some few feet away. Mihirakula was the commander of Lord Damodara's Ye-tai contingents.

"The Ye-tai may loot the bodies of any coin, or jewelry. But the Persians must be exposed with their weapons. Honor demands it."

Mihirakula scowled, but made no verbal protest. He knew that the Malwa commander would accede to Sanga's wishes. The heart of Damodara's army was Rajput, unlike any other of the Malwa Empire's many armies.

"Of course," said Damodara. "If you so wish."

The Malwa commander turned toward one of his other lieutenants, but the man was already moving toward his horse. The man was Rajput himself. He would see to enforcing the order.

Damodara turned back. "There is news," he announced. He gestured toward another man in his little entourage. A small, wiry, elderly man.

"One of Narses' couriers arrived just before the battle ended. With news from Mesopotamia."

Sanga glanced at Narses. There was sourness in that glance. The Rajput King had no love for traitors, even those who had betrayed his enemies.

Still—Narses was immensely competent. Of that there was no question.

"What is the news?" he asked.

"Our main army in Mesopotamia has suffered reverses." Damodara took a deep breath. "*Severe* reverses. They have been forced to lift the siege of Babylon and retreat to Charax."

"Belisarius," stated Sanga. His voice rang iron with certainty.

Damodara nodded. "Yes. He defeated one army at

a place called Anatha, diverted the Euphrates, and trapped another army which came to reopen the river. Shattered it. Terrible casualties. Apparently he destroyed the dam and drowned thousands of our soldiers."

The Malwa commander looked away. "Much as you predicted. Cunning as a mongoose." Damodara blew out his cheeks. "With barely ten thousand men, Belisarius managed to force our army all the way back to the sea."

"And now?" asked Sanga.

Damodara shrugged. "It is not certain. The Persian Emperor is marshalling his forces to defeat his brother Ormazd, who betra—who is now allied with us—while he leaves a large army to hold Babylon. Belisarius went to Peroz-Shapur to rest and refit his army over the winter. After that—"

Again, he blew out his cheeks.

"He marched out of Peroz-Shapur some weeks ago, and seems to have disappeared."

Sanga nodded. He turned toward the many Rajput soldiers who were now standing nearby, gathering about their leader.

"Does one of you have any wine?" He lifted the sword in his hand. "I must clean it. The blood has dried."

One of the Rajputs began digging in the pouch behind his saddle. Sanga turned back to Damodara.

"He will be coming for us, now."

The Malwa commander cocked a quizzical eyebrow.

"Be sure of it, Lord Damodara," stated Sanga. He cocked his own eye at the Roman traitor.

Narses nodded. "Yes," he agreed. "That is my assessment also."

Listening to Narses speak, Sanga was impressed, again, by the traitor's ability to learn Hindi so quickly. Narses' accent was pronounced, but his vocabulary seemed to grow by leaps and bounds daily. And his grammar was already almost impeccable.

But, as always, Sanga was mostly struck by the sound of Narses' voice. Such a deep voice, to come from an old eunuch. He reminded himself, again, not to let his distaste for Narses obscure the undoubted depths to the man. A traitor, the eunuch might be. He was also fiendishly capable, and an excellent advisor and spymaster.

"Be sure of it, Lord Damodara," repeated Rana Sanga.

His soldier handed him a winesack. Rajputana's greatest king began cleaning the blade of his sword.

The finest steel in the world was made in India.

He would need that steel. Belisarius was coming.

Chapter 1

PERSIA
Spring, 532 A.D.

When they reached the crest of the trail, two hours after daybreak, Belisarius reined in his horse. The pass was narrow and rocky, obscuring the mountains around him. But his view of the sun-drenched scene below was quite breath-taking.

"What a magnificent country," he murmured.

Belisarius twisted slightly in the saddle, turning toward the man on his right. "Don't you think so, Maurice?"

Maurice scowled. His gray eyes glared down at the great plateau which stretched to the far-distant horizon. Their color was almost identical to his beard. Every one of the bristly strands, Maurice liked to say, had been turned gray over the years by his young commander's weird and crooked way of looking at things.

"You're a lunatic," he pronounced. "A gibbering idiot."

Smiling crookedly, Belisarius turned to the man on his left. "Is that your opinion also, Vasudeva?"

The commander of Belusarius' contingent of Kushan troops shrugged. "Difficult to say," he replied, in his thick, newly learned Greek. For a moment, Vasudeva's usually impassive face was twisted by a grimace.

"Impossible to make fair judgement," he growled. "This helmet—" A sudden fluency came upon him: "Ignorant stupid barbarian piece of shit helmet designed by ignorant stupid barbarians with shit for brains!"

A deep breath, then: "Stupid fucking barbarian helmet obscures all vision. Makes me blind as a bat." He squinted up at the sky. "It is daylight, yes?"

Belisarius' smile grew more crooked still. The Kushans had not stopped complaining about their helmets since they were first handed the things. Weeks ago, now. As soon as his army was three days' march from Peroz-Shapur, and Belisarius was satisfied there were no eyes to see, he had unloaded the Kushans' new uniforms and insisted they start wearing them.

The Kushans had howled for hours. Then, finally yielding to their master's stern commands—they were, after all, technically his slaves—they had stubbornly kept his army from resuming its march for another day. A full day, while they furiously cleaned and recleaned their new outfits. Insisting, all the while, that invented-by-a-philosopher-and-manufactured-by-a-poet-civilized-fucking caustics were no match for hordes of rampaging-murdering-raping-plundering-barbarian-fucking lice.

Glancing down at Vasudeva's gear, Belisarius privately admitted his sympathy.

He had obtained the Kushans' new armor and uniforms, through intermediaries, from the Ostrogoths. Ironically, although the workmanship—certainly the filth—of the outfits was barbarian, they were patterned on Roman uniforms of the previous century. As armor went, the outfits were quite substantial. They were sturdier, actually, than modern cataphract gear, in the way they combined a mail tunic with laminated arm and leg protection. That weight, of course, was the source of some of the grumbling. The Kushans favored lighter armor than Roman cataphracts to begin with—much less this great, gross, grotesque Ostrogoth gear.

But it was the helmets for which the Kushans reserved their chief complaint. They were accustomed to their own light and simple headgear, which consisted of nothing much more than a steel plate across the forehead held by a leather strap. Whereas these—these—these great, heavy, head-enclosing, silly-horse-tail-crested, idiot-segmented-steel-plate fucking barbarian fucking monstrosities—

They obscured their topknots! Covered them up completely!

"Which," Belisarius had patiently explained at the time, "is the point of the whole exercise. No one will realize you are Kushans. I must keep your existence in my army a secret from the enemy."

The Kushans had understood the military logic of the matter. Still—

Belisarius felt Vasudeva's glare, but he ignored it serenely. "Oh, surely you have some opinion," he stated.

Vasudeva transferred the glare onto the countryside below. "Maurice is correct," he pronounced. "You are a lunatic. A madman."

For a moment, Vasudeva and Maurice exchanged admiring glances. In the months since they had met, the leader of the Kushan "military slaves" and the commander of Belisarius' bucellarii—his personal contingent of mostly Thracian cataphracts who constituted the elite troops of his army—had developed a close working relationship. A friendship, actually, although neither of those grizzled veterans would have admitted the term into their grim lexicon.

Observing the silent exchange, Belisarius fought down a grin. *Outrageous language,* he thought wryly, *from a slave!*

He had captured the Kushans the previous summer, at what had come to be called the battle of Anatha. In the months thereafter, while Belisarius concentrated on relieving the Malwa siege of Babylon, the Kushans had served his army as a labor force. After Belisarius had driven the main Malwa army back to the seaport of Charax—through a stratagem in which their own labor had played a key role—the Kushans had switched allegiances. They had never had any love for their arrogant Malwa overlords to begin with. And once they concluded, from close scrutiny, that Belisarius was as shrewd and capable a commander as they had ever encountered, they decided to negotiate a new status.

"Slaves" they were still, technically. The Kushans felt strongly that proprieties had to be maintained, and they had, after all, been captured in fair battle. Their status had been proposed by Belisarius himself, based on a vision which Aide had given him of military slaves of the future called "Mamelukes."

Vasudeva's eyes were now resting on him, with none of the admiration those same eyes had bestowed on Maurice a moment earlier. Quite hard, those eyes were. Almost glaring, in fact.

Belisarius let the grin emerge.

Slaves, of a sort. But we have to make allowances. It's hard for a man to remember his servile status when he's riding an armored horse with weapons at his side.

"How disrespectful," he murmured.

Vasudeva ignored the quip. The Kushan pointed a finger at the landscape below. "You call this magnificent?" he demanded.

Snort. The glare was transferred back to the plateau. The rocky, ravine-filled landscape stretched from the base of the mountains as far as the eye could see.

"If there is a single drop of water in that miserable country," growled Vasudeva, "it is being hoarded by a family of field mice. A small family, at that."

He remembered his grievance.

"So, at least," he added sourly, "it appears to me. But I am blind as a bat because of this fucking stupid barbarian helmet. Perhaps there's a river—even a huge lake!—somewhere below."

He cocked his head. "Maurice?"

The Thracian cataphract shook his head gloomily. "Not a drop, just as you said." He pointed his own accusing finger. "There's not hardly any vegetation at all down there, except for a handful of oak trees here and there."

Maurice glanced for a moment at the mountains which surrounded them. A thin layer of snow covered the slopes, but the scene was still warmer than the one below. As throughout the Zagros range, the terrain was heavily covered with oak and juniper. The rainfall which the Zagros received even produced a certain lushness in its multitude of little valleys. There, aided by irrigation, the Persian inhabitants were able to grow wheat, barley, grapes, apricots, peaches and pistachios.

He sighed, turning his eyes back to the arid plateau. "All the rain stays in the mountains," he muttered. "Down there—" Another sigh. "Nothing but—"

He finally spotted it.

Belisarius smiled. He, with his vision enhanced by Aide, had see the thing as soon as they reached the pass. "I do believe that's an oasis!" he exclaimed cheerfully.

Vasudeva's gaze tracked that of his companions. When he spotted the small patch of greenery, his eyes widened. "*That?*" he choked. "You call *that* an 'oasis'?"

Belisarius shrugged. "It's not an oasis, actually. I think it's one of the places where the Persians dug a vertical well to their underground canals. What they call their *qanat* system."

The clatter of horses behind caused him to turn. His two bodyguards, Anastasius and Valentinian, had finally arrived at the mountain pass. They had lagged behind while Valentinian pried a rock from one of his mount's hooves.

Belisarius turned back and pointed to the "oasis." "I want to investigate," he announced. "I think we can make it there by noon."

Protest immediately erupted.

"That's a bad idea," stated Maurice.

"Idiot lunatic idea," agreed Vasudeva.

"There's only the five of us," concurred Valentinian.

"Rest of the army's still a day's march behind," added Anastasius. The giant cataphract, usually placid and philosophical, added his own glare to those of his companions.

"This so-called 'personal reconnaissance' of yours," rumbled Anastasius, "is pushing it already." A huge hand swept the surrounding mountains. A finger the size of a sausage pointed accusingly at the plateau below. "Who the hell knows what's lurking about?" he demanded. "That so-called 'plateau' is almost as broken as these mountains. Could be an entire Malwa cavalry troop hidden anywhere."

"An entire *army*," hissed Valentinian. "I think we should get out of here. I *certainly* don't think we should go down—"

Belisarius cleared his throat. "I don't recall summoning a council," he remarked mildly.

His companions scowled, but fell instantly silent.

CONTINUED IN *FORTUNE'S STROKE*
AVAILABLE MAY 2000

Special thanks to

DR. SPENCER ETH AND DR. SHOBA SRINIVASAN

MONSTER

1.

THE GIANT KNEW Richard Nixon.

Towering, yellow-haired, grizzled, a listing mountain in khaki twill, he limped closer, and Milo tightened up. I looked to Frank Dollard for a cue. Dollard appeared untroubled, meaty arms at his sides, mouth serene under the tobaccoed gray mustache. His eyes were slits, but they'd been that way at the main gate.

The giant belched out a bass laugh and brushed greasy hair away from his eyes. His beard was a corn-colored ruin. I could smell him now, vinegarish, hormonally charged. He had to be six-eight, three hundred. The shadow he threw on the dirt was ash-colored, amoebic, broad enough to shade us.

He took another lurching step, and this time Frank Dollard's right arm shot out.

The huge man didn't seem to notice, just stood there with Dollard's limb flung across his waist. Maybe a dozen other men in khaki were out on the yard, most of them standing still, a few others pacing, rocking, faces pressed against the chain link. No groups that I could see; everyone to himself. Above them, the sky was an untrammeled blue, clouds broiled away by a vengeful sun. I was cooking in my suit.

The giant's face was dry. He sighed, dropped his shoulders, and Dollard lowered his arm. The giant made a finger gun, pointed it at us, and laughed. His eyes were dark brown, pinched at the corners, the whites too sallow for health.

"Secret service." He thumped his chest. "Victoria's Secret service in the closet underwear undercover always lookin' out for the guy good old Nixon RMN Rimmin, always rimmin

1

wanting to be rimmed he liked to talk the walk cuttin outta the White House night house doing the party thing all hours with Kurt Vonnegut J. D. Salinger the Glass family anyone who didn't mind the politics heat of the kitchen I wrote *Cat's Cradle* sold it to Vonnegut for ten bucks *Billy Bathgate* typed the manuscript one time he walked out the front door got all the way to Las Vegas big hassle with the Hell's Angels over some dollar slots Vonnegut wanting to change the national debt Rimmin agreed the Angels got pissed we had to pull him out of it me and Kurt Vonnegut Salinger wasn't there Doctorow was sewing the *Cat's Cradle* they were bad cats, woulda assassinated him any day of the week leeway the oswald harvey."

He bent and lifted his left trouser leg. Below the knee was bone sheathed with glossy white scar tissue, most of the calf meat ripped away. An organic peg leg.

"Got shot protecting old Rimmin," he said, letting go of the fabric. "He died anyway poor Richard no almanac know what happened rimmed too hard I couldn't stop it."

"Chet," said Dollard, stretching to pat the giant's shoulder.

The giant shuddered. Little cherries of muscle rolled along Milo's jawline. His hand was where his gun would have been if he hadn't checked it at the gate.

Dollard said, "Gonna make it to the TV room today, Chet?"

The giant swayed a bit. "Ahh . . ."

"I think you should make it to the TV room, Chet. There's gonna be a movie on democracy. We're gonna sing 'The Star-Spangled Banner,' could use someone with a good voice."

"Yeah, Pavarotti," said the giant, suddenly cheerful. "He and Domingo were at Caesars Palace they didn't like the way it worked out Rimmin not doing his voice exercises lee lee lee lo lo lo no egg yolk to smooth the trachea it pissed Pavarotti off he didn't want to run for public office."

"Yeah, sure," said Dollard. He winked at Milo and me.

The giant had turned his back on all three of us and was staring down on the bare tan table of the yard. A short, thick, dark-haired man had pulled down his pants and was urinating in the dirt, setting off a tiny dust storm. None of the other men in khaki seemed to notice. The giant's face had gone stony.

"Wet," he said.

"Don't worry about it, Chet," Dollard said softly. "You know Sharbno and his bladder."

The giant didn't answer, but Dollard must have transmitted a message, because two other psych techs came jogging over from a far corner. One black, one white, just as muscular as Dollard but a lot younger, wearing the same uniform of short-sleeved sport shirt, jeans, and sneakers. Photo badges clipped to the collar. The heat and the run had turned the techs' faces wet. Milo's sport coat had soaked through at the armpits, but the giant hadn't let loose a drop of sweat.

His face tightened some more as he watched the urinating man shake himself off, then duck-walk across the yard, pants still puddled around his ankles.

"Wet."

"We'll handle it, Chet," soothed Dollard.

The black tech said, "I'll go get those trousers up."

He sauntered toward Sharbno. The white tech stayed with Chet. Dollard gave Chet another pat and we moved on.

Ten yards later, I looked back. Both techs were flanking Chet. The giant's posture had changed—shoulders higher, head craning as he continued to stare at the space vacated by Sharbno.

Milo said, "Guy that size, how can you control him?"

"We don't control him," said Dollard. "Clozapine does. Last month his dosage got upped after he beat the crap out of another patient. Broke about a dozen bones."

"Maybe he needs even more," said Milo.

"Why?"

"He doesn't exactly sound coherent."

Dollard chuckled. "Coherent." He glanced at me. "Know what his daily dosage is, Doctor? Fourteen hundred milligrams. Even with his body weight, that's pretty thorough, wouldn't you say?"

"Maximum's usually around nine hundred," I told Milo. "Lots of people do well on a third of that."

Dollard said, "He was on eleven migs when he broke the other inmate's face." Dollard's chest puffed a bit. "We exceed maximum recommendations all the time; the psychiatrists tell us it's no problem." He shrugged. "Maybe Chet'll get even more. If he does something else bad."

We covered more ground, passing more inmates. Untrimmed hair, slack mouths, empty eyes, stained uniforms. None of the iron-pumper bulk you see in prisons. These torsos were soft, warped, deflated. I felt eyes on the back of my head, glanced to the side, and saw a man with haunted-prophet eyes and a chestful of black beard staring at me. Above the facial pelt, his cheeks were sunken and sooty. Our eyes engaged. He came toward me, arms rigid, neck bobbing. He opened his mouth. No teeth.

He didn't know me but his eyes were rich with hatred.

My hands fisted. I walked faster. Dollard noticed and cocked his head. The bearded man stopped abruptly, stood there in the full sun, planted like a shrub. The red exit sign on the far gate was five hundred feet away. Dollard's key ring jangled. No other techs in sight. We kept walking. Beautiful sky, but no birds. A machine began grinding something.

I said, "Chet's ramblings. There seems to be some intelligence there."

"What, 'cause he talks about books?" said Dollard. "I think before he went nuts he was in college somewhere. I think his family was educated."

"What got him in here?" said Milo, glancing back.

"Same as all of them." Dollard scratched his mustache and kept his pace steady. The yard was vast. We were halfway across now, passing more dead eyes, frozen faces, wild looks that set up the small hairs on the back of my neck.

"Don't wear khaki or brown," Milo had said. "The inmates wear that, we don't want you stuck in there—though that would be interesting, wouldn't it? Shrink trying to convince them he's not crazy?"

"Same as all of them?" I said.

"Incompetent to stand trial," said Dollard. "Your basic 1026."

"How many do you have here?" said Milo.

"Twelve hundred or so. Old Chet's case is kinda sad. He was living on top of a mountain down near the Mexican border—some kind of hermit deal, sleeping in caves, eating weeds, all that good stuff. Couple of hikers just happened to be unlucky enough to find the wrong cave, wrong time, woke him up. He tore 'em up—really went at 'em with his bare hands. He actually managed to rip both the girl's arms off and was working on one of her legs when they found him. Some park ranger or sheriff shotgunned Chet's leg charging in, that's why it looks like that. He wasn't resisting arrest, just sitting there next to the body pieces, looking scared someone was gonna hit him. No big challenge getting a 1026 on something like that. He's been here three years. First six months he did nothing but stay curled up, crying, sucking his thumb. We had to IV-feed him."

"Now he beats people up," said Milo. "Progress."

Dollard flexed his fingers. He was in his late fifties, husky and sunburnt, no visible body fat. The lips beneath the mustache were thin, parched, amused. "What do you want we should do, haul him out and shoot him?"

Milo grunted.

Dollard said, "Yeah, I know what you're thinking: good riddance to bad rubbish, you'd be happy to be on the firing squad." He chuckled. "Cop thinking. I worked patrol in Hemet for ten years, woulda said the exact same thing before I came here. Couple of years on the wards and now I know reality: some of them really *are* sick." He touched his mustache. "Old Chet's no Ted Bundy. He couldn't help himself any more than a baby crapping its diaper. Same with old Sharbno back there, pissing in the dirt." He tapped his temple. "The wiring's screwy, some people just turn to garbage. And this place is the Dumpster."

"Exactly why we're here," said Milo.

Dollard raised an eyebrow. "*That* I don't know about. Our garbage doesn't get taken out. I can't see how we're gonna be able to help you on Dr. Argent."

He flexed his fingers again. His nails were yellow horn. "I

liked Dr. Argent. Real nice lady. But she met her end out there." He pointed randomly. "Out in the *civilized* world."

"Did you work with her?"

"Not steadily. We talked about cases from time to time, she'd tell me if a patient needed something. But you can tell about people. Nice lady. A little naive, but she was new."

"Naive in what way?"

"She started this group. Skills for Daily Living. Weekly discussions, supposedly helping some guys cope with the world. As if any of 'em are ever getting out."

"She ran it by herself."

"Her and a tech."

"Who's the tech?"

"Girl named Heidi Ott."

"Two women handling a group of killers?"

Dollard smiled. "The state says it's safe."

"You think different?"

"I'm not paid to think."

We neared the chain-link wall. Milo said, "Any idea why someone in the civilized world would kill Dr. Argent? Speaking as an ex-cop."

Dollard said, "From what you told me—the way you found her in that car trunk, all cleaned up—I'd say some sociopath, right? Someone who knew damn well what he was doing, and enjoyed it. More of a 1368 than a 1026—your basic lowlife criminal trying to fake being crazy 'cause they're under the mistaken impression it'll be easier here than in jail. We've got two, three hundred of *those* on the fifth floor, maybe a few more, 'cause of Three Strikes. They come here ranting and drooling, smearing shit on the walls, learn quickly they can't B.S. the docs here. Less than one percent succeed. The official eval period's ninety days, but plenty of them ask to leave sooner."

"Did Dr. Argent work on the fifth floor?"

"Nope. Hers were all 1026's."

"Besides total crazies and ninety-day losers, who else do you have here?" said Milo.

"We've got a few mentally disordered sex offenders left,"

said Dollard. "Pedophiles, that kind of trash. Maybe thirty of 'em. We used to have more but they keep changing the law— stick 'em here, nope, the prison system, oops, back here, unh-uh, prison. Dr. Argent didn't hang with them, either, least that I noticed."

"So the way you see it, what happened to her couldn't re-late to her work here."

"You got it. Even if one of her guys got out—and they didn't—none of them could've killed her and stashed her in the trunk. None of them could plan that well."

We were at the gate. Tan men standing still, like oversized chess pieces. The faraway machine continued to grind.

Dollard flicked a hand back at the yard. "I'm not saying these guys are harmless, even with all the dope we pump into them. Get these poor bastards delusional enough, they could do anything. But they don't kill for fun—from what I've seen, they don't take much pleasure from life, period. If you can even call what they're doing living."

He cleared his throat, swallowed the phlegm. "Makes you wonder why God would take the trouble to create such a mess."

2.

TWO CORPSES IN car trunks. Claire Argent was the second.

The first, found eight months earlier, was a twenty-five-year-old would-be actor named Richard Dada, left in the front storage compartment of his own VW Bug in the industrial zone north of Centinela and Pico—a warren of tool-and-die shops, auto detailers, spare-parts dealers. It took three days for Dada's car to be noticed. A maintenance worker picked up the smell. The crime scene was walking distance from the West L.A. substation, but Milo drove over to the scene.

In life, Dada had been tall, dark, and handsome. The killer stripped off his clothes, bisected him cleanly at the waist with a tooth-edged weapon, dropped each segment in a heavy-duty black plastic lawn bag, fastened the sacks, stashed them in the Volkswagen, drove to the dump spot, most probably late at night, and escaped without notice. Cause of death was loss of blood from a deep, wide throat slash. Lack of gore in the bags and in the car said the butchery had been accomplished somewhere else. The coroner was fairly certain Dada was already dead when cut in half.

"Long legs," Milo said, the first time he talked to me about the case. "So maybe cutting him solved a storage problem. Or it was part of the thrill."

"Or both," I said.

He frowned. "Dada's eyes were taken out, too, but no other mutilation. Any ideas?"

"The killer drove Dada's car to the dump spot," I said, "so he could've left on foot and lives close by. Or he took the bus

8

and you could interview drivers, see if any unusual passengers got on that night."

"I've already talked to the bus drivers. No memory of any conspicuously weird passengers. Same for taxi drivers. No late-night pickups in the neighborhood, period."

"By 'unusual' I didn't mean weird," I said. "The killer probably isn't bizarre-looking. I'd guess just the opposite: composed, a good planner, middle-class. Even so, having just dumped the VW, he might've been a little worked up. Who rides the bus at that hour? Mostly night-shift busboys and office cleaners, a few derelicts. Someone middle-class might be conspicuous."

"Makes sense," he said, "but there was no one who stuck in any of the drivers' memories."

"Okay, then. The third possibility: there was another car ready to take the killer away. Extremely careful planning. Or an accomplice."

Milo rubbed his face, like washing without water. We were at his desk in the Robbery-Homicide room at the West L.A. station, facing the bright orange lockers, drinking coffee. A few other detectives were typing and snacking. I had a child-custody court appearance downtown in two hours, had stopped by for lunch, but Milo had wanted to talk about Dada rather than eat.

"The accomplice bit is interesting," he said. "So is the local angle—okay, time to do some footwork, see if some joker who learned freelance meat-cutting at San Quentin is out on parole. Get to know more about the poor kid, too—see if he got himself in trouble."

Three months later, Milo's footwork had unearthed the minutiae of Richard Dada's life but had gotten him no closer to solving the case.

At the half-year mark, the file got pushed to the back of the drawer.

I knew Milo's nerves were rubbed raw by that. His specialty was clearing cold cases, not creating them. He had the highest solve rate of any homicide D in West L.A., maybe the entire department for this year. That didn't make him any more popular; as the only openly gay detective on the force, he'd never be invited to blue-buddy barbecues. But it did provide insurance, and I knew he regarded failure as professionally threatening.

As a personal sin, too; one of the last things he'd said before filing the murder book was "This one deserves more. Some felonious cretin getting bashed with a pool cue is one thing, but this . . . The way the kid was sliced—the spine was sheared straight through, Alex. Coroner says probably a band saw. Someone cut him, neat and clean, the way they section meat."

"Any other forensic evidence?" I said.

"Nope. No foreign hairs, no fluid exchange. . . . As far as I've been able to tell, Dada wasn't in any kind of trouble, no drug connections, bad friends, criminal history. Just one of those stupid kids who wanted to be rich and famous. Days and weekends he worked at a kiddie gym. Nights he did guess what."

"Waited tables."

His index finger scored imaginary chalk marks. "Bar and grill in Toluca Lake. Closest he got to delivering lines was probably 'What kind of dressing would you like with that?' "

We were in a bar, ourselves. A nice one at the rear of the Luxe Hotel on the west end of Beverly Hills. No pool cues, and any felons were wearing Italian suits. Chandeliers dimmed to orange flicker, spongy carpets, club chairs warm as wombs. On our marble-topped drink stand were two leaden tumblers of Chivas Gold and a crystal pitcher of iced spring water. Milo's cheap panatela asserted itself rudely with the Cohibas and Churchills being sucked in corner booths. A few months later, the city said no smoking in bars, but back then, nicotine fog was an evening ritual.

All the trim notwithstanding, the reason for being there was to ingest alcohol, and Milo was doing a good job of that.

I nursed my first scotch as he finished his third and chased it with a glassful of water. "I got the case because the Lieutenant assumed Dada was gay. The mutilation—when homosexuals freak, they go all the way blah blah blah. But Dada had absolutely no links to the gay community, and his folks say he had three girlfriends back home."

"Any girlfriends out here?"

"None that I've found. He lived alone in a little studio place near La Brea and Sunset. Tiny, but he kept it neat."

"That can be a dicey neighborhood," I said.

"Yeah, but the building had a key-card parking lot and a security entrance; the landlady lives on the premises and tries to keep a good clientele. She said Dada was a quiet kid, she never saw him entertain visitors. And no signs of a break-in or any burglary. We haven't recovered his wallet, but no charges have been run up on the one credit card he owned—a Discover with a four-hundred-dollar limit. The apartment was clean of dope. If Dada did use, he or someone cleaned up every speck."

"The killer?" I said. "That fits with the clean cut and the planning."

"Possibly, but like I said, Dada lived neat. His rent was seven hundred, he took home twice that a month from both jobs, sent most of his money back home to a savings account." His big shoulders dropped. "Maybe he just ran into the wrong psychopath."

"The FBI says eye mutilation implies more than a casual relationship."

"Sent the FBI the crime-scene data questionnaire, got back double-talk and a recommendation to look for known associates. Problem is, I can't locate any friends Dada had. He'd only been out in California for nine months. Maybe working two jobs prevented a social life."

"Or he had a life he hid."

"What, he *was* gay? I think I would've unearthed that, Alex."

"Not necessarily gay," I said. "Any kind of secret life."

"What makes you say that?"

"Model tenants just don't walk out on the street and get sawed in half."

He growled. We drank. The waitresses were all gorgeous

blondes wearing white peasant blouses and long skirts. Ours had an accent. Czechoslovakia, she'd told Milo when he asked; then she'd offered to clip his cigar, but he'd already bitten off the tip. It was the middle of the summer, but a gas fire was raging under a limestone mantel. Air-conditioning kept the room icy. A couple of other beauties at the bar had to be hookers. The men with them looked edgy.

"Toluca Lake is a drive from Hollywood," I said. "It's also near the Burbank studios. So maybe Dada was trying to make acting connections."

"That's what I figured. But if he got a job it wasn't at a studio. I found a want ad from the *Weekly* in the pocket of one of his jackets. Tiny print thing, open casting call for some flick called *Blood Walk*. The date was one month before he was killed. I tried to trace the company that placed the ad. The number was disconnected, but it had belonged at that time to some outfit called Thin Line Productions. That traced to a listing with an answering service, which no longer serviced Thin Line. The address they had was a POB in Venice, long gone, no forwarding. No one in Hollywood's heard of Thin Line, the script's never been registered with any of the guilds, no evidence a movie ever got made. I talked to Petra Connor over in Hollywood. She says par for the course, the *industry's* full of fly-by-nights, most casting calls go nowhere."

"*Blood Walk,*" I said.

"Yeah, I know. But it was a full month before, and I can't take it any further."

"What about Richard's other job? Where's the kiddie gym?"

"Pico and Doheny."

"What'd he do there?"

"Played games with toddlers. Irregular work, mostly birthday parties. The gym owner said he was great—patient, clean-cut, polite." He shot back whiskey. "Goddamn Boy Scout and he gets bisected. There has to be more."

"Some homicidal toddler who resented waiting in line for the Moon Bounce."

He laughed, studied the bottom of his glass.

"You said he sent money home," I said. "Where's that?"

"Denver. Dad's a carpenter, Mom teaches school. They came out for a few days after he was killed. Salt of the earth, hurting bad, but no help. Richard played sports, got B's and C's, acted in all the school plays. Did two years in junior college, hated it, went to work for his father."

"So he's got carpentry skills—maybe he met the killer at some woodworking class."

"He never went to classes of any type that I can find."

"A carpenter's kid and he gets band-sawed," I said.

He put down his glass, careful to do it silently. His eyes fixed on me. Normally startling green, they were gray-brown in the tobacco light. His heavy face was so pale it looked talced, white as his sideburns. The acne pits that scored his cheeks and chin and brow seemed deeper, crueler.

He pushed black hair off his forehead. "Okay," he said very softly. "Besides exquisite *irony,* what does it mean?"

"I don't know," I said. "It just seems too cute."

He frowned, rolled his forearm along the edge of the table as if rubbing an itch, raised his glass for a refill, thanked the waitress when he got it, sipped his way through half the whiskey, and licked his lips. "Why are we even talking about it? I'm not gonna close this one soon, if ever. I can just feel it."

I didn't bother arguing. His hunches are usually sound.

Two months later, he caught the Claire Argent homicide and called me right away, sounding furious but sparked by enthusiasm.

"Got a new one, some interesting similarities to Dada. But different, too. Female vic. Thirty-nine-year-old psychologist named Claire Argent—know her, by any chance?"

"No."

"Home address in the Hollywood Hills, just off Woodrow Wilson Drive, but she was found in West L.A. territory. Stripped naked and stashed in the trunk of her Buick Regal, back of the loading dock behind the Stereos Galore in that big shopping center on La Cienega near Sawyer."

That side of La Cienega was West L.A.'s eastern border. "Barely in your territory."

"Yeah, Santa loves me. Here's what I know so far: the shopping center closes at eleven, but there's no fence at the dock; anyone can pull in there. Real easy access because an alley runs right behind. West of the alley is a supplementary indoor lot, multiple levels, but it's closed off at night. After that, it's all residential. Private homes and apartments. No one heard or saw a thing. Shipping clerk found the car at six A.M., called for a tow, and when the driver winched it up he heard something rolling around inside and had the smarts to worry about it."

"Was she cut in half?" I said.

"No, left in one piece, but wrapped in two garbage bags, just like Dada. Her throat was slashed, too, and her eyes were mangled."

"Mangled how?"

"Chopped into hamburger."

"But not removed."

"No," he said irritably. "If my storage theory about Richard is correct, it would explain why she wasn't cut in half. Dr. Argent was five-five, folded easily into the Buick. And guess where she worked, Alex: Starkweather Hospital."

"Really," I said.

"Ghoul Central. Ever been there?"

"No," I said. "No reason. None of my patients ever killed anyone."

3.

IN THE SPRING of 1981, Emil Rudolph Starkweather died in his bed in Azusa at the age of seventy-six, unmarried, leaving no heirs, having dedicated fifty years to public service, ten as a Water and Power engineer, forty as a state senator.

Tightfisted in every other regard, Starkweather campaigned relentlessly for mental-health funding and pushed through construction of scores of community treatment centers throughout the state. Some said living with and caring for a psychotic sister had made him a one-issue humanist. The sister died five months before Starkweather's massive nocturnal coronary. Soon after her burial, Starkweather's health seemed to rot away.

Not long after his funeral, state auditors discovered that the veteran senator had systematically embezzled four decades of campaign funds for personal use. Some of the money had been spent on the sister's twenty-four-hour nursing care and medical bills, but most went into real estate: Starkweather had amassed an empire of over eleven thousand California acres, primarily vacant lots in run-down neighborhoods that he never developed.

No racehorses, no Swiss accounts, no secret mistresses. No apparent profit motive of any kind. People started questioning Emil Starkweather's mental health.

The rumors intensified when the will was made public. Starkweather had bequeathed everything to the State of California, with one proviso: at least one hundred acres of "his" land was to be used for construction of a "major mental hygiene facility that takes into account the latest research and progress in psychiatry and allied disciplines."

Legal experts opined that the document was probably worthless, but the knots Starkweather had tied might take years to unravel in court. Yet, in one sense, the timing was perfect for the newly elected governor. No admirer of Starkweather—whom he'd long considered an annoying, eccentric old fart—he'd campaigned as a crime-crusher, condemning revolving-door justice that spat dangerous maniacs back onto the street. Frenzied consultations with legislative bosses produced a plan that cut through the morass, and aides were dispatched from Sacramento to search for worthless publicly owned real estate. The perfect solution emerged quickly: a long-unused parcel of county land well east of the L.A. city line, once a gas company fuel station, then a garbage dump, now a toxic swamp. Poisoned soil, pollutants seeping past bedrock. Only eighty-nine acres, but who was counting?

Through a combination of executive order and rammed-through legislation, Starkweather's purloined plots reverted to the state, and construction of a "major mental hygiene facility" for criminals judged incompetent to stand trial was authorized. Secure housing for spree murderers, blood drinkers, cannibals, sodomizers, child-rapers, chanting zombies. Anyone too crazy and too dangerous for San Quentin or Folsom or Pelican Bay.

It was an odd time to build a new hospital. State asylums for the retarded and the harmlessly psychotic were being closed down in rapid succession, courtesy of an odd, cold-hearted alliance between right-wing misers who didn't want to spend the money and left-wing ignoramuses who believed psychotics were political prisoners and deserved to be liberated. A few years later, a "homeless problem" would appear, shocking the deacons of thrift and the social engineers, but at the time, dismantling an entire inpatient system seemed a clever thing to do.

Still, the governor's storage bin for maniacs went up in two years.

He stuck the old fart's name on it.

* * *

Starkweather State Hospital for the Criminally Insane was one main building—a five-story cement-block and gray stucco tower hemmed by twenty-foot-high electrified barbed-wire chain link, streaked with mineral deposits and etched by pollutive grime. Punitively ugly.

We'd gotten off the 10 Freeway, sped past Boyle Heights and several miles of industrial park, traversed a series of dormant oil wells frozen like giant mantis specimens, greasy-gray slaughterhouses and packing plants, abandoned freight yards, several more empty miles that stank of stillborn enterprise.

"Here we go," said Milo, pointing to a narrow tongue of asphalt labeled Starkweather Drive. Another sign said STATE FACILITY AHEAD.

The road drew the unmarked into a gray-green fringe of eucalyptus maybe seventy trees deep that blessed us with mentholated shade before we reemerged into the August sun and a white glare so piercing it rendered my sunglasses useless.

Up ahead was the high fencing. Electric cables thick and black as water snakes. A collection of English and Spanish warning signs in approved state colors presaged a glassed-in booth and a steel gate arm. The guard was a chunky young man of indeterminate mood who slid open a window, listened to Milo's explanation, took his time coming out. He examined our I.D. with what seemed like pain, took all the papers back to his glass closet, returned, asked how many firearms or knives we were carrying, and confiscated Milo's service revolver and my Swiss Army knife.

Several minutes later, the gate opened very slowly and Milo drove through. He'd been unusually quiet during the trip. Now he looked uneasy.

"Don't worry," I said. "You're not wearing khaki, they'll let you out. If you don't say too much."

He snorted. What he was wearing was an old maroon hop-sack blazer, gray wide-wale cords, gray shirt, wrinkled black poly tie, scuffed beige desert boots with soles the color of pencil erasers. He needed a haircut. Black cowlicks danced atop his big head. The contrast with the now-white sideburns was too strong. Yesterday, he'd made some comment about being Mr. Skunk.

The road tilted upward before flattening. We came to an outdoor parking lot, nearly full. Then more chain link, broad stretches of earth, yellow-tinged and sulfurous. Behind the fence stood a solid-looking man in a plaid sport shirt and jeans. The sound of the unmarked made him turn and study us.

Milo said, "Our welcoming party," and began searching for a spot. "Why the hell would anyone want to work here?"

"Are you asking in general or about Dr. Argent?"

"Both. But yeah, her. What would make her choose this?"

It was the day after he'd called me, and I hadn't yet seen the Argent file. "There's something for everyone," I said. "Also, managed care's tightened things up. Could be she had no choice."

"She had plenty of choice. She quit a research position at County General, neuro-something."

"Maybe she was doing research here, too."

"Maybe," he said, "but her job title was Psychologist II, pure civil service, and the director—some guy named Swig—didn't mention research. Why would she quit County for this?"

"You're sure she wasn't fired?"

"Her ex-boss at County told me she quit. Dr. Theobold."

"Myron Theobold."

"Him you know?"

"Met him a few times at faculty meetings. What else did he say?"

"Not much. Like he didn't know her well. Or maybe he was holding back. Maybe you should talk to him."

"Sure."

He spotted an opening, swung in sharply, hit the brakes hard. Yanking off his seat belt, he looked through the windshield. The man in the plaid shirt had unlocked the second fence and come closer. He waved. Milo returned the gesture. Fifties, gray hair and mustache.

Milo pulled his jacket from the backseat and pocketed his

keys. Gazed beyond the man in the plaid shirt at the chain-link desert. "She spent eight hours a day here. With deranged, murderous assholes. And now she's dead—wouldn't you call this place a detective's happy hunting ground?"

4.

DOLLARD UNLOCKED THE rear gate and took us out of the yard and across a short cement path. The gray building appeared like a storm cloud—immense, flat-roofed, slab-faced. No steps, no ramp, just brown metal doors set into the block at ground level. Small sharp-edged letters said STARKWEATHER: MAIN BLDG. Rows of tiny windows checked the cement. No bars across the panes. The glass looked unusually dull, filmed over. Not glass. Plastic. Thick, shatterproof, wind-whipped nearly opaque. Perhaps clouded minds gained nothing from a clear view.

The doors were unlocked. Dollard shoved the right one open. The reception area was cool, small, ripe with a broiled-meat smell. Pink-beige walls and black linoleum blanched under blue-white fluorescence. Overhead air-conditioning ducts emitted a sound that could have been whispering.

A heavyset, bespectacled woman in her thirties sat behind two old wooden desks arranged in an L, talking on the phone. She wore a sleeveless yellow knit top and a picture badge like Dollard's. Two desk plaques: RULE ONE: I'M ALWAYS RIGHT. RULE TWO: REFER TO RULE ONE. And L. SCHMITZ. Between them was a stack of brochures.

Her phone had a dozen lines. Four lights blinked. On the wall behind the desk hung a color photo of Emil Starkweather flashing a campaign smile full of bridgework. Above that, a banner solicited employee contributions for Toys for Tots and the United Way. To the left, a small, sagging shelf of athletic trophies and group photos trumpeted the triumphs of "The Hurlers: Starkweather Hosp. Staff Bowling Team."

First prize for seven years out of ten. Off to the right stretched a long, bright hallway punctuated by bulletin boards and more brown doors.

Dollard stepped up to the desk. L. Schmitz talked a bit more, finally got off. "Morning, Frank."

"Morning, Lindeen. These gentlemen are Mr. Swig's ten o'clock."

"He's still on a call, should be right with you. Coffee?"

"No, thanks," said Dollard, checking his watch.

"Should be soon, Frank."

Milo picked up two brochures and gave one to me. Lindeen watched him, then got back on the phone and did a lot of "uh-huh"ing. The next time she put down the receiver, she said, "You're the police about Dr. Argent, right?"

"Yes, ma'am," said Milo, hovering by the desk. "Did you know her?"

"Just hello and good-bye. Terrible thing." She returned to the phone.

Milo stuck around for a few more minutes. Lindeen looked up once to smile at him but didn't interrupt her conversation. He gave me a pamphlet. We both read.

Brief history of Starkweather State Hospital, then a bold-type "Statement of Purpose." Lots of photos: more shots of Emil the Embezzler; the governor breaking ground with a gold-tipped shovel, flanked by nameless dignitaries. Construction chronology from excavation to completion. Cranes, earth movers, hard-hatted worker ants. Finally a long view of the building set against a gorgeous sky that looked as false as Starkweather's chompers. The block walls were already stained. The hospital had looked weary on its birthdate.

The mission statement was written by William T. Swig, MPH, Director, and it stressed humane treatment of inmates while safeguarding the public. Lots of talk about goals, directives, objectives, interfaces. Who taught bureaucrats how to write?

I folded the brochure and slipped it in my pocket just as Lindeen said, "Okey-doke, he's free."

We followed Dollard down the hall. A few of the brown

doors bore name signs in slide-out slots; most were blank. The bulletin boards were layered with state paper: notices, legislation, regulation. No other people walked the corridor. I realized the place was silent except for the sibilance from the ducts above us.

Swig's door was no different from the rest, his sign no more permanent. Dollard knocked once and opened without waiting for a reply. Outer office. Another receptionist, older and heavier than Lindeen—"Go right in, Frank." Three vases of huge yellow roses, obviously homegrown, sat on her desk. Her PC monitor featured a Mona Lisa screen saver. Smiling, frowning, smiling, frowning . . .

Dollard pushed through to the inner sanctum. Swig was on his feet with his hand out as we entered.

He was younger than I'd expected, maybe thirty-five, sparely built, with a soft, round baby face under a bald dome and several ominous moles on his cheeks and chin. What little hair he did have was blond and cottony. He wore a short-sleeved blue shirt, plaid tie, navy slacks, moccasin loafers.

"Bill Swig." Introductions all around. Swig's hand was cool and small-boned. His desk was a bit larger than his secretary's, but not by much. No joke plaques here, just a pen-and-pencil set, books and folders, several standing picture frames, their felt backs to us. A photo on the right-hand wall showed Swig in a dark suit with a curly-haired, pointy-chinned woman and two pretty girls around four and six, both Asian. A few books and lots of rubber-banded paper in a single case. Swig's plastic window offered an oily view of the yard.

Dollard said, "Anything else?"

Swig said, "No thanks, Frank," and Dollard hurried out.

"Please, sit. Sorry to keep you waiting. Tragedy, Dr. Argent. I'm still shocked."

"I guess you'd be a hard one to shock, sir," said Milo.

Swig looked confused.

"Working here," said Milo. "The things you see."

"Oh. No, not really, Detective Sturgis. This is generally a peaceful place. Probably safer than the streets of L.A. Especially since the air-conditioning's fixed. No, I'm as shockable as anyone."

"The air-conditioning?"

"We had a problem," said Swig. "The condensers went out a few years ago. Before I arrived." He raised his hands, palms up. "My predecessor couldn't get them fixed. As you might imagine, the comfort of our patients isn't a high priority in Sacramento. Staff attrition's what finally did it. People started quitting. I filed a report, we finally got a new system. Today's a perfect example—can you imagine it without A.C.?"

"How did the inmates handle it?"

Swig sat back. "It was a bit of a . . . challenge. So . . . how can I help you?"

"Any ideas about Dr. Argent's murder?"

Swig shook his head. "I can understand your thinking it might be work-related, but I term that impossible. Because of one simple fact: Dr. Argent's patients are here, and she was murdered out there." He pointed at the window. "Add to that the fact that her tenure was totally trouble-free, and there's nothing to work with, is there?"

"Model employee?"

"I was very impressed with her. Calm, level, thoughtful. Everyone liked her. Including the patients."

"That makes the patients sound rational," said Milo.

"Pardon?"

"The patients liked her, so they wouldn't hurt her. I thought the men here didn't operate out of any logical motive pattern. So what's to say one of them didn't hear a voice telling him to cut Dr. Argent's throat?"

No mention of the eyes. He was keeping that confidential.

Swig tightened his lips. "Yes. Well, they are psychotic, but most of them are very well maintained. But what's the difference? The main point is, they don't leave here."

Milo took out his pad and scrawled for a while. That almost always gets a reaction. Swig raised his eyebrows. They were pale blond, nearly invisible, and the movement created two crescent-shaped wrinkles above his clear blue eyes.

Milo's pen stopped moving. He said, "No one *ever* gets out?"

Swig shifted in his chair. "I won't tell you never. But *very, very* rarely."

"How rare?"

"Only two percent even attempt to obtain release, and most of those never make it past our review committee. Of those who are reviewed, perhaps five percent succeed in obtaining conditional release. That means placement in well-supervised board and care, regular outpatient treatment, and random urinalysis to monitor medication compliance. Additionally, they must continue to show absolutely no symptoms of dangerous decompensation. Any minor infraction lands them back here. Of those who do leave, the revocation rate is still eighty percent. Since I've been here, never has a released patient committed a violent felony. So, for all practical purposes, it's a non-issue."

"How long have you been here?"

"Five years."

"Before that?"

"Before that, there were a few problems."

"So," said Milo, scanning his notes. "With so few men released, it should be easy enough to track those who've gotten out."

Swig clapped his hands together very softly. "Yes, but that would require a court order. Even our men have rights—for example, we can't monitor their mail without clear evidence of infraction."

"You can dose them, but no snooping?"

"The difference is that dosing them is for their own good." Swig wheeled his chair forward. "Look, I'm not trying to make your job difficult, Detective, but I really don't get this line of questioning. I can understand your initial assumption: Dr. Argent worked with dangerous individuals, and now she's been murdered. On the face of it, that's logical. But as I said, it's probably safer at Starkweather than on your beat."

"So you're telling me I need to file papers to find out who's been released."

"I'm afraid so. Believe me, if there was some obvious risk, don't you think I'd let you know? If only for our sake. We can't afford errors."

"Okay," said Milo with an ease that made me glance at him. "Let's move on. What can you tell me about Dr. Argent's personality?"

"I didn't know her well," said Swig, "but she was competent, quiet, businesslike. No conflicts with staff or patients." He picked up a folder and scanned the contents. "Here's something I *can* give you. Her personnel file."

"Thank you, sir." Milo took it and handed it to me and resumed jotting notes. Inside were Claire Argent's job application, an abbreviated résumé, and a headshot photo. The resumé was five pages thick. Several published studies. Neuropsychology. Reaction time in alcoholics. Solid journals. A clinical appointment as a lecturer. Why *had* she quit to come here?

The picture revealed a pretty, slightly broad face brightened by a shy half-smile. Thick, dark hair, shoulder-length, flipped at the edges, feathery bangs, white hairband, baby blue crewneck top. Clear skin, very little makeup, big dark eyes. The first adjective that came to my mind was "wholesome." Maybe a little too ingenue for someone her age, though she looked closer to thirty than the thirty-nine established by her birthdate.

No date on the photo, so maybe it had been snapped years earlier. She'd gotten her Ph.D. ten years ago. Graduation shot? I continued to study her face. The eyes were lustrous, warm—her best feature.

Now mangled. Someone's trophy?

"I'm afraid I can't tell you much," said Swig. "We've got a staff of over a hundred, including more than twenty psychologists and psychiatrists."

"The others are psych techs like Mr. Dollard?"

"Techs, nonpsychiatric physicians, nurses, pharmacists, secretaries, cooks, plumbers, electricians, custodians."

"And you don't know if any of them had some kind of relationship with Dr. Argent away from work?"

"I'm afraid not."

"Did she work with any staff members consistently?"

"I'd have to check on that."

"Please do."

"Certainly. It will take a few days."

Milo took the file from me, opened it, flipped pages. "I appreciate your letting us have this, Mr. Swig. When I saw her she looked quite different."

As if warding off the comment, Swig turned to me. "You're a psychologist, Dr. Delaware? Forensic?"

"Clinical. I do occasional consulting."

"Have you worked much with dangerous psychotics?"

"I rotated through Atascadero as an intern, but that's about it."

"Atascadero must have been pretty tough back then."

"Tough enough," I said.

"Yes," he said. "Before us, they were the toughest place. Now they're handling mostly MDSO's—sex offenders." His tone was dismissive.

"You have some of them, too, right?" said Milo.

"A few," said Swig. "Incorrigibles who happened to come up for sentencing when the law-of-the-week said hospitalization. Nowadays, they go to jail. We haven't accepted any in years."

That made the hospital sound like a college. I said, "Are the sex offenders housed with the regular population or up on the top floor with the 1368's?"

Swig touched one of his moles. "Regular population. The 1368's are a completely different situation. They're boarders, not residents. The court orders us to screen them. We keep them totally isolated on the fifth floor."

"Bad influences on the 1026's?" said Milo.

Swig laughed. "I don't think the 1026's can be influenced too easily. No, it's all the traffic and the escape risk. They come in and out on sheriff's buses—what they really want isn't treatment, it's out." He sat back, touched some of the moles on his face. Fingering them carefully, like a blind man reading braille. "We're talking about malingering criminals who think they can drool and avoid San Quentin. We evaluate them, ship them back."

His voice had climbed and his skin had pinkened.

"Sounds like a hassle," I said.

"It's a distraction from our main goal."

Milo said, "Managing the 1026's."

"Treating insane murderers and keeping them invisible. From the public. Every one of our men has committed the proverbial 'senseless crime.' On the outside, you hear non-sense like 'Anyone who kills has to be crazy.' Doctor, you of course know that's garbage. Most murderers are perfectly sane. Our men are the exception. They terrify the public—the apparent randomness of their crimes. They have motives, but not the kind the public can relate to. I'm sure you understand, Dr. Delaware."

"Voices in the head," I said.

"Exactly. It's like sausage making. The less the public knows about what we do, the better off we and the public are. That's why I hope Claire's murder doesn't put us in the spotlight."

"No reason for that," said Milo. "The sooner I clear the case, the faster I'm out of your life."

Swig nodded and worried another mole. "Is there anything else?"

"What, specifically, did Dr. Argent do here?"

"What any psychologist would do. Behavior modification plans for individual patients, some counseling, some group work—truthfully, I don't know the details."

"I heard she ran a group called Skills for Daily Living."

"Yes," said Swig. "She asked permission to start that a few months ago."

"Why, if the men don't get out?"

"Starkweather's also an environment. It needs to be dealt with."

"How many men were in the group?"

"I have no idea. The clinical decisions were hers."

"I'd like to meet with them."

"Why?"

"In case they know something."

"They don't," said Swig. "How could they—no, I'm afraid I can't let you do that. Too disruptive. I'm not sure any of them even realize what happened to her."

"Are you going to tell them?"

"That would be a clinical decision."

"Made by who?"

"The clinician in charge—probably one of our senior psychiatrists. Now, if that's all—"

"One more thing," said Milo. "Dr. Argent had a good position at County Hospital. Any idea why she switched jobs?"

Swig allowed himself a small smile. "What you're really asking is why would she leave the glorious world of academic medicine for our little snakepit. During her job interview she told me she wanted a change of pace. I didn't discuss it further. I was happy to have someone with her qualifications come aboard."

"Did she say anything else during the interview that would help me?"

Swig's mouth puckered tight. He picked up a pencil and tapped the desktop. "She was very quiet—not shy. More like self-possessed. But pleasant—very pleasant. It's a terrible thing that happened to her."

He stood. We did, too. Milo thanked him.

"I wish I could do more, Detective."

"Actually," said Milo, "we wouldn't mind taking a look around—just to get a feel for the place. I promise not to disrupt anyone clinically, but maybe I could chat with some of the staff Dr. Argent worked with?"

The white eyebrows climbed again. "Sure, why not." Swig opened the door to the front room. His secretary was arranging roses.

"Letty," he said, "please call Phil Hatterson down. Detective Sturgis and Dr. Delaware are going to get a little tour."

5.

PHIL HATTERSON WAS short, pear-shaped, middle-aged, with Silly Putty features and thinning brown hair. His mouse-colored mustache was feathery and offered no shelter to plump, dark lips.

"Pleased to meet you," he said, offering the firm, pumping handshake of a club chairman.

His eyes were hazel, alert, and inquisitive, but soft—like those of a tame deer.

His shirt and pants were khaki.

We followed him at a distance.

"First floor's all offices," he said cheerfully. His walk was odd—small, neat, dancelike steps that forced us to slow down. "Not docs' offices, just administration. The docs circulate through offices on the wards."

His smile begged for approval. I managed an upturned lip. Milo wasn't having any part of it.

Toward the end of the hall, at the right, were two double-width elevators, one key-operated that said STAFF ONLY, the other with a call button, which Hatterson pushed. Milo watched Hatterson intently. I knew exactly what he was thinking: *The inmates run the asylum.*

The elevator didn't respond but Hatterson was unbothered, bouncing on his feet like a kid waiting for dessert. No floor-number guide above the doors, no grinding gears. Then a voice came out of the wall—out of a small square of steel mesh surrounding the button.

"Yes?" Male voice, electronically detached.

"Hatterson, Phillip Duane."

"I.D."

"Five two one six eight. You just let me down to see Administrator Swig. Administrator Swig just called to authorize me back up."

"Hold on." Three beats. "Where you heading?"

"Just up to Two. I've got two gentlemen taking a tour—a police officer and a doctor."

"Hold on," the voice repeated. Seconds later, the elevator doors slid open. Hatterson said, "After you, sirs."

Wondering whom I was turning my back on, I complied. The lift was walled with thick foam. Interior key lock. Sickly-sweet disinfectant permeated the foam.

The doors closed. As we rose, Hatterson said, "Up up and away." He was standing in the middle of the car. I'd pressed myself into a corner, and so had Milo.

The elevator let us out into another pink-beige hallway. Brown double doors with plastic windows. Key locks. Wall speaker similar to that near the elevator. A sign above the door said A WARD. Hatterson pushed a button, talked to someone, and the doors clicked open.

At first glance, the second floor resembled any hospital ward, except for a nursing station completely encased by plastic. A sign said MED LINE FORM HERE, NO PUSHING. Three white-uniformed women sat inside, talking. Nearby, a gurney was pushed to the wall. Brown stains on white cotton sheeting.

The same black linoleum and brown doors as the first floor. Very low ceilings—no higher than seven feet. Khaki'd figures roamed the halls. Many of the taller inmates stooped. So did some short men. A few inmates sat on white plastic benches. Bolted to the floor. Others rocked in place; several just stood there. The arms of the chairs were drilled through with one-inch-diameter holes. Handcuff slots.

I tried to look around without being conspicuous.

Black men, white men, brown men, yellow men.

Young men with surfer-blond hair and testosterone posture, callow enough for acne but ancient around the eyes. Old men with toothless, caved-in faces and hyperactive tongues.

Gape-jawed catatonics. Ragged, muttering apparitions not much different from any Westside panhandler. Some of the men, like Hatterson, looked relatively normal.

Every one of them had destroyed human life.

We passed them, enduring a psychotic gauntlet, receiving a full course of stares. Hatterson paid no notice as he dance-stepped us through.

One of the young ones smirked and took a step forward. Patchy hair and chin beard, swastika tattoo on his fore-arm. White welted scars on both wrists. He swayed and smiled, sang something tuneless, and moved on. A Hispanic man with a braid dangling below his belt drank from a paper cup and coughed as we neared, splashing pink liquid. Someone passed wind. Someone laughed. Hatterson sped up a bit. So many brown doors, marked only by numbers. Most bore small, latched rectangles. Peephole covers.

Halfway down the hall, two black men with matted hair—careless dreadlocks—faced each other from opposite sides. From a distance their stance mimicked a conversation, but as we got closer I saw that their faces weren't moving and their eyes were distant and dead.

The man on the right had his hand in his fly and I could see rapid movement beneath the khaki. Hatterson noticed it too, and gave a prissy look. A few feet away, an avuncular type—seventyish, white-haired as Emil Starkweather, wearing rim-less eyeglasses and a white cardigan sweater over his beige shirt—leaned against the wall reading *The Christian Science Monitor*.

Someone cried out. Someone laughed.

The air was frigid, a good deal colder than down in Swig's office. We passed an obese, gray-haired man sitting on a bench, soft arms as thick as my thighs, face flushed and mis-shapen, like an overripe melon. He sprang up and suddenly his face was in mine, blowing hot, sour breath.

"If you're lost, that's the way out." He pointed to one of the brown doors.

Before I could respond, a young woman appeared and took him by the elbow.

He said, "If you're lost—"

The woman said, "It's okay, Ralph, no one's lost."

"If you're lost—"

"That's enough, Ralph." Sharp voice now. Ralph hung his head.

The woman wore a green-striped badge that said H. OTT, PT-I.

Claire's group-therapy tech. She wore a long-sleeved chambray shirt, rolled to the elbows and tucked into snug jeans that showed off a tight shape. Not a large woman—five-six and small-boned. She looked maybe twenty-five, too young to wield authority. Her dishwater hair was gathered in a tight knot, exposing a long face, slightly heavy in the jaw, with strong, symmetrical features. She had wide-set blue eyes, the clear, rosy complexion of a farm girl. Ralph had six inches and at least a hundred and fifty pounds on her. He remained in her grasp, looking remorseful.

"Okay, now," she told him, "why don't you go rest." She rotated him. Her body moved smoothly. Taut curves, small bust, long smooth neck. I could see her playing volleyball on the beach. What did the men in khaki see?

Ralph tried again: "If you're lost, that's the way . . ." His voice caught on the last word.

Heidi Ott said, "No one's lost." Louder, firmer.

A tear fell from Ralph's eye. Heidi Ott gave him a gentle push and he shuffled off. A few of the other men had watched, but most seemed oblivious.

"Sorry," she said to us. "He thinks he's a tour guide." The blue eyes settled on Hatterson. "Keeping busy, Phil?"

Hatterson drew himself up. "I'm giving them a tour, Miss Ott. This is Detective Sturgis from the LAPD, and this is a doctor—sorry, I forgot your name, sir."

"Delaware."

Heidi Ott said, "Pleased to meet you."

Hatterson said, "The thing about Ralph is, he used to cruise the freeways, pick up people having car trouble. He'd offer to help them and then he'd—"

"Phil," said Heidi Ott. "You know we respect each other's privacy."

Hatterson let out a small, tight bark. Pursed his lips. Annoyed, not regretful. "Sorry."

Heidi Ott turned to Milo. "You're here about Dr. Argent?" Her lips pushed together and paled. Young skin, but tension caused it to pucker.

"Yes, ma'am," said Milo. "You worked with her, didn't you?"

"I worked with a group she ran. We had contact about several other patients." The blue eyes blinked twice. Less force in her voice. Now she seemed her age.

Milo said, "When you have a chance, I'd like to—"

Screams and thumps came from behind us. My head whipped around.

The two dreadlocked men were on the floor, a double dervish, rolling, punching, clawing, biting. Moving slowly, deliberately, silently. Like pit bulls.

Other men started to cheer. The old man with *The Christian Science Monitor* slapped his knee and laughed. Only Phil Hatterson seemed frightened. He'd gone white and seemed to be searching for a place to hide.

Heidi Ott snapped a whistle out of her pocket, blew hard, and marched toward the fighters. Suddenly, two male techs were at her side. The three of them broke up the fight within seconds.

The dreadlocked men were hauled to their feet. One was bleeding from his left cheek. The other bore a scratch on his forearm. Neither breathed hard. Both looked calm, almost serene.

The old man with the newspaper said, "By golly fuck!"

Heidi took the bleeder by the arm and led him to the nurses' station. Button-push, click, and she received something from a slot in the front window. Swabs and antibiotic cream. As she ministered to the bleeder, some of the men in khaki began to come alive. Shifting position, flexing arms, looking in all directions.

The hallway smelled of aggression. Phil Hatterson sidled closer to Milo. Milo stared him still. His hands were fisted.

One of the male techs, a short, husky Filipino, said, "Okay, everyone. Just settle down *now*."

The hallway went quiet.

Hatterson gave out a long, loud exhalation. "I hate when stupid stuff happens. What's the point?"

Heidi hustled the bleeder around the nursing station and out of sight.

Hatterson said, "Gentlemen?" and we resumed our tour. Most of his color had returned. I wouldn't have picked him for any pathology worse than oily obsequiousness—Eddie Haskell misplaced among the lunatics, annoying but coherent. I knew many psychotics were helped mightily by drugs. Could this be chemistry at its best?

He said, "Here's my favorite place. The TV room."

The ward had ended and we were facing the open doorway of a large bright space filled with plastic chairs. A big-screen TV stood at the front like an altar.

Hatterson said, "The way we choose what to watch is with democracy—everyone who wants to vote, votes. The majority rules. It's pretty peaceful—picking shows, I mean. I like news but I don't get to watch it too often, but I also like sports and almost everyone votes for sports, so it's okay. There's our mailbox."

He pointed to a hard plastic box fastened to the wall. Rounded edges. Chain-locked. "Our mail's private unless there's a mitigating circumstance."

"Such as?" I said.

The question frightened him. "Someone acts out."

"Does that happen often?"

"No, no." His eyelids fluttered. "The docs do a great job."

"Dr. Argent, too?" said Milo.

"Sure, of course."

"So you knew her."

Hatterson's hands made tiny circular motions. He licked his lips and turned them the color of raw liver. "We didn't do any counseling together, but I knew who she was. Very nice lady." Another lip-lick. "I mean, she seemed very smart—she was nice."

"Do you know what happened to her?"

Hatterson stared at the floor. "Sure."

"Does everyone?"

"I can't speak for anyone, sir. It was in the paper."

"They let you read the paper?" said Milo.

"Sure, we can read anything. I like *Time* magazine, you get all the news in a neat little package. Anyway, that's it for A Ward. B and C are mostly the same. There's a few women on C. They don't cause any problems."

"Are they kept to themselves?" I said.

"No, they get to mingle. There's just not too many of them. We don't have problems with them."

"What about the fifth floor?" said Milo.

"Oh," said Hatterson. "The 13's. Naw, we never see them except to look out the window when a sheriff's bus brings them in. They wear jail blues, go straight up their own elevator. They're . . ."

He shrugged.

"They're what?" I said.

"Fakers. Got no stake here. Anyway, we've got some pretty nice rooms, let me show 'em to you—here's an open one we can take a look at."

The space was generous, totally bare, clean as a Marine barracks. Four beds, one for each corner: mattresses set into white molded-plastic frames attached to the floor. Next to each one, a nightstand of the same material.

A single clouded window offered a few square inches of cottony light.

Three of the beds were made up neatly, top sheets tucked tight. One was jumbled. No closets. A doorless entry led to a tiny white lav. Lidless white toilet, white sink. No medicine cabinet, no toiletries, no toothbrushes. Anything was a potential weapon.

"They give us disposables," said Hatterson, as if following my thoughts. "Aftershave, brushes, shaving cream, safety razors under supervision. Guys who want to shave use electrics that are sterilized and reused." He looked disapprovingly at the unmade bed. "Someone must be having a bad day. . . . We can't hang anything on the wall because it could be set on fire. So there's no family pictures or anything like that. But it's not bad, right?"

Milo grunted.

Hatterson flinched, but persisted: "We get our three squares, the food's pretty tasty."

Chapter president of the Starkweather Chamber of Commerce. I could see why Swig had picked him. He led us out of the room. "And that's about all she wrote, folks."

"Are all the rooms multiple occupancy?" I said, wondering how roommates were chosen.

"Except for the S&R's—Suppression and Restraint. Those come one to a customer. You can tell which ones they are because they have an S after the number." He pointed. "They're basically the same, except smaller, 'cause it's only one patient."

"Does Suppression and Restraint mean straitjackets?" said Milo. "Padded walls like the elevator?"

Hatterson's mustache vibrated. "No padding, but sure, if someone needs a straitjacket, we've got 'em. But hopefully, if you behave yourself after you earn an S&R, you earn out of there in a jif. I couldn't say from direct experience, but that's what I imagine."

Pride of ownership; he gave denial new meaning. I saw the revulsion in Milo's eyes.

We stood in the empty room as Hatterson prattled on about the food. Fridays were still fish, even though the pope said meat was okay. Vitamin pills, too. The patients were well taken care of.

An operator; there's one in every setting. A gossip, too, eager to tell us about Ralph's criminal history. Was he Swig's stoolie? Risky business on a ward full of murderers.

Might as well take advantage. I said, "What wards did Dr. Argent work on?"

Hatterson stopped. "I guess she worked all over the place. The docs all do—they move around. Most of them don't even have permanent offices, they just share desks for charting."

"Where are the charts kept?"

"In the nursing station."

"What exactly did Dr. Argent do here?" I said.

"I guess counseling."

"What do you know about her group—Skills for Daily Living?"

"Just that she started it a few months ago. Picked some weird guys for it."

"Weird in what way?"

"Messed-up guys," said Hatterson. He tapped his temple. "You know, low-functioning guys."

Milo said, "What was the point? No one gets out of here, right?"

Hatterson whitened. His head began to droop and remained low, as if straining under impossible weight. The plump lips rotated.

"Right," he said.

"It's not right?"

"No, no, yes it is."

"Did joining Dr. Argent's group help someone *earn* release?" said Milo.

"Not that I heard, sir."

"Did any of the group members get out?"

Hatterson shook his head. "No, it was just about—learning to do things for yourself. I guess Dr. Argent wanted to help them feel better about themselves."

"Improve their self-esteem," said Milo.

Hatterson brightened. "You got it. You can't love others 'less you love yourself. She knew what she was doing, the docs here are smart. Okay, I'll call and get us up to B."

The two upper wards were laid out identically to A. On C the hallway teemed, but no female inmates were in sight. We walked through quickly. No fights, nothing untoward; the same mix of degraded muscles, stupor and self-absorption, occasional dark stares rife with paranoia, a few serpentine tongue-flicks and jumpy muscles that said phenothiazine drug side effects. Hatterson moved us through quickly, no more happy chatter. He seemed defeated, almost peevish.

With his chatter gone, the corridors were stripped of conversation. No discourse among the inmates.

Here, every man *was* an island.

I supposed Swig was right; his charges would be easier to control than simple criminals. Because once the violent impulses were held in check, psychosis was a custodian's friend, neurochemically suppressing and restraining as the disease blunted initiative, squelched the spark of freshness and novelty.

Medication helped, too. To handle violent psychotics, the trick was to find a drug that soothed the occasional fried synapse, squelched rage, hushed the little voices that commanded mayhem.

But take away the violence and you didn't have serenity. What remained were what psychiatrists labeled the negative symptoms of psychosis: apathy, flat mood, deadened voice, blunted movement, impoverished thinking, language stripped of nuance and humor. An existence devoid of surprise and joy.

That explained the ambient silence. The lack of noise wasn't peaceful. The ward felt like a crypt.

A psych tech came by wheeling a food cart. I found myself welcoming the jangle.

Hatterson took us to the C Ward elevator. Milo said, "Let's go up to Five."

"Sorry," said Hatterson. "I'm not authorized. No one is, not even the docs unless they get an order to evaluate a 13."

"You know a lot about this place," I said.

Hatterson shrugged. As we waited for the lift to arrive, I peered through the plastic panels on the door and watched the traffic on the ward. Techs moving around confidently, unarmed; a black nurse emerging from the station with a clipboard and making her way down the corridor with a high-hipped trot. Inmates not doing much of anything.

I thought of how Heidi Ott had handled Ralph and the fighters. In a jail, a skirmish like that could have led to full-scale rioting.

So Starkweather was indeed a tight ship. Full of one-way passengers.

Meaning the chance that Claire Argent's work had anything to do with her murder *was* remote.

But had the system broken down somehow? A released man "acting out" in the worst way?

Maybe Heidi could tell us. She'd worked with Claire Argent on the Living Skills group . . . low-functioning men, according to Hatterson. What had Claire had in mind when setting up the sessions?

Why had she *come* here?

Hatterson said, "Here's some docs."

Three men came through the door. Shirts and ties, no white coats, badges with yellow bars. No outward sign that a colleague had been slashed to death and stuffed in a car trunk.

Milo said, "Excuse me," showed his badge, explained his purpose. The man in the middle was tall, sandy-haired, weathered-looking, in his sixties. Green plaid shirt, yellow knit tie. He said, "Terrible thing. I wish you luck." V. N. Aldrich, M.D., Psychiatrist III.

Milo said, "If there's anything anyone can tell me that might help . . ."

No responses. Then a bald, dark-bearded man said, "Claire seemed very nice, but I can't say I knew her." C. Steenburg, Ph.D.

The third man was short and ruddy. D. Swenson, M.D. He shook his head. "She was comparatively new, wasn't she, Vern?"

Aldrich said, "Just a few months. I was her nominal supervisor on a few cases. Her work was fine."

"Nominal?" I said.

"I'm the senior psychiatrist on day shift, so, officially, she reported to me. But she didn't need much supervision. Very bright. I'm terribly sorry about what happened. We all are."

Nods all around.

"What kind of work did she do here?" I said.

"Mostly behavior modification—setting up contingency

schedules—rewards for good behavior, withdrawal of privileges for infractions. That kind of thing." Aldrich smiled. "I won't claim to be an expert on her work product. We're pretty autonomous around here. Claire was very well trained, used to work at County General."

"Any idea why she transferred?" I said.

"She said she needed a change. I got a sense she didn't want to talk about it. My feeling is that she'd simply had enough of what she was doing. I used to be in private practice, retired, got bored with golf, came here."

"Did you get the sense that she needed more human contact than neuropsych provided?" I asked. It was a psychologist's question, not a cop's, and Aldrich studied me.

"I suppose," he said. "In any event, I don't imagine any of this has much to do with what happened to her."

"Why's that?" said Milo.

"She got killed out there." Aldrich pointed to a wall. "The wonderful, democratic, *normal* world." He looked over at Hatterson as if first noticing the little man, laced his hands behind his back, scanned Hatterson from toe-tip to head. "Circulating, Phil?"

"Mr. Swig asked me to show them around, Dr. Aldrich."

"I see. Well, do that, then." Aldrich faced Milo. "I wish we could help you, Detective, but we're all stymied."

"So you've discussed what happened?"

The three of them exchanged looks.

"Yes, of course," said Aldrich. "We were all upset. What we found out is that none of us knew Dr. Argent. It spurred us to be more social with each other. Good luck getting to the bottom of it."

"One more thing," said Milo. "The group Dr. Argent ran, Skills for Daily Living. Would it be possible to meet with the patients?"

"You'd have to check with administration on that," said Aldrich.

"Would you see a problem with it? Medically speaking."

Aldrich tugged at his tie. "Let me look into that. I want to make sure we don't . . . upset anything."

"Appreciate it, Doctor." Milo gave him and the others business cards.

The elevator arrived. Aldrich said, "You three ride down first. We'll catch it next time."

As we descended, Hatterson said, "Dr. Aldrich is very, very smart."

Milo said, "How long have you been here, Phil?"

Hatterson's head drew back like that of a turtle poked with a stick. His reply was inaudible.

"What's that, Phil?"

Hatterson began smoothing his mustache. Chomped his lower lip with his upper teeth. "A long time."

He stayed in the car and waved us out.

"Goddamn weenie," said Milo, as we walked back toward the reception area. "Didn't get a chance to speak with the Ott girl—better get her home number and follow up. Everyone here spouts the same line: 'This place is as safe as milk.' You buy it?"

"They broke up that fight pretty fast."

"Yeah, okay, let's assume they've got the lunatics well controlled. You see anything that would lure Claire away from County?"

"Maybe all the structure," I said. "No more applying for grants or having to play the academic game. Aldrich said she talked about needing a change."

"Structured or not, the place creeps me out. . . . We didn't even scratch the surface, did we?"

"Maybe there's nothing below the surface."

He didn't answer. We passed Swig's office. The door was closed. "Okay, I'll get Ms. Ott's number, then we fly out of here. If you've got time, I can show you Argent's house. Out in the evil, messy, *normal* world. The longer I stay here, the more I crave the insanity out there."

Lindeen Schmitz was back on the phone and she barely looked up. Milo stationed himself in front of her desk and leaned forward, imposing on her space. Where does a frustrated, six-three, 240-pound cop stand? Anywhere he wants.

She tried to "uh-huh" her way through a conversation that was clearly personal, finally said, "Gotta go," and hung up.

"Yes, sir?"

Milo grinned down at her. "I need to do some follow-up with one of your staffers. Heidi Ott. May I have her home number, please?"

"Um, I'm not sure I can do that without authorization. And Mr. Swig's gone— Oh, what the hey, you're the police. You can always get it anyway, in one of those backwards directories, right?" Batting her lashes, she left her desk, sashayed up the hall to the closest brown door, came back with a message blank, and gave it to Milo. Neatly printed name and number, 213 area code.

Milo gave a small bow. "Thank you, ma'am."

"No problem, *sir.*" More eyelash aerobics. "I hope you find whoever did it."

Milo thanked her again and we headed for the main doors.

Lindeen said, "Why do you want to speak to Heidi?"

"She worked with Dr. Argent."

Lindeen picked up a pencil and tapped the edge of her desk. "I don't think they were friends or anything. Dr. Argent didn't have any friends that I saw. Real quiet. When a bunch of us went for margaritas or something we asked her along, but she always said no, so we stopped asking. I figured she was shy. But still, it's so horrible what happened to her. When I heard, I just couldn't believe it, someone you see every day and then they're just . . ." She snapped a finger. "She used to walk right past me every morning at eight, pronto, say good morning, walk on like she had a big plan for the day. It's so . . . horrible."

"Yes it is," said Milo. "So she didn't have any pals at all?"

"Not that I saw. She always seemed like work, work, work. Nice, but work, work, work. Hope you solve it."

She reached for the phone. Milo said, "Pardon me, ma'am. Just one more thing I'm curious about."

Her hand rested on the receiver. "What's that?"

"The guy who took us around—Hatterson. What's he in for?"

"Oh, *him,*" she said. "Why, was there some kind of problem?"

"No. Does he cause problems?"

She snorted. "Not hardly."

"The reason I'm asking is, he didn't seem very crazy. I'm just wondering what kind of guy gets to be a tour guide."

"Phil," she said, pronouncing the name with distaste. "Phil raped a child so bad she needed reconstructive surgery."

6.

FRANK DOLLARD WAS waiting for us, outside. He walked us across the yard without comment. Giant Chet stood in a corner, staring at chain link. Sharbno the urinator was gone. A few men palsied, a few men sat in the dirt. The sun was even hotter.

Dollard waited as we retrieved Milo's gun and my knife. The outer gate swung open.

Milo said, "Let me ask you a question, Frank. A guy like Hatterson—in prison he'd be lunch meat."

Dollard smiled. "So what's his status here? Low. Same as everyone. For all I know, the other guys don't even know what he did. They don't care much about each other—that's the point. They're not *connected*."

Driving through the eucalyptus grove, Milo began to laugh.

"What?" I said.

"How's this for a story line: we catch the bad guy; he's some joker they let out by mistake. He pleads insanity, ends up right back here."

"Sell it to Hollywood—no, not stupid enough."

We left the grove, passed into white light. "Then again, you tell me our boy probably doesn't act or look crazy, so maybe I should forget about this place."

"My guess is our boy is probably more like a fifth-floor resident."

"So do I bother looking for a recently released Stark-weather alum? And what's with that group Claire ran? Why do low-functioning guys need daily living skills? Unless she had a notion some of them would end up on the outside."

"Maybe it was altruism," I said. "Misguided or otherwise. Heidi Ott might be able to shed some light on it. She'd also be able to tell you if any of Claire's patients have been released recently."

"Yeah, she's definitely high on my list. Tough kid, the way she handled that Ralph guy. Can you imagine a female coming in here, day in and day out?" He drove off Starkweather Drive and back onto the connecting road. The bare gray acreage appeared, then the first of the packing plants, gigantic and soot-stained. Behind the shadowy columns, the blue sky seemed like an insult.

Milo said, "I'm neglecting basic detective dogma: Lay your foundation. Get to know the vic. Trouble is, I'm getting the same feeling about Claire that I did about Dada. Grabbing air. She lived alone, no obvious kinks so far, no pals I can locate, no local family. You heard the way everyone at Starkweather described her: nice, did her job, stayed to herself. Offended no one. Richard's spiritual sister. So what do we have here, a psychopath who goes after *inoffensive* people?"

"Assuming the cases are related, maybe someone who goes after lonely people."

"Then half of L.A.'s at risk."

"Where is Claire's family?"

"Pittsburgh. Just her parents—she was an only child." He chewed his cheek. "I did the notification call. You know the drill: I ruin their lives, they cry, I listen. They're coming out this week; maybe I'll get more than I did over the phone, which was: Claire had no enemies, terrific daughter, wonderful girl. They're always wonderful girls."

We cut through industrial wasteland. Mounds of rotting machinery, slag heaps, muddy trenches, planes of greasy dirt. Under a gray sky, it could have passed for hell. Today, it just looked like something you kept from the voting public.

Milo wasn't noticing the scenery. Both his hands were back on the wheel, tight-knuckled, white.

"Lonely people," he said. "Let me show you her house."

* * *

He drove much too fast all the way to the freeway. As we swooped up the on-ramp, he said, "I was up there for a good part of yesterday, checking out the street, talking to neighbors. Home's the big killing spot for females, so I told the crime-scene guys to take their time. Unfortunately, it looks like time ill spent. Got some prelims this morning: no blood or semen, no evidence of break-in or disruption. Lots of prints all over the place, which you'd expect in anyone's house, but so far, the only matches are to Claire's. Final autopsy's scheduled for tomorrow if we're lucky and no drive-bys stuff up the pipeline."

"What did the neighbors have to say?"

"Take a guess."

" 'She kept to herself, never caused problems.' "

"I'm hanging with the Answer Man." He pressed down on the accelerator. "No one spoke two words to her. No one even knew her name."

"What about visitors?"

"None that anyone saw," he said. "Just like Richard. She did have an ex-husband, though. Guy named Joseph Stargill. Lawyer, lives down in San Diego now. I put a call in to him."

"How'd you find him?"

"Came across some divorce papers she kept in her home office. I called Dr. Theobold this morning; he'll be happy to engage in shrink talk with you. He had some vague recollection of Claire getting divorced. Only reason he found out is each year staff members update their résumés. In the past, Claire had put 'Married' in the marital-status blank. This year she whited it out and typed 'Divorced.' "

"So it was recent," I said. "Theobold didn't ask her about it?"

"He said she just wasn't the type you got personal with."

"Maybe that's why she took the job at Starkweather."

"What do you mean?"

"Great escape. Show up on time, don't make waves, no one bugs you. Like Dr. Aldrich said, the staff gets leeway. Maybe she wanted to do clinical work but was afraid of having to relate to patients. Surrounding herself with psychotics took the pressure off, and as long as none of her patients got violent, she could do what she wanted with them. The perfect escape."

"Escape from what?"

"Academia. And emotional entanglement. Her divorce was recent. Just because she didn't talk about it doesn't mean she wasn't still hurting. People going through life changes sometimes try to simplify."

"You see Starkweather as simple."

"In a sense, it is."

He didn't answer, put on even more speed.

A few miles later, I said, "On the other hand, she got entangled with *someone*. The person who cut her throat."

The house was like so many others.

Single-story white stucco aged to a spoiled-milk gray, roofed with black composite shingle. Attached single garage, double parking space instead of a front yard. One of those unadorned late-fifties hillside knockups posing as intentionally contemporary but really the product of a tight construction budget. The street was called Cape Horn Drive—a short, straight afterthought of a slit into the north side of Woodrow Wilson, dead-ending at a huge tipu tree. Matching trees tilted over the pavement. The sidewalk was bleached and dry where the branches didn't hover.

Second lot in, third from the end. Eight neighboring residences in all, most like Claire Argent's, with minor variation. Very few cars at the curb, but closed garage doors made it hard to assess what that meant. No major intersections or nearby commercial district. You'd have to intend to come up here.

This high, the air was moving. In the summer light, the tipu trees were filmy, their fern-shaped leaves swishing in the breeze. Contrary creatures: they lost their leaves in the spring, when everything else bloomed. When other branches began to shed, the tipus were a riot of yellow blossoms. Not yet. The only sparks of color shot from flower boxes and potted plants. Other houses, not Claire's.

We made our way up to the front door. Nice views all around. The freeway was miles away, but I could hear it. Nowadays, you always seem to hear it.

LAPD seal on the door. Milo had a key and let us in. I followed him into a tight, bare space too small to be called an entry hall. Two white walls right-angled us into the living room.

Not a lived-in room.

Unmarked walls, empty hardwood floors, not a single piece of furniture.

Milo took three echoing steps and stood in the center. Over his head was a light fixture. Cheap frosted dome; it looked original.

Chenille drapes browned the windows. The walls looked clean but were turning the same gray-white as the exterior.

The floors caught my attention—lacquered shiny, free of scuff marks, dents, drag furrows. As if the inhabitants had floated, rather than walked.

I felt short of breath. The house had no odor—neither the stench of death nor the aromas of tenancy. No food, sweat, perfume, cut flowers, air freshener. Not even the must of disuse.

A *vacant* place; it seemed airless, incapable of sustaining life.

I made myself take a deep breath. Milo was still in the center of the room, fingers drumming his thighs.

"Cozy," I said, understanding why he'd wanted me to see it.

He turned very slowly, taking in the open area to the left that led to a small kitchen. A single oak stool at an eat-in counter. White Formica laced with a gold threadlike design, also bare except for black fingerprint-powder smudges. Same for the other counters and the cabinets. On the far wall hung an empty wooden spice rack. Four-burner white stove at least twenty years old, refrigerator of matching color and vintage. No other appliances.

He opened the fridge, said, "Yogurt, grapes, two apples,

baking soda . . . baking soda for freshness. She liked things neat. Just like Richard . . . simplifying."

He began opening and closing cabinets. "White ironstone dishes, Noritake, service for four . . . Ditto stainless-steel utensils . . . Everything full of fingerprint powder . . . One skillet, one saucepan, containers of salt, pepper, no other spices . . . Bland life?"

On to the stove burners. Lifting the grill, he said, "Clean. Either she never cooked or she was really compulsive. Or somebody else was."

I stared back at the empty front room. "Did Crime Scene take furniture back to the lab?"

"No, just her clothing. This is the way we found it. My first thought was someone cleaned the place out, or she'd just moved in or was in the process of moving out. But I can't find evidence of her leaving, and her deed says she's been here over two years."

I pointed to the virgin floor. "Either she was planning to re-decorate or never bothered to furnish."

"Like I said, grabbing air. C'mon, let's take a look at the rest of the place."

A hall to the left led to one bath and two small bedrooms, the first set up as an office. No carpeting, the same pristine hard-wood, harsh echoes.

Milo kneeled in the hallway, ran his finger along the smooth, clean oak. "Maybe she took off her shoes. Like in a Japanese house."

We started with the bedroom. Box spring and mattress on the floor, no headboard, four-drawer pecan-veneer dresser, matching nightstand. On the stand were a tissue box and a ce-ramic lamp, the base white, ovular, shaped like a giant co-coon. Swirls of white fingerprint powder, the telltale concentrics of latent prints.

"Her linens are at the lab," said Milo, "along with her clothes."

He moved the mattress around, slid his hand under the box spring, opened the closet. Empty. Same for the dresser.

"I watched them pack her undies," he said. "No hidden stash of naughty things, just your basic white cotton. Small wardrobe: dresses, sweaters, skirts, tasteful stuff, Macy's, some budget-chain stuff, nothing expensive."

He righted the mattress, looked up at the ceiling, then back at the empty closet. "She wasn't moving out, Alex. This is where she lived. If you can call it that."

In the office, he put his hands together prayerfully and said, "Give me something to work with, Lord."

"Thought you already went through it."

"Not thoroughly. Couldn't, with the criminalists buzzing around. Just that box." He pointed to a cardboard file on the floor. "That's where I found the divorce papers. Near the top."

He approached the desk and studied the books in the cheap plywood cases that covered two walls. Shelves stuffed and sagging. Volumes on psychology, psychiatry, neurology, biology, sociology, bound stacks of journals arranged by date. White powder and prints everywhere.

Milo had emptied the top drawer of staples and paper clips, bits of paper and lint, was into the second drawer, rummaging. "Okay, here we go." He waved a red leather-ette savings account passbook. "Century Bank, Sunset and Cahuenga . . . Well, well, well—looks like she was doing okay."

I went over and looked at the page he held out. Balance of $240,000 and some cents. He flipped to the front of the booklet. The initial transaction had taken place three years ago, rolled over from a previous passbook, when the balance had been ninety-eight thousand less.

Accrual of nearly a hundred thousand in three years. The deposit pattern was repetitive: no withdrawals, deposits of three thousand at the end of each month.

"Probably a portion of her salary," I said.

"Theobold said her take-home was around four, so she probably banked three, took out a grand for expenses. Looks like it didn't change during the time she worked at Stark-weather. Which makes sense. Her civil service job classification puts her at a comparable salary."

"Frugal," I said. "How'd she pay her bills? And her taxes? Is there a checking account?"

He found it seconds later, in the same drawer. "Monthly deposits of five hundred . . . last Friday of the month—same day she deposited into the savings account. The woman was a clock. . . . Looks like she wrote mostly small checks— probably household stuff. . . . Maybe she had a credit card, paid the rest of her bills in cash. So she kept five hundred or so around the house. Or in her purse. To some junkie that could be a sizable score. And the purse hasn't been found. But this doesn't feel like robbery, does it."

I said, "No. Still, people have been killed for a lot less. Without her purse, how'd you identify her?"

"Car registration gave us her name. We ran her prints, matched them to her psychologist's license. . . . A stupid junkie robbery, wouldn't that be something? She's out shopping, gets mugged for her cash. But what junkie mugger would bother stashing her in trash bags, driving her to a semi-public spot, and leaving her car behind, when he could have thrown her somewhere dark, gotten himself some wheels for the night? Then again, most criminals take stupid pills. . . . Okay, let's see what else she left behind."

He got to work on the rest of the desk. The money showed up in a plain white envelope, pushed to the back of the left-hand bottom drawer. Nine fifty-dollar bills, under a black leatherette appointment book issued as a gift by a drug company. Three-year-old calendar, blank pages in the book.

"So maybe she had fifty or so with her," he said. "Big spender. This does *not* feel like robbery."

I asked him for the bankbook, examined every page.

"What?" he said.

"So mechanical. Exact same pattern, week in, week out. No sizable withdrawals also means no vacations or unpredictable splurges. And no deposits other than her salary implies she got no alimony, either. Unless she put it in another account. Also, she maintained her individual account throughout her marriage. What about her tax return? Did she file jointly?"

He crossed the room to the cardboard file box. Inside were two years of state and federal tax returns, neatly ordered. "No outside income other than salary, no dependents other than herself . . . nope, individual return. Something's off. It's like she was denying being married."

"Or she had doubts from the beginning."

He came up with a stack of stapled paper, started flipping. "Utility bills . . . Ah, here's the credit card. . . . Visa . . . She charged food, clothing, gasoline for the Buick, and books. . . . Not very often—most months there're only three, four charges. . . . She paid on time, too. No interest."

At the bottom of the stack were auto insurance receipts. Low premium for no smoking and good driving record. No financing on the Buick meant she probably owned the car. No way for her to know it would end up being a coffin on wheels.

Milo scribbled notes and placed the paper back in the carton. I thought of what we hadn't found: mementos, photographs, correspondence, greeting cards. Anything personal.

No property tax receipts or deductions for property tax. If she rented, why no record of rent checks?

I raised the question. Milo said, "So maybe the ex paid the mortgage and taxes. Maybe that was his alimony."

"And now that she's gone, he's off the hook. And if he's maintained some ownership of the house, there's a bit of incentive for you. Any idea who gets the two hundred forty? Any will show up?"

"Not yet. So you like the husband?"

"I'm just thinking about what you always tell me. Follow the money."

He grunted. I returned to the bookcase, pulled a few books out. Foxed pages, neatly printed notes in margins. Next to five years' worth of *Brain* was a collection of journal reprints.

Articles Claire Argent had authored. A dozen studies, all related to the neuropsychology of alcoholism, funded by the National Institutes of Health. The writing was clear, the subject matter repetitive. Lots of technical terms, but I got the gist.

During graduate school and the five years following, she'd filled her hours measuring human motor and visual skills under various levels of intoxication. Easy access to subjects: County Hospital was the treatment center of last resort for physically wasted alcoholic paupers who used the emergency room as their private clinic. E.R. docs called them GOMER's—Get Out of My Emergency Room.

Her results had been consistent: booze slowed you down. Statistically significant but hardly profound. Lots of academics drudged through undistinguished careers with that kind of stuff. Maybe she *had* tired of the grant game.

One interesting fact: she'd always published solo—unusual for academic medicine, where chairmen commonly stuck their names on everything underlings produced.

Maybe Myron Theobold had integrity.

Letting Claire do her own thing.

Claire going it alone from the very beginning.

A rattling sound made me turn. Milo had been handling the objects on the desktop and a pen had dropped. He retrieved it and placed it next to a small calendar in a green plastic frame. Another drug company giveaway. Empty memo pad. No appointments, no indentations on the pad.

Such a spare life.

Several books trumpeting the virtues of serene simplicity had recently gone best-seller. I wondered if the newly rich authors practiced what they preached.

This house didn't seem serene, just blank, hollow, null.

We left the office and moved to the bathroom. Shampoo, soap, toothpaste, multiple vitamins, sanitary napkins, Advil. No birth control pills, no diaphragm. The travertine deck around the tub was clear of niceties. No bath beads or bubble bath or loofah sponge—none of the solitary pleasures women sometimes crave. The porcelain was streaked with amber.

Milo said, "Luminol. No blood in the tub or the drain. No semen on the towels or sheets, just some sweat that matches Claire's blood type."

Wondering if anyone but Claire had ever set foot in this

house, I thought of the work pattern she'd chosen for herself. Five years with drunks, six months with dangerous psychotics. Perhaps, after days immersed in delusion and warp, she'd craved silence, her own brand of Zen.

But that didn't explain the lack of letters from home, not even a snapshot of parents, nieces, nephews. Some kind of *contact*.

The ultimate Zen triumph was the ability to lose identity, to thrive on nothingness. But this place didn't bespeak any sort of victory. Such a sad little box . . . or was I missing something? Projecting my own need for attachment?

I thought of what Claire *had* hoarded: her books and her articles.

Maybe work had been everything and she *had* been content.

Yet she'd abandoned her first job impulsively, relinquishing grant money, trading dry but durable science for the chance to school psychotic murderers in the art of daily living.

To what end?

I kept searching for reasons she'd traded County for Starkweather, but the shift continued to bother me. Even with comparable salaries, a civil service position was a comedown from the white-coat work she'd been doing at County. And if she'd craved contact with schizophrenics, County had plenty of those. Dangerous patients? The jail ward was right there.

If she was tired of the publish-or-perish grind, then why not do some private practice? Neuropsych skills were highly prized, and well-trained neuropsychologists could do forensic work, consult to lawyers on injury cases, bypass the HMO's and earn five, ten times what Starkweather paid.

Even if money hadn't been important to her, what about job satisfaction? Why had she subjected herself to shift after shift in the ugly gray building? And the drive to Starkweather—day after day past the slag.

There had to be some other reason for what I couldn't stop thinking of as a self-demotion.

It was almost as if she'd punished herself.
For what?
Or had she been fleeing something?
Had it caught up with her?

7.

IT WAS JUST after two P.M. when we left the house. Outside, the air felt alive.

Milo connected to Laurel Canyon, headed south to Sunset, drove west on the Strip. An accident near Holloway and the usual jam of misery ghouls slowed us, and it was nearly three by the time we crossed through Beverly Hills and over to Beverly Glen. Neither Milo nor I was saying much. Talked out. He zoomed up the bridle path to my house. Robin's truck was in the carport.

"Thanks for your time."

"Where are you headed?"

"Hall of Records, look for real estate paper, see what else comes up on Mr. Stargill. Then a call to Heidi Ott."

He looked tired, and his tone said optimism was a felony. I said, "Good luck," and watched him speed away.

I walked up to my new house. Three years, and I still thought of it as a bit of an interloper. The old house, the one I'd bought with my first real earnings, had been an amalgam of redwood and idiosyncrasy. A psychopath out to kill me torched it to cinders. Robin had supervised the construction of something white, airy, a good deal more spacious and practical, undeniably charming. I told her I loved it. For the most part, I did. One day, I'd stop being secretly stodgy.

I expected to find her out back in her studio, but she was in the kitchen reading the morning paper. Spike was curled up at her feet, black-brindle pot-roast body heaving with each snoring breath, jowls flowing onto the floor. He's a French bulldog, a miniature version of the English breed, with up-right bat ears and enough vanity for an entire opera troupe. He lifted one eyelid as I entered—*Oh, you again*—and let it drop. A subsequent sigh was laden with ennui.

Robin stood, spread her arms, and squeezed me around the waist. Her head pressed against my chest. She smelled of hardwood and perfume, and her curls tickled my chin. I lifted a handful of auburn coils and kissed the back of her neck. She's a charitable five three but has the long, swanlike neck of a fashion model. Her skin was hot, slightly moist.

"How'd it go?" she said, putting her hand in my hair.

"Uneventful."

"No problem from the inmates, huh?"

"Nothing." I held her closer, rubbing the taut musculature of her shoulders, moved down to delicate vertebrae, magical curves, then back up to the clean line of her jaw and the silk of her eyelids.

She stepped away, took my chin in one hand. "That place made you romantic?"

"Being out of there makes me romantic."

"Well, I'm glad you're back in one piece."

"It wasn't dangerous," I said. "Not even close."

"Five thousand murderers and no danger?"

"Twelve hundred, but who's counting."

"Twelve hundred," she said. "How silly of me to worry." At the last word, her voice rose a notch.

"Sorry," I said. "But really, it was fine. People go to work there every day and nothing happens. Everyone seems to think it's safer on the wards than out on the streets."

"Sounds like rationalization to me. Meanwhile, that psychologist gets stuffed in a car trunk."

"There's no indication, so far, that her work had anything to do with it."

"Good. The main thing is, you're back. Have you eaten yet?"

"No. You?"

"Just juice in the morning."

"Busy day?"

"Pretty busy, trying to finish that mandolin." She stretched to her full height. She had on a red T-shirt and denim overalls, size six Skechers. Small gold hoops glinted from her ears. She took them off when she worked. Not planning to return to the studio.

"I'm hungry now," she said. "Hint, hint."

"Let's go out," I said.

"A mind reader!"

"Just call me the Answer Man."

We gave Spike a chewbone and drove to an Indian buffet in Santa Monica that was open all afternoon. Rice and lentils, kulcha bread stuffed with onions, curried spinach with soft cheese, spicy eggplant, hot milky tea. Some sort of chant played in the background—a single male voice keening, maybe praying. The two ectomorphs in the next booth got up and left and we were the only patrons. The waiter left us alone.

Halfway through the pile on her plate, Robin said, "I know I'm harping, but next time you go somewhere like that, please call the minute you get out."

"You were really that worried?"

"Ax murderers and vampires, Lord knows what else?"

I covered her hand with mine. "Rob, the men I saw today were submissive." Except for the bearded fellow on the yard who'd come toward me. The fight in the hall. Plastic windows, S&R rooms.

"What makes them submit?"

"Medication and a structured environment."

She didn't seem comforted. "So you learned nothing there?"

"Not so far. Later we went to Claire Argent's house." I described the place. "What do you think?"

"About what?"

"The way she lived."

She drank tea, put the cup aside, thought awhile. "Would I want to live like that? Not forever, but maybe for a short stretch. Take a nice vacation from all the complications."

"Complications," I said.

She smiled. "Not you, honey. Just . . . circumstances. Obligations, deadlines—life piling up. Like when I was handling all the construction. Or now, when the orders stack up and everyone wants results yesterday. Sometimes life can start to feel like too much homework, and a little simplicity doesn't sound bad at all."

"This was more than simplicity, Robin. This was . . . bleak. Sad."

"You're saying she was depressed?"

"I don't know enough to diagnose her," I said. "But the feeling I got from the place was—inorganic. Blank."

"Did you see any evidence she was neglecting herself?" she said.

"No. And everyone describes her as pleasant, dependable. Distant, but no obvious pathology."

"So maybe inwardly she was fine, too."

"Maybe," I said. "The only things she did amass were books. Maybe intellectual stimulation was what turned her on."

"There you go. She trimmed things down to concentrate on what mattered to her."

I didn't answer.

"You don't think so," she said.

"Pretty severe trim," I said. "There was nothing personal in the entire house. Not a single family photo."

"Perhaps she wasn't close to her family. Or she had problems with them. But even so, how different does that make her from millions of other people, Alex? She sounds to me more like . . . someone cerebral. Living in her head. Enjoying her privacy. Even if she did have social problems, what does any of that have to do with her murder?"

"Maybe nothing." I spooned more rice onto my plate, played with grains of basmati, took a bite of bread. "If she wanted intellectual stimulation, why switch from a research job to Starkweather?"

"What kind of research was she doing?"

"Alcoholism and how it affects reaction time."

"Anything earth-shattering?"

"Not to me." I summarized the studies. "Actually, it was pretty mundane."

"Could be she came to a realization: she'd been a good little girl, doing what was expected of her since grad school. She got tired of hacking it out. Wanted to actually help someone."

"She didn't pick a very easy group to help."

"So it was the challenge that motivated her. That, and tackling something new."

"The men at Starkweather don't get cured."

"Then I don't know. All out of guesses."

"I'm not trying to be contentious," I said. "She just really puzzles me. And I think there's a good deal of truth in what you're saying. She got divorced within the last year or so. Maybe she was trying to cut free on several levels. Maybe for someone who'd been grinding out studies year after year, Starkweather seemed novel."

She smiled and stroked my face. "If knitted brows are any kind of measure, Milo's getting his money's worth out of you."

"The other thing I wonder about is the first case—Richard Dada, the would-be actor. On the surface, he and Claire have little in common. But what they do seem to share is negative space—an absence of friends, enemies, quirks. Both of them were very neat. *No* entanglements. Maybe we're talking about loneliness and an attempt to fill the void. Some sort of lonely-hearts hookup with the wrong person."

"A man and a woman?" she said. "A bisexual killer?"

"That would make Dada gay, and Milo never found any indication of that. Or maybe it had nothing to do with sex—just companionship, some kind of common-interest club. On the other hand, the cases could be unrelated."

I raised her hand to my lips, kissed the fingertips one by one. "Mr. Romantic. I'd better switch gears before I drive *you* into isolation."

She grinned, waved languidly, kissed air, put on her Bette Davis voice. "Pass me the spinach, dahling. Then you can pay the check and sweep me off my feet to the nearest Baskin

Robbins for some jamoca almond fudge. After that, hi-ho all the way home, where you ah cawjully invited to add some entanglement to my life."

8.

AT EIGHT P.M. Milo called. "Am I interrupting anything?"

He'd missed interrupting by an hour. Robin was reading in bed and I'd taken Spike for a short walk up the canyon. When the phone rang, I was sitting out on the terrace, trying to rid my mind of question marks, struggling to concentrate on the sound of the waterfall that fed the fishpond. Grateful because I couldn't hear the freeway.

"Not at all. What's up?"

"Got the info on Claire and Stargill. Married two years, divorced nearly two, no kids. I reached Stargill. He says the split was amicable. He's a partner in a ten-lawyer firm, remarried three months ago. He just learned about Claire. San Diego papers didn't carry it, but one of his partners was up here, read about it."

"What was his demeanor?"

"He sounded pretty upset over the phone, but what the hell does that mean? Said he doubted there was anything he could add but he'd talk to me. I set up an appointment for tomorrow morning at ten."

"San Diego?"

"No, he's driving up."

"Very cooperative fellow."

"He has business here anyway. Some commercial property closings—he's a real estate lawyer."

"So he comes up to L.A. regularly."

"Yeah, I made note of that. Let's see what he's like face-to-face. We're meeting at Claire's house. Which she owns. It was his bachelor place, but after the divorce he signed it over to

62

her and agreed to pay the mortgage and taxes in lieu of alimony and her dipping into his stocks and bonds."

"Who inherits the property now?"

"Good question. Stargill wasn't aware of any will, and he claims neither of them took out insurance on the other. I never came across any policies; Claire was thirty-nine, probably wasn't figuring on dying. I suppose a lawyer would know how to play the probate process—he might make a case for mortgage payment constituting partial ownership. But my guess her parents would come first. What do you think a place like that is worth?"

"Three hundred or so. How much is equity?"

"We'll find that out tomorrow if Mr. Cooperative stays cooperative. . . . Maybe he got tired of paying her bills, huh?"

"It could chafe, especially now that he's remarried. Especially if he's got money problems. Be good to know what his finances are like."

"If you want to meet him, be there at ten. I left a message with Heidi Ott's machine, no callback yet. And the lab sent another report on the prints: definitely only Claire's. Looks like she really did go it alone."

The next morning I called Dr. Myron Theobold at County Hospital, left a voicemail message, and drove to Cape Horn Drive, arriving at 9:45. Milo's unmarked was already there, parked at the curb. A deep-gray late-model BMW sedan sat in front of the garage, ski clamps on the roof.

The house's front door was unlocked, and I entered. Milo had reassumed his position at the center of the empty living room. Near the kitchen counter stood a man in his forties wearing a blue suit, white shirt, yellow pin-dot tie. He was just shy of six feet, trim, with short, curly red hair and a matching beard streaked with gray. Skinny gold watch on his left wrist, wedding band studded with small diamonds, shiny oxblood wingtips.

Milo said, "This is Dr. Delaware, our psychological consultant. Doctor, Mr. Stargill."

"Joe Stargill." A hand extended. Dry palms but unsteady

hazel eyes. His voice was slightly hoarse. He looked past me, into the empty room, and shook his head.

"Mr. Stargill was just saying the house looks pretty different."

Stargill said, "This wasn't the way we lived. We had wall-to-wall carpeting, furniture. Over there was a big leather sofa; that wall held a chrome cabinet—an étagère, I think it was called. Claire taught me that. I'd bought a few things when I was single but Claire filled it in. Pottery, figurines, macramé, all that good stuff." He shook his head again. "She must have gone through some major changes."

"When's the last time you spoke to her, sir?" said Milo.

"When I U-Hauled my things away. Maybe a half-year before the final decree."

"So you were separated before the divorce."

Stargill nodded, touched the tip of his beard.

Milo said, "So your last contact would be around two and a half years ago."

"That's right."

"You never talked about the divorce?"

"Well, sure. A phone call here and there to wrap up details. I thought you meant a real conversation."

"Ah," said Milo. "And after the divorce you never came back to visit?"

"No reason to," said Stargill. "Claire and I were over—we'd been over long before we made it official. Never really started, actually."

"The marriage went bad quickly."

Stargill sighed and buttoned his jacket. His hands were broad, ruddy, coated with beer-colored hair. "It wasn't a matter of going bad. The whole thing was essentially a mistake. Here, I brought this. Found it this morning."

He fished out a crocodile wallet and removed a small photo, which Milo examined, then handed to me.

Color snapshot of Claire and Stargill arm in arm, "Just Married" banner in the background. He wore a tan suit and brown turtleneck shirt, no beard, eyeglasses. His nude face was bony, his smile tentative.

Claire had on a long, pale blue sleeveless dress printed with lavender pansies, and she carried a bouquet of white roses. Her hair was long, straight, parted in the middle, her face leaner than in the headshot I'd seen, the cheekbones more pronounced.

Full smile.

"Don't really know why I brought it," said Stargill. "Didn't know I even had it."

"Where'd you find it?" said Milo.

"In my office. I went in early this morning before driving up here, started going through all the paperwork Claire and I had in common: divorce documents, transfer of ownership for the house. It's all out in the car—take whatever you want. The picture popped out from between some pages."

Stargill turned to me. "Guess a psychologist could interpret that—still having it. Maybe it does mean something on a subconscious level, but I sure don't remember holding on to it intentionally. Seeing it again was bizarre. We look pretty happy, don't we?"

I studied the photo some more. A flimsy-looking altar flecked with glitter was visible between the newlyweds. Glittering red hearts on the walls, a pink Cupid figurine with Dizzy Gillespie cheeks.

"Vegas?" I said.

"Reno," said Stargill. "Tackiest wedding chapel you ever saw. The guy who officiated was an old geezer, half blind, probably drunk. We got into town well after midnight. The geezer was closing up and I slipped him a twenty to do a quickie ceremony. His wife had already gone home, so some janitor—another old guy—served as witness. Afterward Claire and I joked that they were both senile—it probably wasn't legal."

He placed his hands on the counter, stared blankly into the kitchen. "When I lived here, we had appliances all over the place—juicer, blender, coffee maker, you name it. Claire wanted every gizmo invented. . . . Wonder what she did with the stuff—looks like she was stripping everything away."

"Any idea why she'd do that?" I said.

"No," he said. "Like I said, we weren't in touch. Truth is, even when we were together I couldn't have told you what made her tick. All she ever really liked was going to the movies—she could see a flick a night. Sometimes it didn't seem to matter what was on the screen, she just liked being in the theater. Beyond that, I never knew her at all."

"Where'd the two of you meet?"

"Another major romantic story: hotel cocktail lounge. Marriott at the airport, to be specific. I was there to meet a client from the Far East who never showed up, and Claire was attending a psychology convention. I'm sitting at the bar, irritated because this guy does this to me all the time, and now I've wasted half a day. Claire glides in looking great, sits a few stools down."

He pointed at the picture. "As you can see, she was an eyeful back then. Different from my usual type, but maybe that's what did it."

"Different, how?" I said.

"I'd been dating legal secretaries, paralegals, a few models, wannabe actresses—we're talking girls who were into fashion, makeup, the whole body-beautiful thing. Claire looked like exactly what she was: a scholar. Great structure, but she didn't mess with herself. That afternoon she was wearing granny glasses and one of those long print dresses. Her whole wardrobe was those dresses and some jeans and T-shirts. No makeup. No high heels—open sandals, I remember looking down at her feet. She had really pretty feet, adorable white toes. She saw me staring and laughed—this low chuckle that struck me as being really sexy, and then I started to look past the glasses and I realized she was great-looking. She ordered a ginger ale, I was well into the Bloody Marys. I made some crack about her being a wild party girl. She laughed again and I moved closer and the rest is history. We got married two months later. At the beginning, I thought I'd died and gone to heaven."

He had a redhead's typical milky complexion and now it pinkened.

"That's the whole sordid story," he said. "I don't know why I came here, but if there's nothing else—"

"Died and gone to heaven?" said Milo.

Pink turned to rose. "Physically," said Stargill. "I don't want to be vulgar, but maybe this will help you in some way. What drew Claire and me together was one thing: sex. We ended up getting a room at the Marriott and stayed there till midnight. She was— Let's just say I'd never met anyone like her, the chemistry was incredible. After her, those other girls seemed like mannequins. I don't want to be disrespectful, let's leave it at that."

I said, "But the chemistry didn't last."

He unbuttoned his jacket, put a hand in his pocket. "Maybe it was too much too quickly. Maybe every flame burns out, I don't know. I'm sure some of the blame was mine. Maybe most. She wasn't my first wife. I'd gotten hitched in college— that one lasted less than a year; obviously I wasn't good at the matrimony thing. After we started living together, it was like . . . something sputtered. No fights, just . . . no fire. Both of us were really into our work, we didn't spend much time together."

The beard hair under his lip vibrated a bit. "We never fought. She just seemed to lose interest. I think she lost interest first, but after a while it stopped bothering me. I felt I was living with a stranger. Maybe I had been all along."

The other hand went in a pocket. Now he was slouching. "So here I am, forty-one, working on my third. Happy honeymoon so far, but who knows?"

I noticed that he tended to shift the focus to himself. Self-centered, or an intentional distraction?

I said, "So Claire was really into her work. Did that ever change?"

"Not that I saw. But I wouldn't have known. We never talked about work. We never talked about anything. It was weird—one moment we're getting hitched, having hurricane sex, then we're each going about our business. I tried. I invited her to the office a couple of times, but she was always too busy. She never invited me to her lab. One time I dropped in on her anyway. What a zoo, all those drunks lurching around. She didn't seem happy to see me—like I was intruding. Eventually, we were avoiding each other completely. Easy to do when you're both working seventy hours a week. I'd get home when she was already asleep; she'd wake up early, be over at the hospital by the time I was in the shower. Only reason we stayed married for two years is each of us was too busy—or too lazy—to file the papers."

"Who ended up filing?" I said.

"Claire did. I remember the day she announced it to me. I came home late, but this time she was up, in bed doing a crossword puzzle. She pulls out a stack of papers, says, 'I thought it was about time, Joe. How do you feel about it?' I remember feeling relieved. But also hurt. Because she didn't even want to try to work it out. Also, for me it was the second time, and I was wondering if I'd ever pull off the whole relationship thing. I moved out, but she didn't actually file for six months."

"Any idea why?" said Milo.

"She said she hadn't gotten around to it."

"What was the financial agreement?" said Milo.

"Polite," said Stargill. "No hassles; we worked the whole thing out with one phone call. I give Claire big points for fairness, because she refused to hire a lawyer, let me know she had no intention of cleaning me out. And I was the vulnerable one, I had the assets—investments, pension plan, I had some real estate things cooking. She could've made my life miserable, but all she asked was for me to deed her the house, finish paying it off, and handle the property taxes. Everything else was mine. I left her the furniture, walked away with my clothes and my law books and my stereo."

He rubbed an eye, turned away, tried to speak, cleared his throat. "The paperwork was easy—we never filed a joint tax return. She never changed her name. I thought it was a feminist thing, but now I wonder if she ever intended to stay with me."

"Did that bother you?" said Milo.

"Why should it? The whole marriage didn't feel like a marriage. More like a one-night stand that stretched out. I'm not saying I didn't respect Claire as a person. She was a terrific woman. Considerate, kind. That was the only downer: I *liked* her—as a person. And I know she liked me. My first wife was twenty when she left me, we'd been together eleven months and *she* tried to enslave me for the rest of my life. Claire was so damn decent. I wouldn't have minded remaining her friend. But it just didn't go down that way. . . . I can't understand why anyone would want to hurt her."

He rubbed his eyes.

"When did you move to San Diego?" said Milo.

"Right after the divorce. A job opportunity came up, and I'd had it with L.A., couldn't wait to get out."

"Fed up with the smog?" said Milo.

"The smog, the congestion, the crime. I wanted to live near the beach, found myself a little rental near Del Mar. The first year, Claire and I exchanged Christmas cards, then that stopped."

"Did Claire have any enemies you were aware of?" said Milo.

"No way. I never saw her offend anyone—maybe some nutcase at County got an idea in his head, stalked her or something. I still remember those drunks leering, smelling of barf, leaking all over the place when they walked. I couldn't see how Claire could work with them. But she was real businesslike about it—giving them these tests, doing research. Nothing grossed her out. I'm no expert, but I'd concentrate on County."

He folded his handkerchief and Milo and I used the split second to exchange glances. Stargill didn't know about the job switch to Starkweather. Or wanted us to think he didn't.

Milo shook his head. *Don't bring it up now.*

He said, "How much is owed on the house, Mr. Stargill?" Quick change of context. It throws people off balance. Stargill actually stepped backward.

"Around fifty thousand. By now the payments are mostly principal; I was thinking of paying it off."

"Why's that?"

"Not much of a tax deduction anymore."

"Who gets the property in the event of Dr. Argent's death?"

Stargill studied him. Buttoned his coat. "I wouldn't know."

"So you and she didn't have any agreement—in the event of her demise, it reverts to you?"

"Absolutely not."

"And so far, no will's turned up—do you have a will, sir?"

"I do. Why is that relevant, Detective Sturgis?"

"Just being thorough."

Stargill's nostrils expanded. "I'm the ex, so I'm a suspect? Oh, come on." He laughed. "What's the motive?" Laughing again, he stuffed his hands in his pockets and rocked on his heels—a courtroom gesture. "Even if I did get the house, three hundred thousand equity, tops. One of the things I did when I moved to S.D. was invest in seaside property. I've got a net worth of six, seven million, so murdering Claire for another three, before taxes, would be ludicrous."

He walked to the bare kitchen counter and rubbed the Formica. "Claire and I were never enemies. I couldn't have asked for a better ex-wife, so why the hell would I hurt her?"

"Sir," said Milo, "I have to ask these questions."

"Sure. Fine. Ask. Hearing about Claire made me sick to my stomach. I felt this stupid urge to do something—to be useful. That's why I drove up, brought you all the documents. I should've figured you'd see me as a suspect, but still it's . . ." Shrugging, he turned his back on us. "All I can say is, glad it's your job and not mine. Anything else you want to quiz me on?"

I said, "What can you tell us about Claire's family background, her social life?"

"Nothing."

"Nothing about her family?"

"Never met her family. All I know is she was born in Pittsburgh, did undergrad at the University of Pittsburgh, went to Case Western for her Ph.D. Only reason I know that is I saw her diplomas in her office. She refused to talk about her past."

"Refused, or avoided?" I said.

"Both."

"And she never talked at all about her family?"

Stargill pivoted and stared at me. "That's right. She was a closed book. Claimed she had no brothers and sisters. Her parents ran some kind of store. Other than that, I don't know a *thing*."

He shook his head. "I talked plenty about my family, and she listened. Or pretended to. But she never met my side, either. *My* choice."

"Why's that?" I said.

"Because I don't like my family. My mother was okay—a quiet drunk—but by the time I met Claire, she was dead. My father was a violent, drunken sonofabitch I wouldn't have tossed a stick at, let alone introduced to my bride. Same for my brother."

He gave a sick smile. "Get it? I'm one of those adult children of alcoholics et cetera, et cetera. Never developed a drinking problem myself, but I watch myself, went through the whole therapy thing after my mother killed herself. When I saw Claire with that ginger ale I wondered if maybe she had some history with alcohol, maybe we had something in common. I ended up telling her about my colorful background." The smile acquired teeth. "Turned out, she just liked ginger ale."

"Not a mention of her family in two years of marriage," I said. "Amazing."

"Like I said, it wasn't your typical marriage. Every time I tried to get personal, she changed the subject." He rubbed his scalp and the corners of his mouth curled up—outward trappings of another smile, but his mood was hard to read. "And she had an interesting way of changing the subject."

"What's that?" I said.

"She took me to bed."

9.

STARGILL WAS EAGER to leave but Milo convinced him to tour the rest of the house. The bathroom provoked no comment. In the office he said, "Now, this looks exactly the same. This was Claire's place, she spent all her time here."

"Where was your office?" said Milo.

"I didn't like bringing work home, used a small desk in the bedroom."

That room widened his eyes. "No memories left here. We had a king-size bed, brass headboard, down comforter, antique nightstands. Claire must have really wanted a change."

His expression said he still took that personally. He looked into the empty closet. "Where are all her clothes?"

"At the crime lab," said Milo.

"Oh, man . . . I've got to get out of here." Grabbing his beard for support, he left the room.

Outside, he got the carton of documents from his BMW, handed them over, revved noisily, and barreled down the hill.

"What's your take on the guy?" said Milo.

"He's got his share of problems, but no bells are ringing. And unless Claire wasn't as financially benevolent as he made out—or he's not as rich—where *is* the motive?"

"Three hundred even after taxes is still serious bread. And guys with big net worth can still get into trouble. I'm going to take a crash course on his finances. What do you mean, problems?"

"Bleeding in public—telling us his life history. Maybe

that's what attracted Claire to him. Someone so self-absorbed he wouldn't try to get into *her* head. Their marriage sounds like a passion-with-a-stranger fantasy gone stale. That shows an impulsive side to Claire, sexually and otherwise. Stargill says they avoided each other for most of the marriage, meaning both of them could've had multiple affairs. Maybe Claire's been dating strangers for years, and finally met the wrong one."

"The neighbors never saw anyone."

"Neighbors don't notice everything. Pick someone up in a bar, bring them back in your car late at night, who's to know? Or she had liaisons away from home. That would fit with no prints except hers in the house.

"Stargill described her the same way everyone else has: nice but detached," I went on. "But there's one thing he did add: a touch of dominance. She moves into his house, takes over the office; he gets a desk in the bedroom. He shares *his* past, but she refuses to reciprocate. When she tires of him, *she* decides they're going to divorce. And what the settlement is going to be. The fact that Stargill didn't press her on anything tells us something about him."

"A submissive lawyer? That's a novel concept."

"Some people keep work and play separate. Think of the specifics of the settlement: Claire ends up with the house, gets him to carry the mortgage and the taxes, and he feels grateful because she didn't take more. Even their first meeting has that same lopsided feel: she's sober, he isn't. She's in *control,* he isn't. He spills his guts about his drunken father and brother, alcoholic tendencies of his own that he keeps in check. The guy's her polar opposite: turns every conversation into therapy. Some women might be put off. Claire goes upstairs with him and gives him the time of his life. Later on, whenever she wants to shut him up, she uses sex. She was clearly drawn to people with serious problems. Maybe she left County because she needed a bigger dose of pathology."

"So," he said, "maybe she found a nutcase who'd gotten out of the hospital, tried to dominate him, pushed the wrong button—I've got to see if anyone was released from Stark-weather during the last six months. But if nothing turns up, then what?"

He looked worn out. I said, "You ask me to theorize, I theorize. It could still turn out to be a carjacking gone really bad."

We walked to the Seville.

"Something else," he said. "The big taboo she had on talking about her family. To me that says rotten background. Only, unlike Stargill, she kept the bandage on."

"When are her parents coming out?"

"Couple of days. Why don't you meet them with me?"

"Sure." I got in the car.

He said, "She starts out as your basic nice lady, and now we're thinking of her as some kind of dominatrix. . . . So all I have to do is find some highly disturbed joker with sadistic tendencies who held on to her credit card. Speaking of which, better call Visa."

He looked back at the house. "Maybe she did have visitors no one saw. Or just one sicko loverboy . . . Her living room woulda been a great playpen, wouldn't it? Plenty of space to roll around in—those floors are baby smooth. No body fluid traces on the wood, but who knows?"

"What's easier to clean than lacquered hardwood?" I said.

"True," he said. "Carpet would have yielded something."

"Stargill said she took the carpeting out."

He rubbed his face. "Ex-patient or ex-con, some bad boy she thinks she can control."

"Both would fit with the fact that she was found in her own car. Someone without his own wheels."

"Putting her in the driver's seat, again." Faint smile. "A late-night pickup—we know from Stargill that she wasn't opposed to being picked up. They go somewhere, things go bad. No semen in her, so it never got to hanky-panky. . . . Bad Boy cuts her, puts her in the trash bag, stashes her in the trunk and drives her over to West L.A. Doesn't steal the car, because that's a sure way to get busted. Smart. Meticulous. Not a

Starkweather fellow." He grimaced. "Meaning I'm wasting my time over there. Back to square one."

His cell phone chirped. Snapping it off his belt, he said, "Sturgis . . . Oh, hi. . . . Yes, thank you— Oh? How so? Why don't you just tell— Okay, sure, that would be fine, give me directions."

Cradling the phone under his chin, he produced his pad, wrote something down, clicked off.

"That," he said, "was young Miss Ott. She does the night shift today at Starkweather, wants to talk before work."

"Talk about what?"

"She wouldn't say, but I know scared when I hear it."

She'd asked to meet at Plummer Park in West Hollywood. I followed Milo, connecting to Laurel, turning east on Melrose. On the way, I passed a billboard advertising a kick-boxing gym: terrific-looking woman in a sports bra drawing back a glove for a roundhouse. The ad line was "You can rest when you're dead." Theology everywhere.

The park was scrubby, crowded, more Russian spoken than English. Most of the inhabitants were old people on benches, heavily garbed despite the heat. A sprinkle of kids on bicycles circled a dry oval of grass in the center, sleepy-looking dog walkers were led by the leash, a few scruffy types in designer T-shirts and cheap shoes hung out near the pay phones trying to radiate Moscow Mafia.

Heidi Ott stood by herself under a sad-looking carrotwood tree, arms crossing her chest, checking out the terrain in all directions. When she spotted us, she gave a small wave and headed for the only vacant bench in sight. A pile of fresh dog turd nearby explained the vacancy. Wrinkling her nose, she moved on and we followed her to a shady spot near the swing set, under an old Chinese elm. The surrounding grass was bruised and matted. A lone young woman pushed her toddler in a gently repeating arc. Both she and the child seemed hypnotized by the motion.

Heidi leaned against the elm and watched them. If I hadn't been looking for the fear, I might not have noticed it. She wore it lightly, a glaze of anxiety, hands knotting then releasing, eyes fixing too intently on the swinging child.

"Thanks for meeting with us, ma'am," said Milo.

"Sure," she said. "My roommate's sleeping, or I would've had you come to my place."

She moistened her lips with her tongue. She wore low-slung jeans, a ribbed white T-shirt with a scalloped neck and high-cut sleeves, blunt-toed brown boots. Her hair was drawn back, just as it had been at Starkweather, but in a ponytail, not a tight bun. Dangling earrings of silver filigree, some eye shadow, a smear of lip gloss. Freckles on her cheeks that I hadn't noticed on the ward. Her nails were clipped short, very clean. The T-shirt was form-fitting. Not much meat on her, but her arms were sinewy.

She cleared her throat, seemed to be working up the courage to speak, just as a tall, thin man with long hair came loping by with a panting mutt. The dog had some Rottweiler in it. The man wore all black and his coarse hair was a dull ebony. He stared at the ground. The dog's nose was down; each step seemed to strain the animal.

Heidi waited until they passed, then smiled nervously. "I'm probably wasting your time."

"If there's anything you can tell me about Dr. Argent, you're not."

Squint lines formed around her eyes, but when she turned to us they disappeared. "Can I ask you one thing first?"

"Sure."

"Claire—Dr. Argent—was anything done to her eyes?"

Milo didn't answer immediately, and she pressed herself against the tree trunk. "There was? Oh my God."

"What about her eyes concerns you, Ms. Ott?"

She shook her head. One hand reached back and tugged her ponytail. The man with the dog was leaving the park. Her eyes followed him for a second before returning to the swinging child. The boy squalled as the young woman pulled him off, struggled to stuff him into a stroller, finally wheeled away.

Just the three of us now, as if a stage had been cleared. I

heard birds sing; distant, foreign chatter; some traffic from Fuller Avenue.

Milo was looking at Heidi. I saw his jaw loosen deliberately and he bent one leg, trying to appear casual.

She said, "Okay, this is going to sound weird but . . . three days ago, one of the patients—a patient Dr. Argent worked with—said something to me. The day before Dr. Argent was killed. It was at night, I was double-shifting, doing bed check, and all of a sudden he started talking to me. Which by itself was unusual, he's barely verbal. Didn't talk at all until Dr. Argent and I began—"

She stopped, pulled the ponytail forward so that it rested on her shoulder, played with the ends, squeezed them. "You're going to think I'm flaky."

"Not at all," said Milo. "You're doing exactly the right thing."

"Okay. This is the situation: I'm just about to leave his room and this guy starts mumbling, like he's praying or chanting. I pay attention because he hardly ever talks—never really talks at all. But then he stops and I turn to leave again. Then all of a sudden, he says her name—'Dr. A.' I say, 'Excuse me?' And he repeats it a little louder. 'Dr. A.' I say, 'What *about* Dr. A?' And he gives this strange smile—till now, he never smiled either—and says, 'Dr. A bad eyes in a box.' I say, 'What?' Now he's back to looking down at his knees the way he always does and he's not saying anything and I can't get him to repeat it. So I leave again and when I reach the door he makes this sound I've heard him make a few times before— like a bark—*ruh ruh ruh.* I never knew what it meant but now I get the feeling it's his way of laughing—he's laughing at *me*. Then he stops, he's back in space, and I'm out of there."

Milo said, " 'Dr. A bad eyes in a box.' Have you told anyone about this?"

"No, just you. I planned to talk to Claire about it, but I never got to see her because the next day . . ." She bit her lip. "The reason I didn't mention it to anyone at the hospital was because I figured it was just crazy talk. If we paid attention every time someone talked crazy, we'd never get any work done. But the next day, when Claire didn't come to work, and later in the afternoon I heard the news, it freaked me out. I still didn't say anything, because I didn't know where to go with it—and what connection could there be? Then when I read the paper and it said she'd been found in her car trunk, I'm like, ' "Boxed up" could be a car trunk, right? This is freaky.' But the paper didn't mention anything about her eyes, so I thought maybe by 'bad eyes' he meant her wearing glasses, it probably *was* just crazy talk. Although why would he say something about it all of a sudden when usually he doesn't speak at all? So I kept thinking about it, didn't know what to do, but when I saw you yesterday, I figured I should call. And now you're telling me something *was* done to her eyes."

She exhaled. Licked her lips.

Milo said, "I didn't exactly say that, ma'am. I asked why Dr. Argent's eyes concerned you."

"Oh." She slumped. "Okay, so I'm making a big deal. Sorry for wasting your time." She started to walk away. Milo placed a big hand on her wrist.

"No apologies necessary, Ms. Ott. You did the right thing." Out came his pad. "What's this patient's name?"

"You're going to *pursue* it? Listen, I don't want to make waves—"

"At this point," said Milo, "I can't afford to eliminate anything."

"Oh." She picked some bark from the tree trunk and examined a fingernail. "The administration doesn't like publicity. This is not going to earn me gold stars."

"What's the problem with publicity?"

"Mr. Swig believes in no-news-is-good-news. We depend on politicians for funding and our patients aren't exactly looked upon kindly, so the lower the profile, the fewer the budget cuts." She flicked bits of bark from under her nail. Slender fingers twirled the ponytail again. Shrug. "I opened the can, what did I expect. No big deal, I've been thinking about leaving anyway. Starkweather's not what I expected."

"In what way?"

"Too repetitious. Basically, I baby-sit grown men. I was looking for something a little more clinical. I want to go back to school to become a psychologist, thought this would be a good learning experience."

"Dr. Delaware's a psychologist."

"I figured that," she said, smiling at me. "When Hatterson said he was a doctor. You wouldn't exactly be taking a surgeon around on the ward, would you?"

"This patient," I said. "Is there any particular reason he'd pay attention to Dr. Argent?"

"Not really, except she worked with him. I was helping her. We were trying to raise his verbal output, getting him to interact more with his surroundings."

"Behavior modification?" I said.

"That was the ultimate goal—some kind of reward system. But it didn't get that far. Basically, she just talked to him, trying to build up rapport. She had me spending time with him, too. To bring him out of his isolation. No one else bothered with him."

"Why's that?"

"Probably no one wanted to. He's got difficult . . . personal habits. He makes noises in his sleep, doesn't like to bathe. He eats bugs when he finds them, garbage off the floor. Worse stuff. He doesn't have roommates because of that. Even at Starkweather, he's an outcast."

"But Claire saw something workable in him," I said.

"I guess," she said. "She told me he was a challenge. And actually, he did respond a bit—the last few weeks, I got him to pay attention, sometimes nod when I asked yes-or-no questions. But no real sentences. Nothing like what he said that day."

" 'Dr. A. bad eyes in a box.' "

She nodded. "But how could he know? I mean, it doesn't make sense. This is nothing, right?"

"Probably," I said. "Did this man associate with anyone who could've planned to hurt Claire? Maybe someone who's been discharged?"

"No way. He didn't associate with anyone, period. And no one's been discharged since I've worked there. No one gets out of Starkweather."

"How long have you worked there?"

"Five months. I came on right after Claire did. No, I wouldn't be looking for any friends of this guy. Like I said, no one hangs out with him. On top of his mental problems, he's physically impaired. Tardive dyskinesia."

Milo said, "What's that?"

"Side effects. From the antipsychotic drugs. His are pretty bad. His walk is unsteady, he sticks his tongue out constantly, rolls his head. Sometimes he gets active and marches in place, or his neck goes to one side, like this."

She demonstrated, straightened, kept her back to the tree trunk. "That's all I know. I'd like to go now, if that's okay."

Milo said, "His name, ma'am."

Another tug on the ponytail. "We're not supposed to give out names. Even *our* patients have confidentiality. But I guess all that changes when . . ." Her arms went loose and her hands joined just below her pubis, fingers tangling, remaining in place, as if protecting her core.

"Okay," she said. "His name's Ardis Peake, maybe you've heard of him. Claire said he was notorious, the papers gave him a nickname: Monster."

10.

MILO'S JAW WAS too smooth: forced relaxation. "I've heard of Peake."

So had I.

A long time ago. I'd been in grad school—at least fifteen years before.

Heidi Ott's calm was real. She'd been a grade-school kid. Her parents would have shielded her from the details.

I remembered the facts the papers had printed.

A farm town named Treadway, an hour north of L.A. Walnuts and peaches, strawberries and bell peppers. A pretty place, where people still left their doors unlocked. The papers had made a big deal out of that.

Ardis Peake's mother had worked as a maid and cook for one of the town's prominent ranch families. A young couple. Inherited wealth, good looks, a big old frame house, a two-story house—what was their name? Peake's name was immediately familiar. What did that say?

I recalled snippets of biography. Peake, born up north in Oregon, a logging camp, father unknown. His mother had cooked for the tree men.

As far as anyone could tell, she and the boy had drifted up and down the coast for most of Ardis's childhood. No school registrations were ever found, and when Peake and his mother Greyhounded into Treadway, he was nineteen and illiterate, preternaturally shy, obviously different.

Noreen Peake scrubbed tavern floors until landing the job at the ranch. She lived in the main house, in a maid's room off the kitchen, but Ardis was put in a one-room shack behind a peach orchard.

He was gawky, mentally dull, so quiet many townspeople thought him mute. Unemployed, with too much time on his hands, he was ripe for mischief. But his sole offenses were some paint-sniffing incidents out behind the Sinclair store, broad-daylight acts so reckless they confirmed his reputation as retarded. The ranch owners finally gave him a job of sorts: rat catcher, gopher killer, snake butcher. The farm's human terrier.

His territory was the five acres immediately surrounding the house. His task could never be completed, but he took to it eagerly, often working late into the night with pointed stick and poison, sometimes crawling in the dirt—keeping his nose to the ground, literally.

A dog's job assigned to a man, but by all accounts Peake had found his niche.

It all ended on a cool, sweet Sunday morning, two hours before dawn.

His mother was found first, a heavy, wide woman sitting in a faded housedress at the kitchen table, a big plate of Granny Smith apples in front of her, some of them cored and peeled. A sugar bowl, white flour, and a stick of butter on a nearby counter said it would have been a pie-baking day. A pot roast was in the oven and two heads of cabbage had been chopped for coleslaw. Noreen Peake was an insomniac, and all-night cooking sprees weren't uncommon.

This one ended prematurely. She'd been decapitated. Not a neat incision. The head lay on the floor, several feet from her chair. Nearby was a butcher knife still flecked with cabbage. Another knife from the same cutlery set—heavier, larger— had been removed from the rack.

Bloody sneaker prints led to a service staircase. On the third floor of the house, the young rancher and his wife lay in bed, covers tossed aside, embracing. Their heads had been left on, though severed jugulars and tracheas said it wasn't for lack of effort. The big knife had seared through flesh but failed at bone. Facial crush wounds compounded the horror.

A gore-encrusted baseball bat lay on the floor in front of the footboard. The husband's bat; he'd been a high school slugger, a champ.

The papers made a big deal about how good-looking the couple had been in life—what was their *name* . . . Ardullo. Mr. and Mrs. Ardullo. Golden couple, everything to live for. Their faces had been obliterated.

Down the hall, the children's bedrooms. The older one, a five-year-old girl, was found in her closet. The coroner guessed she'd heard something and hid. The big knife, badly bent but intact, had been used on her. The papers spared its readers further details.

A playroom separated her room from the baby's. Toys were strewn everywhere.

The baby was an eight-month-old boy. His crib was empty.

Fading sneaker prints led back down to the laundry room and out a rear door, where the trail lightened to specks along a winding stone path and disappeared in the dirt bordering the kitchen garden.

Ardis Peake was found in his shack—a wood-slat and tar-paper thing rancid with the stink of a thousand dogs. But no animals lived there, just Peake, naked, unconscious on a cot, surrounded by empty paint cans and glue tubes, flasks bearing the label of a cheap Mexican vodka, an empty filled with urine. A plastic packet frosted with white crystal residue was found under the cot. Methamphetamine.

Blood smeared the rat catcher's mouth. His arms were red-drenched to the elbows, his hair and bedding burgundy. Gray-white specks in his hair were found to be human cerebral tissue. At first he was thought to be another victim.

But he stirred when prodded. Later, everything washed off. Fast asleep.

A scorching smell compounded the reek.

No stove in the shack, just a hot plate powered by an old car battery. A tin wastebasket serving as a saucepan had been left on the heat. The metal was too thin; the bottom was starting to burn through, and the stench of charring tin lent a bitter overlay to the reek of offal, putrid food, unwashed clothes.

Something else. Heady. A stew.

The baby's pajamas on the floor, covered by flies.

Ardis Peake had never been one for cooking. His mother had always taken care of that.

This morning, he'd tried.

Heidi Ott said, "I never heard of him till I came to Starkweather. Way before my time."

"So you know what he did," said Milo.

"Killed a family. It's in his chart. Claire told me about it before she asked me to work with him, said he'd been nonviolent since commitment but I should know what I was dealing with. I said fine. What he did was horrible, but you don't end up at Starkweather for shoplifting. I took the job in the first place because I was interested in the endpoint."

"The endpoint?"

"The extreme—how low people can go."

She turned to me, as if seeking approval.

I said, "Extremes interest you?"

"I think extremes can teach us a lot. What I'm trying to say is, I wanted to see if I was really cut out for mental-health work, figured if I could handle Starkweather, I could cope with anything."

Milo said, "But the job ended up being repetitious."

"There's a lot of routine. I guess I was naive, thinking I was going to see fascinating things. Between their medication and their disabilities, most of the guys are pretty knocked out—passive. That's what I meant by baby-sitting. We make sure they get fed and stay reasonably clean, keep them out of trouble, give them time out when they pull tantrums, the same as you'd do with a little kid. Same thing over and over, shift after shift."

"Dr. Argent was new to the job," I said. "Any idea if she liked it?"

"She seemed to."

"Did she talk about why she'd transferred from County General?"

"No. She didn't talk much. Only work-related stuff, nothing personal."

"Was she assigned to Ardis Peake, or did she choose to work with him?"

"I think she chose to—the doctors have a lot of freedom. We techs are pretty much bound by routine."

"Did she say why she wanted to work with Peake?"

She stroked her ponytail, arched her back. "All I remember her saying about him was that he was a challenge. Because of how low-functioning he was. If we could increase his behavioral repertoire, we could do it for anyone. That appealed to me."

"Learning from the extreme."

"Exactly."

"What about the Skills for Daily Living group?" I said. "What was her goal there?"

"She wanted to see if the men could learn to take better care of themselves—grooming, basic manners, paying attention when someone else spoke. Even with their psychosis."

"How were men picked for the group?"

"Claire picked them. I was just there to assist."

"See any progress?"

"Slow," she said. "We only had seven sessions. Tomorrow would've been eight." She swiped at her eyes.

"Any particular disciplinary problems in the group?"

"Nothing unusual. They have their moods; you have to be firm and consistent. If you're asking if any of them resented her, not at all. They liked her. Everyone did."

Tug. She chewed her cheek, arched her back again. "It really stinks. She was a good teacher, very patient. I can't believe anyone would want to hurt her."

"Even though she didn't get personal," said Milo, "did she tell you anything about her life outside work?"

"No. I'm sorry—I mean, you just didn't sit down for coffee with her."

Yet she referred to Claire by her first name. The instant familiarity of Gen X.

She said, "I really wish I could tell you more. The thing about Peake—it's nothing, right?"

"Probably nothing," said Milo. "But I will want to talk to him."

She shook her head. "You don't talk to him. Not in any normal way. Most of the time he's totally spaced. It took Claire and me months just to get him to pay attention."

"Well," said Milo, "we'll see what happens."

She reached back, pulled a leaf from the tree, and ground it between her fingers. "I guess I expected that. Better brace myself for a lecture from Swig. I probably should've gone through him first."

"Want me to run interference for you?"

"No, I can handle it. At least I know I did the right thing— time to move on, anyway. Maybe do some work with children."

"How much more school do you have?" I said.

"One more year for a bachelor's, then graduate work. I'm paying for it all, so it'll take time. One thing about Stark- weather, the pay's good. But I'll find something."

Milo said, "So you're definitely leaving?"

"Can't see any reason not to."

"Too bad. You might be able to help some more."

"Help how?"

"By trying to draw Peake out again."

Her laugh was skittish. "No thanks, Detective Sturgis. I don't want to get any more involved. And he doesn't really talk to me, either."

"He did the day before Claire was killed."

"That was—I don't know what that was all about," she said.

Milo smiled. "I can't convince you, huh?"

She smiled back. "I don't think so."

"Think of it as learning more about extremes—a challenge."

"If I want a challenge now, I rock-climb."

"A climber," said Milo. "I'm afraid of heights."

"You get used to it. That's the point. I like all sorts of chal- lenges—physical things—climbing, parasailing, skydiving.

Getting physical's especially important when you work in a place like Starkweather. Having to watch yourself all the time, but no exercise, no movement. Anyway . . ." She looked at her watch. "I'd really like to go now, okay?"

"Okay."

She shook our hands, walked away with an easy athletic stride.

Milo said, "So what the hell is this thing with *Peake* all about?"

"Probably nothing," I said. "He muttered something; normally Heidi wouldn't have noticed. After Claire was murdered, she got scared."

"Little Ms. Daredevil?"

"Jumping out of planes is one thing. Murder's another."

" 'Dr. A bad eyes in a box,' " he said. "What if it's not pure gibberish? What if Peake had a buddy who got out? Someone who told him he was gonna do something bad to Claire?"

"It doesn't sound as if Peake has buddies. Heidi said he rooms alone, no one wants to associate with him. But maybe. Let's have a closer look at him."

"Ardis Peake," he said. "Long time since he did his thing. Sixteen years ago. I know exactly, because I'd just started Homicide, first thing they hand me is a screwed-up whodunit, I'm sweating over it, not getting anywhere, wondering if I went into the wrong line of work. A few days later Peake does his thing over in Whateverville, some local yokel sheriff solves it the same day. I remember thinking some people have all the luck: asshole just hands himself over on a platter with garnish. Few years later, when I took that VICAP course at Quantico, the Fibbies used Peake as a teaching case, said he was typical of the disorganized spree killer, just about defined the profile: raving lunatic with poor hygiene, mind coming apart at the seams, no serious effort to hide the crime. 'Bad eyes in a box'—so now he's gone from psycho to prophet?"

"Or he overheard another patient say something and repeated it. I just can't see him involved in Claire's murder. Because he *is* disorganized. Borderline intelligence. And whoever murdered Claire—and Richard—planned meticulously."

"That's assuming Peake really is that messed up."

"You think he's been faking all his life?"

"You tell me—is it possible?"

"Anything's *possible,* but I'd say it's highly unlikely. You're saying he's part of some murderous duo? Then why would he brag about it? On the other hand, a guy like that, withdrawn, never talks, someone might figure he's not tuned in, let down their guard around him, say something interesting. If that's what happened, maybe Peake can focus enough to tell you who it was."

"Back to Bedlam," he said. "Peachy."

We headed out of the park, toward our cars.

I said, "One thing's consistent with what we were just saying about Claire. Picking Peake as a project because she wanted serious pathology. But what if something else happened along the way? In her attempt to open Peake up, she opened *herself* up—had the poor judgment to talk about herself. In therapist jargon, it's called self-disclosure, and we're taught to be careful about it. But people mess up all the time—focusing on themselves instead of the patient. Claire's specialty was neuropsych. As a psychotherapist, she was a novice."

"She never got personal, but with Peake she related?"

"Precisely because Peake couldn't relate *back.*"

"So," he said, "she tells him something about a box, bad eyes . . . whatever the hell that means, and he spits it back."

"Maybe a box refers to some kind of bondage game."

"Back to dominance . . . You really see her that way?"

"I'm just throwing out suggestions," I said. "Maybe Claire selected Peake out of some great sense of compassion. Robin disagrees with my impression of Claire's house. She says it just sounds like Claire wanted privacy."

"Something else," he said. "Something that made my little heart go plink-a-plink when Heidi mentioned Peake's name. At Quantico, his case summary was passed around. I remember relatively seasoned guys looking at the photos and groaning; a couple had to leave the room. It was beyond butchery, Alex. I wasn't a hardened bastard yet. All I could do was skim."

He stopped so suddenly that I walked past him several steps.

"What?" I said.

"One of the photos," he said. "One of the kids. The older one. Peake took the eyes."

11.

WILLIAM SWIG SAID, "You think that *means* something?"

It was just after four P.M. and we were back in his office. Milo's unmarked was low on gas, so he left it at the park and I drove to Starkweather.

On the way, he made two calls on the cell phone. An attempt to reach the sheriff of Treadway, California, resulted in a rerouting to the voicemail system of a private security firm named Bunker Protection. Put on hold for several minutes, he finally got through. The brief conversation left him shaking his head.

"Gone," he said.

"The sheriff?"

"The whole damn town. It's a retirement community now, called Fairway Ranch. Bunker does the policing. I talked to some robocop with an attitude: 'All questions of that nature must be referred to national headquarters in Chicago.' "

The call to Swig connected, but when we arrived at the hospital's front gate, the guard hadn't been informed. Phoning Swig's office again finally got us in, but we had to wait awhile before Frank Dollard showed up to walk us across the yard. This time he barely greeted us. Impending evening hadn't tamed the heat. Only three men were out on the yard, one of them Chet, waving his huge hands wildly as he told stories to the sky.

The moment we passed through the end gate, Dollard stepped away and left us to enter the gray building alone. Swig was waiting just inside the door. He hurried us in to his office.

Now he tented his hands and rocked in his desk chair. "A box, eyes—this is obviously psychotic rambling. Why would you take it seriously, Doctor?"

"Even psychotics can have something to say," I said.

"Can they? I can't say I've found that to be the case."

"Maybe it's no big lead, sir," said Milo, "but it does bear follow-up."

Swig's intercom buzzed. He pressed a button and his secretary's voice said, "Bill? Senator Tuck."

"Tell him I'll call him back." Back to us: "So . . . all this comes via Heidi Ott?"

"Does she have credibility problems?" said Milo.

Another beep. Swig jabbed the button irritably. The secretary said, "Bill? Senator Tuck says no need to call him back, he was just reminding you of your aunt's birthday party this Sunday."

"Fine. Hold my calls. Please." Rolling back, Swig crossed his legs and showed us his ankles. Under his blue trousers he wore white sweat socks and brown, rubber-soled walkers. "State Senator Tuck's married to my mother's sister."

"That should help with funding," said Milo.

"On the contrary. State Senator Tuck doesn't approve of this place, thinks all our patients should be hauled outside and shot. His views on the matter harden especially during election years."

"Must make for spirited family parties."

"A blast," Swig said sourly. "Where was I . . . yes, Heidi. The thing to remember about Heidi is she's a rookie, and rookies can be impressionable. Maybe she heard something, maybe she didn't, but either way I can't believe it matters."

"Even though it's Ardis Peake we're talking about?"

"Him or anyone else. The point is, he's here. Locked up securely." Swig turned to me: "He's withdrawn, severely asocial, extremely dyskinesic, has a whole boatload of negative symptoms, rarely leaves his room. Since he's been with us he's never shown any signs whatsoever of any high-risk behavior."

"Does he receive mail?" said Milo.

"I'd tend to doubt it."

"But he might."

"I'd tend to doubt it," Swig repeated. "I'm sure when he was first committed there was some of the usual garbage— screwed-up women proposing marriage, that kind of thing. But now he's ancient history. Obscure, the way he should be. I'll tell you one thing: in the four years I've been here he's never received a visitor. In terms of his overhearing something, he has no friends among the other patients that I or anyone else on the staff is aware of. But what if he did? Anyone he might have overheard would be confined here, too."

"Unless someone's been released recently."

"No one's been released since Claire Argent came on board. I checked."

"I appreciate that."

"No problem," said Swig. "Our goal's the same: keep the citizens safe. Believe me, Peake's no threat to anyone."

"I'm sure you're right," said Milo. "But if he was receiving mail or sending it, no one on the staff would be monitoring it. Same with his phone calls—"

"No one would *officially* be monitoring content unless Peake acted out, but—" Swig held up a finger, punched four digits on his phone. "Arturo? Mr. Swig. Are you aware of any mail—letters, packages, postcards—anything arriving recently for Patient Three Eight Four Four Three? Peake, Ardis. Even junk mail . . . You're sure? Anything at all since you can remember? Keep an eye out, okay, Arturo? No, no authority for that, just let me know if anything shows up. Thanks."

He put the phone down. "Arturo's been here three years. Peake doesn't get mail. In terms of phone calls, I can't prove it to you, but believe me, nothing. He never comes out of his room. Doesn't talk."

"Pretty low-functioning."

"Subterranean."

"Any idea why Dr. Argent chose to work with Peake?"

"Dr. Argent worked with lots of patients. I don't believe

she gave Peake any special attention." His finger rose again. Springing up, he left the office, closing the door hard.

Milo said, "Helpful fellow, even though it kills him."

"As Heidi said, he thinks publicity's the kiss of death."

"I was wondering how such a young guy got to be in charge. Now I know. Uncle Senator may not approve of this place, but how much you wanna bet he had something to do with nephew getting the gig."

The door swung open and Swig bounded in, carrying a brown cardboard folder. Bypassing Milo, he handed it to me and sat down.

Peake's clinical chart. Thinner than I'd have predicted. Twelve pages, mostly medication notes signed by various psychiatrists, a few notations about the tardive dyskinesia: "T.D., no change." "T.D. intensifies, more lingual thrust." "T.D. Unsteady gait." Immediately after arriving at Starkweather, Peake had been placed on Thorazine, and for fifteen years he'd been kept on the drug. He'd also received several medications for the side effects: lithium carbonate, tryptophan, Narcan. "No change." "No behav. change." Everything but Thorazine had been phased out.

The last two pages bore four months of nearly identical weekly entries written in a small, neat hand:

"Indiv. sess. to monitor verb., soc., assess beh. plan. H. Ott assist. C. Argent, Ph.D."

I passed the chart to Milo.

"As you can see, Dr. Argent was monitoring his speech, not treating him," said Swig. "Probably measuring his response to medication, or something like that."

"How many other patients was she monitoring?" said Milo.

Swig said, "I don't know her total load, nor could I give you specific names without going through extensive review procedures." He held out his hand for the folder. Milo flipped pages for a second and returned it.

Milo said, "Did Dr. Argent seek out severely deteriorated patients?"

Swig rolled forward, placed his elbows on the desk,

expelled a short, pufflike laugh. "As opposed to? We don't house mild neurotics here."

"So Peake's just one of the guys."

"No one at Starkweather's one of the guys. These are dangerous men. We treat them as individuals."

"Okay," said Milo. "Thanks for your time. Now, may I please see Peake?"

Swig flushed. "For what purpose? We're talking barely functioning."

"At this point in my investigation, I'll take what I can get." Milo smiled.

Swig made the puffing sound again. "Look, I appreciate your dedication to your job, but I can't have you coming in here every time some theory emerges. Way too disruptive, and as I told you yesterday, it's obvious Dr. Argent's murder had nothing to do with Starkweather."

"The last thing I want to do is disrupt, sir, but if I ignored this, I'd be derelict."

Swig shook his head, poked at a mole, tried to smooth the fluff atop his bald head.

"We'll keep it short, Mr. Swig."

Swig dug a nail into his scalp. A crescent-shaped mark rose on the shiny white skin. "If I thought that would be the end of it, I'd say sure. But I get a clear sense you're hell-bent on finding your solution here."

"Not at all, sir. I just need to be thorough."

"All right," Swig said with sudden anger. He seemed to hurl himself upward. After fiddling with his tie, he took out a chrome ring filled with keys.

"Here we go," he said, jangling loudly. "Let's peek in on Mr. Peake."

On the ride up the elevator, Milo said, "Heidi Ott's not in any hot water, is she, sir?"

"Why would she be?"

"For telling me about Peake."

Swig said, "Am I going to be vindictive? Christ, no, of

course not. She was doing her civic duty. How could I be anything other than a proud administrator?"

"Sir—"

"Don't *worry,* Detective Sturgis. Too much worry is bad for the soul."

We got out on C Ward. Swig opened the double doors and we walked through.

"Room Fifteen S&R," he said. The halls were still crowded. Some of the inmates moved aside as we approached. Swig paid them no attention, walked briskly. Midway down the hall, he stopped and inspected the key ring. He was wearing short sleeves, and I noticed how muscled his forearms were. The bulky, sinewed arms of a laborer, not a bureaucrat.

Double dead bolts fastened the door. The hatch was also key-locked.

Milo said, "Fifteen S&R. Suppression and Restraint?"

"Not because he needs it," said Swig, still shuffling through the keys. "The S&R rooms are smaller, so when a patient lives alone we sometimes use them. He lives alone because his hygiene's not always what it should be." Swig began shoving keys up the ring. Finally, he found what he was looking for and stabbed both locks. The tumblers clicked; he held the door open six inches and looked inside.

Swinging it back, he said, "He's all yours."

Six-by-six space. Unlike the hallways, generous ceilings—ten feet high or close to it.

More of a tube than a room.

High on the walls were mounted thick metal rings—fasteners for the iron shackles now coiled up against the plaster like techno-sculpture.

Soft walls, pinkish white, covered with some kind of dull-looking foam. Faint scuff marks said the material couldn't be ripped.

Dim. The only light came through a tiny plastic window, a skinny, vertical rectangle that aped the shape of the room. Two round, recessed ceiling bulbs under thick plastic covers were turned off. No internal switch, just the one out in the hall. A lidless plastic toilet took up one corner. Precut strips of toilet paper littered the floor.

No nightstand, no real furniture, just two plastic drawers built into the foam walls. Molded. No hardware.

Music came from somewhere in the ceiling. Sugary strings and belching horns—some long-forgotten forties pop tune in a major key, done by a band that didn't care.

On a thin mattress attached to a raised plastic platform sat . . . something.

Naked from the waist up.

Skin the color of whey, blue-veined, hairless. Ribs so deeply etched they evoked a turkey carcass the day after Thanksgiving.

Khaki pants covered his bottom half, bagging on stick legs, stretching over knees as knobby as hand-carved canes. His feet were bare but dirty, the nails untrimmed and brown. His head was shaved clean. Black stubble specked his chin and cheeks. Very little stubble on top said he'd gone mostly bald.

His cranium was strangely contoured: very broad on top, the hairless skull flat at the apex, furrowed in several places, as if a child's fingers had dragged their way through white putty. Under a bulging shelf of a brow, his eyes were lost in moon-crater sockets. Gray lids, caved-in cheeks. Below the zygomatic arch, the entire face tapered radically, like a too-sharpened pencil.

The room smelled foul. Vinegary sweat, flatulence, burning rubber. Something dead.

The music played on, nice bouncy dance tune in waltz time.

"Ardis?" said Swig.

Peake's head stayed down. I bent low, caught a full view of his face. Tiny mouth, pinched, lipless. Suddenly it filled: a dark, wet tongue tip showing itself as a liver-colored oval. The tongue retreated. Reappeared. Peake's cheeks bellowed, caved in, inflated again. He rolled his neck to the left. Eyes closed, mouth open. Lots of teeth missing.

Swig stepped closer, came within three feet of the bed.

Peake's head dropped and he looked down at the floor

again. His nose was short, very thin—not much more than a wedge of cartilage—and bent up to the left. More putty, the child twisting capriciously. Large but lobeless ears flared battishly. Narrow, vein-encrusted hands ended in tentacle fingers that curled over his knees.

Living skeleton. I'd seen a face like that somewhere. . . .

Peake's tongue darted again. He started to rock. Moved his head from side to side. Rolled his neck. Blinked spasmodically. More tongue thrusts.

The mouth had flattened, gone two-dimensional. Moistened by saliva, the lips materialized—port-wine slash in the center of the triangle, vivid against the doughy skin.

It opened again and the tongue extended completely—thick, purplish, mottled, like some cave-dwelling slug.

It hung in the air. Curled. Wagged from side to side. Zipped back.

Out again. In again.

More neck-rolling.

I knew where I'd seen the face. Poster art from my college days. Edvard Munch's *The Scream*.

Hairless melting man clutching his face in primal mental agony. Peake could have posed for the painting.

His hands remained in his lap, but his upper body swayed, trembled, jerked a few times, seemed about to topple. Then he stopped. Righted himself.

Looked in our direction.

He'd butchered the Ardullos at age nineteen, making him thirty-five. He looked ancient.

"Ardis?" said Swig.

No reaction. Peake was staring in our direction but not making contact. He closed his eyes. Rolled his head. Another two minutes of tardive ballet.

Swig gave a disgusted look and waved his hand, as if to say, "You asked for it."

Milo ignored that and stepped closer. Peake began rocking faster, licking his lips, the tongue emerging, curling, retreating. Several toes on his left foot jumped. His left hand fluttered.

"Ardis, it's Mr. Swig. I've got some visitors for you."

Nothing.

Swig said, "Go ahead, Detective."

No response to "Detective."

I bent and got down at Peake's eye level. Milo did, too. Peake's eyes had remained closed. Tiny waves seemed to ruffle—eyeballs rolling behind gray skin. His chest was white and hairless, freckled with blackheads. Gray nipples— a pair of tiny ash piles. Up close the burning smell was stronger.

Milo said, "Hey," with surprising gentleness.

A few new shoulder tics, tongue calisthenics. Peake rolled his head, lifted his right hand, held it in midair, dropped it heavily.

"Hey," Milo repeated. "Ardis." His face was inches from Peake's. I got closer myself, still smelling the combustion but feeling no heat from Peake's body.

"My name's Milo. I'm here to ask you about Dr. Argent."

Peake's movements continued, autonomic, devoid of intent.

"Claire Argent, Ardis. Your doctor. I'm a homicide detective, Ardis. Homicide."

Not an errant eyeblink.

Milo said, "Ardis!" very loud.

Nothing. A full minute passed before the lids lifted. Halfway, then a full view of the eyes.

Black slots. Pinpoints of light at the center, but no definition between iris and white.

"Claire Argent," Milo repeated. "Dr. Argent. Bad eyes in a box."

The eyes slammed shut. Peake rolled his head, the tongue explored air. One toe jumped, this time on the right foot.

"Bad eyes," said Milo, nearly whispering, but his voice had gotten tight, and I knew he was fighting to keep the volume down. "Bad eyes in a box, Ardis."

Ten seconds, fifteen . . . half a minute.

"A box, Ardis. Dr. Argent in a box."

Peake's neuropathic ballet continued, unaltered.

"Bad eyes," Milo soothed.

I was looking into Peake's eyes, plumbing for some shred of soul.

Flat black; lights out.

A cruel phrase for mental disability came to mind: "no one home."

Once upon a time, he'd destroyed an entire family, speedily, lustily, a one-man plague.

Taking the eyes.

Now his eyes were twin portholes on a ship to nowhere.

No one home.

As if someone or something had snipped the wires connecting body to soul.

His tongue shot forward again. His mouth opened but produced no sound. I kept staring at him, trying to snag some kind of response. He looked through me—no, that implied too much effort.

He was, I was. No contact.

Neither of us was really there.

His mouth cratered, as if for a yawn. No yawn. Just a gaping hole. It stayed that way as his head craned. I thought of a blind newborn rodent searching for its mother's nipple.

The music from the ceiling switched to "Perfidia," done much too slowly. Ostentatious percussion that seemed to lag behind wah-wah trumpets.

Milo tried again, even softer, more urgent: "Dr. Argent, Ardis. Bad eyes in a box."

The tardive movements continued, random, arrhythmic. Swig tapped his foot impatiently.

Milo stood, knees cracking. I got to my feet, catching an eyeful of the chain on the wall. Coiled, like a sleeping python.

The room smelled worse.

Peake noticed none of it.

No behav. change.

12.

Outside the room, Swig said, "Satisfied?"

Milo said, "Why don't we give Heidi a try with him?"

"You've got to be kidding."

"Wish I was, sir."

Swig shook his head, but he hailed a tech standing across the hall. "Get Heidi Ott, Kurt."

Kurt hustled off and we waited among the inmates. Patients. Did it make a difference what you called them? I started to notice lots of tardive symptoms—a tremor here, lip work there—but nothing as severe as Peake's. Some of the men seemed oriented; others could have been on another planet. Shuffling feet in paper slippers. Food stains on clothing.

Swig went into the nursing station, used the phone, glanced at his watch. He was back just as Heidi Ott came through the double doors.

"Hello, Heidi."

"Sir?"

"Because of the information you provided, Detective Sturgis has been trying unsuccessfully to communicate with Ardis Peake. Since you've got a track record, why don't you give it a shot?"

"Sir, I—"

"Don't worry," said Swig. "Your sense of duty is beyond reproach. The main thing is, let's get to the bottom of this."

"I—"

100

"One thing before you go in there. You're sure Peake actually spoke to you—real words, not just grunts."

"Yes, sir."

"Tell me exactly what he said."

Heidi repeated the story.

"And this was the day before Dr. Argent died?"

"Yes, sir."

"Had Peake talked to you before?"

"Not about Dr. Argent."

"What did he say?"

"Nothing much. Mostly mumbles. Yeah, no, nods, grunts. When we asked him questions." Tug on the ponytail. "Nothing, really. That's why I paid attention to when he did start—"

"You were monitoring his speech."

"Yes, sir. Dr. Argent was hoping she might be able to increase his verbal output. His behavioral output in general."

"I see," said Swig. "Any particular reason she wanted to do that?"

Heidi glanced at us. "Like I told these gentlemen, she said he was a challenge."

A faint, scraping sound grew louder, and we all turned. Paper soles on linoleum. A few of the men in the hall had drifted closer. Swig looked at them and they stopped. Retreated.

He smiled at Heidi. "Looks like you've got the challenge, now."

She went in alone, stayed for twenty minutes, emerged, shaking her head. "How long do you want me to try?"

"That'll be enough," said Swig. "It was probably just an isolated incident. Meaningless rambling. For all we know, he does that when he's alone. Thanks, Heidi. You can get back to work. We'd all better get back to work."

As I drove off the grounds, Milo said, "What the hell turns a human being into *that*?"

"Answer that and you've got the Nobel," I said.

"But we've got to be talking biology, right? No amount of

stress can do that." The air-conditioning was on, but sweat dripped off his nose and spotted his trousers.

"Even in concentration camps people rarely went mad from suffering," I said. "And schizophrenia has the same prevalence in nearly every society—two to four percent. Cultural factors influence how madness is expressed, but they don't cause it."

"So what is it—brain damage, genetics?"

"The highest risk factor is having a relative with schizophrenia, but only a very small percentage of schizophrenics' relatives become ill. Slightly more schizophrenics are born during winter and spring, when virus levels are higher. Some studies have implicated prenatal influenza. It's all speculation."

"Hell," he said, "maybe it's just bad luck."

He wiped his face with a tissue, pulled out a panatela, unwrapped it, and jammed it in his mouth, but didn't light up.

"I had a couple crazy relatives," he said. "Two aunts—my mother's cousins. Loony Letitia had this thing for baking, did it nonstop. Cookies every day, hundreds of them. She ended up spending all her money on flour and sugar and eggs, started neglecting herself, trying to steal ingredients from the neighbors. They finally put her away."

"Sounds more like manic behavior than schizophrenia," I said. "Anyone ever try her on lithium?"

"This was years ago, Alex. She died in the asylum—choked on her dinner, how's that for a bad joke? Then there was Aunt Renee, stumbling around the neighborhood, looking like a mess. She lived till she was pretty old, died in some county facility."

He laughed. "That's my pedigree."

"I had a schizophrenic cousin," I said. Brett, two years my senior, son of my father's older brother. As children we'd played together. Brett had competed fiercely, cheated chronically. During college he metamorphosed from a Young Republican to an SDS honcho. By his senior year he was an unwashed, silent recluse who accumulated narcotics arrests, dropped out of sight for five years, finally ended up in an Iowa board-and-care home. I assumed he was still alive. There'd been no contact between us for over two decades. Our fathers hadn't been close. . . .

"There you go," said Milo. "Tainted stock. Starkweather, here we come."

"Starkweather's only for the chosen few," I said.

"Bad little madmen. So what makes crazy people violent?"

"Another Nobel question. The main ingredients seem to be alcohol and drug use and a strong delusional system. But not necessarily paranoia. Psychotics who kill usually aren't trying to protect themselves from attack. They're more likely to be acting on some paranormal or religious delusion—waging war against Satan, battling space aliens."

"Wonder what Peake's mission was."

"God only knows," I said. "Dope and booze were obviously in play. Maybe he thought the Ardullos were mantises from Pluto. Or nineteen years of twisted sexual impulses finally exploded. Or a random circuit in his brain shorted out. We just don't know why some psychotics blow."

"Great. I'll never be out of work." His voice drifted off.

"In one sense," I said, "Peake's typical. Schizophrenic breaks occur most frequently in young adulthood. And long before Peake fell apart, he'd been showing signs of schizotypy—it's a fancy name for oddness. Low mental skills, social ineptitude, poor grooming, eccentricities. Some eccentrics stay mildly strange, others move on to full-blown schizophrenia."

"Oddness," he said. "Take a walk in the park, walk out of a restaurant, there're some *odd* guys wanting spare change. Which one's gonna start wielding the cleaver?"

I didn't answer.

He said, "If Peake had any sort of thought system, he must have been in a helluva lot better shape than what we saw today."

"Probably. Though behind all the tardive symptoms there could still be some thinking going on."

"What does 'tardive' mean, exactly?"

"Late-onset. It's a reaction to Thorazine."

"Is it reversible?"

"No. At best, he won't get worse."

"And he's still crazy. So what good's the Thorazine doing him?"

"Neuroleptics are best at controlling delusions, hallucinations, bizarre behavior. What psychiatrists call the positive symptoms of schizophrenia. The negatives—poor speech, flat mood, apathy, attentional problems—don't usually respond. Drugs can't put back what's missing."

"Well-behaved vegetables," he said.

"Peake's an extreme case, possibly because he didn't start out with that much intellect. His T.D.'s also very severe. Though he's not getting that much Thorazine. Despite what Dollard told us about high-dosing, Peake's prescription has remained at five hundred milligrams, well within the recommended range. They probably haven't needed to high-dose him because he behaves himself. Behaves very little. Psychologically, he's disappeared."

Milo removed the cigar, placed it between his index fingers, and sighted over the tobacco bridge. "If Peake was taken off Thorazine, would he be able to talk more?"

"It's possible. But he could also fall apart, maybe even revert to violence. And don't forget, he was on Thorazine when he talked to Heidi. So he's capable of speech while medicated. Are you still taking this in-a-box stuff seriously?"

"Nah. . . . I guess I can't get away from the eye thing—hey, maybe *I'm* delusional and Peake's a true prophet. Maybe Satan *has* dispatched the Pluto Mantises."

"Maybe," I said, "but would he inform Peake?"

He laughed, chewed the cigar some more. " 'Bad eyes in a box.' "

"For all we know, Claire tried talking to him about his crime and sparked some kind of memory. 'In a box' could mean his own incarceration. Or something else. Or nothing at all."

"Okay, okay, enough of this," he said, pocketing the cigar. "Back to basics: check out Claire's finances and Stargill's. Go over Richard's file again, too. For the hundredth time, but maybe there's something I missed. And if you're not jammed, now's as good a time as any to go see Dr. Theobold at County. Maybe one of us will come up with something remotely resembling a factoid."

He grinned. "Lacking that, I'll settle for some juicy delusions."

13.

I called Dr. Myron Theobold's office and got an appointment for ten-fifteen the next morning. By nine-forty-five I was clearing my head in the fast lane of the 10 East, enduring the crawl to the interchange, moving with the smog stream toward San Bernardino. I got off a few exits later, on Soto Street in East L.A., drove past the county morgue, and pulled into the main entrance of the dun-colored metropolis that was County General Hospital.

Perenially underfunded and overstressed, County's a wonder: first-rate medicine for the tired and the poor, last stop for the hopeless and the addled. I'd done some clinical training here, taught occasional seminars, but it had been two years since I'd set foot on the hospital campus. Outwardly, little had changed—the same sprawl of bulky, homely buildings, the constant parade of people in uniforms, the halting march of the ill.

One of those hot, overcast days that makes everything look decayed, but after Starkweather, County seemed fresh, almost perky.

Theobold's office was on the third floor of Unit IV, one of the half-dozen no-frills annexes sprouting at the rear of the complex like afterthoughts. Dazed-looking men and women in open-backed pajamas wandered white-tiled halls. Two grim nurses escorted a heavy black woman toward an open door. IV's in both her arms. Tears marked her cheeks like dew on asphalt. In an unseen place, someone retched. The overhead pager recited names emotionlessly.

Theobold's secretary occupied a space not much bigger

than Peake's cell, surrounded by gunmetal filing cabinets. A stuffed Garfield clung to the handle of one drawer. Empty chair. A note said, "Back in 15 min."

Theobold must have heard me enter because he stuck his head out of the rear doorway. "Dr. Delaware? Come on in."

I'd met him a few years ago, and he hadn't changed much. Sixtyish, medium height and build, graying fair hair, white beard, large nose, close-set brown eyes behind aviator specs. He wore a wide-lapeled herringbone sport coat the color of iced tea, a beige vest checked with blue, a white shirt, a blue tie.

I followed him into his office. He was a psychiatry vice-chairman and a respected neurochemistry researcher, but his space wasn't much more generous than the secretary's. Haphazardly furnished with what looked like castoffs, it sported another collection of file cases, brown metal furniture, a storm of books. An attempt to freshen things up with a faux-Navajo rug had failed long ago; the rug's threads were unraveling, its color bands fading. The desk supported a turbulent swirl of paperwork.

Theobold squeezed behind the desk and I took one of the two metal chairs wrinkling the fake Navajo.

"So," he said. "It's been a while. You're still officially faculty, aren't you?"

"Courtesy faculty," I said. "No salary."

"How long since you've been down here?"

"Couple of years," I said. His attempts at cordiality were deepening the lines on his face. "I appreciate your seeing me."

"No problem." He cleared the area around the phone. Papers flew. "I had no idea you led such an interesting life—police consultant. Do they pay well?"

"About the same as Medi-Cal."

He managed a chuckle. "So what have you been up to, otherwise? Still at Western Peds?"

"Occasionally. I do some consulting, mostly legal work. A few short-term treatment cases."

"Able to deal with the HMO's?"

"I avoid them when I can."

He nodded. "So . . . you're here about poor Claire. I suppose that detective thought I'd confide secrets to you that I withheld from him, but there's really nothing more to tell."

"I think he felt it was more a matter of knowing the right questions to ask."

"I see," he said. "Persistent type, Sturgis. Smarter than he lets on. He tried to disarm me by playing to class consciousness—'I'm the humble working-class cop, you're the big smart doctor.' Interesting approach. Does it work?"

"He's got a good solve rate."

"Good for him. . . . The problem is, he was wasting his acting talents on me. I wasn't holding back. I have no inside information about Claire. I knew her as a researcher, not as a person."

"Everyone seems to say that about her."

"Well, then," he said, "at least I'm consistent. So no one has much to offer about her?"

I nodded.

"And here I thought it was me—the way I run my projects."

"What do you mean?"

"I like to think of myself as a humane administrator. Hire good people, trust them to do their jobs, for the most part keep my hands off. I don't get involved in their personal lives. I'm not out to parent anyone."

He stopped, as if expecting me to pass judgment on that.

I said, "Claire worked for you for six years. She must have liked that."

"I suppose."

"How'd you find her?"

"I'd put in for my grant and she applied for the neuropsych position. She was completing a postdoc at Case Western, had published two papers as a grad student, sole author. Nothing earth-shattering, but encouraging. Her interest—alcoholism and reaction times—meshed with mine. No shortage of alcoholics here. I thought she'd be able to attract her own funding, and she did."

All facts I'd read in Claire's résumé.

"So she worked with you and on her own research."

"Twenty-five percent of her time was her research; the rest she spent on my longitudinal study of neuroleptic outcomes— NIMH grant, three experimental drugs plus placebo, double-blind. She tested the patients, helped organize the data. We just got renewed for five more years. I just hired her replacement—bright kid from Stanford, Walter Yee."

"Who else worked on the study?" I said.

"Three research fellows besides Claire—two M.D.'s, one Ph.D. pharmacologist."

"Was she friendly with any of them?"

"I wouldn't know. As I said, I don't meddle. It's not one of those situations where we fraternize after hours."

"Five-year renewal," I said. "So there was no financial reason for her to leave."

"Not in the least. She probably could've renewed her own study, too. She had substance-abuse money from NIH, completed the final study before she left. Inconclusive results, but well run, very decent chance. But she never applied." He glanced upward. "Never even told me she was allowing the grant to lapse."

"So she must have been intending to leave for some time."

"Looks that way. I was pretty irritated at her. For not wanting to follow through. For not communicating. Irked at myself, too, for not staying in touch. If she'd come to me, most likely I'd have been able to raise her to full-time, or to find her something else. She was very good at what she did. Dependable, no complaints. I managed to get Dr. Yee on full-time. But she never bothered to— I suppose you're right. She wanted to leave. I have no idea why."

"So she never complained."

"Not once. Even the way she told me she was leaving—no personal meeting; she just sent in a summary of her data with a note that the grant was finished and so was she."

That reminded me of the way she'd divorced Joe Stargill.

"Who'd she work with on her own grant?"

"She got part-time secretarial help from the main pool, ran

all her own studies, analyzed her own data. That was also irksome. I'm sure she could've applied for ancillary funding, brought more money into the department, but she always wanted to work by herself. I suppose I should be grateful. She took care of herself, never bothered me for anything. The last thing I need is someone who requires hand-holding. Still . . . I suppose I should've paid more attention."

"A loner," I said.

"But all of us are. In my group. I didn't think I'd been hiring antisocial types, but perhaps on some level . . ." Wide smile. "Did you know I started as an analyst?"

"Really."

"You bet, classical Freudian, couch and all. This"—he touched the beard—"used to be a very analytic goatee. I attended the institute right after residency, got halfway through—hundreds of hours cultivating the proper 'hmm'—before I realized it wasn't for me. Wasn't for anyone, in my estimation, except possibly Woody Allen. And look at the shape *he's* in. I quit, enrolled in the biochem Ph.D. program at USC. I'm sure those choices mean something psychodynamically, but I'd rather not waste time trying to figure out what. Claire seemed to me the same way—scientific, focused on reality, self-possessed. Still, she must have been terribly unhappy here."

"Why do you say that?"

"Leaving for a place like *that*. Have you been there?"

"Yesterday."

"What's it like?"

"Highly structured. Lots of high-dose medication."

"Brave new world," he said. "I can't see why Claire would have wanted that."

"Maybe she craved clinical work."

"Nonsense," he said sharply. Then he smiled apologetically. "What I mean is, she could've had all the clinical work she wanted right here. No, I must have missed something."

"Could I talk to the other fellows?" I said.

"Why not? Walt Yee didn't know her, of course, and I don't believe Shashi Lakshman did, either—he's the pharmacologist, has his own lab in a separate building. But maybe she interfaced with the M.D.'s—Mary Hertzlinger and Andy Velman. Let me call Shashi first."

A few seconds on the phone confirmed that Dr. Lakshman had never met Claire. We took the stairs down to a second-floor lab and found Doctors Hertzlinger and Velman typing at personal computers.

Both psychiatric fellows were in their thirties and had on white coats. Mary Hertzlinger wore a short brown dress under hers. She was thin, with cropped platinum-blond hair, ivory skin, well-formed but chapped lips. Andrew Velman's coat was buttoned up high, revealing a black shirt collar and the tight knot of a lemon-yellow tie. He was short, broad, with black wavy hair, a gold stud in his left ear.

I asked them about Claire.

Velman spoke first, in a clipped voice. "Virtual stranger. I've been here two years and maybe we exchanged twenty sentences. She always seemed too busy to hang out. Also, I do the structured clinical interviews on the study and she did the neuropsych testing, so at any given time, we'd be with different patients."

"Did she ever say why she was leaving to work at Starkweather?"

"No," he said. "I didn't even know about that until Mary told me." He glanced at Hertzlinger. So did Theobold.

She held her coat closed with one hand and said, "She told me a few days before she left." Low, smooth voice. "I had a really small office on the floor below, and she asked me if I wanted hers. I went to look at it and said yes, helped her carry some boxes to her car. She said her grant had run out and she hadn't tried to renew it. She'd just written a note informing Dr. Theobold."

Theobold said, "What reason did she give you, Mary?"

"None."

"What was her mood when she told you?" I said.

"Pretty calm. Not agitated or upset . . . I'd have to describe her as calm and deliberate. As if she'd planned it for a while, was at peace with it."

"Time to move on," said Velman.

"Did you socialize with her?" I asked Hertzlinger.

She shook her head. "Same thing as Andy—we had almost no contact. I've only been here a year. We saw each other in the cafeteria and had coffee. Maybe three, four times. Never lunch. I never saw her *eat* lunch. Sometimes when I was on my way out to the caf, I'd pass her office and her door would be open and she'd be at her desk working. I remember thinking, *What a work ethic, she must be extremely productive.*"

"The times you did have coffee," I said, "what did you talk about?"

"Work, data. After I found out what happened to her, I realized how little I knew about her. It's so grotesque—do the police have any idea who did it?"

"Not yet."

"Terrible," she said.

Velman said, "Had to have something to do with Starkweather. Look at the patient population she got herself involved with."

I said, "Only problem is, the patients don't get out."

"Never?"

"So they claim."

He frowned.

"Did she tell either of you that she was going to Starkweather?"

Velman shook his head.

Mary Hertzlinger said, "She told me. The day we moved the boxes. It surprised me, but I didn't question her—she was like that. You didn't get personal with her."

"Did she give a reason?" I said.

"Not really a reason," she said. "But she did say something . . . uncharacteristically flippant. We'd just loaded the car. She thanked me, wished me luck, and then she smiled. Almost *smugly.*"

"What was funny?" said Theobold.

"Exactly," said Hertzlinger. "I said something to the effect that 'I'm glad you're pleased about your plans.' That's when she said it: 'It's not a matter of being pleased, Mary. So many madmen, so little time.' "

14.

"SHE WAS IN a big damn hurry to work with psychotics?" said Milo.

It was noon. We were standing next to the Seville, on Butler Avenue, across from the West L.A. station.

"She had plenty of psychotics at County," I said. "She wanted *madmen*."

"Why? To squeeze a few more syllables out of them? To hell with all that, Alex, I'm concentrating on the boring stuff for now. Located a safe-deposit box at her bank, actually managed to finagle my way in with the death certificate. No cash, no dope, no B&D videos, no drooling letters from psycho pen pals. Stone empty. So if she did have some secret life going, she kept it very well wrapped."

"Maybe we should go back further—grad school, the years before she moved to L.A. I can try talking to someone at Case Western."

"Sure, but tomorrow you'll have a chance at something better. Her parents are arriving on the red-eye tonight. I have a date with them at eight A.M. down at the morgue. No need for them to view the body, tried to talk them out of it, but they insisted. After all that fun, I'll try to sit down with them. I'll give you a call where and when. Probably be late afternoon."

Several young officers walked by. He watched them for a while, stared at the roof of the Seville, flicked dirt off the vinyl. "Reviewing Richard's file was sobering. Not as much of a file as I remembered. The only people I spoke to were Richard's landlady and parents and the staff at the restaurant where he worked. No listings in the 'Known Associates' column. Sound familiar? I made another try at locating the film outfit that Richard might've auditioned for—Thin Line. Still can't find a trace of them. You'd think even a rinky-dink outfit would make a mark somewhere."

"Something about the movie bothers you?"

"They've got carpenters on movie sets, right? All sorts of tools, including saws."

"Plenty of knives in restaurants, too."

"Maybe I'll go back there."

"One possible angle on Thin Line," I said. "Even fly-by-nights need equipment. A small outfit would be likely to rent rather than own. Why not check some of the leasing companies?"

"Very good," he said. "Thank you, sir." He laughed. "Any other case I wouldn't consider the film thing half a lead. But these two—you don't wanna blame the victim, Alex, but the least they could've done is *relate* to someone."

I wanted another look at Claire's résumé, so the two of us crossed over to the station and walked upstairs to the detectives' room. Milo retrieved the box of material he'd taken from Claire's house. He hadn't booked it into the evidence room, meaning he'd planned some review himself. He left to get a cup of coffee while I searched.

I found the résumé near the middle, neatly typed and stapled. The Wite-Out in the "Marital Status" slot was a chalky lozenge. She'd been born in Pittsburgh, lived there through college before moving to Cleveland to attend Case Western.

Thousands of miles from Richard Dada's Arizona childhood, little chance of a connection there.

I scrounged until I found the first study she'd published— the student research that had impressed Myron Theobold.

Solo author, just as he'd said, but at the bottom of the first page, in very small print, were acknowledgments and thanks: "To the Case Western Graduate Fund for supplies and data analysis; to my parents, Ernestine and Robert Ray Argent, for their unwavering support throughout my education; and to my dissertation chairman, Professor Harry I. Racano, for his thoughtful guidance."

One P.M. in L.A. was four in Cleveland. Using Milo's phone, I dialed 216 Information. None of the other detectives paid notice to a civilian using city equipment. Scrawling the number for Case Western's psychology department, I called and asked for Professor Racano.

The woman at the other end said, "I'm sorry, but there's no one here by that name."

"He used to be on the faculty."

"Let me check our faculty directory." Several moments passed. "No, I'm sorry, sir, not in the current directory or the emeritus list."

"Is there anyone around who worked in the department ten years ago?"

Silence. "Hold on, please."

Another five minutes before another woman said, "May I ask what this is about?"

"I'm calling from the Los Angeles Police Department." Literally. "Unfortunately, one of your alumnae, Dr. Claire Argent, was murdered, and we're trying to locate anyone who might have known her back in Cleveland."

"Oh," she said. "Murdered. . . . My God, that's terrible. . . . Argent. No, I've only been here six years, she must have been before my time—how terrible, let me check." I heard paper shuffling. "Yes, here she is, on the alumni roster. And she was Professor Racano's student?"

"Yes, ma'am."

"Well, I'm sorry to tell you Professor Racano's deceased as well. Died right after I came on. Cancer. Nice man. Very supportive of his students."

Racano's tolerance of Claire's solo launch suggested an easygoing nature.

"Is there anyone who might have known Dr. Argent, Ms. . . . ?"

"Mrs. Bausch. Hmm, I'm afraid there aren't too many people in the building right now. There's a big symposium going on over at the main auditorium, one of our professors just won a prize. I can ask around and get back to you."

"I'd appreciate that." I gave her Milo's name. Just as I put the phone down, it rang. Milo was nowhere in sight so I took the call. "Detective Sturgis's desk."

A familiar voice said, "I'd like to leave a message for Detective Sturgis."

"Heidi? It's Dr. Delaware."

"Oh . . . hi—listen, I'm sorry I couldn't get anything out of Peake today."

"Don't worry about it."

"It didn't help my credibility with Swig, either. After you were gone he called me into his office and made me go over the whole thing again: what Peake said, when he said it, was I sure I heard right."

"Sorry for the hassle."

"It would've sure been nice to be able to prove it. . . . Anyway, I just wanted to call to let Detective Sturgis know I've decided to leave Starkweather in a couple of weeks, but if there's anything else he needs, he can call me."

"Thanks, Heidi. I'll tell him."

"So," she said, "you actually work there? Right at the police station?"

"No. I just happen to be here today."

"Sounds interesting. Meanwhile, I'll keep trying with Peake, maybe something will come up."

"Don't put yourself in any jeopardy."

"What, from Ardis? You saw his condition. Not exactly dangerous. Not that I let my guard down—do you think Claire did?"

"Don't know," I said.

"I keep thinking about her. What happened to her. It seems so strange that anything could touch her."

"What do you mean?"

"She seemed like one of those people—caught up in their own worlds. Like she was happy being alone. Didn't *need* anyone else."

15.

I CALLED HOME before leaving the station. Robin was out, and all that awaited me was paperwork—final reports on custody cases that had already been decided. I told my own voice on the message machine that I'd be back by five.

Talking to myself.

Put a cell phone in a psychotic's hand and he could fake normalcy.

The encounter with Ardis Peake had stayed with me.

Monster.

Hard to connect that mute, emaciated husk with someone capable of destroying an entire family.

What better endorsement for Mr. Swig's highly structured system?

What turns a human being into that?

I'd given Milo the short-version lecture and he'd been gracious enough not to complain. But I had no real answers; no one did.

I wondered what questions had led Claire to Starkweather. And Peake. She'd gravitated to him shortly after taking the job. Why, of all the madmen, had *he* been the one whose pathology had drawn her in?

The other thing that troubled me was Peake's assault on the eyes of the little Ardullo girl. Had I been too hasty minimizing his gibbering at Heidi?

Or perhaps it was simple: Claire had learned about the eyes and discussed it with him. Had it elicited something in him—guilt, excitement, a horrible nostalgia?

Bad eyes in a box. Was the box a coffin? Peake's imagery of

118

the dead child. Reliving the crime and feeding off the memory, the way lust killers did?

It all hinged on learning more about Claire, and so far her ghost had avoided capture.

No entanglements, no known associates. Not much impact on her world.

Ardis Peake, on the other hand, had been a star in his day.

I drove to Westwood and used the computers at the U's research library to look up the Ardullo massacre. The murders had been covered nationally for one week. The periodicals index offered half a page of citations, and I went looking for microfiche.

Most of the articles were nearly identically worded, lifted intact from wire service reports. An arrest headshot showed a young Peake, stick-faced, hollow-cheeked, sporting a full head of long, stringy, dark hair.

Wild-eyed, startled, a cornered animal. The Edvard Munch screamer on jet fuel.

A large bruise spread beneath his left eye. The left side of his face swelled. Rough arrest? If so, it hadn't been reported.

The facts were as I remembered them. Multiple stab wounds, crushing skull fractures, extensive mutilation, cannibalism. The articles filled in names and places.

Scott and Theresa Ardullo, thirty-three and twenty-nine, respectively. Married six years, both UC Davis agricultural grads. He, "the scion of a prosperous farming family," had developed an interest in winegrowing but concentrated on peaches and walnuts.

Brittany, five years old.

Justin, eight months.

Next came the happier-times family photo: Scott hand in hand with a restless-looking little girl who resembled her mother, Theresa holding the baby. Pacifier in Justin's mouth, fat cheeks ballooning around the nipple. Ferris wheel in the background, some kind of fair.

Scott Ardullo had been muscular, blond, crew-cut, grinning with the full pleasure of one who believes himself blessed.

His wife, slender, somewhat plain, with long dark hair held in place by a white band, seemed less certain about happy endings.

I couldn't bear another look at the children's faces.

No picture of Noreen Peake, just an account of the way she'd been found, sitting at the kitchen table. My imagination added the smell of apples, cinnamon, flour.

A ranch superintendent named Teodoro Alarcon had found Noreen's body, then discovered the rest of it. He'd been placed under sedation.

No quote from him.

Treadway's sheriff, Jacob Haas, said: "I served in Korea and this was worse than anything I ever saw overseas. Scott and Terri took those people in out of the goodness of their hearts and this is how they get repaid. It's beyond belief."

Anonymous townspeople cited Peake's strange habits— he mumbled to himself, didn't bathe, cruised alleys, pawed through garbage cans, ate trash. Everyone had known of his fondness for sniffing propellants. No one had thought him dangerous.

One other attributed quote:

" 'Everyone always knew he was weird, but not that weird,' said a local youth, Derrick Crimmins. 'He didn't hang out with anyone. No one wanted to hang with him because he smelled bad and he was just too weird, maybe into Satan or something.' "

No other mention of satanic rituals, and I wondered if there'd been any follow-up. Probably not, with Peake out of circulation.

Treadway was labeled a "quiet farming and ranching community."

" 'The worst things we usually have,' said Sheriff Haas, 'are bar fights, once in a while some equipment theft. Nothing like this, never anything like this.' "

And that was it.

No coverage of the Ardullos' funeral, or Noreen Peake's.

I kept spooling, found a three-line paragraph in the L.A.

Times two months later reporting Peake's commitment to Starkweather.

Using "Treadway" as a keyword pulled up nothing since the murders.

Quiet town. Extinct town.

How did an entire community die?

Had Peake somehow killed it, too?

Milo called in a message while I was out on my morning run:

"Mr. and Mrs. Argent, the Flight Inn on Century Boulevard, Room 129, one P.M."

I did some paperwork, set out at twelve-thirty, taking Sepulveda toward the airport. Century's a wide, sad strip that cuts through southern L.A. Turn east off the freeway and you might end up in some gang gully, carjacked or worse. West takes you to LAX, past the bleak functionalism of airport hotels, cargo depots, private parking lots, topless joints.

The Flight Inn sat next to a Speedy Express maintenance yard. Too large to be a motel, it hadn't passed through hotel puberty. Three stories of white-painted block, yellow gutters, cowgirl-riding-an-airplane logo, inconspicuous entry off to the right topped by a pink neon VACANCY sign. The bi-level self-park wrapped itself around the main building. No security in the lot that I could see. I left the Seville in a ground-floor space and walked to the front as a 747 roared overhead.

A banner out in front advertised king-size beds, color TV, and discount coupons to happy hour at someplace called the Golden Goose. The lobby was red-carpeted, furnished with vending machines selling combs and maps and keychains with Disney characters on the fobs. The black clerk at the counter ignored me as I strolled down the white-block hall. Fast-food cartons had been left outside several of the red doors that lined the corridor. The air was hot and salty, though we were miles from the ocean. Room 129 was at the back.

Milo answered my knock, looking weary.

No progress, or something else?

The room was small and boxy, the decor surprisingly

cheery: twin beds under blue quilted floral covers that appeared new, floating-mallard prints above the headboard, a fake-colonial writing desk sporting a Bible and a phone book, a pair of hard-padded armchairs, nineteen-inch TV mounted on the wall. Two black nylon suitcases were placed neatly in one corner. Two closed plywood doors, chipped at the bottom, faced the bed. Closet and bathroom.

The woman perched on a corner of the nearer bed had the too-good posture of paralyzing grief. Handsome, early sixties, cold-waved hair the color of weak lemonade, white pearlescent glasses on a gold chain around her neck, conservative makeup. She wore a chocolate-brown dress with a pleated bottom, and white piqué collar and cuffs. Brown shoes and purse. Diamond-chip engagement ring, thin gold wedding band, gold scallop-shell earrings.

She turned toward me. Firm, angular features held their own against gravity. The resemblance to Claire was striking, and I thought of the matron Claire would never become.

Milo made the introductions. Ernestine Argent and I said "Pleased to meet you" at exactly the same time. One side of her mouth twitched upward; then her lips jammed shut—a smile reflex dying quickly. I shook a cold, dry hand. A toilet flushed behind one of the plywood doors and she returned her hands to her lap. On the bed nearby was a white linen handkerchief folded into a triangle.

The door opened and a man, drying his hands with a hand towel, struggled to emerge.

Working at it because he could barely fit through the doorway.

No more than five-seven, he had to weigh close to four hundred pounds, a pink egg dressed in a long-sleeved white shirt, gray slacks, white athletic shoes. The bathroom was narrow and he had to edge past the sink to get out. Breathing deeply, he winced, took several small steps, finally squeezed through. The effort reddened his face. Folding the towel, he tossed it onto the counter and stepped forward very slowly, rocking from side to side, like a barge in choppy water.

The trousers were spotless poly twill, held up by clip-on

suspenders. The athletic shoes appeared crushed. Each step made something in his pocket jingle.

He was around the same age as his wife, had a full head of dark, curly hair, a fine, almost delicate nose, a full-lipped mouth pouched by bladder cheeks. Three chins, shaved close. Brown eyes nearly buried in flesh managed to project a pin-point intensity. He looked at his wife, studied me, continued to lumber.

Mentally paring away adipose, I was able to visualize handsome structure. He pressed forward, perspiring, breathing hard and raspy. When he reached me, he stopped, swayed, righted himself, stuck out a ham-hock arm.

His hands were smallish, his grip dry and strong.

"Robert Ray Argent." A deep, wheezy voice, like a bass on reverb, issued from the echo chamber of his enormous body cavity. For a second, I imagined him hollow, inflated. But that fantasy faded as I watched him struggle to get to the nearer bed. Every step sounded on the thin carpeting, each limb seemed to shimmy of its own accord. His forehead was beaded, dripping. I resisted the urge to take his elbow.

His wife got up with the handkerchief and wiped his brow.

He touched her hand for an instant. "Thanks, honey."

"Sit down, Rob Ray."

Both of them with that soft, distinctive Pittsburgh drawl.

Moving slowly, bending deliberately, he lowered himself. The mattress sank down to the box spring and creaked. The box spring nearly touched the carpet. Rob Ray Argent sat, spread-legged, inner thighs touching. The gray fabric of his pants stretched shiny over dimpled knees, pulled up taut over a giant pumpkin of a belly.

He inhaled a few times, cleared his throat, put his hand to his mouth, and coughed. His wife stared off at the open bathroom door before walking over, closing it, sitting back down.

"So," he said. "You're a psychologist, like Claire." Dark circles under his armpits.

"Yes," I said.

He nodded, as if we'd reached some agreement. Sighed and placed his hands on the apex of his abdomen.

Ernestine Argent reached over and handed him the hand-kerchief and he dabbed at himself some more. She pulled another white triangle from her purse and pecked at her own eyes.

Milo said, "I was just telling Mr. and Mrs. Argent about the course of the investigation."

Ernestine gave a small, involuntary cry.

"Honey," Robert Ray said.

She said, "I'm okay, darling," almost inaudibly, and turned to me. "Claire loved psychology."

I nodded.

"She was all we ever *really* had."

Rob Ray looked at her. Parts of his face had turned plum-colored; other sections were pink, beige, white—apple-peel mottle caused by the variable blood flow through expanses of skin. He turned to Milo. "Doesn't sound like you've learned much. What's the chance you find the devil who did it?"

"I'm always optimistic, sir. The more you and Mrs. Argent can tell us about Claire, the better our chances."

"What else can we tell you?" said Ernestine. "No one disliked Claire; she was the nicest person."

She cried. Rob Ray touched her shoulder with his hand.

"I'm sorry," she finally said. "This isn't helping. What do you need to know?"

"Well," said Milo, "let's get a basic time frame, for starters. When was the last time you saw Claire?"

"Christmas," said Rob Ray. "She always came home for Christmas. We always had a nice family time, no exception last Christmas. She helped her mother with the cooking. Said in L.A. she never cooked, too busy, just ate things out of cans, takeout."

Consistent with the kitchen at Cape Horn Drive.

"Christmas," said Milo. "Half a year ago."

"That's right." Rob Ray flexed his left foot.

"That would be right around the time Claire left County Hospital and moved to Starkweather Hospital."

"Guess so."

Milo said, "Did she talk about changing jobs?"

Headshakes.

"Nothing at all?"

More silence.

Ernestine said, "She never talked about her work in specifics. We never wanted to be nosy."

They hadn't known. I watched Milo hide his amazement. Rob Ray tried to shift his weight on the bed. One leg cooperated.

Milo said, "Did Claire talk about any sort of problems she might be having? Someone who was giving her difficulty—at work or anywhere else?"

"No," said Rob Ray. "She had no enemies. That I can tell you for sure."

"How did she act during her Christmas visit?"

"Fine. Normal. Christmas was always a happy time for us. She was happy to be home, we enjoyed having her."

"How long did she stay?"

"Four days, like always. We went to a bunch of movies; she loved her movies. Saw the Pittsburgh Ice Extravaganza, too. When she was a little girl, she skated. The last day, she came into our store, helped us out a bit—we're in giftware, have to stay open somewhat during the holiday season."

"Movies," I said. Joseph Stargill had said the same thing.

"That's right—the whole family loves 'em," said Rob Ray.

"She was happy, had no problems," said Ernestine. "The only problem for us was we didn't see her enough. But we understood, what with her career. And travel's hard for us. The business."

"No buck-passing when it's yours," said Rob Ray. "Also, I don't travel well—my size. But so what? This had nothing to do with Claire's trip home or her problems. There'd be no reason for anyone to hate her; this had to be some maniac on the loose—somewhere from that place she worked." His skin had deepened to scarlet and his words emerged between rough inhalations. "I tell you, I find out anyone put her in danger, I'll— Let's just say a lot of lives are going to be made miserable."

"Darling," said his wife, patting his knee. To us: "What my

husband's saying is, Claire was kind and generous and sweet. No one could've hated her."

"Generous to the nth," Rob Ray agreed. "Back in high school, she was always the first to volunteer to help others. Old people at the hospital, animals at the shelter—didn't matter, she was there at the head of the line. She loved animals especially. We used to have a dog, a little Scottie. You know how kids never take responsibility with pets, it's always the parents who end up with it. Not our situation. Claire did everything, feeding it, cleaning up after it. She was always trying to fix things—broken wings on bugs, anything. We knew she'd be some kind of doctor, I would've guessed a veterinarian, but psychologist was fine. She always got good grades—it doesn't make sense, Detective Sturgis. At the morgue—what we just saw—I just don't . . . It had to be a maniac—this Starkweather place is nothing but maniacs?"

"Yes, sir," said Milo. "It's the first thing we looked at. So far, no leads. Apparently the inmates never get out."

"Sure," said Rob Ray. "Isn't there always some screwup that lets someone out? Some stupid *mistake*?" Tears began coursing silently down the jelly of his cheeks.

"You're right, sir," said Milo. "But so far I haven't come up with anything."

His tone had gentled; suddenly he seemed like a much younger man.

"Well," said Rob Ray. "I can tell you're good people. Where you from originally? Your folks, I mean."

"Indiana."

Satisfied nod. "I know you're trying."

Suddenly one log-arm moved with astonishing speed, slamming upward to the big man's face, as he ground the handkerchief to his eyes.

"Oh, Rob," said his wife, and she was crying again, too.

Milo went into the bathroom and brought them water.

Rob Ray Argent said, "Thanks, I'm supposed to drink a lot, anyway. For my joints, keep them lubricated." Half a shrug made his sloping shoulders jiggle. He plucked shirt fabric out of a fat fold.

Milo said, "So Claire visited only on Christmas."

"Yes, sir."

"Is that since she moved to Los Angeles or since she went to graduate school in Cleveland?"

"Los Angeles," said Rob Ray. "When she was at Case Western she came home for Thanksgiving, Easter, summers. She helped us out in the store, summers."

"Once she moved to L.A., how often did she write?"

Silence.

"We're phoners, not writers," said Ernestine. "Long distance is so economical nowadays. We have one of those calling plans."

I remembered Claire's phone bills. No recent calls to Pittsburgh. Had she dialed her parents from the office? Or had she become a stranger to them? Adding them to the club of strangers we'd encountered at every turn?

"So she called," said Milo.

"That's right," said Ernestine. "Every so often."

Milo scribbled. "What about her marriage? And the divorce. Anything I should know about that?"

Ernestine lowered her eyes. Her husband took a long, noisy breath.

"She said she'd gotten married in Reno," he said. "Soon after. One of her calls."

"So she told you over the phone," said Milo. "Did she seem happy about it?"

"I'd say yes," said Ernestine. "She apologized for not telling us before, said it was one of those sudden things— love at first sight. She said the husband was a nice fellow. A lawyer."

"But you never met him."

"I'm sure we would've, but Claire didn't stay married to him very long."

Two years, no contact.

"So she visited on Christmas while she was married."

"No," said Ernestine. "Not during the marriage. Last Christmas she was divorced already."

Milo said, "Did she explain why she got divorced?"

"She called after it happened, said she was fine, everything was friendly."

"She used that word?" said Milo. " 'Friendly.' "

"Or something to that effect. She was trying to reassure *me*. That was Claire. Take care of everyone else."

She glanced at her husband. He said, "I know this sounds weird to you—our not meeting him. No big white wedding. But Claire always needed her freedom. She— It was— That's just the way she was. Give her her freedom and she got straight A's. She was always a good kid—a great kid. Who were we to argue? You do your best, who knows how your kids are going to turn out? She turned out great. We gave her freedom."

Focusing on me during most of the speech. I nodded.

"We asked to meet him," he said. "The husband. She said she'd bring him by, but she never did. I got the feeling it didn't work too well from the beginning."

"Why's that?"

"Because she never brought him out."

"But she never actually complained about the marriage," said Milo.

"She never said she was unhappy," said Rob Ray, "if that's what you're getting at. Why? Do you suspect him of having anything to do with it?"

"No," said Milo. "Just trying to learn what I can."

"You're sure?"

"Absolutely, sir. At this point, he's not a suspect. No one is, unfortunately."

"Well," said Rob Ray, "I know you'd tell us if it was different. The only mention she made of him was sometimes at the end of a conversation, she might say, 'Joe sends his regards.' She did say he was a lawyer, not a courtroom lawyer, a business lawyer. When she called he was never home. I got the feeling he was always working. She was, too. One of those modern marriages. That's probably what happened, they were too busy for each other."

Ernestine said, "She did send us a picture. Of the wedding—the chapel. So we knew what he looked like. A redhead.

I remember joking to Rob Ray about little ginger-haired grandchildren."

She started to cry again, checked it, apologized under her breath.

Rob Ray said, "You'd have to know the kind of girl she was to understand. Very independent. She always took care of herself."

"Took care of others, too," I said.

"Exactly. So you can see why she'd need to unwind. And she unwinds by going off by herself to the movies. Or reading a book. Privacy's a big thing with her, so we try to respect that. Mostly she does things by herself. Except when we go out to the movies together. She likes doing that with me— we're both crazy for the movies."

The lapse into present tense made my own eyes begin to ache.

He might've realized it, too. His shoulders lowered suddenly, as if someone had pushed down upon them, and he stared at the bedcovers.

"Any particular kind of movies?" I said.

"Anything good," he mumbled. His face stayed down. "It was something we did together. I never pushed her to do sports. Tell the truth, being large, I wasn't exactly ready to run around, myself, so I was glad she was that kind of kid, could sit still and watch a movie."

"Even when she was tiny," said Ernestine, "she could amuse herself. She was the sweetest little thing. I could leave her in her playpen, go about my housework, and no matter what was happening all around her, she'd just sit there and play with whatever you put in there."

"Creating her own world," I said.

Her smile was sudden, unsettling. "Exactly, Doctor. You put your finger right on it. No matter what was happening all around her, she created her own world."

No matter what was happening all around her. Second time she'd used the phrase within seconds. Did it imply some kind of family turmoil?

I said, "Privacy as an escape."

Rob Ray looked up. Uneasiness in his eyes. I tried to engage him. He turned away. Ernestine watched him, twisted the handkerchief.

"About the way Claire got married," she said. "Rob Ray and I *had* a big church wedding, and it put my father in debt for two years. I always thought one of Claire's intentions was to be considerate."

"What put a light in her eyes," said Rob Ray, "was consideration. Helping people."

"Before Mr. Stargill," said Milo, "did Claire have any other boyfriends?"

"She dated," said Ernestine. "In high school, I mean. She wasn't some social butterfly, but she went out. Local boys, nothing steady. A fellow named Gil Grady took her to the prom. He's a fire lieutenant now."

"What about later?" said Milo. "College? Graduate school?"

Silence.

"How about once she moved to L.A.?"

"I'm sure," said Ernestine, "that when she wanted to date, she had her pick. She was always very pretty."

Something—probably her most recent memory of her daughter, gray, damaged, laid out on a steel table—caused her face to collapse. She hid herself behind both hands.

Her husband said, "I can't see where this is leading us anywhere."

Milo looked at me.

"Just one more thing, please," I said. "Did Claire ever get involved in arts and crafts? Painting, woodwork, that kind of thing?"

"Crafts?" said Rob Ray. "She drew, like any other kid, but that's about it."

"Mostly she liked to read and go to the movies," said Ernestine. "No matter what was happening all around her, she could always find some quiet time for herself."

Rob Ray said, "Excuse me." Lifting himself laboriously, he began the trudge to the bathroom. The three of us waited until the door closed. Running water sounded through the wood.

Ernestine began speaking softly, frantically: "This is so hard on him. When Claire was growing up, children made fun of him. Cruel children. It's glandular; sometimes he eats less than I do."

She stopped, as if daring us to debate. "He's a wonderful man. Claire was never ashamed, never treated him any way but respectful. Claire was always proud of her family, no matter what—"

The last word ended too abruptly. I waited for more. Her lips folded inward. As she bit down on them, her chin shuddered. "He's all I've got now. I'm worried about what this will do to him—"

Another toilet flush. Several moments later, the door opened and Rob Ray's big head appeared. Repeat of the laborious exit, the huffing trek to the bed. When he finally settled, he said, "I don't want you to think Claire was some strange kid, all locked up in her room. She was a tough kid, took care of herself, wouldn't fall in with anything bad for her. So this had to be an abduction, some kind of maniac."

Talking louder, more forcefully, as if he'd refueled.

"Claire was no fool," he went on. "Claire knew how to take care of herself—had to know."

"Because she lived alone?" I said.

"Because— Yes, exactly. My little girl was independent."

Later, sitting in a coffee shop on La Tijera with Milo, I said, "So much pain."

"Oh, man," he said. "They seem like good people, but talk about delusions. Making like it's one happy family, yet Claire never bothers to bring the husband around, never calls. She cut them off, Alex. Why?"

"Something the mother said made me wonder about family chaos. She used the phrase 'no matter what was happening all around her' three times. Emphasizing that Claire coped well. Maybe there was turmoil. But they're sure not going to tell you now. Pretty memories are all they've got. And why would it matter?"

He smiled. "All of a sudden the past isn't relevant?"

"It's always relevant to someone's life," I said. "But it may not have had a thing to do with Claire's death. At least, I don't see it."

"A maniac, like the old man said."

"He and his wife might be holding back family secrets, but I don't think they'd obstruct you," I said. "Claire's been out here for years. I think L.A.'s more relevant than Pittsburgh or Cleveland."

He gazed past me, toward the cash register, waved for service. Other than two red-eyed truckers at separate booths, we were the only customers.

A waitress came over, young, nasal, eager to please. When she left with our sandwich order, I said, "If she grew up with disruption, wanted her adult life quiet, that empty living room makes a bit more sense. But how it helped make her a victim, I don't know."

Milo tapped a front incisor. "Dad's size alone would've been disruptive. Kids making fun of him, Claire having to deal with it." He drank coffee, peered through the coffee shop's front window. An unseen jetliner's overhead pass shook the building.

"Maybe that's it," I said. "Growing up with him could also've made her comfortable with folks who were different. But when it came to her personal life, she drew a clear line: no fuss, no mess. Escaping to solitude, just as she had as a child."

The waitress brought the sandwiches. She looked disappointed when Milo said there'd be nothing else. He took a bite of soggy ham as I assessed my burger. Thin, shiny, the color of dry mud. I put it aside. One of the truckers tossed cash on the table and hobbled out the front door.

Milo took two more gulps of his sandwich. "Nice how you worked the arts-and-crafts question in. Hoping for some wood-shop memories?"

"Wouldn't that have been nice."

He bit down on something disagreeable and held the bread at arm's length before returning it to the plate. "Some scene at the morgue. The coroner did his best to put her back together, but it was far from pretty. I tried to discourage them again from viewing. They insisted. Mom actually handled it okay; it was Dad who started breathing real hard, turned beet red, braced himself against the wall. I thought we'd end up with another corpse. The morgue attendant's been staring at the poor guy like he's some freak-of-the-week, now he's really gawking. I got them out of there. Thank God he didn't collapse."

Neither of us talked for a while. Ever the prisoner of my training, I lapsed into thoughts of Claire's childhood. Escape from . . . something . . . finding refuge in solitude . . . because solitude spun layers of fantasy . . . theater of the mind. Real theaters.

I said, "Claire's love of movies. That's something both the parents and Stargill mentioned. What if it led beyond just watching? Caused her to have acting aspirations? What if she answered a casting call—the same one Richard Dada answered?"

"She likes flicks, so all of a sudden she wants to be a star?"

"Why not?" I said. "It's L.A. Maybe Claire did a bit on *Blood Walk,* too. There's your link with Richard. The killer met both of them on the set."

"Everything we've learned about this woman tells us she's a privacy nut. You think she'd put herself in front of a camera?"

"I've known actors who were extremely shy. Taking on someone else's identity allowed them to cut loose."

"I guess," he said doubtfully. "So they both meet some loon on the set and he decides to pick them off for God knows what motive. . . . Then why the time lapse between the murders?"

"Maybe there are other murders in between that we don't know about."

"I looked for similars. Anything in car trunk, anything with eye wounds or saw marks. Nothing."

"Okay," I said. "Just a theory."

The waitress came over and asked if we wanted dessert.

Milo's barked "No thanks" made her step backward and hurry away.

"I understand about role-playing, Alex, but we're talking Ms. Empty Room, her big thrill was being alone. I can see her taking in a matinee by herself, pretending to be Sharon Starlet, whatever. But going to the movies isn't *being* in the movies. Hell, I still can't believe there's no link to *Starkweather*. The woman worked with homicidal *murderers*, for God's sake, and I'm expected to take it on faith that none of them got out and hunted her down. Meanwhile, we sit here wondering about some hypothetical *acting* gig."

He pressed both temples, and I knew a headache had come on.

The waitress brought the check and held it out at arm's length. Milo shoved a twenty at her, asked for aspirin, ordered her to keep the change. She smiled and hustled away looking frightened.

When she brought the tablets, he swallowed them dry. "To hell with Swig and his court orders. Time to get with State Parole, see what they can tell me about Starkweather creeps flewing the coop since Claire went to work there. After that, sure, the movie thing, why not? Equipment rentals, like you suggested."

Crumpling the aspirin packet, he dropped it into an ashtray. "Like you said, it's L.A. Since when has logic ever meant a damn thing here?"

16.

IN THE COFFEE-SHOP parking lot, he cell-phoned Sacramento, billing through LAPD. Authorization took a while. So did being shunted from clerk to supervisor to clerk. Every few seconds a plane swooped down to land. I stood around as he burned up calories keeping his voice even. Finally, his patience earned him the promise of a priority records search from State Parole.

"Which means days instead of weeks," he said, walking over to a nearby phone booth and lifting a chained Yellow Pages from its shelf. Dried gum crusted the covers. "One thing the supervisor did confirm: Starkweather guys do get out. Not often, but it happens. She knows for a fact because there was a case five years ago—some guy supposed to be on close supervision returned to his hometown and shot himself in the local barbershop."

"So much for the system," I said. "Maybe that's why Swig was nervous."

"The system is bullshit. People aren't machines. Places like Quentin and Pelican Bay, there's all kinds of trouble. Either you cage them completely or they do whatever the hell they please." He began paging through the phone directory. "Okay, let's find some rental outfits, play cinema sleuth."

Most of the film equipment companies were in Hollywood and Burbank, the rest scattered around the Valley and Culver City.

"Hollywood first," he said. "Where else?"

It was just after three P.M. when I followed Milo's unmarked onto the 405 and over to the 101. We got off at Sunset. Traffic was mean.

The Hollywood outfits were in warehouse buildings and large storefronts on the west end of the district, between Fairfax and Gower. A concentration on Santa Monica Boulevard allowed us to park and cover half a dozen businesses quickly. The mention of Thin Line Productions and *Blood Walk* evoked baffled stares from the rental clerks, most of whom looked like thrash-metal band castoffs.

On the seventh try, at a place on Wilcox called Flick Stuff, a bony, simian-looking young man with a massive black hair extension and a pierced lip slouched behind a nipple-high counter. Massively unimpressed by Milo's badge. Maybe twenty-one; too young for that level of world-weariness. Behind him were double doors with an EMPLOYEES ONLY sign. In the background, a female vocalist shouted over power chords. Joan Jett or someone trying to be her. Big Hair wore a tight black T-shirt and red jeans. A slogan on the shirt: "*No Sex Unless It Leads to Dancing.*" His arms were white and hairless, more vein than muscle. Lumpy fibroid dope scars in the crooks said he'd probably had police experience.

Milo said, "Were you working here twenty months ago, sir?"

"Sir" made the kid smirk. "Off and on." He managed to slouch lower.

Price lists were tacked to the surrounding walls. Day rates for sandbags, Western dollies, sidewalls, Magliners, wardrobe racks, Cardellini lamps, Greenscreens. Surprisingly cheap; a snow machine could be had for fifty-five bucks.

"Remember renting to an outfit called Thin Line Productions?"

I expected a yawn, but Big Hair said, "Maybe."

Milo waited.

"Sounds familiar. Yeah, maybe. Yeah."

"Could you check your files, please?"

"Yeah, hold on." Hair opened the double doors and disappeared, returned waving an index card, looking ready to spit. "Yeah, now I remember them."

"Problems?" said Milo.

"Big problems." Hair wiped his hands on the black T-shirt. The grubby steel ring through his upper lip robbed his expression of some of the injured dignity he was trying to project.

"What'd they do?" said Milo.

"Stiffed us fourteen grand worth."

I said, "That's a lot of equipment."

"Not for Spielberg, but for assholes like that, yeah. We gave 'em everything. Mikes, props, fake blood, filters, misters, eye chamois, coffee makers, cups, tables, the fuckin' works. The big items were a dolly and a couple of cameras—old gear, no studio would touch 'em, but still they cost. Supposed to be a ten-day rental. They had no history with us and it was obviously like a virgin voyage, so we demanded double deposit and they gave us a check that we verified was covered. I got I.D., everything by the book. Not only didn't they pay up, they fucking split with the equipment. When we tried to cash the deposit check, guess what?"

He bared his teeth. Surprisingly white. Behind them, something glinted. Pierced tongue. No click when he talked—the voice of experience. Were pain thresholds rising among the new generation? Would it make for a better Marine Corps?

I said, "What made you think it was a virgin voyage?"

"They putzed around, didn't know what they were doing. What pisses me off is I guided them, man, told them how to get the most for their money. Then they go and screw me."

"You got blamed?"

"Boss said I did the transaction, I was assigned to find 'em, try to recover. I couldn't find shit."

"You say 'they,' " said Milo. "How many people are we talking about?"

"Two. Guy and a girl."

"What'd they look like?"

"Twenties, thirties. She was okay-looking, blond hair—light blond, like Marilyn Monroe, Madonna, when she was like that. But long and straight. Nice body, but nothing special. Okay face. He was tall, older than her, trying to play hip."

"How old?" said Milo.

"Probably in his thirties. She was maybe younger. I wasn't really paying attention. She didn't say much, it was mostly him."

"How tall was he?" said Milo.

"About your size, but skinny. Not as skinny as me, but nothing like you either." Smirk.

"Hair color?" said Milo.

"Dark. Black. Long."

"Like yours?"

"He wished, man. His was curly, like a perm, maybe went to here." He touched his shoulders.

"Platinum blond for her," said Milo, writing. "Long and curly for him. Maybe wigs?"

"Sure they were," said Hair. "It's not exactly hard to tell, man."

"What kind of clothing did they wear?"

"Regular. Nothing special."

"Any other distinguishing marks?"

Hair laughed. "Like '666' on their foreheads? Nope, unh-uh."

"Could you identify them if you saw them again?"

"I dunno." The pierced tongue slid between his upper and lower teeth. The mannerism formed his mouth into a tragedy-mask frown. "Probably not. I wasn't really paying attention to their faces. I was concentrating on getting them the most for their money."

"But maybe you could recognize them?"

"Why, you have a picture?"

"Not yet."

"Well, bring one if you get it. Maybe, no promises."

"The fact they were wearing wigs," said Milo. "That didn't bother you?"

"Why should it?"

"Maybe they were hiding something."

Hair laughed. "Everyone in the industry hides something. You never see a chick with a natural rack anymore, and half the guys are wearing wigs and eye shadow. Big fucking deal—maybe they were acting in their own flick, doing it all. That's the way it is with a lot of these indie things."

"They tell you anything about the flick?"

"Didn't ask, they didn't say."

"*Blood Walk,*" said Milo. "Sounds like a slasher flick."

"Could be." Boredom had returned.

"They rented fake blood."

"Couple gallons. I picked out the best we had, nice and thick. Then they butt-ream me like that. Boss *loved* that."

"Any hint it might've been porn?"

"Anything's possible," said Hair. "I know most of the porn people, but there's always new assholes trying to break in. I don't think so, though. They didn't have that virgin porn feel."

"What's the virgin porn feel?"

"Stoned-happy on Ecstasy, big fucking adventure. They didn't say much—thinking about it, they didn't say hardly nothing at all."

"Boss take it any further than having you look for them?" said Milo.

"What do you mean?"

"Did he run a trace on them? Hire a collection agency?"

"He put 'em out to collection and when that didn't work, he wrote it off. We had a good year, I guess he can piss away fourteen grand."

"Does this kind of thing happen all the time?"

"Getting ripped off? Not all the time, but yeah, it happens. But not usually for this much. And usually we collect something."

"Do you still have their file?"

"I didn't throw it out."

"Could we please see it, Mr. . . . ?"

"Bonner. Vito Bonner." He wiped his hands again. "Let me go back and check. They rip someone else off? That why you're here?"

"Something like that."

"Man," said Bonner. "Talk about stupid. We warned the other companies in the neighborhood. Burbank and Culver, too." A black sprig of false hair tickled his chin and he slapped it away. "I think we warned the Valley, too. So anyone who rented to them after that deserves to get cornholed."

We sat in the unmarked and studied the file. The tab read THIN LINE: BLOOD WALK, *BAD DEBT*. The first page was a letter from an Encino collection agency reporting an extensive search, no results. Next came the rental application. Thin Line's address was listed on Abbot Kinney Boulevard in Venice. Venice phone exchange with the notation that it traced to a pay phone.

"Bit of a drive to Hollywood," I said. "Especially with rental outfits close by in Santa Monica. They didn't want to foul their own nest."

Milo pored over the form, nodding. The signature at the bottom was hard to read, but a black business card stapled to the file folder said:

Griffith D. Wark
PRODUCER AND PRESIDENT
THIN LINE PRODS

The pay-phone number in the lower left corner. White printing on black. Old-fashioned camera logo in the lower right-hand corner.

"Bogus phone," he said. "Scam from the get-go . . . Wark. Sounds like a phony moniker."

"Griffith D. W.," I said. "Ten to one it's an inversion of D. W. Griffith. I'll also bet the W in 'D. W.' was Wark. Not very subtle, but old Vito didn't catch it."

"Old Vito probably knows more about Maglites than film history." He flipped to the next page. "Here's the bank verification on the deposit check—B. of A. branch out in Panorama City. These guys were all over the place."

He studied his Timex. "Too late to call the manager. I'll drive by the Venice address, see if they really did have a place there; then I'll get the file over to the lab just in case some old latents from known bad guys show up. Tomorrow, it's on the horn to every other prop house in the county, see if Mr. Wark talked anyone else out of gear."

"You like the film thing now," I said.

"Work with what you've got," he said. "I'm an old stink-hound: when something smells bad, I go nosing."

"The casting ad could have been another scam—get wannabes to pay for auditioning."

"Wouldn't surprise me. Hollywood's one big scam, anyway—image *über alles*. Even when it's supposedly legit. One of my first cases, back when I was doing Robbery, was—" He named a well-known actor. "Got his start as a student, doing artsy stuff using gear he stole from the university's theater arts department. When I caught up with him he was a real fresh-mouth, no remorse. Finally, he agreed to return everything and the U decided not to take it any further. A few years later, I'm watching TV and this asshole's up for an Oscar, some social-issues film about prison reform, making a holier-than-thou speech. And what about—" He named a major director. "I know for a fact he got *his* foot in the door by selling coke to studio execs. Yeah, this Wark found the right business for a psychopath. The only question is how relevant his mischief is to *my* cases."

I got home just after six. Robin's truck was in the car-port. The house smelled wonderful—the salty bouquet of chicken soup.

She was at the stove, stirring a pot. Her hair was loose, tumbling down her back; black sweats accentuated the auburn. Her sleeves were pushed up to her elbows and her face looked scrubbed. Steam from the soup had brought up some sweat. Down by her feet, Spike squatted, panting, ready to pounce for a scrap. The table was set for two.

When I kissed her, Spike grumbled. "Be a good sharer," I said.

He grumbled some more and waddled over to his water bowl.

"Winning through intimidation," I said.

Robin laughed. "Thought we'd eat in. Haven't seen enough of you lately."

"Sounds great to me. Want me to prepare something?"

"Not unless there's something else you want."

I looked into the pot. Golden broth formed a bubbling home for carrots, celery, onions, slivers of white meat, wide noodles.

"Nothing," I said, moving behind her, cupping her waist, lowering my hands to her hips. I felt her go loose.

"This," I said, "is one of those great fantasies—he chances upon her as she cooks and, lusty stallion that he is . . ."

She laughed, let out two soft breaths, leaned back against me. My hands rose to her breasts, loose and soft, unfettered by the thin fleece of the sweats. Her nipples hardened against my palms. My fingers slipped under the waistband of her pants. She inhaled sharply.

"You shrinks," she said, placing her hand over mine. Guiding it down. "Spending too much time on fantasy, not enough on reality."

17.

I WOKE UP the next morning thinking about Mr. and Mrs. Argent's claim that Claire had chosen psychology because she wanted to nurture people. Yet she'd opted for neuropsychology as a specialty, concentrating on diagnostics, avoiding treatment. On research diagnostics, charts and graphs, the hieroglyphics of science. She'd rarely ventured out of her lab. On the face of it, she'd nurtured nothing but data at County.

Until six months ago and the shift to Starkweather. Maybe Robin was right, and the move represented getting in touch with her altruism.

But why *now*? Why *there*?

Something didn't fit. My head felt like a box full of random index cards. I circled the office, trying to collate. Robin and Spike were out, and the silence chewed at me. There had been a time, long ago, when I was content living alone. The knots and liberties of love had changed me. What had Claire experienced of love?

The phone ring was glass shattering on stone.

"Small stuff first," said Milo. "Joseph Stargill's not quite as rich as he claimed, because some of his properties are mortgaged, but he still comes out over four mil in the black. His law practice brings in around a hundred and eighty K a year. If he's a greedy psychopath or he hated Claire's guts, I suppose three hundred K might motivate him, but I can't find evidence of either, and a probate lawyer tells me Stargill would have a hell of a time getting hold of that property. With no will, the state takes most of it and Claire's parents get the rest. Stargill's not off the suspect list completely; I still have to nose around about any bad investments he might have. But he's been kicked down several notches.

"Item Two: no other prop company reports being bilked by Mr. Wark or Thin Line, so maybe he wasn't out for a big-time equipment rip-off, just wanted to supply his own shoot, decided to keep the gear when they were through. No progress finding Wark. The *Blood Walk* script has definitely not been registered with any of the guilds, no one's heard of Thin Line, and there's no evidence the film was ever released. I contacted film-developing labs, because if there was ever footage it might've been processed somewhere. Nada. At the B. of A. in Panorama City, no dice over the phone, I have to come in, present a warrant to get a look at the Thin Line account."

"Busy day," I said.

"With zippo to show for it. I'm thinking this whole movie angle is a distraction. Especially with Item Three: the clerk from State Parole called me, God bless her. Turns out a Starkweather inmate *was* released, seven months ago. A guy named Wendell Pelley. Three weeks before Claire went to work there. It's a narrow window, but Pelley could've learned about Claire from some buddy still in there. Or Claire actually had contact with him. Think about it: her official start date was three weeks after Pelley got released, but what's to say she didn't go to Starkweather before then? To take a look, see if it was right for her. Let's say she runs into Pelley by accident—he's about to be sprung, so they make him a trusty—a tour guide, like Hatterson. She's coming there to help people, and here's a success story. It could be appealing to her, right?"

"Sure," I said, "but seven months ago means Pelley was released one month *after* Richard Dada's murder."

"So someone else did Dada. That's always been a possibility."

His tone said not to push it. "What's Pelley's background?" I said.

"White male, forty-six, got committed twenty-one years ago for shooting his girlfriend and her three little kids up in the Sierras—gold country. Apparently Pelley was trying to do some mining, brought the rest of them along to be one happy family, got drunk, convinced himself they were trying to rob his claim, and went berserk. Diagnosis of paranoid schizophrenia, drug and booze history, too wacky for trial."

"Why'd they let him out?"

"Staff recommendation from Starkweather is all State Parole had."

"Swig approved the release," I said. "So he held back plenty."

"Shmuck. Never liked him. Gonna look into *his* background, but right now Pelley's whereabouts are my main concern."

"He's on the run?" I said. "Released inmates are supposed to get counseling and random drug tests."

"Funny thing 'bout that, isn't it? Pelley was bunking in a halfway house near MacArthur Park. The operators haven't seen him for a *month*. They claim they notified his parole officer right away. I tried to reach the P.O., no callback yet."

"Whom would the parole officer be obligated to notify?"

"The local police. Ramparts Division. They can't find any record of notification. The system, huh?"

"Would Swig be notified?"

"Maybe. If so, it's something else he held back on. Not that he's any use to us at this point. Pelley wouldn't be likely to run back to Starkweather."

"So what's next?" I said. "A statewide alert?"

"Nah," he said. "That's for TV. Officially, Pelley hasn't done anything bad yet, so no way does State Parole or anyone else want to get the press on it, panic the public. If Ramparts does get notified, all it means is Pelley's face and stats go up on a bulletin board in the station, maybe if the desk's feeling real cooperative they issue photo memos for the squad car dashboards. Meaning if Pelley acts up publicly and a uniform gets there in time, he's busted. But if he doesn't cause problems, he can probably fade into the woodwork."

"Out on the streets three weeks before Claire joins the staff at Starkweather," I said. "You could be right. She met Pelley and he became her outpatient project."

"Hey," he said, "she told that psychiatrist she was ripe for it. 'So many madmen, so little time.' "

"And maybe Pelley and Peake maintained some sort of communication. Maybe Peake talked to him because they had some kind of rapport. They had one important thing in common: they both murdered families."

"As good a basis for friendship as I've ever heard." He cursed.

"Heidi never mentioned Pelley's release. But she came on staff after Claire, might not have heard about it."

"I want to talk to Heidi again, anyway," he said. "So far she's the only one in that place showing any desire to help. She's due on shift at three. I'm gonna be out on the road all day, trying to trace Pelley, so I left a message with your number as backup. Okay?"

"Okay. I can also try that head psychiatrist at Starkweather—Aldrich—see what he knows about Pelley."

"No, not yet—I need to be discreet. If it turns out Pelley's our bad guy, whoever okayed his release is gonna be up the creek. No reason to warn them, give them time to get their defenses up. Give Swig a chance to get on the horn with Uncle Senator and unleash a paper barrier."

He sounded angry but exhilarated.

"You have a good feeling about this," I said.

"Don't know about that, but I will tell you one thing: this is a helluva lot more to my liking than movies and all that hocus-pocus about Peake's gibberish. This is the world as I know it: bad guy gets out on the street, bad things happen. . . . Guess my faith in crappy endings has been validated once again."

I heated up some of the leftover soup and chewed on a hard roll as I thought about Milo's enthusiasm for Wendell Pelley.

In addition to his being clear for the Dada murder, Pelley had used a gun, not a knife. But maybe twenty-one years had changed his killing style. And he *had* bolted the halfway house.

Still, Milo was relying on what he hated most: theory. If

he'd looked at it coldly, he might've tempered his enthusiasm. I hadn't said a thing. I'd continue to keep my doubts to myself. One thing doing therapy had taught me: timing is all.

My service rang at three-twenty-three. I'd been expecting a call from Heidi Ott, but the operator said, "It's a Dr. Hertzlinger, from County General Hospital. She says it's about Dr. Argent."

"Put her on."

Click. "Dr. Delaware? Mary Hertzlinger. I was calling Detective Sturgis, but someone at the station gave me this number."

"He's out, asked me to take some messages. What's up?"

"After you and he left, I found myself thinking more about Claire. And I began to wonder if I'd misspoken. About that strange parting shot—'So many madmen, so little time.' You asked me if Claire seemed upset when she said it, and I said no, she was actually smiling. But the more I considered it, the more I realized how unlike Claire the remark was. Because she'd never joked before. Never displayed any sense of humor, really. I don't mean that unkindly—she was just a very serious person. Off the job, I try not to analyze people, but you know how it is. Anomalies attract me."

"Me, too. Occupational hazard."

She laughed softly. "Anomalies also make me wonder about anxiety."

"You think Claire was anxious about switching jobs?"

"It's just speculation," she said, "but she just rattled off that line as if she'd rehearsed it. Had been reciting it to herself. Because, let's face it, it *was* a strange thing to do. Claire's job was secure, Dr. Theobold liked her. To just pick up and leave for a place like Starkweather? She'd never worked with patients, let alone homicidal psychotics. It really doesn't make sense."

"Maybe after doing all that research, she wanted to help people directly."

"Then why Starkweather? Who gets help there?"

"So you're saying the decision scared her but she went ahead, anyway," I said.

"Yes, but that doesn't make sense, either, does it? If she was nervous, why do it? I'll bet if she'd marched into Dr. Theobold's office and announced she'd changed her mind, he'd have taken her back in a flash, no questions asked. So it's confusing. I tried to think back, what her demeanor had been as we cleaned out those boxes. What we'd been talking about. I couldn't remember much, but I *did* recall something: she mentioned leaving some material behind in the office closet, said she'd be back for it later in the afternoon. But I was in the office all day and she never returned. Ever. After I met you, I went to check, and sure enough, there it was, back in a corner. Two cartons with her name on them. The flaps were closed but not sealed, so I opened one up—I hope I didn't ruin anything by doing that?"

"No," I said. "Find anything interesting?"

"Mostly they were journal reprints. Claire's own publications and some articles related to her alcoholism research. But there was also a plastic bag full of newspaper clippings. Photocopies, actually, and when I read them, I knew I had to call Detective Sturgis. They were all about a mass murder that took place sixteen years ago—"

"The Ardullo family," I said. "Ardis Peake."

Silence. "So you already know."

"Peake's at Starkweather. He was one of Claire's patients."

"Oh, my . . . So Claire was interested in him before she went there—maybe he was one of the reasons she took the job. But why would that be?"

"Good question," I said. "Where are the clippings now?"

"Right here in front of me—I won't touch another thing, haven't even gone near the second box. Someone can pick them up any time before eight tonight, and I'll be back in around seven A.M."

"Thanks," I said. "And thank you for calling. Soon as I can reach Detective Sturgis, I'll let him know."

"This Peake," she said. "He's still in there—incarcerated?"

"Yes."

"So it couldn't have been him," she said, sounding relieved. "I started to read the clippings. The things he did . . . Anyway, that's it."

"One more thing," I said. "Did Claire ever mention loving the movies?"

"Not to me. Why?"

"We've been told it was a main form of recreation for her."

"I suppose that wouldn't surprise me," she said. "Sure. I could see that—losing herself in fantasy."

"You saw her as someone with an active fantasy life?"

"I saw her as someone who might've *depended* upon an active fantasy life. Because she didn't—I don't want to be cruel, but the truth is, she just didn't seem to have much of a *real* life."

Interested in Peake before she'd taken the job.

Her project. Trying to increase his verbal output.

Or so she'd claimed. What about him had really caught her interest?

Stashed the clippings along with her research data.

Because she considered the *clippings* data?

Why would an alcoholism researcher raised in Pittsburgh and schooled in Cleveland be concerned with a sixteen-year-old atrocity in a California farm town?

A town that no longer existed.

I thought about the abolition of Treadway. An entire community obliterated. What role had been played by Ardis Peake's savage night?

Peake's blood walk . . . I wrestled with it some more. Claire, a researcher, coming upon something . . .

It was three-forty, and Heidi Ott still hadn't called. I checked out with my service and drove back to the library.

18.

First I photocopied and reviewed the murder articles I'd pulled up yesterday. No new insights. Using "Ardullo" and "Ardis Peake" as keywords, I went back twenty years before the crimes and pulled up five references, all from the L.A. *Times*.

November 24, 1929:

ARDULLO LEADS INDIANS
TO GRIDIRON VICTORY
Red Schoen, *Times* sportswriter

Two fourth-quarter record-breaking runs by star quarterback Henry "Butch" Ardullo led the Stanford Indians to a 21–7 victory over the UC Bears in last Sunday's cliffhanger game.

Ardullo, already renowned for his passing, showed his leg-stuff, accomplishing a pair of unimpeded Mercury imitations to the touchdown line, 70 and 82 yards respectively. The capacity crowd showed its appreciation with a standing ovation, and professional scouts, alerted to Ardullo's stellar performance all season, were reputed to be eyeing the husky junior. No one will be surprised when Butch is tapped on the shoulder for stardom, maybe even while still in his cap and gown. More important to assembled Palo Alto stalwarts and alums, a Rose Bowl place for the Redskins is all but assured.

December 8, 1929:

INJURY SIDELINES GRIDIRON STAR
Red Schoen, *Times* sportswriter

A broken femur suffered during practice yesterday led to Stanford great Henry "Butch" Ardullo being carried from the field on a stretcher.

Ardullo, the Pacific College League's high-scoring quarterback, had been expected to lead the Indians in their upcoming Rose Bowl game with USC. Doctors treating the injured junior have pronounced his football career over.

August 12, 1946:

FARMERS GROUP SAYS IMMIGRANT LABOR NECESSARY TO FEED STATE
John M. D'Arcy, *Times* staff writer

A consortium of California fruit growers met with Deputy Agriculture Secretary Clement W. Chase in Washington this week to request relaxation of immigration laws in order to permit increased numbers of "wetback" laborers from Mexico.

The Affiliated Agricultural Network claims that tighter immigration laws will raise labor costs to the point of "severe abuse of the domestic consumer," according to AAN president Henry Ardullo, a peach and walnut grower from Treadway, California.

"These people," said Ardullo, "can come up here and earn ten times what they can down in Mexico and still give us excellent labor value. They do jobs no one else wants, so American workers don't get hurt. Meanwhile, Mrs. Housewife gets to go to the grocery store and stock up on the finest, most nutritious produce ever grown on this planet at a price that makes healthful eating the only logical choice."

Anti-immigration groups oppose the variance. Secretary Chase said he will consider the petition and issue a ruling.

January 14, 1966:

RESIST LAND BOOM LURE, SAYS GROWER
Stephen Bannister, *Times* business writer

Farmers need to resist the temptation to sell their land at high market prices, says a prominent Kern County fruit grower, because the future of the family farm is at stake.

"Quick profits pose a difficult temptation, and Lord knows farming can be difficult, what with all the government restrictions," said Henry Ardullo, a walnut and peach farmer from Treadway, California, and past president of the Affiliated Agricultural Network, a group representing the interests of independent growers. "But the farm is the soul of California. This state is America's breadbasket, and if we cut off the hand that feeds us in the name of easy money, what are we leaving to our children? Golf courses and country clubs are pretty, but try feeding your family with turf grass."

Ardullo's comments were made at a GOP fund-raiser at the Fairmont Hotel in San Francisco, where he shared the dais with State Senators William Greben and Rudy Torres, and real estate developer Sheridan Krafft.

March 5, 1975:

OBITUARIES
HENRY ARDULLO, COLLEGE GRIDIRON STAR
AND AGRICULTURAL EXEC

Henry "Butch" Ardullo died at his ranch in Treadway, California, this past Wednesday. Renowned as a quarterback at Stanford University, where he broke several records for running and passing, Ardullo received a B.A.

*in business in 1930. He had been widely expected to
enter professional football until an injury ended his athletic career.*

*Upon graduation, he joined the family enterprise, a
large walnut and peach plantation begun by his father,
Joseph (Giuseppe) Ardullo, an immigrant from Naples
who came to California in 1883, found work as a fruit
vendor in San Francisco and invested his profits in real
estate in and around the Kern County community of
Treadway, where he planted hundreds of fruit trees from
stock acquired in England, Italy and Portugal.*

*Upon Joseph Ardullo's death in 1941, Henry Ardullo
took over the business, Ardullo AA Fruit, which he re-
named and incorporated as BestBuy Produce, and continued to purchase land, amassing large private real estate
holdings in the lower central valley region. Elected as president of Affiliated Agricultural Network, a post World War II
consortium of independent growers, in 1946, Ardullo represented grower interests in Washington, including a successful petition for relaxation of immigration laws to
allow increased numbers of farm laborers into California.
He was a member of Kiwanis, the Treadway Chamber of
Commerce, and the Farm League and a contributor to the
Republican party; he served as central valley chairman of
United Way from 1953 to 1956.*

*He married Stanford classmate Katherine Ann Steth-
son, daughter of a Palo Alto department store owner, in
1933. She died in 1969. A son, Henry Ardullo, Jr., died in
a mountain climbing accident in Nepal, in 1960. The senior Ardullo is survived by his other son, Scott Stethson
Ardullo of Treadway, vice president of BestBuy Produce.*

The farm is the soul of California.

It had taken the rampage of a madman to bring Henry
Ardullo's nightmare home.

A family obliterated. An entire town wiped off the map.
Once sentimentality had been taken care of, high real estate
values had done the rest.

Sad, but I couldn't see any connection to Claire or the demons hissing in Ardis Peake's head.

Could she have had a family connection to the Ardullos? Her parents hadn't mentioned it. There seemed no reason for them to conceal history. Still, people often hid their reasons. I found a pay phone just outside the reading room, phoned the Flight Inn, and asked for the Argents' room. Rob Ray's familiar rumble said, "Yes?"

"Mr. Argent? Dr. Delaware."

"Oh. Hello."

"Sorry to bother you again, sir, but I had one more question."

"Lucky you caught us," he said. "We're on our way out the door and back home."

"I'll be quick, Mr. Argent. Do you have any relatives in California? Specifically, in the farming business?"

"Farming? Nope."

"Does the name Ardullo mean anything to you?"

"No again. I thought you might be calling about some progress—what's this all about?"

"The Ardullos were a family Claire showed some interest in—she'd read up on them, held on to some newspaper clippings."

"*Were* a family?" he said. "Something happened to them?"

"Unfortunately, they were murdered. Fifteen years ago, and Claire seemed to be interested in the case."

"Murdered. The whole family?" He nearly choked on the last two words. "So what— I don't mean, so what they were murdered. So what about Claire? No, I don't know them, never did. It was probably just something . . . professional. Doing her work. Have to go, good-bye."

"Have a good flight," I said.

"Oh, yeah," he said. "It's going to be a great flight—at least I'm getting out of your lousy city."

His anger rang in my head and I hung up feeling foolish and intrusive. What had I hoped to accomplish? What did big money and land deals have to do with Claire's murder?

Now that I was thinking straight, I realized there was a

simple explanation for the clippings: knowing she was trans-
ferring to Starkweather, Claire had plugged the hospital's
name into some data banks, come across the description of
Peake's bloody night. Once she got there, she looked him up,
found him near vegetative. A challenge.

So many madmen, so little time.

After all those years in the lab, she was hungry for clinical
raw meat—for a firsthand look at astounding criminal madness. Maybe she'd even intended to write Peake up, if she
made some kind of progress.

She'd entered the world of madness, but—Milo's enthusiasm for Wendell Pelley aside—I wondered if that had anything to do with her death. Right at the beginning, my gut had
told me someone organized—twisted but sane—had cut her
throat, stashed her in the car trunk, made off with the bit of
cash in the as yet undiscovered purse. Left no clues.

Maybe the same person who'd bisected Richard Dada,
maybe not. Any similarities between the two cases could
be explained by abnormal psychology: psychopaths weren't
that original. Confront enough evil and you smell the same
garbage over and over.

No voices in the head here. Maybe Pelley was now
sane enough to pull it off, maybe not. In any case, I couldn't
help thinking we were up against something coldhearted,
orchestrated.

Murder for fun. A production.

There was nothing more I could do, so I drove home, spent
some time outdoors, weeding, pruning, feeding the fish, net-
ting leaves out of the pond.

Just before five, my service patched Heidi Ott through.

"Doctor?" She sounded buoyant. "I can't believe it, but
Peake's talking again, and this time Swig can't accuse me of
being hysterical. I got it on tape!"

19.

"*Tuh.*"

"*What's that, Ardis?*"

Tape buzz. I clocked it. Twenty-two seconds—

"*What did you say, Ardis . . . ? You just said something . . . because you want to talk to me, right, Ardis . . . ?*"

Thirty-two seconds.

"*Ardis? Could you open your eyes . . . please?*"

A minute. Ninety seconds, a hundred . . . Heidi Ott held up her finger, signaling us to be patient.

It was just before midnight, but her eyes were bright. She and Milo and I were in an interrogation room at the station—a hot, Lysol-smelling yellow closet barely large enough for the three of us. Heidi's hair was tied back and styled with a shark clip. She'd come straight from Starkweather and the clip of her I.D. badge protruded from a breast pocket. The recorder was a tiny black Sony.

"Just a bit more," she said, tapping her fingers on the steel table.

Her voice on the tape said, "*Okay, Ardis. Maybe tomorrow.*"

Thirty-three seconds. Footsteps.

"*Tuh.*"

"*Tuh, Ardis? Two? Two what?*"

Twenty-eight seconds.

"*Ardis?*"

"*Tuh guh.*"

"*To go?*"

"*Tuh guh choo choo bang bang.*"

"*To go choo choo bang bang? What does that mean, Ardis?*"

156

Fifteen seconds.

"Choo choo bang bang, Ardis? Is that some sort of game?"

Eighteen seconds.

"Ardis? What's choo choo bang bang?"

Thirty seconds, forty, fifty.

"What does it mean, Ardis?"

Eighty-three seconds. Click.

She said, "At that point, he turned away from me, wouldn't open his eyes. I waited awhile longer, but I knew it was all I was going to get out of him."

" 'Choo choo bang bang,' " said Milo.

She colored. "I know. It's pretty stupid, isn't it? I guess I shouldn't have gotten so jazzed. But at least it's something, right? He's talking to me. Maybe he'll keep talking."

"Where'd you keep the recorder?" I said.

"In my pocket." She pointed to the navy photographer's vest she'd draped over her chair. "I tried yesterday, too, but nothing happened."

" 'Choo choo bang bang,' " said Milo. " 'Bad eyes in a box.' "

"I've been trying to figure out some connection," said Heidi. Suddenly, she looked very tired. "Probably wasting your time. Sorry."

"No, no," said Milo. "I appreciate your help. I'd like to keep the tape."

"Sure." She popped it out of the machine, gave it to him, placed the recorder back in the vest pocket, collected her purse, and stood.

Milo held out a hand and they shook. "Thanks," he said. "Really. Any information is helpful."

She shrugged. "I guess. . . . Want me to keep taping?"

"I don't want you to do anything that violates regulations."

"Never heard of any regulation against taping."

"It's generally illegal to tape anyone without their knowledge, Heidi. Jail prisoners lose the presumption of privacy, but whether or not that applies to the men at Starkweather, I don't know."

"Okay," she said. "So I won't do it anymore." Shrugging, she moved toward the door. "Kind of strange, isn't it? Protecting *them*. That's another reason I don't want to stick around."

"What's that?"

"Swig talks all the time about humane care, how they're human beings, too. But I just can't find much sympathy for them, and I'd rather work with people I care about. —At least they can't leave. I guess that's the main thing."

"Speaking of which," said Milo. "One of them did get out."

Her knuckles whitened around the purse handle. "I never heard that. When?"

"Before you came on staff."

"Who? What was his name?"

"Wendell Pelley."

"No," she said. "Never heard of him—why, is he some sort of suspect in Claire's murder?"

"No," said Milo. "Not yet. I'm just trying to cover all bases. Anything you could find out about Pelley would be useful. Like, did he and Peake associate with each other."

"I can try . . . long as I stay at Starkweather."

"Two more weeks."

"Yes, but if there's something you think I can . . . Are you saying this Pelley is what Peake's little speeches are all about? Pelley's been communicating with Peake? Sending him messages, and Peake's babbling them back at me?"

"I wish I knew enough to theorize, Heidi. Right now I'm simply looking into everything."

"Okay . . . I'll do what I can." Sharp tug of the ponytail. Looking troubled, she opened the door. Milo and I walked her downstairs to the street. Her car was parked at the curb, half-lit by a streetlamp. Old, dented Chrysler minivan. A bumper sticker read, "Climbers Get High Naturally."

Milo said, "What's the highest mountain you ever tackled?"

"I'm more of a wall person than a mountain person. Sheer surfaces, the more vertical the better." She smiled. "Promise you won't tell? The best one wasn't exactly legal. Power sta-

tion near the Nevada border. We did it at three A.M., then para-
chuted down."

"Adrenaline high," said Milo.

"Oh, yeah." She laughed, got in the van, and drove away.

"Got your junior G-woman on the job," I said. "I think
she's found a new source of adrenaline."

"Yeah, she's a little hyper, isn't she? But at least someone's
cooperating. . . . So, what do you think about Peake's latest
soliloquy?"

"If there's some deep psychological meaning, it's elud-
ing me."

" 'Choo choo bang bang.' " He laughed. "Talk about loco
motives."

We returned to the Robbery-Homicide room. A Dunkin'
Donuts takeout box dominated Milo's desk. He said, "Shouldn't
you be getting home to Robin?"

"I told her it might take a while."

He studied the notes he'd scrawled in the interrogation
room. "Heidi," he said. "Our little mountain girl. Too bad
everything she's come up with is probably worth a warm
bucket of spit. . . . 'Choo choo bang bang.' What's next?
Peake reads selections from Dr. Seuss?"

He rubbed his eyes, stacked some papers, squared the corners with his thumbs.

"You think it was poor judgment?" he said. "Asking her to
check on Pelley?"

"Not if she's discreet."

"Worse comes to worst, Swig finds out, gets all huffy. He
can't afford to make too big a deal of it—bad publicity."

"Anything new on Pelley's whereabouts?" I said.

"Zilch. Ramparts *was* notified by the P.O., so there's something positive. Other than that, the P.O. wasn't very helpful.
Caseload in the hundreds; to him, Pelley was just another
number. I doubt he could point him out in a crowd."

He pulled a folded sheet out of his jacket pocket and
handed it to me. LAPD Suspect Alert. Pelley's vital statistics
and a photo so dark and blurry I couldn't see it being useful

for anything. All I could make out was a round, clean-shaven Caucasian face smudged with indeterminate features. Thin, light-colored hair. Serious mouth. The crime was failure to report.

"This is what they're using?" I said, placing the paper on the desk.

"Yeah, I know—not exactly Cartier-Bresson. But at least they're looking. I did some looking, too. Driving around the neighborhood, checking out MacArthur Park, Lafayette Park, alleys, con bars, some other bad-guy spots I know. Visited the halfway house, too. Old apartment building, cons out in front, some Korean guy running the place—sincere enough, told me he'd been a social worker in Seoul. But he barely speaks English, and basically all he does is warehouse the residents, do random drug tests maybe four times a year. Counseling consists of asking the cons how they're doing. The ones I saw hanging around didn't look at all insightful. As for Pelley, all the Korean could say was that he'd been quiet, hadn't caused problems. None of the cons remembered a damn thing about him. Of course."

He reached for a piece of stale cinnamon roll. "He could be a thousand miles away by now. I didn't do much better with Stargill's investment records. The Newport money managers wouldn't talk to me, and they informed him I'd been asking around. He calls me, all irate. I tell him I'm just trying to clear him, how about he voluntarily gives me a look at his stock portfolio. If everything checks out, we call it a day. He says he'll think about it, but I could tell he won't."

"Hiding something?" I said.

"Or just guarding his privacy—everyone gets privacy, right? Even guys who cook and eat babies. Everyone except citizens who get laid out on steel tables, some white-coat peeling off their face, doing the Y-cut, playing peekaboo with their internal organs. No privacy there."

20.

ROBIN DIDN'T STIR when I slipped into bed beside her at one A.M. Visions of Peake's crimes and the knowledge that I hadn't helped Milo much kept me up for a while, heart beating too fast, muscles tight. Deep-breathing myself into an uneasy torpor, I finally slipped off. If dreams intruded, I had no memory of them in the morning, but my legs ached, as if I'd been running from something.

By nine A.M., I was drinking coffee and catching what passes for TV news in L.A.: capped-toothed jesters hawking showbiz gossip, the latest bumblings of the moronic city council, the current health scare. Today, it was strawberries from Mexico: everyone was going to die from an intestinal scourge. Back when I'd treated children, the news had frightened more kids than any horror flick.

I was about to switch off the set when the grinning blonde gushed, "And now more on that train accident."

The story merited thirty seconds. An unidentified man had lain across the MetroRail tracks just east of the city limits, squarely in the path of an empty passenger train. The engineer spotted him and put on the emergency brake, but not in time.

Choo choo.

I called Milo.

He picked up right away. "Yeah, yeah, the little train that couldn't. Probably nothing. Or maybe Peake really is a prophet and we should be worshiping him instead of keeping him locked up. Nothing much else on my plate, so I called the coroner. The deceased is one Ellroy Lincoln Beatty, male black, fifty-two. Petty criminal record—mostly possession and drunk and disorderly. The only thing that intrigued me was that Beatty spent some time in a mental hospital. Camarillo, thirteen years ago, back when they were still open for that kind of business. No mention of Starkweather, but you never know. The accident happened in Newton Division. I wish Manny Alvarado had the case, but he retired and the new guy isn't great about returning calls. I figured I'd head over to the morgue before lunch. Feel free to join me. If it gets you hungry, we can have lunch later. Like a big rare steak."

"Basically, the head and the lower extremities," said the attendant. He was a short, solidly built Hispanic named Albert Martinez, with a crew cut and goatee and thick-lensed glasses that enlarged and brightened his eyes. The crucifix around his neck was gold and hand-tooled, vaguely Byzantine.

The coroner's office was two stories of square, smooth, cream stucco, meticulously maintained. Back in East L.A. Back at County Hospital. Claire's old office was a few blocks away. I hadn't realized it before, but she'd come full circle.

"The rest of him is pretty much goulash," said Martinez. "Personally, I think it's amazing we got what we did. The train must have hit him at what—forty, fifty miles per?"

The room was cool, immaculate, odorless. Empty steel tables equipped with drain basins, overhead microphones, a wall of steel lockers. A junior high student would recognize all of it; too many TV shows had dimmed the shock. But television rarely offered a glimpse at the contents of the lockers. Dead people on TV were intact, clean, bloodless props resting peacefully.

I hadn't been down here since internship, wasn't enjoying the experience.

"How'd you identify him?" said Milo.

"Welfare card in his pocket," said Martinez. "The lower extremities still had pieces of pants on and the pocket was in one piece. All he had on him was the card and a couple of bucks. The interesting thing is, you could still smell the booze on him. Even with all the other fluids. I mean, it was really strong. Only other time I smelled it that strong was this woman, died in childbirth, must have drunk two bottles of wine that night and she arrested on the delivery table. Her amniotic fluid was red—wine-red, you know? Almost purple. She must have been saturated with Thunderbird or whatever. The baby was dead, obviously. Probably lucky."

Martinez touched his crucifix.

"When's Beatty's autopsy scheduled?" said Milo.

"Hard to say. It's the usual backlog. Why?"

"It might be related to something. So you're saying Beatty must have been pretty juiced."

"To smell that strong? Sure. My guess would be way over the limit. He probably got blasted, wandered onto the tracks, lay down for a nap, and boom." Martinez smiled. "So, could I be a detective?"

"Why bother?" said Milo. "Your job's more fun."

Martinez chuckled. "Those tracks—they really should do something about them, no fence, no guardrail when they get close to the train yard. I grew up around there, used to play on the tracks, but they weren't running trains back then. You remember last month? The little kid who wandered on, walking home from school? Not far from where Beatty got hit. That kid, we didn't get anything recognizable on him. They should put a fence up, or something. . . . So, anything else?"

"I'd like to look at Beatty."

"Really? How come?"

"I want to think of him as a person."

Martinez's thumb and forefinger closed around the bottom of the crucifix. "A person, huh? Well, maybe looking at him isn't the right way to do that, you know?"

Milo said, "Humor me."

Martinez walked over to a locker, slid the drawer out silently, drew back white sheeting.

The face was gray, surprisingly intact except for a thatch of lacerations on the left cheek. Ash gray, because in life Ellroy Beatty had been black. White lint of kinky beard stubble, maybe four, five days' worth. Untrimmed mass of gray hair. The eyes were open, dull, dry, the lips caked with pinkish crust. That vacant look common to all dead faces. No matter what your IQ in life, when the soul flies, you look stupid.

Below the neck was empty space. Clean decapitation except for a few fringes of trachea and jugular, meaty muscle fibers protruding. Two feet down the table was a white-wrapped package that Martinez needlessly explained was "the lower extremities."

Milo stared at the ashen chunk that had once borne the consciousness of Ellroy Beatty. Not blinking, not moving. I wondered how many times he'd been down here.

Just as Martinez said, "Okay?" the door opened and a man strode in. He wore scrubs, a hairnet, paper slippers, a loose mask around his neck. About Beatty's age, tall, stoop-shouldered with a deeply tanned face and a thick black beard.

He glanced at us, read the index card in his right hand, and headed for one of the steel lockers, two rows away.

Then he saw Ellroy Beatty's head and flushed with anger. "What the hell's going on here?"

Martinez said, "Some kind of problem, Dr. Friedman?"

"I'd sure as hell say so. Who cut up my D.B.?"

"Your D.B.?" said Martinez.

"That's what I said. Are you *deaf,* Albert?" Friedman turned to Milo. "And who the hell are you?"

"LAPD."

"I thought Willis Hooks was on this one."

"No," said Milo. "Hooks is Central. This is a Newton case, the detective's Robert Aguilar."

"What?" said Friedman, jabbing the card. "The paperwork says Central, Hooks. How long have you been doing this, Mr. Aguilar?"

Milo said, "I'm Sturgis, Doctor. West L.A."

Friedman blinked. "What the hell—" He stepped closer to Ellroy Beatty's head. "Let me tell you, Detective, someone's in deep dirt. I had this D.B. scheduled for a post and someone cut his goddamn head off! And what's he doing in *that* drawer when he's supposed to be over here?" Friedman waved the card.

"No one moved him, Dr. Friedman," said Martinez. "He got put here right away. And no one cut him, this is the—"

"*Bullshit,* Albert! Bullshit on *toast*—bullets don't sever your damn head! Bullets don't—"

"This is D.B. Beatty," said Martinez. "The one who was hit by a—"

"I know who he *is*, Albert!" Another wave of the card. "Beatty, Leroy. Gunshot wound to the head, brought in last night—"

"Beatty, Ellroy," said Martinez.

"*Leroy*, Albert. Says so right here." The card was thrust at Martinez's face. "Case number 971132; Time of Delivery: three-sixteen A.M."

Martinez rolled up some of the sheeting covering Beatty's legs. Pulling out a toe tag, he read, "Ellroy Beatty, hit by a train. TOD three-forty-two A.M., case number 971135."

Friedman looked down at the head. Then the card. Then the numbers on the steel drawers. He yanked one open.

Inside was an intact body, naked, gray.

Exact same gray as Ellroy Beatty.

Same face.

All four of us stared.

I looked from corpse to corpse. Minor discrepancies materialized: Leroy Beatty had slightly less hair on top than Ellroy, but more on the bottom. A full white beard. No scratches on his face, but a keloid scar puckered the right jawline, probably an old knife wound.

The neat, blackened hole in his forehead looked too innocuous to have killed him. The impact had caused facial distortion—swelling around the nose, puffiness under the eyes. Bloodred eyeballs, as if he'd stared too long into the fires of hell.

Friedman's head was swiveling now, too.

"Twins," said Martinez. "Brother Ellroy, meet Brother Leroy."

Friedman turned on him. "Don't joke, Albert. What the hell's going on?"

"Good question," said Milo.

*   *   *

It took two hours to put it all together. Dr. Friedman left long before then, muttering about having to work with incompetents.

I sat with Milo in a morgue conference room. Detective Robert Aguilar from Newton showed up first. Young, good-looking, with a sleek black pompadour, he wore a gray pin-striped suit tailored to his trim frame. Manicured nails. He spoke very crisply, a little too fast, tried to come across light-hearted but couldn't pull it off. Milo'd told me he was new to the division, a Detective I. For all I knew, this was his first case.

Last to arrive was Willis Hooks from Central. I'd met him when he worked Southwest. A series of killings of handicapped people that had given me a glimpse of a cowardly new world.

Hooks was in his early forties, black, five-nine, heavy, with a clean head, bulldog jowls, and a thick, drooping mustache. His navy blazer had that baggy, too-long look you sometimes see with big-chested men. His shoes were dusty.

"Milo," he said, sitting down. "Dr. Delaware. Fate keeps putting us in the same room."

Aguilar watched and listened, trying, I guessed, to gauge Hooks's mood. To know with whom to align himself.

"Fate or just plain bad luck, Willis," said Milo.

Hooks laughed hoarsely and spread pudgy fingers on the table.

Milo said, "Willis, this is Robert Aguilar."

"Newton Division," said Aguilar.

"Charmed," said Hooks. "Yours is the train?"

"Yup," said Aguilar. "Ellroy Lincoln Beatty, male black, fifty-two."

"Mine's Leroy Washington Beatty, male black, fifty-two. Think they could be distantly related?"

Before Aguilar could answer, Hooks winked and said, "Mine went down around three A.M., give or take."

"Mine, too," said Aguilar.

"How 'bout that?" Hooks turned to Milo. "It appears

someone's got it in for the Beatty family. Maybe we should find out if they've got any other siblings. Maybe there's some more Beatty 187's all over town—hell, this could be a Beatty Holocaust. If not, least we should do is warn them."

Aguilar frowned. Taking out a gold Cross pen, he began writing in his pad.

Hooks said, "Got some ideas, Detective?"

Aguilar looked up. His lips were tight. "Just charting the data flow."

Hooks pursed his lips and his mustache bristled. "Well, that's good. So tell me, Detective Sturgis. What's your connection to the Bobbsey twins?"

"You're not going to believe this," said Milo.

We left the morgue at twelve-thirty P.M. Mission Road was alive with pedestrians. The air smelled like fried chicken.

"Grease," said Milo. "Yum. Lunch?"

"Not in the mood," I said.

"Such strength of character."

He'd left the unmarked in the red zone turnaround in front of the building along with other police vehicles. I'd used a nearby lot. A white-and-blue coroner's van circled past us and cruised out to the street.

Milo said, " 'Choo choo bang bang.' A train and a gun." He rested a foot on the unmarked's front bumper. " 'Bad eyes in a box.' Both times Peake spouts off the day before. So when does the bastard go on the Psychic Hotline and start raking in serious money?"

"If the news got out, I'm sure agents would be doing lunch with him at Spago."

He huffed. "So what the hell does it mean, Alex?"

"Two homeless men, a psychologist, a waiter," I said. "Wide range of ages, both sexes, blacks, whites. If there's a connection, I don't see it. Maybe Wendell Pelley's behind some of it. But he didn't do Dada. So if Dada's part of the mix, it means more than one killer. Same if the Beatty brothers really were killed simultaneously."

"Fine, fine, there's a psycho army out there. For all we

know, Peake spouted off about Richard, too, but till Claire showed up, no one was around to listen. The question is how the hell does Peake know?"

"The only logical possibility," I said, "is that he has some link to the outside."

"Got to be Pelley," he said. "Or another Starkweather alum. Guys like that would know all the boozehound places like the train tracks, the alley where Leroy was shot. Booze and mental illness, you said so yourself: bad combination. And Pelley's history fits: he was blind drunk when he shot his girlfriend and her kids. Now he's living on the streets again. The Beattys are just the kind of people he'd run into."

"Why use the train?" I said. "Why not shoot both of them?"

"The guy's crazy. Maybe a voice told him to do it that way. Choo choo goddamn bang bang. The main thing is, there's some pattern here."

I didn't reply.

He said, "You have a problem with Pelley?"

"No," I said. "I just can't see any conceptual link, even eliminating Richard Dada from the mix, between Claire and the Beattys."

"The Beattys were alcoholics," he said. "Claire worked with alcoholics. Maybe they were her patients."

"They'd fit the County profile," I said, "but that still doesn't offer any motive to kill them. It had to have something to do with Peake. His crimes—those clippings Claire held on to. She targeted him because there was something she wanted to learn about him. Or *from* him. I went back into the newspaper files and got some background on the Ardullo family. Scott's father was a major agricultural figure, adamant about not selling farmland to developers—he'd been wooed for years, but refused. Then he died, Scott and his family got murdered, and all the Ardullo land was sold. Be interesting to know who inherited."

"What?" he said. "We're running off in a whole other direction? The Ardullos were eliminated for *profit*, and Peake's some corporate *hit* man? C'mon, Alex, I'm more likely to believe Peake can flow through walls at will, off people, and return to his beddy-bye at the Loon Farm."

"I know Peake's disorganized, but big money always adds another dimension. Maybe you should at least visit Treadway—Fairway Ranch. Maybe someone will be around who remembers."

"Remembers what?"

"The crime. Something. Just to be thorough."

"Right now being thorough means finding Wendell Pelley."

He placed both hands on the hood of the unmarked and gazed over at the coroner's building, then up at the milky sky. Behind us were Dumpsters, water pumps, the rears of two antique hospital buildings. Sculpted cornices and ornate moldings topped crumbling brick. More Victorian London than East L.A. Jack the Ripper would've found it cozy.

"Okay," I said. "Let's stick with here-and-now. I can even give you a motive. The Beatty twins died at around the same time. That has a ritual flavor to it—a game. My vote is slaughter for fun. That also fits with the second-killer scenario. Plenty of precedent: Leopold and Loeb, Bianchi and Buono, Bittaker and Norris. It could return Richard Dada to the victim list. Pelley's buddy killed Dada before Pelley was released. But only a month before—the crime would still be psychologically fresh. Maybe the buddy's descriptions of how he did it turned Pelley on, got him back in the murder game."

"And the other bastard could be some nutcase Pelley hooked up with at the halfway house, Alex. I saw the guys living there. Not the Kiwanis Club. Okay, I'm going back, gonna be a little more assertive. Gonna continue patrolling Ramparts on my own, too. Keep checking the bum haunts. Play more phone tag with other divisions, neighboring cities, in case Pelley and/or Nut Buddy has been a bad boy somewhere else. Though the site of the Beattys' murders says they're still local. Which makes sense. They probably have no wheels, can't hit the freeway."

That reminded me of something. "The first time we discussed Richard, we talked about someone without a car. Maybe a bus rider. Same for Claire's phantom boyfriend."

"There you go," he said. "Bus-riding lunatics. You said he wouldn't look crazy. How do you feel about that, now?"

"Pretty much the same," I said. "All four murders were planned and meticulous. Whoever killed Richard and Claire had the sense not to steal their cars. And murdering the Beattys on the same night adds another level of calculation. Choreography. So if Pelley is involved, he's probably not actively psychotic. At least not externally. Don't forget, they let him out. He must've appeared coherent."

"When he kills, he's neat. That makes me feel a whole lot better." Shaking his head, Milo reached for the car door.

I said, "So the Treadway thing's off the table, completely?"

"You don't want to let go of it?"

"Those clippings bother me, Milo. Whatever Pelley's role in all this, something went on between Claire and Peake. She sought him out, made him a project. He predicted her murder. Sixteen years ago, he took out Brittany Ardullo's eyes. Claire's eyes were also targeted. It's almost as if he'd been trying to connect the two crimes—somehow relive his past, using a surrogate."

"The Beattys' eyes weren't messed with."

"But Richard's eyes *were* taken. Too much variation, too much that doesn't fit. Peake's the only link. If we understand more about him—his history—it may get us closer to Pelley. And whoever else is involved."

He swung the door open. "I just don't have the time, Alex. But if you want to go out there, fine. I appreciate the effort— I'll even phone Bunker Protection, see if I can get them to be cooperative. Meanwhile, I go nut-hunting right here on the streets."

"Good luck," I said.

"Luck doesn't seem to be cutting it." He withdrew his hand from the door and placed it on my shoulder. "I'm being a cranky bastard, aren't I? Sorry. Not enough sleep, too much futility."

"Don't sweat it."

"Let me apologize anyway. Contrition's good for the soul. And thanks for all your time on this. I mean it."

"My thanks will be your getting good grades and cleaning your room."

He laughed. Much too loudly. But maybe it helped.

21.

TWENTY MILES NORTH of L.A., everything empties.

I'd stopped at home long enough to pick up and scan the articles I'd photocopied at the library, gulp down some coffee, and get back on the freeway. The 405 took me to the 101 and finally Interstate 5, this time headed north. The last fast-food signs had been five miles back and I shared the freeway with flatbeds hauling hay, long-distance movers, the odd car, a few Winnebagos lumbering in the slow lane.

I had a heavy foot, speeding past brown, rumpled-blanket mountains, groves of scrub oak and pine and California pepper trees, the occasional grazing horse. The heat hadn't let up, but the sky was awash with pretty clouds—lavender-gray swirls, satin-shiny, as if an old wedding dress had been draped over the world.

The clippings had given me three possible contacts: Teo-doro Alarcon, the ranch superintendent who'd found the bodies; Sheriff Jacob Haas; and the only other person to comment on Ardis Peake's strange behavior without protection of anonymity, a kid named Derrick Crimmins. No listings on Alarcon or Crimmins, but a Jacob B. Haas had an address at Fairway Ranch. I called his number and a hearty male voice on a machine told me Jake and Marvelle were unavailable, but feel free to leave a message. I said I'd be in town on LAPD business and would appreciate it if Sheriff Haas could spare me some time.

The highway forked, the truck route sprouting to the right and draining the traffic from three lanes. Radar surveillance warnings were all around, but the eternity of open road before me was too seductive and I kept the Seville at 85, zipping past Saugus and Castaic, the western ridge of Angeles Crest National Forest, the Tejon Pass, then the Kern County border.

Shortly after eleven, I exited at Grapevine and bought some gas. My freeway map showed me how to get to Fairway Ranch, but I confirmed directions with the sleepy-looking attendant.

"That's for old people," he said. He was around nineteen, crew-cut, tan, and pimpled, with four earrings in his left lobe.

"Visiting Grandma," I said.

He looked up and down the Seville. "It's pretty nice there. Rich people, mostly. They play a lot of golf." The minitruck with the huge wheels and the Radiohead bumper sticker parked near the garbage cans was probably his. Freshly waxed. His eyes narrowed as he continued to stare at the Seville. I try to keep the car in good shape, but it's a '79 and there are limits.

"Used to be another town around here," I said.

His stare was dull.

"Treadway," I said. "Farms, ranches, peaches, and walnut groves."

"Oh, yeah?" Profound indifference. "Cool car."

I thanked him and left, taking a narrow northeastern road toward the Tehachapi Mountains. The range was gorgeous—high and sharp, peaks of varying height laid against one another masterfully, more perfectly arranged than any artist's composition could ever be. The lower hills were dun, the upper ridges the precise ash-gray of the Beatty brothers' dead faces. Some of the more distant crests had faded to a misty purple. Wintry colors even at this time of year, but the heat was more intense than in L.A., burning through the clouds as if they were tissue paper.

The road rose sharply. This was subalpine terrain. I couldn't imagine it as farmland. Then ten miles in, a sign reading FAIRWAY RANCH: A PLANNED COMMUNITY directed me down a left-hand pass that cut sharply through walls of granite. Another sign—STEEP GRADE: REDUCE SPEED—came too late; I was already hurtling down a roller-coaster chute.

A good two miles of chute. At the bottom was flat green patchwork centered by a diamond-bright aquamarine lake. The lake was amorphous—too perfectly shapeless, it shouted man-made. Two golf courses hugged the water, one on each side, fringed by lime-colored trees with feathery tops—California peppers. Red-topped houses were grouped in premeditated plots. Spanish tile on cream stucco, interspersed with trapezoids of green. The entire layout—maybe five miles wide—was outlined in white, as if drawn by a child too fearful to go outside the lines.

As I got closer I saw that the white was waist-high beam-and-post fencing. An exact duplicate of the "planned community" sign appeared a hundred yards later, over a smaller plaque that said Bunker Protection patrolled the premises.

No gates, just a flat, clean road into the development. Fifteen MPH speed limit and warnings to watch for slow-moving golf carts. I obliged and crawled past stretches of perfect rye grass. Lots more pepper trees, shaggy and undulating, sub-planted with beds of multicolored impatiens.

A thousand feet in, another dozen signs on a stout, dark tree trunk that might have been walnut offered a crash course in the layout of Fairway Ranch.

Balmoral Golf Course to the north, White Oak to the south, Reflection Lake straight ahead. The Pinnacle Recreation Center and Spa to the north, Walnut Grove Fitness Center to the south. In the center, Piccadilly Arcade.

Other arrows pointed to what I assumed were six different housing subdivisions: Chatham, Cotswold, Sussex, Essex, Yorkshire, Jersey.

The mountains were two or three miles away but seemed to be closer. Sparkling color and knife-edge detail said the air was pure.

Beyond the tree post was a small single cube of a building. The rounded edges and blatant texture of pseudo-adobe. More Spanish tile.

Letting the Seville idle, I looked around. Acres of grass and scores more California peppers, a few clumps of peach trees with curling leaves. A handful of larger trunks with bark that matched the color and texture of the signpost and had to be walnuts. No fruit or blossoms. Dead branches and truncated tops.

Imagining the stink of fertilizer, the grind of machinery, pickers moving through sun-dappled rows, I thought of Henry Ardullo's resolve never to sell out.

In the distance I could see assortments of houses—sugar cubes with red tile roofs. Not a hint of half-timber, brick, slate, or wood shingle.

Sussex, Essex . . . English monikers, Southwest architecture. In California, escape from logic was sometimes construed as freedom.

I heard an engine start. A pale blue Ford sedan with black-wall tires was parked next to the cube. Now it drove forward very slowly and stopped right next to me. Understated shield logo on the driver's door. Crossed rifles above "BP, Inc. A Security Corporation." No cherry on top, no conspicuous display of firearms.

At the wheel was a mustachioed young man wearing a pale blue uniform and mirrored shades.

"Morning, sir." Tight smile.

"Morning, Officer. I'm here to visit Jacob Haas on Charing Cross Road."

"Charing Cross," he said, stretching it out so he could appraise me. "That's all the way over in Jersey."

I resisted the temptation to say, "Atlantic City or Newark?"

"Thanks."

He cleared his throat. "New around here?"

"First time," I said.

"Relative of Mr. Haas?"

"Acquaintance. He used to be the sheriff. Back when it was Treadway."

He hesitated a moment before saying, "Sure." The same dullness I'd seen on the gas jockey's face. Treadway meant nothing to him, either. He knew nothing of the area's history. How many people did? I looked past him at the peach and walnut trees, now just woody memorials. Nothing else from the ranching days remained. Certainly not a hint of the blood-bath at the Ardullo ranch. If Jacob Haas wasn't in, or if he refused to see me, I'd wasted my time. Even if he talked, what could I hope to learn?

The security guard's car phone buzzed and he picked up, nodded, told me, "Jersey's way at the end—go straight through to the lake, turn right. You'll see a sign pointing to the White Oak golf course. Just keep on and it'll be there."

I drove away, watched him through my rearview mirror as he performed a three-point turn and headed toward Balmoral.

Piccadilly Arcade was a small shopping center due east of the security office. Grocery with a post office and ATM, dry cleaner, two clothing shops leaning toward golf togs and velour jogging suits. A sign outside the second said the movie tonight was *Top Gun*.

My drive to Jersey took me past perfectly appointed public buildings—the clubhouse, the spa—tennis courts, swimming pools. The houses looked better from a distance.

They varied in size by development. Essex was the high-rent district—detached split-levels and two-story haciendidas on postage-stamp lots, some landscaping, lots of Cadillacs and Lincolns, a few satellite dishes. Clear views of the lake. Fit-looking white-haired people in activewear. Further inland, Yorkshire was mock-adobe town houses clumped in fours and fives. A little skimpier in the flower-and-shrub department, but still immaculate.

The lake was obscured, now, by peppers. The trees were hardy, drought resistant, clean. They'd been brought into the San Fernando Valley years ago by the truckload, taking over the chaparral and contributing to the death of the native oaks. A quarter-mile of shaded road before Jersey appeared.

Mobile homes in an open lot. The units were uniformly white and spotless, with plenty of greenery camouflage at the base, but clearly prefab. Just a few trees on the periphery and no direct access to the lake, but majestic views of the mountains.

The few people I saw also looked in good shape, perhaps a

bit more countrified. Parked in front of the mobiles were Chevys, Fords, Japanese compacts, the occasional RV. The road that split the subdivision was freshly asphalted. No-frills, but the overall feel was still cleanliness, good maintenance, seniors settled in contentment.

I parked in one of the ten public spaces at the end and found Charing Cross Road easily enough—first street to the right.

Jacob and Marvelle Haas announced ownership of their Happy Traveler with a wood-burned sign over the front door. Two vehicles—a Buick Skylark and a Datsun pickup—so maybe someone was home. Some improvements had been added to the unit: green canvas window awnings, an oak door that looked hand-carved, a cement porch stacked up to the entrance. Potted geranium and cactus at the top, along with an empty fishbowl still housing a carbon filter. The door knocker was a brass cocker spaniel. Around its neck hung a garland of tiny cowries.

I lifted the dog and let it concuss against the door.

A voice called out, "One minute."

The man who opened was younger than I'd expected—younger than any of the residents I'd seen, so far. Sixty, if that, with iron-gray hair brushed straight back, and very acute eyes the same color. He wore a short-sleeved white knit shirt, blue jeans, black loafers. His shoulders were broad, but so were his hips. A lip of fat curled over his belt buckle. His arms were long, hairless, thin except at the wrists, where they picked up some heft. His face was narrow, sun-spotted in places, cinched around the eyes, and sagging around the bone lines, but his skin had a sheen, as if someone had buffed him lovingly.

"Dr. Delaware," he said in that same hearty voice. But his expression didn't match—cautious, tentative. "Got your message. Jacob Haas."

When we shook hands, his grip seemed reluctant—bare contact, then quick pressure around my fingers before he pulled away and stepped back inside.

"C'mon in."

I entered a narrow front room that opened to a kitchenette. A window air conditioner hummed. The interior wasn't cool, but the worst of the heat had been kept at bay. No knotty pine, no framed homilies, no trailer-park clichés. Deep gray berber carpeting floored the mobile. White cotton sofa and two matching easy chairs, glass-and-brass coffee table, blue-and-white Chinese garden bench serving as a perch for daffodils in a deep blue vase.

Picasso prints hung on panel walls painted pale salmon. Black lacquer bookshelves held paperbacks and magazines, a thirty-five-inch TV with VCR and stereo setup, and a skinny black vertical rack full of CD's. The Four Seasons, Duane Eddy, the Everly Brothers, Tom Jones, Petula Clark.

Rock and roll was old enough to retire.

The room smelled of cinnamon buns. The woman on the sofa got up and said, "Marvelle Haas, so pleased to meet you." She wore a navy polo shirt, white slacks, white sandals, looked to be her husband's age. More wrinkled than he, but a trim figure. Short, wavy hair dyed mahogany.

Her grip was strong. "Have a nice drive up from L.A.?"

"Very nice. Beautiful scenery."

"It's even more beautiful when you live here. Something to drink?"

"No, thanks."

"Well, then, I'll be shoving off." She kissed her husband's cheek and put her arm around his shoulder—protectively, I thought. "You boys be good, now."

"Now, that's no fun," Haas said. "Drive carefully, hon."

She hurried to the door. Her hips rotated. Years ago, she'd been beautiful. She still was.

When the door closed after her, Haas seemed to get smaller. He motioned toward the chairs. We both sat.

"She decided to visit her sister in Bakersfield," he said, "because she didn't want to be here when you were."

"Sorry—"

"No, not your fault. She doesn't like unpleasantness." Crossing his legs, he plowed his hair with one hand and studied me. "I'm not sure I want to be doing this, myself, but I guess I feel obligated to help the police."

"I appreciate that, Sheriff. Hopefully it won't be unpleasant."

Haas smiled. "Haven't been 'Sheriff' for a while. Quit right after the Ardullos, started selling insurance for my father-in-law. Two years later, there was no need for a sheriff—no more town."

"Who closed it down?"

"Group called BCA Leisure bought all the land. One of those multinational deals—Japanese, Indonesian, British. The American partners are a development group out in Denver. Back then they were buying up land right and left."

"Was there any resistance from the residents?"

"Not a peep," he said. "Farming's always been a tough life, and in Treadway only two families made a serious living from it, the Ardullos and the Crimminses. Between them, they owned ninety percent of the land. The rest of us were just here to keep their businesses going—like sharecroppers. So once they sold out, it wasn't much of a brainer. The sheriff job was only part-time, anyway. I was already living up in Bakersfield, near my in-laws. Doing bookkeeping for my father-in-law."

"When did you move back here?"

"Five years ago." He smiled again. "Like I said, it was near my in-laws. Seriously, I decided to pack it in when I figured I had enough policies tucked away to be comfortable. And Bakersfield was starting to look like L.A. We were thinking out of state, maybe Nevada, then this unit came up—a lucky deal, because Fairway units don't stay vacant very long. We said, why not. The air's great, terrific fishing, they show movies, you can do all your shopping right here. We travel half the year, a small place is perfect. We don't go mobiling, this thing's as rooted as any regular house. We fly. Vegas, when there's a show we want to see. Alaska, Canada. This year, we did a big one. London, England. Saw the Chelsea Flower Show because Marvelle likes flowers. Beautiful country. When they say green, they mean it."

His tone had relaxed. I hated what I had to do, decided to

approach the task indirectly. "The Ardullos and the Crimminses. A boy named Derrick Crimmins was quoted in an article I read about the crime."

"Carson Crimmins's son. The younger one—he had two boys, Derrick and Carson Junior, Cliff. Yeah, I remember both of them hanging around the crime scene, along with a bunch of other kids. I don't remember Derrick talking to the press, but sure, I can see him shooting off his mouth, he always had a mouth on him. —So, tell me, why do the police send a psychologist to talk about the Monster? Don't tell me it's some kind of evaluation, they're thinking of letting him out."

"No," I said. "He's locked up tight, no release in sight. I just saw him. He's pretty deteriorated."

"Deteriorated," he said. "Like what, a vegetable?"

"Close to."

"Well that's good. He shouldn't be alive. . . . *Deteriorated*—the village idiot, that's how everyone saw him. Myself included. He was treated with kindness, pity, it's a big-city lie that small-town people are prejudiced and intolerant, like those morons you see on *Jerry Springer.* The Monster received more kindness in Treadway than he ever would've in L.A. Him *and* his mother. A couple of drifters, not a penny in their pockets, they just showed up one day and got taken in."

Haas stopped, waited for comment. I just nodded.

He said, "She was no charm-school gal, Noreen. And *he* was certainly no prize. But no one let 'em starve."

"Was she a difficult person?"

"Not difficult, but not exactly pleasant, either. She was sloppy-looking, kind of puffy in the face, like she cried all night. You'd try talking to her and she'd hang her head and mutter. Not as crazy as Ardis, but if you ask me they were both retarded. Him more than her, but she was no genius. It was nothing but kindness on the Ardullos' part, taking her and Ardis in. She could cook, but Terri Ardullo was a fine cook herself. It was charity, pure and simple. Done it in a way to give them some dignity."

"Scott and Terri were charitable people."

"Salt of the earth. Scott was a nice fellow, but it was Terri had the ideals. Religious, involved in all the church activities. The church was on land donated by Butch Ardullo—Scott's dad. Presbyterian. Butch was born a Catholic, but Kathy—his wife—was Presbyterian, so Butch converted and built the church for her. *That* was a sad thing. Demolishing that church. Butch and his crew built it themselves—beautiful little white-board thing with carved moldings and a steeple they had made by some Danish fellow over in Solvang. Butch's house was something, too. Three stories, also white board, with a big stone porch, land stretching out in all directions. They grew walnuts and peaches commercially but kept a small citrus grove out in back. You could smell the blossoms all the way out to the main road. They gave most of the oranges and lemons away. The Crimmins place was almost as big, but not as tasteful. Two mansions, opposite sides of the valley."

His eyes clouded. "I remember Scott when he was a kid. Running around the groves, always cheerful. The house was happy. They were rich folks, but down-to-earth."

He got up, filled a glass with bottled water from the fridge. "Sure you don't want a drink?"

"Thanks, I will."

He brought both tumblers to the coffee table. Two gulps and his was empty.

"Refill time," he said. "Don't want to parch up like a raisin. Need more BTUs on the A.C."

Another trip to the kitchenette. He drained the glass, ran his finger around the rim, set off a high-pitched note. "You still haven't told me why you're here."

I began with Claire's murder. Her name drew no look of recognition. When I recounted Peake's babbling, he said, "I can't believe you came all the way up here because of that."

"Right now, there's very little else to go on, Mr. Haas."

"You just said he's deteriorated, so who cares what he says? Now, what is it exactly you think I can help you with?"

"Anything you can tell me about Peake. That night."

His hands flew together and laced. Fingertips reddened as

they pressed into knuckles. Nails blanched the color of clotted cream.

"I've spent a long time trying to forget that night, and it doesn't sound like you've got any good reason to make me go through it again."

"I'm sorry," I said. "If it's too difficult—"

"Damn thirst," he said, springing up. "Must be going diabetic or something."

22.

HAAS RETURNED LOOKING no happier, but resigned.

"It happened at night," he said, "but no one found out till the morning. I was the second to know. Ted Alarcon called me—he was one of Scott's field supervisors. Scott and Ted were supposed to drive up early to Fresno, take a look at some equipment. Scott was going to pick up Ted, and when he didn't, Ted called the house. No answer, so he drove over, went in."

"The door was open?" I said.

"No one locked their doors. Ted figured Scott had over-slept, maybe he should go upstairs and knock on the bedroom door. That shows you the kind of guy Scott was—a Mexican supervisor felt comfortable going upstairs. But on the way, Ted passed through the kitchen and saw it. Her." He licked his lips. "After that, God only knows how he had the strength to go upstairs."

"The papers said he followed the bloody sneaker prints."

"Ted was a gutsy guy, Vietnam vet, saw combat."

"Any idea where I can locate him?"

"Forest Lawn," he said. "He died a couple years later. Cancer." He patted his sternum. "Fifty years old. He smoked, but nothing will convince me the shock didn't break down his health."

He sat up straighter, as if affirming his own robustness.

I said, "So Ted went upstairs, saw the rest of it, and called you."

"I was still in bed, the sun had just come up. The phone rings and someone's breathing hard, gasping, sounding crazy,

I can't make head nor tail out of it, Marvelle's saying, 'What's going on?' Finally, I recognize Ted's voice, but he's still not making any sense, I hear 'Mr. Scott! Miss Terri!' " He shook his head. "I just knew something bad had happened. When I got there, Ted was on the front porch with a big pool of vomit in front of him. He was a dark-skinned fellow, but that morning he was white as a sheet. He had blood on his jeans and shoes, at first I thought *he'd* done something crazy. Then he started throwing up some more, managed to stand up, just about collapsed. I had to catch him. All the while he's crying and pointing back at the house."

Putting his knees together, Haas hunched and sank lower on the couch. "I took my gun out and went in. I didn't want to mess anything up, so I was careful where I stepped. The light was on in the kitchen. I saw Noreen Peake sitting on a chair—I mean you couldn't really tell it was her, but I knew. Maybe it was the way she was dressed—" His hand waved stiffly. "Ted's boot prints were in the blood—he wore Westerns—but so were others. Sneakers. I still didn't know if anyone was up there, so I moved really quietly. The lights were on wherever he'd—like he was showing off what he'd done. Scott and Terri were next to each other—hugging each other. I ran across the hall . . . found the little girl. . . ."

He emitted a low-pitched noise, like poorly oiled gears grinding. "The FBI interviewed me, wrote it up for their research. Get your bosses at LAPD to find you a copy."

I nodded. "What led you to Peake's shack?"

"The damn blood, it was obvious. The trail had thinned but it ran down the back stairs and out the back door. Specks and spots but you could still see bits of sneaker prints. It kept going maybe twenty yards on the pathway; then it died completely. At that point, I didn't know I was looking for Peake, only that I should head back to the shack. The sneakers were right inside Peake's door. Clerk over at the five-and-dime said Peake had tried to shoplift 'em a few weeks before and when she caught him, he mumbled and paid something and she let him keep the damn things."

Haas glared. "That was the trouble. Everyone was too nice

to him. He stumbled around town looking dumb and spooky; we didn't have any real crime in Treadway, didn't recognize him for what he was. It was a peaceful place, that's why a part-timer like me could be the law. Mostly what I did was help people fix stuff, check on shut-ins, make sure someone didn't get in his car when he was blind drunk. More of a damn social worker. But Peake . . . he was always strange. We were all too damn trusting."

His hands were working furiously. Time to give him some breathing room. I said, "When Treadway closed down, what happened to all the town records?"

"Boxed and shipped up to Bakersfield. But forget about finding anything there. We're talking maps, plot plans, and not much of it, at that. Sounds to me like you're digging a dry hole, Doctor. Why don't you go back to L.A. and tell your bosses to forget all this psychological stuff. Peake's locked up, that's the main thing."

He looked at his wrist. No watch. He got up and found it on one of the bookshelves, put it on, checked the dial.

I said, "I appreciate your spending the time. Just a few more things. The article I read said you found Peake sleeping."

"Like a—" His mouth trembled. "I was going to say like a baby. Christ—yeah, he was asleep. Lying on his back, hands folded over his chest, snoring, face all smeared with blood. At first I thought he'd been killed too, but when I looked closer I could see it was just stains, and that made me jam the cuffs on him."

He wiped sweat from his cheeks. "That place. I'd seen it from the outside but never been inside before. A sty— smelled worse than a dog run. What little stuff Peake owned was all jumbled and thrown around. Spoiled food, armies of bugs, empty bottles of booze, cans of spray paint, glue tubes, porno magazines he must've gotten somewhere else, 'cause that garbage wasn't sold in Treadway. No one recalls Peake traveling, but he must've. For the dope, too. He had all kinds of pills—speed, downers, phenobarbitol. The prescription pharmacist was over in Tehachapi, and they had no record of any prescriptions. So it must have been street stuff. Scum like Peake can get any sort of thing."

"Was he stoned that night?"

"Had to be. Even after I cuffed him and screamed in his face, stuck my gun right under his nose, I could barely rouse him. He kept fading in and out, got this real dumb smile on his face, and then he'd close his eyes and be in Never-Never Land again. It was all I could do not to shoot him right there. Because of what he did—what I found in his shack." He turned away. "On his hot plate. He'd taken the knife with him, the one he used on the little girl, grabbed that baby boy out of the crib, and—"

He sprang up again. "Hell, no, I won't go there. Took me too damn long to erase those pictures from my head. Goodbye, Doctor—don't say another word, just good-bye."

He hurried to the door, held it open. I thanked him for his time again.

"Yeah, sure."

"Just one more thing," I said. "Who inherited Scott and Terri's estate?"

"Bunch of relatives all over the state. Her folks were from Modesto, and Scott still had family up in San Francisco, on his mother's side. The lawyer in charge said there were two dozen or so heirs, but no one was fighting. None of them gave a damn about inheriting, they were all broken up about how the money came to them."

"Do you remember the lawyer's name?"

"No. Why the hell would it matter?"

"I'm sure it doesn't," I said. "And Scott's mother was already deceased."

"Years before. Heart condition. *Why?*"

"Just being thorough."

"Well, you're sure being that." He started to close the door. I said, "Mr. Haas, is there anyone else around here who might be willing to talk to me?"

"What?" he said, furiously. "This wasn't enough?"

"As long as I'm up here, I might as well cover all bases—you were a lawman, you know what it's like."

"No, I don't. And I don't want to. Forget it. There's no one from the old days. Fairway's for old city folk looking for peace and quiet. I'm the only Treadway hick in the place. Which is why they stuck me out with the trailers." His laugh was cold.

I said, "Any idea where Derrick Crimmins—"

"The Crimminses are as gone as anyone else. After Carson Senior and his wife got their money out of the land, they moved to Florida. I heard they bought a boat, did all this sailing, but that's *all* I know. If they're alive, they'd be old. At least he would."

"His wife was younger?"

"She was a second wife."

"What was her name?"

"I don't remember," he answered too quickly. His voice had hardened and he had closed the door till only a five-inch crack remained. The half-face I saw was grim. "Cliff Crimmins is also gone. Motorcycle accident in Vegas—it made the papers. He was into that motocross stuff, stunt driving, parachuting, surfing, anything with speed and danger. Both of them were like that. Spoiled kids, always had to be the center of attention. Carson bought them all the toys they wanted."

The door closed.

I'd raised someone else's stress level. Some psychologist.

No end to justify the means, either.

Had he reacted with special vehemence when the topic was the second Mrs. Crimmins, or had I already primed his emotional pump so that anything I said raised his blood pressure?

Walking back to the car, I decided upon the former: how likely would he be to forget the name of one of the richest women in town? So something about Mrs. Crimmins bothered him . . . but big deal. Maybe he'd hated her. Or loved her. Or lusted for her without satisfaction.

No reason to think it related to anything I was after.

I didn't even know what I was after.

Dry hole.

It was still before noon, and I felt useless. Haas claimed no Treadway residents were around, and maybe he was telling the truth. But I felt unsettled—something about his demeanor—why had he agreed to see me, started off amiable, then turned?

Probably just horror flashbacks.

Still, as long as I was up here . . . I'd already exhausted the major news sources on the Ardullo murders, but small towns had local papers, and Treadway's might've covered the carnage in detail. The records had all been shipped to Bakersfield. Not much of it, Haas claimed. But city libraries appreciated the value of old news.

As I reached the Seville, a baby blue security sedan nosed through the trailer park. Different guard at the wheel, also young and mustachioed. Maybe that was the Bunker Protection image.

He cruised alongside me, stopped the way the first man had. Staring. No surprise. He'd been told about me.

I said, "Have a nice day."

"You too, sir."

On my way out, I tripled the speed limit.

Back at the Grapevine gas station, I made a few calls and learned that the main reference library for Kern County was Beale Memorial, in Bakersfield.

Another forty-five minutes of driving. I found Beale easily enough, a ten-year-old, modernistic, sand-colored structure in a nice part of town, backed by a two-hundred-vehicle parking lot. Inside was a fresh-smelling atrium and the feel of efficiency. I told the smiling librarian at the reference desk what I was after and she directed me to the Jack Maguire Local History Room, where another pleasant woman checked a computer database and said, "We've got twenty years of something called the *Treadway Intelligencer*. Hard copy, not microfiche."

"Could I see it, please?"

"All of it?"

"Unless that's a problem."

"Let me check."

She disappeared behind a door and emerged five minutes later pushing a dolly bearing two medium-sized cardboard boxes.

"You're in luck," she said. "It was a weekly, and a small one, so this is twenty years. You can't take it out of the room, but we're open till six. Happy reading."

No raised eyebrows, no intrusive questions. God bless librarians. I wheeled the dolly to a table.

A small one, indeed. The *Intelligencer* was a seven-page green sheet and the second carton was half empty. Copies, beginning with January 1962, were bound by the dozen and bagged in plastic. The publisher and editor-in-chief was someone named Orton Hatzler, the managing editor Wanda Hatzler. I copied down both names and started to read.

Wide-spaced text and a few photos with surprisingly good clarity. Weather reports on the front page, because even in California weather mattered to farmers. High school dances, bumper crops, science projects, 4-H Club, scouting expeditions, gleeful descriptions of the Kern County Fair ("Once again, Lars Carlson has shown himself to be the peach-pie-eating champion of all time!"). Page two was much the same, and three was reserved for wire-service snips abstracting the international events of the day and for editorials. Orton Hatzler had been a strong hawk on Vietnam.

Butch Ardullo's name cropped up frequently, mostly in stories related to his leadership in the farm organization. A photo of him and his wife at a Fresno charity ball showed a big man with a bulldog face and a gray crew cut hovering over a willowy, refined-looking, dark-haired woman. Luck-of-the-draw genetics had favored Scott with his father's build and his mother's facial features.

Scott had inherited athletic skills, as well. The first time I found his name was under one of those football-hero group shots—players selected for the Kern County all-star game kneeling and beaming in front of a goalpost. Scott had played halfback for Tehachapi High, acquitted himself honorably.

No pictures of Terri Ardullo, which made sense. She wasn't a Treadway native, had grown up in Modesto.

Carson Crimmins's name showed up regularly, too. The other rich man in town. From what I could make out, Crimmins had started out as Butch Ardullo's ally in the fight for the family farm, but had switched course by the early seventies, expressing his frustration with low walnut prices and the rising cost of doing business, and advertising his willingness to sell "to the highest serious bidder."

No pictures of him. No comments from Butch Ardullo. The *Intelligencer* avoided taking sides.

March 1969. An entire issue devoted to Katherine Stethson Ardullo's funeral. References to a "lingering illness," and to the hiking death, years before, of the oldest son, Henry Junior. The article was augmented by old family snapshots and pictures of Butch and Scott at graveside, heads hung low.

August 10, 1974. Orton Hatzler mourned Nixon's resignation.

The following December, a hard frost damaged both the Ardullo and the Crimmins crops. Butch Ardullo said, "You've got to be philosophical, ride out the bad times with the good." No comment from Carson Crimmins.

March 1975. The death of Butch Ardullo. Two extra pages in a memorial issue. This time, Scott stood alone in the cemetery. Carson Crimmins said, "We had our differences, but he was a man's man."

June 1976. Announcement of Crimmins's marriage to "the former Sybil Noonan, of Los Angeles. As we all know, Miss Noonan, a thespian who has acted under the name Cheryl Norman, met Mr. C. on a cruise to the Bahamas. The nuptials took place at the Beverly Wilshire Hotel in Beverly Hills. Maid of honor was the bride's sister, Charity Hernandez, and co–best men were Mr. C.'s sons, Carson Jr. and Derrick. The newlyweds are honeymooning in the Cayman Islands."

Two photos. Finally a look at Carson Crimmins. Black tie. In the first shot, he and his new wife cut a five-tiered cake. He looked to be around sixty, tall, stooped, bald, with a too-small face completely overpowered by a beak of a nose. The nose bore down upon a fleshless upper lip. A pencil mustache added movie-villain overtones. Tiny, dark eyes glanced somewhere to the left—away from the bride. His smile was painful. A wary owl in a tuxedo.

The second Mrs. Crimmins—she who'd narrowed Jacob Haas's eyes and hardened his voice—was in her late thirties, short, with full arms and a lush body packed into a tight silk sheath of a sleeveless wedding dress. What looked to be a deep tan. Spiky tiara perched upon a pile of platinum hair. Lots of teeth, lipstick, and eye shadow, a generous offering of cleavage. No ambivalence in her thousand-watt smile. Maybe it was true love, or perhaps the rock on her finger had something to do with it.

The second picture showed the Crimmins boys flanking the newlyweds. On the left was Carson Junior, around seventeen. Haas had said Derrick was younger, but that was hard to tell. Both boys were thin, rangy, with prominent noses and a touch of their father's avian look. Better-looking than their father—stronger chins, broader shoulders. The same thin lips. Carson Junior was already his father's height, Derrick slightly taller. Junior's hair was wild, blond, curly, Derrick's dark and straight, hanging past his shoulders. Neither boy seemed to share the joy of the day. Both projected that immovable sullenness unique to teenagers and mug-shot criminals.

April 1978. The front-page story was a visit to Treadway by representatives of a company called Leisure Time Development. Carson Crimmins's invitation. Scott Ardullo said, "It's a free country. People can sell what's theirs. But they can also show some guts and hold fast to the farming tradition." No follow-up progress reports.

July 1978. The wedding of Scott Ardullo and Theresa McIntyre. The bridal gown, a "flowing affair complete with 10-foot train and hand embroidery, including Belgian lace and freshwater pearls, was imported from San Francisco." No cleavage here; Theresa Ardullo had favored long sleeves and full cover.

I moved on to the next batch of papers.

A half-year after the developers' visit, there was still no

mention of land sales or negotiation, offers from other companies.

Crimmins's overtures rejected because Scott Ardullo had refused to sell out and no one wanted to deal for half a loaf?

If so, Crimmins wasn't commenting on the record. In July 1978, he and Sybil took a cruise to the Bahamas. Snapshots of her on deck, doing justice to a flowered bikini, a tall, iced drink in one hand. The text said she'd "entertained the other guests with lilting renditions of show tunes and Broadway classics."

Nothing of interest till January 5, 1980, when I came across an account of "The Farm League New Year's Ball and Fund-raiser" at the Silver Saddle Lodge in Fresno.

Mostly pictures of people I didn't recognize. Till the bottom of page four.

Scott Ardullo dancing, but not with his wife.

In his arms was Sybil Crimmins, white-blond hair long and flowing over bare tan shoulders. Her gown was black and strapless; her breasts were barely tucked into its skimpy bodice as they pressed against Scott's starched white chest. Her fingers were laced with his and her big diamond ring sparkled between his digits. He looked down at her, she gazed up at him. Something different in his eyes—at odds with the solid-young-businessman image—too much heat and light, a hint of stupidity.

Dopey surrender.

Maybe it was too many drinks, or the novelty of holding someone who wasn't your wife, feeling her warm breath against your face. Or maybe a big party had offered the two of them the chance to flaunt something they'd been savoring in dark, musky rooms.

It could be why Jacob Haas had tightened up when talking about Sybil Crimmins. Scott, a boy he'd long admired, straying with a platinum-haired strumpet from L.A.?

As I stared at the picture, it seemed to give off waves of heat. Worth well more than a thousand words. I was surprised the *Intelligencer* had published it.

I found an editorial three weeks later that might've explained that:

After much soul-searching, as well as witnessing, first-hand, the triumphs and the travails of those noble enough—and some would say sufficiently quixotically inclined—to brave the elements of Nature as well as the much more malignant Forces of Big Government, this newspaper must weigh in on the side of rationality and self-preservation.

It's all fine and well for those born with silver spoons in their mouths to pronounce righteously about abstract ideals such as the Sanctity of the Family Farm. But to the bulk of the populace, those hardy but bowed men entrusted with the day-to-day, backbreaking labor that keeps the ground fertile, the branches laden, and the trucks loaded with Bounty, the story is quite another one.

Joe Average in Treadway—and, we'd venture to wager, any agricultural community—toils day after day for fixed wages, with no promise of security or profit, or long-term investment. In most cases, his meager plot of backyard and his domicile are all he owns, and sometimes even that is tethered to some Financial Institution. Joe Average would love to plan for the Future, but he's usually too overwhelmed by the Present. So when Good Fortune smiles in the form of rising land values, offering said Mr. Average the chance of Real Gain, he cannot be condemned for seizing the opportunity to afford his family the same safety and comfort that the more fortunate regard as their birthright.

Sometimes good sense and the rights of individuals must prevail.

At our last Kiwanis luncheon, Mr. Carson Crimmins said it best: "Progress is like a jet plane. Fly with it or stand on the runway and you risk getting blown away."

Those of more fortunate lineage but less vision would do well to realize this.

Times change, and change they must. The history of this

great country is based upon Free Will, Private Property, and Self-reliance.

Those who resist the voice of the future may find themselves in that Godless state known as Stagnation.

Times change. Brave and smart men change along with them.

Humbly, O. Hatzler

Scott Ardullo, fallen out of editorial good graces. Still, wouldn't the picture have embarrassed Carson Crimmins as well?

I read through subsequent issues, waiting for Scott's written response to the editorial. Nothing. Either he hadn't bothered, or the *Intelligencer* had refused to print his letter.

Five weeks later, Orton and Wanda Hatzler's names were gone from the paper's masthead. In their place, in ornate, curlicued typescript:

Sybil Crimmins
Publisher, Editor and Chief Writer

A pink sheet now, and cut back to three pages, flimsy as a supermarket mailer. No more wire-photo material. In its place, gushing movie reviews that seemed copied from press releases, barely literate accounts of local events, and amateurishly drawn cartoons with no apparent point. The too-large signature: "Derrick C."

Three barely filled pages, even twenty months later, when the headline screamed:

Slaughter At The Ardullo Ranch!
Ratcatcher Peeke Arrested!
by Sybil Noonan Crimmins
Publisher, Editor and Chief Writer

Treadways darkest hour has arrived, or so it seemed when Sheriff Jacob Haas was called by Best Buy Produce Supervisor Teodoro "Ted" Alarcon to the ranch

*and found a horrible massacre of unbelievable propor-
tion. Their in the house, Sheriff Jacob Haas found several dead bodies, namely the ranch cook, Miss Noreen
Peeke who was subjected to unbelievable and unhumane
treatment at the hand of a dark fiend. Upstairs, were the
other bodies, the ranch owner Scott Ardullo who got the
place from his dad, Butch Ardullo, Scott's wife Terri and
their daughter little Brittany who was around five years
old. It was all horrible. But no sign of one other member
of the family. The baby—Justin. All of us remember how
Terri had such a hard labor with him and it would've
been great for him to be okay.*

*But the terror continued. Sheriff Haas followed the
blood and walked all the way to the back of the house
where Noreen Peeke's son Ardith was living at the time
and their he found Justin. Good taste says we won't go
into detail but let's just say whoever did that to a tiny
little infant is a fiend of unbelievable satan-like propor-
tion. We are sick over this.*

*Ardith Peeke was drunk and stoned on all sorts of
drugs. He was the ratcatcher on the ranch, going after
all sorts of rodents and other pests, as well. So he
probably had all sorts of weapons and poisons but we
don't know yet what he used on those poor people.*

*Its really terrible and unbelievable, that something
like this could happen in a small, peaceful place like
ours but that seems to be the way the world is going,
look at the Manson Family and how they attacked
people who thought they were safe because they had
money and lived behind gates. And the music of today,
no one sings about love and romance, it's all nasty stuff
and getting worse.*

*So the message, I guess is, trust in God, only He can
protect you.*

*Sheriff Haas called in the FBI and the Bakersfield po-
lice to consult on this because its way out of what he
usually deals with. He told me he was in Korea but never
saw anything like this.*

My sources tell me Ardith Peeke has always been weird. Sometimes people tried to help him—I know my sons Cliff and Derrick sure did, trying to get him involved in some athletic activities and whatnot, theater projects, you name it. Anything to bring him out of his shell, because they figured he was lonely. But he wouldn't hear of it. He just stayed by himself snorting paint and glue and whatnot. My sources tell me he was too into himself to relate to other people, some sort of severe mental illness.

Why did he suddenly do such a terrible thing?

Will we ever know?

Everyone loved the Ardullos, they were here so long, working hard even when it wasn't sure that would help because crop prices were so low. But working hard because that's what they believed in, they were salt of the earth people, they just loved to work.

HOW COULD THIS HAPPEN HERE—IN TREADWAY!?

IN AMERICA!!!!???

But that's what happens when the mind goes I guess.

I wish I had the answers but I'm only a journalist not an oracle.

I wish God worked in ways that we could understand— why should babies and children suffer like that? What makes a guy just go crazy like that?

Questions, questions, question.

When I get some answers, I'll keep you posted.

S.N.C.

She never did.

Last edition of the *Intelligencer*.

23.

RETURNING TO THE main reference room, I pulled up San Francisco, Bakersfield, and Fresno microfiche on the Ardullo slayings. Nothing that hadn't been covered down in L.A.

In the Modesto *Bee* I found an obituary for Terri McIntyre Ardullo. Her death was described as "untimely," no mention of homicide. The bio was brief: Girl Scout, volunteer for the Red Cross, honor student at Modesto High, member of the Spanish Club and the Shakespeare Society, B.A. from UC Davis.

She'd been survived by her parents, Wayne and Felice McIntyre, and sisters Barbara McIntyre and Lynn Blount. A Wayne McIntyre was listed in Modesto. Feeling like a creep, I dialed and told the elderly woman who answered that I was conducting a search for relatives of the Argent family of Pennsylvania, in anticipation of the first Argent reunion, to be held in Scranton.

"Argent?" she said. "Then why us?"

"Your name came up on our computer list."

"Did it? Well, I'm afraid your computer got it wrong. We're not related to any Argents. Sorry."

No anger, no defensiveness.

No idea what had interested Claire about Peake.

I pictured him in his room, grimacing, twitching, rocking autistically. Nerve endings firing randomly as Lord knew what impulses coalesced and scrambled among the folds of beclouded frontal lobes.

The door opens, a woman enters, smiling, eager to help.

A new doctor. The first person to show any interest in him in sixteen years.

She kneels down beside him, talks soothingly. Wanting to help him . . . help he doesn't want. Help that makes him angry.

Put her in a box. Bad eyes.

I went searching in Miami newspapers for items about the Crimminses. Obituaries were the daily special: the *Herald* informed me that Carson and Sybil Crimmins had died together twelve years ago, in a yacht explosion off the coast of south Florida. An unnamed crew member had perished as well. Carson was listed as a "real estate developer," Sybil as a "former entertainer." No pictures.

Next came a *Las Vegas Sun* reference to Carson Crimmins, Jr.'s, death in a motocross accident, two years later, near Pimm, Nevada. Nothing on the younger brother, Derrick. Too bad; he'd talked on record once. Maybe he'd be willing to reminisce, if I found him.

Former *Intelligencer* publisher Orton Hatzler was memorialized in a back-page paragraph of the *Santa Monica Evening Outlook*. He'd died in that beach town of "natural causes" at the age of eighty-seven. Just a few miles from my house. Memorial services at the Seaside Presbyterian Church, donations to the American Heart Association, in lieu of flowers. The surviving widow: Wanda Hatzler.

Maybe she still lived in Santa Monica. But if I found her, what would I ask about? I'd uncovered a financial battle between the Ardullo and Crimmins clans, had played Sherlock with a single photograph that suggested another type of competition. But nothing suggested that the slaughter of the Ardullos had resulted from anything other than one madman's blood feast.

I thought of the suddenness of the attack. Asian cultures had a word for that kind of unprovoked savagery: *"amok."*

Something about Peake's amok had caught Claire Argent's interest, and now she was dead. Along with three other men . . . and Peake had predicted the murders of two of them.

Prophet of doom in a locked cell. There had to be a common thread.

I abandoned the periodicals indexes and searched computer databases for Wanda Hatzler and Derrick Crimmins. Find-A-Person coughed up a single approximation: Derek Albert Crimmins on West 154th Street in New York City. I used a library pay phone, called, and participated in a confused ninety-second conversation with a man who sounded very old, very gentle, and, from his patois, probably black.

W. Hatzler was listed in Santa Monica, no address. The woman's voice on the tape machine was also elderly, but hearty. I gave her machine the same spiel I'd offered Jacob Haas, told her I'd stop by later today.

Before I left Bakersfield, I phoned Milo. He was away from his desk and not answering his cell phone. Route 5 clogged up just past Newhall. An accident had closed the northbound lanes and caused rubberneck spillover in the opposite direction. A dozen flashing red lights, cop cars from several jurisdictions and ambulances parked diagonally across the freeway, news copters whirring overhead. An overturned truck blocked the mouth of the nearest on-ramp. Inches from its front wheels was a snarled mass of red and chrome.

A highway patrolman waved us on, but inertia slowed us to a snail slide. I turned on KFWB. The accident was a big story: some sort of altercation between two motorists, a chase off the ramp, then an abrupt U-turn that took the pursuing vehicle the wrong way. Road rage, they were calling it. As if labeling changed anything.

It took over two hours to get back to L.A., and by the time I reached the Westside the skies had darkened to charcoal splotches underlaid with vermilion. Too late to drop in on an old woman. I bought gas at Sunset and La Brea and called Wanda Hatzler again.

This time, she answered. "Come on over, I'm expecting you."

"You're sure it's not too late?"

"Don't tell me you're one of those morning people."

"As a matter of fact, I'm not."

"Good," she said. "Morning people should be forced to milk cows."

I called home to say I'd be late. Robin's message said she'd be in Studio City till eight, doing some on-site repairs at a recording session. Synchrony of the hyperactive. I drove to Santa Monica.

Wanda Hatzler's address was on Yale Street, south of Wilshire, a stucco bungalow behind a lawn of lavender, wild onions, thyme, and several species of cactus. An alarm company sign protruded from the herbs, but no fence surrounded the property.

She was at the curb by the time I finished parking, a big woman—nearly six feet, with healthy shoulders and heavy limbs. Her hair was cut short. The color was hard to make out in the darkness.

"Dr. Delaware? Wanda Hatzler." Brisk shake, rough hands. "I like your car—used to have a Fleetwood until Orton couldn't drive anymore and I got tired of supporting the oil companies. Show me some identification just to play it safe, then come inside."

Inside, her house was cramped, warm, bright, ash-paneled and filled with chairs covered in at least three variations of brown paisley cotton. Georgia O'Keeffe prints hung on the walls, along with some muddy-looking California plein-air oils. An open doorway peeked into the kitchen, where soft dolls were arranged on the counter—children in all sorts of native costumes propped up sitting, a tiny stuffed kindergarten. Old white two-burner stove. A saucepan sat above dancing blue flames, and a childhood memory hit me: the cold-afternoon fragrance of canned vegetable soup. I tried not to think of Peake's culinary forays.

Wanda Hatzler closed the door and said, "Go on, make yourself comfortable."

I sat in a paisley armchair and she stood there. She wore a deep green V-neck pullover over a white turtleneck, loose gray pants, brown slip-on shoes. The hair was black well salted with silver. She could've been anywhere from seventy to eighty-five. Her face was broad, basset-hound droopy, crumpled as used wrapping paper. Moist blue-green eyes seemed to have suction power over mine. She wasn't smiling but I sensed some sort of amusement.

"Something to drink? Coke, Diet Coke, hundred-proof rum?"

"I'm fine, thanks."

"What about soup? I'm going to have some."

"No, thanks."

"Tough customer." She went into the kitchen, filled a mug, came back and sat down, blew into the soup, and drank. "Treadway, what a hole. Why on earth would you want to know anything about it?"

I told her about Claire and Peake, emphasizing a therapeutic relationship gone bad, keeping prophecy out of it, omitting the other murders.

She put the mug down. "Peake? I always thought he was retarded. Wouldn't have pegged him for violence, so what do I know? The only psychology I ever studied was an introductory course at Sarah Lawrence back in another century."

"I'll bet you know plenty."

She smiled. "Why? Because I'm old? Don't blush, I *am* old." She touched one seamed cheek. "The truth is in the flesh. Didn't Samuel Butler say that? Or maybe I made it up. Anyway, I'm afraid I can't give you any ideas on Peake. Never had a feel for him. Now you're going to leave. Too bad. You're good-looking and I was looking forward to this."

"To talking about Treadway?"

"To maligning Treadway."

"How long did you live there?"

"Too long. Never could stand the place. At the time of the murders, I was working in Bakersfield. Chamber of commerce. Not exactly a cosmopolis but at least there was some semblance of civilization. Like sidewalks. At night I helped my husband put the paper to bed. Such as it was."

She lifted the mug and drank. "Have you read the rag?"

"Twenty years' worth."

"Lord. Where'd you get hold of it?"

"Beale Memorial Library."

"You *are* motivated." She shook her head. "Twenty years' worth. Orton would be shocked. He knew what he'd come down to."

"He didn't like publishing?"

"He liked publishing fine. He would've preferred running the *The New York Times*. He was a Dartmouth boy. The *Intelligencer*—doesn't that reek of East Coast sensibilities? Unfortunately his politics were somewhere to the right of Joe McCarthy, and after the war that wasn't very fashionable. Also, he had a little problem." She pantomimed tossing back a drink. "Hundred-proof rum—developed a taste for it when serving in the Pacific. Lived to eighty-seven, anyway. Developed palate cancer, recovered, then leukemia, went into remission, then cirrhosis, and even that took years to kill him. His doctor saw an X ray of his liver, called him a medical miracle—he was oodles older than me."

Laughing, she finished the soup, got up, poured a refill, came back. "The *Intelligencer* was Orton hitting bottom. He began his career at *The Philadelphia Inquirer* and proceeded to embark on a downward slide for the rest of his life. Treadway was our last stop—we bought the rag for next to nothing and settled into a life of crushing tedium and genteel poverty. Gawd, I hated that place. Stupid people everywhere you looked. Social Darwinism, I suppose: the smart ones leave for the big city, only the idiots remain to breed." Another laugh. "Orton used to call it the power of positive backpedaling. He and I decided not to breed."

I made sure not to look at the dolls in the kitchen.

She said, "The only reason I stayed there was because I loved the guy—very good-looking. Even handsomer than you. Virile, too."

She crossed her legs. Were those eyelashes batting?

I said, "The Ardullos don't sound stupid."

She gave a dismissive wave. "Yes, I know: Butch went to Stanford—he told anyone who'd listen. But he got in because of football. Everyone else liked him, but I didn't. Pleasant enough, superficially. One of those fellows who's convinced he's a magnet for females, puts on the Galahad act. Too much confidence in a man is not an endearing trait, particularly when it's unjustified. Butch had no fire—stolid, straight-ahead as a horse with blinders. Point him in a direction and he went. And that wife of his. An oh-so-delicate Victorian relic. Taking to her bed all the time. I used to think it was phony baloney, called her Little Miss Vapors. But then she surprised me and actually died of something."

She shrugged. "That's the trouble with being malicious—occasionally one is wrong, and a nasty little urge to repent seeps in."

"What about Scott?"

"Smarter than Butch, but no luminary. He inherited land, grew fruit when the weather obliged. Not exactly Einstein, eh? Which isn't to say I wasn't shocked and sickened by what happened to him. And his poor wife—sweet thing, liked to read, I always suspected there might be an intellectual streak hidden somewhere."

Her lip trembled. "The worst thing was those babies. . . . By the time it happened, Orton and I had just sold the paper and moved down here. When Orton read about the murder in the *Times*, he vomited, sat down at his desk, and wrote a story—as if he were still a journalist. Then he ripped it up, vomited again, drank daiquiris all night, and passed out for two days. When he woke up, he couldn't feel his legs. Took another day to convince him he wasn't dying. Great disappointment for him. He cherished the idea of drinking himself to death, sensitive soul. His big mistake was taking the world seriously—though I guess in a case like that you'd have to. Even I cried. For the babies. I wasn't good with children—found them frightening, too much vulnerability, a big girl like me never seemed suited to those little twig bones. Hearing what Peake had done confirmed all that. I didn't sleep well for a long time."

She brandished the mug. "I haven't thought about it in years, wondered if raking it up might bother me, but apart from thinking about the babies, this is rather fun. For twenty years we lived above the newspaper office, scrounged for advertising, took extra jobs to get by. Orton did people's bookkeeping, I tutored incredibly stupid children in English and wrote press releases for the yahoos at the C of C."

"So you never had much contact with Peake."

"I knew who he was—rather conspicuous fellow, lurching around in the alleys, going through the garbage—but no, we never exchanged a single sentence." She recrossed her legs. "This is good. Knowing I can still remember a few things— some juice in the old machine. What else would you like to know?"

"The Crimmins family—"

"Morons." She sipped more soup. "Worse than the Ardullos. Vulgarians. Carson was like Butch—uncreative, obsessed by the dollar—but minus the charm. In addition to walnuts, he grew lemons. Orton used to say he looked as if he'd been weaned on them. Never seemed to take pleasure in anything— I'm sure you have a word for it."

"Anhedonia."

"There you go," she said. "I should've taken Intermediate Psychology."

"What about Sybil?"

"Slut. Gold digger. Dumb blonde. Right out of a bad movie."

"Out for Crimmins's money," I said.

"It sure wasn't his looks. They met on a cruise line, faw-gawdsakes, what a horrid cliché. If Carson had had a brain in his head he'd have jumped overboard."

"She caused him problems?"

Pause. Eyeblink. "She was a vulgar woman."

"She claimed to be an actress."

"And I'm the Sultan of Brunei."

"What kind of difficulties did she cause?" I said.

"Oh, you know," she said. "Stirring things up—wanting to run everything the moment she hit town. Transform herself into a *star*. She actually tried to get a theater group going. Got Carson to build a stage in one of his barns, bought all sorts of equipment. Orton laughed so hard telling me about it, he nearly lost his bridgework. 'Guess who moved in, Wanda? Jean Harlow. Harlow in Horseshit.' "

"Who did Sybil plan on acting with?"

"The local yokels. She also tried to rope in Carson's boys. One of them, I forget which, had a minor knack for drawing, so she put him to work painting sets. She told Orton they both had 'star quality.' I remember her coming into the office with her ad for the casting call."

Leaning toward me, she spoke in a chirpy, little-girl voice: " 'I tell you, Wanda, there's hidden talent all over the place. Everyone's creative, you just have to bring it out.' She even thought she'd rope Carson in, and just being civil was a performance for him. Guess what play she had planned? *Our Town.* If she'd had a brain, you could have credited her with some irony. *Our Dump,* she should've called it. The whole thing fell apart. No one showed up at the audition. Carson helped that along. The day before the ad was supposed to run, he paid Orton double not to print it."

"Stage fright?"

She laughed. "He said it was a waste of time and money. He also said he wanted the barn back for hay."

"Was that pretty typical?" I said. "Crimmins buying what he wanted?"

"What you're really asking is, Was Orton corrupt when he dealt with wealth and power?, and the answer is, Absolutely." She smoothed her sweater. "No apologies. Carson and Butch ran that town. If you wanted to survive, you played along. When Butch died, Scott took over his half. It wasn't even a town. It was a joint fiefdom with the rest of us serfs balancing on a wire between them. Orton was caught right in the middle. By the late seventies, we decided we were getting the heck out, one way or the other. Orton had qualified for Social Security and mine was about to kick in, plus I'd inherited a small annuity from an aunt. All we wanted was to sell the printing equipment and get something for ownership of the paper. Orton approached Scott first, because he thought Scott would be easier to deal with, but Scott wouldn't even listen."

Beating her chest, she put on a gorilla face. " 'Me farmer,

me do nothing else.' Straight ahead and pigheaded, just like his father. So Orton went to Carson, and to his surprise, Carson said he'd consider it."

"Surprise because Carson was uncreative?"

"And because everyone knew Carson wanted to get out of Treadway himself. Each year there'd be talk of some new real estate deal."

"How long had that been going on?"

"Years. The main problem was Scott wouldn't hear of it, and half the land wasn't very attractive to the developers. The approach Orton used with Carson was to suggest the paper might be a good activity for Sybil, to keep her out of trouble." She snapped her fingers. "That did the trick."

Now I understood the *Intelligencer*'s sudden editorial shift toward Crimmins.

"What other kind of trouble was Sybil getting into?" I said.

She smiled archly. "What do you think?"

"I saw a picture of her and Scott at a dance."

The smile faltered, then changed course, growing wider, fuller, ripe with glee.

"Oh, that picture," she sang. "We might as well have published them naked. Orton wasn't going to print it, a gentleman to the last. But that night, he was sloshed to the gills, so I put the paper to bed."

Breathing in deeply, she savored the exhalation.

I said, "What was the fallout?"

"Nothing public. I suppose there was tension among those directly concerned. Terri Ardullo always impressed me as tightly wound, but she didn't run around after Sybil with a hatchet. The Ardullos were never the type to air their laundry in public. Same for Carson."

"What did the serfs have to say about it?"

"Nothing that I heard. Doesn't pay to antagonize the nobility if you want to eat. And it wasn't as if everyone didn't already know about Scott and Sybil."

"The affair was public knowledge?" I said.

"For months. Certainly since Sybil's production fell apart. I suppose she needed another role." She shook her head. "The two of them adopted a flimsy cover: First, Scott's truck would speed out of town. An hour later, the slut's little Thunderbird would zoom away. She'd always return first, usually with shopping bags. Sometimes she'd visit the peasants in the local stores, showing off what she'd acquired. Then, sure enough, Scott's truck would zip past. Ludicrous. How could they possibly think they were getting away with it?"

"So Carson had to know."

"I don't see how he couldn't have."

"And no reaction at all? He never tried to stop it?"

"Carson was much older than Sybil. Maybe he couldn't cut the mustard, didn't mind someone else keeping her busy from time to time. Perhaps that's why he bought Orton's line about finding Sybil recreation. We were certainly trying to exploit him—did you read the rag after she took over?"

"Borderline coherent."

"You're a charitable young man." She stretched. "My, this *is* great fun."

"What can you tell me about Jacob Haas?" I said.

"Well-meaning but a boob. Before he became sheriff, he'd been working as a bookkeeper in Bakersfield. He got the job because he'd served in Korea, took some law enforcement courses in junior college, didn't offend anyone."

"Meaning he wasn't aligned with either Butch or Carson."

"Meaning he never put their kids in jail."

"Was that ever a possibility?" I said.

"Not with Scott, but with the Crimmins boys, sure. Two obnoxious little buggers—spoiled rotten. Carson gave them fast cars, which they proceeded to race down Main Street. It was common knowledge that they drank and took drugs, so it was only luck they never killed anyone. One of them paid for his recklessness a few years later—died motorcycling."

"Any other offenses besides drunk driving?"

"General bad character. They treated the migrants like dirt. Chased the migrant girls. When the picking season was over, they switched gears and bothered the local girls. I remember one night, very late, I'd just finished with the paper, walked outside to get some air, when I saw a car screech to a stop down the block. One of those souped-up things with stripes on the side, I knew right away whose it was. The back door opened, someone fell out, and the car sped away. The person lay there for a second, then got up and started walking down the middle of Main Street very slowly. I went over. It was a little Mexican girl—couldn't have been older than fifteen, and she spoke no English. Her face was all puffy from crying and her hair and clothes were messed and torn. I tried to talk to her but she just shook her head, burst into tears, and ran away. The street ended a block later and she disappeared in the fields."

"Whose fields?" I said.

Her eyes narrowed, then closed. "Let me think about that. . . . North. That would have been Scott's alfalfa field."

"So no consequences for Cliff and Derrick?"

"None."

"How did they get along with their stepmother?"

"Are you asking if they slept with her?" she said.

"Actually, my imagination hadn't carried me that far."

"Why not? Don't you watch talk shows?"

"You're saying Sybil—"

"No," she said. "I'm not saying anything of the sort. Merely musing. Because she was a slut and they were healthy big boys. To be fair—something I generally detest—I never picked up an inkling of anything quite so repellent, but . . . How'd they get along? Who loves a stepmother? And Sybil wasn't exactly the maternal type."

"But she managed to get them involved in her theatrical production."

"Only one of them—the one who drew."

"Derrick," I said. "She wrote about it in the *Intelligencer*. Still, spoiled adolescents don't do things they hate."

She turned quiet. "Yes . . . I suppose he must have enjoyed it. Why all these questions about the Crimmins clan?"

"Derrick Crimmins's name came up in newspaper accounts of the murders. Commenting about Peake's oddness. Other than Haas, he was the only person to speak on the record, so I thought I'd track him down."

"If you find him, don't send regards. Of course he'd jump at the chance to ridicule Peake. He and his brother delighted in tormenting Peake—another bit of their delinquency."

"Tormenting how?" I said.

"What you'd expect from rotten kids—teasing, poking. More than once I saw the two of them and a gang of others they ran with collecting in the alley that ran behind our office. Peake used to hang around there, too. Inspecting garbage cans, looking for paint cans and God knows what. The Crimmins brats and their friends must have been bored, gone after some sport. They circled him, laughed, cuffed him around a bit, stuck a cigarette in his mouth but refused to light it. The last time, I'd had enough, so I stepped out into the alley using some blue language and they dispersed. Not that Peake was grateful. Didn't even look at me, just turned his back and walked away from me. I never bothered again."

"How'd Peake react to the ridicule?" I said.

"Just stood there like this." Her facial muscles slackened and her eyes went blank. "The boy was never all there."

"No anger?"

"Nope. Like a zombie."

"Were you surprised when he exploded into violence?"

"I suppose," she said. "It wouldn't surprise me, today, though. What do they always say—'It's the quiet ones'? Can you ever tell about anyone?"

"Any theories about why he killed the Ardullos?"

"He was crazy. You're the psychologist, why do crazy people act crazy?"

I started to thank her and moved to stand but she waved me still. "You want a theory? How about bad luck, wrong time, wrong place. Like walking off a curb, getting hit by a bus."

Her lips worked. She looked ready to cry. "It's not easy—surviving. I keep waiting for something to happen to me, but my luck keeps running in the black. Sometimes it's infuriating—yet another day, the same old routine." Another wave. "All right then, be off. Abandon me. I haven't helped you, anyway."

"You've been very helpful—"

"Oh, please, none of that." But she reached over and took

my hand. Her skin was cold, dry, so smooth it seemed inorganic. "Bear that in mind, Doctor: Longevity can be hell, too. Knowing things will inevitably go bad, but not knowing when."

24.

WHEN I LEFT, just after eight P.M., Wilshire was a pretty stream of headlights under a black-pearl sky. My head hurt—stuffed with history and hints. More hatred and intrigue in Treadway than I'd counted on. But still no connection to Claire Argent. Ready to end the workday, I called my service from the pay booth in the parking lot.

An earful: Robin would be delayed till ten, and a particularly obnoxious Encino attorney wanted my help on a festering custody case. He knew I worked only for the court, not as a hired gun, and he hadn't paid his bill for a consultation I'd done last year. Delusions were everywhere.

The fifth message was from Milo: "I'll be at my desk by seven-thirty, get in touch."

The operator said, "He sounded pretty irritated, your detective friend."

I drove to the station, announced myself at the desk, waited as the clerk called up to the Robbery-Homicide room. Uniforms passed in and out. No one paid me any attention as I scanned the Wanted posters. A few minutes later the stairwell door opened and Milo bounded out, brushing hair off his forehead.

"Let's go outside, I need air," he said, not bothering to stop. His suit was the color of curdled oatmeal, the right lapel stained with something green. His tie was tight, his neck was suffering, and he looked like a poster boy for National Hypertension Week.

We reached the sidewalk and started walking up Butler.

Dry, acidic heat hung in the air and I wished I'd stopped for a cold drink.

"Nothing on Pelley, yet," he said, "so don't ask. It's the Beatty twins who've been occupying my day. Brother Leroy told people he had an acting gig."

"Which people?"

"His fellow juiceheads. Willis Hooks and I were down at the murder scene this evening. Not far from a liquor store where Leroy used to hang, along with some other grapesuckers. Couple of them said Leroy had bragged about becoming a movie star."

"How long ago was this?" I said.

"Time isn't a strong concept with these guys, but they figure three, four months. Leroy also told his drinking buds he was gonna get his brother involved with the movie—said once the director found out he had a twin, he offered to pay more. The winos thought he was just running his mouth, 'cause Leroy tended to do that when he got sufficiently drunk. They didn't even believe Leroy *had* a twin. He'd never mentioned Ellroy."

"Did Leroy report back after the filming?"

"No. He returned a week later, cranky, refusing to talk about it. If he'd gotten hold of any cash, no one saw it. His buddies figured he'd gone on a bender, flushed it all down his gullet."

"Or Mr. Griffith D. Wark stiffed someone else," I said. Now my mind was racing. Fragments of history coming together . . . pieces fitting . . .

"I thought of that," he said. "None of them saw any tall white guy chatting up Leroy."

"Did Ellroy's drinking pals have anything to say about the movie?"

"Aguilar hasn't found any pals for Ellroy yet. He seems to have been the loner twin, lived by himself near the train tracks. One of the conductors remembers seeing him from time to time, stumbling around. Figured he was crazy because he was always talking to himself."

He scratched the side of his nose. "So here I am, stuck with the movie angle again. Maybe it's a link between Dada and the twins, but still no tie-in with Claire. Except for the fact that she *went* to the movies. Hell, can't you see me explaining *that* to her parents? I showed her picture to the bums and they didn't recognize her. No surprise, why would she have gone down to some South Central wino kip? I'm gonna head back tonight to that place in Toluca Lake where Richard used to wait tables—the Oak Barrel. It's a long shot, but maybe Claire dined there. For all we know, Mr. Wark picked up both of 'em there—and incidentally, you were right about Wark being D. W. Griffith's middle name. I looked it up. So this ass-hole sees himself as a cinema hotshot."

He scratched his head. "This is exactly the kind of flaky bullshit I hate dealing with. Why would Wark—or anyone else—bump off his cast?"

"Keeping the budget low?" I said.

"Better not give the studios any ideas. Seriously, what's going on here? And how—and *why*—would a robot like *Peake* be clued in?"

"Maybe Wark's filming murder."

"A snuff thing?"

"That, or a variant—not necessarily a sexual angle. A chronology of unnatural death—a literal blood walk. For the underground market. That would explain why the script's never been registered and why Wark used a fake name to rent his equipment and cut out on the bill. It could also explain the diversity of victims and methods. And the ritualism. We could be dealing with someone who sees himself as a splatter auteur. Playing God by setting up characters—real people— then bumping them off. Psychopaths depersonalize their victims. Wark could be accomplishing the ultimate degradation: reducing his 'cast' to prototypes: The Twins, The Actor, that kind of thing. It's cruel, primitive thinking—exactly the way kids play out their anger. Some angry kids never grow up. As far as Peake is concerned, he could be involved because Wark wants him involved. Because Wark's someone out of Peake's past. Wark's mightily affected by Peake's crimes. Now he's creating his own production, wants to integrate Peake into the process. And I've got a possible candidate for Wark: a fellow named Derrick Crimmins."

I told him everything I'd learned about Treadway. The longtime conflict between the Ardullos and the Crimminses, Scott's affair with Sybil, the Crimmins boys' antisocial behavior, Derrick's involvement with Sybil's abortive theater group.

"He had no special love for his stepmother, Milo, but he stayed involved with her. Because the whole notion of theater—of production—grabbed him personally. He also matches the physical description Vito Bonner gave us of Wark—tall, thin—and his age fits. Derrick would be in his mid-thirties now."

Milo took a long time to think about that. We were walking dark residential streets, shoes slapping the pavement. "So all the Crimminses except this Derrick are dead?"

"Father, stepmother, brother, all by accidental death. Interesting, isn't it?"

"Now he's a family murderer, too?"

"Rigging accidents can also be seen as a form of production—setting up scenes. Derrick was far from a model citizen. Wanda Hatzler described him and his brother as spoiled bullies and possible rapists."

I stopped.

"What?" he said.

"Something else just occurred to me. Sheriff Haas told me that after the murder Peake was found with lots of different drugs in his shack, including some illegal prescription pills, phenobarbital. None was missing from the pharmacy in Treadway and no one in the Ardullo household had obtained a prescription for it. So Haas was certain it had to have been obtained out of town. But no one ever saw Peake leave Treadway. So maybe he had a dope source in town. Wanda saw Derrick and his friends hanging around with Peake, mostly to harass him. Peake offered no resistance, was extremely passive. What if the Crimmins boys were the ones who supplied him with drugs—having fun with the village idiot? The night of the massacre, Peake got massively stoned, his psyche broke down, and he slaughtered the Ardullos. And Derrick and his brother realized they'd played an indirect role in it. Someone else might be horrified by that, but the Crimmins boys had plenty of reason to hate Scott Ardullo. His refusal to sell his land had obstructed their father's big development deal for years. And Scott was sleeping with their stepmother. What if they were *pleased* with what Peake had done? Took some vicarious *credit* for it? And, in a sick sense, it was a successful production: the land deal went through, the family became rich again. That kind of high could've been powerful stuff for a kid who'd already shown some serious antisocial tendencies. A few years later, Derrick tries his hand at something more direct: blowing up Daddy and Stepmom's boat. And, once again, he gets away with it."

"Or," he said, "the boat thing really was an accident, someone else gave Peake his dope, Wark's not Derrick, and Derrick's just some playboy drinking piña coladas in Palm Beach while working on his melanoma."

"All that, too," I said. "But as long as we're being contentious, I'll go you one further: Derrick and Cliff's involvement was more than vicarious. They fed Peake dope and played on his delusions intentionally. *Prodded* him to kill the Ardullos. They were dominant, aggressive; Peake was passive, impressionable. Maybe they learned that Peake harbored some resentment of his own toward the Ardullos, and they used that. Perhaps they never really expected it to happen—idle teenage dope talk—and when Peake ran amok, they were frightened, initially. Then amazed. Then pleased."

He knuckled his eyes. "What happened during your childhood to make you think this way?"

"Too much spare time." *Alcoholic father, depressed mother, dark hours alone in the basement fighting to escape the noise upstairs, struggling to create my own world . . .*

"My, my, my."

"At the very least," I said, "wouldn't it be good to find out where Derrick lives, what his financial situation is, does he have some sort of police record?"

"Fine," he said. "Fine."

Back in Robbery-Homicide, he played with the computer. No wants or warrants out on Derrick Crimmins, no listings on the sex offender rosters or the FBI's VICAP file, and as far as we could tell, he wasn't occupying space in any California jail.

A call to the Department of Motor Vehicles police info line revealed zero current registrations under that name.

Same for Griffith D. Wark. Find-A-Person yielded several D. Crimminses but no Derricks. No G. D. Wark.

Milo said, "I'll follow up with Social Security tomorrow. I'll even check out the death certificates for the Crimmins family, just to show you I care. Where exactly did the boat thing go down?"

"All I know is, out on the water off the coast of south Florida," I said. "Brother Cliff crashed on a motocross run in Pimm, Nevada."

He scribbled, closed his pad, got up heavily. "Whoever this Wark is, how's he contacting Peake?"

"Maybe with ease," I said. "Maybe he works at Starkweather."

He grimaced. "Meaning I need to get a look at personnel records. My old pal Mr. Swig . . . If this *Blood Walk is* a mega-snuff, you think Wark's actually hoping to sell it?"

"Or he just wants to keep it around for his own amusement. If he's Derrick and he inherited a bundle and doesn't need money, it could be one big, sick diversion."

"A game."

"I always thought the murders had a gamelike quality to them."

"If only," he said, "you were a stupid guy and I could kiss off your fantasies. . . . Okay, back to Planet Earth. The Oak Barrel."

"I'll come with, if you want."

He checked his Timex. "What about hearth and home?"

"Too hot to light a fire in the hearth, and the home's empty for a couple more hours."

"Suit yourself," he said. "You drive."

* * *

Toluca Lake's a pretty secret sandwiched between North Hollywood and Burbank. The main drag is a curving eastern stretch of Riverside Drive lined with low-profile shops, many with their original forties and fifties facades. The housing ranges from garden apartments to major estates. Bob Hope used to live there. Other stars still do, mostly those leaning toward the GOP. Lots of the great Western flicks were shot nearby, at Burbank Studios and up in the surrounding foothills. The Equestrian Complex is just a short drive away, as is NBC headquarters.

A quick turn on either side of Riverside takes you onto quiet streets emptied at night by permit-only parking and an attentive police force. Toluca Lake restaurants tend to be dim and spacious, leaning toward that unclassifiable fare known as continental cuisine, once an L.A. staple, now nearly extinct west of Laurel Canyon. White hair doesn't elicit sneers from the wait staff, martinis aren't the retro craze of the minute, piano bars endure.

From time to time I testify in a Burbank court and find myself down here, thinking about the perfect suburbia of black-and-white TV shows: moderne furniture, fat sedans, dark lipstick. Jack Webb tippling steely-eyed at a vinyl-padded bumper, winding down after a long day on the set. Nearby might be the guy who played Ward Cleaver, whatever his name was.

I'd been to a few of the Riverside Drive restaurants, but not the Oak Barrel. It turned out to be a modest stack of bricks and stucco squatting on a southeastern corner, half-lit by streetlamps, the cask-and-tankard logo discreetly outlined in green neon above the porte cochere. A parking lot twice the size of the restaurant put the construction date at late forties, early fifties. No valet, just a well-lit asphalt skillet with scores of spaces, a quarter of them occupied. Lincolns, Cadillacs, Buicks, more Lincolns.

The front door was oak inlaid with a panel of bubbled glass. We walked in, confronted a lattice screen, stepped around it into a small reception area backed by the cocktail lounge. Four drinkers flashing elbow. TV news winking above a wall full of bottles. No sound on the set. The air was icy, seasoned with too-delicate piano music, the lighting barely strong enough to let us make out colors. But the maître d's bright green jacket managed to work its way through the gloom.

He was tall, at least seventy, with slicked white hair, Roman features, and black-rimmed eyeglasses. A reservation book was spread out before him on the oak lectern. Plenty of open slots. The lattice blocked a view of the main dining room to his left, but I could hear silverware clatter, conversational thrum. The pianist was turning "Lady Be Good" into a minuet.

The maître d' said, "Good evening, gentlemen." Capped smile, clear diction peppered by an Italian accent. As we came closer, he said, "Ah, Detective. Nice to see you again." A small gold rectangle on his jacket was engraved LEW.

"Hey, you remember," said Milo, with joviality that might've been real.

"I still got a memory. And we don't get too many police, not here. So this time you come to eat?"

"To drink," said Milo.

"This way." A green sleeve flourished. "You making any progress on Richard?"

"Wish I could say I was," said Milo. "Speaking of which, has this woman ever been here?" A photo of Claire had snapped into his hand like a magician's dove.

Lew smiled. " 'Speaking of which,' huh? You here to drink anything but information?"

"Sure. Beer, if you carry that."

Lew laughed and peered at the picture. "No, sorry, never saw her. Why? She know Richard?"

"That's what I'd like to know," said Milo. "Tell me, is there anything else that came to mind since the last time I was here?"

The maître d' handed back the photo. "Nah. Richard was a good boy, quiet. Good worker. We don't usually hire the so-calleds, but he was okay."

"The so-calleds," I said.

"So-called actors, so-called directors—mostly they're punks, think they're overqualified for everything, doin' you a big favor to show up. Nine times outta ten they can't handle carrying a bread plate or they end up mouthing off to some regular and I gotta untangle everybody's shorts."

He reached behind his back and tugged upward.

"We prefer old guys," he said. "Classy pros. Like me. But Richard was okay for a kid. Polite—'madam' and 'sir,' not that goddamn 'you guys.' Nice boy, very nice boy, that's why even though he wanted to be an actor I hired him. Also, he begged me. Said he really needed the money. And I was right about him. Good worker, got the orders right, no complaints—c'mon, let's go over, get you gents a nice drink."

The bar was an enormous lacquered walnut parabola rimmed with red leather. Brass bar, red stools with brass legs. The four drinkers were all glassy-eyed middle-aged men wearing sport coats. One necktie, three sport shirts with open collars spread over wide lapels. Plenty of space between them. They stared into tall glasses on paper coasters, dipped thick hands into dishes of nuts, olives, roast peppers, sausage chunks, pink curls of boiled shrimp pierced by red plastic toothpicks. The bartender was pushing sixty, dark-skinned, with luxuriant hair and the face of a carved tiki god. He and a couple of the drinkers looked up as Lew showed us to the end of the bar, but a second later, everyone had settled back into booze hypnosis.

Lew said, "Hernando, bring these gents . . ."

"Grolsch," said Milo. I asked for the same and Lew said, "Some of that sauterne for me, the reserve stuff, but just a little."

Hernando's hands moved like a chop-sockey hero. After he'd delivered the drinks and returned to the center of the bar, Milo said, "You ever get a customer named Wark?"

"Work?"

"Wark." Milo spelled it. "Mid to late thirties, tall, thin, dark hair, could be curly. Claims to be a film producer."

The maître d's eyes were merry. "Plenty of claims-to-be's, but no, I don't recall any Wark."

Milo sipped his beer. "What about Crimmins? Derrick Crimmins. He might have come in with a woman, younger, long blond hair."

" 'Might,' 'maybe'—this is still about Richard?"

"Maybe," said Milo.

"Sorry, no Crimmins either, but people come in without reservations, we don't know their names."

"We're talking eight, nine months ago. Would you remember every name—even with an excellent memory?"

Lew looked hurt. "You want me to check the reservation books, I'm happy to do it, but I can tell you right now, weird names like that I'd definitely remember." He closed his eyes. "Tall and skinny, huh? Richard's customer?"

"Could be."

"I am thinking of one guy, never gave me a name, just waltzed in expecting to be seated—but no girl, just him. I remember him clearly because he caused problems. Monopolized Richard's time to the point where the other customers weren't getting their food. They start complaining to the busboys, the busboys gripe to me, I have to deal with it. Another reason I remember was it was the only time I had any kind of problem with Richard. Not that he gave me any lip—it wasn't *his* problem, it was the guy's, just kept gabbing to Richard and Richard didn't know what to do. He'd just been working here for a few weeks. We drum into 'em, The customer's always right, so this musta put Richard in a situation, know what I mean? So I have to deal with it, doing my best to be polite, but the guy is not polite about it. Gives me the look, like who am *I* to tell *him*, know what I mean?"

"Did Richard say what the guy was talking to him about?"

"No, but the guy did. Something like, 'Hey, I could be his meal ticket, you think he wants to work here for the rest of his life?' Richard's off at another table, looking at me out of the corner of his eye, letting me know this isn't his idea. I offered the guy some comp wine, but he just said something nasty, threw down money, and left. Barely covered the check, not much left over for Richard. Caesar salad, veal parmigiana, German chocolate cake."

"So tell me," said Milo, "what song was the piano playing?"

Lew grinned. "Probably 'You Talk Too Much.'" He shrugged. "I'm just lucky, always had a memory, never bother with that elderberry stuff, Ginkgo biloba, any a that. Tell the truth, sometimes it's not fun. I got two ex-wives I wouldn't mind forgetting." His laugh was phlegmy. "You got pictures of this Wark guy, I can tell you right away if it's the same one."

"Not yet," said Milo. "Can you describe him?"

"Six-two, maybe -three, skinny, those all-black clothes like they do now, the so-calleds. My day, that was going to a funeral."

"Hair?"

"Long, dark. Not curly, though. Straight down—like a wig. Come to think of it, it probably *was* a wig. Big nose, little eyes, skinny little mouth. Not a good-looking guy. Hungry like, know what I mean? And tan—like he baked himself under a lamp."

"How many times did he come in here?"

"Just that once. One thing that might help, I saw his car. Corvette. Not a new one—the style with the big swoop in front? Bright yellow. Like a taxicab. I saw it because after he left, I cracked the door, made sure he was really leaving. You're saying he had something to do with Richard getting killed? Sonofabitch."

"Don't know," said Milo, finishing his drink. "You've been very helpful. I appreciate it. Is there anyone else working tonight who might remember the guy?"

Lew ran his finger around his wineglass. The sauterne was brassy gold. He hadn't touched it. "Maybe Angelo—I'll check. Want a refill?"

"No, thanks. You didn't happen to get a look at the Corvette's license plate? Even a few numbers."

"Ha," said the maître d'. "You're one a those cockeyed optimists, huh? Like in the song—think I'll go tell Doris to play that."

25.

ANGELO WAS A short, bald waiter of the same vintage as Lew, rushing flush-faced between two large tables. When the maître d' beckoned him away, his frown turned a pencil mustache into an inverted V and he approached us, muttering under his breath. Milo had talked to him, too, months ago, but he recalled the interview only vaguely. The troublemaker in black evoked nothing from him but a shrug.

"This is concerning Richard," said Lew.

"Richard was a nice kid," said Angelo.

Milo said, "Is there anything else you can tell us about him?"

"Nice kid," Angelo repeated. "Said he was gonna be a movie star—gotta get back, everyone's bitching about not enough mushrooms in the sauce."

"I'll talk to the kitchen," said Lew.

"Good idea." Angelo left.

Lew said, "Sorry 'bout that, his wife's sick. Give me your card and I'll call you when I have a chance to look at those books."

Driving back to the city, I said, "Maybe the meeting at the Oak Barrel was Richard's audition. Richard answers the casting ad, Wark says let me meet you where you work. See you in your natural habitat. Like a hunter sighting prey. It would also eliminate the need for Wark to have a formal casting location."

"Pretty gullible of Richard."

"He wanted to be a star."

He sighed. "Curly wig, straight wig—this is starting to feel nasty. Now all we have to do is find Mr. W., have a nice little chat."

"You've got a car now. A yellow Corvette isn't exactly inconspicuous."

"DMV doesn't list colors, only make, model, and year. Still, it's a start, if the 'Vette wasn't stolen. Or never registered . . . Big fenders—probably a seventies model." He sat up a bit. "A 'Vette could also explain why Richard was stashed in his own car. 'Vettes don't have trunks."

"Someone else to think about," I said. "The blond girlfriend. She fits the second-driver theory. She waits nearby until Wark's ditched Richard's VW, picks Wark up, they drive away. Untraceable. No reason to connect the two of them with Richard."

"Every producer needs a bimbo, right? Her I don't even have a *fake* name for." Taking out a cigar, he opened the window, coughed, and thought better of it. He closed his eyes, and his fleshy features settled into what might have passed for stupor. I stayed on Riverside, going west. By Coldwater Canyon, he still hadn't spoken. But his eyes opened and he looked troubled.

"Something doesn't fit?" I said.

"It's not that," he said. "It's the movie angle. All these years sweeping the stables and I finally break into showbiz."

I didn't hear from him in the morning and Robin and I went for breakfast down by the beach in Santa Monica. By eleven, she was back in the shop with Spike and I was taking a call from the obnoxious Encino attorney. I listened to one paragraph of oily spiel, then told him I wasn't interested in working with him. He sounded hurt, then he turned nasty, finally slammed down the phone, which provided a bit of good cheer.

Two seconds later, my service phoned. "While you were on the line, Doctor, a Mrs. Racano called from Fort Myers Beach, Florida."

Florida made me think of the Crimmins boating accident.

Then the name clicked in: Dr. Harry Racano, Claire's major professor. I'd called Case Western two days ago, asking about him. I copied down the number and phoned. A crisp-voiced woman answered.

"Mrs. Racano?"

"This is Eileen."

"It's Dr. Alex Delaware from Los Angeles. Thanks for calling."

"Yes," she said guardedly. "Mary Ellen at Case told me you called about Claire Argent. What in God's name happened to her?"

"She was abducted and murdered," I said. "So far, no one knows why. I was asked to consult on the case."

"Why did you think Harry could help you?"

"We're trying to learn whatever we can about Claire. Your husband's name showed up on one of her papers. Faculty advisers can get to know their students pretty well."

"Harry was Claire's dissertation chairman. They were both interested in alcoholism. We had Claire at the house from time to time. Sweet girl. Very quiet. I can't believe she's been murdered."

Talking faster. Anxious about something?

"Claire worked on alcoholism here," I said, "but a few months before she was killed, she quit her job somewhat abruptly and took a position at Starkweather Hospital. It's a state facility for the criminally insane."

Silence.

"Mrs. Racano?"

"I wouldn't know about any of that. Claire and I hadn't been in contact since she left Cleveland."

"Did she ever show an interest in homicidal psychotics?" I said.

Her sigh blew through the phone like static. "Have you met her parents?"

"Yes."

"And . . . But of course they wouldn't say anything. Oh, Dr. Delaware, I suppose you'd better know."

* * *

She gave me the basic facts. I got the details back at the research library newspaper files.

The Pittsburgh *Post-Gazette,* twenty-seven years ago, but it could've been any major paper. The story had been covered nationally.

FAMILY SLAIN IN YOUTH'S RAMPAGE

Responding to calls from concerned neighbors, police entered a west Pittsburgh home this morning and discovered the bodies of an entire family, and, hiding in the basement, the youth who is alleged to have murdered them.

James and Margaret Brownlee, and their children, Carla, 5, and Cooper, 2, had been stabbed and beaten to death with a knife and a tenderizing mallet obtained from the kitchen of their Oakland home. Brownlee, 35, was a delivery supervisor for Purity Bottled Water, and his wife, 29, was a homemaker. Both were described as early risers with regular habits, and by noon yesterday, when Mr. Brownlee hadn't left for work and none of the other family members had appeared, neighbors called the police.

The suspect, Denton Ray Argent, 19, was found crouching near the furnace, still clutching the murder weapons and drenched with blood. Argent, who lived with his parents and a younger sister three doors down from the Brownlees, was termed odd and reclusive, a high school dropout whose personality had changed several years before.

"He was around fourteen when it started," said a woman who declined to be identified. "Even before then, he wasn't very social—quiet, but the whole family was, they kept to themselves. But when he got to be a teenager he stopped taking care of himself, real sloppy. You'd see him walking around, talking to himself, waving his hands around. We all knew he was strange, but no one thought it would ever come to this."

Reports that Denton Argent had worked briefly as a gardener for the Brownlees have not been confirmed. Argent was taken into custody at central jail, pending booking and further investigation.

Plugging Denton Argent's name into the computer pulled up several more stories that reiterated the crime. Then nothing for a month until a page-three item appeared:

FAMILY KILLER COMMITTED TO HOSPITAL

Alleged mass murderer Denton Argent has been judged legally insane and incapable of assisting in his own defense by three court-appointed psychiatrists. Argent, accused of slaying Mr. and Mrs. James Brownlee and their two small children in a homicidal spree that shocked the quiet Oakland neighborhood and the entire city, was evaluated by doctors hired by both the prosecution and the defense.

"It was pretty clear," said Assistant District Attorney Stanley Rosenfield, assigned to prosecute the case. "Argent is severely schizophrenic and completely out of touch with reality. No purpose would be served by going to trial."

Rosenfield went on to say that Argent would be committed to a state hospital for an indefinite term. "Should he ever regain competence, we'll haul him into court."

One week after that:

MURDERER'S FAMILY STAYS PUT—AND MUM

The parents of family killer Denton Argent have no plans to move from the Chestnut Street address where, three doors from their well-kept house, their son slew all four members of a neighboring family.

Argent, 19, was judged criminally insane and incapable of assisting in his own defense against the charges of murdering James and Margaret Brownlee and their two young children, Carla, 5, and Cooper, 2. His parents, Robert Ray and Ernestine Argent, owners of a local gift shop, have refused to talk to the press, but neighbors report they have stated an unwillingness to "run from what Denton did." Their shop was closed for three weeks but later reopened, reportedly with a substantial drop in business. But the general attitude of the neighborhood was charitable.

"These are decent people," said another neighbor, Roland Danniger. "Everyone knew Denton was strange, and maybe they should've tried to help him more, but how could they know he'd turn violent? If I feel sorry for anyone, it's the little sister; she's always kept to herself, now you don't see her at all."

The reference was to Argent's younger sister, Claire, 12, who was removed from her public junior high school and is reportedly being tutored at home.

Five years later:

FAMILY SLAYER DIES IN ASYLUM
Mass murderer Denton Argent has died of a brain seizure in his cell at Farview State Hospital, authorities reported today.

Argent, 24, murdered an entire family during a bloody early-morning spree five years ago. Judged mentally incompetent, he was committed to the state facility, where he has resided without incident. The seizure, possibly due to a previously undiagnosed epileptic condition, or to psychiatric medication, caused Argent to pass out in his locked cell and to choke on his own vomit in the middle of the night. His body was discovered the following morning. Hospital authorities report no suspicions of foul play.

"Harry never found out until Claire's last year in grad school," Eileen Racano had said. "It was a shock. The poor thing, carrying around that burden."

"How did she bring it up?"

"It was during the time she was working on the final draft of her dissertation. That's always a stressful period, but Claire seemed to be having an especially hard time. Writing didn't come easily to her, and she was a perfectionist, drafting and redrafting. She told Harry she was worried she wouldn't pass her orals."

"Was that a possibility?" I said.

"Her grades were excellent and her research was solid."

I let the unspoken "but" hang in the air.

"Back then, personality issues couldn't be considered," she said.

"So your husband had reservations about Claire's temperament."

"He thought she was a sweet young woman, but . . . too closed off. And to grow up under a shadow like that . . . Harry felt she hadn't dealt with it. That it might cause her problems later on."

"How exactly did he find out?" I said.

"One morning he came in to the lab and found Claire there. She looked awful; it was obvious she'd been working all night. Harry asked her why she was driving herself so hard and she said she had no choice, she just *had* to pass, it was everything she'd lived for. Harry said something to the effect that there was life beyond grad school, and Claire fell apart—sobbing, telling Harry he didn't understand, that becoming a psychologist was all that mattered, she *had* to do it, she wasn't like other students. Harry asked in what way, and that's when it all came out. Afterward, Claire just curled up on the chair, shivering. Harry gave her his jacket and stayed with her until she calmed down. After that, we reached out more to Claire, invited her over for dinner. Harry was a wonderful man. His students all loved him. Years after he went emeritus, we'd still get letters and cards and visits. Not from Claire, though. After that one episode, she closed up, refused to talk about it. Harry couldn't demand that she receive therapy, but he suggested it strongly. Claire promised she would, but she never confirmed that she had."

"So she passed her exams, received her doctorate, and went her own way."

"Believe me," she said, "it troubled Harry. He even debated holding her up—he was in real conflict, Dr. Delaware. But ethically, he knew he couldn't. Claire had fulfilled all the requirements for graduation, and he felt she'd never trust anyone again if he went public with her story. The funny thing was, at her orals, she was the picture of confidence. Charming, in control, as if nothing had ever happened. Harry chose to take that as a sign that she'd gotten help. But once she had her degree in hand, she shut us out completely. Even after she received the fellowship right here at Case Medical School we never heard from her. A year later, we heard she got a job in Los Angeles. Harry said, 'Claire's going off to the Wild West.' The whole incident bothered him. He wondered if he should've been more forceful in getting her to deal with the guilt."

"She felt guilty about what her brother had done?"

"Unjustified guilt, but yes, that's the way Harry saw it, and his insights were almost always correct. He saw neuropsychology as an escape for Claire. Testing, numbers, lab work, no need to get into feelings. He wondered if she'd ever leave the field, and now you tell me she did."

"Her brother died of a seizure," I said. "Did your husband wonder if Claire's career choice might have been related to her seeking an organic basis for Denton's crimes?"

"That, too. But he worried that someday that defense would crumble. Because she wouldn't find any simple answers, might grow disillusioned. Harry was a neuropsychologist himself, but he was also a master psychotherapist. Along with his alcoholism research, he worked with MADD, treating the families of drunk-driving victims. He tried to teach his students the value of maintaining emotional balance."

"Claire didn't get the message."

"The Claire we knew didn't. She was such a . . . distant girl. Seemed to be punishing herself."

"In what way?"

"All work, no play, never attending department functions,

no friendships with the other students. I'd bet the dinners at our home were her main social contacts. Even the way she furnished her room, Dr. Delaware. Student housing's never gorgeous, but most students try to do something with what the university gives them. One night it was especially cold, and Harry and I drove her home. The way she lived shocked us. All she had was a bed, a desk, and a chair. I told Harry it looked like a jail cell. He wondered if she might be trying, symbolically, to share her brother's fate."

Now I knew why Claire had refused to talk about her family to Joe Stargill.

Now I understood Rob Ray and Ernestine's willingness to let Claire shut them out of her life: monumental shame.

No matter what was happening around her . . .

I'd wondered about family chaos, but my imagination hadn't stretched far enough.

Like so many people who enter the helping fields, Claire had been trying to heal herself. Approaching it from a distance, at first, as she hid behind hard data and lab work. Working for Myron Theobold, a man who'd abandoned psychoanalysis for a Ph.D. in biochemistry. *I see myself as a humane administrator. . . . I don't get involved in their personal lives. I'm not out to parent anyone.*

Staying with Theobold all those years because he allowed her to remain a stranger.

Then something changed.

Professor Racano had suspected professional escape wouldn't work forever, and he'd been right. Last year, Claire had gone looking for answers—going about it with characteristic academic detachment, scanning library files for rampages similar to her brother's.

Why at that point in her life? Perhaps something had weakened her defenses. . . . The only thing that came to mind was the divorce. Because marrying Joe Stargill had been another sad stab at normalcy, and it had failed.

I thought of how she and Stargill had met. That afternoon in the Marriott bar, impulsive, just like the Reno wedding. Yet ultimately, Claire's motivation for pairing up with Stargill had been anything but hasty, most probably unconscious. She'd preserved the secrecy with which she'd encrusted herself since adolescence by selecting a self-absorbed child of alcoholics who could be counted upon to concentrate on his own problems and keep his nose out of hers.

Casual pickup, incredible sex. The semblance of physical intimacy, unencumbered by exploration. Stargill had described the marriage as the parallel movement of two busy roommates.

Claire had made a brief stab at decorating her home and her life. After Stargill moved out, she stripped the house bare. Not for serenity. Back to the cell.

Punishing herself, just as Professor Racano had suspected. Trying, once again without consciously realizing it, to replicate Denton Argent's bleak fate in order to bond, somehow, with the brother who'd polluted her formative years.

She'd been twelve when Denton slaughtered the Brownlees. But maybe much younger when she realized there was something different—maybe dangerously different—about her only sibling. Did she blame herself for not telling someone?

Or was she simply ashamed to be linked genetically to a monster?

I thought of how the Argents had refused to move. Remaining on the same block had to have been wrenching for them. For the entire neighborhood. Had Claire been shunned for the rest of her childhood?

When Denton seized fatally, she'd been seventeen, still living at home. An upbringing capped at both ends by trauma, shame, and loss. Adolescence was hallmarked by the quest for identity. What had happened to Claire's sense of self?

Had she ever visited Denton at the asylum, or had her parents forbidden contact? Had she planned, at some point, to talk to her brother about his crimes? Tried to make sense of events that defied explanation?

If so, Denton's death had killed any hope.

Years later, she decided to look for answers anyway.

Learning about the Ardullo murders must have seemed like salvation.

The parallels between the two cases chilled my blood. I could only imagine how Claire had felt, spooling microfiche, only to come upon Denton's doppelgänger in Ardis Peake.

First, shock. Then sickening, spreading familiarity, empathy in its worst incarnation.

Finally, a glimmer of reprieve: one last chance to tackle the Big Why.

Now that I knew what I did, Claire's move to Starkweather, her zeroing in on Ardis Peake, wasn't puzzling at all.

So many madmen, so little time.

Not a choice, really. A psychologically preordained dance backed by the choreography of pain.

A dead certainty.

26.

"NO LUCK," SAID Milo.

"On what?"

"Anything. The Corvette, any sort of locale on either Wark or Derrick Crimmins. No Social Security on Wark, and Crimmins's last tax filing was ten years ago. In Florida. Didn't get to take it any further 'cause I was tied up in the courthouse. Trying to get three separate judges to okay warrants on Peake's mail and his phone calls. No go. Prophecy didn't impress them. The third one laughed me out of chambers and told me to consult a palm reader."

It was nearly five. He'd pulled up in my driveway a few minutes ago. Now he was scrounging in the fridge, bent sharply as he eyed a lower shelf, the ridges and bulges of his service revolver protruding through his too-tight tweed jacket.

"Claire's relationship to Peake didn't matter?" I said.

He shook his head, pulled out mayonnaise, mustard, a packet of corned beef I'd forgotten about, got some corn rye of similar vintage from the bread box. Slapping together a limp-looking sandwich, he sat down, chomped out a semicircle.

" 'Gobbledygook' was the operative word," he said. "And 'psychotic meanderings.' They all said Peake was, at most, a material witness. If that. Also, his mental state rendered him unlikely to provide significant materiality, so the entire rationale falls apart."

Another chunk of sandwich disappeared. "I didn't do any better on getting into Wark's B. of A. account. A fictitious

233

person only remotely and theoretically associated with an eight-month-old homicide doesn't cut the evidentiary mustard."

"Mommy," I said, "I wanna be a policeman when I grow up."

His grin was savage. "Now for the happy news: Wendell Pelley is no longer a suspect. At least not for the Beatty brothers. Wendell Pelley is deceased. For well over a week—before choo choo bang bang. His body showed up in a county garbage dump in Lennox six days ago. Sheriff's deputy happened to read the wire I put out and called. The dump's organized, so they were able to pinpoint what load Pelley came in on. Commercial container behind an industrial laundry. It was collected three days before he was found, but the maggot feast indicates Pelley could have been in there a while before that. No sign of violence to the corpse. Looks like he fell asleep in the Dumpster and got shipped out with the trash."

"Crushed to death?"

"No, they spotted him before compaction—what was left of him. Cause of death was extreme dehydration and malnutrition. The sonofabitch starved himself. I called the Korean who runs the halfway house. He said yeah, Pelley hadn't been eating much before he split. Probably weighed a hundred and twenty back then. No, he didn't see that as reason for alarm, Pelley wasn't causing problems."

"Talk about self-punishment," I said. "Pelley made it all the way from Ramparts to Lennox on foot?"

"He probably walked through alleys in some not-nice neighborhoods, found his final resting place, curled up, and died."

"Not a trace of foul play?"

"Nothing, Alex. They filed it as a definite suicide. I read the report and it's pretty clear. Desiccation, cachexia, low hemoglobin count, something about his liver chemistry that said he hadn't received adequate nutrition for a long time. No wounds, no broken bones; his neck bones were intact, and so was his skull. The only damage was what the maggots had done."

Staring at what was left of the sandwich, he hesitated, gulped it down, wiped his face, got himself a beer.

"Think about that, Alex. Feeling so low that you throw yourself out in the garbage."

"He could still be good for Claire," I said.

"If I could show that he and Claire ever met, maybe. But now that he's dead? Also, given the fact that he's *not* good for Dada or the Beattys, my enthusiasm for him has faded considerably. I got carried away. Like Mr. Dylan said, too much of nothing."

He returned to the fridge, got an apple, bit down noisily.

"Maybe I can throw you a little cheer," I said. "For what it's worth, I know why Claire sought out Peake."

I told him about Denton Argent's rampage. His chewing slowed. When I finished, he put the apple down. "Her brother. Never heard of the case."

"Me, neither. It happened twenty-seven years ago."

"I was in Vietnam. . . . So what was she hoping to learn by glomming on to Peake?"

"Her conscious motive was probably wanting to understand psychotic violence. Being a psychologist—and a researcher— legitimized it. But I think she was really trying to understand why her family—her childhood—had been shattered."

"And Peake could've told her that?"

"No," I said. "But she would've denied her motives."

"So she attaches herself to Peake, tries to get him to open up about what he did."

"Maybe she did more than try," I said. "If anyone could pry him open, it would've been Claire. Because she was the only person to spend any significant time with him during his commitment. She *cared*. What if she succeeded, and Peake told her something that put her in danger?"

"Such as?"

"He hadn't acted alone. He'd been prodded by the Crimmins brothers. Or believed he had. Alternatively, Peake's still in contact with Crimmins and told him Claire was getting too nosy. Crimmins decided to fix the problem. That's how Peake knew about Claire's murder the day before it happened."

"*If* he knew," he said. " 'Bad eyes in a box' ain't exactly evidence. As I was reminded three times today." He picked up the apple, twirled it by the stem. "Very creative, Alex, but I don't know. It all hinges on Peake having conversations. Faking out being a veg."

"What if his mental dullness isn't all due to psychosis?" I said. "What if the bulk *is* caused by his medication? The severity of his tardive symptoms and the fact that he's never had his dosage altered from five hundred milligrams show he reacts strongly to moderate amounts of Thorazine. Let's say Claire decided to experiment, withdrawing pills in order to restore some clarity. And it worked."

"She tampered on the sly?"

"We're talking intense motivation. A woman who gave up her job just to get next to Peake. If she thought easing up on his Thorazine would open him up, why not? She could've rationalized that it was for his own good—the meds were increasing his neurological problems, he could get by on less. The obvious risk would have been an increase in his violent impulses, but she might've felt confident she could deal with that."

"Heidi was working with him, too," he said. "She wouldn't suspect?"

"Heidi's medically and psychologically unsophisticated. Claire told her what she wanted her to know. Any changes may have been subtle—a few sentences here and there. And they may have occurred only in response to Claire's prodding. Claire was spending intense one-on-one time with Peake, probing very deliberately. She knew what she wanted: a window into Peake's violence. And, by extension, Denton's. Even if Peake did say something to Heidi, there'd be no reason for her to comprehend. Or care. She'd dismiss it as gibberish, just as she did with the 'bad eyes' recitation until Claire turned up dead."

"And with Claire gone, Peake gets his full dosage again."

"And lapses into incoherence."

"Okay," he said. "Let me take this all in. . . . Peake blabs, Claire finds out someone else was involved . . . and Wark enters the picture because he and Peake are somehow in contact—"

"Because Wark works at Starkweather—"

"Yeah, yeah, let me put this in order. . . . Peake wakes up—maybe he does get more violent. Or at least belligerent with Wark. He makes threats—'I've got this doctor who's really interested in me. I told her you turned me into a monster, she believes me, she's gonna get me out of here.' Even if Claire never said that, Peake could believe it—delusional. He's still crazy, right?"

I nodded.

"Still," he said, "that's an awful lot of gabbing for old Monster."

"Unless he's been faking."

"I brought that up at the beginning. You said it was unlikely."

"The context has changed."

He shot out of his chair, paced the room, buttoned and unbuttoned his coat. "If Wark was threatened, why not kill Peake?"

"Why bother?" I said. "Back on a full dose—or a higher one, if someone's tinkering in the opposite direction—Peake's no threat. He'll live out his life in his S&R room, the tardive symptoms will intensify until he's neurologically cooked, one day someone will walk in and find him dead. Just like Denton."

"Claire could just do that?" he said. "Pull pills with nobody noticing?"

"Starkweather gives its staff plenty of latitude. Dr. Aldrich was Claire's nominal supervisor, and he didn't seem to know much about her cases. Neither did Swig. In that respect, working at Starkweather was similar to her job with Theobold—plenty of solitude. The style to which she'd become accustomed since childhood."

"So," he said, "I waltz in there again and ask to look at the personnel files. Swig's gonna roll out the carpet."

"You can use the publicity threat—filing for warrants, the media getting hold of it. No reason for him to know the judges haven't cooperated. Ask to meet with the men in

Claire's group. That's certainly reasonable. While you're there, try to work in the personnel records."

He circled some more. "One more thing. The Beatty brothers. Why would Crimmins/Wark tell Peake about killing them? On the contrary, if Peake's hassling him, the last thing he'd want would be for Peake to know anything."

"Good point," I said. "So maybe it's Column A: Peake and Crimmins still *are* colluding. Carrying on the alliance that led to Peake's original blood walk. Having fun with it—recording it on film." My gut tightened. "I just thought of something. The eye wounds. What's a camera lens?"

He stopped pacing. "An eye."

"An all-seeing eye. Invisible, omniscient, director as god. These crimes are about power and control. Actors as subjects. *Subjected*. Camera observation goes only one way. I see, you don't. No eyes for *you*."

"Then why weren't the Beattys' eyes messed with?"

"Maybe because they were already impaired. Drunk—blind drunk?"

"Nutso," he said. "Back to the booby hatch. Maybe while I'm there I'll rent a room. . . . Okay, I'll set it up for tomorrow. I'd like you there, see what else you can pick up. Meanwhile, I'll do more tracing on Crimmins, see if I can find out the last time he surfaced under his own name, learn more about those family accidents."

A big finger poked the expanse of wash-and-wear that covered his heart. He winced.

"You okay?" I said.

Laboriously, he stood up. "Just gas—serve me something healthier next time."

27.

GLOSSY WALLS PAINTED a peach pink that managed to be unpleasant. A dozen blond fake-wood school desks lined up in two rows of six. The facing wall was nearly spanned by a spotless blackboard. Rounded edges blunted the plastic frame; no chalk, two soft erasers.

Directly in front of the board was an oak desk, bolted to the floor. Nothing atop the surface. The right-hand wall bore two maps of the world, equal-area and Mercator projection. Posters taped to the walls offered treatises on table manners, nutrition, the basics of democracy, the alphabet in block and cursive, a chronology of U.S. presidents.

Duct tape fastened the posters: no thumbtacks.

The American flag in the corner was plastic sheeting atop a plastic rod, also bolted.

Outward trappings of a classroom. The students wore khaki uniforms and barely fit behind the blond desks.

Six of them.

Up front sat an old man with beautiful golden-white hair. Kindly granddad on a laxative commercial. Behind him were two black men in their thirties, one mocha-toned, freckled, and heavy, with Coke-bottle glasses and a rashlike beard, the other lean, with a hewn-onyx face and the glint-eyed vigilance of a hunter surveying the plains.

At the head of the next row was a very thin creature in his twenties with hollow cheeks, haunted eyes, and blanched lips. Gray fists knuckled his temples. He sat so low his chin nearly touched the desktop. Stringy brown hair streamed from under a gray stocking cap. The hat was pulled down to his eyebrows and made his head appear undersized.

Behind him was giant Chet, yawning, flexing, sniffing, exploring the interior of his mouth with his fingers. So big he had to sit sideways, giraffe legs stretched into the aisle. No hint of the bony horror concealed by khaki trousers. He recognized Milo and me right away, winked, waved, blew a raspberry, said, "Yo bro my man whus shakin and bakin baked Alaska Juneau you know hot cold tightass don't sneeze on me homey you too homely homo fuck me up the ass." The lean black man glared.

When we'd seen Chet the first day, Frank Dollard hadn't mentioned he'd been part of Claire's group. Today, Dollard wasn't saying much of anything; he stood in a corner and glared at the inmates.

The last man was a small, sallow Hispanic with a shaved head and a grease-stain mustache. The room was air-conditioned to meat-locker chill, but he sweated. Rubbed his hands together, craned his neck, licked his lips.

More tardive symptoms. I scanned the room for other signs of neurological damage. Grandpa's hands trembled a bit, but that could've been age. Probably the freckled black man's gaping mouth, though that might have been psychotic stupor or a twisted daydream . . .

Frank Dollard swaggered to the front of the room and positioned himself behind the oak desk. "Morning, gentlemen."

No more warmth in his voice than fifteen minutes ago, when he'd met us at the inner gate, arms folded across his chest.

"Here again," he'd finally said, making no move to free the lock.

Milo said, "Just couldn't stay away, Frank."

Dollard huffed. "What exactly are you trying to accomplish?"

"Solve a murder, Frank." Milo's hand grazed the lock.

Dollard took a long time pulling out his key ring, locating the right key, inserting it in the lock, giving one sharp turn.

The bolt released. Several more seconds were taken up in pocketing the key. Finally, Dollard shoved the gate open.

Once we were in, he smiled sourly. "Like I said, what exactly are you trying to accomplish?" Not waiting for an answer, he smoothed his mustache and began walking across the yard. The dirt stretched ahead of us, brown and smooth as butcher's paper.

Milo and I started to follow. Dollard increased the distance between us. The heat and the light were punishing. Inmates stared. If one of them had come from behind, Dollard would have been no use at all.

Three techs stood watch on the yard. Two Hispanics and a blocky white man, nothing close to Derrick Crimmins's physical description.

Dollard unlocked the rear gate and we approached the main building. Instead of entering, he stopped several feet from the door and rattled his key ring.

"You can't see Mr. Swig. Not here."

"Where is he?" said Milo.

"Hospital business. He said to give you fifteen minutes access to the Skills for Daily Living group. That's it."

"Thanks for your time, Frank," said Milo, too mildly. "Sorry to be such a bother."

Dollard blinked, pocketed the keys. Gazing back at the yard, he clicked his teeth together. "These guys are like trained animals, you can't vary the stimulus-response too much. Your coming in here is disruptive. Top of that, it's pointless. No one here had anything to do with Dr. Argent."

"Because no one gets out."

"Among other things."

"Wendell Pelley got out."

Dollard blinked again. His tongue rolled under his lower lip. "What does that have to do with the price of eggs?"

"A nutcase gets out, a few weeks later one of his shrinks is dead?"

"Dr. Argent was never one of Pelley's shrinks. I doubt she ever ran into him."

"Why was Pelley released?"

"You'd have to ask one of the doctors."

"You have no idea, Frank?"

"I don't get paid to have ideas," said Dollard.

"So you said the first time," said Milo. "But we both know that's crap. What'd Pelley do to get out?"

Dollard's leathery skin reddened and his shoulders rose. Suddenly, he chuckled. "More like what he didn't do. Act crazy. He hadn't been crazy for a long time."

"Medical miracle?" said Milo.

"My opinion, the guy was never really psychotic in the first place, just a drunk. I'm not saying he faked anyone out. People who knew him when he was first committed said he was all over the place—hallucinating, acting wild, at one point they had to put him in restraints. But then a month or two later, that all stopped, even without meds. So, my opinion, it was severe alcohol poisoning and he got detoxed."

"Then why wasn't he sent back to trial?"

"Because when he got arrested we were still doing not guilty by reason. He was off the hook."

"Lucky him," said Milo.

"Not so lucky—he still got cooped up here for twenty-odd years. Longer than he would've been in prison. Maybe it wasn't just alcohol. Pelley'd been mining for years; he could've got some kind of heavy-metal poisoning in his system. Or he was just a short-term crazy, freaked out and got better. Whatever, he never needed any neuroleptics, just some antidepressants. Year after year, he's hanging around, no symptoms, guess they thought it didn't make sense."

"Antidepressants," said Milo. "Sad sack?"

"Why all the interest? He cause problems on the outside?"

"Only for himself, Frank. Starved himself to death."

Dollard's mouth twitched. "He never liked to eat. . . . So where'd they find him?"

"In a garbage dump."

"Garbage dump," said Dollard, as if visualizing it. "This is gonna sound bleeding-heart, but he wasn't really that bad of a guy. At least when I talked to him, he really felt remorse for what he'd done to his girlfriend and those kids. Didn't even wanna get out. Which don't excuse what he did, but . . ." He shrugged. "What the hell, we all have to go sometime."

"Who was his doctor?" I said.

"Aldrich. Not Argent."

"You're sure he had no contact with Dr. Argent?"

Dollard laughed. "Can't be sure of anything but death and taxes. And to answer your next question, he wouldn't a known Peake, either. Pelley was on B Ward, Peake's always been on C."

"What about out on the yard?" I said.

"Neither of them ever went out onto the yard that I saw. Peake never leaves his damn *room*."

"So who did Peake have contact with?"

Dollard's eyes got cold. "I answered that last time you were here, doc. No one. He's a damn zombo." He looked at his watch. "And you're wasting my time. Let's get this over with."

Turning, he stomped past the big gray building, bull neck pitched forward. A well-trodden dirt path veered to the right. When we reached the west side of the building, the dirt kept snaking to a group of three low, single-story beige structures cooking in the full sun.

A sign said ANNEXES A, B, AND C. Behind the smaller buildings sprawled another brown yard, as wide as the one in front, locked and empty. Then more chain link and a bulk of forest. Not eucalyptus, like at the entrance. Denser, green-black, some kind of pine or cedar.

"Where does that lead?" said Milo.

"Nowhere."

"Thought there was only one building."

"These aren't buildings, they're annexes," said Dollard, smiling. He hurried us past A. Double-locked door, plastic windows. Darkness on the other side of the panes, no signs of habitation. Outside were a few plastic picnic benches and a cement patio swept clean. The silence was punctured by occasional shouts from the main yard. No birdsongs, no insect chitters, not even the faintest stutter of traffic.

Annex B was empty, too. I sensed something behind me,

glanced over my shoulder. The main building, shielded from the morning sun, had darkened to charcoal.

Then the illusion of movement danced in a corner of my right eye, and my head buzzed, seized by split-second vertigo that passed just as quickly.

I looked back without stopping. Nothing. But for that brief interval, the entire structure had seemed to tilt forward, as if straining on its foundation. Now it was immobile as a building had to be, rows of windows dull and black, blank as a series of empty scorecards.

Dollard hurried to Annex C, stopped at the door, nodded at the pair of techs standing guard. Two black men. No Wark. They checked us out before stepping back. Dollard used his key, opened the door wide, peeked in, let the steel-reinforced panel swing back in Milo's face as he charged in.

"Morning, gentlemen," Dollard repeated.

None of the men returned the greeting. He said, "Let's do the pledge," and began reciting. No one stood. Dollard's tone was bored. Chet and Grandpa and the lean black man joined in.

"Hey, all you patriots," said Dollard when it was over.

"Born in the U.S.A.," said Chet. To us: "Top of the morning to ya morning becomes Elektra electrified all those ions ioning boards gotta keep everything smooth, pressed, even the French cuffs, fisticuffs cuffing up Rodney King yo bro."

The lean black man angled his head toward Chet and shook it disgustedly. No one else seemed to pay attention to the giant's ramblings, though the old man's hands were shaking more conspicuously.

"Okay," said Dollard, perching on the edge of the oak desk. "It's been a while since you guys got together because Dr. Argent no longer works here but—"

"Fuck her," said the sweating Hispanic. "Fuck her in the ass."

"Paz," said Dollard in a tight voice. "Keep it clean."

"Fuck her," said Paz. "Giving us her pretty-face attention and then cutting out on us."

"Paz, I explained to you that she didn't quit, she was—"

"Fuck her," Paz insisted. Sweat dripped from his chin. He appeared on the verge of tears. "Fucking fucked *up*, man . . . no fair." He looked at his classmates. None of them paid attention.

"Fuck her," he said weakly. "Can't mother*fucking* treat *people* like that."

"Fuck you," said Chet, cheerfully. "Fuck everyone everything the old Kama Sutra pretzel bake about time we had some fun around here oral love oral roberts oral hygiene."

"Fuck her," said Paz sadly. He closed his eyes. His chest vibrated with every exhalation. The vibrations slowed. Within seconds, he appeared to be sleeping.

"Nighty-night," Chet said. "Fuck everyone equality for all rights and responsibilities and participatory democracy with liberty under God livery too riding a pale horse—"

"Enough," said the lean black man. Weary voice, but clear, calm, almost parental.

"Good point, Jackson," said Dollard. To Chet: "Enough, big man."

Chet remained cheerful. His yellow beard was littered with crumbs and his eyes were bloodshot. He gave a throaty, equine laugh. "Enough is too much enough is never enough unless which is a paradox so enough can be anything depending on the dimension of—"

"Hey, man," said Jackson, sitting up straighter, "we all know you went to school, you're a genius, but hey. *Okay?*" Baring his teeth at Chet.

Chet said, "I'm no genius I'm the genus and the species and the—"

"Yeah, yeah, yeah, the mama, the son, and the Holy Roller Ghost," said Jackson. "Hey, okay. Chill out, okay?" His grin was pantherish.

Chet said, "Hey hey hey bro muhfuh you know whu hey hey hey I be okay you be—"

Jackson moved forward in his chair.

"Chet," said Dollard.

"Chet," said Jackson.

"Chet," giggled Chet. Slapping his desk, he reached down, bared his ruined leg, ran his hand along the pole of skin-sheathed bone.

Dollard said, "Cover that up."

Jackson had disengaged, was staring at the ceiling. Kindly Grandpa twiddled his thumbs and smiled sweetly.

Paz let out a loud belching snore.

Chet continued to finger-walk up and down his own leg. A smile spread slowly, bristling the yellow beard.

Another snore from Paz.

"Cover it," said Dollard.

Chet laughed and complied.

The heavy, freckled black man's head lolled; he seemed to be sleeping, too. Grandpa caught my eye and favored me with a smile. His cheeks were fresh apples. The comb tracks in his hair were drafting-table precise.

The only one who hadn't moved was the pale, thin man in the stocking cap. His fists remained glued to his temples.

Dollard said, "Gentlemen, these guys are from the po-lice. And speaking of Dr. Argent, they want to ask you some *questions* about her."

Only Grandpa and Chet observed Milo's walk to the desk. Dollard remained in place for a moment, as if unwilling to cede ground; then he stepped aside.

"Po-lice," said Chet. "Good man gendarme right to bear two arms got to guard society from the dregs and the dross and the eggs and the boss born in the U.S.A.! I was po-lice myself po-lite Poe Edgar Allan lite trained with Special Forces me and Chuck Yeager and Annabel Lee and Bobby McGee—"

"Good," said Milo. "We need all the help we can get. About Dr. Argent—"

A harsh whisper cut through the introduction: *"The Jews did it."*

Stocking Cap. He hadn't moved. His face had all the life of bleached driftwood.

"Got a point, there," said Chet. "Karl Marx violent overthrow all those other semites semiotics antibiotics no that was Fleming no Jew a Scot—"

"The Jews did it," Stocking Cap repeated.

Dollard said, "Enough of that, Randall."

Chet said, "Maybe valid Jack the Ripper writing on the wall the Jews are the men who didn't not do it or somesuch doubletriplenegative which in the alternate universe parallel systems parallelograms dodecahedrons you never know anything's possible—"

"Randall's a racist asshole," said Jackson. "He don't know shit and neither do you." He showed teeth again, began picking at his cuticles.

Dollard glared at us. *Look what you've done.*

"Randall's a racist motherfucker," said Jackson matter-of-factly.

Randall didn't react. Paz and the freckled black man remained asleep.

"One more word out of you, Jackson," said Dollard, "and it's S&R."

Jackson fidgeted wildly for several seconds, but he kept silent.

Dollard turned to Milo: "Finish up."

Milo looked at me. I moved next to him. "So, Dr. Argent was working with you guys."

Kindly Grandpa said, "Would you be so kind as to inform us exactly what exactly happened to the poor woman?"

Dollard said, "We've already been through that, Holtzmann."

"I realize that, Mr. Dollard," said Holtzmann. "She was murdered. How tragic. But perhaps if we knew the details we could assist these police officers."

Gentle voice. Twinkly blue eyes. Coherent. What had gotten him in here?

"I gave you all the details you need to know," said Dollard.

Paz's eyes opened. And closed. Someone passed wind and the stink floated through the room, then dissipated.

Randall's head raised an inch. His fists began grinding into his skull. The stocking cap was filthy. The hand slipped down a bit and I saw that the skin around his temples was red and raw, scabbed in places.

I said, "If there's anything—"

"How did it happen?" said Grandpa Holtzmann. "Was she shot? If so, was it a handgun or a long gun?"

"She wasn't shot," said Dollard. "And that's all you need to—"

"Stabbed, then?" said Holtzmann.

"What does it matter, Holtzmann?"

"Well," said the old man, "if we're to be of assist—"

Chet said, "The modus is always a clue signature profile-wise psychological penmanship so to speak to squeak—"

"*Was* she stabbed?" said Holtzmann, pressing forward so that the desk bit into his trunk.

"Holtzmann," said Dollard, "there's no reason for—"

"She *was* stabbed!" the old man exclaimed. "Fileted to the bone, hallelujah!" Working at his zipper with both hands, he exposed himself, began masturbating frantically. Singing out in a fine rich baritone: "Stabbed, stabbed, stabbed, glory be! Gut the bitch in pieces three!"

Dollard took him roughly by the shoulders and shoved him toward the door.

To us, "You, too. Out. Meeting over."

As we exited, Chet shouted, "Wait I've solved it cherchez la femme cherchez la femme—!"

Outside, Dollard locked the door to the annex and handed Holtzmann over to the other two techs. The old man simpered but looked thrilled.

The taller tech said, "Tuck yourself in. *Now.*"

Holtzmann obeyed, dropped his hands to his side.

"Nice to meet you." Kindly Grandpa again. "Mr. Dollard, if I've offended—"

"Don't say another damn word," Dollard ordered him. To the techs: "Keep them in there while I deal with *these* two. I'll send Mills back to help you."

The techs moved Holtzmann to the wall, had him face the stucco. "Don't budge, old man." Pointing at the door, one of them said, "They okay in there, Frank?"

"Chet Bodine's running his mouth like a broken toilet and

Jackson's ticked at him. At Randall, too—he's doing the Aryan crap."

"Really?" said the tech lightly. "Haven't heard that in a while, thought we had it under control."

"Yeah," said Dollard. "Something must have tensed them all up."

When we were back at the main building, he said, "Now, that was a good expenditure of taxpayers' money."

Milo said, "I want to see Peake."

"And I want to fuck Sharon Stone—"

"Take me to Peake, Frank."

"Oh, sure, just like that. Who the hell do you think—" Again, Dollard checked his anger. Chuckled. "That requires authorization, Detective. Meaning Mr. Swig, and, like I said, he's not—"

"Call him," said Milo.

Dollard bent one leg. "Because you order me to do it?"

"Because I can be back here in an hour with serious backup and a warrant on you for obstruction of justice. My bosses are antsy about this one, Dollard. Maybe Swig will eventually be able to protect you, but seeing as he's not here, he won't stop you from going through the process. I'm talking Central Booking. You were a cop, you know the drill."

Dollard's face was the color of rare steak. His words came out slow and clipped. "You have no idea what kind of deep shit you're getting yourself into."

"I have a real good idea, Frank. Let's play the media game. Bunch of TV idiots with sound trucks and cameras. The slant I'll give them is the police were saddled with a stroke-inducing whodunit homicide and you did everything in your power to impede. I'll also throw in a nice little sidebar about how you geniuses judged a mass murderer sane and qualified for release and then he proves how sane he is by turning himself into garbage. When all that hits the fan, Frank, think Uncle Senator's gonna help Swig, let alone you?"

Dollard's jaw jutted. He toed the dirt. "Why the hell are you doing this?"

"Just what I was going to ask you, Frank. Because this change of attitude on your part puzzles me. Ex-cop, you'd expect something different. Makes me wonder, Frank. Maybe I should be looking closer at you."

"Look all you want," said Dollard, but his head drew back and his voice lacked conviction. Squinty eyes examined the sky. "Do your thing, man."

"Why the change, Frank?"

"No change," said Dollard. "The first time you were here was courtesy, the second time tolerance. Now you're a disruption—look at what you just did to those guys."

"Murder's a disruption," said Milo.

"I keep telling you, *this* murder had nothing to— Forget it. What the *hell* do you want from me?"

"Take me to Peake. After that, we'll see."

Dollard's toe stirred up more dirt. "Mr. Swig's in a serious budget meeting and can't be—"

"Who's second in command?"

"No one. Only Mr. Swig authorizes visits."

"Then leave him a message," said Milo. "I'll give you five minutes; after that, I'm outta here and it's a whole different game. When's the last time you had your fingers rolled for prints?"

Dollard looked up at the sky again. Someone on the yard howled.

Milo said, "Okay, Doc, we're outta here."

Dollard let us walk ten paces before saying, "Screw it. You get ten minutes with Peake, in and out."

"No, Frank," said Milo. "I get what I want."

28.

WE ENTERED THE main building. Milo got to the door first, throwing off Dollard's rhythm. Lindeen Schmitz was at the front desk, talking on the phone. She began to smile up at Milo, but a glance from Dollard stopped her.

We rode up to C Ward in silence. On the other side of the double doors, four inmates idled. I could see the nurses in the station chatting cheerfully. Laughter, shallow and grating, spilled from the TV room.

Dollard stomped to Peake's room, unlocked the peep hatch, flipped the light switch, frowned. He released both bolts and opened the door cautiously. A brief look inside. "Not here." Trying to sound annoyed, but puzzlement took over.

"How about that," said Milo. "He never leaves his room."

"I'm telling you," said Dollard, "he never does."

"Maybe he's watching TV," I said.

We went over to the big room, scanned the faces. Two dozen men in khaki stared at the screen. Canned yuks poured out of the box—a sitcom. No one in the room was laughing. Peake wasn't in the audience.

Back in the corridor, Dollard had flushed again. The rage of a dogmatist proven wrong. "I'll get to the bottom of this." He was heading for the nursing station when a sluggish, abrasive sound stopped him.

Swish swish . . . swish swish . . . swish swish . . . Like a snare drum bottoming a slow dance. Seconds later, Peake stepped out from around the left side of the station.

Swish . . . Paper slippers shuffling on linoleum.

251

Heidi Ott held his elbow as he stumbled forward, eyelids half-shut, each step causing his triangular head to bob like that of a rear-window stuffed dog. In the merciless fluorescence of the hallway, the bits of stubble on his head and face looked like random blackheads. The furrows on his skull seemed painfully deep. He was bent over sharply, as if his spine had given way. As if gravity would have pulled him down but for Heidi's grip.

Neither of them noticed us as she propelled him, whispering encouragement.

Dollard said, "Hey," and she looked up. Her hair was drawn back in a tight bun, her expression bland. Peake could've been any kind of invalid, she his long-suffering daughter.

She held him back. Peake swayed, opened his eyes, but still didn't seem to be aware of our presence. He rolled his head. His purple-slug tongue oozed out, curled, remained suspended for several seconds before retreating.

"What's going on?" said Dollard.

"Taking a walk," said Heidi. "I thought some exercise might help."

"Help with what?" said Dollard. His thick arms snapped across his chest, fingers digging into stout biceps.

"Is something wrong, Frank?"

"No, everything's great, terrific—*they* want to see him again. Be nice if he was where he's supposed to be."

"Sorry," said Heidi, glancing my way. "Is he on room restriction? I didn't hear about it."

"Not yet he isn't," said Dollard. "Go on, put him back." To Milo: "Do your thing, I'll be back in fifteen."

Arms still folded, he walked off.

Heidi smiled uneasily—a teenager embarrassed by Dad's outburst. "Okay, Ardis, exercise time's over." One of Peake's eyes opened wider. Bleary, unfocused. He licked his lips, extended his tongue again, rolled his shoulders.

"No one bothers to get him out," said Heidi. "I thought it might help with . . . you know."

"Verbal output," I said.

She shrugged. "It didn't seem like a bad idea. C'mon, Ardis, let's get you back."

She guided him across the hall to his room, led him to his bed, sat him down. He stayed exactly where she put him. For several seconds, no one said anything. Peake didn't budge for a while. Then the tongue-thrusts renewed. Both eyes fluttered, struggled to stay open, couldn't.

Heidi said, "Could one of you please turn off the light? I think it bothers him."

I flipped the switch and the room turned gray. Peake sat there, licking and rolling his head. The same reek of intestinal gas and charred wood seemed to press forward, a putrid greeting triggered by our entry.

Heidi turned to Milo. "Why was Frank so bugged? Is something wrong?"

"Frank's not in a good mood. So tell me, has Peake been talking at all since you taped him?"

She shook her head. "No, sorry. I've been trying, but nothing. That's why I thought some exercise . . ."

Peake rolled his head. Rocked.

Milo motioned us away from the bed. We moved toward the doorway.

Milo said, "So no elaboration on 'choo choo bang bang.' "

Heidi's eyes widened. "Does that actually mean something?"

Milo shrugged. "Let me ask you, did Peake ever mention anything else—like a name?"

"What name?" she said.

"Wark."

She repeated it very slowly. "Doesn't really sound like a name . . . more like a bark."

"So he might've blurted it and you would've thought it was just gibberish?"

"Maybe . . . But no, he never said that." She reached to tug her ponytail. Nothing there. Her hand rose to the tight bun. "Wark . . . No, he never said that. Why? Who is it?"

"Maybe a friend of Peake's."

"He doesn't have any friends."

"Old friend," said Milo. "Are you still taping?"

"I tried . . . when I could. Why's Frank so uptight?"

"Frank doesn't like being told what to do."

"Oh," she said. "And you've got him actually working."

"Frank doesn't like to work?"

She hesitated. Moved closer to the door, looked out through the hatch. "This may not be true, but I heard he got fired from some police department for sleeping on the job. Or something like that."

"Who'd you hear it from?" said Milo.

"Just talk on the wards. He's also a sexist—treats me like I don't belong. You saw his attitude—I mean, what's wrong with taking someone who never gets out for a walk? All the other patients are watching TV, it's not like anyone's getting neglected."

I said, "Has Frank been giving you other problems?"

"Basically what you just saw—attitude. Swig likes him, so he doesn't have to do too much scut."

She glanced back at Peake. He continued to sit and rock and lick air. "You're saying Peake actually has a friend? From his past?"

"Hard to believe?" I said.

"Sure is. I've never seen him make contact with anyone."

Milo said, "No mail?"

"Not that I know about. Same with phone calls. He never leaves his room."

"Till today," I said.

"Well, yeah. I was trying to help out. What's this Wark done? What's going on?"

"Probably nothing," said Milo. "Just working all the angles. You drill a bunch of wells, hope for a trickle every now and then."

"Sounds too slow for me," said Heidi. "No offense."

"Not like jumping off power stations."

She smiled. "Very few things are."

We left Peake's room and she locked the door.

Milo said, "Any idea where I could get a personnel list?"

"I guess in the front office. Why?"

"To see who else I should talk to."

"If it's about Peake," she said, "I'm the only one worth talking to. No one else pays attention to him, now that Claire's gone."

"How much time exactly did she spend?" I said.

"Hmm. Hard to say. There were times when I was on shift when she'd be in there as long as an hour. Sometimes every day. Usually every day. She was like that—involved."

"With everyone?"

"No," she said. "Not really. I mean she spent more time with her patients, in general, than the other docs. But Peake was . . . she seemed to be especially interested in him."

"Speaking of her patients," I said, "we just met the men in the Living Skills group. Low-functioning, just like you said. Any idea what criteria she used to pick them?"

"We never discussed that. I was just the tech. Mostly I stood guard, got supplies. To be honest, the group never really went anywhere. Claire seemed to be . . . observing them more than training. The group only met seven times before she was . . ." Shaking her head. Stroking the bun. "Sometimes it just hits me. What actually *happened* to her."

"Do you have any background information on the men? What they did to get here?"

"Let's see . . . there's Ezzard Jackson—skinny black guy. He killed his wife. Tied her up in their house and burned it down. Same with Holtzmann—the old man you'd never think could do anything criminal. He cut his wife up, stored the pieces in the freezer, marked them the way a butcher would—flank, loin. Randall shot his parents—he was into some Nazi stuff, had some delusion they were part of a Zionist plot. . . . Who else . . . The other black guy. Pretty. That's his name—Monroe Pretty. Killed his kids, four of them, little ones. Drowned them in the bathtub, one by one. Sam Paz—the Mexican guy—went bonkers at his brother's wedding. Shot his brother and his mother and a bunch of bystanders. All told, I think six people died. The giant, Chet Bodine, was living like a hermit. Killed some hikers."

So many madmen, so little time . . .

I said, "All except Chet victimized family members."

"Actually, Chet wasn't picked for the group," she said. "He found out about it, asked Claire if he could join. He was so verbal, she thought it might stimulate the others, so she agreed. Yeah, you're right. I never thought about it, but she must've been interested in family killers."

Milo said, "Any idea why?"

She pulled a bobby pin from the bun, slipped it back in. "To be honest, it probably doesn't mean that much. Lots of the guys in here have murdered family members. Isn't that what crazy people usually do when they freak? Like Peake, he started with his mother, right? At least, that's what Claire told me."

"What else did she tell you about Peake's crimes?"

She touched the tip of her nose. "Just what he did. His mom and an entire family. What does any of that have to do with Claire being killed?"

"Maybe nothing," said Milo. "So are you gonna keep working with Peake?"

"I guess. If you want me to. Not that I'm accomplishing much."

"Don't get yourself in trouble, Heidi. I appreciate whatever you do."

"Sure," she said, gnawing her lip.

"Is there a problem?"

"Like I told you before, I was figuring it was time to move on. Was kind of waiting until you got to the bottom of Claire's murder."

"Wish I could tell you it would be soon, Heidi," he said. "Meanwhile, as long as Dr. Delaware's here, he might as well give Peake a try."

"Oh, sure," she said. "Whatever."

The door closed after me with a pneumatic hiss.

I stood halfway between the door and the bed, watching Peake. If he was aware of my presence, he didn't show it.

I watched. He did tongue calisthenics. Rocked, rolled, fluttered his eyes.

Standing there immobile, suspended in gray light, I began to feel formless, weightless. My nose habituated to the stink. Keeping my eyes on Peake's hands, I edged closer. A few more minutes of observation and I thought I'd detected a cadence to his movements.

Tongue-thrust, curl and hover, lingual retreat, neck roll clockwise, then counterclockwise.

Approximately ten-second sequences, six repetitions per minute, played out against the constant rocking of his torso.

I took in other details.

His bed wasn't made. Looked as if it was never made. The hands rested on rumpled, sweat-stained covers. The fingers of the left hand were hooked in the sheeting, half-hidden.

Hands that had wreaked so much ruin . . . I moved to within inches of the bed, standing over him for a while.

No change in the routine. I kneeled. Bringing myself down to Peake's eye level. His eyes were glued shut. Strain-marks at the corners said he was pressing the lids together tightly. A few moments ago, with Heidi, they'd been half-open. Responding to that bit of stimulation? Withdrawing further, once returned to isolation?

I heard a tapping from below. Looked down. His feet. Bare—the paper slippers had come off without my noticing.

Two thin white feet. Oversized feet. Unnaturally long toes. Drumming the floor, faster than the upper-body movements, out of rhythm with the tardive dance.

So much motion, but no flavor of intent—the inanimate dangle of a puppet.

All through it, his eyes remained sealed. This close I could see dry, greenish crust flecking the lashes.

"Ardis," I said.

The beat went on.

I tried again. Nothing.

A few minutes later: "Ardis, this is Dr. Delaware. I want to talk to you about Dr. Argent."

Nothing.

"Claire Argent."

No response. I repeated myself. Peake's eyelids remained

shut, but started to tic—lids contracting and releasing, lateral movement visible under the skin. A few green specks dropped onto his lap.

Reaction? Or random movement?

I sidled closer. Had he wanted to kiss me or claw out my eyes, he could've.

"Ardis, I'm here about Dr. Argent."

Another eyelid tic—a jerky wave traveling beneath the papery skin.

Definite response. On some level, he was able to focus.

I said, "You were important to Dr. Argent."

Tic tic tic.

"She was important to you, Ardis. Tell me why."

His eyelids quivered like a frog in a galvanic experiment. I counted the time in tardive sequences: One T.D., two T.D.'s . . . ten T.D.'s.

Twelve. Two minutes. He stopped.

Subjectively, it seemed longer than a hundred and twenty seconds. I was far from bored, but time was dragging. I started wondering how many minutes Peake's rampage had consumed. Had the Ardullos been fully awake or asleep? Or somewhere in between—a murky semiconsciousness as they died, thinking it was all a bad dream?

I mentioned Claire's name again. Peake's eyes ticced. But nothing more.

I thought back to his arrest photo, the look of terror in *his* eyes. It reminded me of something—a vicious dog from my boyhood. It had drawn lots of blood but, when finally cornered by the dogcatcher, had curled up and whimpered like a starving pup. . . .

How much violence was fear catapulted back at the world? Was all viciousness cowardice at the root?

No, I didn't think so, was still convinced Claire's murderer had acted from a position of power and dominance.

Fun.

Had Peake enjoyed his blood walk? Looking at him now, I found it hard to imagine him extracting enjoyment out of anything.

As I watched at him now, the notion of this husk decapitating his own mother, stalking up the stairs, bloody knife in hand, running from room to room inflicting agony and death, seemed impossibly remote. . . .

As unlikely as kindly Mr. Holtzmann sectioning and freezing his wife.

In this place, logic meant nothing.

I said, "Bad eyes in a box."

No flutter beneath the lids.

"Choo choo bang bang."

Nothing.

I tried it again. Same lack of response.

Back to basics. Claire's name.

"Dr. Argent," I said.

Nothing. Had I turned him off?

"Dr. Argent cared about you, Ardis."

Five T.D.'s, six . . . the eyes ticced.

"Why did Dr. Argent die, Ardis?"

Eleven, twelve . . . tic, tic, tic.

"What about Wark?" Fourteen . . . "Griffith D. Wark."

Sixteen, seventeen. Nothing.

"*Blood Walk.*"

Static eyelids.

Maybe the tics meant nothing, and I'd fooled myself into allowing a random neurological spark to take on meaning.

Delusions were everywhere. . . .

Knowing this might be my last shot with Peake, I decided to keep going. Keep it simple.

Moving close enough to whisper in his ear. "Dr. Argent. Claire Argent."

The eyelids jumped spasmodically and I retreated with a pounding heart.

He froze. No more T.D. for several seconds.

The eyes opened, revealing a sliver of gray white.

Looking at me. Seeing me? I wasn't sure.

They closed.

"Dr. Argent cared," I said.

No eye movement—but the cords of his neck tightened; he craned toward me. Again, I drew back involuntarily.

Unable to see me but turning toward me, and I couldn't help feeling he was . . . engaging me. His mouth gaped wider. No tongue visible, and now he was making a gagging sound, as if choking on it. Suddenly, his head thrust forward, a snake darting, the eyelids fluttering once again, wildly.

I stared in fascinated horror as he tilted his head upward, neck stretched so tight it seemed to elongate impossibly. What little mandible he had pointed up at the ceiling.

I took another step backward. His arms began climbing. Slowly. Painfully.

His eyes opened. Remained open. Wide, very wide. Fixed on the ceiling.

As if heaven resided in the plaster . . . as if he were *praying* to something.

He gurgled, gagged some more. How far had he retracted the slug of muscle into his gullet?

His arms rose higher. Supplication . . .

He coughed, made no sound. The neck rolls resumed, more frantic than ever, epileptically rapid. More gagging. His sunken chest heaved. I thought of Denton Argent, dead in his cell, brain burned out from seizing, and wondered if I should do something.

But Peake seemed to be breathing fine. Not a seizure. New pattern of movement.

He began rocking faster. His scrawny buttocks lifted from the mattress as he thrust his chest upward.

Offering himself.

His right hand sank to his mouth. Four fingers jammed inside.

He withdrew them and the tongue appeared—yanked free—flapped like a fish on deck, curled, hovered. . . .

Return of the initial T.D. sequence: thrust, curl, hover, retract. But his rear remained inches above the bed, feet barely touching the ground. Unnatural—it had to strain—did he even *feel* pain?

Then, suddenly, it was over, and his head had lowered to its usual slump, his arms were back in the bedcovers, and the beat went on. . . .

One T.D., two T.D.'s . . .

I sat there with him for five more minutes, whispering, coaxing, to no effect.

Now Claire's name left him silent as paint. Maybe a new approach would startle him into another outburst.

"The Beatty brothers," I said. "Ellroy. Leroy."

Zero.

"Choo choo bang bang."

Nothing.

"One with a gun, one run over by a train."

Deaf, blind, mute.

Still, Claire's name had stimulated him. I needed more time with him, knew I wouldn't get much.

Keep going.

One T.D., two . . .

I whispered: "The Ardullos."

No change.

"The Ardullos—Scott Ardullo, Terri—" Yes, yes, yes there it was: the eyelid tic, faster than before, much faster, a churning of the lids as if the eyeballs were rotating at jet speed.

"Terri and Scott Ardullo," I said.

The eyes opened. Alive now.

Fixed on mine.

Awake.

Clear intent. To do what?

He stared at me. Didn't move at all.

Paying close attention? To me.

Success, but I felt as if a scorpion were cakewalking along my spine.

I checked his hands. *Those* hands. Both knotted in the sheets.

Keep a look out for sudden movement.

"Scott and Terri Ardullo," I said.

The stare.

"Scott and Terri. Brittany and Justin."

The stare.

"Brittany and Justin."

He blinked. Once, twice, six times, twenty, forty—eyelid convulsions, which wouldn't—or couldn't—cease.

Metronomic, hypnotic. I felt myself being drawn in. *Avoid that, watch his hands. . . .*

His arms rose again. Fear stabbed me and I stood up quickly, backed away.

He didn't seem to notice.

Stood, himself.

Unsteadily, but managing to remain upright. Stronger than he'd appeared out in the hallway, in Heidi's grasp.

Still staring. Hot stare. Hands curling slowly into fists.

Straightening his spine.

Stepping toward me.

Okay, you've done it, Delaware. Success!

He moved another step closer. I braced myself, plotted my defense. How much damage could he do, unarmed, so thin, so feeble?

Another step. His arms reached out, inviting embrace.

I retreated toward the door.

His mouth opened, contorted—no tongue-thrusts, just the excruciating labor of the lipless orifice struggling to change form, fighting to talk or scream . . . working so hard, working working—

Suddenly, a shrill, dry sound escaped. Soft, wispy, echoing—soft, but it pounded my ears—

His arms began to climb again, very slowly. When they were parallel with his shoulders, they flapped. Birdlike. Not a bird of prey, something thin, deliberate, delicate—a crane.

Without warning, he turned his back on me and hobbled—still flapping, miming flight—to the far corner of the room.

Pressing his back to the wall, keeping the arms stretched. Head tilted to the right.

Above him, the metal restraint hooks embedded in the wall hovered like warnings.

Eyes still open—wide open—*stretched* open; I could see

wet pink borders all around. *Wet* eyes. Tears welling, over-flowing, streaming down sunken cheeks.

His left leg crossed over its mate so that he was standing on one leg.

More avian posturing—no, no, something else—

Posing.

Unmistakable pose.

His body had formed a cross.

Crucifixion on an unseen scaffold.

Tears flooded his face. Uncontrollable, silent sobs, brutally paroxysmic, each gush seizing ownership of his fragile body and shaking it like a wet kitten.

Weeping Jesus.

29.

HE STAYED THAT way, just stayed that way.

How long had I been in there? Surely Dollard, hostile and impatient, would be returning soon and ordering me out.

Five minutes later, it hadn't happened.

Peake remained against the wall. The tears had slowed, but they hadn't stopped.

The stink had returned. My skin itched. Senses returning, heightening. I wanted out.

Knocking on the brown steel door produced only a feeble thump. Could it be heard out in the hall? No sounds from the outside made their way inside the cell. I tried the hatch. Locked. Released only from the outside. The door hatch opened from the outside. Sensory deprivation. What did that do to already damaged minds?

Another knock, louder. Nothing.

Peake stayed frozen in the cruciform pose, pinioned by invisible spikes.

The names of his victims had loosened his tears. Remorse or self-pity?

Or something I could never hope to understand?

I thought of him entering the Ardullo kitchen, spotting his mother, the strength it had taken to saw through the cervical spine. . . . Upstairs, swinging Scott Ardullo's baseball bat.

The children . . .

Their names had triggered the Jesus pose.

Martyr pose.

No remorse at all?

Seeing himself as a *victim*?

264

Suddenly, the absurdity and futility of what I was doing hit me—trying to pry information from a diseased mind that smoothly morphed sin and salvation. What use could this be to anyone?

Had Claire prodded Peake the same way? Died, somehow, because of her curiosity?

The narrow room started to close in on me. I was up against the door, couldn't get far enough away from the white, dangling creature.

Just a trickle of tears, now.

Crying for himself.

Monster.

Serene in his suffering.

His head rotated very slowly. Lifted a bit. Faced me. Something surfaced in his eyes that I hadn't seen before.

Sharpness. Clarity of purpose.

He nodded. Knowingly. As if the two of us shared something.

I pressed my back against the door.

The space opened behind me and I tumbled back.

Heidi said, "Sorry! I should've opened the hatch and warned you, first."

I regained my balance, took a breath, smiled, tried to look composed. Milo watched me, along with Dollard and the trio of doctors—Aldrich, Steenburg, and Swenson. All in sport shirts, as if they'd just gotten in from the golf course. Nothing playful on their faces.

Heidi started to close the door, looked into the room, went pale. "What's he doing? What's going on?"

The others rushed over and stared. Peake had returned to the full Jesus pose, head cocked to the right. But no tears.

I said, "He got up a few minutes ago, positioned himself that way."

Aldrich said, "My, my . . . Has he done this before, Heidi?"

"No. Never. He never gets off the bed." She sounded scared. "Dr. Delaware, you're saying he actually moved on his own?"

"Yes."

Steenburg and Swenson looked at each other. Aldrich said, "Interesting." The gravity of his tone bordered on comical. Trying to assume authority on a case he knew nothing about.

Frank Dollard said, "What'd you say to him to get him that way?"

"Nothing," I said.

"You didn't talk to him?"

Milo said, "What's the big deal? He used to think he was a vegetable, now he's evolved into Jesus."

Dollard and doctors glared at him.

"Psychosis is a disease," said Aldrich. "It's unseemly to ridicule."

"Sorry," said Milo.

Swenson said, "Has he ever talked about religious themes, Heidi?"

"No. That's what I'm trying to tell you. He doesn't talk much, period."

Swenson turned contemplative, laced his hands over his belt buckle. "I see. . . . So it's something altogether new."

Dollard jutted his head in my direction. "You'd better tell us what you were talking to him about. We need to know, in case he starts acting out."

Aldrich said, "Is there some problem, Frank?"

"These people are a problem, Dr. Aldrich. They keep coming in here, disrupting, going at Peake. Mr. Swig authorized only fifteen minutes with the SDL group, no time with Peake." He pointed through the door. "Look at that. Guy like that, who knows what could happen? And for what? He couldn'ta had anything to do with Dr. Argent. I told 'em that, you told 'em that, Mr. Swig told 'em that—"

Aldrich turned to Milo. "What *is* your purpose here, Officer?"

"Investigating Dr. Argent's murder."

Aldrich shook his head. "That's not an answer. Why are you questioning *Peake*?"

"He said something that might have predicted Dr. Argent's murder, Doctor."

"Predicted? What in the world are you talking about?"

Milo told him.

" 'In a box,' " said Aldrich. He faced Heidi. Steenburg and Swenson did the same. "When did he *say* this to you?"

"The day before it happened."

"An oracle?" said Steenburg. "Oh, please. And now he's Jesus—am I the only one who sees a trend toward irrelevance?"

Swenson said, "At least it's original. Relatively, that is. We don't get a lot of Jesuses anymore." He smiled. "Plenty of Elvises but not that many Jesuses. Maybe it's the godless state of our culture."

No one else seemed amused.

Swenson wouldn't give up. "We can always do what Milton Erickson did with his Jesuses—give him carpenter's tools and have him fix something."

Aldrich scowled and Swenson looked the other way.

"Officer," said Aldrich, "let me get this clear: on the basis of this supposed . . . utterance, you're back here?"

"It's an unsolved homicide, Dr. Aldrich."

"Even so . . ." Aldrich moved closer to the doorway and peered inside. Peake hadn't budged. He closed the door.

Dollard said, "They caused a ruckus in SDL, too. Herman Randall's all worked up, shouting Nazi stuff in his room. We might think of upping his meds."

"Might we?" said Aldrich. He turned to Heidi. "How about you and I meeting after lunch to review Mr. Peake's file. Make sure what we're seeing in there isn't some kind of regression."

"I'd think just the opposite," I said. "He's showing more mobility and affective response."

"Affective response?"

"He was crying, Dr. Aldrich."

Aldrich took another look inside. "Well, he's not crying now. Just hanging there looking pretty regressed. Looks like catalepsy to me."

I said, "Is there any chance of reducing his meds?"

Aldrich's eyes bugged. "Why in the world would we do *that*?"

"It might loosen him up verbally."

"Loosen him up," said Swenson. "Just what we need, a loose Jesus."

A couple of figures in khaki had drifted out of the TV room. The inmates stared at us, began heading our way. Swenson and Steenburg stepped forward. The men turned, reversed direction, collected near the door to the TV room, returned inside.

Aldrich said, "Thank you for your opinion, Doctor. However, you and Officer Sturgis must leave immediately. No further contact with Mr. Peake or any other patients until cleared by myself or Mr. Swig." To Steenburg and Swenson: "We'd better get moving. The reservation's at one."

Crossing the yard, Dollard walked even farther ahead. Big Chet was on the yard and he started to come over, gesticulating and laughing, tugging at his hair like a toddler.

Dollard's palm shot out. "Stay back!"

The giant halted, pouted, yanked a clump of hair out of his head. The yellow filaments floated to the ground like dandelion petals.

His expression said, *Look what you made me do.*

"Idiot," Dollard growled.

Chet's eyes slitted.

Dollard waved and two techs jogged over from across the yard. Chet saw them, froze, finally skulked away. Four steps later, he stopped, looked at us over his shoulder.

"Mark my words," he bellowed. "Cherchez la femme Champs Elysées!"

Dollard threw the gate open, slammed it after us, left without a word.

As we waited to get Milo's gun and my knife, I said, "Something sure yanked his shorts."

"Makes you wonder, doesn't it?" he said. The moment we got in the Seville, he was on the cell phone, asking for the number of the Hemet police department. I let the car idle as he talked. The car seat was a griddle and I cranked the air-conditioning to an arctic blast. Milo got transferred half a dozen times, maintained collegial cheer through every step, but he looked as if he'd swallowed something slimy. The air inside the car cooled, hit my face, turned my sweat icy. Milo was drenched.

He hung up. "Finally got a supervisor who'd talk. Heidi was right. Dollard was a major-league goldbrick: ignored calls in his zone, took unauthorized leaves, put in for unjustified overtime. They couldn't prove anything serious enough to prosecute him—probably didn't want to. Easier just to ask him to leave."

"How long ago was this?"

"Four years ago. He went straight to Starkweather. Supervisor made a crack about nutcases being perfect for Frank, no one to complain when he slacked off."

"Swig likes him," I said. "Tells you something about Swig."

"High standards, all around."

I drove out of the parking lot. Convection waves rose from the asphalt.

"What *did* you do to get Peake to play Jesus in the school play?"

"Mentioned the Ardullos' names. After I got a response to Claire's name—eye tics, tensing up. When I whispered Brittany's and Justin's names into his ear he jumped up, ran to the wall, assumed the pose. I'd been thinking of him as lethargic, stuporous, but he can move fast when he wants to. If he'd jumped me, I'd have been unprepared."

"So he's *not* a total veg. Maybe he's a sneaky bastard, playing all of us. Makes sense when you think about how he walked in on his mother. She's sitting there coring apples, he gets behind her, she has no idea what he's going to do."

"He surprised the Ardullos, too," I said. "Sheriff Haas said they left their doors unlocked."

"Everyone's nightmare. Right out of a splatter flick."

The eucalyptus forest appeared, a big gray bear split by a yawning mouth of road.

"So," he said, "was he crying real tears?"

"Copiously. But I'm not sure it was remorse. When he turned and stared at me, I started to feel something else: self-pity. The Jesus pose fits that, too. As if he sees himself as a martyr."

"Sick bastard," he said.

"Or maybe," I said, "hearing the kids' names evoked an overpowering memory. Recall of not acting alone. Of taking the rap for something the Crimmins brothers put him up to. Maybe he communicated that to Claire. I didn't see anything close to speech, but with a lowered dosage . . ."

He cooled his hands on the air-conditioning vent. "Why do you think Dollard turned so hostile?"

"Antsy about our return visit. Something to hide."

Milo didn't answer. We exited the forest and summer light whitened the windshield. The trees shimmered as they broiled. I could sense the heat trying to claw its way in.

"What about some kind of hospital scam?" I said. "Financial mismanagement. Or trafficking in prescription drugs. Claire found out about it and that's what put her in jeopardy. Maybe Peake knew, too. Learned someone was going to hurt Claire and the 'prophecy' was his way of warning her."

We were free of the hospital grounds, heading toward the sludge yards and the freight barns. I wondered where the rear forest behind the annexes led, was unable to see the tall dark trees from here.

"How would Peake find out?" he said.

"Loose lips. Everyone assumes he's vegetative, can't process. I saw enough today to convince me that's not true. If Dollard was involved in something illegal, he might've said or done something that Peake noticed."

"That careless?"

"How many cases have you closed because someone was careless?"

"Peake warns Claire," he said. "Now he's a hero?"

"Maybe on some level, he bonded with Claire. Appreciated the attention Claire was giving him."

"Then why warn Heidi?"

"Claire wasn't at work that day, so Peake did the next best thing: told her assistant. Not a clear message, because he was struggling to talk through the Thorazine haze and his neurological problems."

"Everyone treats Peake like he's wallpaper, but he's sucking up information."

"He's *functioned* like wallpaper for sixteen years. It wouldn't be hard to get complacent. That could be why Dollard was so upset when he saw Peake playing Jesus. Now *he* realizes Peake's capable of more. He's nervous, doesn't want us back there. Look how he bad-mouthed us to Aldrich. And Aldrich played into it. Or Aldrich is part of it."

"Big-time staff racketeering?"

"Like you said, it's not a tight ship. Either way, Dollard just got what he wanted. We won't get through those gates again without a court order."

" 'Bad eyes in a box,' " he said. "That has Peake knowing someone is gonna gouge Claire's eyes and stash her somewhere closed. I might be able to buy Dollard blabbing to some compadre in general terms about getting Claire, but I *can't* see him laying it out in detail."

I had no answer for that. He pulled out his pad, made some notes, closed his eyes, seemed to doze. We reached the freeway. I floored the Seville, crossed over to the fast lane, sped to the interchange, headed west on the 10, past the old brick buildings on the fringes of downtown, surprise survivors of the big quake. A huge blowup of a movie poster had been painted on one of them. Some hypertrophied bionic cop flashing fire from gun-barrel knuckles. If only it were that easy.

Milo said, "Dollard a scamster . . . our Mr. Wark, his partner. But what about Richard, the Beatty twins? How do they connect to any hospital racket?"

"Don't know," I said. "But if Wark *is* Derrick Crimmins, his working there makes sense on another level: he was drawn by Peake's presence, just as Claire was. Because Peake's rampage made a major impression on him. And if my guess about his being Peake's drug source sixteen years ago is right, that would fit with the racket being a dope thing. Dollard smuggles out pharmaceuticals, hands them over to Wark, who sells them on the street. Wark had enough money in that Bank of America account to cover the gear rental when Vito Bonner called to validate the check. So he's got some sort of cash source. Being the outside man would also make Wark the perfect choice for ambushing and murdering Claire. Dollard alerts Wark, gives Wark Claire's address from personnel files; Wark stalks her, kills her in West L.A., dumps her in her own car. No reason for anyone ever to connect it to Starkweather. What's the mantra everyone there keeps reciting? 'It couldn't be related to her work.' I looked around the hospital today to see if anyone fit Wark's physical description. The only one tall and thin enough is Aldrich, but he's too old, and I doubt Wark would masquerade as a doctor—too risky. But there are over a hundred people on staff and we've run into maybe twenty."

"And we get no access to the personnel records." Milo punched the dashboard lightly. Keeping his arm stiff; I knew he wanted to hit much harder.

"How about approaching it another way?" I said. "Let's assume Peake's presence is what attracted Wark to Starkweather initially. But he also needed money, and the job had to be something he could qualify for quickly. That would eliminate anything with extensive training—doctor, psychologist, nurse, pharmacist—and leaves lower-level positions: cooks, custodians, gardeners, psych techs. A would-be producer down on his luck might see the first three as beneath him. Psychiatric technician, on the other hand, has some cachet, could be construed as almost-a-doctor. And psych techs are licensed by the state. The medical board keeps a roster."

Milo's smile spread very slowly. "Worth a try."

The movie-poster mural flashed in my head. "Another reason for Wark to take the job: if he sees himself as some dark-side cinema auteur, what better place to dredge up bloody plots than Starkweather? *That* could explain Richard and the Beatty twins: they're part of Wark's film game."

"The snuff extravaganza, again—we're all over the place with this."

"Like you said, drill a few wells . . ."

He massaged his temples. "Okay, okay, enough talk, I need to *do* something. I put calls in to Miami and Pimm, Nevada, this morning. When we get back, I'll see if anyone called. And the psych board for that tech list. Though for it to be of any use, Wark would've had to register under that name or Crimmins, or something close." He rubbed his face. "Long shots."

"Better than nothing," I said.

"Sometimes I wonder."

30.

WE WERE BACK in the detectives' room by two P.M.

Friday. Most of the desks were empty. Del Hardy's was next to Milo's, and Milo waved me to Del's chair. Del had partnered with Milo years ago—an early alliance cemented by mutual respect and shared alienation. Del had been one of the first black D's to get an assignment west of La Brea. Now he had plenty of black colleagues, but Milo remained a one-man show. Maybe that had wedged them apart, or perhaps it was Del's second wife, a woman with strong views on just about everything. Milo never talked about it.

I used Del's phone to call the state psychiatric board, got put on hold electronically. Milo's desktop was clear except for a message slip taped to the metal. He peeled it loose and read it, and his eyebrows arched.

"Callback from Orlando, Florida. Some guy named Castro 'happy to talk about Derrick Crimmins.' "

He punched numbers, loosened his tie, sat down. A recorded voice of indeterminate gender told me my call would be accepted as soon as an operator was free. I watched Milo's shoulders bunch as his call came through.

"Detective Sturgis for Detective Castro," he said. "Oh, hi. Thanks for calling back. . . . Really? Well that's interesting— listen, could I put someone else on the line? Our psychological consultant . . . Yeah, occasionally we do. . . . Yeah, it's been helpful."

Placing a hand over the mouthpiece, he said, "Hang up and punch my extension number."

The recorded voice broke in, thanking me for my patience.

274

I cut it off, made the conference adjustment, introduced myself.

"George Castro," said a thick voice on the other end. "We all set now?"

"Yeah," said Milo. "Dr. Delaware, Detective Castro was just saying he's been waiting for someone to call him about Derrick Crimmins."

"Waiting a long time," said Castro. "This is like Christmas in the summer. Tell the truth, I gave up, figured he might be dead."

"Why's that?"

"Because his name never showed up in any crime list I could find, but bad guys don't just give up. And that kid was real bad. Got away with multiple murder."

"His parents," said Milo.

"You got it," said Castro. "Him and his brother—Cliff. Cliff was older, but Derrick was smarter. What a pair. Kind of a pre-Menendez Menendez, only the Crimminses didn't even come close to getting arrested. It was my curse. It's been jammed in my craw ever since. Tell me what you have him on, the little bastard."

"Nothing definite," said Milo. "Can't even find him. So far it looks like scamming and homicide."

"Well, that's our boy, to a T. I got to tell you, this really takes me back. I was new to Miami Beach. Did a year on Bunco, then Homicide. Moved down the year before from Brooklyn for the sun, never thought about what being named Castro would mean in Miami." He stopped, as if waiting for laughter. "And I'm Puerto Rican, not Cuban. Anyway, I worked some pretty ugly stuff up north. Bed-Stuy, Crown Heights, East New York. But none of the scum I met ever bothered me as much as those brothers. Killing your own folks for dough—dad and stepmother, actually. It was a Coast Guard case, because the boat blew up in the water—half a mile offshore—but we did the land work. No doubt at all about it being dirty. Someone rigged a pipe bomb to the fuel tank, and the whole thing turned into sawdust. Three people died, actually. Old man Crimmins, his wife, and some Cuban kid they'd hired to captain. They were out marlin fishing. Boom. Shreds of bone, and that's about it."

"Did the Crimmins boys build the bombs?"

"Doubtful. We had some theories about that—down here there's quite a few characters with explosives experience floating around. Mobbed-up types, druggies, Marielitos. Alibis narrowed it down to half a dozen scrotes; we hauled 'em all in, but no one talked. And no one's bank account had suddenly gotten fat. I had my eye on two of them in specific—pair of Dominicans with a dry-cleaning joint as cover. They'd been busted before on a nearly identical explosion in a clothing warehouse, weaseled out on lack of evidence. We pulled in every informant we had, couldn't shake a rumor loose. That tells me the payoff was big bucks."

"The boys had money?"

"Big allowances—fifty grand a year, each. Back then you could have someone taken out for a hundred bucks. One to five thousand would get you someone competent, fifteen a stone pro. We scoured the brothers' bank accounts, found some nice-sized cash withdrawals during the weeks before the explosion, but we couldn't make anything outa that because that's the way they lived in general: the old man gave 'em the fifty at the beginning of the year, they took out play money as they needed it—four, five a month. Spent every penny. So there was no change in pattern. They used a smart-mouthed lawyer, he didn't give us an extra syllable."

"You focused on them right away 'cause of the inheritance angle?"

"You bet," said Castro. "First commandment, right? Follow the honey trail. With the stepmother gone, they were the old man's sole heirs, figured to get millions. Also, their alibis were too damn perfect: both out of town, they made sure to let us know that first thing. It was like one minute of phony grief, then, 'Oh, by the way, we were in Tampa, riding motorcycles.' Showing us some admission ticket to a race they'd been in—all ready with it. And smirking—rubbing *my* face in it. Because we'd had contact before. Back when I was on Bunco. Which is the third thing that nailed them in my mind: they'd been bad boys before. Fraud. Like I said, murder and cons, perfect fit."

"What was the con?" said Milo.

"Nothing brilliant. They cruised the beach, picked up senile old people, drove them out to some swampland that they pitched as vacation lots. Then they'd head over to the marks' bank, wait while the marks withdrew cash for a down payment, hand them some bullshit deed of trust, and split. They preyed on real deteriorated old folk. Most of the time, the marks didn't even know they'd been fleeced. And the withdrawals weren't huge—five, six hundred bucks—so the banks didn't notice. It ended when some old lady's son got wind of it—local surgeon. He waited with his mom on the beach until she pointed out Derrick."

"They serve time?"

"Nah," said Castro angrily. "Never even got charged. Because Daddy hired a lawyer—the same smart-mouth who shielded them on the boat thing. The weakness was the identification angle. The lawyer said he'd have fun with the old people on the stand—show they were too demented to be reliable witnesses. The D.A. didn't want to risk it. A couple of bank tellers thought they could make an I.D. but they weren't sure. Because Derrick and Cliff wore disguises—wigs, fake mustaches, glasses. Stupid stuff, amateurish, they coulda dressed up like Fidel for all the marks noticed. We couldn't trace the phony deeds back to them, either—primitive shit, mimeographed jobs. The whole thing was so low-level it woulda been funny if it hadn't been so cruel. In the end, the old man made restitution, case closed."

"How much restitution?"

"I think it was six, seven thou. Not a major con, but remember, we're talking a one-month period and two kids in their early twenties. That's what I found scary: so young and so cold. My experience was you got plenty violent kids at any age, but it usually takes a few years to season a frosty con like that. It wasn't like they were so bright—neither of them went to college, both just bummed around on the beach. Cliff was actually kind of a cabbage-head. But they had that con edge.

They were lucky, too. One good I.D. and they mighta gone down—at least probation."

He laughed again. "Lucky bastards. The excuse they gave was the stupidest thing of all: big misunderstanding, the old folk were too mentally disturbed to know the difference between reality and fantasy, the land thing was never supposed to be taken seriously. It was all part of some movie they were doing on con games. They even showed us the outline of a script. One page of bullshit—scam games and hot cars—something like *The Sting* meets *Cannonball Run*. They claimed they were gonna sell it to Hollywood." He laughed again. "So they actually got out there, huh?"

"Derrick made it," said Milo. "Cliff died a few years after Daddy and Stepmom. Motocross accident near Reno."

"Oh boy," said Castro. "Interesting."

"Very."

"Like I told you, cold. I always saw Derrick as the idea guy. Cliff was a party dude. Better-looking than Derrick, nice tan, expert water-skiier, pussy hound. And, yeah, motorcycles, too. He had a bunch of them. A collection. They both did. So Derrick might very well know how to rig one. . . . I figured if anyone cracked, it'd be Cliff, my plan was to split them apart, see if I could play one against the other. But the lawyer wouldn't let me get close. I'll never forget the last time I talked to them. I'm asking questions, faking being civil, and those two are looking at their lawyer and he's telling me they don't have to answer and they're smirking. Finally, I leave, and Derrick makes a point of walking me to the door. Big old house, tons of furniture, and he and his brother are gonna get it all. Then he smiles at me, again. Like, '*I* know, *you* know, fuck you, Charlie.' The only comfort I got out of it was they didn't get as rich as they thought they would."

"How much they get?" said Milo.

"Eighty grand each, mostly from the sale of the house. The place was heavily mortgaged, and by the time they paid estate taxes, commission, all that good stuff, there wasn't much left. They were figuring the old man was sitting on big-time cash, but turns out he'd made some bad investments—land deals, as a matter of fact—which is funny, don't you think? Leveraged up the Y.Y. He'd even cashed in his insurance policies as collateral for some loans. The only other assets were the furniture, pair of three-year-old Caddies, golf clubs and a golf cart, and the stepmom's jewelry, half of which turned out to be costume and the rest new stuff, which doesn't maintain its value once you take it out of the store. The other funny thing was, the boat *hadn't* been borrowed on. Apparently the old man loved it, kept up with his slip fees and maintenance. Nice-looking thing, from the pictures. The old man had stuffed fish all over the house." He laughed louder. "Fifty grand worth of boat, minimum, free and clear, and that they blew up. So tell me more about what Derrick did out there."

Milo kept it sketchy.

"Whoa," said Castro. "Creepy murder, that's a whole new level. . . . Makes sense, I guess. Keep getting away with it, you start thinking you're God."

"The thing that interests me," said Milo, "is from what we can tell, Derrick isn't living well. No car registrations, no address in any swank neighborhood that we can find, and he may have taken a low-paying job under an alias. So he must not have invested that eighty grand."

"He wouldn't. He'd plow right through it, just like any other sociopath."

"I can't find any Social Security for him except when he lived in Miami," said Milo. "So no jobs under his own name. Any idea what he's been doing all these years?"

"Nah," said Castro. "He left town nine or ten months after the murder, they both did, left no trail. The case was officially open, but no one was really working on it. In my spare time, I kept following the money, drove by some clubs they hung out at. Then one day a source at County Records called me—I'd asked to be told when the estate was settled. That's when I learned how little they were gonna get. The address on the transfer was in Utah. Park City. I traced it. POB. It was winter by then. I figured the little fucks went skiing with the death money."

* * *

"Scams, murder, movies," I said. "No known address. Need a closer fit?"

Milo shook his head. I felt sparked by what we'd just learned but he seemed dejected.

"What is it?"

"First Derrick offs his parents, then his brother, probably for Cliff's share of the eighty grand. This is professional evil."

"What was left of Cliff's share," I said. "Like Castro said, they probably chewed right through it. Maybe Derrick chewed faster."

"Derrick the dominator . . . arrogant, just like you've been saying."

"Good criminal self-esteem," I said. "And why not? He does bad things and gets away clean. And maybe he had practice with family elimination."

"The Ardullos," he said. "Spurring Peake on—well, your guesses have been pretty right on, haven't they?"

"Aw shucks," I said. "Now all we need to do is find Derrick. Let me get back on the line with the psychiatric board."

"Sure. I'll hit Pimm again. And Park City. Maybe Derrick tried a land scam there, too."

"If you want, I'll give you some other possibilities."

"What?"

"Aspen, Telluride, Vegas, Tahoe. This is a party boy. He goes where the fun is."

The dejected look returned. "Those kinds of record checks could take weeks," he said. "The guy's right here, polluting *my* city, and I can't put a finger on him."

It took several calls to learn that psychiatric tech licenses were granted for periods ranging from thirteen to twenty-four months. Individual names could be verified, but sending the entire list was unheard-of. Finally, I found a supervisor willing to fax the roster. Another twenty minutes passed before paper began spooling out of the sorry-looking machine across the room.

I read as it unraveled. Page after page of names, no Crimmins, no Wark.

Another alias?

Griffith D. Wark. Scrambling a film maestro. Manipulative, pretentious, arrogant. And strangely childlike—playing pretend games.

Seeing himself as a major Hollywood player. The fact that he'd never produced anything was a nasty bit of potential dissonance, but the same could be said of so many coutured reptiles occupying tables at Spago.

Psychopaths could deal with dissonance.

Psychopaths had low levels of anxiety.

Besides, there were other types of productions.

Blood Walk.

Bad eyes in a box.

Something else about human snakes: they lacked emotional depth, faked humanity. Craved repetition. *Patterns.*

So maybe Wark had co-opted other major directors. I was no film expert but several names came to mind: Alfred Hitchcock, Orson Welles, John Huston, John Ford, Frank Capra. . . . I scanned the tech list. None of the above.

But Wark was D. W. Griffith's *middle* name. What was Hitchcock's?

I called the research library at the U, asked for the reference desk, and explained what I needed. The librarian must have been puzzled, but odd requests are their business and, God bless her, she didn't argue.

Five minutes later I had what I needed: Alfred Joseph Hitchcock. John no middle name Huston. Frank NMN Capra. George Orson Welles. John NMN Ford; real name, Sean Aloysius O'Feeney.

Thanking her, I turned back to the tech list. No Capras, four Fords, one Hitchcock, no Hustons, no O'Feeneys . . . no obviously cute manipulations of Hitchcock or Ford. . . . Then I saw it.

G. W. Orson.

Co-opting a genius.

Delusions were *everywhere.*

31.

"CITIZEN CREEP," SAID Milo, looking at the circled name.

"G. W. Orson got licensed twenty-two months ago," I said. "That's about all I could get except for the address he put on his application form."

He studied the address slip. "South Shenandoah Street . . . around Eighteenth. West L.A. territory . . . only a few blocks from the shopping center where Claire was dumped."

"The center's far from Claire's house, so why would she shop there? Unless she went with someone else."

"Crimmins? They had a relationship?"

"Why not?" I said. "Let's assume Orson—and Wark—are both Crimmins aliases. We have no employment records yet, but Crimmins is a psych tech, so it's not much of a leap to assume he works at Starkweather, or did in the past. He ran into Claire. Something developed. Because they had two common interests: the movies and Ardis Peake. When Claire told Crimmins she'd picked Peake as a project, he decided to find out more. When Crimmins learned Claire was uncovering information potentially threatening to him, he decided to cast her in *Blood Walk*."

"Kills her, films her, dumps her," he said. "It holds together logically; now all I have to do is prove it. I canvassed the shopping center, showed her picture to every clerk who'd been working the day she was killed. No one remembered seeing her, alone or with anyone else. That doesn't mean much, it's a huge place, and if I can get a picture of Crimmins, I'll go back. But maybe we can get a look at him in person."

282

He waved the address slip. "This helps big-time. First let's see if he registered his 'Vette."

The call to DMV left him shaking his head. "No G. W. Orson cars anywhere in the state."

"Lives in L.A., but no legal car," I said. "That alone tells us he's dirty. Try another scrambled director's name."

"Later," he said, pocketing the address. "This is something real. Let's go for it."

The block was quiet, intermittently treed, filled with plain-wrap, single-story houses set on vest-pocket lots that ranged from compulsively tended to ragged. Birds chirped, dogs barked. A man in an undershirt pushed a lawn mower in slo-mo. A dark-skinned woman strolling a baby looked up as we passed. Apprehension, then relief; the unmarked was anything but inconspicuous.

Years ago, the neighborhood had been ravaged by crime and white flight. Rising real estate prices had reversed some of that, and the result was a mixed-race district that resonated with tense, tentative pride.

The place G. W. Orson had called home twenty-two months ago was a pale green Spanish bungalow with a neatly edged lawn and no other landscaping. A FOR LEASE sign was staked dead center in the grass. In the driveway was a late-model Oldsmobile Cutlass. Milo drove halfway down the block and ran the plates. "TBL Properties, address on Wilshire near La Brea."

He U-turned, parked in front of the green house. A stunted old magnolia tree planted in the parkway next door cast some shade upon the Olds. Nailed to the trunk was a poster. Cloudy picture of a dog with some Rottweiler in it. Eager canine grin. "Have You Seen Buddy?" over a phone number and a typed message: Buddy had been missing for a week and needed daily thyroid medication. Finding him would bring a hundred-dollar reward. For no reason I could think of, Buddy looked strangely familiar. Everything was starting to remind me of something.

We walked to the front of the green house, stepping around

a low, chipped stucco wall that created a small patio. The front door was glossy and sharp-smelling—fresh varnish. White curtains blocked the front window. Shiny brass door knocker. Milo lifted it and let it drop.

Footsteps. An Asian man opened the door. Sixties, angular, and tanned, he wore a beige work shirt, sleeves rolled to the elbows, matching cotton pants, white sneakers. Creepily close to Starkweather inmate duds. I felt my hands ball and forced them to loosen.

"Yes?" His hair was sparse and white, his eyes a pair of surgical incisions. In one hand was a crumpled gray rag.

Milo flashed the badge. "We're here about George Orson."

"Him." Weary smile. "No surprise. Come on in."

We followed him into a small, empty living room. Next door was a kitchen, also empty, except for a six-pack of paper towel rolls on the brown tile counter. A mop and a broom were propped in a corner, looking like exhausted marathon dancers. The house echoed of vacancy, but stale odors—cooked meat, must, tobacco—lingered, battling for dominance with soap, ammonia, varnish from the door.

Vacant, but more lived-in than Claire's place.

The man held out his hand. "Len Itatani."

"You work for the owner, sir?" said Milo.

Itatani smiled. "I am the owner." He produced a couple of business cards.

TBL Properties, Inc.
LEONARD J. ITATANI, PRES.

"Named it after my kids. Tom, Beverly, Linda. So what did Orson do?"

"Sounds like you had problems with him, sir," said Milo.

"Nothing but," said Itatani. He glanced around the room. "Sorry there's no place to sit. There's some bottled water, if you're thirsty. Too hot to be cleaning up, but summer's prime rental time and I want to get this place squared away."

"No thanks," said Milo. "What did Orson do?"

Itatani pulled a square of tissue paper from his shirt pocket and dabbed a clear, broad forehead. No moisture on the bronze skin that I'd noticed. "Orson was a bum. Always late with his rent; then he stopped paying at all. Neighbor complained he was selling drugs, but I don't know about that, there was nothing I could do. She said all kinds of cars would show up at night, be here a short time, and leave. I told her to call the police."

"Did she?"

"You'd have to ask her."

"Which neighbor?"

"Right next door." Itatani pointed south.

Milo's pad was out. "So you never talked to Orson about selling drugs?"

"I was going to, eventually," said Itatani. "What I did try to talk to him about was the rent. Left messages under the door—he never gave me a phone listing, said he hadn't bothered to get one. That should've warned me." Another swipe at the dry brow. "Didn't want to scare him off with any drug talk until he paid the rent he owed me. Was *this* close to posting notice. But he moved out, middle of the night. Stole furniture. I had his first and last and damage deposit in cash, but he trashed more than was covered by the deposit—cigarette burns on the nightstands, cracked tiles in the bathroom, gouges in the wood floors, probably from dragging cameras around."

"Cameras?"

"Movie cameras—big, heavy stuff. All sorts of stuff in boxes, too. I warned him about the floors; he said he'd be careful." He grimaced. "Had to refinish a hundred square feet of oak board, replace some of it totally. I told him no filming in the house, didn't want any funny business."

"Like what?"

"You know," said Itatani. "A guy like that, says he's making movies but he's living here. My first thought was something X-rated. I didn't want that going on here, so I made it clear: this was a residence, not a budget studio. Orson said he had no intention of working here, had some kind of arrangement with one of the studios, he just needed to store some equipment. I never really believed that—you get a studio contract, you don't live here. I had a bad feeling about him from the beginning—no references, he said he'd been freelancing for a while, working on his own projects. When I asked him what kind of projects, he just said short films, changed the subject. But he showed me cash. It was the middle of the year, the place had been vacant for a long time, I figured a bird in the hand."

"When did he start renting, sir?"

"Eleven months ago," said Itatani. "He stayed for six months, stiffed me for the last two."

"So it's been five months since he left," said Milo. "Have you had other tenants since?"

"Sure," said Itatani. "First two students, then a hairdresser. Not much better, had to evict them both."

"Did Orson live alone?"

"Far as I know. I saw him with a couple of women; whether or not he moved them in, I don't know. So what'd he do to get you down here?"

"A few things," said Milo. "What did the women look like?"

"One was one of those rock-and-roll types—blond hair, all spiky, lots of makeup. She was here when I showed up to ask about the overdue rent. Said she was a friend of Orson's, was out on location, she'd give him the message."

"How old?"

"Twenties, thirties, hard to tell with all that makeup. She wasn't tough or anything—kind of polite, actually. Promised to tell Orson. Nothing happened for a week, I stopped by again but no one was here. I left a note, another week passed, Orson sent me a check. It bounced."

"Remember what bank it was from?"

"Santa Monica Bank, Pico Boulevard," said Itatani. "Closed account, he'd only had it for a week. I came over a third time, looked through the window, saw he still had his stuff here. I could've posted right there, but all that does is cost money for filing. Even if you win in Small Claims, try collecting. So I left more messages. He'd call back, but always late at night when he knew I wasn't in." He ticked his fingers. " 'Sorry, been traveling.' 'There must be a bank mixup.' 'I'll get you a cashier's check.' By the next month, I'd had it, but he was gone."

"What about the second woman?" said Milo.

"Her I didn't meet, I just saw her with him. Getting into his car—that's another thing. His car. Yellow Corvette. Flashy. *That* he had money for. The time I saw the second woman was around the same time—five, six months ago. I'd come by to get the rent, no one was home. I left a note, drove away, got halfway up the block, saw Orson's car, turned around. Orson parked and got out. But then he must've seen me, because he got back in and drove off. Fast, we passed each other. I waved but he kept going. She was on the passenger side. Brunette. I'd already met the blonde, remember thinking *He can't pay the rent but he can afford two girlfriends.*"

"You figured the brunette was his girlfriend."

"She was with him, middle of the day. They were about to go into the house."

"What else can you tell me about her?"

"I didn't get much of a look at her. Older than the blonde, I think. Nothing unusual. When she passed me, she was looking out the window. Right at me. Not smiling or anything. I remember thinking she looked confused—like why was Orson making a getaway, but . . . I really can't say much about her. Brunette, that's about it."

"How about a description of Orson?"

"Tall, skinny. Every time I saw him he wore nothing but black. He had these black boots with big heels that made him even taller. And that shaved head—real Hollywood."

"Shaved head," said Milo.

"Clean as a cueball," said Itatani.

"How old?"

"Thirties, maybe forty."

"Eye color?"

"That I couldn't tell you. He always reminded me of a

vulture. Big nose, little eyes—I think they were brown, but I wouldn't swear to it."

"How old was the brunette in the car?"

Itatani shrugged. "Like I said, we passed for two seconds."

"But probably older than the blonde," said Milo.

"I guess."

Milo produced Claire's County Hospital staff photo.

Itatani studied the picture, returned it, shaking his head. "No reason it *couldn't* be her, but that's as much as I can say. Who is she?"

"Possibly an associate of Orson. So you saw the brunette with Orson five, six months ago."

"Let me think. . . . I'd say closer to five. Not long before he moved out." Itatani dabbed his face again. "All these questions, he must've done something really bad."

"Why's that, sir?"

"For you to be spending all this time. I get burglaries at some of my other properties, robberies, it's all I can do to get the police to come out and write a report. I knew that guy was wrong."

Milo pressed Itatani for more details without success; then we walked through the house. Two bedrooms, one bath, everything redolent of soap. Fresh paint; new carpeting in the hallway. The replaced floorboards were in the smaller bedroom. Milo rubbed his face. Any physical evidence of Wark's presence had long vanished.

He said, "Did Orson keep any tools here—power tools?"

"In the garage," said Itatani. "He set up a whole shop. He kept more movie stuff in there, too. Lights, cables, all kinds of things."

"What kind of tools did he have in the shop?"

"The usual," said Itatani. "Power drill, hand tools, power saws. He said he sometimes built his own sets."

The garage was flat-roofed and double-width, taking up a third of the tiny backyard. Outsized for the house.

I remarked on that.

Itatani unlocked the sliding metal door and shoved it up. "I enlarged it years ago, figured it would make the place easier to rent."

Inside were walls paneled in cheap fake oak, a cement floor, an open-beam ceiling with a fluorescent fixture dangling from a header. The smell of disinfectant burned my nose.

"You've cleaned this, too," said Milo.

"First thing I cleaned," said Itatani. "The hairdresser brought cats in. Against the rules—he had a no-pets lease. Litter boxes and those scratch things all over the place. Took days to air out the stink." He sniffed. "Finally."

Milo paced the garage, examined the walls, then the floor. He stopped at the rear left-hand corner, beckoned me over. Itatani came, too.

Faint mocha-colored splotch, amoebic, eight or nine inches square.

Milo knelt and put his face close to the wall, pointed. Specks of the same hue dotted the paneling. Brown on brown, barely visible.

Itatani said, "Cat pee. I was able to scrub some of it off."

"What did it look like before you cleaned it?"

"A little darker."

Milo got up and walked along the back wall very slowly. Stopped a few feet down, wrote in his pad. Another splotch, smaller.

"What?" said Itatani.

Milo didn't answer.

"What?" Itatani repeated. "Oh—you don't— Oh, no . . ." For the first time, he was sweating.

Milo cell-phoned the crime-scene team, apologized to Itatani for the impending disruption, and asked him to stay clear of the garage. Then he got some yellow tape from the unmarked and stretched it across the driveway.

Itatani said, "Still looks like cat dirt to me," and went to sit in his Oldsmobile.

Milo and I walked over to the south-side neighbor. Another Spanish house, bright white. The mat in front of the door said

GO AWAY. Very loud classical music pounded through the walls. No response to the doorbell. Several hard knocks finally opened the door two inches, revealing one bright blue eye, a slice of white skin, a smudge of red mouth.

"What?" a cracked voice screeched.

Milo shouted back, "Police, ma'am!"

"Show me some I.D."

Milo held out the badge. The blue eye moved closer, pupil contracting as it confronted daylight.

"Closer," the voice demanded.

Milo put the badge right up against the crack. The blue eye blinked. Several seconds passed. The door opened.

The woman was short, skinny, at least eighty, with hair dyed crow-feather black and curled in Marie Antoinette ringlets that reminded me of blood sausages. A face powdered chalky added to the aging-courtesan look. She wore a black silk dressing gown spattered with gold stars, three strings of heavy amber beads around her neck, giant pearl drop earrings. The music in the background was assertive and heavy—Wagner or Bruckner or someone else a goose-stepper would've enjoyed. Cymbals crashed. The woman glared. Behind her was a huge white grand piano piled high with books.

"What do you want?" she screamed over a crescendo. Her voice was as pleasing as grit on glass.

"George Orson," said Milo. "Is it possible to turn the music down?"

Cursing under her breath, the woman slammed the door, opened it a minute later. The music was several notches lower, but still loud.

"Orson," she said. "Scumbag. What'd he do, kill someone?" Glancing to the left. Itatani had come out of his car and was standing on the lawn of the green house.

"Goddamn absentee landlords. Don't care who they rent to. So what'd that scumbag do?"

"That's what we're trying to find out, ma'am."

"That's a load of double-talk crap. What'd he *do*?" She slapped her hands against her hips. Silk whistled and the dressing gown parted at her neckline, revealing powdered wattle, a few inches of scrawny white chest, shiny sternal knobs protruding like ivory handles. Her lipstick was the color of arterial blood. "You want info from me, don't hand me any crap."

"Mr. Orson's suspected in some drug thefts, Mrs.—"

"*Ms.*," she said. "Sinclair. *Ms.* Marie Sinclair. Drugs. Big boo-hoo surprise. It's about time you guys caught on. The whole time that lowlife was here there'd be cars in and out, in and out, all hours of the night."

"Did you ever call the police?"

Marie Sinclair looked ready to hit him. "Jesus Almighty—only six times. Your so-called officers said they'd drive by. If they did, lot of good it accomplished."

Milo wrote. "What else did Orson do to disturb you, Ms. Sinclair?"

"Cars in and out, in and out wasn't enough. I'm trying to practice, and the headlights keep shining through the drapes. Right there." She pointed to her front window, covered with lace.

"Practice what, ma'am?" said Milo.

"Piano. I teach, give recitals." She flexed ten spidery white fingers. The nails were a matching red, but clipped short.

"I used to do radio work," she said. "Live radio—the old RKO studios. I knew Oscar Levant, what a lunatic—another dope fiend, but a genius. I was the first girl pianist for the Cocoanut Grove, played the Mocambo, did a party at Ira Gershwin's up on Roxbury Drive. Talk about stage fright—George *and* Ira listening. There were giants back then; now it's only mental midgets and—"

"Orson told Mr. Itatani he was a film director."

"Mr. Ita*whosis*"—she sneered—"doesn't give a damn *who* he rents to. After the scumbag moved out, I got stuck with two sloppy kids—real pigs—then a fag cosmetologist. Back when I bought this house—"

"When Orson lived here, did you ever see any filming next door?" said Milo.

"Yeah, he was Cecil B. DeMille—no, never. Just cars, in

and out. I'm trying to practice and the damn headlights are glaring through like some kind of—"

"You practice at night, ma'am?"

"So what?" said Marie Sinclair. "That's against the law?"

"No, ma'am, I was just—"

"Look," she said. Her hands separated from her hips, clamped down again. "I'm a night person, as if it's any of your business. Just woke *up*, if it's any of your *business*. Comes from all those years of clubbing." She stepped onto the porch, advanced on Milo. "Nighttime's when it comes alive. Morning's for suckers. Morning people should be lined up and shot."

"So your basic complaint against Orson was all the traffic."

"*Dope* traffic. Those kinds of lowlifes, what was to stop someone from pulling out a gun? None of those idiots can shoot straight, you hear about all those colored and Mexican kids getting shot in drive-bys by accident. I could've been sitting in there playing Chopin, and *pow!*"

She squeezed her eyes shut, punched her forehead, jerked her head back. Black ringlets danced. When her eyes opened, they were hotter, brighter.

Milo said, "Did you ever get a good look at any of Orson's visitors?"

"Visitors. Hah. No, I didn't look. Didn't want to see, didn't want to know. The headlights were bad enough. You guys never did a damn thing about them. And don't tell me to turn the piano around, because it's a seven-foot-long Steinway and it won't fit in the room any other way."

"How many cars would there be on an average night, Ms. Sinclair?"

"Five, six, ten, who knows, I never counted. At least he was gone a lot."

"How often, ma'am?"

"A lot. Half the time. Maybe more. Thank God for small blessings."

"Did you ever talk to him directly about the headlights?"

"What?" she screeched. "And have him pull out a gun?

We're talking *scumbag*. That's *your* job. I *called* you. Lot of good it did."

"Mr. Itatani said Orson had a machine shop out in the garage. Did you ever hear sawing or drilling?"

"No," she said. "Why? You think he was manufacturing the dope back there? Or cutting it, whatever it is they do to that crap?"

"Anything's possible, ma'am."

"No, it's not," she snapped. "Very *few* things are possible. Oscar Levant will not rise from the dead. That cancer in George Gershwin's genius brain will not— Never mind, why am I wasting my time. No, I never heard *drilling or sawing*. I never heard a damn thing, because during the day, when I sleep, I keep the music on—got one of those programmable CD players, six discs that keep repeating. It's the only way I can go to sleep, block out the damn birds, cars, all that daytime crap. It was when I was up that he bothered me. The lights. Trying to get through my scales and the damn headlights are shining right on the keyboard."

Milo nodded. "I understand, ma'am."

"Sure you do," she said. "Too late, too little."

"Anything else you can tell us?"

"That's it. Didn't know I was going to be tested."

Milo showed her Claire's picture. "Ever see her with Orson?"

"Nope," she said. "She looks like a schoolteacher. Is she the one he killed?"

The crime-scene crew arrived ten minutes later. Itatani sat in his Oldsmobile, looking miserable. Marie Sinclair had gone back inside her house, but a few other neighbors had emerged. Milo asked them questions. I followed as he walked up and down the block, knocking on doors. No new revelations. If George Orson had been running a dope house, Marie Sinclair had been the only one to notice.

A pleasant old woman named Mrs. Leiber turned out to be the owner of Buddy, the missing dog. She seemed addled, disappointed that we weren't here to investigate the theft.

Convinced Buddy had been dognapped, though an open gate at the side of her house indicated other possibilities.

Milo told her he'd keep his eyes open.

"He's such a sweetie," Mrs. Leiber said. "Got the courage but not any meanness."

We returned to the green house. The criminalists were still unpacking their gear. Milo showed the stains in the garage to the head tech, a black man named Merriweather, who got down and put his nose to it.

"Could be," he said. "If it is, it's pretty degraded. We'll scrape. If it *is* blood, should be able to get a basic HLA typing, but DNA's a whole other thing."

"Just tell me if it's blood."

"I can try that now."

We watched him work, wielding solvents and reagents, swabs and test tubes.

The answer came within minutes:

"O-positive."

"Richard Dada's type," said Milo.

"Forty-three percent of the population," said Merriweather. "Let me scrape around here and inside the house, it'll take us the best part of the day, but maybe we can find you something interesting."

Back in the unmarked, Milo phoned DMV again, cross-referencing vehicle registrations with the Shenandoah address. No match.

Gunning the engine, he pulled away from the curb, tires squealing. Less urgency than frustration. By the time we were back on Pico, he'd slowed down.

At Doheny, we stopped for a red light and he said, "Richard's blood type. Orson's cutting out on the rent could explain why Richard was cut in half and Claire wasn't. By the time he did her, he'd lost his machine shop, didn't have the time—or the place—to set up. . . . All that stolen movie junk. He has to keep it somewhere. Time to check out storage outfits. . . . Be nice if Itatani could've I.D.'d Claire as the woman in the car."

"If she was, Itatani saw her shortly before she was murdered. Maybe she and Orson did go shopping at the center, and that's why he dumped her there. What stores are there?"

"Montgomery Ward, Toys 'R' Us, food joints, the Stereos Galore she was found behind."

"Stereos Galore," I said. "Might they sell cameras?"

He looked in his rearview mirror, hung an illegal U-turn.

The front lot was jammed and we had to park on the far end, near La Cienega. Stereos Galore was two vast stories of gray rubber flooring and maroon plastic partitions. Scores of TV's projected soundlessly; blinking, throbbing entertainment centers spewed conflicting backbeats; salespeople in emerald-green vests pointed out the latest feature to stunned-looking customers. The camera section was at the rear of the second floor.

The manager was a small, dark-skinned, harried-looking man named Albert Mustafa with a precise black mustache and eyeglasses so thick his mild brown irises seemed miles away. He shepherded us into a relatively quiet corner, behind tall displays of film in colorful boxes. The cacophony from below filtered through the rubber tiles. Marie Sinclair would have felt at home.

Claire Argent's picture evoked a blank stare. Milo asked him about substantial video purchases.

"Six months ago?" he said.

"Five or six months ago," said Milo. "The name could be Wark or Crimmins or Orson. We're looking for a substantial purchase of video equipment or cameras."

"How much is substantial?" said Mustafa.

"What's your typical sale?"

"Nothing's typical. Still cameras range from fifty dollars to nearly a thousand. We can get you set up with basic video for under three hundred, but you can go high-tech and then you're talking serious money."

"Every sale is in the computer, right?"

"Supposed to be."

"Do you categorize your customers based upon how much they spend?"

"No, sir."

"Okay," said Milo. "How about checking video purchases over one thousand dollars, four to six months ago. Start with this date." He recited the day of Claire's murder.

Mustafa said, "I'm not sure this is legal, sir. I'd have to check with the home office."

"Where's that?"

"Minneapolis."

"And they're closed by now," said Milo.

"I'm afraid so, sir."

"How about just spooling back to that one day, Mr. Mustafa, see what comes up."

"I'd really rather not."

Milo stared at him.

"I don't want to lose my job," said Mustafa. "But the police help us . . . Just that day."

Eight credit-card purchases of video equipment that day, two of them over a thousand dollars. No Crimmins, Wark, or Orson, or Argent. Nothing that brought to mind a scrambled director's name. Milo copied down the names and the credit card numbers as Mustafa looked on nervously.

"What about cash sales? Would you have records of those?"

"If the customer purchased the extended warranty. If he gave us his address so we could put him on the mailing list."

Milo tapped the computer. "How about scrolling back a few days."

Mustafa said, "This isn't good," but he complied.

Nothing for the entire week.

Mustafa pushed a button and the screen went blank. By the time Milo thanked him, he'd walked away.

32.

A FEW MORE detectives had returned to the Robbery-Homicide room. I pulled a chair up next to Milo's desk and listened as he called Social Security and the Franchise Tax Board. Two hits: tax refunds had been sent to George Orson. Place of employment: Starkweather State Hospital.

"The checks were sent to an address on Pico—ten thousand five hundred. Commercial zone, ten to one a mail drop. Also, close to Richard's dump site . . . Okay, okay, something's happening here. I need to get more specific, find out if he still works at Starkweather."

"What about Lindeen the receptionist?" I said. "She likes you. Must be that masculine cop musk."

He grimaced. "Yeah, I'm a musk ox. . . . Okay, why not?" He jabbed the phone. "Hello, Lindeen? Hi, it's Milo Sturgis. Right . . . Oh, muddling along, how 'bout you. . . . Well, that's terrific, yeah I've heard about those, sounds like fun, at least you get to solve something. . . . Uh, well, I'm not sure I have anything to . . . Think so? Well, okay, if I can get some free time—after I clear Dr. Argent's case. . . . No, wish I could say I was. . . . Speaking of which, does a psych tech named George Orson still work there?" He spelled the surname. "Nothing major, but I heard he might've been a friend of Dr. Argent's. . . . I know she didn't, but his name came up from another party, they said he worked at Starkweather and knew her. . . . No?" He frowned. "Could you? That'd be great."

He lowered the mouthpiece. "The name's a little familiar, but she can't connect it to a face."

297

"Hundred employees," I said. "What's the barter?"

He started to answer, moved the phone back under his mouth. "Yup, still here. . . . Did he? When was that? Any forwarding address?" His pen was poised, but he didn't write. "So how long was he actually on staff?" Scribble. "Any idea why he left? No, I wouldn't call him *that*, just checking every lead. . . . What's that? That soon? I wish I could say yes, but unless the case clears, I'm pretty— Pardon? Yeah, okay, I promise. . . . Yeah, it should be fun. Me, too. Thanks, Lindeen. And listen, you don't need to bother Mr. Swig about this. I've got everything I need. Thanks again."

He hung up. "The barter is I come give a talk to some murder-mystery club she belongs to. They stage phony crimes, give out prizes for solving them, eat nachos. She wanted me next month but I deferred to their big bash at Christmas."

"Playing Santa?"

"Ho ho fucking ho."

"I tell you it's the musk."

"Yeah, next time I'll shower first. . . . The deal on Orson is, he joined Starkweather fifteen months ago, left after ten months of full-time employment."

"Five months ago," I said. "A month after Claire got there. So they had plenty of time to get acquainted."

"The brunette in the car," he said. "Itatani's three-second observation isn't much, but with this . . . maybe. Orson's file says he worked primarily on the fifth floor, with the criminal fakers—how's that for a match made in hell? But he did do some overtime down on the regular wards, so that gives him access to Peake. No infractions, no problems, he quit voluntarily. His photo's missing from the file, but Lindeen thinks she *might* remember him—maybe he had light brown hair. Probably being overly helpful. Or the guy's got a wig collection."

"Little dip into the costume box," I said. "He produces, directs, *and* acts. Five months ago is also shortly after Richard Dada's murder. Right when Orson closed up shop at Shenandoah, packed up the machine shop. He keeps himself a moving target. Saves money on rent and gets off on the thrill of the con."

"His relationship with Claire. You think it could've gone beyond an interest in Peake?"

"Who knows? Castro said he wasn't very smooth in Miami, but he's had time to polish his act. For all her love of privacy, Claire might've been lonely and vulnerable. And we know she could be sexually aggressive. Maybe her interest in pathology went beyond the workday. Or Orson promised to put her in pictures."

He knuckled his eyes, let out air very slowly. "Okay, let's check out that Pico address."

As we left the building, I said, "One thing in our favor, he may trip himself up. Because there's rigidity and childishness to his technique. The way he scripted his Miami con. I'll bet he's done the same here. The way he stays in comfort zones, dumping Claire near one of his addresses, Richard near another. He sees himself as some creative wizard, but he always returns to the familiar."

"Sounds about right," he said, "for a showbiz guy."

Mailbox Heaven. Northeast corner of a scruffy strip mall just west of Barrington, a stuffy closet lined with brass boxes and smelling of wet paper. A young woman came out from the back room, redheaded, bright-eyed, brightening as Milo showed her his badge. Opining that police work was "cool."

George Orson's box had been rented to someone else for over a year and she had no records of the original transaction.

"No way," she said. "We don't keep stuff. People come and go. That's who uses us."

We got back in the unmarked. On the way to the station, we passed the spot where Richard Dada's VW had been abandoned. Small factories, auto mechanics, spare-parts yards. Just another industrial park—a cleaner, more compact version of the desolate stretch presaging Starkweather.

Comfort zones . . .

We sat, parked at the curb, not talking, watching men with rolled-up sleeves hauling and driving, loafing and smoking.

No gates around the enclosure. Easy entry after hours. Empty, dark acres: the perfect dump site. A flatbed full of aluminum pipe rumbled past. A catering truck with rust-specked white sides sounded a clarion and men marched forward for burritos of dubious composition.

The noise had never abated, but now I heard it for the first time. Compressors snapping and popping, metal clanging against cement, whining triumph as saw blades devoured wood . . .

I accompanied Milo as he visited shop after shop, asking questions, encountering boredom, confusion, distrust, occasional overt hostility.

Asking about a tall, thin, bald man with a bird face who did woodwork. Maybe a wig, black or brown, curly or straight. A yellow Corvette or an old VW. Two hours, and all the effort bought were lungfuls of chemical air.

Milo drove me back to the station and I headed home, thinking, suddenly and inexplicably, of a missing dog with a nice smile.

Nighttime can be so many things.

Shortly after eight P.M., Robin and I were eating pizza on the deck, tented by a starless purple sky. Just enough dry heat had lingered to be soothing. The quiet was merciful.

Robin had driven up an hour before. Feeling guilty about returning to Starkweather without informing her, I'd filled her in.

"No need for confession. You're here in one piece."

She'd looked tired, soaked in the tub while I drove into Westwood to get the pizza. I took the truck, playing Joe Satriani very loud. Not minding the traffic, not minding much of anything at all. A couple of beers when I got back didn't raise my anxiety. The bath had refreshed Robin, and staring at her across the table as she worked on a second slice seemed a great way to pass the time.

I'd allowed myself to feel pretty good by the time the unmarked zoomed up in front of the house.

The headlights made my head hurt. Tonight, Marie Sinclair and I were kindred spirits.

The car stopped. Spike barked. Robin waved. I didn't budge.

Milo stuck his head out the passenger's window. "Oh. Sorry. Nothing earth-shattering. Call me tomorrow, Alex."

Spike had cranked up the volume, and now he was baying like an insulted hound. Robin got up and leaned over the railing. "Don't be silly. Come up and eat something."

"Nah," he said. "You lovebirds deserve some quality time."

"Up, young man. *Now.*"

Spike hurled himself down the stairs, sped to the car, stationed himself at Milo's door and began jumping up and down.

"How do I interpret this?" said Milo. "Friend or foe?"

"Friend," I said.

"You're sure?"

"Psychologists are never sure," I said. "We just make probability judgments."

"Meaning?"

"If he pees on your shoes, I was wrong."

He claimed to have grabbed a sandwich, but one and a half beers later, he started to observe the pizza with interest. I slid it over to him. He got down four slices, said, "Maybe it's good for me—the spice, cleanses the body."

"Sure," I said. "It's health food. Detoxify yourself."

He got to work on a fifth slice, Spike curled at his feet, lapping the scraps that fell from his dangling left hand, Milo maintaining a poker face, thinking Robin and I weren't noticing the covert donations.

Robin said, "Dessert?"

"Don't put yourself out—"

She patted his head and went into the house.

I said, "So what's not earth-shattering?"

"Found four more George Orson bank accounts. Glendale, Sylmar, Northridge, downtown. All the same pattern: he plants cash for a week, withdraws right after writing checks."

"Checks for what?"

"Haven't been able to look at them yet. After a certain amount of time—no one seems to know how long—bad paper's destroyed and the data's sent to some computer in the home office."

"In Minnesota," I said.

"No doubt. These guys are addicted to paperwork, don't seem to wanna help themselves."

"Glendale, Sylmar, Northridge, downtown," I said. "Orson's spreading himself all over the city. It might also mean he's a restless driver. Consistent with a fun-killer. Anyone remember him?"

"Not a one. The crimes were duly documented, police reports were filed, but no one bothered to check for similars, no one spent much energy following up. Next item: the lab has complete HLA typing from the stains in the garage. I sent over samples of Richard's blood for comparison. Nothing showed up in the rest of the house. Too many cleanings by Mr. Itatani—where are negligent slumlords when you need them?"

Spike emitted a pulsating, froglike croak. Milo's left hand slid across the table. Slurp, munch.

"Finally: the lovely and outgoing Ms. Sinclair did indeed report the nighttime traffic at the house. A dozen complaints, cruisers were sent out seven times, but all the blues saw were some cars in the driveway, no dope transactions. I spoke to one of the sergeants. He considers Sinclair a crank. I have cleaned up his language. Apparently, bitching's her main hobby. One time she called in at two A.M. about a mockingbird in a tree she claimed was singing off-key intentionally—some bird plot to throw off her piano playing. In the warrant application I thought it best not to describe her psychological status in too much detail, called her a 'neighborhood observer.' But what a whack job; you guys will never be out of work."

"Too bad Mrs. Leiber didn't notice anything," I said.

"Who's Mrs. Leiber?"

"The lady with the lost dog."

"Oh, her. All she cared about was the dog."

"I keep thinking about the dog."

"What do you mean?"

"His face stays with me. Don't know why. It's as if I've seen him before."

"In a past life?"

I laughed because it was the right thing to do. Milo slipped Spike a long strip of mozzarella.

Robin came out with iced coffee and chocolate ice cream. Milo finished the pizza and joined us sipping and spooning. Soon, he'd slid down in his chair, nearly supine, eyes closed, head hanging over the back of the chair.

"Ah," he said, "the good life."

Then his beeper went off.

33.

"SWIG," HE SAID, returning from the kitchen.

"Someone told him about Peake's Jesus pose," I said, "and he's going to make your life a living hell if you don't stay away."

"On the contrary. He offered a personal invitation to come over. Now."

"Why?"

"He wouldn't say, just 'Now.' Not an order, though. A polite request. He actually said please."

I looked at Robin. "Have fun."

She said, "Oh, please. You'll be pacing the house, end up having one of your sleepless nights." To Milo: "Take care of him, or no more beer."

He crossed his heart. I kissed her and we hurried down to the car.

As he sped down to the Glen and headed south, I said, "Were you shielding Robin, or did he really not say?"

"The latter. One thing I *didn't* say in front of her. He sounded scared."

Ten P.M. The night was kind to the industrial wasteland. A hospital security guard was waiting on the road just outside the turnoff, idly aiming a flashlight beam at the ground. As we drove up, he illuminated the unmarked's license plate and waved us forward hurriedly.

"Straight through," he told Milo. "They're waiting for you."

"Who's they?"

"Everyone."

304

* * *

The guard in the booth flipped the barrier arm as we approached. We drove through without being questioned.

"No surrendering the gun?" I said. "When do they unfurl the red rug?"

"Too easy," said Milo. "I hate it when things go too easy."

At the parking lot, a black tech with salt-and-pepper hair pointed out the closest parking space. Milo muttered, "Now I have to tip him."

When we got out of the car, the tech said, "Hal Cleveland. I'll take you to Mr. Swig."

Hurrying toward the inner fence without waiting. Running ahead the way Dollard had done, he kept checking to see if we were with him.

"What's the story?" Milo asked him.

Cleveland shook his head. "I'll leave that to Mr. Swig."

At night, the yard was empty. And different, the dirt frosty and blue-gray under high-voltage lights, scooped in places like ice cream. Cleveland half-jogged. It was nice being able to cross without fear of some psychotic jumping me. Still, I found myself checking my back.

We reached the far gate and Cleveland unlocked it with a quick twist. The main building *didn't* look much different—still ashen and ugly, the clouded plastic windows gaping like an endless series of beseeching mouths. Another guard blocked the door. Armed with baton and gun. First time I'd seen a uniform—or weapons—inside the grounds. He stepped aside for us, and Cleveland hurried us past Lindeen's cleared desk, past the brassy flash of bowling trophies, through the silent hallway. Past Swig's office, all the other administrative doors, straight to the elevator. A quick, uninterruped ride up to C Ward. Cleveland wedged himself in a corner, played with his keys.

When the elevator door opened, another tech, big and thick and bearded, was positioned right in front of us. He stepped back to let us exit. Cleveland stayed in the lift and rode it back down.

The bearded tech took us through the double doors.

William Swig stood midway up the corridor. In front of Peake's room. Peake's door was closed. Another pair of uniformed guards was positioned a few feet away. The bearded man left us to join two other techs, their backs against the facing wall.

No men in khaki. But for the hum of the air conditioner, the ward was silent.

Swig saw us and shook his head very hard, as if denying a harsh reality. He had on a navy polo shirt, jeans, running shoes. The filmy strands atop his head puffed at odd angles. Overhead fluorescents heightened the contrast between his facial moles and the pallid skin that hosted them. Dark dots, like braille, punctuating the message on his face.

Nothing ambiguous about the communication: pure fear.

He opened Peake's door, winced, gave a ringmaster's flourish.

Not that much blood.

A single scarlet python.

Winding its way toward us from the far right-hand corner of the cell. About three feet from the spot where Peake had played Jesus.

Otherwise the room looked the same. Messy bed. Wall restraints bolted in place. That same burning smell mixed with something coppery-sweet.

No sign of Peake.

The blood trail stopped halfway across the floor, its point of origin below the body.

Stocky body, lying facedown. Plaid shirt, blue jeans, sneakers. A head full of coarse gray hair. Arms outstretched, almost relaxed-looking. Thick forearms. The skin had already gone grayish-green.

"Dollard," said Milo. "When?"

"We don't know," said Swig. "Someone discovered him two hours ago."

"And you called me forty-five minutes ago?"

"We had to conduct our own search first," said Swig. He picked at a mole, brought a rosy flush to its borders.

"And?"

Swig looked away. "We haven't found him."

Milo was silent.

"Look," said Swig, "we *had* to do our own search first. I'm not even sure I should've called you. It's sheriff's jurisdiction—actually, it's our jurisdiction."

"So you did me a favor," said Milo.

"You had an interest in Peake. I'm trying to cooperate."

Milo stepped closer to the body, kneeled, looked under Dollard's chin.

"Looks like one transverse cut," he said. "Has anyone moved him?"

"No," said Swig. "Nothing's been touched."

"Who found him?"

Swig pointed to one of the three techs. "Bart did." The man stepped forward. Young, Chinese, delicately built, but with the oversized arms of a bodybuilder. His badge photo was that of a stunned child. B. L. Quan, Tech II.

"Tell me about it," Milo told him.

"We were in lockdown," said Quan. "Not because of any problems; we do it during staff meetings."

"How frequent are staff meetings?"

"Twice a week for each shift."

"What days?"

"It depends on the shift," said Quan. "Tonight was for the eleven-to-seven. Six-thirty. Friday night, the weekly summary. The patients go in lockdown and the staff goes in there." He pointed to the TV room.

"No staff on the ward?" said Milo.

"One tech stays outside. We rotate. There's never been any problem, the patients are all locked up tight."

Milo looked at the body.

Quan shrugged.

"And Dollard was scheduled to be the outside guy tonight."

Quan nodded.

"But your beeper never went off."

"Right."

"So what made you look for him?" said Milo.

"The meeting was over, I was doing a double, and Frank was supposed to talk to me about some patients. Give me the transfer data—meds, things to watch out for, that kind of thing. He didn't show up, I thought he forgot."

"Was that typical?" said Milo. "Frank forgetting?"

Quan looked uncomfortable. He glanced at Swig.

"Don't worry," said Milo. "You can't embarrass him anymore."

Quan said, "Sometimes."

"Sometimes what?"

Quan shifted his feet. Milo turned to Swig.

"Tell him anything you know," said Swig. His voice had turned hoarse. He rolled his fingers, rubbed another mole.

"Sometimes Frank forgot things," said Quan. "That's why I didn't make any big deal out of it. But then, when I went to get the charts I couldn't find one of them—Peake's. So I checked out Peake's room."

"You ever find the chart?"

"No."

"What else?" said Milo.

"That's it. I saw Frank, Peake was gone, I locked the door, put out a Code Three alert. Easy, we were already in lockdown. Mr. Swig came in, we brought outside guards onto the wards, and a bunch of us searched everywhere. He's got to be somewhere, it makes no sense."

"What doesn't?" said Milo.

"Peake disappearing like that. You don't just disappear at Starkweather."

Milo asked for a key to Peake's room, got Swig's, closed the door and locked it, then moved out of earshot and used his cell phone to call the sheriff. He talked for a long time. None of the guards or techs budged.

The silence seemed to amplify. Then it began to falter—with sporadic knocks from behind some of the brown doors; muffled scuffs, faint as mouse steps. Cries, moans, escalating gradually but steadily into ragged shards of noise that could only be human voices in distress.

A chorus of cries. The guards and techs eyed one another. Swig seemed oblivious.

"Shit," said the bearded tech. "Shut the hell up."

Swig moved farther up the hall. No one attempted to stop the noise.

Louder and louder, frantic pounding from within the cells. The inmates knew. Somehow, they knew.

Milo pocketed the phone and returned. "Sheriff's crime-scene team should be here shortly. Squad cars will be searching a five-mile radius outside the hospital grounds. Tell your men in front not to hold anyone up at the gate."

Swig said, "We need to keep this under wraps until— What I mean is, let's find out exactly what happened before we jump to—"

"What do *you* think happened, Mr. Swig?"

"Peake surprised Frank and cut his throat. Frank's a strong man. So it had to be a sneak attack."

"What did Peake use to cut him?"

No answer.

"No guesses?" said Milo. "What about Dollard's own knife?"

"None of the techs are armed," said Swig.

"Theoretically."

"Theoretically and factually, Detective. For obvious reasons we have strict—"

Milo cut him off: "You have rules, an ironclad system. So tell me, are techs and doctors required to check in weapons at the guardhouse the way we were?"

Swig didn't answer.

"Sir?"

"That would be cumbersome. The sheer number of . . ."

Milo looked over at the three techs. No telltale evasive gestures. The big bearded man stared back defiantly.

"So everyone *but* staff is required to surrender weapons?"

"Staff knows not to *bring* weapons," said Swig.

Milo reached into his jacket, pulled out his service revolver, dangled it from his index finger. "Dr. Delaware?"

I produced my Swiss Army knife. Both guards tensed.

"No one checked us tonight. I guess the system breaks down from time to time," said Milo.

"Look," said Swig, raising his voice. He exhaled. "Tonight is different. I told them to facilitate your entry. I had full knowledge—"

"So you're willing to bet Dollard wasn't carrying the blade that killed him?"

"Frank was very trustworthy."

"Even though he tended to *forget* things?"

"I've never heard that," said Swig.

"You just did," said Milo. "Let me tell you about Frank. Hemet P.D. fired him for malfeasance. Ignoring calls, false overtime—"

"I had absolutely *no* knowledge of—"

"So maybe there are other things you have no knowledge of."

"Look," Swig repeated. But he added nothing, just shook his head and tried to smooth down his filmy hair. His Adam's apple rose and fell. He said, "Why bother? You've already got your mind made up."

Milo turned to the techs. "If I frisk any of you guys, am I going to turn up something?"

Silence.

He walked across the hall. Bart Quan's feet spread, as if ready for combat, and the other two men folded their arms across their chests—the same resistant stance Dollard had adopted yesterday.

"Tell them to cooperate," said Milo.

"Do what he says," said Swig.

Quickly, efficiently, Milo patted down the techs. Nothing on Quan or the tech who hadn't spoken—an older man with droopy eyes—but the jeans of the heavy, bearded man produced a bone-handled pocketknife.

Milo unfolded the blade. Four inches of gracefully honed steel. Milo turned it admiringly.

"Steve," said Swig.

The heavy man's face quivered. "So what?" he said. "Work with these *animals,* you take *care* of yourself."

Milo kept examining the blade. "Where'd you get it, Home Shopping Network?"

"Knife show," said Steve. "And don't worry, man, I haven't used it since I went hunting last winter."

"Kill anything?"

"Skinned some elk. Tasty."

Folding the knife, Milo dropped it in his jacket pocket.

"That's mine, man," said Steve.

"If it's clean, you'll get it back."

"When? I want a receipt."

"Quiet, Steve," ordered Swig. "You and I will talk later."

The bearded man's nostrils opened wide. "Yeah, right. If I even want to stay in this dump."

"That's up to you, Steve. Meanwhile, the state's still paying your salary, so listen up: Go down to A and B Wards, make sure everything's in order. Complete foot circuits, constant surveillance including door checks. No breaks till you're notified."

The bearded man gave Milo one last glare and stomped around the left side of the nursing station.

"Where's he heading?" said Milo.

"Staff elevator."

"We didn't see any elevator when we toured."

"The door's unmarked, staff only," said Swig. "We need to keep searching. Can I free these guards?"

"Sure," said Milo.

"Go," Swig told the uniformed men.

"Where?" said one of them.

"Every damn where! Start with the outer grounds, north and south perimeters. Make sure he's not hiding somewhere in the trees." Swig turned to the two remaining techs. "Bart, you and Jim search the basement again. Kitchen, laundry, every storage room. Make sure everything's as tight as it was the first time we looked."

Barking orders like a general. When everyone had dispersed, Swig turned to Milo. "I know what you're thinking. We're a bunch of civil-service bumblers. But this is absolutely the first time since I've run this place that we've had anything close to an escape. As a rule, nothing ever—"

"Some people," said Milo, "live for the rules. Me, I deal with the exceptions."

We walked up and down C Ward as Milo inspected doors. Several times, he had Swig unlock hatches. As he peered inside, the noise from within subsided.

"Can't see the entire room through these," he said, fingering a hatch door.

"We've gone over every room," said Swig. "First thing. Everything checks out."

I said, "That unmarked staff elevator door. I assume the inmates know about it."

"We don't make a point of explaining it," said Swig. "But I suppose—"

"Reason I mention it is that yesterday Peake and Heidi came from that direction. It was the first time anyone remembers Peake leaving his room for any length of time. I'm wondering if he saw someone enter the elevator, got an idea. Does it stop on every floor?"

"It can," said Swig.

"Has anyone checked it?"

"I assume."

Milo bore down on him. "You assume?"

"My orders were to check everywhere."

"Your orders were not to carry weapons."

"I'm sure," said Swig, "that— Fine, to hell with it, I'll show you."

Brown door, slightly wider than those that sealed the inmates' cells. Double key locks, no intercom speaker. Swig keyed the upper bolt and a latch clicked. The door swung open, revealing yet another brown rectangle. Inner door. No handle. Single lock in the center of the panel. The same key operated it, and a flick of Swig's wrist brought forth rumbling gear noise that vibrated through the walls. A few feet away was a smaller door, maybe two feet wide and twice as high.

"Where's the car coming from?" said Milo.

"No way to tell," said Swig. "It's a little slow, should be here soon."

"The first time we were here," I said, "Phil Hatterson called upstairs, spoke to someone, and got the elevator sent down. You can't do that with this one."

"Right," said Swig. "The call box for the main elevator is in the nursing station. A tech's in there at all times to monitor meds. Part of station duty's also monitoring inter-floor transport."

"Did Frank Dollard ever have that duty?"

"I'm sure he did. The staff circulates. Everyone does a bit of everything."

"When the elevators are keyed remotely, what determines where they stop?"

"You leave the key in until the elevator arrives. When an approved person—someone with a key—rides up, he can release the lock mechanism and punch buttons in the elevator."

"So once the lock's been released, this operates like any other elevator."

"Yes," said Swig, "but you can't release anything without a key, and only the staff has keys."

"Do you ever remaster the locks?"

"If there's a problem," said Swig.

"Which never happens," said Milo.

Swig flinched. "It doesn't take something of *this* magnitude to remaster, Detective. Anything out of the ordinary—a key reported stolen—and we change the tumblers immediately."

"Must be a hassle," said Milo. "All those keys to replace."

"We don't have many hassles."

"When's the last time the tumblers were changed, Mr. Swig?"

"I'd have to check."

"But not recently, that you can recall."

"What are you getting at?" said Swig.

"One more thing," said Milo. "Each ward is sectioned by those double doors. Every time you walk through, you have to unlock each one."

"Exactly," said Swig. "It's a maze. That's the point."

"How many keys do the techs need to carry to negotiate the maze?"

"Several," said Swig. "I never counted."

"Is there a master key?"

"I have a master."

Milo pointed to the key protruding from the inner elevator door. The rumbling continued, louder, as the lift approached. "That it?"

"Yes. There's also a copy in the safe in one of the data rooms on the first floor. And yes, I checked it. Still there, no tampering."

The door groaned open. The compartment was small, harshly lit, empty. Milo looked in. "What's that?"

Pointing to a scrap on the floor.

"Looks like paper," said Swig.

"Same paper as the sandals the inmates wear?"

Swig took a closer look. "I suppose it could be—I don't see any blood."

"Why would there be blood?"

"He cut Frank's throat—"

"There were no bloody footprints in Peake's room," said Milo. "Meaning Peake did a nice clean job of it, stepped away as he cut. Not bad for a crazy man."

"Hard to believe," said Swig.

"What is?"

"Just what you said. Peake mobilizing that much skill."

"Close this elevator," said Milo. "Keep it locked, don't let anyone in. When the crime-scene people come, I want them to remove that paper first thing."

Swig complied. Milo pointed to the smaller door. "What's that?"

"Disposal chute for garbage," said Swig. "It goes straight down to the basement."

"Like a dumbwaiter."

"Exactly."

"I don't see any latches or key locks," said Milo. "How does it open?"

"There's a lever. In the nursing station."

"Show me."

Swig unlocked the station. Three walls of glass, a fourth filled with locked steel compartments. The room felt like a big telephone booth. Swig pointed to the metal wall. "Meds and supplies, always locked."

I looked around. No desks, just built-in plastic counters housing a multiline phone, a small switchboard, and an intercom microphone. Set into the front glass was a six-inch slot equipped with a sliding steel tray.

"Too narrow to get their hands through," said Swig, with defensive pride. "They line up, get their pills, nothing's left to chance."

"Where's the lever?" said Milo.

Reaching under the desk, Swig groped. A snapping sound filled the booth. We left the station and returned to the hall. The garbage chute had unhinged at the top, creating a small metal canopy.

"Big enough for a skinny man." Milo stuck his head in and emerged sniffing. "Peake wasn't exactly obese."

Swig said, "Oh, come on—"

"What else is in the basement?"

"The service areas—kitchen, laundry, pantry, storage. Believe me, it's all been checked thoroughly."

"Deliveries come through the basement level?"

"Yes."

"So there's a loading dock."

"Yes, but—"

"How can you be sure Peake's not hiding out in a bin of dirty laundry?"

"Because we've checked and double-checked. Go see for yourself."

Milo tapped the elevator door. "Does this go up to the fifth floor, too—where the fakers are kept?"

Swig looked offended. "The 1368's. Yes."

"Does the main elevator go there, too?"

"No. The fifth floor has its own elevator. Express from ground level to the top."

"A third elevator," said Milo.

"For Five only. Security reasons," said Swig. "The 1368's come in and out. Using the main elevator for all that traffic would create obvious logistical problems. The jail bus lets them off around the back, at the 1368 reception center. They get processed and go straight up to Five. No stops—they have no access to the rest of the hospital."

"Except for the staff elevator."

"They don't use the staff elevator."

"Theoretically."

"Factually," said Swig.

"If you want to segregate the fifth floor completely, why even have the staff elevator go there?"

"It's the way the hospital was built," said Swig. "Logical, don't you think? If something happens on Five and the staff needs backup, we're ready for them."

"Ready," said Milo, "by way of a slow elevator. How often does something happen on Five?"

"Rarely."

"Give me a number."

Swig rubbed a mole. "Once, twice a year—what does it matter? We're talking temporary disruption, not a riot. Some 1368 trying too hard to impress us with how crazy he is. Or a fight. Don't forget, plenty of the evaluees are gang members." Swig sniffed contemptuously. Every society had its castes.

"Let's have a look at Five," said Milo. "Through the reception center. I don't want anyone to touch that piece of paper."

"Even if it is an inmate slipper," said Swig, "that wouldn't make it Peake's. All the inmates are issued—" He stopped. "Sure, sure, staff only—what was I thinking?"

On the way down, he said, "You think I'm some bureaucrat who doesn't give a damn. I took this job because I care about people. I adopted two orphans."

We got out on the first floor, exited the way we'd come in, followed Swig around the left side of the building. The side we'd never seen. Or been told about.

Identical concrete pathway. Bright lights from the roof yellowed five stories, creating a giant waffle of clouded windows.

Another door, identical to the main entrance.

The structure was two-faced.

A painted sign said INTAKE AND EVALUATION. A guard blocked the entry. Ten yards away, to the left, was a small parking lot, empty, separated from the yard by a chain-link-bordered path that reminded me of a giant dog run. The walkway veered, bled into darkness. Not visible as you crossed the main yard. Not accessible from the main entry. So there was another way onto the grounds, an entirely different entry.

Off to the right I saw the firefly bounce of searchlights, the outer borders of the uninhabited yard we'd seen yesterday, hints of the annex buildings. Unlit, too far to make out details. The search seemed to be carrying on beyond the annexes, fireflies clustering near what had to be the pine forest.

"How many roads enter the hospital grounds?" I said.

"Two," said Swig. "One, really. The one you've taken."

"What about there?" I pointed to the small parking lot.

"For jail buses only. Special access path clear around the eastern perimeter. The drivers have coded car keys. Even staff can't access the gates without my permission."

I indicated the distant searchlights. "And that side? Those pine trees. How do you get in there?"

"You don't," said Swig. "No access from the western perimeter, it's all fenced." He walked ahead and nodded at the guard, who stepped aside.

The intake center's front room was proportioned identically to that of the hospital entrance. Front desk, same size as Lindeen's, gunboat gray, bare except for a phone. No bowling trophies, no cute slogans. Lindeen's counterpart was a bullet-headed tech perched behind the rectangle of county-issue steel. Reading a newspaper, but when he saw Swig, he snapped the paper down and stood.

Swig said, "Anything unusual?"

"Just the lockdown, sir, per your orders."

"I'm taking these people up." Swig rushed us past a bare hall, into yet another elevator and up. Fast ride to Five, during which he used his walkie-talkie to check on the search's progress.

The door slid open.

"Keep on it," he barked, before jamming the intercom into his pocket. His armpits were soaked. A vein behind his left ear throbbed.

Two sets of double doors, over each a painted sign: I AND E, RESTRICTED ACCESS. As opposed to what?

Where the nursing station would have been was empty space. The ward was a single hall lined with bright blue doors. Higher tech–inmate ratio: a dozen especially large men patrolled.

Milo asked to look inside a cell.

Swig said, "We went room-to-room here, too."

"Let me see one, anyway."

Swig called out, "Inspection!" and three techs jogged over.

"Detective Sturgis wants to see what a 1368 looks like. Open a door."

"Which one?" said the largest of the men, a Samoan with an unpronounceable name on his tag and a soft, boyish voice.

"Pick one."

The Samoan stepped to the closest door, popped the hatch, looked inside, unlocked the blue panel, and held it open six inches. Sticking his head in, he opened the door fully and said, "This is Mr. Liverwright."

The room high and constricted, same dimensions as Peake's. Same bolted restraints. A muscular young black man sat naked on the bed. The sheets had been torn off a thin, striped mattress. Torn into shreds. Royal blue pajamas lay rumpled on the floor next to a pair of blue paper slippers. One of the slippers was nothing but confetti.

I stepped closer and was hit by a terrible stench. A mound

of feces sat in a drying clot near the prisoner's feet. Several pools of urine glistened. The walls behind the bed were stained brown.

He saw us, grinned, cackled.

"Clean this up," said Swig.

"We do," said the Samoan calmly. "Twice a day. He keeps trying to prove himself."

He flashed Liverwright a victory V and laughed. "Keep it up, bro."

Liverwright cackled again and rubbed himself.

"Shake it but don't break it off, bro," said the Samoan.

"Close the door," said Swig. "Clean him up *now*."

The Samoan closed the door, shrugging. To us: "These guys think they know what crazy is, but they overdo it. Too many movies." He turned to leave.

Milo asked him, "When's the last time you saw George Orson?"

"Him?" said the Samoan. "I dunno, not in a while."

"Not tonight?"

"Nope. Why would I? He hasn't worked here in months."

"Who are we talking about?" said Swig.

"Has he visited since he quit?" Milo asked the Samoan.

"Hmm," said the Samoan. "Don't think so."

"What kind of guy was he?" said Milo.

"Just a guy." The Samoan favored Swig with a smile. "Love to chat, but got to clean up some shit." He lumbered off.

"Who's George Orson?" said Swig.

"One of your former employees," said Milo. Watching Swig's face.

"I can't know everyone. Why're you asking about him?"

"He knew Mr. Peake," said Milo. "Back in the good old days."

Swig had plenty of questions, but Milo held him off. We rode the fifth-floor elevator down to the basement, took a tense, deliberate tour of the kitchen, pantry, laundry, and storage rooms. Everything smelled of slightly rotted produce. Techs and guards were everywhere. Helping them search were orange-jumpsuited janitors. White-garbed cooks in the kitchen stared as we passed through. Racks of knives were in full view. I thought of Peake passing through, deciding to sample. The good old days.

Milo found four out-of-the-way closet doors and checked each of them. Key-locked.

"Who gets keys besides clinical staff?" he asked Swig.

"No one."

"Not these guys?" Indicating a pair of janitors.

"Not them or anyone else not engaged in patient care. And to answer your next question, nonclinical staff enter through the front like anyone else. I.D.'s are checked."

"Even familiar faces are checked?" said Milo.

"That's our system."

"Do clinical staffers take their keys home?"

Swig didn't answer.

"Do they?" said Milo.

"Yes, they take them home. Checking in scores of keys a day would be cumbersome. As I said, we change the locks. Even in the absence of a specific problem, we remaster every year."

"Every year," said Milo. I knew what he was thinking: George Orson had left five months ago. "What date did that fall on?"

"I'll have to check," said Swig. "What exactly are you getting at?"

Milo walked ahead of him. "Let's see the loading dock."

Sixty-foot-wide empty cement space doored with six panels of corrugated metal.

Milo asked a janitor, "How do you get them open?"

The janitor pointed to a circuit box at the rear.

"Is there an outside switch, too?"

"Yup."

Milo loped to the box and punched a button. The second door from the left swung upward and we walked to the edge of the dock. Six or seven feet above ground. Space for three or four large trucks to unload simultaneously. Milo climbed down. Five steps took him into darkness and he disappeared, but I heard him walking around. A moment later, he hoisted himself up.

"The delivery road," he asked Swig, "where does it go?"

"Subsidiary access. Same place the jail bus enters."

"I thought only the jail buses came in that way."

"I was referring to people," said Swig. "Only jail bus transportees come in that way."

"So there's plenty of traffic in and out."

"Everything's scheduled and preapproved. Every driver is preapproved and required to show I.D. upon demand. The road is sectioned every fifty feet with gates. Card keys are changed every thirty days."

"Card keys," said Milo. "So if they show I.D., they can open the gates on their own."

"That's a big if," said Swig. "Look, we're not here to critique our system, we want to find Peake. I suggest you pay more attention to—"

"What about techs?" said Milo. "Can they use the access road?"

"Absolutely not. Why are you harping on this? And what does this Orson character have to do with it?"

Shouts from the west turned our heads. Several fireflies enlarged.

Searchers approaching. Milo hopped down off the deck again and I did the same. Swig contemplated a jump but remained in place. By the time I was at Milo's side, I could make out figures behind the flashlights. Two men, running.

One of them was Bart Quan, the other a uniformed guard.

Suddenly, Swig was with us, breathing audibly. "What, Bart?"

"We found a breach," said Quan. "Western perimeter. The fence has been cut."

Half-mile walk to the spot. The flap was man-sized, snipped neatly and put back in place, wires twisted with precision. It had taken a careful eye to spot it in the darkness. Milo said, "Who found it?"

The uniform with Quan raised his hand. Young, thin, swarthy.

Milo peered at his badge. "What led you to it, Officer Dalfen?"

"I was scoping the western perimeter."

"Find anything else?"

"Not so far."

Milo borrowed Dalfen's flashlight and ran it over the fence. "What's on the other side?"

"Dirt road," said Swig. "Not much of one."

"Where does it lead?"

"Into the foothills."

Milo untwisted the wires, pulled down the flap, crouched, and passed through. "Tire tracks," he said. "Any gates or guards on this side?"

"It's not hospital territory," said Swig. "There has to be a border, somewhere."

"What's in the foothills?"

"Nothing. That's the point. There's no place to go for a good three, four miles. The county clears trees and brush every year to make sure there's no cover. Anyone up there would be visible by helicopter."

"Speaking of which," said Milo.

By the time the choppers had begun circling, nine sheriff's cars and the crime-scene vans had arrived. Khaki uniforms on the deputies; I saw Swig tense up further, but he said nothing, had started to isolate himself in a corner, muttering from time to time into his walkie-talkie.

Two plainclothes detectives arrived last. The coroner had just finished examining Dollard, searching his pockets. Empty. Milo conferred with the doctor. The paper scrap in the staff elevator had been retrieved and bagged. As a criminalist carried it past, Swig said, "Looks like a piece of slipper."

"What kind of slipper?" said one of the detectives, a fair-haired man in his thirties named Ron Banks.

Milo told him.

Banks's partner said, "So all we have to do is find Cinderella." He was a stout man named Hector De la Torre, older than Banks, with flaring mustaches. Banks was serious, but De la Torre grinned. Unintimidated by the setting, he'd greeted Milo with a reminder that they'd met. "Party over at Musso and Frank's—after the Lisa Ramsey case got closed. My buddy here is good pals with the D who closed it."

"Petra Connor?" said Milo.

"She's the one."

Banks looked embarrassed. "I'm sure he cares, Hector." To Milo: "So maybe he rode down in that elevator."

"No inmates allowed," said Milo. "So there's no good reason for there to be a slipper in there. And Dollard's key ring is missing, meaning Peake lifted it. The rest of the techs were in a meeting, so Peake could've easily ridden down to the basement, found a door out, and hightailed it. On the other hand, maybe it's just a scrap that got stuck on the bottom of someone's shoe."

"No blood in the elevator?" said Banks.

"Not a drop; the only blood's what you just saw in the room."

"Clean, for a throat cut."

"Coroner says it wasn't much of a cut. Peake nicked the carotid rather than cut it, more trickle than spurt. Came close to not being fatal; if Dollard had been able to seek help right away, he might've survived. Looks like he went into shock, collapsed, lay there bleeding out. No spatter—most of the blood pooled under him."

"Low-pressure bleedout," said Banks.

"A nick," said De la Torre. "Talk about bad luck."

"Peake didn't have much muscle on him," said Milo.

"Enough to do the trick," said De la Torre. "So who cut the fence? Where'd Peake get tools for that?"

"Good question," said Milo. "Maybe Dollard carried the blade he was cut with. Maybe one of those Swiss Army deals with tools. Though there'd be no way for Peake to know that, unless Dollard had gotten *really* sloppy and let him see it. The alternative's obvious. A partner."

Banks said, "This is some big-time premeditated deal? I thought the guy was a lunatic."

"Even lunatics can have pals," said Milo.

"You got that right," said De la Torre. "Check out the next city council meeting."

Banks said, "Any ideas about who the buddy might be?"

Milo eyed Swig. "Please go down to your office and wait there, sir."

"Forget it," said Swig. "As director of this facility, I have jurisdiction and I need to know what's going on."

"You will," said Milo. "Soon as we know something, you'll be the first to find out, but in the meantime—"

"In the meantime, I need to be—" Swig's protest was cut short by a beeper. He and all three detectives reached for their belts.

Banks said, "Mine," and scanned the readout. A cell phone materialized and Banks identified himself, listened, said, "When? Where?," wiggled his fingers at De la Torre, and was handed a notepad. Tucking the phone under his chin, he wrote.

The rest of us watched him nod. Emotionless. Clicking off the phone, he said, "When we got your call I told our desk to keep an eye out for any psycho crimes in the vicinity. This isn't exactly in the vicinity, but it's pretty psycho: woman found on the Five near Valencia." He examined his notes. "White female, approximately twenty-five to thirty-five, multiple stab wounds to torso and face, really messy. Coroner says within the last two hours, which could fit if your boy has wheels. Tire tracks nearby said someone did. She wasn't just dumped there—lots of blood: it's almost certain that's where she got done."

"What kind of facial wounds?" said Milo.

"Lips, nose, eyes—the guy at the scene said it was really brutal. That fits, right?"

"Eyes," said Milo.

"My God," said Swig.

"Was she found on the northbound Five?" I said.

"Yes," said Banks.

Everyone stared at me.

"The road to Treadway," I said. "He's going home."

34.

THE LAST BIT of news deflated Swig. He looked small, crushed, a kid with a man's job.

Milo paid him no attention, spent his time on the phone. Talking to the Highway Patrol, informing the sheriffs of the towns neighboring Treadway, warning Bunker Protection. The private firm must have given him problems, because when he got off, he snapped the phone shut so hard I thought he'd break it.

"Okay, let's see what shakes up," he told Banks and De la Torre. To Swig: "Get me George Orson's personnel file."

"It's downstairs in the records room."

"Then that's where we're going."

The records-room treasures were concealed by one of the unmarked doors bordering Swig's office. Tight space, hemmed by black file cabinets. The folder was right where it should have been. Milo examined it as the sheriff's men looked over his shoulder.

Missing photo, but George Orson's physical statistics fit Derrick Crimmins perfectly: six-three, 170, thirty-six years old. The address was the mail drop on Pico near Barrington. No phone number.

"What else exactly did this guy do?" said Banks.

"Series of cons, and he probably killed his dad and mom and brother."

Swig said, "I can't believe this. If we hired him, his credentials had to be in order. The state fingerprints them—"

"He has no arrest record we know of, so prints don't mean

much," said Milo, taking the file and flipping pages. "Says here he completed the psych tech course at Orange Coast College. . . . No point following that up, who cares if he bogused his education." To Swig: "Would there be any record if he actually returned his keys?"

"His file's in order. That means he did. Any irregularity—"

"Is picked up by the system. I know. Of course, even if he did return them, seeing as he got to take them home every day, he had plenty of chances to make copies."

"Each key is clearly imprinted 'Do Not Duplicate.' "

"Gee," said De la Torre. "That would scare *me*."

Swig braced himself against the nearest file. "There was no reason to worry about that. The risk wasn't someone breaking *in*. Why don't you look for him, instead of *harping*? Why would he come *back*?"

"Must be the ambience," said Milo. "Or maybe the new air-conditioning." He looked up at a small grilled grate in the center of the ceiling. "What about the ductwork? Wide enough for someone to fit?"

"No, no, no," said Swig, with sudden conviction. "Absolutely *not*. We considered that when we installed, used narrow ducts—six inches in diameter. It caused technical problems, that's why the work took so long to—" He stopped. "Peake's my only concern. Should we keep searching?"

"Any reason to stop?" said Milo.

"If he killed that woman on the freeway, he's miles away."

"And if he didn't?"

"Fine—exactly—got to go, need to supervise."

"Sure," said Milo. "Do your thing."

Outside the main building, the fireflies continued to dance, fragmented sporadically by the downslanting beams of circling helicopters. Milo yelled at a guard to get us out of there.

He and I and the sheriff's detectives reconvened in the parking lot, next to the unmarked. The white coroner's van was still in place, as were the squad cars and a pea-green sedan that had to be Banks and De la Torre's wheels.

Banks said, "So what's the theory here? This Orson, or

whatever his real name is, snuck in somehow and got Peake loose? What's his motive?"

Milo flourished an open palm in my direction.

"Unclear," I said. "It may have had something to do with Peake's original rampage. Crimmins and Peake go way back. It's possible—now I'd say probable—that Crimmins was involved somehow. Either by directly urging Peake to kill the Ardullos or by doing something more subtle." I described the long-term conflict between the Crimminses and the Ardullos, described Peake's prophecies.

"Money," said De la Torre.

"That's part of it, but there's more. The root of all this is power and domination—criminal production. Orson—Derrick Crimmins—sees himself as an artist. I think he views the massacre as his first major creative accomplishment. He's been working on something called *Blood Walk*. At least three people associated with the film are dead; there may very well be others. I think Crimmins has reserved a role for Peake, but I can't say what it is. Now he's decided it's time to put Peake in the spotlight."

"Sounds nuts," said De la Torre.

Banks looked back at the yard. "Funny 'bout that, Hector." To me: "So Crimmins is crazy, too? They hired a psychotic to work here?"

"Crimmins comes across as a classic psychopath," I said. "Sane but evil. Sometimes psychopaths fall apart, but not usually. Fundamentally, he's a loser—can't hold on to money, can't stick with anything, has had to take jobs that he considers below him. On some level, that enrages him. He takes out his anger on others. But he's fully aware of what he's doing—has been careful enough to shift identities, addresses, pull off one scam after another. All that spells rationality."

"Rational," said De la Torre, "except he likes to kill people." He stretched both wings of his mustache, distorting the lower half of his face. Releasing the hair, he allowed his lips to settle into a frown. "Okay, now Peake. Basically, you're saying he was a head-case blood freak who turned into a vegetable here because they overdosed him. But for him to cooperate in the escape, he'd have to be significantly better put together than a summer squash. You think he could've been faking how crazy he is?"

"The guys on Five do it all the time," said Milo.

"And rarely succeed," I said. "But Peake's a genuine schizophrenic. For him, it wouldn't be a matter of either-or, it'd be the intensity of his psychosis. At an optimal level, it's possible Thorazine made him more lucid. Clear enough to be able to cooperate in the escape. Crimmins could have played a role, too. He was a significant figure in Peake's life. Who knows *what* fantasies his showing up on the ward could have stimulated."

"The good old days," said Milo. "Like some damn re-union. And once Crimmins got here, he'd have seen right away how rinky-dink the system was. Pure fun. Betcha he had keys to every door within weeks. We know he floated overtime on Peake's ward. Meaning he could wear his badge, drop in whenever he wanted, arouse no suspicion." He shook his head. "Peake must've seen it as *salvation*."

"Crimmins dominated him before, knows he's passive," I said. "Slips him a knife. No one bothers to check Peake's room for weapons because he's been nonfunctional for sixteen years. Crimmins cues Peake that the time's right; Peake sneaks up on Dollard, cuts his throat, leaves on the staff elevator. Dollard was a perfect target: lax about the rules. And if he was involved in a drug scam with Crimmins, that would be another reason to hit him. You asked Swig if Dollard had access to the drug cabinet, so you were thinking the same thing. Or maybe Crimmins sneaked in and did the cutting himself. Showed up on the ward during the staff meeting, knowing he had only Dollard to contend with."

"What drug scam?" said Banks.

Milo explained the theory, the cars in the driveway that had bedeviled Marie Sinclair. "What's better than pharmaceutical grade? Dollard's the inside man, Crimmins works the street. That's why Dollard got so antsy when we kept coming back. Idiot was afraid his little side biz would be blown. He shows his anxiety to Crimmins, tips Crimmins that he can't be counted on to stay cool, and signs his own death warrant. Crimmins has a history of tying up loose ends, and Dollard's starting to unravel."

"This," said Banks, "is . . . colorful."

"Lacking facts, I embroider," said Milo.

"Whatever the details," I said, "the best guess is that Crimmins managed to get Peake down in that elevator. I think he entered the hospital grounds tonight through that cut in the fence, made his way across the rear yard, maybe hid in one of the annexes. Easy enough, no one uses them. Coming in through the foothills wouldn't be much of a problem. Crimmins used to race motocross. He could've brought a dirt bike or an off-roader."

"Where does your vic come in?" said Banks. "The Argent woman?"

Milo said, "She could've come across the drug scam. Or found out something from Peake she wasn't supposed to."

"Or, she was part of the drug scam."

Silence.

"Why," said De la Torre, "did Peake start prophesying?"

"Because he's still psychotic," I said. "Crimmins made the mistake of divulging what he was going to do, figuring Peake would keep his mouth shut. Don't forget, Peake's been mum for sixteen years about the Ardullo murders. But recently something—probably the attention Claire paid him—opened Peake up. He got more verbal. Started to see himself as a victim—a martyr. When I brought up the Ardullos, he assumed a crucifixion pose. That could make *him* a threat to Crimmins. Maybe the role Crimmins has in mind for him is victim."

"Not if he's the one sliced that woman up on the I-Five."

"Not necessarily," I said. "In this case monster and victim aren't mutually exclusive."

Banks ran his hands down his lapels, looked up at the helicopters.

"One more thing," said Milo. "That fence wasn't cut tonight. There was some oxidation around the edges."

"Well rehearsed," I said. "Just like any other production.

That's the way Crimmins sees life: one big show. He could've come anytime, set the stage."

"What a joke," said Banks. "Place like this and they take keys home."

"Not that it matters," said De la Torre. To Milo: "You ever seen a maximum-security prison that wasn't full of dope and weapons? Other than my mother-in-law's house."

"Can't stop inhuman nature," said Banks. "So now Crimmins and Peake are heading back to the hometown? Why?"

"The only thing I can think of is more theater. A script element. What I don't get is why Crimmins would leave that woman on the freeway. It's almost as if he's directing attention *to* Treadway. So maybe he's deteriorating. Or I'm totally wrong—the escape's a one-man operation and Peake's fooled everyone. He's a calculating monster who craves blood, is out to get it any way he can."

Banks studied his notes. "You're saying the Ardullo thing might've been financial revenge. Why kill the kids?"

"You ruin my family, I ruin yours. Primitive but twisted justice. Derrick might have planned it, but at twenty he lacked the will and the stomach to carry out the massacre himself. Then Peake entered the picture and everything clicked: the village lunatic, living right there on the Ardullo ranch. Derrick and Cliff started spending time with Peake, became his suppliers for porn, dope, booze, glue, paint. Psychopaths lack insight about themselves, but they're good at zeroing in on other people's pathology, so maybe Derrick spotted the seeds of violence in Peake, put himself in a position to exploit it. And it was a no-risk situation: if Peake never acted, who'd ever know the brothers had prodded him? Even if he said something, who'd believe him? But he did follow through, and it paid off, big-time: Carson Crimmins was able to sell his land; the family got rich and moved to Florida, where the boys got to be playboys for a while. That's one big dose of positive reinforcement. That's why I called Peake a major influence on Crimmins."

"Crimmins didn't worry about Peake blabbing back then," said Milo, "but now it's different. Someone's listening."

"Maybe Claire *was* involved in the drug scam," I said, "but unless we find evidence of that, my bet is she died because she'd learned from Peake that he hadn't acted alone. And she believed him. Believed *in* him. Because what she was really after was finding out something redeeming about her brother. Symbolically."

"Symbolically," said De la Torre. "If she suspected Crimmins, what was she doing getting in that Corvette?"

"Maybe she got involved with Crimmins before Peake started talking. Crimmins held himself out as a cinematic hotshot, a struggling independent filmmaker trying to plumb the depths of madness or some nonsense like that. He calls his outfit Thin Line—as in walking the border between sanity and insanity. Maybe he asked her to be a technical adviser. The guy was a con; I can see her falling for it."

"Something else," said Milo. "If Peake's blabbing to Claire, he's telling her about Derrick Crimmins. The guy she knows is George Orson."

That made my heart stop. "You're right. Claire could've told Crimmins everything. Fed him the very information that signed her death warrant."

"Eye wounds," said Milo. "Like the Ardullo kids. Only *he* sees. No one else." He rubbed his face. "Or he just likes carving people's eyes."

"Evil, evil, evil," said Banks, in a soft tight voice. "And no idea where to find him."

The helicopters' sky-dance had shifted westward, white beams sweeping the foothills and whatever lay behind them.

"Waste of fuel," said De la Torre. "He's got to be on the road."

35.

MILO AND THE sheriffs did more cell-phone work. Better suits and they might have looked like brokers on the make. The end result was more nothing: no sightings of Peake.

Milo looked at his watch. "Ten-fifty. If any reporters are playing with the scanner, this could make the news in ten minutes."

"That could be helpful," said Banks. "Maybe someone'll spot him."

"I doubt Crimmins has him out in the open," I said.

"If he's with Crimmins."

Milo said, "CHP says the vic from the freeway was transported. I thought I'd hit the morgue."

"Fine," said Banks. "Let's exchange numbers, we'll keep in touch."

"Yeah," said Milo. "Regards to Petra."

"Sure," said Banks, coloring. "When I see her."

In the past, Milo had sped through the eucalyptus grove. Now he kept the unmarked at twenty miles per, used his high beams, glancing from side to side.

"Stupid," he said. "No way they're anywhere near here, but I can't stop looking. What do you call that, obsessive-compulsive ritualism?"

"Habit strength."

He laughed. "You could euphemize anything."

"Okay," I said. "It's canine transformation. The job's turned you into a bloodhound."

"Naw, dogs have better noses. Okay, I'll drop you off."

"Forget it," I said. "I'm coming with."

"Why?"

"Habit strength."

The body lay covered on a gurney in the center of the room. The night attendant was a man named Lichter, paunchy and gray-haired, with an incongruously rich tan. A Highway Patrol detective named Whitworth had filled out the papers.

"Just missed him," said Lichter. The bronze skin gave him the look of an actor playing a morgue man. Or was I just seeing Hollywood everywhere?

"Where'd he go?" said Milo.

"Back to the scene." Lichter placed his hand on a corner of the gurney, gave the sheet a tender look. "I was just about to find a drawer for her."

Milo read the crime-scene report. "Gunshot wound to the back of the head?"

"If that's what it says."

Folding the sheet back, Milo exposed the face. What was left of it. Deep slashes crisscrossed the flesh, shearing skin, exposing bone and muscle and gristle. What had been the eyes were two oversized raspberries. The hair, thick and light brown where the blood hadn't crusted, fanned out on the steel table. Slender neck. Blood-splashed but undamaged; only the face had been brutalized. The eyes . . . the slash wounds created a crimson grid, like a barbecue grilling taken to the extreme. I saw freckles amid the gore, and my stomach lurched.

"Oh, boy," said Lichter, looking sad. "Hadn't looked at it yet."

"Look like a gunshot to you?"

Lichter hurried to a desk in the corner, shuffled through piles of paper, picked up some stapled sheets, and flipped through. "Same thing here . . . single wound to the occipital cranium, no bullet recovered yet."

Gloving up, he returned to the gurney, rolled the head carefully, bent, and squinted. "Ah—see."

A distinct ruby hole dotted the back of the skull. Black

crust fuzzed the edges and black dots peppered the slender neck.

"Stippling," said Lichter. "I'm just a body mover, but that means an up-close wound, right?" He released the head carefully. Another sad look. "Maybe she got shot first and then they used a knife on her. More like a hatchet or a machete—a thick blade, right? But I better not say more. Only the coroners have opinions."

"Who's the coroner tonight?"

"Dr. Patel. He had to run out, should be back soon with some genuine wisdom."

He began to cover the face, but Milo took hold of the sheet. "Shooting, then slashing. Right on the side of the freeway."

"Don't quote me on anything," said Lichter. "I'm not allowed to speculate."

"Sounds like a good guess. Now all we have to do is find out who she is."

"Oh, we know that," said Lichter. "They pulled prints on her right away. Easy, the fingers were fine. Detective Whitworth said she came right up on PRINTRAK—hold on."

He ran back to the desk, retrieved more papers. "She had a record . . . drugs, I think. . . . Yup, here we go. Hedy Lynn Haupt, female Caucasian, twenty-six . . . arrested two years ago for P.C. 11351.5—that's possession of cocaine for use or sale, right? I know it by heart, because we get lots of that in here. Got an address on her, too."

Milo covered the distance between them in three strides and took the papers from him.

"Hedy Haupt," I said, leaning down for a look at the face.

Putting my face inches from the ruined flesh. Smelling the copper-sugar of the blood, the sulfur of released gases . . . something light, floral—perfume.

The skin that unique green-gray where it wasn't blood-rusty.

Most of the head had been turned into something unthinkable, the mouth kissed by a smear of blood, the upper lip split diagonally. Yet the overall structure remained somewhat recognizable. Familiar . . . freckles across the nose and forehead. The ear that hadn't been hacked to confetti, an ashen seashell.

I peeled back the sheet. Plaid blouse. Blue jeans. Even in death the body retained a trim, tight shape. Something protruded from the breast pocket of the blouse. Half a loop of white elastic. Ponytail band.

"I think I know who this is," I said.

Milo wheeled on me.

I said, "Hedy Haupt, Heidi Ott. The age fits, the hair's the right color, the body's the right length—look at the right jaw, that same strong line. I'm sure of it. This is her."

Milo's face was next to mine, exuding sweat and cigar residue.

"Oh, man," he said. "Another cast member?"

"Remember what big Chet kept shouting at us?" I said. "Both in group, and as we walked across the yard? 'Cherchez la femme.' Search for the woman. Maybe he was trying to tell us something. Maybe maniacs are worth listening to."

36.

MILO WANTED TO examine the body closely and to go over the paperwork in detail. Figuring I could do without either, I left, bought scalding, poisonous coffee from a machine, and drank it out in the waiting area facing the autopsy room. The coffee didn't do much for my stomach, but the chill that had taken hold of my legs started to dissipate.

I sat there, thinking about Heidi, executed and mutilated on the I-5.

Everyone associated with Peake and Crimmins was being discarded like garbage. It stank of a special malevolence.

Monsters.

No; Peake's moniker notwithstanding, these were people, it always came down to people.

I pictured the two of them, bound together by something I was really no closer to understanding, stalking, severing, hacking, shooting.

Crimmins's production, the worst kind of documentary. For the sake of what? How many other victims lay buried around the city?

Crisp, rapid footsteps made me look up. A perfectly groomed Indian in his forties passed me wordlessly and entered the autopsy room. Dr. Patel, I assumed. I found a pay phone, called Robin, got the answering machine. She was asleep. Good. I told the machine I'd be back in a few hours, not to worry. I finished the coffee. Cooler, but it still tasted like toasted cardboard sautéed in chicory gravy.

Heidi. A narcotics record. That started me off in a whole new direction.

Viewing life through a new set of glasses . . . The door swung open and Milo shot out, wiping his forehead and waving a sheet of paper full of his cramped, urgent handwriting. Body-outline logo at the top. Coroner's gift-shop stationery.

"Heidi's home address," he said. "Let's go."

We headed for the elevator.

"Where'd she live?" I said.

"West Hollywood, thirteen hundred block of Orange Grove."

"Not far from Plummer Park, where we met with her."

"Not far from my own damn house." He stabbed the elevator button. "C'mon, c'mon, c'mon."

"Who's in charge?" I said. "Sheriff or Highway Patrol?"

"Highway Patrol on the killing itself," he said. "I reached Whitworth at the scene. He said feel free to check out her house. He's staying there, wants to make sure they scrape whatever physical evidence they can off the road before traffic thickens up."

"They shot her and butchered her right there on the freeway?"

"Turnoff. Wide turnoff. Far enough and dark enough for cover."

"Crimmins would know the road well," I said. "Growing up in Treadway. But still, it was risky, right there in the open."

"So they're loosening up—maybe losing it, like you said. Peake's massacre wasn't exactly well thought out. He left goddamn bloody footprints. Maybe Crimmins is starting to freak, too."

"I don't know. Crimmins is a planner. The escape says he's still pretty organized."

He shrugged. "What can I tell you?" The elevator arrived and he threw himself in.

"Did the coroner have anything to add?" I said.

"The bullet's still in there, he'll go digging. Ready for me to drop you off now?"

"Not a chance," I said.

"You look wiped out."

"*You're* not exactly perky-fresh."

His laugh was short, dry, reluctant. "Want some chewing gum?"

"Since when do you carry?" I said.

"I don't. The attendant—Lichter—gave me a pack. Says he started doing it for any cops who come in. Says he's gonna retire next year, feels like spreading good cheer and fresh breath."

Outside the morgue, the air was warm, thick, gasoline-tinged. Even at this hour, the freeway noise hadn't abated. Ambulances shrieked in and out of County General. Derelicts and dead-eyes walked the street, along with a few white-coated citizens who didn't look much better off. Above us, on the overpass, cars blipped and dopplered. A few miles north, the interstate was quiet enough to serve as a killing ground.

I imagined the car pulling abruptly to the side—not the yellow Corvette; something large enough to seat three.

Crimmins and Peake. And Heidi. Riding along.

A captive? Or a passenger.

The dope conviction.

I thought of the meeting at Plummer Park.

My roommate's sleeping, or I would've had you come to my place.

Would a live roommate be waiting for us at the Orange Grove address? Or . . .

My mind flashed back to the freeway kill. Heidi out of the car, surprised, asking Crimmins what was up. Or immobilized—bound, gagged—and terrified.

Crimmins and Peake haul her out. She's a strong girl, but they control her easily.

They walk her as far as they can from the freeway. To the edge of the turnoff, everyone swallowed by darkness now.

Last words or not?

Either way: *pop.* A searing burst of light and pain.

What was the last thing she'd heard? A truck whizzing by? The wind? The racing of her pulse?

They let her fall. Then Crimmins gives a signal and Peake steps forward.

Blade in hand.

Summoned.

Camera. Action.

Cut.

My guts pogoed as I got in the unmarked, wanting to sort it all out, to make sense of it before I said anything to Milo. He started up the engine, sped through the morgue lot, and turned left on Mission. We roared off.

Orange Grove showed no signs of ever having hosted citrus trees. Just another L.A. street full of small, undistinguished houses.

The house we came to see was hidden behind an untrimmed ficus hedge, but the green wall didn't extend to the asphalt driveway and we had a clear view all the way to the garage. No vehicles in sight. Milo drove a hundred feet down and we returned on foot. I waited by the curb as he made his way up the asphalt, gun in hand, back to the garage, around the rear of the wood-sided bungalow. Even in the darkness I could see scars on the paint. The color was hard to make out, probably some version of beige. Between the house and the ficus barrier was a stingy square of dead lawn. Sagging front porch, no shrubbery other than the hedge.

Milo came back, gun still out, breathing hard. "Looks empty. The back door's Mickey Mouse, I'm going in. Stay there till I tell you."

Another five minutes, ten, twelve, as I watched his penlight bounce around behind shaded windows. A single firefly. Finally, the front door opened and he waved me inside.

He'd gloved up. I followed as he turned a few lights on, exposing a poverty of space. First we did an overall check of the house. Five small, shabby rooms, including a dingy lavatory. Grimy yellow walls; the window shades crazed, gray oilcloth patched in spots by duct tape.

Colorless rental furniture.

Where the space allowed. The bungalow was filled with crisp-looking cardboard boxes, most of them sealed. Printed labels on the outside. THIS SIDE UP. FRAGILE. Scores of cartons of TV's, stereos, video gear, cameras, PC's. Cassettes, compact discs, computer discs. Glassware, silverware, small appliances. Stacks of video cartridges and Fuji film. Enough film to shoot a thousand birthday parties.

In a corner of the larger bedroom, squeezed next to an unmade queen-size mattress, stood a pile of smaller boxes. The labels claimed Sony minirecorders. Just like the one Heidi had used to tape Peake.

"The movie stuff's out in the garage," said Milo. "Dollies, booms, spotlights, crap I couldn't identify. Tons of it, piled almost to the ceiling. Didn't see any saws, but they could be buried under all the gear. It'll take a crew to go through it."

"She was in on it," I said.

He'd moved into the bathroom, didn't answer. I heard drawers opening, went over to see him remove something from the cabinet beneath the sink.

Glossy white shoe box. Several more just like it stacked next to the pipes.

He lifted the lid. Rows of white plastic bottles nesting in Styrofoam beds. He extracted one. "Phenobarbital."

All the other bottles in that box were labeled identically. The next box yielded an assortment, and so did all the others.

Chlorpromazine, thioridazine, haloperidol, clozapine, diazepam, alprazolam, lithium carbonate.

"Candy sampler for a junkie," said Milo. "Uppers, downers, all-arounders."

He inspected the bottom of the box. "Starkweather stamp's still on here."

"Uncut pharmaceuticals," I said. "It ups the price." Then I thought of something.

Milo was looking the other way, but I must have made a sound, because he said, "What?"

"I should've figured it out a long time ago. The missing dog, Buddy. He was sticking in my head because I've seen him before. That day in the park, a tall man in black came by walking a Rottweiler mix. Passed right by where we were sitting with Heidi. Heidi was aware of him. She watched him.

He was her roommate. The one she'd claimed was sleeping. Their little joke. They were playing with us right from the beginning. So much for powers of observation. Lot of good it does us now."

"Hey," he said, recording the drug inventory in his notepad. "I'm the so-called detective, and I never noticed the dog."

"Crimmins stole him from Mrs. Leiber. Taking what he wanted. Because he could. For him, it's all about power."

He stopped writing. "No sign of any dog here," he said. "No food or bowl anywhere in the house."

"Exactly."

"Heidi," he said, suddenly sounding tired.

"It casts a whole new light on her story," I said. "Peake's prophecy. Peake's supposed prophecy."

His hand tightened around his pen. He stared at me. "Another scam."

"Has to be. The only evidence we ever had was Heidi's account."

" 'Bad eyes in a box.' 'Choo choo bang bang.' "

"The tape, too," I said. I led him back to the larger bedroom. Pointed at the stack of Sonys. "The tape was nothing but mumbles. Unrecognizable mumbles, could've been anyone. But we *know* who it was."

"Crimmins."

"Dubbing the soundtrack," I said. "George Welles Orson. Like I said, he's an auteur: produces, directs, acts."

He cursed violently.

"He murdered Claire," I went on, "then set Peake up as a phony oracle to spice up his story line—who knows, maybe he thought he'd be able to use it one day. Write a screenplay, sell it to Hollywood. We took it seriously—great fun, once again he's screwed the Law. Just like he did back in Florida. And Nevada. And Treadway. So when he eliminated the Beatty brothers, he did it again. Used Heidi, again. Once again, no risk; nothing he does with Peake bears any risk. No one's heard Peake talk in almost two decades—who's to say it's not his voice on the tape? The first time we met Heidi, she let us know she was going to quit the hospital. That allowed her to do you a favor by sticking around. Gave her instant credibility—personally invited by the police. From that point, no one was going to suspect anything she did with Peake."

"Except maybe Chet."

" 'Cherchez la femme,' " I said. "Maybe Chet noticed something—something off about Heidi. Maybe the way she related to Peake. Or he saw her steal dope from the nursing station. Or get a little handoff from Dollard. But once again, who'd pay attention to *his* ramblings? Heidi was free to continue as Crimmins's inside woman. She was there in the first place because Crimmins wanted her—she joined the staff right after he left. He gave her multiple assignments: work with Dollard to keep the drugs flowing, make sure Dollard didn't rip them off, and attach herself to Claire so she could report back what Claire was saying about Peake. Because he *had* to have discussed Peake with Claire. That was the basis of *their* relationship."

" 'Cherchez la femme,' " he said. "The guy collects *femmes*." He looked around at the piles of contraband. "Heidi traveling with him and Peake tonight probably means she was in on the escape. Her being the inside woman would *smooth* the escape, wouldn't it? Yesterday, the last time we ran into her, she was walking Peake right near that service elevator. Dry run for tonight."

"Has to be. She and Crimmins needed to rehearse, because whatever the state of Peake's psyche, he'd been cooped up for sixteen years, was unpredictable. It's also possible the time-table for the escape was sped up because you were getting too close. That same day, you asked Heidi if Peake had mentioned Wark's name, and she hesitated for a second. Probably shocked that you'd gotten on to the alias, but she stayed cool. Said it was a funny name, didn't really sound like a name. Edging us away from Wark and diverting our attention to Dollard by letting us know he'd been fired for malfeasance. Because Dollard had become a liability. He'd always been the expendable member of the dope scam. Crimmins and Heidi came up with a kill-two-birds plan: get rid of Dollard and break Peake loose. Something else: right after Heidi told us about Dollard, she returned the conversation to Wark, started asking questions. Who was he, was he actually Peake's friend? Why would she care? She was trying to find out exactly what we knew, and we didn't notice because we saw her as an ally."

"Actress," he said.

"Calm under pressure—a very cold young woman. The moment we were gone, she was probably on the phone to Crimmins. Informing him you were on to his alter ego. He decided to act."

"Cool head," he said. "Lot of good it did her head."

"Cool but also reckless," I said. "A coke conviction didn't stop her from stealing dope at Starkweather. Flirting with danger was also behind her attraction to Crimmins. She told us she was a thrill seeker. Rock climbing, skydiving off power stations—making sure to let you know that was illegal. Think of it: telling a cop she'd committed a crime. Smiling about it. Another little game. Getting off on danger is probably also the way she hooked up with Crimmins in the first place. Castro told us Derrick and brother Cliff were thrill chasers, liked speed. Derrick and Heidi probably met at some kind of daredevil club."

"Going for the adrenaline rush," he said. "Then it gets old, so they move on to a different kind of high."

"Crimmins's crimes have a profit motive, but I've been saying all along that thrill's the main ingredient. Crimmins's thing is creating a twisted world and controlling it. He scripts the action, casts the players, moves them around like pawns. Gets rid of them once they've finished their scenes. For a psychopath, it would be pretty damn close to heaven. Heidi had similar motivations, but she wasn't in Crimmins's league. It was a fun ride for her, but her mistake was thinking of herself as a partner when she was just another extra. She must have been confused when Crimmins pulled off the I-Five and told her to get out."

I didn't feel like laughing, but there I was, doing it.

"What?" he said.

"Just thought of something. If Crimmins had been lucky enough to really break into Hollywood, maybe none of this would've happened."

He took in the room and I followed his eyes. Cramped, dingy, nothing on the walls. For Heidi and Crimmins, interior decorating had meant something else, completely. Cruel puzzles, bloody scenes, embroidery of the mind . . .

"Let me sort out the escape," he said, very softly. "Double entry to Starkweather: Crimmins enters the grounds from the back, through that hole in the fence; Heidi drives right in through the front gate, like she would any other night. She waltzes right on to C Ward, heads over to Peake's room, gets him ready. All the techs are at the weekly meeting, except Dollard, who's patrolling. Heidi lures Dollard into Peake's room—no big challenge, all she has to do is tell him Peake is sick, or freaking out—assuming the Jesus pose again. Dollard goes in, locks the door behind him—basic procedure—goes over to check on Peake. Maybe Peake jumps him, maybe not. In either case, Heidi gets Dollard and cuts his throat. Or *she* distracts Dollard and *Peake* does the cutting . . . She makes sure the coast is clear, hustles Peake over to the staff elevator, no floor guide to tell anyone where it's going . . . Down to the basement, over and out."

"And Crimmins, hiding in one of the annexes, or nearby, meets up with them," I said. "Heidi and Crimmins lead Peake out the back fence. Heidi returns and leaves the hospital the way she came in, through the front, while Crimmins and Peake escape into the foothills, where they've got a vehicle waiting that can handle the terrain. Peake's not in great condition, but Crimmins is a climber, already knows the hills; it wouldn't be a problem dragging Peake along. Heidi as Dollard's cutter would also explain why the artery was only nicked, not slashed clear through. She was a strong girl without much of a conscience. But if she'd never actually cut anyone's throat before, her inexperience could've showed. It takes will to saw through someone's neck. And there's the gush factor. She would've wanted to avoid getting blood-stained, had to coordinate cutting and stepping back in time—I can see Crimmins rehearsing her. So she wounded Dollard just deeply enough to open the jugular. Dollard collapsed, so she thought she'd finished him off. He went into shock, lay there draining. Once again, they were lucky—no one found him soon enough to save him."

"Crimmins seems to have lots of luck."

"No sin unrewarded," I said. "That's why he keeps doing bad things."

"The nick could also mean Peake did it," he said. "Atrophied muscles from all those years in the loony bin."

"Not if he chopped up Heidi's face. Those gashes took force. What do you figure, a hatchet?"

"Patel said that, or some kind of cleaver. Yeah, you're probably right. . . . Heidi cut Dollard, and Peake cut Heidi."

"Her murdering Dollard would serve another purpose: no need to hide a weapon in Peake's room, risk discovery. Techs carry. You just proved that."

He pulled out his phone, called Ron Banks, told him about the drugs and the stolen goods, Heidi's involvement. "Yeah, looks like she was. . . . Listen, I'm gonna snoop around her house some more, but it's West Hollywood, so you might as well get some of your guys over here to tape it off. Tell 'em I'm here, what I look like, so there's no misunderstandings. . . . Thanks. Anything new over there? . . . Yeah, sometimes the job is boring. . . . Yeah, I think I will. Chippie's still over there. . . . Whitworth. Michael Whitworth."

Milo started to search in earnest. The bedroom closet held blue jeans, blouses, and jackets in women's small and medium sizes, and men's black jeans, 34 waist, 35 length, black XL T-shirts, sweaters, and shirts.

"Home sweet home," he said, shining his light on the floor. Three plastic cartons full of rumpled underwear and socks sat next to a jumble of battered running shoes and several pairs of thick-soled, dirty-looking boots. In the corner were four olive-drab packages the size of seat cushions, festooned with straps. U.S. Army stencil. Next to them, scuba gear, a single set of skis, a box of amyl nitrate—poppers. Another box full of polyester hair. Four woman's wigs: long and blond; short, spiky, and blond; raven black; tomato red and curly. Three male toupees, all black, two curly, one straight. Labels inside from a theatrical makeup store on Hollywood Boulevard.

"Toys," said Milo. "When you were over at Fairway Ranch, see any good climbing spots?"

"The entire development is backed by the Tehachapi mountains. But a short walk through foothills is one thing, serious climbing's another. Crimmins would be limited by Peake's condition. Even if Peake's vegetable act's a fake, he's no Edmund Hillary. Also, if Crimmins has returned to Treadway, it's because it has psychological meaning for him. So maybe he'll stick close to home."

"What kind of psychological meaning?"

"Something to do with the massacre—maybe he's reworking it. For his movie. Rescripting—re*living*—a major triumph. Back when he lived there, Treadway was essentially divided between the Ardullo and the Crimmins ranches. Wanda Hatzler told me the Mexican girl Derrick and Cliff threw out of their car ran toward the Ardullo property. On the north side. That could narrow things down."

"But which way would he go? To the Ardullo side because that's where the massacre went down, or to his daddy's place?"

"Don't know," I said. "Maybe none of the above."

"What's there now? Where the ranches were."

"Homes. Recreational facilities. A lake."

"Big homes?" he said. "Something that might remind Crimmins of the Ardullo place?"

"I didn't get that close a look. It's an upscale development. Whether or not that will trigger anything in Crimmins's head, I can't say."

"Any obvious place to hide out?"

"It's pretty open," I said. "Two golf courses, the lake. If they break into someone's home, there'll be plenty of cover. But even if Crimmins is loosening up mentally, that seems downright stupid. . . . Maybe outside the development.

Somewhere at the base of the Tehachapis. If Derrick climbed as a kid, he could have a special hiding place."

Milo got back on the phone, called Bunker Protection. Once again, his side of the conversation was tense. "Idiot rent-a-cops. No sign of any disturbance, no disreputables have driven through tonight, yawn, yawn . . . Okay, let me toss the rest of this palace."

The second bedroom, the space where Heidi and Derrick Crimmins had slept, was narrow, also devoid of personal touches, with barely enough space for the queen-size mattress and two cheap nightstands. In the top drawer of the stand on the right were a half-empty box of tampons, three gold-wrapped Godiva chocolates, two energy bars, a baggie of marijuana. The bottom compartment held woman's underwear, an empty Evian bottle, some white powder in a glassine envelope.

"The 11351.5 didn't make much of an impression," I said.

"First offense—she probably got probation. If that."

"More fuel for her confidence. Coke and poppers would've helped, too."

He checked under the mattress, in the pillowcases, moved around to Crimmins's nightstand. Pack of Kools, two foil-wrapped condoms, two matchbooks, and a thin red paperback book entitled *Finding Fame and Fortune in Hollywood: Writing Your Screenplay,* "by the editors of the Fame and Fortune Series."

The publisher was an outfit called Hero Press, POB address in Lancaster, California. The flyleaf said others in the series included *Buying Real Estate with Nothing Down, Options and Commodities Trading with Nothing Down, Start Your Own Business with Nothing Down,* and *Live to 120: The Herbal Way to Longevity.*

"The scammer finally gets scammed," said Milo, kneeling in front of the lower compartment.

Inside was a black vinyl looseleaf. He pulled it out, turned to the title page.

Typed at the top was

BLOOD WALK

A TREATMENT FOR A MAJOR MOTION PICTURE
By
D. Griffith Crimmins***

***PRESIDENT AND CEO, DGC PRODUCTIONS, THIN LINE PRODUCTIONS, ENTERPENEUR, DIRECTOR, PRODUCER, AND CINEMATOGRAPHER

The next page, soiled and smudged, bore several up-slanting lines written in ballpoint. Curious, sharp-edged penmanship, full of angles and peaks that reminded me of hieroglyphics.

Equip. No prob. Obviosly.
Casting: wrd of mth? Ad? Pickups? Special effects:
   fakeout, double-bluff
Figure out the cameras or use video? Worth the hassle?
   Viedo can work good enough
Titles: Blood Walk. Bloodwalkers. Walk of Blood. Blood-
   bath. The Big Walk
Alternetive titles: 1. The Monster Returns   2. Bag-
   ging the Monster   3. Daredevil Avenger—justice for
   all.   4. Saturday The 14th   5. Return of the Moster
   6. Horror On Palm Street   7. Maniac   8. Psycho-
   Drama   9. The Ultamite Crime   10. Genius and In-
   sanity   11. The Thin Line—who's to say whos crazy
   and whos not.

"Another plot outline, just like in Florida," I said. "Reads like a twelve-year-old's diary—look at the third alternative title. 'Daredevil Avenger—justice for all.' Superman fantasies. He sees *himself* as a risk taker, is thinking of himself as the hero who saves the world from Peake."

Milo shook his head. "Number eleven's the one he actually used for the name of his company—who's to say who's nuts, asshole? *I* say. And you *are*." He turned to the next page. Blank.

"Guess he ran out of ideas," he said. "This kind of brilliance, he *definitely* could've gotten a legit job at the studios."

The light changed in the room. Something yellowing the window shades.

Headlights. A car idling next to the house. In the driveway.

I thought of Marie Sinclair, cranky and paranoid. Pays to listen to everyone.

Milo moved quickly, killing the room lights, replacing the looseleaf, pulling out his gun.

The headlights dimmed; the engine dieseled for several seconds before quieting. The whoosh-and-click of the car door closing. Footsteps scraping the driveway.

Diminishing footsteps.

Milo raced through the house, made it to the front door, said something to me.

Stay put, he explained later, but I never processed it and I stayed on his heels.

He cracked the door, looked outside, flung it open, ran.

In the driveway sat a lemon-yellow Corvette.

We ran past the ficus hedge. A man was fifty feet up the street, to the north. Walking casually, arms swinging.

Tall man. Thin. A too-big head—much too big. Some kind of hat.

Milo set out after him. Closed the gap, bellowed.

"Policefreezedon'tmovepolicefreezefreeze!"

The man stopped.

"Stay right there hands behind your head."

The man obeyed.

"Lie down slowly face to the sidewalk—get your hands back there again—up up behind your head."

Total compliance. As the man lay down, his hat fell off.

In a flash, Milo had his cuffs out, was bending the man's arm behind his back.

That easy.

Time for someone else to have some luck.

"Where's Peake?" Milo demanded.

"Who?" High, tight voice.

"Peake. Don't fuck with me, Crimmins—"

"Who—"

Keeping his gun trained on the back of the man's head, Milo fished out the penlight and tossed it to me. "Shine it on his face—lift up your face!"

Before the man could respond, Milo grabbed a handful of hair and helped him along. The man gasped in pain. I moved around in front and aimed the beam at his face.

Thin face. Framed by long blond hair. He had hat head from the watch cap that lay a few feet away on the pavement.

A few lights went on in neighboring houses, but the street remained quiet.

Milo held the man's chin as I illuminated scared pale eyes. Weak chin, cottony with fledgling beard growth.

Pimples.

Adolescent acne.

A kid.

37.

HIS NAME WAS Christopher Paul Soames and he had I.D. to prove it.

An obviously phony California Identification Card and a student card from Bellflower High, dated three years ago. He'd been a sophomore then, with shorter hair and clearer skin. Had dropped out the following summer, because "it sucked and I had a job."

"Where?" said Milo. He'd dragged Soames onto the lawn behind the ficus hedge, emptied the boy's pockets.

"Lucky's."

"Doing what?"

"Box boy."

"How long did you work there?"

"Two months."

"After that?"

Soames's shrug was inhibited by the cuffs.

He had a twenty-dollar bill in his pocket, a marijuana roach, a partially crushed bag of Peanut M&M's, no driver's license. "But I know how to, my brother taught me before he went into the Marines."

Milo pointed to the Corvette. "Nice wheels."

"Yeah—can you take these off me, man?"

"Run your story by me one more time, Chris."

"Can I at least get off the grass? It's wet, I'm getting my ass wet."

Milo lifted him by a belt loop and hauled him over to the bungalow's front porch. The interrogation had been going on for nearly ten minutes. No sign of any sheriff's cars yet.

Soames shifted his shoulders. "These hurt, man. Lemme loose, I din't do nothin'."

"Didn't steal the car?"

"No way, I tole you."

"You didn't find an address in the car and drive over to rob the house?"

"No way."

"How'd you get the keys?"

"Dude gave 'em to me, I tole you."

"But you don't know the dude's name."

"Right."

"Dude just hands you the keys to his 'Vette, just like that."

"Yeah." Soames sniffed. A bony knee started shaking.

"Where'd this fairy tale take place?" said Milo.

"Ivar and Lexington, like I tole you."

Hollywood back streets. The boy had a hollow-cheeked look that screamed too much Hollywood.

Milo said, "He just came up to you on the corner and gave you his keys."

"Right."

"What were you doing on Ivar and Lexington?"

"Nothin'. Hangin'."

"And he drove up in the 'Vette and—"

"No, he walked up. The 'Vette was parked somewhere else."

"Where?"

"Coupla blocks away."

"So you figured him for a john."

"No—I don' do that shit. That's all that happened, man."

"What'd the dude look like, Chris?"

"Don' know."

"Dude gives you his car keys, and you don't know what he looks like."

"It was dark—it's always dark there, that's why— Go look for yourself, it's always dark there."

"Dude you don't know and whose face you can't see just hands you the keys to his 'Vette, tells you to drive it home for him, gives you twenty bucks for the favor."

"That's right," said Soames.

"Why would he want to do that?"

"Ask him."

"I'm asking you, Chris."

"He had another car."

"Ah," said Milo. "Something you forgot to tell me the first time around."

"He— I—" Soames's mouth snapped shut.

"What, Chris?"

"Nothing."

"Part of the twenty was the dude told you not to say anything to anybody, right?"

Silence.

"Did he say anything about bailing you when you get busted for grand theft auto?"

Silence.

Milo got down on one knee, eye level with Soames. "What if I told you I believe you, Chris? What if I told you *I* know what this guy looks like? Tall, skinny, big nose like a bird's beak. Dresses all in black. Black hair, or maybe light brown. As in, wig."

Soames blinked.

"How'm I doing?"

Soames looked away.

"What if I told you you're a very lucky kid, Chris, because this is a very, very, *very* bad individual and you might be mixed up in something extremely heavy."

Soames's nose wrinkled. Dried snot crusted one nostril. His eyes were runny. His clothes smelled dirty, old, strangely metallic.

"Something *unbelievably* heavy, Chris."

"Right."

"Think I'm kidding you, Chris? How else would I know what he looks like? Why do you think I'm here at his house?"

Soames gave another abbreviated shrug.

"Accessory to murder, Chris," said Milo.

"Right."

"Hundred percent right. This guy likes to kill people. Likes to make it hurt."

"Bullshit."

"Why would I bullshit you, Chris?"

Soames said, "You—he— You better be bullshitting."

"I'm not."

Soames's eyes had turned wet. His lip was shaking.

"You know something, Chris?"

"You *better* be bullshitting," Soames whined. "I let him take *Suzy.*"

Susanna Galvez. Female Hispanic, black and brown, five-two, 116. A DOB that made her fourteen years and seven months old. Missing-persons report filed eighteen months ago at the Bellflower substation.

"Parents suspect she's with her boyfriend," said Milo, pocketing his phone. "Male Caucasian, blond and blue, six to six-two, a hundred forty-five, goes by the name of Chris. No last name."

To Soames: "So, Mr. No Last Name, she ran away with you when she was twelve?"

"She's fourteen now."

Milo grabbed his collar. "You want her to make fifteen, tell me the rest of it, Chris. *Now,* you stupid little shit."

"Okay, yeah, yeah, I've seen the guy before, but I don' know him, that's the truth, man. Not a john, that was true, he just usually cruises. No name, he never told me no name."

"No name and he cruises Hollywood in the 'Vette," said Milo.

"No, no," Soames said impatiently. "Not the 'Vette, never saw the 'Vette before, the other car, this black Jeep. Suzy and I used to call him Marilyn, like Marilyn Manson, 'cause he's tall and weird-looking like Marilyn Manson."

"What's he cruise for?"

Soames's nose bubbled. Milo pulled out a handkerchief, wiped it, took hold of Soames's face again and stared into the boy's eyes. "What's his business, Chris?"

"Sometimes people—not me—score dope from him. Pills.

He's got boocoo pills, prescription shit. Not for me, Suzy either. I just seen him sell pills to other dudes. He has this girlfriend, white hair, all punked up, they both sell pills—"

"What happened tonight?"

"Me and Suzy were hangin' out, what time I don't know, we don't have watches, don't give a shit about time, had a couple burgers at Go-Ji's, we were headed back to this place where we camp—no B&E, it's like an empty squat, we camp there all the time, this guy Marilyn comes up and says he needs me to drive the 'Vette to his house, he knows I'm straight he can trust me, he just wants me to drive it there, put the keys in the mailbox, and take the bus back to 'Wood. Twenty bucks now and fifty more when he sees me tomorrow morning at Go-Ji's."

"What time tomorrow morning?"

"Ten. He's gonna meet me in the parking lot and give me the fifty and also give Suzy back."

"Give her back from where?" said Milo.

"I don't know," said Soames. He whimpered.

"He just took her and didn't tell you where or why?"

"He borrowed her, man."

"To make a movie, right? Guess what kind of movies he makes?"

Soames's shaking knee locked. He began to cry. Milo shook him out of it. "What else, Chris?"

"Nothing, that's it—you think he really could hurt her?"

"Oh, yeah," said Milo. "So think back, genius. Where did he say he was taking her?"

"I don't know! Oh, man!" said Soames. "Oh man, oh man—after we arranged about the 'Vette, he looked at Suzy and said she was real pretty and he could use her in this movie he was making, he's a producer. He didn't say nothing about where, I thought, *Oh, man, her dad's gonna kill me.*"

"Why?"

"'Cause a the movie—you know."

"You assumed he was making a fuck film," said Milo.

"No," said Soames. "I wouldn'ta— He said, 'Don't worry, no one's gonna mess with her, it's just a movie.' "

"What kind of movie? You handed her over and didn't ask him *anything*?"

"I— He— I think he said it was a thriller, she was gonna be like a main character, he needed to film her at night. 'Cause it was a thriller. He was gonna give us—her—a hundred bucks."

"In addition to the fifty?"

"Yeah."

"Generous."

"He said it was a big part."

"And he said he'd give you every penny of it, right?"

"It was for both of us, man. We hang together, but Suzy don't hold no money, I'm more responsible."

The deputies finally arrived. Milo let them take custody of Soames, and he and I hurried to the unmarked.

He pulled away fast, sped north.

"Two cars means two drivers," I said. "Before the escape, Crimmins and Heidi arranged a meet. Somewhere in Hollywood. But Crimmins knew Heidi wouldn't live out the evening, and with her out of the way, he needed someone to drive the second car. Most Hollywood streets have parking regulations; he couldn't risk a ticket. Also, the 'Vette's conspicuous."

"Why would he trust an idiot like Soames to transport it?"

"The idiot followed through, didn't he? Like I said, Crimmins is good at reading people. Or maybe he didn't care— was finished with the 'Vette."

"Just like that? He walks away from a car? And why would he be finished with it?"

"Because tonight marks a new stage in his life," I said. "And money's not his thing, it never was. The moment he has any, he lets it slip through his fingers. He grew up with fast toys, easy come, easy go. Easy to replace, too. He steals movie equipment, boosting another car's no big deal. The Jeep's not registered under any of the names we know about, either. For all we know, he's got a fleet stashed somewhere."

"Supercriminal. Daredevil Avenger."

"Let's face it, Milo, you don't have to be a genius to get away with felonies in L.A."

He growled, raced to Sunset, turned right. I closed my eyes and sat back, knowing exactly where he was headed. Moments later, I felt the car swerve, opened my eyes to see a freeway signpost. The 101 North. Very little traffic this late, and the I-5 interchange was only minutes away. He pushed the unmarked up to ninety, a hundred.

"Susanna Galvez," he said. "That Hatzler woman told you Derrick and his brother had a thing for Mexican girls."

"Nostalgia," I said. "Exactly. This whole thing's about reliving the good old days."

38.

THE SPOT WHERE Heidi Ott had been executed wasn't hard to find.

The rosy incandescence of Highway Patrol flares was visible half a mile away, starbursts fallen to the horizon.

As we got closer, a tapering row of red cones cordoned off the right-hand lane. Milo drove between them, showed his badge to a uniformed officer, received a wary appraisal. Two CHP cruisers, a CHP bike, and a sleek, nonregulation Harley-Davidson were parked on the turnoff.

The officer said, "Okay."

"Mike Whitworth?"

"There." A thumb indicated a huge man in his thirties standing near an embankment. Several arc lights cast focused glare on a taped-off area. The white body outline was at the far edge of the turnoff, inches from the merging of asphalt and dirt embankment. Full-scale version of the morgue gift-shop logo; life imitates art.

Whitworth stood just outside the cones. Young and in good shape, but he looked tired. His ruddy baby-face was centered by a small, blond mustache. His hair was buzzed so short the color was hard to determine. He wore a peanut-butter-colored leather jacket, white shirt, dark tie, gray slacks, and black boots, and he carried a motorcycle helmet.

Milo introduced himself.

Whitworth shook his hand, then mine. He pointed at the ground. Several ruby blotches, the largest over a foot wide. "We found some bone bits and cartilage, too. Probably part of her nose bone. We get gore all the time, plenty of bad stuff in garbage bags, but this kind of damage . . ." He shook his head.

Milo said, "I think the guys who did her are about to do another one." He gave Whitworth a breakneck account of Derek Crimmins's history, Peake's escape, Heidi's possible involvement, ended with Christopher Soames's account. The recruitment of Suzy Galvez.

"Out in the Tehachapis?" said Whitworth.

"Best guess. The Tehachapis behind his hometown. It's a place called Fairway Ranch, now. Know it?"

"Never heard of it," said Whitworth. "I live in Altadena, do most of my work closer to the city. Before Grapevine or past?"

"Right there," I said.

"Crimmins probably has some climbing experience," said Milo, "but Peake doesn't, and if they've got the girl with them, it's not gonna be any Everest thing. They could even be right on the development—commandeering someone's house. The private cops who patrol Fairway say no, but that doesn't convince me. If they *are* in the mountains, I'm figuring right at the base, maybe some kind of sheltered spot—a cave, an outcropping. Either way, we've got to take a look."

"Who're the private cops and what's their problem?" said Whitworth.

"Bunker Protection, out of Chicago. Every time I try to convince them there's something to worry about, they don't wanna know. Keep handing me this public relations crap— 'Nothing ever goes wrong here.' "

"Till it does," said Whitworth, massaging his belt buckle. "Okay, let's get going. I don't know about the jurisdictional aspect, but to hell with all that." He glanced back at the body outline. "We're just about wrapped up, so I can get you these four troopers right now, call for more with ETA's of less than half an hour. I'm on my bike—I was going off duty when the call came in; I'll ride solo, meet you there. If the Bunker yahoos give you a hard time, we'll bulk-intimidate them. What about choppers?"

Milo turned to me. "What do you think? Would noise and lights stop him or egg him on?"

"Depends what's in the script," I said.

"The script?" said Whitworth.

"He's following some sort of story line. In terms of how he'll react to a direct threat, the problem is we don't know enough about his arousal level to predict safely."

"Arousal? This is a sex thing?"

"His general physiological state," I said. "Psychopaths tend to function at a quieter level than the rest of us—low pulse rates and skin conductance, high pain thresholds—except when tension builds up. Then they can be extremely explosive. If we confront Crimmins when he's still relatively calm—scheming, planning, taking control—it's possible he'll fold his tents and run, or just give up. But if we catch him at a peak moment, he might just go for the big ending."

"Pull a Koresh," said Whitworth. "How old's that girl?"

"Fourteen."

"Course, there's nothing to say he hasn't already done her."

Milo said, "Put the choppers on standby. Get me two, three more cars. Along the same lines, we drive into Fairway quietly, no lights, no sirens." To me: "Where do the Bunker people hang out?"

"There's a guardhouse right past the entrance."

"Okay," he said to Whitworth. "Meet you at the main entrance. Alex, give him directions. You're the only one who's actually been there."

39.

THE MEN IN the powder-blue shirts weren't happy.

Three guards, surprised as they sat in the mock-Spanish guardhouse. Soft music on stereo. The shirts freshly pressed.

Neat, clean building, outside and in, cozy interior: spotless kitchenette, oak table set with four matching chairs, blue hats on a rack. On the table were the remains of takeout Mexican food. Taco Fiesta, Valencia address. Next to a half-eaten burrito, a Trivial Pursuit board. Three little plastic pies, blue, orange, brown, the last half-filled with tiny plastic wedges.

The door had been unlocked. When Milo and Mike Whitworth and I entered, all three guards had stood up, grabbed for guns that weren't there. Across the room, a metal locker said WEAPON DEPOSITORY. Next to it was a plaque with the crossed-rifles logo of Bunker Protection.

Now we were all outside in the peach-scented air, under a sky surprisingly deprived of stars. The Bunker guards kept their eyes on the CHP cruisers that blocked the entrance to Fairway Ranch. Inside the cars, the barest outline of men behind night-darkened windshields.

As we'd driven in, Milo had eyed the low white fence, muttered, "No gate. They could've cruised right in."

Moments later, Mike Whitworth coasted up on his Harley and said something to the same effect.

"So you haven't searched yet," Milo said to the tallest guard. "E. Cliff." The one who'd protested loudest until Milo hushed him with a scolding index finger.

"No," he said. "It's past two in the morning, we're not going to wake up the residents. No reason to."

"You'd know if there *was* a reason?" said Whitworth.

"Absolutely," said Cliff. Adding a barked "*Sir.*"

Whitworth stepped closer to him, using his size the way Milo does. "The way you're set up, anyone could get in—is it Ed?"

Cliff tried to smile as he backed away. "Eugene. *Not* correct. Anyone entering can be spotted from the guardhouse."

"Assuming the drapes are open."

Cliff's head jerked toward the building. "They usually are."

Milo said, "I'm *usually* charming." He moved in on Cliff, too. "So tell me, what category would two murderers driving right past you fall into? Sports and Leisure? Arts and Entertainment?"

"Sir!" said Cliff. "There's no reason to get disrespectful. Even with the drapes closed we see headlights."

"Assuming there *were* headlights—I know, there usually are."

"There's no reason—"

Milo stepped closer. Cliff was over six feet, but reedy, an elk confronting bears. He looked at the other two Bunker guards. Both just stood there.

Milo said, "There's *every* reason to search the premises, friend, and we're going to do it, right now."

"I'm sorry, sir, in terms of your jurisdiction . . ." Cliff began. Milo's nose moved a half-inch from his, and the voice tapered. "At the least, I'll have to clear it with headquarters."

Milo smiled. "In Minneapolis?"

"Chicago," said one of the other guards. Nasal voice. "L. Bonaface."

"Call," said Milo. "Meanwhile, we start. Give me a map of this place."

"There isn't one," said Cliff.

"None at all?"

"Not a real map, with coordinates. Just a general layout."

"Jesus," said Milo. "This isn't arctic exploration, hand it over. *Before* you call."

Cliff looked at Bonaface. "Go get it for him." Bonaface

went inside the guardhouse and returned with several sheets of paper.

"I brought a bunch," he said.

Milo grabbed the maps and distributed them. A single page of crude, computer-generated diagram. English street names printed in Gothic, the shops and golf courses, Reflection Lake dead center. No indication a mountain range loomed to the east.

Whitworth said, "Except for the golf courses, it's a small area—that's in our favor . . . Already divided into six zones, and I've got five officers plus me. How's that for karma?"

"Karma's for believers," said Milo, "but yeah, do the golf courses first, then the public buildings and the lake, then door-to-door at each residence. Prioritize any place with anything Jeep-like parked nearby. If the vehicle's got any film equipment in the back, get really careful. If we're right about Crimmins trying to film something, there may be telltale lights."

I said, "In his notes he debated learning how to use the film cameras or sticking with video. He's not one for honest labor, so I'll bet on video. That means he may just be using a hand-held cam, keeping it very low-key. Also, I doubt he'd be on either of the golf courses. Too open."

"Assuming he's even *here*," said Cliff.

"*I'm* assuming you've got golf carts," Whitworth told him.

"Sure, but they're the property of—"

"Law enforcement." Whitworth turned to Milo. "You're doing the mountains?"

"If I can get out there. We'll stay in radio contact."

"How're you going to travel?"

"Got a four-wheeler?" Milo asked Cliff.

The guard didn't answer.

"Hard of hearing, Eugene?"

"We have basically one Samurai, over behind the golf shop, with the carts. It's a relief vehicle, just in case."

"In case of what?"

"In case we have to go out back. Like an old person getting

lost. But that's never happened yet. We don't use it, I can't even say if the tires have air or if it's gassed up—"

"So you'll inflate and siphon," said Milo. "Bring it over."

Cliff didn't respond.

Milo bared his teeth. "Pretty *please*, Eugene."

Cliff snapped, "Go," at Bonaface. Again, Bonaface hurried away.

Milo asked Whitworth the helicopters' estimated time of arrival.

"I could only get one," said Whitworth. "They're holding it at Bakersfield—five, ten minutes."

"Eugene, is there a road leading from Fairway out to the mountains?"

"Not much of one."

"*How* much of one?"

Cliff shrugged. "It's maybe a quarter-mile long. It was supposed to be for hiking, but none of the residents hike. It goes nowhere, just ends, and then all you've got is dirt and rocks." He gave a small smirk, decided to hide it by covering his mouth with his hand.

Whitworth drew Milo and me away from him. "The Ott girl was shot, so they've got some kind of firepower. We have vests; how about you?"

"One," said Milo. He looked at me. "None for you. Sit this out."

"Love to," I said, "but you'd better consider using me. It's a hostage situation with two hostage takers, each with a different psychological makeup, in both cases poorly understood. I'm as close to an expert on Peake and Crimmins as you're going to get."

"Makes sense," said Whitworth. "I think we've got an extra vest."

Milo shot him a sharp look.

Whitworth said, "Not that I want to tell you how to—"

"I've been through worse," I said, knowing what was going on in Milo's mind. An undercover situation last year had gone very bad. He blamed himself. I kept telling him I was fine, the worst thing he could do for me was treat me like an invalid.

"Robin will kill me," he said.

"Only if I get scratched. Right now it's Suzy Galvez who's got something at stake."

He looked up at the sky. Out past the development at high, black, unknowable mountains.

"Fine," he finally said. "If there's a vest."

Whitworth trotted over to one of the cruisers, returned with a bulky black package. I slipped the vest on. Scaled for someone Milo's size, it felt like a giant bib.

"Stylish," said Milo. "Okay, let's get going."

"One place you might check right away," I told Whitworth, "is Sheriff Haas's trailer. Jacob and Marvelle Haas. He arrested Peake for the original massacre, is a major link to the past."

"He lives *here*?"

"Right over in Jersey." I pointed south. "Charing Cross Road."

Whitworth said to Eugene Cliff, "Get me the exact address—no, take me there personally."

Cliff jabbed his own chest. "What about me? No protection?"

Whitworth looked ready to pound him into the ground. "Take me within fifty yards and scram."

"All of a sudden I work for *you*?"

Whitworth's arm shot up and for a second I thought he'd hit Cliff. Cliff believed it, too. He recoiled, raised his own arm protectively. Whitworth's arm kept going. Smoothing his buzz cut. He jogged to his bike, pulled another vest out of the storage box, and slipped it on.

Cliff's mouth was still trembling. He forced it back into smirk mode. "Big-time SWAT attack."

"You find this funny?" said Milo.

"I find it a waste of time. And I'm calling Chicago, now." He took a step, waited for debate, got none, and walked away. The remaining guard followed. Ten steps later, Cliff stopped and looked back. "Remember: these are seniors. Try not to give anyone a heart attack. They pay a lot to live here."

"And look where it gets them," said Milo. "Just a little mindless violence, and gracious living bites the dust."

The Samurai was open-roofed, powder blue, and noisy. An after-market roll bar arced over the front seats. Bonaface left the motor chugging and got out. "It's got half a tank. But hell if I'd use it out there. Makes a shitload of noise, and your lights'll be spotted a mile away."

Milo checked the tires.

"Those are okay," said Bonaface. He had a smooth pink face, blond hair, monkey features, big blue eyes. "Wouldn't use that buggy out there: too easy to spot."

Milo straightened. "You know the area?"

"Not this exact area. Grew up in Piru, but out to the mountains it's the same thing all over. Full of rocks and pits. Plenty of shit to tear up the undercarriage."

"Any caves at the base of the mountains?"

"Never been out there, but why not? So who are these guys, and why would they be here?"

"It's a long story," said Milo, getting behind the wheel and adjusting the driver's seat. I climbed in next to him.

Bonaface looked miffed. "You're using headlights?" He turned at the sound of his name. Cliff barking from the doorway of the guardhouse.

"Asshole," muttered Bonaface. He stared at the vest. Smiled at me. "That thing's way too big for you."

40.

WE DROVE THROUGH the center of the development, passing the gentle swell of Balmoral, the northern golf course, behind twelve-foot chain link. Moving slowly while trying to keep the Samurai as quiet as possible. Tricky, because low gear was the loudest.

I could hear the low hum of the golf carts, but the vehicles were invisible, except for an occasional suggestion of shadows shifting on the green. Headlights off. Same for the Samurai. The Victorian streetlights glowed a strange, muddy tangerine color, barely rescuing us from depthless black.

We reached the end of the road: the pepper trees that rimmed Reflection Lake. The growth here was luxuriant, fed by moist earth. Miserly light from a distant quarter-moon turned the foliage into gray lace. In the empty spaces, the water was still and black and glossy, a giant sunglass lens.

Milo stopped, told me to stay put, took his nine-millimeter in one hand and his flashlight in the other, and climbed out. He walked to the trees, looked around, parted a branch, and peered through, finally disappeared into the gray fringe. I sat there, absently rubbing one thumb against the warm wooden stock of the rifle he'd placed in my lap. No animal sounds. No air movement. The place felt vacuum sealed. Maybe another time I'd have found it peaceful. Tonight it seemed dead.

I was alone for what seemed like a long time. Then scraping sounds from behind the trees tightened my throat. Before I could move, Milo emerged, holstering his gun.

"If anyone's out there, I can't see them." He looked at the

rifle. Unconsciously, I'd raised the weapon and pointed it in his direction.

I relaxed my hands. The rifle sank. He got behind the wheel.

When we were rolling again, he said, "It's pretty open once you get past the trees, just some reeds and other low stuff on the other side. No Jeep or any other car in sight; no one's filming." Grim smile. "Unless it's an underwater shoot—new twist on *Creature from the Black Lagoon*. . . . For all we know, they've already been here and gone, did what they wanted to do, dumped the girl in the water. Or they never came here in the first place."

"I think they did," I said. "No other reason to kill Heidi on the route that leads straight up to Fairway. And Crimmins paid the Soames kid to take the Corvette home—just a mile or two from Hollywood. If he was in the city, he could've driven the Jeep home himself, walked back in half an hour, and gotten the 'Vette. Why bother with Soames unless he was planning to be far away?"

"Because he has plans for Soames? Nice little screen test?"

"That, too. Tomorrow morning. But there'd be no reason to entrust him with the car."

"Why'd he kill Heidi?"

"Because he had no more use for her," I said. "And because he could."

He chewed his lip, squinted, lowered his speed to ten miles per. The map had indicated a service road that hugged the southern end of the White Oak golf course and led to the rear of the development. The streetlamps were less frequent now, visibility reduced to maddeningly subtle shades of gray.

Milo missed the road, and we found ourselves at the sign marking the entrance to Jersey. Lights out in all the mobile homes. I remembered the street bisecting the subdivision as freshly asphalted. In the darkness, it stretched empty and smooth, so perfectly drafted it appeared computer generated. Resumption of the tangerine light. Deep orange on black; every night was Halloween.

"This is where Haas lives?" he said.

"First street to the right. I can show you the trailer."

He cruised past the trailers.

"Up there is parking for visitors," I said. "No visitors tonight . . . There's Charing Cross. Haas's place is four units in. Look for a cement porch, a Buick Skylark, and a Datsun truck."

He stopped two houses away. Only the truck was parked in front, backed by Mike Whitworth's Harley.

Lights out. No sign of Whitworth, and I saw Milo's face tighten up. Then the Highway Patrol man came out from behind the trailer and headed for the bike.

Milo stage-whispered, "Mike? It's Milo."

Whitworth stopped. Turned toward us, focused, came over.

"In the neighborhood," said Milo, "so we dropped by."

If Whitworth was offended by being second-guessed he didn't show it. "No one home, nothing funny. I spotted some unopened mail on the table—a day's worth, maybe two."

"One of their cars is gone," I said. "They have family in Bakersfield. Probably traveling."

"You see any justification for breaking in?" said Whitworth.

Milo shook his head.

"I'm not comfortable with it either. Okay, let me go see if any of my guys hit a hole in one. You ready for the mountains yet?"

"On our way," said Milo.

Whitworth looked out at the black peaks, barely discernible against the onyx sky. Country skies were supposed to be crammed with stars. Why not tonight?

"Must be pretty during the day," said Whitworth, kick-starting the Harley. "Sure you want to go it alone?"

"I'd better," said Milo. "Gonna be hard enough to avoid being spotted with one vehicle." He brandished his cell phone. "I'll keep in touch."

Whitworth nodded, took another glance at the Tehachapis. Keeping his engine low, he rolled away.

Turning the Samurai around, Milo drove back through Jersey. Lights went on in one of the mobiles as we passed, but so far we'd avoided attracting undue attention. Milo coasted without gas, looking for the service strip. Almost missing it again.

Unmarked, just a car-wide break in the peppers, topped by arcing branches.

Letting the Samurai idle, Milo got out and shined his light on the ground. "Hardpack . . . maybe degraded granite . . . tire tracks. Someone's been here."

"Recently?"

"Hell if I know. Jeb the Tracker I ain't."

He got back in and turned onto the road. The passage was unlit and lined on the north side by more chain link, on the south by a high berm planted with what looked and smelled like oleander. The Samurai traveled well below the berm level, as if we were tunneling.

The four-by-four rode rough, every irregularity in the road vibrating through the stiff frame, Milo's head bouncing perilously close to the roll bar. Nothing changed for the next half-mile: more chain link and shrubbery. Then the road ended without warning and we were faced with the sudden shock of open space, as if tumbling out of a chute.

No more gray, just black. I saw nothing through the windshield, wondered how Milo could navigate. He began wrestling with the wheel. Pebble spray snare-drummed against the undercarriage, followed by deeper sounds, hollow, like hoofbeats. Larger rocks. The Samurai began swaying from side to side, seeking purchase on the grit. Beneath the floorboard, the chassis twanged.

The next dip slammed Milo's head against the bar.

He cursed and braked.

"You okay?" I said.

He rubbed his crown. "If I had a brain in here I might be in trouble. What the hell am I doing? I can't drive like this. Visibility's zilch; we hit a big enough rock, this thing flips and we break our goddamn necks."

Locking the parking brake, he stood on the seat and stared over the windshield.

"Nothing," he said. "Whole lot of nothing."

I took the flashlight, got out, faced away from the mountains, cupped my hand over the lens, and tried to examine the ground with the resultant muffled light.

Dry, compacted soil, inlaid with sharp-edged stones and desiccated plants. Matted flat and embroidered by chevron-shaped corrugations. "The tracks are still going."

He got down beside me. "Yeah . . . maybe someone went off-roading. That wild ol' California lifestyle." He laughed very softly. "They're supposed to be the crazy ones, but they probably did it with headlights, or at least low beams. Meanwhile, I blind myself. And even without lights we're vulnerable. All the empty space, this thing's probably audible clear to the mountains." Standing, he squinted at the Tehachapis. "How far does that look to you?"

"Two miles," I said. "Maybe three. You're saying it's time to go it on foot?"

"I don't see any choice. If you're up for it, that is—scratch that, stupid question. Of course you're up for it. You're the one who thinks running is fun."

He tried to call Whitworth, got no connection, walked a hundred feet back, tried again, same result. Switching off the phone, he put it in his pocket along with the car keys. The flashlight went into another pocket. He took the rifle, gave me the nine-millimeter.

"Handing a civilian my gun." He shook his head.

"Not just any civilian," I said.

"Even worse. Okay, let me get rid of this thing." He yanked off his tie and tossed it in the car. "And this." In went his jacket. Mine, too.

We began walking, trying to follow the tracks.

Moving on leather-soled shoes ill-equipped for the task. Nothing to guide us but the hint of the crisp peaks I'd seen during my daytime visit. The quarter-moon looked sickly, degraded, a child's rendering erased here and there to tissue-paper consistency. Set high and well behind the mountains, the filmy crescent appeared to be fleeing the galaxy. What little light filtered down to earth offered no wisdom about anything below the mountaintops.

The lack of spatial cues made it feel as if we'd entered a

huge, dark room as big as the world; every step was tinged by the threat of vertigo.

Reduced to stiff, small movements, I edged forward, feeling the rocks rolling under my shoes. Larger, sharper fragments caught on the leather, like tiny parasites attempting to burrow through. As the stones grew progressively larger, contact became painful. I got past the discomfort but remained unable to orient myself. Clumsy with indecision, I stumbled a few times, came close to falling, but managed to use my arms for balance. Several feet in front of me, Milo, encumbered by the rifle, had it worse. I couldn't see him but I heard him breathing hard. Every so often the exhalations choked off, only to resume harsher, faster, like a labored heart making up for skipped beats.

Ten more minutes seemed to bring us no closer. No lights up ahead. *Nothing* up ahead but walls of rock, and I started to feel I'd been wrong about Crimmins returning to the scene. A fourteen-year-old in his grasp, and we were baby-stepping toward nothing.

What else was there to do but continue?

Three times we paused to risk a quick, cupped flash-lighting of the path. The tracks endured, and immense boulders started appearing, sunk deeply into the ground, like fallen meteorites. But no rocks directly in front of us, so far. This was a well-used clearing.

We kept moving at a pitiful pace, shuffling like old men, enduring the loss of orientation in angry silence. Finally, the moonlight obliged a bit more, revealing folds and corrugations in the granite. But I still couldn't see two feet in front of me, and each step remained constricted, tension coursing up my tailbone. Finally, I got a handle on walking by pretending I was weightless and able to float through the night. Milo's breath kept cutting off and rasping. I got closer behind him, ready to catch him if he fell.

Another hundred yards, two hundred; the peaks enlarged with a suddenness that shook me, as if I'd taken my eyes off the road and were headed for collision.

I reassessed the distance between Fairway's eastern border

and the Tehachapis. Less than two miles, maybe a mile and a half. In daylight, nothing more than a relaxed nature stroll. I was sweating and breathing hard; my hamstrings felt tight as piano wire, and my shoulders throbbed from the odd, stooped posture that maintaining balance had imposed on me.

Milo stopped again, waited till I was at his side. "See anything?"

"Nothing. Sorry."

"What are you apologizing for?"

"My theory."

"Better than anything else we've got. I'm just trying to figure out what we do if we get there and it's still nothing. Head straight back, or trail along the mountains just in case they dumped a body?"

I didn't answer.

"My shoes are full of rocks," he said. "Let me shake them out."

A few thousand baby steps. Now the mountains were no more than a half-mile away, reducing the sky to a sliver, dominating my field of vision. The contours along the rock walls picked up clarity and I could see striations, wrinkles, dark gray on darker gray against black.

Now, something else.

A tiny white pinpoint, fifty, sixty feet to the left of the track.

I stopped. Squinted for focus. Gone. Had I imagined it?

Milo hadn't seen it; his footsteps continued, slow and steady.

I walked some more. A few moments later, I saw it again.

A white disc, bouncing against the rock, widening from sphere to oval, paling from milk white to gray to black, then disappearing.

An eye.

The eye.

Milo stopped. I caught up with him. The two of us stood there, searching the mountainside, waiting, watching.

The disc appeared again, bouncing, retreating.

I whispered, "Camera. Maybe she's still alive."

I wanted to run forward, and he knew it. Placing a hand on my shoulder, he whispered softly but very quickly: "We still don't know what it means. Can't give ourselves away. Backup would be great. One last try to reach Whitworth. Any closer and it's too risky."

Out came the phone. He punched numbers, shook his head, turned off the machine. "Okay, slow and quiet. Even if it feels like we'll never get there. If you need to tell me something, tap my shoulder, but don't talk unless it's an emergency."

Onward.

The disc reappeared, vanished. Circling the same spot to the left.

Focused on what? I yearned to know, didn't want to know.

I stayed close behind Milo, matching my steps to his.

Our footfalls seemed louder, much too loud.

Walking hurt and silence fed the pain. The world was silent.

Silent movie.

Images flooded my head: herky-jerky action, corseted women, men with walrus mustaches, mugging outrageously over a plinkety-manic piano score. White-lettered captions, framed ornately: "So it's carving you want, sir? I'll show you carving."

Stop, stupid. Keep focused.

Fifty yards from the mountain. Forty, thirty, twenty.

Milo stopped. Pointed.

The white disc had appeared again, this time with a tail—a big white sperm sliding along the rock, wriggling away.

Still no sounds. We reached the mountain. Cold rock fringed with low, dry shrubs, larger stones.

Holding the rifle in front of him, Milo began edging to the left. The nine-millimeter was heavy in my hand.

The disc materialized overhead. White and creamy, bouncing, lingering, bouncing. Gone.

Now a sound.

Low, insistent.

Flash. Whir. Click.

On. Off.

No human struggle. No voices. Just the mechanics of work.

We moved along the mountain undetected, got to within twenty yards before I saw it.

A high, ragged rock formation—an outcropping of sharp-edged boulders, sprouting like stalagmites from the base of the parent range. Clumped and overlapping, ten to fifteen feet high, pushed out twenty feet.

Natural shield. Outdoor studio.

The sound of the camera grew louder. We crept closer, hugging the rock. New sounds. Low, unintelligible speech.

Milo stopped, pointed, hooked his arm, indicating the far end of the boulders. The wall had acquired convexity, continuing in a smooth, unbroken semicircle. No breaks in sight, meaning entry had to be at the far north.

He pointed again and we edged forward inch by inch, bracing ourselves with palms against the rock. The wall curved radically, killing visibility, transforming every step into a leap of faith.

Twelve steps. Milo stopped again.

Something jutted out from the rock. Square, bulky, metallic.

Rear end of a vehicle. From the other side of the granite wall, *flash, whir.* Mumbles. Laughter.

We edged to the vehicle's rear tires, squatted, swallowed breath.

Chrome letters: Ford. Explorer. Black or dark blue. Sand spray streaked the rear fender. No license plate. A partially shredded bumper sticker commanded: ENGAGE IN RANDOM ACTS OF KINDNESS.

One-third of the vehicle extended past the rock walls, the rest nosed inside. Milo straightened and peered through the rear window. Shook his head: tinted. Crouching again, he secured his grip on the rifle, moved around the Explorer's driver's side. Waited. Pointing his rifle at whatever was in front of him.

I joined him. The two of us remained pressed against the truck.

Partial view of the clearing. Plenty of light now, from a spotlight on a pole. An orange extension cord connected the lamp to a gray battery pack. The bulb was aimed downward, well short of the fifteen-foot walls that created the staging area.

Forty-foot stage, roughly circular, set on flat gray earth rimmed by the high, seamed rock. A few boulders were scattered in the corners, like sprinkles of pebbles where the mountain had given way.

Natural amphitheater. Derrick Crimmins had probably discovered it as a youth, driving out with his brother to stage God knew what.

The good old days, when he'd designed sets for his stepmother, acquired a taste for production.

Tonight, he'd gone minimalist. Nothing in the clearing but the single light, a tackle box, and several videocassettes off to the side. Three white plastic folding chairs.

The chair to the left was off by itself, twenty feet from its neighbors. On it sat a young, brown-skinned, plain-faced girl, arms and legs bound by thick twine, dark hair tied in pigtails. Pink baby-doll pajamas were her sole costume. A pink spot of blush on each cheek, red lipstick on a frozen mouth. A wide leather belt secured her to the chair, cinching her cruelly at the waist, pushing her rib cage forward. Not a belt—a hospital restraint, the same kind they used at Starkweather.

Her head hung to the right. Livid bruises splotched her face and breasts, and dried blood snaked from her nose down to her chin. A shiny red rubber ball was jammed into her mouth, creating a nauseating cartoon of gee-whiz amazement. Her eyes refused to go along with it: open, immobile, mad with terror.

Staring straight ahead. Refusing to look at what was going on to her left.

The center chair held another woman captive: older, middle-aged, wearing a pale green housedress torn down the middle. The rip was fresh, fuzzed by threads, exposing white underwear, loose pale flesh, blue veins. Auburn hair. The same kind of bruises and scratches as the girl's. One eye purple and swollen shut. Red ball in her mouth, too.

Her other eye undamaged, but also closed.

The gun jammed against her left temple was small and square-edged and chrome-plated.

Next to her, in the right-hand chair, sat Ardis Peake, holding the weapon. From our vantage, only half his body was visible. Long white fingers around the trigger. He had on his Starkweather khakis. White sneakers that looked brand-new. Big sneakers. Oversized feet.

Tormenting the auburn-haired woman, but showing no sign he enjoyed it. His eyes were closed, too.

Beyond enjoyment into reverie?

The man holding the video camera prodded him. Hand-held camera, compact, dull black, not much larger than a hardcover book. It sprayed a beam of creamy-white light.

Peake didn't budge, and the cameraman gave him a sharper prod. Peake opened his eyes, rolled them, licked his lips. The cameraman got right in front of him, capturing each movement. *Whir.* Peake slumped again. The cameraman let the camera drop to his side. The lens tilted upward and the beam climbed, hitting the upper edges of the rock and projecting the eye-dot onto the mountainside. The cameraman shifted and the dot-eye died.

Milo's jaw bunched. He edged around to get a fuller view. I stayed with him.

No one else in the clearing. The cameraman kept his back to us.

Tall, narrow, with a small, white, round, shaved head that glowed with sweat. Black silk shirt, buccaneer sleeves rolled to the elbows, black jeans, dusty black boots with thick rubber soles. Some kind of designer label ran diagonally across the right patch pocket of the jeans. From the left patch dangled the butt of another chrome automatic.

Milo and I sidled farther. Froze as gravel spat under us. No reaction from the cameraman. Too busy mumbling and cursing and prodding Peake.

Manipulating Peake.

Sitting Peake up straighter. Poking Peake's face, trying to mold expression. Adjusting the gun in Peake's hand.

Adhering to Peake's hand.

Strips of transparent tape bound the weapon to Peake's spindly fingers. Peake's arm was held unnaturally rigid by a tripod that had been rigged to support the limb. Tape around the arm.

Forced pose.

Milo narrowed his eyes, raised his rifle, aimed, then stopped as the cameraman moved suddenly.

Half-turning, touching something.

A tight, downslanting line that cut through night-space.

Nylon fishing filament, so thin it was virtually invisible from this distance.

Running from the gun's trigger to a wooden stake hammered into the dirt.

Slack line. One sharp tug would force Peake's finger backward on the trigger, propel the bullet directly into the auburn-haired woman's brain.

Special effects.

The cameraman ran a fingertip along the line, stepped back. Peake's gun arm remained stiff but the rest of him was rubbery. Suddenly a wave of tardive symptoms took hold of him and he began licking his lips, rolling his head, fluttering his eyelids. Moving his fingers just enough to twang the line.

The cameraman liked that. Focused on the woman. The gun. Back to the woman. Seeking the juicy shot.

Peake stopped moving. The line sagged.

The cameraman cursed and kicked Peake hard in the shins. Peake didn't react. Slumped again.

"Go for it, fucker." Low-pitched gravel voice. "*Do* it, man."

Peake licked his lips. Stopped. His legs began to shake. The rest of him froze.

"Okay! Keep those knees going—don't stop, you psycho piece of shit."

Peake didn't react to the contempt in the cameraman's tone.

Somewhere else, completely. The cameraman walked over

and slapped him. The auburn-haired woman opened her eyes, shuddered, closed them immediately.

The cameraman had stepped back, was focused on Peake. Peake's head whipped back, bobbled. Drool flowed from his mouth.

"Fucking meat puppet," said the cameraman.

The sound of his voice brought a whimper from the auburn-haired woman. The crepe around her uninjured eye compressed into a spray of wrinkles as she bore down, struggling to block out the moment. The cameraman ignored her, preoccupied with Peake.

No other movements in the clearing. The brown-skinned girl was in a position to see us, but she showed no sign of recognition. Frozen eyes. Fear paralysis or drugs or both.

Milo trained the rifle on the back of the cameraman's head. Thick fingers around his trigger. But the cameraman was only inches from the fishing line. If he fell the wrong way, the gun would fire.

Tucking the camera under his arm, the filmmaker positioned Peake some more. Peake's arms dangled; he threw his head back. More drool. He inhaled noisily, coughed, blew snot through his nose.

The cameraman yanked the camera up and filmed it. Slapped Peake again, said, "Some monster you are."

Peake's head dropped.

Unbound. Free to leave the chair, but constrained by something stronger than hemp.

The cameraman filmed, shifting attention from the woman to the gun to Peake, still inches from the rigged line.

More lip-licking and head-rolling from Peake. His eyelids slammed upward, showcasing two white ovals.

"Good, good—more eye stuff, give me eye stuff."

The cameraman was talking louder now, and Milo used the sound for cover, charging out into the clearing, raising his rifle.

The cameraman's right thigh nudged the line. Made it bob. He realized it. Laughed. Did it again, watched the pull on Peake's hand.

Peake was able to pull the trigger, but even tardive movement hadn't caused him to do so.

Resisting?

Again, his head dropped.

The cameraman said, "Where's good help when you need it?" Taking hold of Peake's ear, he shoved Peake's head upward, filmed the resultant gaping stare. Caressing the line with his own index finger as the camera panned the length of Peake's body, moving slowly from furrowed skull to oversized feet.

Disproportionate feet. *Puppet.*

I understood. Insight was worthless.

I readied my gun, but stayed in place. Milo had inched closer to the cameraman, fifteen or so feet to his rear. With exquisite care, he lifted the rifle to his shoulder, trained it once again on the cameraman's neck. Sniper's target: the medulla oblongata, lower brain tissue that controlled basic body process. One clean shot and respiration would cease.

The cameraman said, "All right, Ardis, I've got enough background. One way or the other, let's *do* the cunt."

The auburn-haired woman opened her good eye. Saw Milo. Moved her mouth around the red ball, as if trying to spit it out. I knew who she was. Sheriff Haas's wife—Marvelle Haas.

Mail on the table, one day, maybe two. One car gone, the wife left alone.

She began shivering violently.

The young girl remained glazed.

The cameraman turned toward Marvelle, gave us a full view of his profile. Deep lines scored the sides of a lipless mouth. Grainy, tanned skin, several shades darker than the white, hairless head. The head accustomed to wigs. Small but aggressive chin. Beak nose sharp enough to draw blood. No facial fat, but loose jowls, stringy neck. Forearms wormed by veins. Big hands. Dirty nails.

Derrick Crimmins was turning steadily into his father.

His father had been a sour, grasping man, but nothing said he'd been anything other than a flawed human being.

Here in front of me was monstrosity.

Yet open him up and there'd be unremarkable viscera. Bouncing around the vault of his skull would be a lump of gray jelly, outwardly indistinguishable from the brain of a saint.

A man—it always came down to just a man.

Marvelle Haas closed her eyes again. Whimpers struggled to escape from behind the red ball. All that emerged were pitiful squeaks. Milo crouched, ready to shoot, but Crimmins was still too close to the line.

"Open your eyes, Mrs. Haas," said Crimmins. "Give me your eyes, honey, come on. I want to catch your expression the moment it happens."

He checked the tape around Peake's hand. Adjusted the gun barrel so that it centered on Marvelle Haas's left temple.

She squeaked.

He said, "Come on, let's be professional about this." Moved toward her. Away from the fishing line.

"Used to fish," he said, arranging her hair, parting her housedress. Slipping a hand under the fabric and rubbing, pinching. "Look what I caught here."

Still within arm's reach of the line.

"Back when I fished," he said, "a tug on the line meant you'd caught something. This time it means throwing something away."

She turned away from him. He moved to the left, focusing, filming.

Away from the line. Far enough away.

"Don't move! Drop your hands! Drop 'em drop 'em now!"

Derrick Crimmins froze. Turned around. The look on his owlish face was odd: surprised—betrayed.

Then the flush of rage. "This is a private shoot. Where's your pass?"

"Drop your hand, Crimmins. Do it now!"

"Oh," said Crimmins. "You talk so I'm supposed to listen, asshole?"

"Drop it, Crimmins, this is the last time—"

Crimmins said, "Okay, you win."

He shrugged. The lipless mouth curved upward. "Oh, well," he said.

He lunged for the fishing line.

Milo shot him in the smile.

41.

THE EXPLORER SHOWED up on a Hollywood Division want list. Stolen from a strip mall at Western and Sunset two months before. In the rear storage area were five sets of license plates, three phony registrations, two videocams, a dozen cassettes, candy wrappers, soda cans. Wedged in the spare-tire case, barbiturates, Thorazine, methamphetamine.

Hedy Haupt was traced to a family in Yuma, Arizona. Father's whereabouts unknown, Welfare Department clerk mother, one brother who worked for the Phoenix fire department. Hedy had earned a B average during her first three years at Yuma High, played a starring role on the track and basketball teams. After she "fell in with a bad crowd" during her senior year, her grades had plummeted and she'd dropped out, earned a GED, gotten a job at Burger King, run away. During the ensuing eight years, her mother had seen her twice, once for Christmas five years ago, then a one-week visit last year, during which she'd been accompanied by a boyfriend named Griff.

"Had a bad feeling about him," Mrs. Haupt told Milo. "Carried a camera around and did nothing but take our picture. Wore nothing but black, like someone died."

Milo and Mike Whitworth found the tapes while excavating the mounds of stolen goods in the garage at Orange Drive. Sixteen cassettes in black plastic cases, buried under thousands of dollars' worth of motion picture gear that Derrick Crimmins had lacked the will, or the ability, to master.

Sixteen death scenes.

The first recognizable victim was the fourth we viewed.

384

Richard Dada, young, handsome, talking animatedly about his career plans, unaware of what lay ahead. Cut to the next scene: Richard's head yanked back by the hair, exposed for the throat slash. The body bisected with a band saw. The dark-sleeved arms of the murderer visible, but no face. The camera was stationary, making it possible for one person to murder and film. Other tapes featured a roving lens that necessitated two killers. The log on the tape said Dada had been killed at one A.M.

Ellroy Beatty's tape featured two segments, an initial shot of the homeless man sucking a bottle near the train tracks, then, four months later, Beatty prone and unconscious on those same train tracks, followed by a long shot of an approaching express. Poor technique; the camera jumped around and the moment of impact was just a blur. Next came brother Leroy, also in two installments. Smiling drunkenly as he talked about wanting to be a blues singer. Four months later, a similar smile, cut short as a black hole snapped onto his forehead like a decal and he collapsed.

Both brothers killed the same night. Ellroy first, his death mandated by the train schedule. Leroy's turn two hours later.

Midway through the stack was Claire Argent's final day on earth: like the others, she'd been unprepared. Crimmins had filmed her in front of a bare white wall. Whether it was her own living room couldn't be determined. She talked about psychology, about wanting to learn more about madness, made allusions to the project she and the cameraman would be starting soon, then said, "Oh, sorry, I'm supposed to forget you're there, right?"

No answer from the cameraman.

Claire talked more about the origins of madness. About not jumping to conclusions, because even psychotics had something to tell us. Then she smoothed an eyebrow—priming for the camera—and smiled some more. Five seconds of shy smile before she was smothered by a pillow. Long shot of her motionless body. Close-up on the straight razor . . .

Twelve other home movies, unlabeled. Seven females: five

teenage girls with the haunted look of street kids, two attractive blond women in their thirties. Five males: a painfully thin goateed boy around sixteen or seventeen and four men, one Asian, one black, two Hispanic.

Folded into an empty box were two sheets of paper.

Title page: **The Monster's Chosen. He Canot Be Stopped.**

Second page: **Cast**

We worked on that for a long time.

The "fag actor" was most likely Dada, the "old-maid profesor," Claire. Other designations included "the wino twins (Monster finds a perfect match)" and three headings—"pompos businessman," "coke whore," and "girl shopping"—for which no conforming tape could be found. "Greaser farm-chick" matched Suzy Galvez, "the sheriff's hotblooded wife" Marvelle Haas. The "teenage pimp" could've been the goateed boy stabbed in the chest, then dismembered. But he fit "street punk," so my guess was Christopher Soames. Never had his audition, lucky lad.

At the bottom of the page: "more?????? definitly. how many????????????"

The job of identifying the unnamed victims was assigned to a six-detective task force from LAPD and the Sheriff's Department. After two months, three of the teenage girls had been matched with runaways on various missing persons rosters; all the girls, it was believed, had been living on the streets of Hollywood. Hedy Haupt would've understood that scene. Two girls and the goateed boy remained nameless, as did the younger of the blond women, probably the "stripper," and the black man (the "nigger stud"). "Greaser 1" and "greaser 2" turned out to be Hernando Alas and Sabino Real, cousins from El Salvador seeking work as laborers by standing outside a paint store in Eagle Rock. Contractors seeking cheap labor cruised the store daily. No one remembered who'd picked up Alas and Real, but family members living in the Union District finally stepped forward to make the identification.

A Korean-American salesman named Everett Kim, bludgeoned with a baseball bat—the "chink"—was traced to the Glendale-based skydiving club where Derrick Crimmins and Hedy had first met. The ex-wife of another member, a dental hygienist from Burbank, turned out to be Allison Wisnowski. "The nurse."

Four months later, no new I.D.'s and only one of the bodies had been found: one of the runaway girls, a sixteen-year-old named Karen DeSantis, discovered by hikers in Bouquet Canyon.

One additional tape was found in the Explorer, the scene barely discernible because of poor light: Hedy Haupt aka Heidi Ott, getting out of the four-wheeler, smiling uneasily. Handing the camera to someone off screen, then turning her back and cocking her hip. Moving slowly, seductively. Vamping. Smiling as she turned to look back.

Saying, "How'm I doing—sexy enough?" just before her head disappeared in a flash. No designation on the list. Perhaps Derrick Crimmins had conceived her as "coke whore," or maybe he had yet to dream up a designation.

Creating characters, killing them off.

Folded in a pocket of Crimmins's black silk shirt was a copy of the *Blood Walk* title page we'd found in his nightstand. On the reverse were several handwritten paragraphs in the same sharp-edged hieroglyphics used for the production notes:

The Monster: combenation of extreme evil-madness and supernatural psychic abilitys to tell the future and to get into peoples heads. Locked up in the high security asylum just like Haniball Leckter he also cant be stopped like Leckter, can go through walls, beam himself around change his moleculs like a StarTrek alien. Exits at will, goes around killing at will. Various people, all types just cause he likes it, gets off on it, not crazy all the time this is just what he does, his job, his callin in life, no one will ever understand it because theyre not in the same dimension. And he canot be stopped anymore than Jason or Freddie Kruger or Michael Meyers.

Except by The Daredeveil Avenger. Who understands him cause He grew up with him and Hes also got the psychic powers but for good not evil. Once Hhe was a kid now He's a man, tall and muscular and silent, a real John Wayne Dirty Harry type but with a sense of humor. True Lies meets James Bond. Doesn't waste action except whem it counts. Women love him the same as James Bond but He has no time for them because only He knows what The Monsters really capible of, so only he can stop The Blood Walk which otherwise would be inevatable.

He wears Black but He's the Good Guy. Keep it different, creative. The actions in the end always between him and the Monster. Prime-evil battle. Only at the end can we know how it turns out. In the last scene the Monster dies the worse death of all. Maybe burning, maybe grinded up in some kind of hamburger machine. Or acid. Either way, he's dead.

Or maybe not.

If it works there's always a sequel.

42.

"WHAT THE HELL was he planning to do with it?" said Milo. "Take a meeting with some studio scrote?"

He stuffed pretzels into his mouth. No answer expected.

We were sitting in a bar on Pacific Avenue on the south end of Venice, not far from the Marina. Jimmy Buffett on tape, sun-roughened faces and zinc noses, sports talk, the pretzels. Mostly calls for beer on tap.

It was Thursday. I'd spent the afternoon just as I had every day this week. Out in Bellflower with Suzy Galvez, trying to break through. Milo had offered my services right after the rescue. Mr. Galvez, a landscaper with a vicious scar running from his left ear to his shoulder blade, had turned him down, growling, "We handle our own problems."

Three weeks later, I got the call from Mrs. Galvez. Meek, halting, slightly accented voice. Apologetic when she didn't need to be. Suzy was still waking up with screaming nightmares. Two days ago, she'd started wetting her bed and sucking her thumb; she hadn't done any of that since the age of six.

I drove out the next day. The house was a brown box behind freshly painted white pickets, too many flowers for the space. Mr. Galvez greeted me at the door, a scar-faced, muscled keg of steam. Shaking my hand too hard. Telling me he'd heard I knew what I was doing. Handing me a mixed bouquet, cut fresh from the garden, when I left.

Marvelle Haas was rumored to be seeing a therapist in Bakersfield. Neither she nor her husband had returned anyone's calls. The task force was still looking for bodies, contacting departments in other cities, other states, trying to figure out how many people Derrick Crimmins had murdered. Cases in Arizona, Oklahoma, and Nevada seemed promising. Evidence on Derrick's brother's motorcycle accident was sketchy, but Cliff Crimmins's name had been added to the victim list.

Milo snarfed more pretzels. Someone shouted for a Bud. The bartender, a black-haired Croatian with four rings in his left ear, palmed the tap. We were drinking single-malt scotch. Eighteen-year-old Macallan. When Milo asked for the bottle, the Croatian's eyebrows lifted. He smiled as he poured.

"What the hell was it all for?" said Milo.

"That's a real question?"

"Yeah, I've used up my ration of rhetorical."

I was sorry he asked. I'd thought about little else, had answers good enough for talk shows but nothing real.

Milo put his glass down, stared at me.

"Maybe it was all for fun," I said. "Or preparation for the movie Crimmins convinced himself he'd write one day. Or he was actually going to sell the tapes."

"We still haven't found any underground market for that kind of crap."

"Okay." I sipped. "So eliminate that."

"I know," he said. "There's an appetite for every damn bit of garbage out there. I'm just saying nothing's turned up linking Crimmins to any snuff-film business deals, and we've looked big-time. No cash hoard, not a single bank account, no meetings with any shifty types in long coats, no ads in weirdo magazines. And the computer Crimmins had in the house wasn't hooked up to the Internet. Nothing but basic software, no files. Our guy says he probably never used it."

"Technologically impaired," I said. "No sweat. Video's as good as film."

"All I'm saying is it doesn't look like he was after the money. Stole all that gear but never tried to sell it. We figure he was probably living off dope sales."

"And Heidi's salary," I said. "Till she became superfluous. No bank accounts means the two of them spent everything as it came in. They weren't living like royalty and they avoided paying rent, so a good deal of it probably went up her nose."

"His, too. Coroner found some coke in his system. A little meth, too. And something called loratadine."

"Antihistamine," I said. "Doesn't make you drowsy. Maybe Crimmins was allergic to the desert, needed to keep his energy level up for the big shoot."

Milo refilled his glass. *"Blood Walk."*

"Whatever his specific motivation," I said, "and he may have had several, in his head it was a major production. It was the process he loved. He got hooked on playing God sixteen years ago."

He downed the scotch. "You really think Crimmins did the Ardullos by himself."

"By himself or with his brother. But not with Peake. Peake was set up. I'll probably never be able to prove it, but the facts support it. Think about Peake's blood test: just a residue of Thorazine. Heidi'd been weaning him off his meds for a while. Just as Claire probably had. But Claire's motive was to get Peake to talk about his crimes. And, unconsciously, she wanted to find some virtue in his soul because that might say something about her brother. Heidi wanted Peake sufficiently coherent so he could cooperate in the escape and—more important—perform on film. Killing Marvelle and Suzy on camera—the Monster finally reveals itself. But it didn't work. He didn't perform. You saw his condition. With or without Thorazine, he's extremely low-functioning, has been for years. At his prime, he had no more than a borderline IQ. Adolescent paint- and glue-sniffing and alcohol knocked off a few more points. Thorazine and tardive dyskinesia numbed him further. He was never in any shape to plan and conduct a crime spree, even the disorganized massacre Jacob Haas found at the Ardullo house. He had nothing to do with Heidi's death or Frank Dollard's. No motive, no means. Same for the Ardullos."

"The Ardullos were your basic senseless crime," he said. "Maniac on the loose, no need for a motive."

"That's what Derrick wanted everyone to think," I said.

"And he got his way. But there's always some kind of motive. Psychotic or otherwise. Peake's no criminal superman, just pathetic. Derrick plotted it all out. Good against evil; Derrick gives, Derrick takes away."

Another drink poured. Milo said, "Daredevil Avenger."

"On some level, Derrick probably started believing his own P.R. Peake as surrogate monster, Derrick as angel of deliverance. But Peake just doesn't fit any type of psychotic killer. He's never shown any indication of a delusional system, bloody or otherwise, never acted violently before the massacre or since. He's a retarded man with advanced schizophrenia, organic brain damage, alcoholic dementia. Crimmins called him a meat puppet and that's exactly what he was, right from the beginning. Derrick and Cliff got him drunk, borrowed his shoes—they were able to even though they were much taller, because Peake's feet are disproportionately large. One or both of them walked through the Ardullo house slashing and bludgeoning. Two killers would have made it easier, quicker. The sneaker prints pointed to Peake and led to his shack. With that kind of proof, why bother looking any further? And don't forget who was in charge: Haas, a parttime cop, absolutely no homicide experience. Then the FBI came in and did an after-the-fact profile."

Milo had two more shots.

"One other thing," I said. "That night, when Peake had his hand taped to the gun, he was experiencing plenty of tardive symptoms. Lots of movement; you'd think he would've pulled the trigger just by chance. But he didn't. And I swear there were times, looking at him, that he seemed to be resisting. Forcing himself to hold back."

He pushed his drink away. Swiveled on his stool and stared.

"He's a hero now?"

"Make of it what you will."

Another shot. He said, "So what are you going to do about it?"

"What can I do? Like you said, no proof. And one way or the other, Peake's going to need confinement. I suppose Starkweather's as good a place as any."

"Starkweather in the post-Swig era," he said. "I heard his uncle found him a job on someone else's staff."

"Swig was a mediocre man trying to do a wizard's job. There're no easy solutions."

"So Peake stays put."

"Peake stays put."

"You're okay with that."

"Do I have a choice?" I said. "Let's say I *do* raise a stink, somehow manage to free him. Some do-gooder will see that he gets out on the street, which'll turn him into just another homeless wretch. He can't take care of himself. He'd be dead in a week."

"So we're putting him away for his own good."

"Yes," I said, surprised at the harshness in my voice. "Who the hell said life was fair?"

He stared at me again.

"That day in his room," I said, "when I talked to Peake about the Ardullo children and he began to cry, I misjudged him. I thought it was all self-pity. But he was feeling real pain. Not just at being blamed for it. At what happened. Maybe he revealed some of that to Claire, and that's what kept her going with him. Or maybe she never saw it. But it was real, I'm sure of it. Right after that is when he jumped up, assumed the Jesus pose. He was telling me he'd been martyred. Suffered for someone else's sins. Not sorry for himself. At peace with it."

"Telling you," he said. "Severely low-functioning, but he's worth listening to?"

"Oh, yeah," I said. "It always pays to listen."

We sat in silence for a long time. Someone else replaced Jimmy Buffett, but I couldn't tell you who.

I threw money on the bar. "Let's get out of here."

He lifted himself with effort. "You going to see him again?"

"Probably," I said.

Coming from Random House in hardcover
in December 2000.

Alex Delaware returns
in another ingenious thriller
by Jonathan Kellerman:

DR. DEATH

To read the first chapter, please turn the page . . . .

Published by Random House, Inc.
Available in hardcover December 2000.

Dr. Death

a novel

by

Jonathan Kellerman

1

Irony can be a rich dessert, so when the contents of the van were publicized, some people gorged. The ones who'd believed Eldon H. Mate to be The Angel of Death.

Those who'd considered him Mercy Personified grieved.

I viewed it through a different lens, had my own worries.

Mate was murdered in the very early hours of a sour-smelling, fog-laden Monday in September. No earthquakes or wars interceded by sundown, so death merited a lead story on the evening news. Newspaper headlines in the *Times* and the *Daily News* followed on Tuesday. T.V. dropped the story within 24 hours but recaps ran in the Wednesday papers. In total, four days of coverage, the maximum in short-attention-span L.A. unless the corpse is that of a princess or the killer can afford lawyers who yearn for Oscars.

No easy solve on this one; no breaks of any kind.

Milo had been doing his job long enough not to expect better.

He'd had an easy summer, catching a quartet of lovingly stupid homicides during July and August—one domestic violence taken to the horrible extreme and three brain-dead drunks shooting other inebriates in squalid west side bars. Four murderers hanging around long enough to be caught. It kept his solve rate high, made it a bit, if not much, easier to be the only openly gay detective in LAPD.

"Knew I was due," he said. It was the Sunday after the murder when he phoned me at the house. Mate's corpse had been cold for six days and the press had moved on.

That suited Milo just fine. Like any artist, he craved solitude. He'd played his part by not giving the press anything to work with. Orders from the brass. One thing he and the brass could agree on: Reporters were almost always the enemy.

What the papers *had* printed was squeezed out of cold biography, the inevitable ethical debates, file photos, old quotes. Beyond the fact that Mate had been hooked up to his own killing machine, only the sketchiest details had been released:

Van parked on a remote section of Mulholland Drive, discovery by hikers just after dawn.

Dr. Death Murdered.

I knew more because Milo told me.

The call came in at 8 p.m., just as Robin and I finished dinner. I was out the door, holding onto the straining leash of Spike, our little French bulldog. Pooch and I both looking forward to a nightwalk up the glen. Spike loved the dark because pointing at scurrying sounds let him pretend he was a noble hunter. I enjoyed getting out because I worked with people all day and solitude didn't bother me, either.

Robin answered the phone, caught me in time, ended up doing dog-duty as I returned to my study.

"Mate's yours?" I said, surprised because he hadn't told me sooner. Suddenly edgy because that added a whole new layer of complexity.

"Who else merits such a blessing?"

I laughed softly, feeling my shoulder humping, rings of tension around my neck. The moment I'd heard about Mate I'd worried. Deliberated for a long time, finally made a call that hadn't been returned. I'd dropped the issue because there'd been no good reason not to. It really *wasn't* any of my business. Now, with Milo involved, all that had changed.

I kept all that to myself. His call had nothing to do with my problem. Coincidence—one of those nasty little overlaps. Or maybe there really are only a hundred people in the world.

His reason for getting in touch was simple: the dreaded W word: whodunit. One with enough psychopathology to make me potentially useful.

Also, I was his friend, one of the few people left in whom he could confide.

The psychopathology part was fine with me. What bothered me was the friendship component. Things I knew but didn't tell him. *Couldn't* tell him.

Dr. Death
by Jonathan Kellerman

Published by Random House, Inc.
Available in hardcover December 2000.

Look for Jonathan Kellerman's
New York Times bestseller

BILLY STRAIGHT

A resourceful runaway alone in the wilds of Los Angeles,
twelve-year-old Billy Straight suddenly witnesses a brutal stabbing in Griffith Park. Fleeing into the night,
Billy cannot shake the horrific memory of the savage
violence, nor the pursuit of a cold-blooded killer. For
wherever Billy turns—from Hollywood Boulevard to
the boardwalks of Venice—he is haunted by the *chuck
chuck* sound of a knife sinking into flesh. As LAPD
homicide detective Petra Connor desperately searches
for the murderer, as the media swarms mercilessly
around the story, the vicious madman stalks closer to his
prey. Only Petra can save Billy. But it will take all her
cunning to uncover a child lost in a fierce urban
labyrinth—where a killer seems right at home. . . .

JONATHAN KELLERMAN

SAVAGE SPAWN

Reflections on Violent Children

What makes children kill?

In such places as Jonesboro, Arkansas; Springfield, Oregon; and Littleton, Colorado, kids are killing kids. In this powerful, disturbing book, bestselling author and noted child psychologist Jonathan Kellerman examines the socio-pathology of today's youth, attempting to make sense of the bloody rampages that have taken over today's headlines. In such chapters as "Dissecting Evil," "The Scapegoat We Love to Hate," and "The Biology of Being Bad," Kellerman discusses the history of childhood violence, takes a hard look at antisocial children, and, most important, offers warning signs and solutions to stop the spread of these devastating tragedies that we all think can—and pray will—ever happen in our town.

**LIBRARY OF
CONTEMPORARY THOUGHT**
Published by Ballantine Books.
Available in bookstores everywhere.